Contents

Love Is Fire

An island in the Hebrides! When her father told her he'd bought a house there, Gail thought he must have lost his mind. It certainly wasn't her idea of a place to spend the summer.

Then an arrogant letter from the island's owner changed her mind. However, the tales she heard about him had not prepared her for their meeting. Callum Black, like his pirate ancestors, was a law unto himself!

CHAPTER ONE

'I've bought a house,' announced Phil Collins as he walked into the kitchen of his London flat one afternoon in July. Sunshine filtered through the terylene net which screened the window, and burnished the golden hair which swirled on the shoulders of his daughter Gail, who was ironing, and who did not bother to look up and acknowledge his entrance.

Phil leaned against the wall inside the door, lit a cigarette and watched her through the smoke he exhaled. She was a puzzle to him, this tall clean-limbed daughter of his, as much an enigma as her mother had been. Phil's heavy-lidded expressive grey eyes narrowed in sudden pain. Even though it was ten years since Eira's death the memory of her still had power to hurt him.

'Where?' asked Gail coolly, turning to look at him at last. She twitched a swathe of her long straight hair back over her shoulder in an eternally feminine gesture which never ceased to tantalize him.

Her question gave him his opportunity to surprise her, to disturb that smooth unruffled façade which she presented to the world. He smiled secretly.

'You'll never guess.'

'No, I don't suppose I shall,' she returned as she folded the ironing board and carried it over to the cupboard where it was stored. She didn't really believe that her father had bought a house. For two years he had been saying he would like to buy a house away from the rush and bustle of the city, but always something else had come along to take his attention and the desire for a house had been shelved.

'It's on an island in the Hebrides,' he said.

Gail shut the cupboard door carefully and turned to look at him. To his delight there was a spark of interest in

9

her clear grey eyes which so often regarded him blankly these days.

'Why so far away?' she asked.

Phil lunged away from the wall and began to pace up and down the room. Six feet tall and weighing more than was good for him, with sandy hair which always looked in need of a good brushing, he often reminded Gail of a great lion pacing its cage, big and handsome in a shaggy way. But unlike a lion he wasn't fierce or dangerous. In fact he was extremely sensitive and vulnerable.

'Because I feel I must get away ... far away from this rat-race,' he was saying. 'I want peace and quiet for a few weeks in the year. I want wide spaces, fresh air, where I can commune with nature and write real music, not just the pot-boilers I've been turning out all these years. That young man ... what's his name? Sorry, love, I get them mixed up ... he was right the other day when he said the true artist can't flourish under the conditions imposed by urban living today.'

'That was Karl,' murmured Gail, hiding a smile as she turned to the sink and began to fill the kettle. Her father's cry was familiar. A teacher of music at a well known girl's school and a successful composer of light music, he had always considered himself capable of composing more serious music if only he had the time.

His hand fell on her shoulder and she was swung round to face him. Water from the kettle slopped to the floor. Phil pushed out his jaw and tried to look fierce.

'You can wipe that supercilious grin off your face, miss. This time I mean it. As soon as the school holidays start we're off to ... to ... Darn it, I can't remember the name of the place.'

He began to search through his jacket pockets, bringing out numerous pieces of paper of all shapes and sizes, most of which were covered with music staves on which notes of music were scribbled.

'We?' queried Gail, as she put the lid on the kettle and placed it on the gas cooker.

'Yes. You'll be coming too.'

Gail shook her head stubbornly. 'No,' she said calmly, and began to take cups and saucers out of a cupboard.

'Ah, here it is.' Phil felt in his breast pocket and brought out a pair of spectacles, pushed them on his nose and peered through them at the paper. 'Stornish, Isle of Sorasay – I think that's how the man pronounced it. It's somewhere near Skye, or was it Mull? Anyway, it's one of those little islands around there somewhere.'

He removed his spectacles, put them away and said with an attempt at severity,

'And what makes you think you're not coming with me?'

'Why should I? It's you who wants the peace and quiet and the wide open spaces. I'm quite happy here in the swinging city. I wouldn't know what to do with myself on an island in the middle of the Atlantic.'

Phil sat down plump on a kitchen chair the expression on his face a mixture of frustration and exasperation.

'It isn't in the middle of the Atlantic!' he roared. Then in a more persuasive tone, 'Who's going to keep house for me if you don't come?'

'I'm sure you'll soon find an excellent housekeeper up there. Judging from what I've read in books, Scotland abounds in good wee bodies who are only too glad to keep house for a widower or a bachelor.'

She was still moving about the room collecting crockery for the table which she had covered with an attractive cloth of bright orange linen. Phil leaned an elbow on the table, put his doubled fist under his chin and watched her while he thought up another way of getting her attention. A battle between him and Gail was nothing new. Usually she won because he was in too much of a hurry or too preoccupied to argue with her.

But this time he was determined to win. For the last few months he had been worried about her. He wanted to get her away from London somehow, away from some of the strange people with whom she had been associating

11

recently. He had tried to speak to her about them, to warn her, but every time he opened the subject she turned off and he knew his advice fell on deaf ears.

He had to get her away from this fellow Karl. He had to do it for Eira's sake. Eira wouldn't have approved of him, he was sure. Oh, he knew that these days the trend was to allow one's children to do their own thing, live their own life, make their own mistakes, but he couldn't stand by and let his only daughter become the victim of a charming scoundrel without putting his spoke in somewhere.

If only Gail wouldn't take up with so many lame dogs. As if being an infant teacher wasn't enough she had to do voluntary work at a local youth club. It was there that she met so many of the young men she brought home. This Karl, for instance, had been there one night covering the club for the magazine of which he was co-editor. It was one of those avant-garde publications full of poetry and weird drawings. God knows where Karl had come from or where he was going, but he'd latched on to Gail, recognizing a good thing when he found it. He believed in moving round the world, he said, but he didn't seem in much of a hurry to move from London, and Phil was pretty sure he knew the reason. Gail was the reason. Already she probably kept the young man supplied with food and cigarettes and maybe even more, and if he was any good at reading signs she would be talking of marriage before the summer was out.

Phil sighed heavily, putting on an act of a badly-done-to father, and immediately Gail glanced at him sharply.

'All right, it was just an idea I had. I thought you'd like to spend the summer up there with me. To wake up in the morning and see the sea and to have all the time in the world to stand and stare ....'

Interest flickered in her grey eyes again.

'What is the house like? Is it on a croft?' she asked.

Phil's heavy eyelids dropped over his eyes in order to hide the triumph he was sure he was showing.

'It's one-storeyed, stone-built. It has five rooms beside the kitchen and bathroom, running water, electricity, and it's completely furnished apart from a piano. And it isn't a croft. Apparently Stornish is a small island off the coast of Sorasay. The bloke who sold the house to me says the climate is mild.'

Gail's eyes widened slightly. 'You've definitely bought it, then?'

He made an impatient gesture which nearly sent his tea-cup spinning from the table.

'You haven't been listening again. I told you when I came in.'

'I thought perhaps it was just another pipe-dream. I thought you'd heard about the house and that you'd bought it . . . in your imagination.'

'This is no pipe-dream, child. I've parted with five thousand pounds for the place.'

'But if you haven't seen it how can you be sure it's what you want?' argued Gail. She was feeling a little uneasy. Phil must be serious after all.

'I've seen pictures of it.'

'Did the man who sold it to you tell you why he wanted to sell?'

'Yes. Financial reasons. He can't afford to keep it as a holiday home any more and the owner of the island is being difficult about the condition of the house.'

'Owner of the island? What has he to do with it?'

'He's a bit of an old tyrant from what I can make out and gets angry when the property on the island isn't kept in good condition. Can't say I blame him. I'd probably behave the same way myself if I owned an island. Where's that book of maps?'

Gail went to fetch the book while Phil poured himself more tea. He'd attracted her interest. Now he must hold it until he'd persuaded her to go there.

She returned with a green-bound book and together they examined the map which showed the west coast of Scotland and the islands.

13

'Oban,' muttered Phil as he placed his glasses on his nose. His forefinger traced the coastline. 'Ah, here. Now west from there along this stretch of water, past Mull. Then south and a bit further west. Here. Here it is. Look, Stornish is marked.'

'It's miles away from anything and anywhere!' she exclaimed.

Phil banged the map book closed and lost his temper suddenly.

'So you don't want to go. Then stay here. As soon as term is over I'm off. I'll go by myself!'

Scattering cigarette ash everywhere, he stood up and marched off into the living-room.

A little startled by her father's unusual display of temper, Gail sipped her tea. Piano notes, clear and syncopated, came from the living-room as Phil rattled out a well-known blues theme in traditional jazz style. He only played jazz when he was disturbed about something.

For a few minutes she sat thinking about her life with Phil during the last ten years since the plane disaster in which her mother had been killed when returning from a concert performance in Berlin. If she closed her eyes she could see again the thick black print of the headline in the newspaper.

'Well-known cellist dies in plane crash'.

She remembered leaving her boarding school to be with Phil, who would have been in the same crash if he had not been otherwise engaged. She remembered comforting the big broken-hearted man, promising that she would stay with him always. Arrangements had been made for her to leave the boarding school and to attend school in London so that she could live with Phil. He had worked hard at the school where he taught and on the side had been very successful with the ballads and film music which he composed.

On her part she had kept house when she wasn't at school and later had been able to train as a teacher without leaving home, and now she taught in a school close by. She enjoyed her work and she also enjoyed the voluntary social work she did in the evenings. She believed she had a good relationship with her father. He had never interfered nor stood in her way, and she had never had cause to worry about him except once when he had seemed very interested in another music teacher called Priscilla Fenson whom he had once met at a Junior Choir Festival. Recently, however, Priscilla seemed to have faded out, or at least Phil had not mentioned her, and Gail assumed he had lost interest in the woman — for which she was very glad, because she had no desire to have a stepmother.

But now Phil had dropped a bombshell. Now he wanted her to go to what seemed the other end of the earth with him even though the Hebrides were part of the British Isles. She had travelled to Europe with Phil, but in Britain she had never been further north than Birmingham, so the north of England and Scotland were foreign parts to her.

How could she drop everything and go with him? How could she go when she had just discovered Karl who could make her pulses leap when he kissed her? If she went away now she would lose Karl. On the other hand he might like to go to the Hebrides too. On sudden impulse she stood up and went into the living-room. Walking over to the piano, she stood by her father and watched his big curved fingers strike the notes. Having punished Ellington's *Mood Indigo* he was now playing a number made famous by the famous blues singer Bessie Smith called *Baby, Won't You Please Come Home* which was a favourite of Gail's.

He stopped playing abruptly and swung round on the piano stool.

'Well? What have you decided?' he asked. His temper had subsided, soothed away by the music.

'I'll come with you, but if I don't like it you'll let me come back before the end of the holidays?'

'There's always the chance that I won't like it either,'

15

he said with a grin. 'But I agree, if you don't like it you can come back.'

'And you'll let me invite a friend to visit me?'

'As long as the friend doesn't stay too long.'

'Can I invite Karl?'

His hesitation was fractional.

'You can ask him. It might be interesting to see how he takes to nature and solitude when he has them thrust upon him. Are you seeing him tonight?'

'Yes?'

'Here?'

'No. His place.'

He stood up and putting his arm around her shoulders squeezed them affectionately.

'Thanks for saying you'll come, ducky ... and don't stay too late tonight.'

It was late when the last of Karl's friends left, so late that Gail felt sure she must leave too, but first she had to tell Karl about the house in the Hebrides.

'Karl, I must talk to you.'

'Talk away, then, but let's sit down and be comfortable.'

Holding her hand, he led her to the sofa, sat down and pulled her against him and kissed her. Gail pulled away from him and sat up.

'Have I annoyed you?' he asked.

'No. But I promised my father I wouldn't be late and if I don't go soon I'll miss the last train home.'

'Do you always have to do what he says?' he queried. 'I thought you were one of those independent sort of women. This is the second half of the twentieth century and daughters don't have to be under the thumbs of their fathers any more. Neither do wives have to obey their husbands. You don't have to live with your father. You could have a place of your own.'

'I know I could. But I like living with him. And anyway, who would keep house for him?'

'He could get a woman of his own. After all, he isn't

16

exactly senile, is he?'

Gail didn't reply. She didn't like Karl when he talked in this way and she had no wish to discuss Phil with him. Phil was too close to her and she loved him too much to discuss him with Karl.

'Where do your parents live?' she asked curiously.

He shrugged carelessly and made a grimace.

'I'm not sure any more. They belong to the past. I'm all for living in the present. Now is all that matters, and this is all that matters now.' He leaned forward and kissed her again.

When she came up for air Gail decided that she'd had enough excitement for one night and stood up.

'I'll have to run to the station,' she said breathlessly, 'or I'll miss that train.'

'Your father doesn't like me,' he muttered.

'Oh, that's not true. I'm sure he doesn't dislike you. Why, he said I could invite you to stay with us in the Western Isles.'

'The Hebrides?' he exclaimed.

'That's what I wanted to tell you. He's bought a house on an island and we're going there for the summer holidays. He says he wants a place of his own, somewhere quiet. I promised I'd go with him and he said I could invite you.'

There was silence for a moment. Then Karl said,

'You don't have to go with him, Gail. You could stay here in London with me. Don't go.'

'I must. I promised,' she replied stubbornly.

'When?'

'End of July.'

His breath was released in a sigh of relief.

'Anything could happen before then. Your father could change his mind. You could change yours.'

He stepped towards her, but Gail's independent spirit, fearing a trap, was already moving out and her body was following.

17

'The train!' she gasped, and grabbing her coat she slung it round her shoulders and made for the door. Up the stairs she ran, along the dimly lit hallway, out of the front door. It had been raining slightly and the dark wet pavements reflected light from the street lamps. Along the road she ran, never looking back. Then she darted down a stairway, her feet clattering, echoing eerily in the deserted entrance to an underground station. She reached the platform just as the District Line train trundled to a stop. Automatic doors swished open, she entered the carriage and sat down on the nearest seat.

There were few passengers on the train and in that particular carriage there were none. Gail stared at her reflection in the dark window opposite and thought of the narrow escape she had just had. Like a moth she had been dazzled by Karl, by his handsome appearance and by his apparent need of her. Like a moth she had flown too close, and tonight she had almost had her wings singed.

Gail grinned at her own comparison and her reflection grinned back. The grin faded as she remembered how Karl's kisses had roused her. He was the first man she had known who could do that. Therein lay the danger of knowing him.

Where did he come from and where was he going? She hadn't liked his reply to her question about his parents. It had been hard and careless. And yet it had been in keeping with everything else she knew about him. Everything he said or wrote rejected authority. Presumably he had rejected his parents and it was obvious that he would like her to reject Phil. Maybe he had reason to reject his, but she had no reason at all to reject hers.

Would he come to the Hebrides? Would she ever see him again? When she had rushed out of his room she had known he wouldn't follow her. She would like to have believed that pride had prevented him from following her, but she had a feeling that Karl did not possess any pride. And she had to come to the reluctant conclusion that it was laziness which had really stopped him from chasing

18

after her. Gail grinned self-mockingly. How like her to be attracted to a man who was too lazy to pursue her!

To her surprise she did see Karl again. He was waiting for her one day outside the school. His smile wide and gay, his blue eyes, his auburn hair made her tummy flutter. He didn't bother to hide his reason for meeting her.

'I haven't a penny in my pockets,' he said, turning the inside of his trouser pockets out to reveal their emptiness, 'and I'm hungry. What are you going to do about it?'

As he had known she would, she responded to that cry at once. Anyone in want or distress appealed to Gail.

'Take you home and feed you, I suppose,' she laughed up at him. The smile left his eyes and they grew wary.

'At your place? Will your father be there?'

'Not until later.'

'That's all right, then.'

They travelled on the tube, standing close together in the crowd, and Gail was very conscious of his nearness and the intense gaze of his blue eyes. At the flat he stood around the kitchen while she cooked, not offering to help but talking all the time about the latest edition of the magazine. After they had eaten Gail cleared away. Again Karl made no offer to help her.

'Are you still set on going to the Hebrides?' he asked casually.

'Phil hasn't said anything about changing his mind. Will you be able to come and see us?'

He didn't reply, nor did he mention the subject when they met again during the next two weeks. Nor did he make love to her again, but managed to show in many subtle ways such as a flick of a finger on her cheek that he was interested in her, so that Gail began to wish more and more that she hadn't promised Phil she would go with him.

Once when she was saying good night to Karl he murmured,

'I don't know what I'll do without you . . . starve, prob-

ably,' she almost said, 'I'm not going. I'll stay with you.'
But something stopped her from saying the comforting
words. Being very feminine and not a little contrary she
would have liked him to come out into the open and de-
clare that he loved her and would never let her go; or
alternatively to say he would follow her to the other ends
of the earth, in this case the Western Isles. He never
would, of course, because he was totally modern in his
attitude to women, believing they had freedom to choose.
So the decision to go or to stay was hers and hers alone.
He wouldn't persuade her to stay, not because he was too
proud but because he didn't think that he should. Which
wasn't very romantic, thought Gail, whose lively independent spirit enjoyed a battle of wills and wits, yet would
have accepted defeat from a superior, more domineering
spirit.

She was beginning to think that Phil had forgotten all
about the house in the Hebrides. He was extremely busy
at school with end-of-term activities as well as composing
the musical score for a new serial to be shown on television. But his attention was drawn to the house and their
fast approaching holidays in a rather dramatic way one
evening, a week before they planned to depart.

The letter addressed to Phil was in the mailbox in the
entrance hall of the flats when Gail arrived home from
work. She glanced at the bold handwriting curiously and
turned the envelope over to read the name and address of
the sender – A. C. Black, Stornish House, Sorasay via
Oban.

Black was the name of the man who owned the island
on which the house Phil had bought was situated. Why
should he be writing? Possibly Phil had been in communication with him unknown to her.

She had to contain her curiosity until her father came
home and opened the letter, which he did while he was
having his pre-dinner whisky and soda as he sprawled in
his favourite chair in the living-room. Sitting opposite
him, Gail waited for him to pass on information. His re-

action to the letter was not what she had expected. He jerked upright suddenly, knocking his glass flying from the arm of the chair on which it had been balanced.

'Good God!' he exploded.

'What's the matter?' asked Gail anxiously as she picked up the glass and set it on a small table.

'It's from that bloke Black whom Sanderson told me about, the man who owns the island. Of all the nerve! He says he doesn't want strangers on Stornish. Calls me a fool for buying the house. Here, read it for yourself while I get a refill to counteract the shock.'

He tossed the letter into her lap and lumbered out of the room into the kitchen, where she could hear him muttering angrily to himself as he poured another drink.

Mr. Black's writing was as dark and uncompromising as his name and his message was brief but left no doubt as to how he felt.

Dear Sir,

It is now almost a month since you were foolish enough to buy Gartbeg, a house situated on this island, from my cousin Ian Sanderson. He sold it to you in defiance of my wishes, and my willingness to buy the house and land from him in order to keep the island intact and free from interlopers. As you have taken no interest in the property to date I am assuming you are regretting having bought it. Therefore I should like to buy it back from you at the same price you gave for it. Believe me, to sell it to me is the best course for you to take as your presence here would not be welcome at this time.

I should be glad if you would contact me immediately to let me know your decision.

Yours faithfully,
A. C. Black.

Gail stared at the bold black signature indignantly. Mr.

Black was in for a shock if he thought the Collins, father and daughter, were going to be frightened away from his island by such a letter.

'You can't let him get away with it,' she asserted when Phil returned to his chair, slumped down in it and sighed.

'Exactly how I feel. But only today I had a call from Bert Colley. He wants me to go to Copenhagen as soon as term finishes. That film, the one about Caractacus, has been entered in the festival there and he thinks it has a good chance of winning an award for the best music composed for a documentary this year, so I'm afraid I'll have to delay my trip to the Hebrides.'

He ruffled his hair perplexedly and took a sip from his drink.

'I could go without you,' said Gail. Judging by the arrogant tone of the letter there was a battle in the offing and she could never resist a fight. 'Sounds to me as if Mr. Black needs putting in his place.'

Phil's eyes brightened.

'That's my girl,' he said. 'I thought you might. We'll ignore this letter and you can arrive on Stornish all innocent-like to take up residence to show that we have an interest in the place. Meanwhile I'll get Jack Tilley, my solicitor, to investigate this Black. I paid five thousand for the place and I'm not letting it go for less, nor am I giving it up until I've seen it. You know, the chances are we've stumbled on a family feud between Black and his cousin.'

Gail's face wore a thoughtful expression. Taking another drink of his whisky, Phil watched her. He knew she had been seeing more of Karl and he had been glad he had taken the plunge and had bought the place in the Hebrides and made arrangements to leave London. He had expected opposition from Gail when he had realized today that it would be impossible for him to go north, but now this abrupt arrogant letter seemed to have roused her as much as it had roused him. A week or even two away

22

from the insidious charm of that scrounger Karl might help Gail to see him as he really was. Besides, there were five thousand pounds at stake.

'Sanderson said the house is fully furnished,' he said. 'Might be a few slates missing and probably it needs decorating, but he assured me that it was inhabitable immediately. Apparently his mother used to live in it, so I don't know why this Black fellow thinks he should have it. I'll join you there as soon as I can.'

'I'll go,' said Gail suddenly impulsively, 'if only to show Mr. Black that we don't like being called interlopers. But you'll have to tell me what to do and say when I get there.'

A week later Gail stood on the quay at Oban where she had arrived the previous day by train from Glasgow. It had rained during the night and the morning air was fresh and cool. Sunlight was reflected on the wet roofs of the houses and the quayside buildings. There was a whirl of activity on the quay around the Royal Mail steamer which was preparing to depart for Tobermory and the Inner Isles. Seagulls laughed caustically as they hovered over the warm air issuing from the steamer's funnel. A small crane creaked as it lifted cargo aboard.

'It's a fine morning,' exclaimed one of the crewmen as he passed Gail, who was already aboard and was leaning over the rail watching the activity, occasionally lifting her eyes to admire the panorama of green hills behind the grey houses of Oban, 'but I doubt we'll be having a storm before sunset,' continued the crewman, shaking his head as he went on his way.

Gail glanced after him, blinking in surprise at his comment. The morning was placid and the sky was clear except for a few streaks of feathery white cloud, so why should he make such an obvious comment?

A chuckle at her side made her turn. A tall plump woman was beside her. She was dressed in a greenish-grey single-breasted burberry raincoat and wore a gaily coloured headscarf over her greying hair.

'I can see you're puzzled, love,' she said. 'So was I when I first came here. They mean "believe" when they say "doubt". He thinks there'll be a storm before the day is over. And being an islander he's probably right.'

'Oh, surely not. The weather looks too clear and settled.'

'You know the old saying about a calm coming before a storm? Well, I've learned that it's true since I came to live in the Western Isles,' answered the woman, her bright grey eyes going over Gail's smart pants suit of green and black tartan. 'You're from London, aren't you? May I ask you where you're going?'

'To Sorasay. Do you know it?'

'I've been to see the tulips in the spring.'

'I didn't know tulips were grown so far north.'

'Yes. The small islands are fairly flat and the Department of Agriculture has been encouraging the industry. On Sorasay and Stornish I believe the bulb plantations are both private enterprise ventures. Aye, the islands grow lovely flowers. You should see the primroses on Barra—a sea of pale gold.'

'You don't belong to the islands either, do you?' asked Gail, curious in her turn.

The woman's rosy-cheeked face creased as she smiled.

'The Lancashire accent is one of the hardest to obliterate,' she said. 'John, my husband, and I bought a cottage on the west coast of Mull about ten years ago. He's an artist. He used to teach pottery at night school. Then one summer we came to Mull for a holiday. We never went back, except to visit relations now and again. The way of life on the islands suited us admirably, so we decided to live there and practise our arts and maybe set up a small business selling paintings of local scenes and pottery made of local clay. We've never regretted coming. Now what brings you here?'

Gail explained about her father buying a house and

24

wanting to spend his holiday far away from London in the hopes of composing music.

The other woman nodded appreciatively.

'I understand only too well, and I hope he finds the place is what he wants. The Hebrides are well named the Isles of Youth. I've just been visiting my sister in Manchester, and here I am returning home four days before my time down there was up, just because I could no longer stand the men and women jostling each other in the mindless commercial system. Every time I return here and see the islands coming up out of the sea I feel the thrill of their promise. You'll see, you'll feel it too.'

Gail gazed in amazement at the plump woman. Who would have thought such a dowdily-dressed (dowdy by London standards, that was) woman could have such sentiments? Here was someone who had put into practice what Karl and his associates were always preaching. Yet she wasn't young. It would seem that the desire for the simple life and to escape from commercialism did not belong to the younger generation only. On impulse she introduced herself to the woman and learned that the other was called Enid Mills.

The steamer was leaving the harbour to the accompaniment of shouts from the crewmen and the men on the quayside. Across the strait of Kerrara it swept smoothly and out into the wider expanse of the Firth of Lorne. Ahead were the dark ramparts of the island of Mull and beyond them was the thickly wooded, darkly mysterious shore of Morven. Between the island and the mainland a strip of glittering water opened up, the Sound of Mull, seaway to the Hebrides.

As the bow of the steamer drove straight towards the shining ribbon of water the bleak outline of a castle appeared on the Mull shore, its square tower dominating the flat promontory on which it was built. Mrs. Mills pointed to it, informing Gail that it was Duart Castle, home of the Macleans, and went on to tell the story associated with the wife of one of the Macleans who was

25

one bound to a stake on the well-known Lady's Rock, which the steamer was just passing, and left to drown there. Fortunately she had been rescued by a passing fishing boat before the high tide had covered the rock.

Mrs. Mills then pointed out the end of the island of Lismore referred to as the Green Island or Great Garden because of the vivid colour of both its grass and its flowers. Behind it another wide arm of the sea opened up and stretched away into the mountains which, Mrs. Mills told Gail, was Loch Linnhe, the route to Fort William and the Caledonian Canal.

Fascinated by the new world of mountains, islands and sea, enchanted by the various myths and legends related to her by her garrulous companion, Gail leaned on the rail of the upper deck and smelt the tang of the isles, the indefinable scent compounded of newly-washed-up seaweed and many flowers. Watching the sunlight tint the grey mountains of Morven a delicate lavender shade above the dark green of thick mixed forest, she felt for the first time the pull of that northern land and heard for the first time its music. Another castle appeared, this time close to the water on the Morven coast and was pointed out by Mrs. Mills.

'That's Ardtornish and just beyond it is the entrance to Loch Aline. White sand is quarried there and is used for the glass industry. Further on is the forest of Fiunary. Morven is fine country for deer and sheep, so I'm told. Now come over to the other side and we'll see Salen Bay.'

From the port side of the deck they watched the coast of Mull curve away into a wide bay on whose distant shore the windows of the town of Salen winked in the sunlight and about which Mrs. Mills had yet another story to tell. Finding her companion so knowledgeable, Gail decided to ask her if she knew anything about the people who lived on Sorasay.

'A little. I know Don Gorrie who keeps the shop. He's a well-known amateur artist and often exhibits in our local art shows.'

26

'Have you ever heard him speak about a man called Black?'

Mrs. Mills wrinkled her forehead as she delved into her memory.

'Black? Yes, I remember hearing something about the Blacks. "Black by name and Black by nature", I think the jingle goes, referring of course to the dreadful deeds committed by members of the family long ago. The family is descended from the original inhabitants of the islands. Picts they'd be, the dark men of history about whom there is so much mystery — pirates and great seafarers. Now the last time I saw Don he mentioned something about Adam Black having died at last and about another Black having come back to live on the island. I think too there was a spot of trouble concerning a young woman. That would be about six years ago. She disappeared while staying on the island and was never seen again. I believe there's always been bad wild blood in the family.'

'Mr. Black owns the island of Stornish except the part my father has bought.'

'Aye, and he probably would like to own it all,' commented Mrs. Mills shrewdly. 'He won't want strangers coming into his domain if I know anything about the islanders. Look, there's Calf Island on the bow. We're nearly at Tobermory. I hope John has remembered to come and meet me. Like most artists he's a wee bit absent-minded. I am myself, for that matter,' she added with a chuckle.

Soon the steamer was sweeping into the deep natural harbour of Tobermory Bay. Placid water reflected the white buildings on the wharf and the hulls and masts of the yachts moored opposite the old stone pier which stretched out into the bay in front of the little town.

'Don't forget, when you reach Sorasay go straight to the shop and tell Don you know me. He'll tell you the best way to get to Stornish. I've a feeling the bus which goes round the island doesn't go near the smaller island,' said Mrs. Mills, and Gail accompanied her to the main deck.

27

As she watched the tall talkative woman walk along the wharf clutching her many parcels and suitcase, Gail felt suddenly lonely, and the feeling was increased when she saw a tall thin man wearing the twin to the greenish-grey burberry Mrs. Mills wore walk up ·to the woman, grasp her suitcase and kiss her. Evidently John had remembered.

Turning away, Gail wandered on to the top deck again to lean on the rail and watch the unloading of mailbags, huge cartons of goods and some sheep. It seemed to her that although it was noon the sun wasn't as bright as it had been, and glancing up at the sky she saw that it had been half-concealed by streaks of dark ragged cloud. There was no wind on the water, however, and all seemed calm. Yet the atmosphere had a strange leaden quality which ·had been absent at Oban. The calm before the storm?

A· storm at sea in a strange place amongst strange people. Gail felt an unusual quiver of apprehension and wished she could have left the steamer with Mrs. Mills and could have gone with that kindly person and her John to the comfort of their cottage. As it was she was going to a house on an island belonging to a man called Black, one of the dark people of history in whose family there was wild bad blood.

In an attempt to shake off the queer sense of foreboding which was wholly alien to her and which she surmised had been induced by Mrs. Mills' stories and the wild and beautiful scenery through which she had passed· that morning, Gail went to have lunch in the small dining-room as the steamer left Tobermory. She hoped she might make another acquaintance with whom she could while away the time, but all the remaining passengers were men; men with craggy weather-worn faces who were dressed in stiff dark suits and who were obviously islanders. They glanced at her shyly and nodded, but made no attempt to converse with her.

After the meal she visited the ladies' room, attended to

her make-up, tied a bright silk scarf over her hair and went up on to the top deck again.

Thin grey clouds were spreading slowly across the sky and the sun was a small round disc. A chilly damp wind twitched at her scarf. When she looked over the rail she saw to her surprise that the water was green, and under its smooth surface there was a regular rolling swell. Glancing up, she saw a lighthouse, high and white, standing alone on the most wicked tumble of rocks she had ever seen, and below the rocks, pale yellow sand gleamed in the eerie grey light. Beyond the lighthouse far in the distance there were mountains with jagged peaks thrusting up out of the rolling greenish-grey sea.

Turning in yet another direction, she looked westward and felt a leap of excitement as she saw the horizon, a curved blue line about which the remnants of blue sky beckoned. There was a dark smudge against the line which might have been a distant island, but visibility was rapidly deteriorating and even as she stared the smudge disappeared to blend with the creeping, all-consuming, greyness.

Then the steamer altered course slightly, turning to the south, and she saw quite clearly the outlines of three islands, like three ships in convoy. Again she felt a tingle of excitement. She had expected nothing like this. The wide expanse of sea and sky broken only by the small humps of land gave her a sense of freedom, a great buoyancy of spirit, and she forgot her earlier sense of foreboding. As Mrs. Mills had said, the way to the isles was a promise of something new, of adventure.

The steamer stopped at the first island, which was Coll, and from her place on the upper deck Gail stared curiously at the low grey cottages of the village of Arinagour huddled on either side of a roadway which wound away to the low hills in the distance. After seeing the mountains of Mull and those other distant mountainous islands she was surprised how low and fairly level Coll was. The next island, Tiree, was even lower, downright flat in fact, and she was sure that the sea, when stormy, would sweep right over it.

By the time the steamer left Tiree and had nosed its way out of Gott harbour and was plunging south in the direction of the dark smudge which was Sorasay, the sky and sea were one colour, grey, and the wind had freshened so that the persistent Atlantic swell was more noticeable. Waves broke incessantly white on grey as far as the eye could see. Gail found the wind too strong for her to stand on deck with any comfort, and went below to discover she was the only passenger left on board.

When the steamer docked at the pier at Portnagour on Sorasay a friendly crewman carried her second suitcase ashore for her and showed her the way to the shop which was just another of the low grey cottages near the landing place. The crewman left her at the door and went off along the road to see his grandmother, he said. Plucking up her courage, Gail lifted the old-fashioned latch and pushed the door open. A bell jangled, startling her and bringing the gaze of the four people assembled in the shop in her direction. During that moment of silence following the noise of the bell she entered the warm atmosphere which was redolent with the smell of oranges, bacon, rubber and leather. For another moment the gaze of four pairs of eyes, two feminine and two masculine, surveyed her highly fashionable pants suit and her now uncovered shining hair and then they were veiled quickly, shyly, and the conversation which she had interrupted continued in a strange guttural language which she realized must be Gaelic.

There was nothing else for her to do but wait until the shopkeeper, a big burly man who was wearing a Harris tweed suit and a brown trilby hat, finished serving his customers. She gazed round the shop. It seemed to stock everything from small refrigerators and vacuum cleaners right through all the grocery items to toothbrushes, men's wellington boots, and cloth by the yard. Every bit of space was used and the counter was so cluttered with displayed goods that the shopkeeper hardly had room to work.

As she looked round she noticed that the other man in the shop was staring at her. He was small and dark and had a big beaky nose and bright blue eyes. He was dressed in farming denims and was slowly edging his way towards her. She smiled at him and nodded, hoping to elicit some show of friendliness. But she received in return only an icy stare. Feeling rebuffed, she looked again at the stuffed shelves and this time found several items which she had not noticed before. Apparently she would not go short of anything while she stayed on the island as long as she could get to the shop.

At last the two women finished their shopping and with many smiles and much laughter they left after smiling shyly at Gail and saying 'Good day' to her. The door had hardly closed behind them when the small man with the fierce blue eyes came right up to her and blurted out, 'You are a Campbell.'

He said every syllable separately so that the name Campbell became two names, the p and the b being given full explosive value. He looked so belligerent that Gail took a step backwards, at the same time shaking her head.

'No, she is not, Willie,' said the man at the counter with a grin.

The little man spun round and hissed, 'She is wearing the Campbell tartan.'

The other man laughed heartily.

'That is the Black Watch tartan she is wearing, right enough, and the Black Watch were founded by the Campbells,' he agreed. 'But that doesn't make her a Campbell. Tartan is fashionable wear for anyone these days. I'm thinking the young lady is from the city and I'm guessing the city is London. Am I right, miss?'

Gail smiled in relief at his friendly approach.

'Yes, you are.'

'If she is not a Campbell she should not be wearing the Campbell tartan,' asserted the small man, then going

31

back to the counter he broke into a flood of Gaelic. When he had been served and had paid for his purchases he went out, passing Gail with another fierce glance at her clothing and a mutter about the Campbells being thieves and traitors.

Don Gorrie, the shopkeeper, chuckled.

'I hope you will not be minding Wullie, miss. He's a MacDonald and he cannot bear the name Campbell. I'm a MacDonald myself, but I like to think we've grown out of the old animosities these days. Now, how can I be helping you?'

Warmed by his beaming hospitality, Gail explained that she wanted to get to Stornish and that Mrs. Mills had suggested she should ask him.

'Ach, now were you after meeting Enid herself? And how is she?' he asked, then without waiting for an answer went on, 'Stornish! Now what would a young lady like yourself be wanting with that place?'

Again Gail had to explain how her father had bought a house on the island and hoped to spend his holidays there.

'And you have come all the way to get the place ready for him,' murmured Don Gorrie, regarding her with suddenly grave brown eyes. He glanced at the big clock on the wall. 'The best way for you to be getting there now is for me to be taking you. Have you all you'll be needing in the way of food?'

Gail had to admit she hadn't, so together they filled a box full of canned goods as well as other useful groceries. She paid him and he set the box by the door and told her to wait until he brought the van round. Then he disappeared through a door in the back of the shop and she heard him calling to someone in Gaelic. He reappeared followed by a girl of about thirteen years of age who had the brightest red hair Gail had ever seen and who smiled shyly at Gail and greeted her in English.

'Manie here will be minding the shop while I'm gone,' said Mr. Gorrie.

'Oh, but I could wait until the shop closes,' said Gail. 'I don't want to take you away from your work.'

'Manie will manage fine. We had better go now before the storm gets any worse. Besides, I have some goods I promised to a customer who is ill and cannot be waiting until Friday for them.'

So he put Gail's luggage in the tall red van which was really a travelling shop and she climbed up to sit beside him in the driving cab.

They left the village with its scattered houses and followed the road inland. The land was very flat and was dotted with cottages set amongst fields in which grain was growing. Beyond the fields Gail could see the sea, storm-grey and wind-tossed.

In answer to her questions Don Gorrie said that the grain was oats and barley, and went on to talk about the other industries of the island.

'We have good healthy cattle producing fine milk, and Sir Morris has encouraged the islanders to set up a cheese-making factory.'

'Sir Morris who?' asked Gail.

'Sir Morris Boyd. He bought the island about twenty years ago and he's been our laird ever since. Ach, the improvements he's introduced! We're all grateful he came for all he's a Lowlander. Thanks to him some of the young people are able to stay.'

'Why have they gone away before?' asked Gail.

'There wasn't enough for them here. Even now we've many men in the Merchant Navy sending home all the money they can and girls in Glasgow helping out.'

He brought the van to a stop outside a typical grey house with dormer windows in its roof. Lights twinkled inside because although it was only half past four on a July afternoon the stormy weather had darkened the sky so much it seemed like a winter's day.

While she waited for Mr. Gorrie to deliver the goods to his customer she stared out of the window at the fields which were divided from each other by a simple fencing

33

of posts and wire. A sudden wild gust of wind shook the van and flung rain against the windscreen and she shivered a little and wondered whether she should have stayed the night at Portnagour instead of trying to reach Stornish.

As soon as Mr. Gorrie was back in the van she asked him how they would cross to the other island.

'Ach, we'll be going over the causeway. It's still low tide, so it's uncovered for another hour yet. But it's not a good place to be crossing in a storm.'

'Is there any other way of getting to the island?'

'Aye. There is a ferry of sorts, but the boat is kept on the Stornish side and Dougie Lean who runs it has to know that you're coming on the bus so that he can be on the Sorasay side to meet you. He wouldn't be knowing you were coming today, would he?'

'No, he wouldn't. Do you know Mr. Black?'

'Aye, I know Callum,' he said shortly.

'Callum? But I thought his first name began with the letter A?'

'So it does. That's for Adam. But all of us have known him as Callum ever since he was a wee bairn coming off the steamer to live with his grandfather. He was called Callum to distinguish him from his grandfather, you see. I knew old Adam better than I know Callum. He was proud and fierce and clannish, unlucky in his children.'

'Oh, why was that?' asked Gail with interest as she sensed another legend similar to those told to her by Mrs. Mills.

'He had a son and a daughter, John and Catriona. John went to sea like so many Blacks before him. He married a girl from the mainland, but she wouldn't come to live on Stornish because she did not want to leave her own family. She died and John, wanting his son to be brought up as a Black, sent young Callum here to live with his grandfather. Later John was lost at sea during the war. As for Catriona—' he paused and sighed. 'You'll forgive the sigh, miss, but Catriona was beautiful and we all loved her. She went away to be an actress. First she was in Perth and then in Glasgow. Ach, there was no one who could sing and dance like Catriona. She came back some years later much changed. She brought her son Ian with her. Old Adam gave her a house to live in, but she was never the same again. She died a few years back of a broken heart. Poor beautiful Catriona!'

Fascinated by the hint of tragedy and by Mr. Gorrie's romantic presentation of his story (whoever believed that people died of broken hearts these days?), Gail found an opportunity to ask a question which had been hovering on her tongue for a while.

'My father bought Gartbeg from Ian Sanderson. Is that the Ian you are talking about?'

He gave her a startled sidelong glance and the van lurched to the side of the road. He righted it and stared intently through the fan of glass wiped clean by the windscreen wiper.

'I was wondering who had sold it to him. I didn't think it would be Callum, because he is the sort of person who holds what he has, if you understand me, and holds fast. I hope you'll not be thinking I'm prying into your business, but does Callum know you've bought the place?'

'Yes, he knows, and my father received a rude letter from him which said we wouldn't be welcome on Stornish.'

Mr. Gorrie, still keeping his eyes on the road and gripping the steering wheel firmly as if afraid the van might lurch to the side of the road again, nodded gravely.

'That sounds like Callum — forthright to a fault, saying what he thinks without any consideration of the effect he might be making. He will not be welcoming you at all, for he's been farming the land belonging to Gartbeg ever since he came back after old Adam died leaving the island divided between his two grandsons. Aye, Callum is one of the people who have come back to the islands and who is using all his learning and skill to improve Stornish and preserve it.'

35

'What learning is that?' asked Gail.

'He's a naturalist. He went away to university to get a degree in Natural History. He was always interested in the wild-life of the islands when he was a boy and he's put his interest to good use.'

'What happened to Ian? What does he do?'

'He had no feeling for Stornish. The island did not speak to him. For all he's an actor, following in his mother's footsteps, he's his father's son and no Black.'

There was a wealth of unspoken criticism of Ian Sanderson in Mr. Gorrie's summing up, and Gail did not ask any more questions, preferring to muse about the information which she had already been given about the Black family. The windscreen wipers clicked rhythmically as they swept the raindrops from the windscreen and the heavy wheels of the van threw up sprays of water as they squelched through puddles on the road.

The road curved over a hill, descended the other side, and Gail saw Stornish for the first time beyond a narrow strait of wind-whipped dark grey water. Through the rain it looked dark, aloof and self-contained. It was fairly long and had a rocky ridge running its full length rather like a backbone. As they approached nearer she could make out a pattern of walls criss-crossing the island, dividing it into fields.

In a few minutes the van was crunching along the rough road which crossed the narrow foreshore and followed the narrow causeway of rock which joined the two islands together at low tide. On either side of the causeway the sea advanced and retreated, seeming to claw with greedy grey fingers at the narrow roadway. The wind funnelling down the narrow strait shook the van so that Gail was glad when they reached the other side and were once more on firm land. The sight of the causeway combined with the tragic story of Catriona had caused the strange feeling of foreboding which she had experienced at Tobermory to return, and she began to wish she had never come to Stornish.

CHAPTER TWO

ONCE on the island of Stornish Mr. Gorrie took the left fork in the road which followed the coast round the end of the island. First it ran close to the muddy shore of the narrow strait of water, then it turned south, rising slightly as it cut across the more rocky tip of the island.

'I'll take you to Stornish House. Callum will be there and he'll be taking you to the other house himself, I'm thinking,' said Mr. Gorrie. He paused and she noticed a rather worried frown crease his forehead. When he spoke again it was with a certain diffidence.

'You'll have to be meeting him some time and explaining who you are, so you may as well see him straight away. I'm thinking he'll not be pleased, but I've never known him be ill-mannered to a woman yet.'

Truly it was what he didn't say about Callum Black which was intriguing, thought Gail.

'I believe you're frightened of him,' she teased.

'You're not far from the truth, miss. I have been knowing Callum for the best part of twenty-five years and yet I'm not knowing him at all. Here we are.'

In the wan light of late afternoon Stornish House looked ghostly and unwelcoming with its white walls and high gables. Set amongst flat dark fields, its gable end faced the sand-dunes beyond which a shore of damp sand was riddled with long channels of water. There were no trees around it, but there were several outbuildings, one of which was a barn.

It was not until she stepped down from the van that Gail knew about the strength of the wind. It slammed into her, almost knocking her over, and she had to turn her back on it quickly. At once her long hair, which she had forgotten to cover, streamed before her and across her face so that she couldn't see.

37

'Step into the porch quickly and knock on the door. I'll be bringing your cases,' yelled Mr. Gorrie.

She hurried, or rather was blown by the gale, towards the porch built over the door in the gable end of the house. She had just managed to open the door and enter the porch when Mr. Gorrie arrived with her two cases. He put them down and fought his way back to the van to return with her box of food. Entering the porch, he closed the door and asked urgently,

'Have you been knocking?'

Gail shook her head. Left alone in the porch listening to the wind wailing and the rain slashing at the windows, her courage had deserted her completely and she had not been able to raise a hand.

Mr. Gorrie regarded her rather impatiently, raised his hand and banged the black cast-iron knocker loudly, waited a few seconds and banged again. Nothing happened.

'Ach, there's nothing else for it,' he muttered, and turning the black doorknob he opened the door and entered the house.

'Callum!' he yelled. 'Is it sleeping you are ... or just dead?' There was no answer.

'He isn't in. If he were, Luran the dog would be barking by now. You'd better come in, miss, and wait for him to return. I must be going before the incoming tide makes the causeway impossible to cross.'

'But won't Mr. Black object to me being in his house alone?' asked Gail, not wanting him to go.

He shook his head slowly and smiled.

'There is a lot you have to be learning about island life. Doors are always left open in case someone calls and people are always walking in and out. Callum must be out walking somewhere away over the fields or the moors. Ach, only a madman would be walking in this weather.' He held out his hand and raised his brown trilby, and Gail reluctantly shook hands with him. His reference to a madman had made her blood freeze.

'We shall be meeting again, miss. Now go in and make yourself at home. Callum will be here before dark, I shouldn't wonder.'

Gail stood in the porch and watched the red van disappear round the bend in the road. For a while she stayed where she was and stared at the sea beyond the sanddunes. It seemed as if the storm was getting worse. It would be impossible for her to set out in such weather to find Gartbeg because she had only a vague idea of where it was. There was nothing else she could do but take Mr. Gorrie's advice and wait in Callum Black's house until he returned.

Only a madman would go out in weather like this. The hairs on her neck prickled and her skin grew chilly with goose pimples. She wished Mr. Gorrie had not said that. In this remote place, miles from anywhere, it was easy to imagine a man going mad if he lived alone.

She shuddered and turning quickly entered the house. She found herself in a wide hallway. The floor was covered with shiny brown linoleum. In the centre of it was a red and blue Persian rug. A tall grandfather clock ticked quietly in a corner and on a small polished antique table there was a telephone.

Cheered by the sight of contact with the outside world, Gail advanced slowly, hearing the wind howling in a chimney and the rain tapping on the window panes. On the table beside the telephone there was a directory and some letters addressed to Mr. A. C. Black. Encouraged by these further signs of communication with the civilized world, she turned and entered the room on her right.

The comfortable casual style of its furnishings made her feel even better. Here was a room in which you could sit at ease. The armchairs and the big chesterfield were covered in flowered cretonne. It was a room in which you could read, for the whole of one wall was a bookcase crammed with books. In fact there were books everywhere, piled beside one of the armchairs, scattered on the low table in front of the old-fashioned fireplace in which a fire was set ready for lighting. It was a room in which you could work, for there was a big desk on which there was a typewriter, piles of paper and more books. Above all it was a room which welcomed you even on a dreary, stormy afternoon.

She left it and feeling a great need for a cup of tea returned to the porch, picked up the box of groceries, then walked the length of the hall to enter what she guessed would be the kitchen. Again, she was pleasantly surprised. It was big, a real living kitchen, and it was all electric.

'A man who has a house like this might be mad, but I don't think he would mind if I make myself a meal to pass the time until he comes,' she said to herself, and was not surprised to hear her own voice. Her feeling of foreboding completely dispersed by what she had seen of the house, she removed her jacket, pushed up the sleeves of her sweater and began to prepare some food.

An hour later, her hunger satisfied, she was still alone, sitting at the big table engrossed in a book which she had taken from the bookcase in the living-room. It was about the legends of the Hebridean islands and she was so absorbed in it that she had not noticed the growing fury of the gale or the passage of time.

A sudden resounding crash brought her to her feet quivering. In the wind-racked, rain-slashed silence which followed the crash the grandfather clock struck the hour, a pleasant mellifluous comforting sound. Seven o'clock and no Callum Black.

Trying to control her trembling, Gail nerved herself to step into the hallway to investigate the crash. She opened the front door. Fingers of wind, damp and icy, reached for her hair and face. The porch door was open, blown back against the shelves on which there were red geraniums in pots. One of the pots had been knocked down and it lay on the tiled floor of the porch. Soil spilled out, rich and dark.

Relief surged through her veins and eased the tension. Closing the door firmly and pushing the bolts at top and bottom home to make sure it would not blow open again, she glanced through the window. Visibility was reduced by driven rain and all she could see was the wind-bent stiff marram grass of the sand-dunes. But she could hear the sea snarling like a frustrated beast, and was glad that the dunes stood between it and the house. Remembering her father's efforts to persuade her that she would like living in the islands because she would wake to see the sea every morning, she grinned. 'Little do you know, Phil, what it can be like in July!' she murmured.

The thought of Phil brought comfort. She would write to him and to Karl. Writing would bring them both close. Quickly she cleared up the mess made by the fallen potted geranium and then went to wash the dishes she had used. She also washed the ones which Mr. Black had carelessly tipped into the sink before he had left the house, and she left the surrounding area looking more sparkling than when she had started. Then she investigated the back door of the house and made sure that it was bolted too in case it had a tendency to blow open. Satisfied that all was tidy in the kitchen, she went to the lovely living-room where she turned on the standard lamp, pulled the curtains across the windows to shut out the storm and sat down at the desk to write her letters, hoping that they would be finished before Mr. Black returned – if he ever did return while the storm raged.

Two hours later, sitting in the glow of lamplight trying desperately to keep her eyes open, Gail was beginning to realize that Mr. Black, wherever he had gone, was not going to return that night. She had written to Phil and she had written to Karl and now she was reading a legend about the sea kelpie of Corryvreckan, the swirling whirlpool between the islands of Scarba and Jura. The description of the kelpie made her think of Karl.

'His flowing locks were auburn bright,
His cheeks were ruddy, his eyes flashed bright.'

It made her wish he was there with her in Stornish House, but when she went on to read that the kelpie enticed a young maid to go with him only to plunge into the whirlpool with her so that she drowned, she decided she'd read enough.

Sleep was calling her and she longed to go to bed. Thoughts of it tantalized her. She hadn't looked upstairs to see how many bedrooms there were, and looking round would be a way of keeping awake and by the time she had finished her tour of the house the owner might be back.

It wasn't until she moved into the hall that she realized it was almost dark. The stairs looked gloomy and it was some time before she could summon sufficient courage to find a switch for the light.

As she went up her feet clattered on the worn wooden stairs which led straight to the upstairs landing. 'Just wide enough to take a coffin,' one of Phil's remarks about staircases, came to her, and she stopped and shuddered. Why did her mind keep running on death and madness? Impatiently she blamed her unusual state of agitation on the book she had been reading plus the storm until she realized that Mr. Gorrie had also mentioned both death and madness in connection with Callum Black.

There were four rooms upstairs. Three bedrooms and a bathroom. Two bedrooms were the same size and the third was smaller. In one of the bigger ones there was a wide double four-poster bed. The posts were heavily carved, but there was no canopy. Apart from the bed there was a chest of drawers on which there was a photograph of an old man. The room was impeccably clean and the wood of the chest and bed shone as if they were frequently polished.

In the other big room there were two single beds and another chest of drawers, and again the same air of cleanliness as if no one ever used it. In the smaller room there was just a single bed and a walk-in cupboard, presumably for clothes, but there as in the other bedrooms there was no visible sign of habitation. That was reserved for the bathroom where the towels had been disturbed, one was actually on the floor, and a man's shaving kit was scattered on the glass shelf under the mirror.

She would sleep in the big double bed if she could find sheets for it, she decided. She had never slept in a four-poster before and it didn't look as if anyone used the room. But when she went back to the room and lifted the bedcover she discovered that there were sheets on it, obviously clean judging by the crisp feel of them. When she looked at the other beds she found they had clean sheets on them too, so it was difficult to deduce which bed was used by Mr. Black. In the end she came to the conclusion that he used the single bed because there were a few books on the bedside table.

Surely he wouldn't object if she went to bed in his house. He must have taken shelter from the storm in someone's house himself, otherwise he would have been back by now, so perhaps he wouldn't mind if she took shelter in his house and slept in one of his beds. There wasn't really anything else she could do, she thought, stifling a yawn.

Having carried her suitcases upstairs she decided that she was too tired for a bath and that a wash would have to do. When she went into the bedroom she peered out of the window before drawing the curtains. There was little to see, but it seemed as if the storm had abated a little. The slates on the roof had stopped rattling and the wind was not blowing so much, although down on the shore the sea still roared and hissed like an angry animal.

Throwing back the covers of the bed, Gail climbed in. It was just as comfortable as she had guessed it would be. She switched off the bedside lamp, wriggled around until she found the right spot in which to curl and was asleep before she could think.

About an hour after Gail had fallen asleep a break appeared in the scurrying clouds and the moon, full and round, peeped out for a few minutes. Its beams glittered uncertainly on the heaving turbulent mass of the sea, struck sparks of light from the scattered wet rocks, gleamed wanly on the wet slates and white walls of the house and glistened eerily on the wet oilskin coat worn by the man who was approaching the house.

The man, who was of medium height and had heavy shoulders, walked with an easy swinging gait as if used to covering long distances. He carried a shepherd's crook in one hand and at his heels a black Labrador retriever not much more than a puppy trailed, damp and miserable.

The man walked up to the back door of the house, turned the knob confidently and pushed. The door did not open. He tried again and this time put his shoulder against the door. It did not budge. The young dog growled softly in its throat and was told in Gaelic to be quiet. The man stared at the door, then shrugged and walked away round the house to the front porch.

Once again he turned the knob of a door and once again the door did not open. Again the dog growled and then began to sniff at the door. The man felt a chill of apprehension raise the hairs on the back of his neck. He put his hand in the pocket of his oilskin coat, pulled out a small torch and flicked it on. Its beam roved over the door and was then flicked off.

'Both doors bolted from the inside, Luran,' the man said softly in English. 'But I'm sure I left both open. We shall have to try the window.'

Going round to the back of the porch, he clicked on the torch and directed its beam at the window. Raising the crook, he used its curved end to smash the window close to the catch which kept it locked.

'An untidy way of breaking and entering, but there's no alternative,' he murmured. 'I've no wish to spend the night out of doors in the condition in which we're in, Luran.'

Again the dog growled. This time the man spoke quietly to it, ordering it to go round and wait by the door. It went, its tail hanging down disconsolately. Then the man put his hand carefully through the hole he had made in the window, released the catch and pushed up the lower part. Heaving himself up, he clambered through the open window and into the porch, knocking down a pot of geraniums on his way. He went at once to the door, unbolted it and let the dog in.

'And now to find out who our unexpected visitor is,' said the man as he opened the door into the house and entered the hallway. The dog followed him gingerly.

The hall light which Gail had forgotten to switch off when she had gone to bed shone down on the polished floor and the slightly askew Persian rug. In the corner the clock ticked benignly. The mail lay where he had left it. All seemed just as it had been when he had gone out early that afternoon except for the light being on.

The man removed the soaking wet tweed hat from his head to reveal jet black hair which was also soaking wet and which fell across his forehead in damp tails. He took a few steps further into the hall, then stood stock still. The dog raised its nose, sniffed and let out a howl.

'So you can smell it too?' murmured the man. 'Perfume. Our guest must be female.'

He closed his eyes momentarily. The faint elusive scent was disturbing. Had Marguerite come back? It would be like her to choose a night like this when the island was lashed by wind and sea. He shook his head impatiently, opened his eyes and went on, his rubber boots squeaking on the linoleum. The idea of Marguerite returning was fantastic. Marguerite belonged to the past. She was dead.

The dog was at his heels when he entered the kitchen and switched on the light. Still growling softly, it slunk across the room to sniff at a chair pushed tidily under the table, then left it to slink across to the electric cooker and sniff around that.

Throwing his hat on to the table and placing the camera he had been carrying beside it, the man shrugged out of his oilskin and flung it over a chair. He sat on another chair and pulled off his boots, then in his stockinged feet he crossed to a cupboard and opened it. He took out a bottle half full of whisky, searched in another cupboard for a glass, took both to the table where he poured a stiff measure of the liquid into the glass. He drank a little of the undiluted spirit, then padded across to the sink to add some water to it. His hand was reaching out to the tap when he noticed that the dishes he had left in the sink had gone and that the sink was clean and shiny. At that point the dog, which had gone out of the kitchen into the hall, let out another hair-raising howl.

The man did not bother to turn the tap but drank the rest of the liquor in one gulp, set the glass down on the draining board and turning slowly walked into the hall.

'What is it, Luran?' he asked the dog.

The animal rolled dark eyes in his direction and looked back up the stairs.

'You think our unexpected guest has gone to bed, do you?' The dog thumped its tail on the floor. 'Then we shall go and search for her together.'

As he walked carefully up the stairs the man felt the spirit he had drunk burning in his empty stomach. It made him feel slightly lightheaded, a condition in which he felt no fear of the unknown. He grinned rather sourly and murmured to himself,

'So it's come to this, Callum. Now you're needing dutch courage to help you face the ghosts of your past!'

He looked into the small bedroom first, flinging open the door and switching on the light. There was no one in the bed. He came out and found the dog hovering around the door to the big front bedroom.

'You'd know which room straight away, of course,' he muttered, and stepped past the animal into the room, his hand going straight to the light switch on the wall. It was down already, which meant that the light had been switched off by someone in the bed. Holding his breath, making no sound with his sock-covered feet, he tiptoed over to the bed and switched on the bedside light. A rosy glow spread over the bed and lit up the golden-coloured

46

hair which was scattered over the pillow and adding a pinkish tint to the delicately moulded oval face, bare white-skinned shoulder, and long slim arm of the woman in bed.

The man's breath came out on a sigh of relief, but the dog, which was looking too, growled in its throat and was kicked gently in the ribs and told to be quiet.

The woman in the bed wasn't Marguerite's ghost. Then who was she? A mermaid swept in from the sea by the storm? Was that a fish tail he could see shaped under the bedclothes?

He shook his head sharply to clear it. The malt whisky had a kick and was playing the devil with his senses. The dog growled unhappily and he patted it absently on the head.

'Shush, Luran. It's Goldilocks herself. But why did she have to choose my bed? In the story she slept in the bed belonging to the smallest bear, and I'm not small by any means.'

He looked around the room. An expensive suitcase of pale grey leather lay flat on a chair and another stood on the floor beside it. He walked over to them and examined the label attached to the handle of one of them. He read,

'Miss G. Collins, c/o Gartbeg, Stornish, Isle of Sorasay.' His mouth tightened grimly. The girl in the bed sighed, muttered something and turned over. He glanced at her. All he could see was a mass of golden hair spilling over the bedclothes which she had hunched around her shoulders.

'How did you get here, Miss G. Collins?' he asked softly. 'And why have you come?'

Just then his eye was caught by two envelopes on the chest of drawers, and still moving silently, he went across to look at them. One was addressed to Mr. P. Collins and the other to Mr. Karl Anders. He noted that the one to P. Collins was care of a hotel in Copenhagen and a puzzled frown creased his forehead. He pushed an impatient hand

47

across his eyes and turned away. The whisky was playing tricks again. He would leave Goldilocks to sleep until morning and sort out the puzzle of her presence when he was less tired. Now he and Luran needed food and sleep.

The dog followed him to the door. Hand on the light switch, he gazed once more at the cloud of spun gold which was the hair of Miss G. Collins and once more the grim expression returned to his face. Then he flicked the light out, closed the door and went downstairs.

In the kitchen he busied himself with feeding the dog and then with preparing some food for himself. But when he was seated at the table he ate little and stared broodingly at the bottle of whisky. Memories which he had thought he had buried decently several years ago came to haunt him. Memories of Marguerite, tall, vivacious, with golden hair and vivid blue eyes. He had brought her to Stornish six years ago this month to meet his grandfather. He had wanted her to see the house on the island which would be his when his grandfather died. He had wanted his grandfather, whose opinion he had valued, to see Marguerite the girl from the city with whom he had fallen in love.

He had left her there for a week while he had returned to the mainland for a conference in Edinburgh. When he had come back Marguerite had gone and so had his cousin Ian. His grandfather had known nothing, could only say that Ian and Marguerite had spent a lot of time together and that one afternoon she had gone out and had not returned. She had left no letter of explanation, only a suitcase full of her clothes. A few weeks later, after he had left Stornish himself, he had received a letter from his grandfather saying that a woman's body had been washed ashore at Portnagour and that he had been to identify it. It had been the remains of Marguerite.

He groaned and pushed the plate of food aside. The dog, which had gone to its bed in a corner of the room, looked up startled.

'It's all right, Luran. Go to sleep.'

Smiling a little, he reached out a hand and picked up the camera. The habit of talking to himself or rather to the dog had increased lately, the result of living alone. After the blow to his hopes of a happy marriage with Marguerite he had immersed himself in his work as a lecturer in Natural History. He had gone on expeditions to various parts of the world and had freelanced as a photographer and writer about wild life. Occasionally he had returned to Stornish to visit his grandfather, but they had never discussed Marguerite. On Callum's side it had been pride which had prevented him from bringing up the subject because he had guessed that his cousin Ian had for once bested him. For Ian, whom he could beat at anything, running or wrestling when they were boys, and whom he had left far behind academically when they had attended school together, had a way with women, an insidious charm inherited from his father who years ago had deserted his mother Catriona. And Ian had stolen Marguerite from him when his back had been turned.

Eventually his work as a naturalist had been recognized and last year he had become a member of the Nature Conservancy Board for Scotland, sitting on a committee concerned solely with the preservation of wild life. His grandfather had died and he had returned to Stornish, making it a base in summer for forays into the outer islands in order to study the wild animals in their natural habitats.

But the island home of his forebears had claimed him more than he had thought it would, and so did its people. He realized that he could not allow years of careful farming and conservation by his grandfather go to waste. Ian had not come back, although the lawyers had found him, and he was aware that the house of Gartbeg and several acres of land surrounding it had been left to him by Adam Black. In his absence Callum had cared for the land and the house and had offered to buy it from his cousin, who had refused to sell. And now Ian had sold his share of the island to the father of the young woman who lay asleep upstairs for far more money than Callum had offered, and the island which generations of Blacks had valued and cared for was divided and open to invasion.

He finished winding the film in the camera, opened the instrument and took out the rolled film. There would be little sleep for him tonight now that his memories had been stirred to life, now that regret stalked his mind. He might as well keep himself occupied by developing the film and perhaps doing a little writing. Leaving the table, he went into the hall and opening a door on his right entered the room which he had converted into a dark-room and closed the door firmly behind him.

Just before she wakened Gail dreamed of Karl. She could see him quite clearly, auburn hair aglow, blue eyes ablaze, as he smiled at her. The image faded as she came awake disturbed by some small noise, but she kept her eyes closed and tried to get back into her dream.

The noise occurred again and she recognized it as the growl of a dog. It was followed by an order in Gaelic spoken by a man and there was the sound of curtain rings rattling on a wooden rod as the curtain was pulled aside. Sunlight, bright and demanding, fell on her closed eyelids making return to her dream impossible. Then the light was blotted out and she opened her eyes quickly, every nerve quivering as she remembered where she was. She looked straight at the man who was about to sit on the end of the bed and whose figure had blotted out the shaft of sunlight.

He sat down and leaned back against the carved post. He looked straight back at her with eyes that were so dark a brown as to be almost black. They were strange eyes, long and narrow and tilted slightly upwards at the outer corners, although their narrowness might have been an illusion caused by the high cheekbones of his lean weath-erbeaten face.

As she stared his gaze wandered downwards from her

eyes to her neck and shoulders and looking down she realized that her flimsy nightdress left rather a lot of her uncovered. Feeling at a definite disadvantage, she pulled the bedclothes up around her and looked up again. He was looking her straight in the eyes again and his face was completely devoid of expression.

Although she had a good idea as to his identity she had to ask, if only to break the silence.

'Who are you?' she asked. 'And what are you doing in here?'

He raised his thick black eyebrows slightly as if he resented her question.

'When in a completely indefensible position always attack first,' he commented quietly. 'You've asked the very question I should be asking. Who are you? And what are you doing in my house?'

Gail blinked. He was not exactly rude, but the impassivity of his manner made his rebuke very effective. She was in the wrong and he had no hesitation in making her feel that way. It was a new sensation for Gail, who had always been able to talk herself out of difficult situations. Added to that she was thrown a little off balance because he was so different from what she had expected. Encouraged by Phil's reaction to the letter and later by the gaps in Mr. Gorrie's description, she had imagined Callum Black to be an older man, slow-speaking, slow-thinking, obstinate perhaps, but countrified and therefore easy for someone like herself to handle. She had imagined he would dress in conventional heavy tweeds and would smoke a pipe.

But the man sitting on the end of the bed watching her while he reached with one hand to tickle the ears of the black Labrador dog which sat on the floor near him was no more than thirty-three or four years of age and there was no sign of grey in his straight black hair. Instead of the heavy tweeds of her imagination he was wearing a turtle-necked sweater and dark pants. He was as inscrutable as the Sphinx, one of the dark people whose history is shrouded in mystery, and looking into his dark opaque

51

eyes Gail found herself suppressing an involuntary shiver.

'I'm Gail Collins,' she said, rushing into speech nervously, afraid that if she didn't answer him immediately he might take dire steps to extract the information from her. 'My father has bought Gartbeg and I've come to get it ready for the holidays. Mr. Gorrie from the shop brought me over yesterday. He couldn't take me to Gartbeg because he hadn't time and he thought I ought to meet you first. You weren't here, so he suggested I waited for you. I waited and waited. I couldn't stay awake any longer and thought that 'perhaps you wouldn't mind if I slept in one of your beds.'

Her explanation made, Gail leaned back against the pillows. It sounded quite clear and logical to her. She couldn't see how he could fail to accept it. But the lack of expression in his eyes intimidated her.

'You chose the wrong bed, Goldilocks,' he remarked drily. As his meaning dawned on Gail a hot blush stained her face and neck. It took her by surprise because she wasn't given to blushing. Forgetting the carefully arranged bedclothes, she sat up suddenly and had to grab them to her as they fell away from her.

'Oh! Is this your bed? I thought ... I assumed that this was a guest room and that the single room was yours,' she stuttered. Then in an attempt to get back her initial advantage she asked, 'You are Mr. Black aren't you? Mr. A. C. Black? You see, you didn't answer my question, so I can't be sure.'

If she had hoped to disconcert him her hope was short-lived. His gaze didn't waver, nor did he move.

'Yes, I'm Callum Black,' he replied calmly. 'You should not have come here and Don Gorrie should have had more sense than to bring you. Strangers aren't welcome on Stornish. I wrote to your father telling him as much. Didn't he receive my letter?'

The direct question accompanied by the direct gaze stumped her. Looking into such dark eyes was like looking into two bottomless wells. They were without reflection. And his mouth, wide and well-shaped, the lower lip slightly fuller than the long upper one, gave nothing away either.

She looked down at the pattern on the bed cover and traced it with one finger. She had a strong desire to tell him he could keep his island to himself, but that would be playing into his hands. She was here because both she and Phil had resented the lofty tone of the letter and were determined to keep what had been bought fairly for a good price. Phil had suggested she should pretend ignorance of the letter, be pleasant but adamant in refusing to give in to Mr. Black's desire to buy Gartbeg and to stay on Stornish until Phil himself arrived to deal with the matter.

So instead of retorting she looked up and smiled.

'What letter? This is the first I've heard of it. I'm sure my father has no intention of selling the place back to you. He's looking forward to staying here for his holidays. When Mr. Sanderson offered the house to him he jumped at the opportunity. He'd been looking for a house far away from the city to which he can escape occasionally.'

She lowered her eyes but managed to watch him surreptitiously from under her eyelashes to see the effect her words had on him. He raised a long-fingered hand tanned brown by exposure to the weather and rubbed it across his eyes rather wearily. When he lowered it she could see quite clearly the dark lines under his eyes caused by sleeplessness.

'Then if your father did not receive my letter how is it you know I offered to buy Gartbeg from him, and how is it you know my initials?' he asked, and the weariness was in his voice.

How could she have been so stupid! How else could she have known he wanted to buy? She searched wildly in her mind for an answer,

'Mr. Gorrie?' she ventured.

'Don't lie again, Goldilocks. You're very bad at it,' he commented. His voice was hard and the curl to the corner of his mouth was unpleasant. Again the hot blood rushed to her face. He was far more astute than she had expected, and already he had made her feel utterly unwanted and unwelcome. She wished she could get up, dress and pack, and go back the way she had come, back to London, back to Karl and his bright smile, away from this dark impassive man. But she had to stay because Phil had asked her to stay put until he came.

Pushing her hair back from her face, she looked directly at him again, the light of battle in her grey eyes.

'All right, my father did receive your letter. It made him furious and if it hadn't been for an engagement in Europe he would have been here now with me. He asked me to come on alone so that you would know he wants the house and intends to use it in spite of your antagonistic attitude. If it isn't too much trouble to you I'd be glad if you would take me to it today. After that, I can assure you, neither I, nor my father when he comes, shall be the slightest bother to you.'

He seemed totally unimpressed by her speech. After surveying her silently for a few moments he murmured,

'That sounds more like the truth.'

Rising slowly to his feet, he walked over to the window to look out, his broad shoulders effectively blocking the light. The dog padded after him and stretching its neck tried to look out too. Gail stared at the man's uncommunicative back, feeling as if she was waiting for him to pass sentence on her. Then to her surprise the sound of a lovely flute-like soprano voice soared up from the lower regions of the house. At the sound Gail caught her lower lip between her teeth. It had never occurred to her that Callum Black might be married.

'Who is singing?' she blurted.

Callum, who had been considering various ways of getting rid of this unwelcome stranger without having to take her over to Gartbeg himself, swung round and

54

walked over to the bed. He stood beside it, hands in his trouser pockets, his glance noting the surprise in the stranger's wide expressive grey eyes. When she wasn't blushing she was very pale, city pale. City bred. His mouth curved derisively. He didn't really need to look for ways to get rid of her and her father. The island would deal with them in its own way, and watching them trying to come to terms with the island might afford him some entertainment. An imp of mischief which was never long dormant within him awoke suddenly, bringing a glint to his dark eyes.

'That is Annie singing,' he said softly and quite truthfully.

'She sings beautifully,' said Gail, equally truthful but trying to placate him by flattery. Then, uncomfortably aware that she had not only kept him out of his bed but probably his wife too, she added apologetically, 'Please tell your wife I'm sorry I chose the wrong bed.'

His quick frown came and went. His eyes narrowed speculatively and the glint of mischief grew stronger. Gail noticed it and felt uneasy.

'Annie is not my wife,' he said. 'But if she finds you in this bed she may have something to say which will be very much to the point and will do your reputation no good at all.'

'Oh!' Gail gasped, and to her annoyance blushed again.

Callum watched the pink spread over her face and throat. The bedclothes had slipped again. As his glance roved further down she noticed and heaved them up round her shoulders. Their eyes met and this time Gail's shone with anger.

'If only you would go I could get up and dress and leave!' she hissed.

He nodded equably.

'I'm going. We'll discuss the matter of Gartbeg while we have breakfast. Do you like porridge?'

'No, I don't. And you don't have to give me any break-

55

fast. I have some food and I can make a meal when I get to Gartbeg. I don't wish to trespass on your hospitality any further, Mr. Black.'

The glint of mischief faded from his eyes. Once more they were blank. She felt he was looking at her yet not seeing her at all.

'Whether you wish to trespass or not has nothing to do with the matter,' he said curtly. 'While you are under my roof, Goldilocks, you'll accept my hospitality and eat my porridge.'

Turning on his heel, he went out of the door and the dog followed. As soon as they had gone Gail threw aside the bedclothes, sprang out of bed, went to the door and closed it just as the unseen Annie began to sing another song. Annie, who was not Mr. Black's wife but who would have something to say if she found Gail in his bed! If she wasn't his wife then who was she? His mistress?

Made thoroughly uncomfortable by her interview, Gail dressed quickly, choosing a pair of gaily patterned flared pants which sat low on her slim hips and topping them with a snug body-hugging short-sleeved scoop-necked knitted sweater. She brushed her hair until it shone and tied a narrow coloured scarf which matched the pants around it to keep it back from her face. She packed the rest of her clothes rapidly, sparing a glance now and then for the scene through the window.

How different from last night! Blue waves danced and glittered beneath a bright sun which shone out of a clear sky. Pale ribbed sand shone wetly beyond the sand-dunes and the long channels of water left by the tide reflected the blue of the sky. It was a lovely morning on which to admire the beauty of sand, sea and rock to the sound of angelic song. Was every morning like this for Mr. Black?

What a disadvantage to be found sleeping in his bed! And to add humiliation to humiliation to be found out in a deliberate lie. What a terrible start to life on this island! She didn't like him, couldn't like him after the way he had treated her.

She snapped the locks on her cases, collected her letters from the chest of drawers and picking up both the suitcases went out of the room. The singing had stopped and she could hear the lazy lilt of Callum Black's voice speaking in Gaelic. He was answered by a woman's laugh.

As she walked down the stairs the singing started again, and when she reached the hall and placed her cases by the front door someone came out of the living-room. Straightening up, Gail turned and braced herself to meet the inquisitive gaze of Annie. Her mouth dropped open in surprise, for Annie was small and stout and was dressed in a flowered wrap-round overall which reached down nearly to her strong, black-laced shoes. Her hair was grey and was snatched back in a bun which perched high on the top of her head. She was just as surprised as Gail and her startled blue eyes stared in turn at Gail's flared pants, low-necked knitted jumper and long smooth hair.

Gail recovered her poise first.

'Good morning,' she said. 'I heard you singing. You have a lovely voice.'

Annie smiled. Her pink cheeks shone and her eyes sparkled.

'Thank you, miss,' she replied in careful English. 'It was a bad storm we were having last night. Ach, I was thinking the very roof was blowing away, but it was only the chicken coop which took to the air and flew across the field.'

'The chicken coop?' asked Gail, mystified.

'Aye. The wind lifted it up and then set it down in another place.'

'Were there hens in it?'

'There were twenty of them. Ach, will you be imagining it! The coop flying across the field and the chickens clucking as they went. It would be enough to frighten the wits out of anyone on a wild night.' She came closer to Gail and added in a quieter voice, 'Would you be telling me now, miss, is it true that all the women are wearing trousers all the time in the cities these days?'

'Many do. It's a popular fashion at present.'

Annie shook her head from side to side.

'Ach, I do not like it. It is always the men who are wearing the trousers here. But I've no time to be standing blethering. I've work to do. Himself is in the kitchen.' She shook her head again. 'It's a strange place for a man to be. Time he had a wife.'

She set off up the stairs nimbly. Gail watched her go with a smile. Annie was not and could not be Callum Black's mistress. She recalled the glint in his eyes as he had implied that Annie would be annoyed to find her in his bed. He had deliberately refrained from explaining who Annie was so that she would draw conclusions about her. Her mouth set determinedly in an expression Phil would have recognized and she walked down the hall to the kitchen.

The room was much more untidy than when she had left it last night. There were a pair of seaboots lying on the floor near the table and an oilskin coat was slung over a chair. Half the big table had been covered by a checked cloth and silver cutlery winked on it. But on the other half of the table there was a bottle half full of liquor, a battered tweed hat and a camera. Looking over in the direction of the sink, she noticed a stack of dirty dishes on the draining board.

The dog came up to her and growled, and Callum Black who was standing by the cooker stirring something in a pan spoke to it sharply. Immediately its tail drooped and it turned as if to slink away. Unused to animals, Gail wasn't sure what she should do, and yet it looked so woe-begone she felt she must make some gesture of friendship so that it wouldn't growl at her any more.

'Hold your fist out to him and let him sniff it,' said Callum. Glancing sideways at him she saw that he had turned from his task and was watching her, his dark fathomless gaze going over her clothes item by item. 'His name is Luran.'

She held out her fist, said, 'Here, Luran,' and the dog turned and eyed her curiously. It came towards her slowly and sniffed at her hand. Then it sat down and looked at her hopefully. Cautiously she put out her hand to pat the top of its head. At once it growled and snapped at her.

'Now you're going too fast for him,' cautioned Callum. 'He isn't trained to make friends with everyone at first meeting. He has to have time to get to know you. Won't you sit down? Which do you prefer, coffee or tea?'

He was very polite, she thought, but it was a cool indifferent politeness, a habit which he could not discard.

'Coffee, please,' she replied, feeling unreasonably disappointed at her unsuccessful attempt to make friends with Luran. 'But you shouldn't be doing that for me. I can cook my own breakfast.'

'Not in my house,' was the not so polite answer. 'I haven't known you long enough.'

She sat down at the table and half-turned to look at him.

'I see. Like master, like dog,' she said, sighing, and felt a flicker of triumph when he sent a sharp glance in her direction. He wasn't as impervious as he made out to be.

'I met Annie in the hall. She was telling me that here in the islands the men wear the trousers and that the kitchen is no place for a man.'

'She must have a very low opinion of both of us, then,' he replied easily as he came to the table and placed a bowl of porridge in front of her.

Gail looked at it with distaste.

'I told you I don't like porridge,' she said.

'You'll like this,' he replied firmly. 'That's real cream in the other bowl. Take a spoonful of porridge and then dip it in the cream. You'll find it very good. You look as if you need feeding up. You're too skinny.'

'Skinny?' The word exploded out of Gail, who prided herself on her fashionably slender figure.

'Yes. Skinny and pale like something found under a stone,' he observed carelessly as he moved back to the cooker for the coffee jug. Gail decided that he wasn't polite after all, and yet she couldn't call him rude. He spoke to her as if she were young and foolish and was in need of advice from someone older. She thought of the horrid pale slimy things she had seen clinging to the underside of stones and her blood boiled. She picked up her spoon, took some porridge, dipped it in the cream and tasted it. It was smooth and delicious. She took another sponful and then another as she realized how very hungry she was.

Callum returned and poured coffee into two big cups. He placed one near to her and then sat down and spooned a little sugar into the other cup and began to stir the liquid. Gail watched the spoon whirl the coffee round and then she said,

'Aren't you having any breakfast?'

'No. Coffee only for me this morning. I don't need to put on weight. When you've finished that, there's bacon and egg.'

'Oh no, I never eat as much as that.'

'You've never had to walk as far as you're going to walk this morning.'

'Are you going to take me to Gartbeg, then?'

'Obviously you can't stay here another night, now that Annie has seen you. But before I take you there I'd like some information from you. Where did your father meet my cousin?'

'I don't know.' Then seeing scepticism in the curl of his mouth she added, 'It's quite true. I don't. Phil came home one day and said he'd bought this house. I didn't believe him at first because he's always had a pipe-dream about buying a house far from the madding crowd. He mentioned your cousin, but he didn't say where he'd met him. Is it important?' -

He raised his hand to his eyes and rubbed them, and again she noticed the dark smudges beneath them. Involuntarily her eyes went to the black coffee and then to the half-full whisky bottle. He noticed her glance and laughed as he got to his feet, the first sign of humour he had shown.

'No, Goldilocks, I'm not suffering from a hangover. I'm just a little short of sleep,' he said, picking up her empty porridge bowl. 'The where and when of your father's meeting is not important in itself, but it strikes me that your father must be remarkably naïve to buy a place he hasn't seen from a man he'd only just met for far more money than the place is worth, that's all.'

She sipped her coffee while he went over to the cooker. His remark about Phil wasn't kind and he was more or less implying that Ian Sanderson was a confidence trickster who had taken her innocent father for a ride. Once again she was tempted to give in, to agree he was right and that neither she nor Phil had any right to stay on Stornish, that Phil should never have brought Gartbeg and should sell it back. But that wasn't what Phil asked her to do.

When Callum came back and set a plate of bacon and egg in front of her she noticed the weariness in his face and her conscience pricked.

'Mr. Black,' she began hesitantly, 'I'm truly sorry I slept in your bed last night. I didn't know....'

He cocked a quizzical eyebrow in her direction as he poured more coffee for himself.

'Are we back to that? You may rest assured it wasn't because you were in bed that I went without sleep. I could have slept in another bed. But the sight of you raised a ghost.'

The morning sun was bright and warm. The wind wasn't howling in the chimney and the rain wasn't slashing at the windows, but her blood ran cold at the mention of ghosts, and she gazed at him with wide troubled eyes.

Callum watched her, noting that her pale face had gone a shade paler. The imp of mischief, fully awake by now, prodded him. He did not care very much for this

61

self-possessed young woman whose outward appearance reminded him of his first love. She was too thin, too fashionable, too quick-tongued, as Marguerite had been, and he did not trust her. He was pleased that having made her blush upstairs he had now made her go pale and he looked for other ways in which he could discomfit her.

'You were reading my book of legends last night, so you'll know by now about the supernatural beings which inhabit the islands, the kelpies, the wee folk, the mer folk and the ghosts of those humans who have met violent deaths. When I saw you in my bed last night I thought for a moment you were a mermaid washed up by a storm and having found a comfortable haven you'd decided to stay and had even locked both back and front doors against me.'

Gail's hand flew to her mouth. She had forgotten the doors. She glanced at him uncertainly. Was he laughing at her? There was no sign of amusement on his face. Was he mad? How did one deal with a madman? She had a vague idea that she had read somewhere that one should always humour them.

'Perhaps you'd have preferred a mermaid,' she said lightly. 'I'm sorry about the doors. The front porch door was blown open by the wind and it knocked one of your plants down.'

'That would be the ghost. She always comes in like that. I suppose she knew you were here and she resented you. She left on a day of storm and often returns on a day of storm,' he murmured, and the sepulchral tone of his voice made her shiver.

'She?' she asked.

He gave her a quick narrowed glance and then stared blankly over her shoulder.

'Yes. Her name is Marguerite and she was here all night.'

'I don't believe you. I didn't see her.'

'No, you wouldn't. But I did.'

Gail gulped her coffee. It was still hot and it burned her throat.

'Are there any other ghosts on the island?' she asked squeakily.

'Yes. Gartbeg has its own particular ghost. Her name is Catriona, and she was my aunt. Marguerite may go there too. I don't know, because I've never stayed there. But she may go to look for Ian.'

'Only a madman would walk about on a day like this.' Mr. Gorrie's observation haunted Gail. Was Callum Black mad? Upstairs she had not thought so, but now, listening to him talk quite seriously about ghosts, she was not sure.

The kitchen door swung open and Annie walked in. She held a pile of sheets in her arms and above their snowy whiteness her rosy face was stern. She tossed the sheets down into a corner and came to the table holding one arm behind her back. She plonked something down on the table in front of Gail. It was a lipstick case.

'I'm thinking this is yours, miss, and I found this lying on the bed.' Disapproval made her voice icy as she brought her arm from behind her back. In her hand she held a foam of blue nylon chiffon which was Gail's night-dress.

Callum's low laughter brought the blood to Gail's cheeks again as she took the nightdress from Annie.

'Thank you, Annie. I must have forgotten it,' she said feebly.

'It was foolish of you to be forgetting, for now I am thinking only one thing,' said Annie. Then turning fiercely on Callum she upbraided him, 'You may laugh, Callum Black, but it's enough to make your grandfather turn over in his grave, and he such a good-living man all his days! I'll wash the sheets again, so if you've finished your breakfast I'll be asking you to leave the kitchen so that I can be getting on with my work and cleaning it for the last time. Then I shall be gone from this house of sin and I'll not be returning.'

'Never, Annie?' asked Callum, mockery spicing his voice as he rose to his feet.

Annie did not answer, but gave him a look which should have seared him. He replied with a grin and picking up the rubber boots from the floor he went out of the room into the hall.

Her lips gripped together grimly, Annie began to clear the dishes from the table with rather a lot of unnecessary clatter. For a moment Gail hesitated thinking to make amends by offering to help, but one glance at the little woman's face decided her against making the offer. Collecting her lipstick and her nightdress, she went after Callum. She found him sitting in the hall chair putting on his rubber boots.

'Can't you explain to her?' she whispered urgently. 'Will she really leave for good?'

His boots on, he stood up. Now that they were side by side she realized that although he wasn't every much taller than she was, not as tall as Phil or Karl, he was so deep-chested and wide-shouldered that he made her feel small.

'Not now,' he replied briefly. 'She isn't in a reasonable mood. There are times when she doesn't approve of my behaviour. You see, although I resemble my grandfather physically my way of life is and has been very different, and she finds that difficult to forgive. But she looked after me when I was a boy and because she was childless I became her child. Now that I've returned to live here she thinks of me as still being her child and believes I'm incapable of doing my own washing and cleaning in my own house. She'll be back tomorrow tut-tutting over the mess I've made and polishing furniture which already has a high gloss.'

He didn't seem mad now. In fact he seemed extremely sane and well-balanced. The kindly understanding humour with which he talked about Annie softened the hardness of his mouth and glowed momentarily in his dark eyes. But even as she looked at him the expression

64

faded and was replaced by a frown.

'It was very careless of you to have your things lying around,' he reprimanded her curtly. 'I warned you she would have something to say if she found you in my bed, and leaving your belongings in the bedroom was almost as bad as being there. But then your whole attitude has been careless and bad-mannered.'

Gail flinched as if he had struck her. No one had ever accused her of being bad-mannered before. He had no right to criticize her! Squaring her shoulders and raising her chin, she glared at him, ready to defend herself.

'And what makes you think that?' she snapped.

'If your father had had the good manners in the first place to answer my letter and inform me that you were coming here I'd have met you off the steamer and taken you to Gartbeg and all this misunderstanding wouldn't have taken place. As it is, you've locked me out of my own house, given me a sleepless night and through your own carelessness acquired a bad reputation.'

Gail took a tight grip on herself and managed to reply in a fairly controlled manner.

'I suppose it's never occurred to you that your letter might be considered abrupt and arrogant, setting us a fine example in bad manners. We certainly didn't get the impression that we'd be met and welcomed with open arms.'

He folded his arms across his chest and raised his eyebrows haughtily.

'All I did was tell your father how I felt about him buying Gartbeg and to offer him a way out. In saying that he would not be welcome I was telling the truth.'

'And you expected us to take your word that selling the house to you was the best course for us to take. Why should we trust you? We'd never met you and knew nothing about you,' retorted Gail, game to the last try.

'Your father was willing to take Ian's word and buy a house he had never seen. Why shouldn't he take mine?' he riposted. 'So you want a reason as to why you're not welcome?' His gaze roved over her and came to rest on her sandals. 'I should have thought the reasons were obvious,' he drawled, and his glance flicked upwards insolently. 'You, and probably your father as well, are totally unsuited to the life of the island.'

There might come a time in the future when she would have to agree with him, but at that moment, facing him in the hallway which smelt of wax polish, hating him for the scolding he had just given her, Gail was fully determined to prove him wrong.

'How can you tell?'

'I can make a few intelligent guesses. You don't know how to farm, you know nothing about animals, domestic or otherwise, and you're afraid of storms. And as far as I can see you don't know how to dress for the place.'

That took her aback. She glanced down at her ribbed top and brightly coloured pants.

'What's wrong with my clothes?' she countered.

'Haven't you anything tougher? You won't get far walking in those shoes this morning.'

'Do I have to walk? Haven't you a car?'

His smile was superior and mocking.

'No, I haven't. I find I can manage very well without one. I have only a tractor and this morning Davie is using it.'

'Davie?' she queried.

'Annie's husband, Davie Rankin. He farms part of the island.'

'But if you haven't a car how do you go anywhere?'

'I walk. The distances aren't great on Stornish. Or I go by boat and on Sorasay I use the bus. Do you still want to go to Gartbeg?'

Her hair shimmered silkily as she tossed her head and her grey eyes sparked defiance.

'Of course I want to go there. But how shall I take my suitcases? They're quite heavy.'

He looked at them. This slim slip of a girl was difficult to put off. For all she was so skinny and pale she had

66

spirit. But another idea had come to him.

'We'll leave them here, then if you don't like the place we won't have to bring them back.'

Gail's breath hissed between her teeth as she drew it in. Her patience was wearing very thin.

'And if I don't like the place what shall I do?'

'I'll make sure you return here in good time to catch Hector McVey, the postman. He'll be here about two o'clock with the mail the steamer brought yesterday and he'll take you back to Portnagour. You can stay in the hotel there until there's a steamer returning to Oban which should be on Thursday.'

Gail had no answer ready. His smile told her more than anything else that for her to leave Stornish this afternoon would give him the greatest pleasure. For a few seconds they stared at each other warily, Gail puzzled and a little hurt by his obvious dislike of her, Callum amused by her sudden speechlessness.

'Well, Goldilocks,' he prodded, 'are you ready to start walking?'

She nodded, and he glanced at her feet again. 'Then I shall go and find some boots for you. The ground will be muddy in parts. While I'm looking perhaps you can find a tougher pair of pants to wear, and a sweater. The sunshine isn't as warm as it looks and the wind is still strong.'

CHAPTER THREE

THAT walk across the island of Stornish was an experience which Gail was never to forget. By the time Callum reappeared with a pair of wellington boots, one size too big for her, and a pair of woollen socks to wear inside them, she had changed into denim jeans and a long-sleeved turtle-necked cotton sweater and had pulled on a bright red poncho. Her host wore a rather battered windcheater over his sweater and carried a shepherd's crook in his hand. Luran the dog was at his heels. Callum waited silently while she put on socks and boots and when she was ready motioned to her to follow him through the front door.

As soon as she stepped outside Gail was struck by the clarity and freshness of the air and by the brilliant colour of grass and sky and sea. Beyond the sand-dunes she could see the tide lapping greedily at the pale sand. Far away the blue line of the horizon divided the deep greenish blue of the water from the paler cloud-streaked sky. Between Stornish and that line there was nothing, not even a distant island or a boat.

But she was not allowed to linger long. Callum ordered her curtly to follow him and they walked round the side of the tall house through the farmyard. A group of hens, objecting to the presence of Luran, ran squawking before them. Passing the end of the big barn, Callum climbed the rough stone wall which protected the farmyard and dropped down into a field in which shaggy, horned Highland cattle were grazing. Luran also disappeared over the wall.

Eyeing the cattle warily and gathering that she wasn't going to receive any help in getting over the wall, Gail searched for footholds in the loosely-piled grey stones, found them and managed to get into a sitting position on

68

top of the wall. Callum was already striding away without bothering to wait and see if she made it. Looking down, she discovered that the field was lower than the farmyard. She tried to turn in order to climb down backwards, using footholds as she had done to climb up, but it wasn't as easy as she had anticipated. Her feet slipped and she fell taking with her one of the stones from the top of the wall. In falling she landed awkwardly on her feet, her left ankle twisted painfully and she sat down. She had just gathered herself together and was able to set off after Callum when she realized he had turned and was shouting to her. She paused and listened.

'Put it back!' he called, and pointed with his crook.

She looked round her and then called back, 'Put what back?'

'The stone you knocked off.'

She was tempted to refuse and shout back, 'Put it back yourself', but he was coming towards her and the irritable expression on his face warned her to be careful. She bent down and lifted the stone, which was quite heavy, walked to the wall, heaved it up into the place from which it had fallen. It balanced precariously for a second and then fell off again into the farmyard. Gail stood quite still blinking stupidly at the wall and waited.

'There's an unwritten law in this ancient land which says that if you knock a stone off a drystone dyke you should always stop and replace it,' said Callum from behind her. 'But not on the other side of the wall, Goldilocks.'

'I'm sorry,' she muttered, and moved forward in order to climb the wall back into the farmyard. The curved end of the crook was hooked round one of her arms and she was pulled back gently but inexorably.

'You can replace it when we return,' said Callum firmly. It seemed he had no doubt that she would be returning this way. 'We must hurry now,' he added, 'or we'll not be back here in time to catch Hector MacVey.'

Gail was becoming tired of his quiet authoritative manner. He seemed to think he could arrange life the way he wanted it without reference to anyone else.

'And that would mean I should have to stay another night in your house, and you wouldn't like that, would you, Mr. Black,' she retorted sweetly, as she unhooked her arm from the crook handle.

His smile had a saturnine quality.

'It's you who would not be liking it,' he replied smoothly, but there was a threat underlying the smoothness. 'Now be careful crossing this field. It's a wee bit marshy after the storm. If you follow me you should be all right.'

He set off again. Conscious that her ankle was painful, Gail began to walk after him. But she was too busy keeping an eye on the nearest Highland bullock to follow directly in his footsteps and before she knew what had happened she was ankle-deep in mud and the bullock was coming straight for her.

Red rag to a bull. That was what she was in her flaming scarlet poncho which she had admired so much and had bought it for its clear uncompromising colour. If only she'd had the sense to wear something green and camouflaging! The trouble was she couldn't move fast because of the mud.

Looking round, wildly aware that the twin horns were coming closer, she noticed what appeared to be a firm piece of ground, and jumped. Her ankle twisted again and she sat down in the marshy grass. Her action surprised the bullock, who stopped advancing and stood and glared at her. Making the most of the opportunity, Gail struggled to her feet and hobbled as fast as she could after Callum, who by now had reached another stone wall and was waiting for her.

As she approached him, mud-spattered and breathless, he raised his eyebrows in surprise.

'What happened?' he asked politely, and she had an uneasy feeling that his bland politeness was a disguise for

70

malicious amusement because there was that glint in his dark eyes.

'I thought the bull was going to attack me,' she gasped, 'and I jumped and fell on some marshy ground. Bulls go for anything red, don't they?'

'Do they?' he asked mockingly. 'That wasn't a bull, it was a heifer – a warm friendly animal who was just curious and wanted to look at you more closely. Do you want to go on or would you like to go back to the house, change your clothes and wait for Hector?'

Dark and somehow devilish and less like a shepherd than anyone she had ever seen, he stood leaning on his crook watching her. Gail experienced a strong primitive urge to pummel him with both fists. Shaken by the violent emotion which she had always considered herself too civilized to experience, she dug down deep into her self-possession and with a semblance of calm replied,

'No, I don't want to change my clothes and wait for Hector. I want to go to Gartbeg and nothing is going to put me off going there. Nothing, do you understand, Mr. Black?'

He inclined his head politely, but the glint was still there.

'I understand, Goldilocks. Can you manage this wall or would you like assistance?'

'I can manage, thank you,' she said haughtily. And she did manage, although she was thankful this time that he waited on the other side until she was over.

They were now in a small plantation of young trees which were planted on the side of the rocky backbone of the island. As they walked up a well-defined path between the rows of trees Gail was pleased that she could recognize some of them even if she didn't know the difference between a bullock and a heifer. They included birch, aspen and rowan, as well as some unexpected species such as beech and elder. In her interest she forgot her antipathy to Callum and hurried to catch up with him to ask about the trees.

71

He seemed surprised by her interest but slowed down his fast pace to answer her, explaining that he was endeavouring to encourage the growth of trees on the island because he believed it had once been afforested. The dry-stone dykes by which the trees were protected saved them from demolition while they were small by weather or animals, and in its turn the resulting woodland would restore the ecological balance of the island by providing a habitat for wild life which had disappeared with the original forest.

'This island has the best of almost all worlds,' he observed as he warmed to his theme. 'It has good soil, sand-dunes, cliffs and rocky beaches plus a small freshwater loch. All that's missing is woodland, and I feel it's my responsibility to provide that. I own this land, or nearly all of it,' he corrected with a certain dryness in his voice, 'and must care for it wisely, remembering always that the natural world was not made for man alone but that we were given the intellectual superiority to respect it and look after it.'

His clearly expressed attitude showed a different aspect of him, and she began to understand a little why he didn't want strangers from the city living on Stornish.

'Is that why you want to buy Gartbeg back from my father? You think that we might not care for the land as well as you would like?'

'That is one of the reasons,' he admitted. 'There is another more personal one.'

'But we aren't destructive,' she defended. 'And Karl and I have often discussed the need for the community as a whole to take more interest in preserving wild life and in conserving the countryside.'

'Have you? And what other contribution have you made besides discussion? What practical action have you taken? Your reaction first to Luran and then to the heifer hardly convinces me that you believe as I do that we are fellow organisms with other living things and that we should accept them as an essential part of the world we live in.'

Gail was silent. It was true she had done nothing to contribute to the preservation of the natural world other than discuss it with Karl and she possessed no knowledge at all about animals. But she could learn.

They had reached the top of the ridge and she could see the long arm of the sea which separated the two islands. It was edged by brown mud and saltmarsh behind which fields planted with grain rose gradually up to the plantation. Away in the distance she could see a cluster of cottages around a small bay. And nearer at hand there was a single white house close to the road which ran along the coast.

Keeping to the stone dyke which protected the plantation from the moorland which covered the rest of the ridge, they began to descend.

'Who is Karl?' asked Callum abruptly.

'A friend,' she replied shortly, and wondered what Karl would think of her now as she hobbled windblown and breathless after the confident Mr. Black.

'Does he live in London?'

'Yes. He's a poet ... and the co-editor of a magazine which publishes poetry and comments by new young writers.'

'He talks about preserving nature and he lives in the city.'

'Oh yes. He's very keen on the idea of everyone returning to live close to nature. He's a great believer in Thoreau's philosophy.'

'Ha!' Callum's crack of laughter was wholly sarcastic. 'I wonder if he's ever "tramped eight or ten miles through deepest snow to keep an appointment with a beech tree or a yellow birch", like Thoreau.'

Gail recognized one of Karl's favourite quotations, but she was sure that Karl had never done such a thing, and somehow, now that she was close to nature herself, horribly aware that her ankle was swelling as she walked through a plantation of young trees to keep an appointment with a house, she could not imagine Karl ever being here or taking an interest in the natural world around him.

'No, I don't think he has. But does he have to prove he's interested?'

'I think so. Otherwise how can he possibly know what he's talking about?'

They had reached the end of the plantation and there was another wall to be climbed. Callum was over it in a couple of lithe movements and this time when Gail was over he steadied her with a hand on her arm as she slid to earth.

They were in a field in which long feathery ears of barley waved in the wind. The field sloped down the road. Beyond the road was the saltmarsh and beyond that was the muddy shore of the inlet of the sea. And on the other side of the water were the shores and fields of Sorasay lifting to heather-brown moorland.

As she limped after Callum along the edge of the field, Gail breathed in deeply, smelling the damp earth, the salty sea and the scents of wild flowers. Over the water white birds with black topped heads too small for seagulls dipped and dived and over the field smaller brown birds which she couldn't name either, swooped and twittered busily. Here on this sea-girdled island with sunlight glinting on water and mud and with the wind shaking the green barley it was difficult to believe that that other world with which she was so familiar existed.

When they reached the road they turned left and walked towards the lone white house. At last she was near Gartbeg. Feeling as if she was at the end of some great pilgrimage, Gail tried to hurry, but her ankle was so sore that it was becoming increasingly difficult for her to put her whole foot on the ground. Not wanting to admit to the superior Mr. Black that she was in pain, she gritted her teeth and hobbled along, watching him forge ahead with his easy swinging walk. He didn't seem to mind that she wasn't with him and presumably thought that she couldn't keep up because she wasn't used to walking. And she wasn't, thought Gail with a rueful grin. Not across hills and fields.

By the time she reached the wall which surrounded the garden in which the house was situated Callum had been up to the front door, had unlocked it and had looked into the house to make sure everything was normal. He had then returned to the gate.

He watched Gail approach, noting that the exercise had brought colour to her face and had dishevelled her hair. The bandbox appearance had been destroyed by the energetic walk, he thought with a private grin. Then he noticed the limp. A blister on her heel, perhaps, caused by the too-big boots. Not an uncommon complaint when one wasn't used to walking.

'Have you a front door key?' he asked.

'Yes, I have.' She put her hand into the pocket of her pants and brought it out, thankful that she had had the presence of mind to bring it.

'Good. I have one too. But I just wondered whether Ian had thought to provide you with one. Annie has been coming regularly during the past six years to keep the place clean and aired and my grandfather kept the roof repaired, but I see that some slates are missing after the storm. Of course, there have been people staying in it from time to time because he used to let it during the summer to families wanting a quiet holiday. Shall we go in?'

Again he was scrupulously polite. He motioned to her to lead the way up the path and she went ahead, very conscious of him pacing slowly behind her as she limped.

When she reached the house she felt a stab of disappointment. It was very ordinary, a simple white bungalow, a square box with a slate roof and plain windows. It had none of the glamour of Callum Black's tall highgabled house which had seemed to hunch its shoulders against the storm the previous night. Nor had it any of the quaint charm of the grey stone houses with their dormer windows which she had noticed on Sorasay. It was a plain twentieth-century bungalow which someone had attempted to soften by planting shrubs around it.

An ugly porch had been built over the front door. The same key for the porch door fitted the glass-fronted house door. She opened it and stepped into the narrow hall. The plain brown linoleum was familiar and was polished to a high gloss. On one wall of the hall there was an old fashioned hat and umbrella stand. Two doors led off the hall, one into a sitting-room furnished with an unobtrusive three-piece suite and the other into a small bedroom furnished with a double bed and a chest of drawers.

A few steps further took Gail straight into the kitchen, which was dark and narrow. From the kitchen another door led into a living-room furnished with a big table, six chairs and a sideboard. As she came out of the room she collided with Callum, who was close behind her.

Trying to hide her disappointment at the size and appearance of the house, she asked,

'Where is the bathroom?'

'This way,' he replied, and going back the way they had come he led her into a narrow passage which branched off the hallway. Down the passage was a bathroom and two more bedrooms.

Standing rather disconsolately in the last bedroom looking round at its pink washed walls and huge furniture which left little space for movement, Gail murmured plaintively.

'It isn't very big, and it's rather ugly.'

Hands in his trouser pockets, Callum leaned a shoulder against the door-jamb. As he had hoped, the small unpretentious house did not appeal to her. She would tell her father she did not like it and he would be glad to sell it and the land that went with it, and once again the whole island would be in the possession of a Black. Then there flashed across his memory a sudden vivid image of his Aunt Catriona, darkly, tragically beautiful, who had been

76

glad to come back to Stornish and hide in this house when life had dealt her an unpleasant blow.

'For some it has been a roof over their heads in time of need. The appearance and size of a house are not important. It's the people who live in it that matter,' he said, rebuking her for her implied criticism.

She flashed a surprised glance in his direction, but he was turning away into the passage. Biting her lower lip against the pain in her ankle, she limped after him, following him into the sitting-room whose window framed a lovely view of sea and shore. Hands on his hips, Callum stood and stared at the view in silence and Gail stood beside him staring too, marvelling once again at the colours.

'Before we go back to Stornish House you'd better take your boot off and we'll see what's making you limp. A blister can be rubbed raw if it doesn't receive attention,' said Callum practically.

Reacting once again to his calm assumption that she wouldn't be staying on Stornish if he could help it, Gail replied defiantly,

'I'm not going back to Stornish House. I'm staying here.'

'But you don't like the house. You've just said so;' he argued.

'And you've just observed that the appearance and size of a house don't matter, it's the people who live in it that matter, and I agree with you. So I'm staying. My father told me to stay here until he arrives.'

He couldn't help admiring how neatly she had turned the tables on him, using his own words. Whatever had led him to speak his thought aloud only to have it used against him by this tall thin girl whose only claims to beauty as far as he was concerned were a mass of heavy hair which glinted and glowed in the sunlight and a pair of wide set grey eyes which looked at him directly and without any suggestion of coyness? It was the expression in her eyes and the determined tilt to her chin which

77

made him murmur suggestively,

'I'm thinking you don't always obey your father, do you?'

'No.' It was out, spoken instinctively before she had time to consider. Quickly she tried to retreat, 'But in this case . . .'

'In this case it suits you to use him as a prop against me,' he put in swiftly. Then his sense of humour got the better of him and he began to smile and then to laugh.

Gail, perturbed by the way he could follow her reasoning, stared at him. The thought that he might be mad flickered to life again. But his laughter was so genuine and infectious that she found herself joining in, laughing at the way they had been sparring with each other all morning. And it seemed as if joy exploded between them there in that dull little sitting-room.

'Far be it for me to encourage you to disobey your father's wishes,' said Callum when he had stopped laughing. 'And since he bought the place my dealing should be with him rather than with you. You may stay and wait for him. In fact I'm thinking you have no alternative but to stay for a few days,' he added seriously, his glance going to her left leg. 'It's time you sat down and took off that boot.'

Knocked off balance by his change of attitude, Gail sat down obediently, glad to take the weight off her ankle, and tried to take off the boot.

'It's no use,' she muttered. 'My ankle is swollen. I think I must have sprained it when I fell off the wall. I felt it give way under me, and when I tried to get away from the bull . . . I mean the heifer, I twisted it again. It's always been rather weak.'

He squatted in front of her and tried to ease off the boot.

'Why didn't you tell me?' he demanded angrily.

'I thought you'd make me go back to your house and that I might never get here. I thought you'd make me go back with Hector MacVey.'

'You're damned right, I would have done,' he grated, as he worked at the boot. 'Are you always so wilful? Your father can't have spanked you enough when you were young. For all we know, you may have damaged your ankle permanently.'

Gail bit her lip and suppressed an urgent desire to weep. It was true that Phil had never raised a hand in punishment, but she had never considered herself wilful, only determined.

'Ouch!' she cried suddenly. 'It's no use, Mr. Black. The boot isn't going to come off.'

He looked up, noticed her blanched cheeks, her bitten lip, the unshed tears in her eyes, and altered course immediately.

'Why so formal?' he challenged. 'My name is Callum, Goldilocks.' That took her mind off the pain, as he hoped it would.

'Well, mine isn't Goldilocks,' she snapped. 'It's Gail...'

'Not knowing what the "G" stood for I had to make up a name. I used the most appropriate, having found you sleeping in my bed. That's the fourth time you've blushed this morning—an unusual accomplishment in a young woman today.'

'What do you know about young women, living here on an island miles away from anywhere?'

'Ah, you'd be surprised at what I know. I'm neither a hermit nor a monk, and I don't stay on Stornish all the time. Also there are some young women living on the islands. They don't all go away from home,' he replied. He plunged a hand into one of his trouser pockets and pulled out a large clasp knife and opened a big shining blade. 'I'll have to cut the boot off,' he said. 'Now keep still.'

Gazing down at the top of his head, Gail tried hard not to move her leg.

'Who farms the island when you're not here?' she asked.

'Davie Rankin, Dougie Lean, Hugie McCaig and his daughter.'

'Daughter?' echoed Gail.

'Yes, Eileen is a shepherdess. She has a grand way with lambs. I expect you'll be seeing her. She lives in the house on the brae overlooking Stornish harbour.'

He was slitting the boot open downwards from top to bottom. When it was open he pulled it gently off her foot and threw it to one side.

'And that's the end of Marguerite's boots,' he muttered, and began to peel the woollen sock from her foot.

'Who was Marguerite?' asked Gail. The sight of her pale swollen ankle between his rough tanned hands made her feel strangely shaky.

'A woman,' he said abruptly, obviously reluctant to answer.

'I guessed that,' she replied tartly. 'Did she die violently?'

'I think she did. She disappeared from Stornish one day. It was about this time of the year and there was a bad storm.' He stopped and she could tell by the grim set of his mouth that he wasn't going to tell her any more.

Marguerite, a ghost who haunted Stornish House and might possibly haunt Gartbeg in search of the missing Ian. Had she been the cause of trouble between the cousins? Had she roused the bad wild blood of the Blacks at which Mrs. Mills had hinted? 'Black by name and Black by nature.' Looking at Mr. Black's lean hawklike face and opaque dark eyes it wasn't hard to imagine the badness and the wildness. And yet there he was squatting before her, handling her swollen ankle gently and looking very concerned about it.

He released her ankle and stood up, closing the clasp knife. 'Your ankle hasn't finished swelling,' he commented impersonally. 'You should rest it. Stand up, put your weight on your other foot, hold on to me and I'll help you to hop over to the couch. You can lie there and watch the tide go out and the light change on the moors.'

She stood up, holding her left foot off the ground. He put an arm round her waist and she put a hand on his shoulder. They moved forward together. One, two hops. The couch seemed a long way away. With an impatient exclamation Callum swept her up into his arms, carried her across the room and set her down on the couch.

'You didn't have to do that,' gasped Gail breathlessly, shaken out of her self-possession. 'I could have hopped.'

He stared down at her with unreflecting dark eyes.

'Skin and bones,' he scoffed. 'The porridge hasn't made any difference to your weight. Of course you could have hopped, but I wanted to make you blush again. Now listen to me, Goldilocks, and don't be arguing with me. You'll stay here and you won't move. I'm going back to Stornish House to fetch your cases and your box of food and an elastic bandage. No more wilfulness on your part or that ankle is not going to get better quickly. I'll leave Luran with you for company and I'll instruct him to snarl at you if you dare to get up and walk about.'

Before she could find breath to object he had left the room and she heard him calling the dog which he had left outside the house. When he returned to the room Luran was at his heels, his tail high wagging with delight at being with his master again. But the dog's delight didn't last long, because Callum ordered him to sit down beside the couch and to stay, which he did with such a mournful expression in his eyes that Gail could not help feeling sympathetic towards him.

'Never mind, Luran. I've had my orders too,' she commiserated, and the dog looked at her hopefully.

'And don't you forget them,' threatened Callum.

'What would you do if I didn't stay put?' she retorted with a flash of her independent spirit.

'I have many methods of punishment passed down to me by my not very pleasant ancestors,' he replied silkily. 'So don't try to bend me too far. I'll leave you now.'

He went from the room and she heard the front door

close behind him. The house was silent, impersonal, hugging the secrets of its past close to it. Gail lay and looked out at the few woolly white clouds which were chasing each other across the sky above the mulberry-coloured moors of Sorasay. As they hovered the moor changed colour, becoming deep purple in patches and then paling to mulberry when they had passed. The water of the strait was sometimes smooth like azure-tinted satin, sometimes dark and ruffled.

After a while Luran, satisfied that she wasn't going to move, lay down with his front legs stretched before him. He laid his head on them and snoozed. Gail glanced at him and smiled to herself. There had been no need for Callum to leave the dog. After having been told in no uncertain manner that she would be punished if she attempted to walk about she had no intention of disobeying. All the same, she was rather surprised at her own obedience and could only attribute it to the slight fear she had of the incalculable Mr. Black.

Yet she had no inclination to move. The walk had tired her and the strange events of the morning had given her plenty to think about. Now that she was at Gartbeg she had no option but to stay until her ankle was better. She grimaced at the dull room with its pale cream walls, overstuffed furniture, shiny glass-fronted cabinet and highly polished occasional tables. It was easy to recognize Annie's handiwork, but the room was very different from that other room where she had sat last night and had waited for the owner of Stornish to return.

Was it only last night that she had waited for him? She had experienced such an emotional upheaval during that time that it seemed longer. Callum's various attempts to put her off staying on Stornish, his cool assumption that she was unsuited to the island, had only increased her desire to defy him and to stay. And where had that defiance landed her? Here on a hard couch which seemed to be springless, lying with a sprained ankle in a miserable silent house.

The house was terrible. It had no character. Her father wouldn't like it she was sure. Where would he put everything? Knowing the disaster he made of any room he entered, she knew he would not have enough space here. Unless it was possible to have some alterations made to it. But then there was the question of land. They couldn't possibly farm it as it had been farmed for generations. Unless they could sell the land only back to Mr. Black.

Although the two alternatives kept presenting themselves as a way of defying Callum Black further she pushed them away, telling herself that the place was too remote. Why, even Callum had admitted that he didn't live on Stornish all the time? Where did he live then? She would ask him when he returned. She would also have liked to ask him more about Marguerite, but guessed she wouldn't get many answers from him. When he had talked of Marguerite's ghost that morning she had received the impression that the woman had been important to him at some time in his life. Had he been in love with her? And why had she disappeared? And where did Ian Sanderson come into the story?

It was difficult to imagine Callum in love. He seemed so self-contained and so very suited to living alone on an island where self-sufficiency and inner resources would be a must. She tried to imagine Karl living in the same circumstances and couldn't. Karl had to have people around him all the time, he had to have an audience, and she didn't think that he would be satisfied with having only a dog for company and with having only the sea, the moors or the trees in the plantation as an audience, for all his much-vaunted idea about everyone returning to live close to nature. As Phil had said, it would be interesting to see how he reacted when he came to stay at Gartbeg.

Yet even though Callum had humiliated her and had made fun of her because she was from the city, he had cooked her breakfast and had shown concern for her ankle, and she could never imagine Karl doing either. He expected her to be able to take care of herself. But she sup-

83

posed that Callum had merely regarded her as a fellow living organism to whom he owed some responsibility. Gail's mouth twitched humorously as she recalled his explanation of his philosophy of life. That was all she was, a fellow living organism no different from Luran or the heifer in the field. She would tell him so when he returned and they would laugh as they had laughed earlier when they had shared an unexpected moment of gaiety.

Gail frowned. In the moment of laughter she had felt very close to him. They had needed no words to explain why they were both laughing. It had been as if their minds had communicated without the help of words; as if their battle of wills and wits had been but a smoke-screen behind which they had both been hiding an awareness of each other which was alarming on such short acquaintance. And close on the memory of the laughter came two other memories of physical contact—the touch of his hands on her foot and the feel of his arms around her as he had carried her to the couch.

She wrenched her thoughts away from Callum and tried to think of Karl again and what they would do together when he came. But all she could think of was how inadequate he would have been today when faced with her swollen ankle.

So the next hour passed for Gail in random and often uncomfortable thought, while Callum, striding back through the plantation of small trees, also thought back over the morning's events. His efforts to frighten Miss G. Collins away from Stornish hadn't worked. Possibly he hadn't been convincing enough, although she had seemed genuinely frightened at the thought of ghosts visiting Gartbeg. The walk through the field of cattle had recoiled on him because it was there she had hurt her ankle. The appearance of the house might have done the trick, but he'd been so annoyed at what he had considered to be a piece of snobbish criticism on her part that he'd been betrayed into saying what he really felt, and she had been quick to pick him up on that.

He smiled to himself. For a skinny city-bred girl she had shown a great deal of spirit when discovered in a very awkward situation in his bed and later had revealed a bred-in-the-bone endurance when in pain. When she had laughed with him he had wished . . . what had he wished? That'd he'd been younger, less marked by the bitter experience of Marguerite? That he wasn't so committed to his present way of life? And when he had lifted her in his arms. . . . Callum's smile faded as he snatched his thoughts back from the direction they were taking.

'Watch it, Callum,' he warned himself. 'That way lies disaster.' He looked round absent-mindedly for the dog and then remembered that he had left it at Gartbeg. He climbed over the wall into his farmyard, replaced the fallen stone and walked on to the house.

He wouldn't go back to Gartbeg, he decided rather grimly. He would send Annie over with Davie. Annie could look after Gail's ankle and help in any other way. That was the best plan. From now on it would be better for his peace of mind if he left Miss G. Collins severely alone and dealt only with her father, because there was really no room for someone like her in his life.

Gail had been at Gartbeg a week and a day before she was able to go walking very far. The swelling of her ankle was down, but she was still wearing an elastic bandage for support. During those eight days Annie had visited her regularly, but she had seen nothing of Callum. She had felt almost as disappointed as Luran had been when instead of his master Annie and her husband had arrived in their old Morris car with her suitcase and her box of food and some books which Callum had provided for her entertainment. But she managed to stifle the unexpected feeling and had told herself he would call again if only out of politeness. So, accepting Annie's explanation that 'himself' had been too busy to return, she was relieved to find the little woman was no longer shocked and critical, and assumed that Callum had explained why there had been a strange woman in his bed the night of the storm.

Annie, who liked nothing better than someone maimed or helpless over whom she could fuss, had sent Luran back with her husband, had made tea and sandwiches for Gail's belated lunch, and then singing at the top of her voice she had bustled about making up the bed in the front bedroom, baking scones and scotch pancakes, and finishing off her visit with the preparation of high tea. Telling Gail she would be back the next morning to help her, she had departed to walk back to her own cottage in the small village.

Callum Black had not come the next day out of politeness, nor had he come any other day, and Annie eventually told Gail that he had gone away for ten days to the Outer Isles.

'He's gone with a friend of his who has a sailing yacht he keeps at Tobermory. They've gone bird-watching, I shouldn't wonder. He's very knowledgeable about wild animals and birds and he's on some committee to do with the preservation of wild life in Scotland. That is why he must be spending some of his time in Edinburgh. Ach, the hours he's after watching the grey seals and the birds which visit the rocks in Aird's Bay at the end of the island. That's where he was the day of the storm and he had to take shelter, which is why he was late returning that night. Have you never heard him talking on the radio nor seen one of his films on the television?'

Gail had to admit that she hadn't, and after that Annie went into a long discourse on what she had been missing.

The only other caller she had during that time of resting her ankle was Mr. Gorrie, who came in his travelling shop after having been told to call by Annie. After a brief preliminary knock he had walked into the house and then into the sitting-room where Gail was still resting her ankle and watching the sea and the moors.

'I'm hearing that you and Callum finally met,' he said, his brown eyes twinkling. 'Annie is full of the story and it'll be told from one end of Sorasay to the next, another legend to be added to those told about the Black family of Stornish.'

Startled by this piece of information, Gail asked,

'What form will the new legend take?'

'All the legends are based on the truth, and this one will be no different. It will be telling of a stormy night and of a young woman with yellow hair who was swept ashore on Stornish and who found shelter in the bed of the owner of the island while he was away from his house. It will also be telling of his surprise at finding himself locked out of his own house when he returned,' chuckled Mr. Gorrie.

Gail could not help going pink, but silently she reviled Callum Black for telling Annie too much of the truth. He must have done so in order to make a laughing stock of her and so drive her away from the place. Well, it would take more than a legend to make her go when she didn't want to go. She managed a feeble smile and said to Mr. Gorrie,

'I didn't make a very good start, did I?'

'Ach, do not be worrying about that,' he comforted. 'There are always tales told about strangers coming to the islands. Some are more fanciful than others depending on the age, sex and appearance of the newcomer. It isn't often we see anyone like yourself hereabouts, so there's bound to be interest taken in you. I hope you won't be minding? It's meant kindly, miss.'

He looked so anxious that she hastened to reassure him that she didn't mind being talked about, although she thought privately that any tale Callum Black told about her would not be meant kindly since he wanted to be rid of her.

'Are there any tales told about another young woman who came to stay on Stornish once? Someone called Marguerite?'

To her surprise Mr. Gorrie's usually florid face lost a little colour and he sat down plump on one of the hard chairs.

'And who was after telling you about her? Annie Rankin?'

'No. Mr. Black mentioned her. He said that there is the ghost of a woman called Marguerite on Stornish, and I thought you might be able to tell me something about her.'

Mr. Gorrie's mouth fell open and his brown eyes went round as he went even paler. Then giving himself a shake he straightened his spectacles unnecessarily and tried to recover a little of his former ebullience.

'Ach, the mischievous scheming devil! That's Callum for you. Wasn't I after warning you he wouldn't be pleased at your coming? That was his way of showing he didn't welcome you. He would be trying to frighten you with a ghost story. I've known him tell a tale at a *ceilidh* and the shivers have been going up and down my spine. He's a grand story-teller, but do not be believing in his ghost, miss.'

'I'll try not to, although he seemed very sure that he'd seen her ghost that night,' said Gail. 'There was a woman called Marguerite, wasn't there?'

'Aye.' Mr. Gorrie looked troubled. 'Callum brought her here. Then he went away for a week and she disappeared. Old Adam didn't like her and when she disappeared he made no effort to find out where she'd gone.'

'But didn't Callum wonder where she was when he returned? Didn't he search for her? Didn't he inform the police?'

'You are knowing who the policeman is on Sorasay?' he asked, looking more troubled than ever.

Gail shook her head.

'I am,' he said almost sadly. 'I'm policeman, mayor and shopkeeper. It's common enough in the islands for one man to hold many positions. I know I should have made inquiries and there were many times I wanted to ask Callum about the young woman in the days after his return, but sometimes when you speak to him and he doesn't like what you're saying he has a way of looking at you as if you aren't there. When he does that my courage fades. So I never asked him and then he went away.'

'Couldn't you have asked his grandfather?'

Mr. Gorrie shook his head.

'You'll be finding this difficult to believe, miss, coming as you do from the city where they have all those clever men from Scotland Yard to ask questions and solve mysteries, but no one ever questioned old Adam. He was a law unto himself, and Callum is becoming more like that too. But the mystery solved itself in a way a few weeks later when Callum had gone.'

'How?'

'The body of a woman was washed up in the harbour at Portnagour. I had to ask old Adam to come and identify it, and to my relief he came. It was Marguerite.'

Gail shuddered. 'She drowned,' she murmured. 'But how? Why?'

Mr. Gorrie wagged his head from side to side. 'I can't be telling you that, and if old Adam knew he took his secret to the grave. And now, miss, I must be providing you with the food.'

Although she had not been able to clear up the mystery surrounding the reasons for Marguerite's drowning Gail felt she had a little more insight into the situation which had existed in Stornish House six years previously. The image of old Adam was coming through clearly and strongly. He had been autocratic, a law unto himself, and he had not liked Marguerite. Was it possible he had been responsible for her drowning? Or had it been an accident? She must find out somehow why he had not liked her, and the person who had a good knowledge of the old tyrant was Annie Rankin.

On that one subject, the character of the old man for whom she had worked, and his likes and dislikes, Annie remained stubbornly uninformative. Twice Gail tried to draw her out on the subject and twice she was firmly rebuffed. The first time she asked a direct question.

'Was Mr. Black very fond of his grandsons?' she asked one morning while Annie was busy at her favourite job of polishing the already shiny furniture.

'He was the kindest man living in the islands, upright and good all the days of his life. He gave both his grandsons the best care any boys could have. There is nothing more I can be telling you about him. It is wrong to speak of the dead.'

Did she mean it was wrong to speak *ill* of the dead, Gail wondered, therefore implying that old Adam had not always been good?

The second time she asked Annie whether she knew any legends about Stornish and after listening to one about a young man who had married a mermaid she managed to lead on to a question about the legend concerning the ghost of the young woman who had drowned six years ago.

'What ghost?' exclaimed Annie, her blue eyes sharp. 'It's the first I've been hearing about a ghost.'

'But there was a young woman who stayed with the Blacks six years ago and who was drowned, wasn't there?' persisted Gail.

'If you mean that flighty piece himself brought here for a holiday. I know nothing of her, and don't wish to know more. I was away at the time visiting my sister in Lewis.'

Then Annie had stalked out of the room huffily, leaving Gail convinced that she knew more than she was prepared to admit, and pondering on Annie's description of Marguerite as 'a flighty piece'. It told her more about the woman in two words than anything Mr. Gorrie or even Callum had said.

The arrival of a letter from her father in reply to the one Callum had posted for her cast down her spirits, which had risen considerably since she had been able to go for short walks. Phil regretted that he was detained in London and could not see his way to travelling to Stornish for a while. He had, however, been in touch with his sister, Gail's Aunt Jane, who had jumped at the chance of a holiday in the Hebrides, so he hoped Gail wouldn't mind staying on Stornish for the time being in order to accommodate Jane. The next mail brought a letter from Aunt Jane stating when she would arrive at Sorasay and asking Gail to meet her off the steamer. As yet there was no letter from Karl saying when he would come to Stornish, so Gail wrote to her aunt asking her to call and see him and to persuade him to travel with her.

Feeling cheered by the thought of having a visitor, Gail celebrated by walking further than she had done before. She was fast discovering the pleasure of walking near the shore when the tide was out. There were always birds to watch and having studied some of the books on the wild life of the islands which Callum had sent to her she was rather pleased with herself when she found she could recognize some of them.

The small plump ones, pale grey with faint dark markings, with black bills and legs and white underparts, were sanderlings. They fed by poking and probing on the muddy flats and they ran about like a stream of hurrying ants. In contrast the greenshanks were slightly bigger and had, of course, green legs and a bluish, slightly up-curved beak. As she approached, a feeding snipe arose suddenly into the air with a hoarse cry and flew off in zig-zag flight, and over the water the white birds with black-topped heads which she knew now were terns dipped or hovered, squealing as they watched for fish.

She walked as far as the small village, waving to Annie who was in her own neat garden pegging clothes to a line. A jetty ran out into the little bay and an open boat was just approaching it. The man in the boat, whom she knew now to be Dougie Lean, waved also and as she walked on following the road as it rose away from the village to the moorland Gail thought how nice it was to go out walking and to be acknowledged.

Today she had decided she would walk as far as the McCaigs' house hoping that she might see a member of that family and make their acquaintance, and as she approached the house, which was set back from the road amongst a cluster of trees, she noticed a young woman dressed in a tweed skirt and jacket with a scarf tied over her head coming down across the moor towards the house. Guessing that she must be Eileen McCaig, the shepherdess, Gail waited at the end of the path which led to the house. It would be a change to talk to someone nearer her own age after being cooped up at Gartbeg.

The young woman saw her and waved, increased her pace and was soon standing before her. Curly-haired and pink-cheeked, with deep blue eyes, she was about twenty-six years of age. She smiled warmly at Gail and held out a hand.

'You're Miss Collins who is staying at Gartbeg,' she said.

'And you are Eileen McCaig the shepherdess. My name is Gail, Eileen.'

'Annie has been telling us about you. We would have called to see you, but we've been busy with the sheep-shearing. Will you come now to the house and have a cup of tea? Ach, I was forgetting, you have a sore ankle.'

'It's much better, thank you. I'd love to come for that tea.'

They were soon in the big comfortable kitchen of the house. Mrs. McCaig, who was tall and dark-haired, greeted Gail courteously and put the kettle on to boil. It wasn't long before the three of them were sitting at the table drinking tea while the musical Hebridean voices of mother and daughter questioned Gail as well as informing her. Soon she knew that Eileen was the youngest of three children. Her brother and sister both worked away from Stornish, Craig being in the fishing fleet which sailed out of Oban and Rose being a nurse in a Glasgow hospital. Eileen had also gone away from home at one time to a domestic science college, but ill-health had driven her back to Stornish to help with the sheep.

'And there is really no place I would rather be,' she told Gail.

'But isn't looking after sheep very hard work?' asked Gail.

'Anything worth doing is hard,' said Mrs. McCaig, 'but she loves being out of doors and it's better for her health than living in the city.'

'The spring is really the hardest,' said Eileen, 'when the sheep come down for the lambing. Then there's little sleep for any of us, especially if the weather is bad, for a lamb will die if it's not on its legs within an hour of its birth.'

'What about social life? Do you have any?' queried Gail.

'Ach, yes, we do so. There's always a *ceilidh* going on in someone's house and there's Highland dancing, and Mother and Annie and I belong to the Sorasay choir.'

'Don't you ever feel cut off from Sorasay?'

'No. We can always go over by boat.'

'But not on a stormy night.'

Eileen giggled. 'No, not on a stormy night like the one on which you arrived. I'd like to have seen Callum's face when he found you asleep in his bed. You must have given him a shock. You'll be knowing that he isn't pleased that Ian sold the house to you?' Eileen queried cautiously.

'Yes, I know. He made no attempt to hide that he doesn't want strangers on Stornish.'

'I'm sure he hasn't anything against you personally,' said Eileen, her pleasant face serious. 'But you see the land, the whole island matters to Callum. He wants to keep it alive. Several people have offered to rent the house knowing that it was empty, but he has refused.'

'You are forgetting it wasn't his to let,' said Mrs. McCaig, her powerful voice breaking in disapprovingly. She had returned to the work which had been occupying her when Eileen and Gail had entered the room and was now kneading the dough for making bread. 'Old Adam should never have divided the island between his grandsons. He should have left it all to Callum and then there would have been no trouble. Gartbeg would have been his and he could have let it to another farmer.'

'Old Adam was trying to be fair, Mother. Give him his due,' said Eileen.

'Fair to whom?' scoffed Mrs. McCaig. 'Not to Callum. You know very well, Eileen, that Ian was always his favourite just because he was Catriona's son. When Ian left and didn't come back he should have had the sense to realize that the rascal wasn't interested in Stornish and should have changed his will. He could have left him money instead of land and a house.'

'Well, Ian has the money now,' said Eileen mildly.

'And we have strangers on Stornish. Coming from the city, what will you have to contribute to the natural society of the island?' asked Mrs. McCaig sternly, looking at Gail.

Gail was inclined to take offence at being questioned in such a way, then she realized suddenly that Mrs. McCaig was stating simply and forthrightly how she felt. Once more, as in the case of Annie, she was surprised to find how educated and intelligent an islander could be. Mrs. McCaig was far further ahead in her thinking than many of her urban counterparts. Like Callum she obviously cared deeply about the island and wished to preserve it.

But Gail couldn't accept the implication that she and Phil would be useless and would contribute nothing, especially when she remembered Mrs. Mills and her husband, who had managed to transplant themselves from the city to the island of Mull.

'Although my father knows nothing about farming he knows a lot about music,' she said.

Eileen turned to her, her blue eyes sparkling.

'Is he knowing anything about conducting a choir?' she asked. 'This year our conductor, Flora Johnson, married the conductor of a choir from Aberdeen and now we've no conductor to train us for the Mod.'

'The Mod? What is that?' asked Gail.

'It's a Gaelic music festival,' said Mrs. McCaig. 'It takes place every year. There are choir competitions and competitions for individual singers, for piping and even

94

for fiddle groups now. It's a great festival of fellowship and friendship and it's been going on since 1892. People are keener on it now than they've ever been, even though Gaelic itself is slowly dying as a language. But it's not for the Gaelic they go. It's for the reunion with old friends.'

'It will be awful if we miss it this year,' mourned Eileen.

'Well, my father conducts the choir of a London girls' school and for years his choirs have won festivals held all over England,' said Gail tentatively.

'Mother, are you listening? Isn't that wonderful? Ach, you cannot be saying now that Mr. Collins couldn't contribute to our society if he lived here. He'd be a great asset!'

Mrs. McCaig smiled at her daughter's enthusiasm.

'But he will be staying here only for his holidays, Eileen. He won't want to be conducting us.'

'No, I suppose not,' sighed Eileen. 'But we'll look forward to meeting him and making him welcome when he comes, and maybe he'll come and hear the choir singing and give us a few hints.'

After that the atmosphere in the kitchen was easier as Mrs. McCaig unbent and seemed to accept Gail more readily. As she accompanied Gail along the road Eileen said rather anxiously,

'I hope you will not be minding my mother. She feels very strongly about Gartbeg being sold because Callum had said that if he could buy it back from Ian he would, and would let it to Ronald Gunn who would come and farm it. Then Ron and I could stay here when we are married. But now with it sold to your father I shall have to be going away to Glasgow.'

'But why?'

'Because that is where Ron is working. He's a policeman, although he did not want to be. His elder brother lives on Sorasay and farms, but there just wasn't enough work for Ron.'

'Oh, Eileen, I am sorry. I'd no idea we'd be causing such an upheaval, believe me,' said Gail, sincerely upset by what she had just learned. 'Nor had my father. We thought Mr. Sanderson had to sell the place because he could no longer keep it and because the owner of the island was complaining that the house was falling into disrepair. My father had always wanted a holiday home in a remote place, so he bought it.'

'Ian Sanderson was lying,' said Eileen angrily. 'But then he was always a liar. I can remember him telling terrible lies about Callum when they were boys just to be getting Callum into trouble with his grandfather. Not that Callum didn't get into trouble often anyway, because he was always up to mischief. Ian lied about the young woman too.'

Gail pricked up her ears. 'Which woman?'

'The one Callum brought for a holiday once. She wasn't unlike you, but she wasn't as friendly, and she didn't talk to any of the islanders. I couldn't understand what Callum saw in her ... but you can never tell what attracts men can you? He brought her here to see if she liked the island. Ian was here at the time staying in Gartbeg, which he'd always used as a hideout ever since his mother had died. He's very attractive, blue-eyed and dark-haired, tall and slim, and he's an actor. Well, Callum, so sure and confident, left Marguerite here in the care of his grandfather while he went over to the mainland for some conference or other and while he was away she visited Ian every day. I know, because I used to see her. Then the day Callum was due to return she disappeared.'

'And so did Ian,' put in Gail.

'Yes. But there was nothing unusual in that because he was always coming and going. Old Mr. Black asked my father if he'd seen Marguerite about and my father asked me. That was the only hint we had that she'd gone without the old man knowing. It seems she had gone out and a storm had blown up and she hadn't returned. Knowing what I did about her movements. I told my father I thought she'd run away with Ian. He told old Adam, who accepted the story and presumably told it to Callum when he came back.'

'What do you think happened?'

'I think she knew that Ian had left and she tried to follow him by walking over the causeway and was caught by the high seas created by the storm.'

Gail realized that at last she had found someone who might know the answer to the questions which had been worrying her ever since she had learned that Marguerite had been drowned.

'But didn't Callum wonder where she'd gone? Didn't he try to find her?'

'No, he didn't,' answered Eileen slowly. 'And the fact that he didn't is like a black mark against him, isn't it? It would make anyone who didn't know Callum suspicious of him. But the reason why he didn't search for her lies deep in his character. He believed she had gone with Ian, that she preferred Ian to him. It was a great blow to his pride—his Black pride, so he never asked a question or referred to her again as far as I know. Pride and appearance are all he and old Adam had in common.'

'And a love of Stornish, too,' suggested Gail softly. 'It's a very strange story.'

'It's a very sad one too,' sighed Eileen. 'Callum is so different from what he used to be. He was lively and gay and sociable when he was younger. Now he's quiet and withdrawn and he rarely joins in any social activity. Sometimes I think he's afraid of committing himself to other people in case he's hurt again. But I have my fingers crossed for him. There's a possibility he might be considering marriage again.'

'Whom will he marry?'

'Alice Boyd, if I have my way. She and Callum have known each other for a long time and since he came back to Stornish they've visited each other often. I hope nothing happens to spoil it.'

CHAPTER FOUR

DURING the time between visiting the McCaigs' house and the arrival of her aunt Gail found herself absorbed into the life of Stornish without actually realizing it. After she had made Eileen's acquaintance no day passed without the young shepherdess coming to visit Gail or inviting her to some social occasion. They went to two *ceilidhs*, one on Stornish at the home of the Leans, and the other on Sorasay at the home of Eileen's Aunt Fiona, a sister of Mrs. McCaig. At both there were a dozen or more people who had met to enjoy stories and songs and sometimes some piping. At both a light meal called a *strupach* was served which usually consisted of scones and jam and biscuits. At both she was surprised how many young people were present and how they mixed easily and unselfconsciously with their elders. They all had something in common. They were bound to the islands by family ties and love of the land.

They also went to a dance in Portnagour. Although Gail's ankle was not strong enough for her to participate in the dancing she was content to watch with surprise and great interest how everyone else exercised with alertness and spirit, whirling round in the intricate reels to the music of an accordion and a fiddle. Every dance was a communal effort and involved three or more couples, and no one seemed to mind that the floor was rough and uneven.

Gail also became used to travelling to Sorasay by boat, crossing the narrow strait in one of Dougie Lean's boats and catching the bus which linked the outlying farms and small villages with Portnagour. As a result of travelling this way she was soon on friendly terms with Dougie, who was also Stornish's fisherman, and with his young shy wife Mairi and their one-year-old son Dougie Beg.

Not only did Gail find she was being accepted by the hospitable islanders but she also found she was beginning to like the island itself. She could not walk very far, but she enjoyed the walks along the seashore as far as the causeway or to Stornish village or up to the moorland where Eileen lived. On fine days the air was very clear and the views were entrancing. On wet days the rain was soft and gentle and so clean that she could walk with her head uncovered, letting the water seep through her hair. Such treatment made her long locks glossier than ever and when she looked at herself in the mirror she could see that her face had lost the paleness at which Callum had scoffed and had taken on a soft brownish pink.

Jane was due to arrive on a Saturday exactly two weeks and three days after Gail's arrival. It was the second week of August and the weather had been calm and warm for several days. Gail travelled to Portnagour with Eileen, who was on her way to another island to take part in the annual Highland Games. Eileen was going to spend the night with her aunt in Portnagour and take the steamer on Saturday. As the bus lurched along the road she told Gail that Callum had participated regularly in the Games when he had been a youth and had been a local champion at putting the shot.

'But of course he hasn't had time to take part these last six years and he won't be taking part tomorrow, which is a pity because he looks as if he still has a good putt in him.'

Remembering Callum's wide shoulders and deep chest Gail was inclined to agree, and wondered vaguely when the elusive Mr. Black would be returning to Stornish.

When they arrived at Portnagour she felt glad that the weather was fine for Jane's voyage from Oban. It was a perfect sunny day with a slight breeze. From the main street in Portnagour she could see for miles across the sea to the mainland where tall mountains lifted their purple, pearl-grey and rose-tinted peaks to the sky.

As the steamer did not arive until the middle of the

afternoon Gail had time to do some shopping at Don Gorrie's shop, which as usual was full of chattering islanders and a fair number of summer visitors. He was as pleasant as ever and persuaded her to take a saddle of lamb for the weekend. By now she knew that the island meat was tender and of delicious flavour on account of the fine grazing which both sheep and cattle had.

Her shopping done, she went to Fiona McKinnon's house for her midday meal with Eileen. After the meal she sat and talked to Eileen while the latter repaired a frill on the lovely blouse which she would be wearing as part of her dance costume, with a kilt made of the MacLeod of Harris tartan because the McCaigs were a sept of the MacLeod clan.

At three o' clock, having wished Eileen luck for the Games, Gail walked down to the pier to wait for the steamer. It was just approaching the entrance to the sea loch, its white superstructure gleaming, the red and black of its funnel making strong splashes of colour amongst the blues and greens of the sky, sea and land.

There were several people waiting by the small white red-roofed harbour building and there was a stir of excitement amongst them. Most of them seemed to be islanders and Gail assumed that they were expecting to meet relatives coming home from the mainland for their summer holidays bringing not only gifts but earnings.

She had learned from Eileen that very few holiday-makers came to Sorasay because there was no car ferry to the island and the steamer could bring only a couple of cars at a time which were usually stowed on the foredeck. This time she knew it would be carrying Jane's car because her aunt had driven as far as Oban from London as she had wanted to visit certain places of historical interest on the way north.

As the steamer came nearer with the usual flock of attendant gulls hovering over its wake, and the sound of its engines a dull throb as they slowed down, the people on the quayside began to wave to individuals standing on the top deck. Greetings were called out and then with a bump the steamer berthed, warps were thrown from bow and stern to the quay and gangways were run ashore.

Gail guessed that her aunt would not be in a hurry to get off the steamer because she would be anxious about her car which would have to be swung in the cargo net on to the quay. So she waited apart from the group of people, recalling her own arrival on that day of storm when she had been the only passenger to step off the boat and there had been no one to greet her. Although interested and amused by the meetings and greetings she couldn't help watching carefully for a tall man with auburn hair, hoping that Karl had travelled with Aunt Jane. In fact she was so busy peering that she was oblivious of the net of cargo which was being swung into the air and over the side in her direction.

A hand seized her and she was pulled roughly aside.

'There's only one person I know on these islands who would be foolish enough to stand in the way of cargo being unloaded, and that person is you, Goldilocks,' said a lazy lilting voice, and she looked up to find Callum Black standing beside her. Then glancing beyond him she saw the net full of enormous cardboard boxes descend on to the spot where she had been standing.

'Oh, I didn't realize.'

'You mean you didn't look. You were miles away ... day dreaming? What are you doing here? The boat doesn't leave for Oban until the morning, so you're a little early for embarkation. Are you so desperate to shake the dust of Stornish from your feet that you can hardly wait to get aboard?'

Listening to his voice, seeing his crooked smile, feeling the strong grip of his hand on her arm, Gail was coping with the most peculiar sensation. If it had been anyone else other than Callum she would have described the sensation as a mixture of pleasure at seeing him and sheer excitement because he had stepped into her life again. But of course she couldn't really feel like that about

Callum Black, so the sensation must be one of shocked reaction to her near escape from having a heap of cargo dumped upon her head.

'No, I'm not leaving,' she retorted. 'I'm surprised you bothered to rescue me if you're so keen to be rid of me! To be crushed beneath a heap of cartons is worthy of one of the more violent deaths dealt out to their enemies by some of your ancestors.'

He smiled. 'Now why didn't I think of that? It has a subtlety worthy of a Black. I could have helped you on your way by shoving you instead of pulling you and no one would have been any the wiser. But seriously, Goldilocks, why are you here? I know it isn't to meet me.'

In his heavy denim trousers and navy blue seaman's sweater he looked tough and weatherbeaten, and the duffle bag at his feet over which was thrown a black oilskin coat reminded her that he had been sailing amongst the Outer Isles.

'No, I haven't. I didn't even know you were due back today. I hope you had a good cruise. I'm here to meet my aunt. She's coming to stay with me for a while.'

His dark eyes narrowed thoughtfully. 'Is your father with her?' he asked.

'No. He's been delayed,' said Gail, and was about to say more when another voice spoke close beside her.

'There you are, Callum. I nearly missed you. I was waiting over by the harbourmaster's office.'

The voice was as soft and as sibilant as the gentle shush of water on the shore on a summer's day. It belonged to a woman of about thirty years of age who now stood beside Callum, her gaze going curiously to his hand which still gripped Gail's arm. Her hair was a dark russet brown and her eyes were a clear greenish blue. She was dressed in a kilt of Royal Stewart tartan which was teamed with a blue blouse open at the neck over which she wore a white cardigan. Although small she was graceful, and her fine-boned face possessed the wonderful complexion which Gail was coming to associate with the women who lived in the islands.

Callum removed his hand from Gail's arm and turned to smile at the newcomer.

'Hello, Alice. I was just making sure that Goldilocks here didn't come to a messy end beneath that pile of cargo or I might have been seeing you sooner.'

An expression of astonishment followed a glint of something not quite so pleasant gleamed in the greenish blue eyes.

'Goldilocks,' repeated Alice. Then glancing at Gail for the first time she asked, 'Is that really your name?'

'No,' said Gail with her sunniest smile. 'You see ... well, I. ...' She looked at Callum and met his rueful yet mirthful glance and stifled a strong desire to laugh. Quickly before he could say anything she added, 'My name is Gail Collins. When I first met Callum he didn't know what the "G" stood for, so he called me Goldilocks.'

She could tell by the way Alice raised her fine eyebrows that her explanation didn't please the woman.

'For obvious reasons,' commented Alice, her gaze going critically over Gail's abundant glowing hair. Alice's own hair was short and wavy and held back from her face by a blue band. Then remembering her manners she held out her hand and said, 'I'm Alice Boyd. I don't think I've seen you before, have I? You don't look or sound as if you belong to the islands.'

'Gail is from London and has recently come to live on Stornish,' put in Callum.

'On Stornish? But how? Why?' exclaimed Alice.

'Ian sold his house and his land to Gail's father,' replied Callum brusquely, the tone of his voice dismissing the subject as one which he did not wish to discuss any further. Turning to Gail, he asked, 'Has your aunt disembarked yet?'

'No, but I think her car has,' replied Gail. 'Oh, there she is!'

Jane Collins, tall, sandy-haired and slightly leonine like

103

her brother, had stalked ashore and was examining her car closely to make sure it hadn't been scratched. Accompanying her was the captain of the steamer, a squat figure in his navy blue uniform and white-topped hat. He also examined the car and they had a few words together, shook hands and the captain returned on board.

'How like Aunt Jane to deal only with the top brass,' murmured Gail as her mind registered the fact that Jane was by herself. Karl hadn't come with her. 'Please come and meet her,' she said, turning to Callum and Alice. 'She has never been to the Hebrides before and I know she'll love being welcomed by you.'

'In Gaelic,' suggested Callum.

'Oh, could you, please? It would make her day,' replied Gail with a smile, and her mind registered another fact, Callum Black could be very charming when he wanted to be.

As they walked towards Jane she turned and saw them. At once she came forward to hug Gail and kiss her on the cheek.

'Gail, how lovely to see you! And how well you look. I've never seen you with so much colour in your cheeks. How's your ankle?'

'Improving slowly,' said Gail, and proceeded to introduce Alice and then Callum who, true to his word, greeted her in Gaelic.

'*Ceud mile failte agus slainte mhath*,' he said politely.

'Wonderful! Like a series of chuckles,' exclaimed Jane. 'But what does it mean?'

'A hundred thousand welcomes and good health,' replied Callum.

'That is very kind of you,' said Jane, her wide slightly short sighted eyes peering at him closely. 'I've heard of you. That film of yours about the bird colonies on St. Kilda was almost perfect.'

'I considered it was perfect,' replied Callum easily.

'I thought you might,' said Jane, her sudden gamin

grin making her seem much younger than her fifty-odd years. 'But I wasn't going to tell you so. And you are also the Mr. Black Gail has written about. Black of Stornish. The Blacks were a bloodthirsty piratical crew, according to the book I've been reading about the islands, no worse, of course, than the other clans who lived here. I hope you haven't been frightening my niece.'

Again Callum's eyes met Gail's in a glance of shared mirth which made her feel close to him.

'Only to make sure she would keep her place,' he replied.

'You mustn't be believing everything you read about the legends of the islands,' said Alice in her soft sighing voice. 'Remember the bloodthirsty deeds took place centuries ago. The Black family is one of the most respected in the islands now. Shall we go, Callum? I promised Father I'd take you back for tea. You know how he likes to have it on time, and he's wanting to hear all about your cruise.'

Was it her imagination or did Callum hesitate before picking up his oilskin and slinging his duffle bag over his shoulder as he agreed to go with Alice? And she was sure Alice was annoyed because he had taken time to talk to Jane and herself.

'We can't give you a lift to your islands, then, Mr. Black?' asked Jane.

'No, thank you. I'll return later by bus and ferry.'

'Then I'll look forward to meeting you again some time. I'm hoping you'll be able to tell me a little about the stone circle at the western tip of your island. It's one of the reasons why I've come. I teach History and I'm a very keen amateur archaeologist.'

The good humour had gone from Callum's face. Impassive, his eyes empty of light, he looked at Jane as if she wasn't there.

'I can tell you nothing about the stones,' he replied coldly. 'And I must warn you not to go wandering about Stornish. Please keep to the road. It is not open to tourists or to amateur archaeologists. And now if you'll please excuse us, Alice and I will be on our way.'

'He's quite right, of course,' said Jane as she manoeuvred the Morris through the narrow street of Portnagour. 'I think if I owned an island I wouldn't want all and sundry wandering about it disturbing the wild life and possibly destroying the vegetation.'

'He might have been a little more pleasant about telling you, though,' replied Gail, who was still seething at Callum's choice of words. Did he think Jane and she would behave like careless sightseers?

'He spoke his mind, that's all. I like a man who does that. I noticed him on the steamer. He seemed to know most of the passengers. I thought then that he looked like a man who knows what he wants. He's quite remarkable in his own field, you know. Haven't you seen any of his films?'

'No, I haven't,' snapped Gail rather crossly. She was tired of being asked that particular question. It always made her feel that she had missed something very important. 'I'd never heard of the man until Phil bought Gartbeg.'

'Well, I suppose that's not unusual. I don't suppose he's ever heard of Phil either. Don't you think it's a coincidence that both of them have been involved with television films? Perhaps they could collaborate on a film about the islands. There what a great idea! Imagine a film about Sorasay and Stornish showing all the wild life, the historical remains (I'd do that bit) and the recent economic developments with background music by Phil. I must mention it to him when he comes and to Mr. Black when I go to see him about the stone circle. He can hardly refuse to take me to see it himself, can he?'

'I wouldn't make any predictions about what Callum will do or not do,' replied Gail shortly, and Jane gave her an amused glance and thought to herself, 'Oho. Like that, is it? Interesting!'

Aloud Jane asked,

106

'Who was the frozen-faced lady of the manor who was with him?'

'Alice Boyd. Her father is Sir Morris Boyd who owns Sorasay,' Jane nodded.

'I've heard of him too. We mustn't antagonize the lady, then, because I simply must meet Sir Morris and look round his gardens. But what's between her and Mr. Black?'

'Eileen McCaig, the shepherdess on Stornish, says they may marry, although there's no official engagement.'

'Nor ever will be, if my judgement of character is right. Mr. Black strikes me as the sort of person who would fall in love violently and deeply and would be impatient of any conventional period of courting. He's not in love with her. She's too prim and organized to suit his hot blood. Am I going the right way, dear?'

Rather astonished by her aunt's forthright summing up of Callum, Gail answered,

'Oh yes. Just follow the road. It goes straight to the causeway. I'm glad it's a fine day as it's rather a nerve-racking idea crossing it in stormy weather.'

'The weather is perfect,' agreed Jane. 'I loved every minute of the sail here. Phil is going to love this place, Gail.'

'Wait until you see the house,' warned Gail. 'You may not think so then.'

But to her surprise Jane was favourably impressed by the house. Sitting at the table in the dining-room while they ate their evening meal looking out at the magnificent view of moorland which backed the village of Stornish, she commented,

'I can see that it's over-furnished and that a little re-decoration wouldn't do any harm, but the building is sound and the situation is delightful.'

'Any ideas where we might put a piano?' asked Gail.

'How would you get one here?'

'MacBraynes would move one for us. I've already asked.'

'Good. Then we've two weeks in which to rearrange the furniture before Phil comes and says where he wants the piano.'

'Two weeks? But I thought he'd be here sooner than that.'

'Somehow I don't think so,' said Jane cautiously, keeping a wary eye on her niece's expressive face. For all her outward glamour and sophistication she knew that Gail was very sensitive.

'Then why must I stay? I only agreed to come because he said he'd follow soon. If I'd known he was going to take so long to come I'd have returned to London as soon as I could put my weight on my ankle, and I'd have told him not to bother with the place.'

'Now why should you tell him that?'

'Because we're not wanted here. Callum Black doesn't want us. He made sure when I arrived that I wasn't welcome.'

'Really! I can't imagine him being so rude.'

'Oh, he wasn't rude. But there was no doubt he resented my arrival on Stornish. Even today he said he hoped I would be leaving on the steamer tomorrow. And Eileen McCaig, although she wouldn't say so, would be very glad if Gartbeg was sold back to Callum because it would mean her fiancé Ron could come back and work on the island and they would be able to stay here when they get married. Oh can't you see Jane, we're intruders here, aliens, depriving someone who is of more use to this community than we are of their chance of livelihood here.'

'Yes, I see. Do you think Mr. Black would buy back the place?' asked Jane.

'I know he would. In fact he offered to buy it back before I came. But Phil and I thought he was being arrogant and difficult. Neither of us knew anything about the real situation.'

Jane considered Gail thoughtfully and came to a decision.

'Gail, I have something to tell you. I was going to wait

until the letter from your father arrived, but perhaps it's better if I anticipate his news. Phil is going to marry Priscilla, next week.'

Wide-eyed and silent, Gail stared at her aunt. Then she stuttered,

'I didn't know ... I thought he had stopped seeing her ... He didn't tell me.'

'Apparently he has been trying to tell you for several weeks, but you turned off every time he broached the subject. Now it's no use looking mutinous, my dear. Phil has been in love with Priscilla for the last few years, but he hesitated to marry again because of you.'

'She can never take the place of my mother,' said Gail stubbornly, gazing out of the window at a small bird doing acrobatics on the washing line which stretched across the small garden.

'Nor does she want to,' replied Jane firmly. 'No one could replace Eira. She was special. But so is Priscilla in her own way. She will make Phil very happy. After all, I don't expect you'll be with him much longer.'

'Do you think she'll like this place?' asked Gail, retreating in the face of Jane's championship of Priscilla.

Jane looked round the homely room at the huge shiny sideboard, at the old-fashioned hand-stitched samplers on the walls. Then she glanced out at the view of the placid strait of water and at the green and brown moorland.

'If Phil likes it I think she will,' she replied. 'Do you like it?'

'I like Stornish far better than I would have believed possible, but I don't think Phil ought to keep Gartbeg considering the problems his ownership have created,' said Gail.

'Then why don't you write to him and tell him so, dear? That's one reason why he asked you to come, to find out about the place. I'm sure once he has heard from you why Mr. Black wants to buy the place back from him he'll be very understanding. Meanwhile we can both enjoy ourselves for the next two weeks.'

'Yes, I'm sure we shall,' murmured Gail, then asked the question which had been uppermost in her mind ever since Jane had arrived. 'Did you go to see Karl as I asked you? Is he going to come up here?'

'Yes, I did, dear,' Jane's voice softened with sympathy. 'He wasn't there and he'd left no forwarding address. He'd moved on. But try to look on the bright side. He may write from his new address.'

Gail shook her head.

'I don't think so,' She sighed. 'I've a feeling that once I was out of his sight I was out of his mind.'

'Then maybe it's just as well you left London when you did,' observed Jane shrewdly as she recalled what Phil had told her about Karl. 'His type of person isn't really for you, dear. You need someone with a stronger will than yours, someone who believes in having and holding.' She grinned rather whimsically. 'You know, in some ways you're rather like me ... independent to a fault, and tending to be sorry for those who seem to be helpless and allowing that pity to blind you to their real intentions. Do you know, I kept thinking today, if only I'd met someone like Mr. Black when I was younger I might have married him.'

'Huh! You'd be welcome. He's the last man I'd want to marry.'

'I thought you'd say that,' said Jane, nodding wisely. 'You think he likes his own way too much and it isn't necessarily your way. I can't see him being happy with Miss Milk-and-Sugar Boyd.'

'What on earth do you mean by milk-and-sugar?'

'She's too sweet and smooth. I would guess that Mr. Black prefers a spicy diet.'

After watching the sun disappear behind Sorasay's purple moors in a spectacular sunset, all crimson streaks of light and feathered grey cloud, Jane went off to her bedroom to finish her unpacking and to prepare for bed.

Feeling restless, Gail decided to go for a walk. Slowly

she strolled along the road towards the small cluster of houses, watching the last crimson light shake across the water and then go out, suddenly leaving the world half-lit, the time of day when all the legends and myths of the Western Isles could easily be believed.

But Gail was not concerned with ghosts and legends. She was thinking about her father. He was going to be married and he hadn't invited her to his wedding. He had tried to discuss the matter with her, but she had turned off every time, Jane had said. The knowledge that she had failed to hear him troubled Gail because she had always thought she and Phil had communicated well. She must have been too absorbed in her own affairs, too engrossed in Karl.

Gail frowned and bit her lip. She found introspection a painful business. Essentially an outgoing person, she rarely analysed her feelings, preferring instinctive action to thoughtful inaction even if that action landed her, as it often did, in hot water. The knowledge that Karl had moved on without contacting her again did not hurt her as much as the information that her father had tried to talk to her and had found her deaf, but it did make her stop to wonder why she always seemed to be beginning relationships with the opposite sex and never getting any further with them. Was it possible, as Jane had pointed out, that she was too independent? If that was the case there was very little she could do about it, and anyway she believed in being loved for what she was, not what anyone thought she should be.

'If thou must love me let it be for nought.
Except for love's sake only,'

she said aloud, then laughed at herself. The twilight was deepening tonight. Glittering stars pinpricked the blue velvet of the sky. In such a setting it did not seem strange to quote one of Elizabeth Barrett Browning's sonnets because the calm starlit Hebridean night was conducive to romantic thoughts.

Voices came from the other side of the strait. She had

noticed before how clearly they carried across water when the weather was good. Then the deep throb of a boat's engine took their place. Dougie must have been out fishing. If she hurried she would reach the jetty as he came alongside and perhaps she would be able to buy some fish from him. Glad to be in action again, thrusting aside all thoughts of Karl, she walked more quickly and reached the jetty as Dougie's boat approached, its port and starboard lights glowing in the still dark air. A man jumped ashore with a rope in his hand which he twisted round a bollard. By the light on the end of the jetty he was easily recognizable as Callum Black. He turned back to the boat to take his duffle bag and oilskin coat from Dougie, who glanced past him, saw Gail and touched his tweed cap.

' 'Tis a fine evening, miss,' said Dougie.

Callum swung round. 'What are you doing here?' he asked curtly.

'I heard the boat coming and I thought Dougie might have some fish to sell.'

'He has,' he replied.

'You'd best be looking them over, miss,' said Dougie, 'and choosing your own. Callum's taken the best.'

'He would!' murmured Gail impishly. Her comment wasn't heard by the fisherman, but Callum heard and laughed,

'It's my prerogative to take the best,' he said.

By the light from Dougie's big torch Gail chose her fish and the fisherman put them in a sou'wester hat and offered it to her as a makeshift basket. She paid him with some change she had in her pants pocket and after saying good night turned to leave.

'I'll walk along the road with you,' said Callum, and turned to say good night to Dougie in Gaelic.

They walked in silence past the few cottages from which small patches of yellow light glowed. Then they were in the starlit darkness and the only sounds were their footsteps and the water sucking and gurgling in the mud.

'You're limping,' observed Callum suddenly. 'I suppose you've been foolish again and have overtaxed your ankle. You shouldn't be out walking.'

'Everything I do seems foolish to you,' she retorted.

'Maybe I used the wrong word. Would impetuous be better? Why take offence? Impetuosity is a sign of youthfulness.'

'I'm twenty-one, almost twenty-two,' she replied haughtily.

'So old?' he mocked. 'But I thought you'd be sitting with your aunt tonight, gossiping, not walking about Stornish in the dark. It isn't safe, you know. The fairies might get you.'

'I don't believe in your fairies any more than I believe in your ghosts.'

'Shush! Never be saying that. They'll hear you and will come to punish you. They return kindness with kindness, but are always prepared to snipe and pinprick those who have taken the land they love, which is what you and your father have done.'

As when he had talked about the ghost of Marguerite his voice carried deep conviction, and in spite of herself Gail looked around her curiously, almost expecting the fairies to come out of the fields. She shivered and drew closer to Callum as if searching for security and protection. Noticing her movement, he put out his free hand and took her free one in it. His clasp was warm and closed firmly over her hand, which was cold. At once her apprehension vanished. With her hand in that strong warm grasp she felt comforted.

'Cold hand, warm heart,' he chanted lightly. 'Is the saying true, I wonder? Is there really a warm heart lurking there beneath the cool sophistication? Is it there hiding behind the haughty glance and the quick tongue?'

The sudden personal twist to the conversation disconcerted Gail for a moment. Was that how she appeared, cool and haughty?

'Why shouldn't there be?' she parried lightly, not wanting him to know that he confused her.

'Experience has taught me to think otherwise. I tend now to believe more readily in that other saying that all that glitters is not gold, which could apply very aptly to you too. One gets a little cynical after having been deceived once by outward appearances,' he replied quietly. The faintly bitter edge to his words added another disturbing factor to her knowledge of him. He had been deceived once by a woman and now he was cautious about all other women. He did not trust her.

'Marguerite?' she queried, and then was rather surprised by her own temerity. It must be the velvet starlit night which made her bold.

At once the comforting hand released hers and she felt unaccountably deserted and alone.

'No doubt you've been hearing all about her,' he commented dryly. If he knew how she had made it her business to find out as much as she could about Marguerite she guessed he would be very angry.

'I know that she was a friend of yours and that she drowned.' She wanted to say how sorry she was that Marguerite had drowned, but hesitated when she remembered Eileen's remarks about Callum having his share of the Black pride, so she quelled her natural impulse to offer sympathy, afraid of having her offer rejected, for some obscure reason.

'Do you know also that I was going to marry her, that I brought her here to see the house and island that I hoped one day would be our home, and that she didn't like the place?' Bitterness made his voice harsh, crowding out the lovely lazy lilt.

'I know only the little Eileen has told me,' she answered truthfully. She was surprised that he had confided so much. Did the darkness affect him in the same way as it did her and create a desire to confide, breaking down barriers and defences which they erected only during the daylight?

'As it turned out Eileen knew more than most. She knew that Marguerite and my cousin met regularly every day after I had introduced them, which I didn't know, or didn't want to believe. How little we know about others! How little we know about people we believe to be close to us, and how easily we can deceive ourselves!'

Although the last few comments were said in an undertone as if he was speaking more to himself than to her Gail felt an almost overwhelming urge to offer comfort again, as she realized how deeply hurt he had been by Marguerite's disloyalty and his cousin's treachery. But once again she quelled it while wondering what had happened to make him break his silence and confide in someone he disliked. After all, she argued, he had Alice Boyd, the woman he was thinking of marrying, and he could presumably confide in her.

Callum, who was regretting having offered to walk along the road with this tall thin girl who spoke to him so directly and had managed without his knowing it to penetrate the barrier of his pride, quickened his step, thinking that by doing so they would both reach Gartbeg sooner and he would be able to leave her. But he had forgotten about her limp. She did not forge ahead with him and something, perhaps it was an old chivalrous impulse, long dormant, made him slow down and wait for her.

'Has your aunt brought news of your father?' he asked politely.

Aware that he had wanted suddenly to be away from her, Gail was surprised when he waited for her. But his cool polite question made her wary. He was interested in her father's whereabouts for one reason only.

'Yes, she has,' she replied. 'He's going to be married next week and he won't be able to come to Stornish until the first week of September.'

'That's a nuisance. I was hoping to get this business of buying Gartbeg back from him settled soon,' he said curtly, then added more gently, 'Were you expecting

115

him to marry again while you were here?'

'No. The news came as a complete surprise. But I should have known, I should have guessed. Jane tells me he tried to tell me, but every time he tried to discuss his marriage with me I turned off.'

It was her turn to confide because she felt, knowing what she knew now he would understand, and she had to confide her bewilderment to someone.

'Did you turn off, as you call it, because you disliked the idea of him marrying again or because you were too absorbed in your own affairs?' he asked, interested in spite of his own warning to himself not to become too involved with her.

'Both, I suppose. I've never liked the idea of having a stepmother. But I feel mean now for not listening to him. You're right, I was too engrossed in my own affairs.'

'And in Karl, perhaps?' he probed quietly, although why he should want to know the answer to that he could not fathom.

The probe hurt a little, but she was surprised he remembered so much about her. His interest had the effect of opening the floodgates and all her bewilderment spilled out into the soft night.

'Yes. And much good that did me,' she wailed. 'He hasn't come as he promised. He's gone, moved on, and I don't know how to get in touch with him.'

They had reached the end of the path which led up to Gartbeg. The light from Jane's bedroom shone out from the side of the house, illuminating the dark shrubs and blanching the grass of the small drying green. They stopped walking and Callum, who had been so determined to walk on once they reached this point allowed his duffle bag to slip from his shoulder to the ground. A frog croaked in the marsh beyond the sea wall and nearer at hand some other animal moved about in the grasses edging the road, causing them to rustle dryly.

'I'm thinking that coming to Stornish has brought you no luck at all,' insinuated Callum softly.

'None at all,' agreed Gail unwittingly. 'If I'd listened to first thoughts I'd have stayed in London. I didn't want to come and stay here.'

'That isn't the impression I received the day we met, Goldilocks,' he observed. 'Then, you were very determined to stay. Have you forgotten?'

Gail bit her lip. His memory was good, too good.

'That was only because you were so determined I shouldn't stay. You even made up a ghost story to frighten me,' she retorted, annoyed to think she had given herself away.

'And you almost believed it,' he taunted. 'Now I know you a little better I realize I was using the wrong tactics. The more I suggested that Stornish was not the place for you the more you wanted to stay, just to defy me. What a mistake that was, and now I'm rueing it. Obviously I should have done the opposite, insisted that you stayed, possibly imprisoned you, and then you'd have wanted to leave. Dare I suggest that you go back to London now to look for Karl?'

'But I can't go. I promised Phil I'd stay until he came and anyway, Jane is here now and looking forward to a holiday here. But I have another suggestion to make, if you're willing to listen,' she said, trying to cope with the utter confusion in her mind which his suggestion that she went to search for Karl created.

'I'll listen,' he agreed.

'If you'd taken the trouble to explain in your letter to him why you wanted to buy Gartbeg back from him it's just possible my father and I would have understood. As it was we had no idea we'd be depriving Ron and Eileen of the chance to live and work here. So now I wonder if you would consider buying back the land only and letting us keep the house. Then you could build another house for Eileen.'

It was too dark to see his face, but she had the impression during the next few seconds he was considering her suggestion seriously. When he spoke, however, her hopes were soon dashed, because his voice was curt and cold.

'No. Buying back the land only will not do. I must have the house too. I seem to have difficulty in making you understand. I don't want any strangers on Stornish, not even for a few months of the year. I don't want your father or you here at all. I thought that was something I'd made clear from the beginning.'

She hadn't moved him an inch. He was rock-like in his adamancy. But being Gail she had to try again.

'Why? What have you against us apart from the facts that we're not farmers and come from the city? In particular why do you dislike me?' she challenged.

She heard him take a deep breath as if he was having to control an emotion which was threatening to get out of control.

'I don't have to answer that, Goldilocks. I don't want you here, that's all,' he snapped angrily. 'Now if you're really interested in helping Eileen and Ron you'll write to your father and you'll tell him that Gartbeg is unsuitable for his needs. You'll tell him that he won't get the peace and quiet he requires because I shall make sure that he won't. You'll tell him also that I'm now willing to buy back the place for more than he gave for it. If you do all that Eileen will be your friend for life and I . . .' Again he took a deep breath and when he continued his voice vibrated with barely-controlled emotion. 'I shall be extremely obliged to you. Good night.'

He picked up his duffle bag and his oilskin and walked away into the night.

In due course Gail received a letter from Phil telling her of his decision to marry again and hoping that she would understand. He said that he and Priscilla had decided on a very quiet civil ceremony and that he did not want to bring her all the way back from Stornish just for that. After a short honeymoon in Italy they would be joining her and Jane for the last two weeks of the holiday.

Having come to terms with herself on the matter of Phil's marriage Gail wrote back to both Phil and Priscilla congratulating them and wishing them happiness, and explaining the situation concerning Eileen and Ron. She told them exactly what Callum had said to her and urged Phil to make an offer to sell the place back to the owner of the island.

She was doing it to help Eileen, she told herself, and not because Callum had asked her. Yet as she was writing she could not help feeling regret at the thought of leaving the island. So far she had enjoyed being there and she was beginning to feel at home. *At home.* Where would her home be now that Phil had married again? As she wrote the familiar London address on her letter to him and Priscilla she experienced a momentary feeling of panic. When Phil was married he would not need her any more. No one needed her. Not Karl, although for a time she had thought he did need her, and least of all Callum Black. He had stated very clearly the last time they had met that he did not want her on his island, not just because she was a stranger but because she was herself. There was something about her which repelled him, that was quite obvious.

Not wanted, not needed. Gail's shoulders slumped as she gazed out at the moorland of Sorasay. Today it was purple and green, placid under a clear blue sky. She would miss this view when she left the island. She would miss everything and everyone. At one time the thought of leaving a place she liked would not have bothered her because always she had returned to the flat in London where her father lived. When one of her slight ineffectual love affairs had fizzled out she had never been unduly troubled because always in the background Phil had been there needing her support and help.

But now her affair with Karl had fizzled out and Phil did not need her any more. She was on her own, free and independent, able to please herself like Jane. And, like Jane, she supposed she could fill her life with interests

119

such as her work at school or with some hobby such as archaeology.

'The air is heavenly today,' said Jane, coming into the living room with a sheaf of wild flowers and grasses in her hand. 'Look what I've collected. You know, Gail, I think Phil got a bargain when he bought this place. Sea air, magnificent views, pleasant people . . .'

'Stone circles,' put in Gail mischievously.

'Yes that as well. I've been thinking it's time I went to see "himself" as Annie persists in calling him to ask his permission to see the stones. I've been here nearly a week and he's had plenty of time to think about it. Shall we walk over to see him this afternoon? We could invite him to come and have dinner with us tomorrow. That would give us an excuse to call.'

They set off after lunch, walking eastwards along the road to the causeway. The tide was in and the island was almost cut off from the larger bulk of Sorasay. Sunbeams danced on the water and in the distance, the mountains of Mull were heather purple. As they walked round the eastern end of the island they admired the clean white sand of the beach which was scattered with lichen-covered rocks and edged with wild fuchsia bushes.

Soon the rocky beach gave way to sand-dunes held together by spiky marram grass which prevented the sand of the shore from creeping over the land so that on the inland side of the road there were flat fields of *machair*, the rich shell-sand grassland which had developed as a result of the protection offered by the sand-dunes.

'This is really very interesting,' commented Jane. 'The difference between this side of the island and the other is amazing. Who would have dreamt you could find such variety of landscape in such a small area? It's truly an island of delight. I suppose that's Mr. Black's house. What does he grow in these fields?'

'I believe Davie Rankin cultivates bulbs in them for spring flowers.'

'Ah yes, of course. Those flat fields must be ideal.'

They turned off the road and walked up to the house. All was peaceful and calm, very different from her first visit, thought Gail. Today the house had none of the ghostly glamour it had possessed the night of the storm. It was just a sturdy farmhouse, plainly built, its white walls dazzling in the sunlight.

She was about to open the porch door when she noticed a movement in the farmyard. Callum was walking away from the house, Luran at his heels, Jane who was totally uninhibited about calling out, cupped her hands round her mouth and shouted,

'Coooeee, Mr. Black! You have visitors!'

Callum who was on his way to Aird's Bay at the western end of the island, heard the shout and recognized the voice. He didn't stop walking because his initial reaction was to pretend he hadn't heard. It was an excellent day for photography and it was just possible he might get some shots of the seals.

Jane shouted again, and this time his habit of courtesy made him stop and turn. The sunshine glinted on the spun gold hair of the younger woman waiting by the house. So Goldilocks had come too. Callum's mouth tightened grimly. Perhaps he should have gone on walking.

Gail noticed the way he hesitated before coming towards her and Jane. She was sure he had heard her aunt's first call. He didn't want to have to talk to them. Reluctance was in every slow stride he made towards them, and the dog looked ridiculously reluctant too.

'Good afternoon,' said Callum looking at Jane.

Oblivious to any tense undercurrents of feeling, Jane gave him her brightest smile.

'Good afternoon, Mr. Black. Wonderful weather we're having. I believe I'm most fortunate to see the islands under these conditions. I just couldn't resist the opportunity to walk over and see this side. It's very interesting. Gail tells me you grow bulbs. Are you successful?'

'We have our problems, but I think the small industry

121

is settling down and we're beginning to compete with other bulb-growing areas,' replied Callum politely.

Out of the corner of his eye he noticed that Gail wasn't wearing any make-up and that the days of sunshine had given her skin a light tan which made her grey eyes seem clearer and her hair more golden. Standing slightly behind her aunt, long-limbed and graceful in her dark blue cotton pants and white shirt, she seemed to him as cool and as unemotional as the mermaid he had first thought her to be, and the challenge she presented stirred his blood.

'I can see that as a naturalist the island must have a great appeal to you,' Jane was saying.

'Then you will appreciate perhaps why I want to protect its value and its beauty as a nature conservancy,' he replied.

'And why you don't want noisy tourists wandering about haphazardly disturbing the wild life. Yes, I appreciate that. But we're keeping you from your photography,' said Jane with an interested glance at the camera slung over his shoulder. 'What sort do you use?'

Callum patiently unslung the camera, unbuttoned the leather case and showed it to her. Gail, aware in every quivering sense of his physical presence, was struggling hard not to look at him, but her glance kept flickering back to linger briefly on the clear-cut severity of his nose and jaw and the curve of his mouth and then to flit on to admire the width of shoulder under the blue sports shirt he was wearing. Disturbed by her reaction to his appearance, she was glad when Luran approached her and sniffed. She cautiously put out her fist and was delighted when the dog showed recognition of her by wagging its tail.

Having examined the camera Jane went on to issue her invitation.

'We won't keep you any longer. Perhaps you would like to come to dinner with us tomorrow evening and we can continue our conversation.'

Callum was fastening the camera case and he did not look up as he declined smoothly.

'Thank you for the invitation. I'm afraid I can't accept. I'm having visitors tomorrow and they'll be here all day.'

'Then what about the next day?'

He looked up, smiled, and shook his head.

'I'm sorry. I shall be busy.'

'Oh, dear. Then I'd better ask you now, because time is going on. I would like your permission to go and look at the stone circle. If you could tell me the best way to get there I can assure you that I wouldn't disturb or damage anything.'

Callum's face was impassive. 'Why do you want to see it?' he asked.

'I've recently been working on a study of stone circles in Britain. I've seen most of the well-known ones, including the one at Callanish on Lewis, but I'd like very much to see this one because as far as I know no archaeologist has yet seen it. I should like to take compass bearings, other measurements and some photographs, if I may.'

'Then I shall take you to it this afternoon. I'm going in that direction.'

His suggestion was so unexpected, so directly in contradiction of his previous attitude, that Gail looked at him in surprise and met his glance for the first time that afternoon.

'Perfect!' Jane was beaming. 'Absolutely perfect, Mr. Black. Except that I haven't brought a compass with me today.'

'I can even provide that,' said Callum calmly, his glance moving downwards from Gail's face to her feet. 'But I'm thinking Gail should stay here because of her weak ankle.'

Gail, who was having difficulty with all sorts of new and conflicting emotions, glared at him.

'My ankle is fine, thank you. I've no wish to stay here

and wait. I'd like to see the stone circle too.'

'It's a long walk over the moors and the going is rough.'

He didn't want her company. It was all part of his dislike of her. If she had any sense or pride she would walk away now and return to Gartbeg. But she wanted desperately to go with him, to walk beside him and listen to his lazy voice.

'I am coming with you,' she said determinedly.

'Very well. But I think you're foolish to do so. Excuse me while I go and get the compass.'

At first they followed a path that was really a continuation of the road. But gradually the sand-dunes gave way to a rocky shore and the path left the coast and went inland, winding up past outcrops of stone.

As they went Jane asked many questions about the various plants and wild-flowers which grew beside the path, and Callum answered easily, often pointing out something she hadn't noticed.

Soon the path grew steeper and more rocky and Gail had to pick her way carefully so that her ankle did not turn on a loose stone. As a result she lagged behind a little. Then the path disappeared altogether and she found herself thigh-deep in heather in full bloom, a sea of purple and brown which stretched ahead of her as far as she could see.

Walking was difficult and she wished she could catch up with Jane and Callum, who had the benefit of his crook with which he could push aside the strong branches of the plant. Once she slipped and sat down. The heather came up to her shoulders and she realized that if she crouched a little lower she would be completely hidden. She was almost tempted to stay and lie there. If she did maybe Callum would miss her and would come back to look for her. It would be a way of drawing his attention.

She sat up sharply and struggled to her feet. How ridiculous could she get? Why should she want his attention? Because you're piqued, she answered herself. Piqued because he agreed to show the stone circle to Jane, but he didn't want you along, and now he's gone ahead with her and left you to lose yourself in the heather.

When she looked round she could not see the other two. They hadn't even missed her. She floundered through the strong crackling bushes hoping that she was going in the right direction. At last the land began to slope downwards and soon she was beside a burn which laughed and danced its way over brown stones under the shade of a few stunted birch and hazel trees. Feeling thirsty, she bent and cupped some clear cold water in her hands and drank.

As she followed the burn she thought of calling out to the others. Then she decided against such an action. Her pride had returned. Not for anything was she going to admit to Callum Black that she was afraid of being lost. How could anyone be lost on an island as small as Stornish?

But as she hurried she forgot to watch the ground and tripped over the exposed root of a tree, twisted her ankle and fell. For a few seconds she sat nursing her ankle and trying to stave off the waves of sickening pain. After a while she got to her feet and limped on.

'Gail! Coooeee! This way!'

At least Jane had no hesitation in calling out. Her voice seemed to be coming from the right. Turning away from the burn, Gail limped up the bank through a small wood. When she came out of it she found herself facing the flat top of a headland jutting into the sea, and set in the long flower-sprinkled grass, eroded by the weather into strange shapes, was the circle of stones.

Beside the stones Jane and Callum looked insignificant. It was difficult to imagine that the great megaliths had been raised by puny human beings who had probably been smaller in stature than modern man. Excited by the sight of them, Gail limped hurriedly towards them.

'Aren't they wonderful?' exclaimed Jane, her eyes

125

ablaze with excitement. 'I must take as many photographs of them as possible. I hope you'll both be patient and wait for me.'

'Take your time,' replied Callum. 'I'm going to be busy down there.' He pointed towards the rocky shore of a small bay. Out in the bay on small rocky islets there were seals basking in the sunshine. 'It's Gail who will be having to be patient waiting for both of us,' he added.

'I didn't know we'd see seals here,' said Gail. 'What sort are they?'

'Grey. They breed here.'

'There, didn't I say that Stornish is an island of delight?' said Jane. 'It has everything, even grey seals. Do you know if those particular animals down there were bred here?'

'That's what I'm hoping to find out. August to September is the time when they start to come in from the feeding grounds to the breeding grounds. I branded some six years ago. They should be returning to breed this year. From now on I shall have to visit this bay every day to count them as they return.' He glanced at his watch. 'I'll be about an hour. Is that long enough for you?'

'Splendid,' said Jane.

Without another word or even a glance at Gail he began to move away from the stone circle to a path which wound down the cliff side to the shore of the bay. Gail glanced at her aunt, at the tall stones and then at the blue water of the bay. Flinging pride to the winds, she hurried after Callum.

'May I come with you to see the seals?' she asked him.

He looked at her, but he didn't stop walking. She assumed he was reluctant to have her company, although he didn't say anything.

'Please,' she appealed. 'I promise not to bother you. I've never seen a seal and this might be my only chance to see one.'

'You will see several, but not closely. We'll have to ob-

126

serve them through the binoculars.'

He hadn't refused. Gail felt a sudden urge to skip with joy, but because of her damaged ankle she contented herself with a smile and a quiet word of thanks.

The path was steep and slippery and she had difficulty in keeping her footing. In front of her, Callum seemed to have no problems and she envied his sure-footed progress.

Eventually they reached the level sea-washed turf which lay behind the shore. Callum pointed to one of the flat-topped islets on which three seals were lying.

'See how they're beginning to collect on the skerries?' he said. 'More and more will come to rest there. At the end of August the adult bulls will start to come ashore. Some of them climb quite high and a long way out of the water to find a territory in a bay like this. Often they lie by a shallow pool where the mating will take place.'

'Do they fight each other?'

'Sometimes. Bulls already in possession of a territory will not trouble each other much. Challenge comes from fresh bulls coming from the sea and looking for territory.' He took out the binoculars and raised them to his eyes and stared intently at the rocky islets. 'There are two more on the farthest skerry. By this time next week there'll be about fifty.'

'As many as that?' exclaimed Gail.

'Didn't you know that the largest part of the world population of grey seals breeds in the British Isles as far as we know at present?' he asked.

'No, I'm afraid I didn't until you told me,' she replied humbly. 'But then I know very little about wild life. May I look at them more closely, please?'

He handed her the binoculars and she raised them to her eyes, reflecting humorously that she knew nothing about binoculars either. All she could see was the sea shimmering brightly and then a wide sweep of sky.

'Where are they?' she asked helplessly.

'You're looking too high. Lower the glasses a little.'

He moved behind her and put his hands over hers which were holding the binoculars, and steadily lowered the glasses. Suddenly the islets swam into her vision.

'Everything looks fuzzy,' she said.

'Then I'll adjust the focus for you.' He fiddled with something on the binoculars and then she could see quite clearly the three bull seals, olive brown in colour, stretched out on the rock.

'They're very big.'

'About eight feet long and five hundred and sixty pounds in weight.'

He was still behind her and his hands were still over hers helping to hold the binoculars steady. The knowledge that she had only to lean back a little to have the support of his shoulders and chest made her shake.

'Are the cows the same colour as the bulls?' she asked.

'No. The most common colour for them is pale steel grey on their upper surfaces and light lemon or deep yellow on their undersides. Some are darker, mole-coloured. When they're young they have a short grey coat. Young bulls are darker, almost jet black, velvety and very beautiful.'

He removed his hands from hers and stepped away from her. Gail lowered the binoculars and handed them to him. Looking round, she noticed a flat-topped rock and limping over to it she sat down on it with relief. She was sure her ankle was swelling, but she hoped that Callum hadn't noticed her limping. If he had he would want to look at it and she did not think she could bear the touch of his hands on her foot.

He followed her over to the rock and put the camera and the binoculars on the stone beside her, dropped his crook on the ground, told Luran to sit. Then he squatted before Gail and said abruptly,

'And now I think it's time I looked at your ankle.'

CHAPTER FIVE

GAIL pulled her legs up and curling them round tucked her feet beneath her.

'No,' she said.

'You've twisted it again, haven't you?'

'A little. I tripped and fell in the heather, then I stumbled near the brook. I was hurrying to catch up with you. You and Jane went on so fast I'd no idea where you were.'

'We had a lot to say to each other.'

'So I noticed,' she said tartly. When she saw mockery gleam in his eyes she wished she'd said nothing. To avoid his intent scrutiny she looked up at the standing stones which loomed against the sky like the petrified trunks of old trees.

Callum put out his hand and touched the rent in the upper part of her shirt sleeve. At once she flinched away and turned a wide-eyed gaze on him.

'You've ripped your shirt,' he said. She looked down and her hand went to the tear. 'Why don't you like being touched?' he added.

Gail looked at the stone circle again. How could she tell him that it was his touch which alarmed her because he had such an odd effect on her?

'I don't mind being touched. I was surprised. I was thinking.'

Callum stood up and sat down on the rock beside her and looked out at the scattered skerries, his eyes narrowed against the bright sea. He noticed that two more bulls had hauled themselves out of the water on to the nearest rock. That made seven bulls all together. He had been waiting for this moment all August and now that they were there the sight of the seals failed to interest him as much as it should, and he did not have far to look for the reason why.

'Were you thinking of Karl, perhaps?' he asked casually. 'I noticed that you haven't taken my advice and gone back to London to find out where he's gone. Have you heard from him?'

'I wasn't thinking of him,' she replied honestly. She could hardly tell him she had been thinking about Callum Black and the curious effect he had on her. 'And he hasn't written. I haven't taken your advice because I think he has left London and searching for him would be useless. Aren't you going to take any photographs?'

'That was my intention, but to tell the truth I find your company distracting,' he replied curtly. 'To watch animals it's essential that one should be completely undisturbed.'

And that was a polite way of telling her he wished she'd get lost, thought Gail miserably. Well, she didn't have to stay with him. She'd seen the seals and now she could climb back up to the headland and see the stone circle with Jane.

'I can easily remedy that,' she said lightly, and uncurling her legs she slid to the ground. She had to bite back a cry of pain as she put her left foot to the ground, but she managed to walk away without much of a limp.

She did not get very far. Callum followed her, overtook her and barred her progress, standing in front of her with his arms crossed over his chest.

'No one admires independence more than I do,' he barked, 'but you go to extremes. Go and sit down on that rock again and I'll look at your ankle.'

Unused to being ordered about in such a peremptory manner, she blinked, swallowed and said huskily but forcibly, 'No!'

A strange reddish light glowed in the depth of his dark eyes. He swore softly and succinctly as if at the end of his patience. Alarm at his reaction kept Gail rooted to the spot and she made no attempt to dodge him when he placed his hands on her waist. He lifted her up as if she had been a small child or a doll and carried her over to the rock and set her down on it. In a few seconds her shoe was off, the leg of her pants had been pushed up and he was examining the blue-veined swelling on her ankle.

Thoroughly shaken by his roughness, Gail tried to appear cool and calm, aware that her heart was beating unevenly,

'Was that to prove to me you were once local champion at putting the shot or was it to demonstrate that the men of the island still wear the pants?' she said.

He released her foot and raised his head slowly. The red glow had gone, leaving his eyes dark and empty. He was his usual impassive self with his emotions well under control again.

'I don't care how you interpret my action,' he retorted coldly. 'As far as I'm concerned I'm treating you as I would treat any other animal in pain.'

He pulled a large clean handkerchief out of his pocket and proceeded to fold it into a triangle.

As she had once thought she meant no more to him than an injured bird or seal. He would probably feel more concern for Luran. Gail bit her lip and once again she hid her real feelings under a flippant remark.

'Oh, yes, I forgot. I'm just a fellow living organism for whom you feel a certain amount of responsibility.'

He didn't laugh as she expected. He had folded the triangle of handkerchief over and over so that now it resembled a long bandage and he was tying it round her ankle and under her foot to give the ankle some support. When he had finished the task he spoke quietly.

'I should like to remind you, Goldilocks, that your own wilful obstinacy has caused this injury. You ignored my suggestion to stay behind and wait for your aunt. You were deliberately defiant as you always are when I tell you what you should do.'

'But I wanted to see the stone circle and the seals.'

'That's no excuse for defying me,' he retorted. 'Didn't it occur to you that I might know what I was talking about? I knew that the way would be rough and a strain on your newly-mended ankle. I wanted to prevent further injury. As it is you'll have to spend another week resting it and so you will not be seeing much of the islands while Jane is here.'

To her dismay she felt tears welling at the back of her eyes. Blinking rapidly, she looked away at the blue sea on which the dark lumps of rock seemed to be floating. She had been wrong again about his motives and this time she had to acknowledge that she'd been wrong.

He was fitting the shoe on her foot over the rough and ready bandage. Gail looked down at the crisp dark hair springing up from his wide forehead and at the thick black lashes which hid his eyes.

'I'm sorry, Callum,' she said in a low voice.

He looked up quickly, his eyes narrowed suspiciously.

'Why?' he demanded.

'I thought you were being deliberately mean and difficult. I though you didn't want me to come with you and Jane because you don't like me.'

Having finished tying the lace of her shoes he stood up slowly and gazed down at her, a faint frown darkening his face. Tears were still glistening in her eyes; wide open honest eyes which gazed back at him with a directness which was wholly sincere. He hadn't liked her at first because she had reminded him of Marguerite. Then he hadn't liked her because she disturbed the quiet routine of his life here on Stornish. Now he knew that she wasn't at all like Marguerite. Again he stretched out a hand and with one finger wiped away a tear which had spilled over on to her cheek.

'I don't dislike you, Goldilocks,' he said softly. 'In fact I'm in danger of liking you too well.'

His gentle gesture and his words had the most peculiar effect on her. Her self-possession was in rags and she was sure he must be able to hear the extra loud thudding of her heart.

'Danger?' she repeated. 'What danger can there pos-

132

sibly be in liking someone too well?'

His smile was self-mocking.

'The explanation is simple. I decided some time ago that there's no room for someone like you in my life.'

No room for her in his life. No room for her on his island. Oh yes, the explanation was very simple and he'd said it many ways ever since their first meeting, but to have it stated again after he had admitted to liking her made her feel completely and utterly rejected. She had been able to accept the fact that he didn't want her on Stornish when she had believed he didn't like her.

Then she remembered Alice Boyd. Of course, he had room only for well-organized, sensible people like Alice who wouldn't distract him when he wanted to take photographs.

The cloudless sky stretched blue over the glittering sea. The patches of white sand gleamed in the sunlight. The seals basked on the ageless rocks. Nothing had changed in that place since Callum had spoken, yet Gail felt that nothing would ever be the same in her life again. Ever since she had set foot on Stornish a subtle influence of this particular island of youth had been at work, softening her outlook, changing her attitudes. She wanted to stay here and be a part of Callum's life, no matter how small. But how could she stay when he didn't want her, when he had the strength to reject her even though he admitted that he was in danger of liking her too much? She would have to leave. The thought jarred her and she stiffened. That was what he wanted. He wanted her to leave. He didn't want strangers on Stornish.

'And no room for me on your island,' she said with a jauntiness she was far from feeling. 'The point has been made and taken many times.'

He did not answer. He had taken out the binoculars and was holding them to his eyes again. They screened his face effectively and she had no way of guessing at his thoughts.

An old hand at concealing his feelings, Callum stared

at the seals. Now there were eight bulls reclining on the skerries, all resting before they came ashore for the breeding season. How uncomplicated life was for them! They followed their natural instincts. Once he had followed his and had brought Marguerite to Stornish. He had been confident that his love for her could overcome any apprehension she had felt about coming to live on the island. Confident, perhaps a little arrogant, he had thought that his love had been returned and he had trusted her. She had betrayed his trust and now he no longer trusted his instinct. If he were to follow it now, for instance? Once again he was forced to pull his errant thoughts back from the direction they were taking. His mouth twisted wryly as he lowered the binoculars. What was instinct, after all? Only a chemical reaction to external stimulus, a mere physical sensation.

'Haven't you found living here lonely?' he asked idly to make conversation while he put the glasses back in their case.

'Oh no. How could anyone be lonely here?' Gail replied. If he thought he could get rid of her that way he was mistaken. Loneliness was something with which she had come to terms long ago.

'People like you from the city often find that they can't live here. They find it difficult to adapt. They miss the bright lights, the hustle and bustle.'

'Some people are often lonely in the middle of the teeming city, but that's because they're unable to relate to other people,' she countered. 'The fault lies in the person, not the place. Once you have learned to live with yourself you should be able to live anywhere.'

He glanced at her with interest because her answer surprised him.

'How wise you are,' he mocked. 'Where did you learn to live with yourself?'

'I've spent many hours alone. My mother died when I was twelve and my father hasn't always been at home.'

'Now that he's married again will you still live with

134

him?'

He had asked the very question which had been bothering her all morning. Now that it had been asked she had to face up to it, to find an answer.

'Phil won't need me any more. He will have Priscilla to look after him,' she said. There was no point in being other than realistic on this matter.

His gaze lingered on the taut proud angle of her chin beneath the slightly tremulous curve of her generous mouth. He had noticed the quivering break in her voice when she had said her father wouldn't need her.

'Is it important to you to be needed?' he asked curiously.

She flashed a startled glance at him. His questions were very near the bone.

'I suppose it is,' she fenced.

'Then what will you do now that your father doesn't need you?'

'I have my work. I've just completed my first year of teaching and I still find I have much to learn about young children.'

'No thoughts about marriage, or are you of the opinion that so many women seem to have today, that it's a trap from which escape is difficult and expensive?'

'I don't regard it as a trap, but I think you have to love a person very much before committing yourself to them in such a binding relationship.'

'And you haven't found anyone yet to whom you would wish to commit yourself?'

'No, I haven't.'

'Not even Karl?'

Her clear eyes clouded with uncertainty. Where were his questions leading? What did he want to know?

'I don't know. I hadn't known him for very long. He was just someone whom I met who seemed to need help, so I tried to help him.'

'A lame dog, and not a very savoury character from all accounts.'

'How do you know?' she demanded. 'Oh, Aunt Jane must have told you. She talks too much. What did she say about Karl?'

'She told me that you have a tendency to be attracted by apparently helpless individuals. She quoted your relationship with Karl as an example. Did you know that your father was very worried about your affair with Karl and that he was relieved when you agreed to come up here because he hoped once you were away from London the affair would die a natural death?'

'No, I didn't. But he never said anything to me about Karl,' she said hotly, furious as she realized again how completely communication between Phil and herself had broken down.

'Perhaps you weren't in a listening mood again. Remember you didn't want to hear about his views on marrying? And when you're infatuated with someone you tend to close your ears to unpleasant information about the subject of your infatuation,' he observed mildly.

She lifted her chin haughtily as she resented his criticism.

'I've no doubt you're speaking from experience,' she countered.

His wide mouth curved upward at one corner as he acknowledged with a certain wry amusement her quick reply.

'I do. I had no father or mother to warn me. But I had a grandfather who never hesitated to give me advice. Like you, there were times when I turned off, especially when I didn't like what he was saying. Perhaps if I'd listened more carefully I wouldn't have been quite so trusting as to leave Marguerite here when Ian was staying at Gartbeg, and perhaps she wouldn't have been drowned.'

So he blamed himself for Marguerite's drowning! How typical of him, how in keeping with his character. He felt he had failed in his responsibility to another living creature. And strangely enough as a result of his description of his own experience of not listening to the advice of his grandfather she felt less annoyed with Phil for having warned her about Karl, with herself for not having listened and with Jane for having told Callum all about it.

'Would you have married Marguerite, if she had lived? Would you have followed her eventually and forgiven her?' she asked curiously.

'I've often wondered,' he admitted. 'Usually I come to the conclusion that I couldn't have married her knowing she had broken trust. I suppose I didn't love her enough, if I loved her at all. Love is fire and should be able to overcome any obstacle in its path. It should conquer pride.'

Gail sat silent, staring out to sea. The close affinity which she felt with Callum at that moment held her tense and inarticulate. If she moved or spoke she would destroy that affinity and it was too precious to destroy. For the first time in her life she had met someone who felt as she did about the highest of human feelings.

Love is fire. How well she knew that sonnet by Elizabeth Barrett Browning in which the poetess observed that just as fire is common to the great cedar tree and the meanest, smallest weed so love can be experienced by and can transfigure the meanest, lowest creature as well as the greatest. But for Callum love was fire because it could overcome all opposition, anything which lay in its way, even pride such as his. And he had not felt like that about Marguerite. Did he now feel like that about Alice Boyd?

She wished she could ask him, but there was no more time for further questions, no time to continue a conversation which had been growing steadily more and more personal because Jane was coming towards them.

She was slightly breathless and overflowing with enthusiasm when she eventually reached them.

'A very good specimen of ancient genius,' she said to Callum. 'Did you know that the people who built those

137

circles, megalithic men, were highly sophisticated beings with a practical knowledge of geometry which would put many twentieth-century people to shame? They even had a common unit of length throughout Britain.'

Callum glanced up at the tall enigmatic stones which he had known intimately since boyhood.

'That piece of information makes me feel even smaller than the stones do,' he said with a smile.

'And so it should,' said Jane. 'They weren't as barbaric as we like to think they were. The circles weren't perfect, however. They are more like ellipses. But we mustn't be deceived into thinking they were built for ritualistic purposes only. They were a practical necessity for accurate timekeeping. You should be very proud to have such a fine example on your land.'

'I hope you won't give it too much publicity,' replied Callum seriously. 'Although I have a great deal of reverence for my not so barbaric ancestors and their wonderful geometric feats I'm really more concerned about the present and future, and I don't want hordes of sightseers invading my island.'

Jane nodded sympathetically.

'I understand, and I can imagine you giving short shrift to anyone who tries to trespass. Now what have you two achieved this afternoon?'

'Very little,' replied Callum smoothly. 'Gail has hurt her ankle again. I'm thinking the quickest way back to Gartbeg for you is by the shepherd's path over there, over the hill and down to the McCaigs' house. Once there you could go ahead and get your car to take Gail the rest of the way. It will mean she won't have to walk so far and I shan't have to carry her much.'

His smile and the glint of mischief in his eyes brought Gail to her feet at once.

'I can walk perfectly well. You won't have to carry me.'

'I'm glad to hear it, because I believe you've taken my suggestion about eating porridge every day seriously and that you've put on weight recently.'

The walk over the hill was easier because there was a well marked path to follow. At first Gail was able to keep up with Aunt Jane. Callum walked a little way behind them with Luran. He had lent his crook to Gail for her to lean on. But once over the hill with the McCaigs' house in view the pain in her ankle increased and she was forced to slow down. Callum walked with her while Jane hurried on now that she could see her way to Gartbeg.

About two hundred yards away from the McCaigs' house Gail had to stop. Immediately Callum offered to carry her, but with a violent shake of her head she refused and began to hobble forward wincingly. He followed her, took the crook from her hand and gave it to the dog to carry in its mouth. Then before she had time to move forward again he swung her up into his arms and strode after the dog.

'I could have managed,' she protested.

'I don't think so.'

'I dislike being carried!'

'I know you do, and I'm wondering is it because being carried makes you feel helpless, which is something you don't like having to admit? Or is it because I'm carrying you?' he asked, and his knowledgeable summing up of how she felt made her seeth.

'Both,' she retorted honestly. 'But mostly because it's you. I loathe masterful men.'.

'Remember, Goldilocks, I'd do this for anyone in pain no matter who or what they are.'

'Even for Annie or Aunt Jane?' she couldn't resist saying, and was immediately subjected to a strange scornful glance.

'Even for them,' he replied. 'Next time I have to carry you I must remember to gag you first. You talk too much.'

'Tyrant!' she hissed, but there was little real rebellion in her protest. No one had ever overruled her in the way that he did, and she was fast discovering how pleasant it

139

was to be overruled by someone stronger than herself.

When they walked into the McCaigs' kitchen there were so many neighbours already that with the addition of Gail and Callum and the knowledge that Jane was on her way, Mrs. McCaig at once declared that it was a *ceilidh* and set about preparing the tea. Gail was instructed to sit on the sofa beside Annie and a chair was found for Callum in a corner by the dresser. Besides Annie, Dougie Lean and his wife and child were also present. They were over to see Ron, Eileen's fiancé, who had just arrived on holiday from Glasgow. Eileen, of course, was sparkling-eyed and pink-cheeked, happy to be reunited with her loved one, who was a quiet, shy six-footer and who possessed the typical bright blue eyes of the Hebridean.

'Now, wasn't I after warning you to be careful where you walked, miss?' chided Annie. 'That ankle will take a deal of nursing before it's properly better.'

'Ach, Gail, you'll not be able to join in the dancing to-morrow night,' wailed Eileen. 'You'll be having to sit and watch again.'

'It would be better if she didn't go to the dance at all. That way she won't be tempted to join in,' said Callum firmly.

'Oh, no, I shall go,' said Gail. 'I wouldn't miss it for anything. Last time I sat and watched.'

'And didn't you find it a dreary way to pass the time?' he asked.

'A lot you know about it! You weren't there,' snorted Eileen. 'Gail enjoyed every minute. For all she wasn't dancing she had plenty of partners wanting to sit out with her. Shall you be going to-morrow night, Callum?'

'I might be,' he replied evasively.

'I'm thinking you haven't been to one in years,' continued Eileen. 'Perhaps you've forgotten how to dance. If you go you'll be taking Miss Boyd, of course.'

'If you say so, Eileen,' he said with a tantalizing grin. 'I know how you like to plan the lives of others.'

140

'You've never said a truer word,' chortled Mrs. McCaig as she busily set out cups and saucers on the kitchen table. 'Aren't I always warning her that man proposes but God disposes?'

'But that's the trouble with Callum. He isn't proposing,' flashed Eileen. 'Why don't you warn him with another of your sayings, Mother? Tell him that he who hesitates is lost and maybe that will move him!'

During the ensuing laughter Jane arrived and her entrance was the signal for the tea to be poured and for the scones and jam to be handed around. Mr. McCaig came in and joined the cheerful relaxed group and soon at the request of Jane, Annie, Mrs. McCaig and Eileen were giving an exhibition of mouth music, after which Ron, who sang in a choir in Glasgow, was persuaded to sing Mrs. McCraig's favourite song, *Land of Heart's Desire*. Listening to the haunting melody by Marjorie Kennedy Fraser which transformed the simple words into a song of nostalgic beauty Gail found in it the perfect expression of her own feelings regarding the island of Stornish, the isle of youth which gleamed in the sunlight under the cloudless sky. During the last verse she looked across at Callum and found he was staring at her with such intensity that she stared back and for a moment was oblivious of the other people in the room. Only the words sung by the beautiful tenor voice penetrated.

> 'There shalt thou and I
> Wander free.
> On sheer white sands
> Dreaming in starlight.'

She was on a shore of gleaming white sands walking hand in hand with Callum and above the stars pinpricked the dark Hebridean night.

'Wake up, Callum!' Eileen's voice was sharp. 'This is no time for dreaming.'

Gail looked away quickly. Had Eileen noticed something which was not in her plans for Callum? She gave herself a little mental shake to bring herself to earth as she heard Callum laugh and say,

'There's always time for dreaming, Eileen. You should try it some time. It's an excellent escape from reality.'

He stood up and crossed the room to the sofa where Gail was now pretending to listen to a conversation Jane was having with Mr. McCaig about sheep. Although she knew Callum was standing in front of her she did not look up at him.

'I'm going now,' he said quietly. 'I hope you will not be trying to walk for a while. If you do I shall be hearing about it and I shall come to Gartbeg and tie you up so that you can't move.'

Shakily aware that their relationship had deepened that afternoon and taken on a new and troubling aspect, Gail tried to answer lightly as she looked up at him at last.

'Will you use chains?' she queried.

'And a padlock of which I shall possess the only key,' he replied with a smile that did her already shattered self-possession no good at all.

'Despot!' she retaliated weakly, and she had the strangest feeling that when he left the room the sunlight departed with him, making it dim and shadowy.

But in spite of Callum's threat Gail went to the dance the following night with Eileen and Ron. Jane took them over to Portnagour in her car, the tide being low, and so Gail did not have to walk very far. After arranging to pick them up later Jane went off to spend the evening with Eileen's aunt and uncle.

As she sat in the village hall watching the energetic antics of the dancers Gail thought it was just as well she hadn't gone full of expectancy hoping to see Callum there, because so far he hadn't put in an appearance, although Alice was there accompanied by a tall stiff-shouldered man of about thirty-five years of age and a younger man whose russet-coloured hair and fine-boned face proclaimed his relationship to Alice.

With a resounding chord from the accordion the dance came to an end and the groups split up. Eileen and Ron came back across the room to sit beside Gail. At once she asked the question which was on the tip of her tongue.

'Who is with Miss Boyd? I thought you hoped that Callum would be with her.'

'Isn't he? Where is she? I didn't know she was here,' said Eileen, her bright glance going quickly over the groups of people standing or sitting around the edge of the floor. 'Ach, look at that now! He's the very reason why Callum should not be hesitating the way he is.'

'But which he?' demanded Gail.

'Major Fraser, the tall man. He used to be in the Army ... the Guards ... but he was invalided out. You'll notice he won't be dancing. He has a limp, the result of an accident when he was playing polo. The other man is Patrick Boyd, her brother. Ach, why hasn't Callum come?'

'Annie was saying to-day that he's very taken up with the seals just now,' offered Ron.

'That's no excuse. He can't count them or take photographs at this time of day. It's too dark,' snorted Eileen. Then she added in an undertone to Gail 'He'll lose her just as he lost the other one because he pays more attention to wild animals, his photography and his writing than he does to the feelings of a woman. If he isn't careful history will repeat itself. Ach, I'm at the end of my patience with him and I don't know what to do!'

'But just because Miss Boyd is with another man it doesn't mean to say she prefers him to Callum,' argued Gail.

'You don't know the Major,' said Eileen. 'Like Ian Sanderson he's one of the charmers of this world. He knows how to talk to a woman, how to make her feel special and needed, and this is the second time this year he's been to stay at Balmore. He was here at Easter. She feels sorry for him because he was hurt and had to give up his career in the Army.'

'Well, the obvious way to prevent her from falling for him is to attract his attention elsewhere,' mused Gail.

Eileen turned and looked at her speculatively. Putting her hand on Gail's arm she patted it gently.

'You could do that if you set your mind to it,' she whispered. There was no chance to question her because the music started again and Ron whisked his fiancée away to take part in a graceful strathspey. Looking across the room, Gail noticed that Alice was partnered by her brother. As they took up their positions Alice glanced round the room. Her gaze rested momentarily on Gail and she smiled and nodded, then her gaze went on searching the crowd. Was she looking for the one person who wasn't there? Was she looking for Callum?

He'll lose her. Eileen's concerned comment worried Gail as she watched Major Fraser. He was a handsome man, very distinguished-looking with a pale narrow face and a white streak in the front of his dark hair. The streak, the limp and the furrows drawn by suffering in his lean cheeks would make an instant appeal to a woman. Would history repeat itself? Would Callum lose Alice whom he intended to marry, to the attractive Major who knew how to make a woman feel special?

'Not if I can help it,' asserted Gail silently, as she recalled the bitterness in Callum's voice whenever he referred to Marguerite. She thought that he was the sort of person who didn't need any help, that he was too strong and self-sufficient. But it was obvious from Eileen's remarks at the *ceilidh* this afternoon and just recently at the dance that Callum had no idea how to win a fair lady. What exactly she could do to help him win Alice she was not quite sure, but encouraged by Eileen's whispered comment before she had gone off to dance, she was determined that Callum should not be made unhappy for a second time by losing to a more superficially attractive man.

When the strathspey finished Eileen lost no time in going up to Alice to speak to her and soon she was bringing her across the room to Gail, followed by the Major and Patrick Boyd. Amused by Eileen's lack of hesitation, Gail played up, smiling at the Major when he was introduced to her and suggesting that he sat beside her while Alice sat on the other side. Patrick, who was a lively young man she judged to be in his early twenties, asked Gail why she wasn't dancing. When she explained he commiserated with her and then with a mocking sidelong glance at Major Fraser he said,

'You and Malcolm can keep one another company, then. He doesn't dance either.' Glancing across at his sister, he called out as the music started up again, 'Come on, Ali. It's an eightsome reel!'

It was almost as if he'd been in the plot, thought Gail, as she watched him go off with Alice, Eileen and Ron. Then she shook herself mentally. What plot? How ridiculous! Just because Eileen had seemed taken up with the idea when she had mentioned that one way of preventing Malcolm Fraser from taking Alice away from Callum was to make sure the handsome Major found alternative attractions while he was staying on Sorasay, she was now imagining all sorts of innuendoes which probably didn't exist.

She glanced at Malcolm. He was watching Alice as she and Patrick made up a circle with three other couples for the eightsome reel. He was smiling faintly and rather wistfully. Immediately Gail went into action.

'Are you staying long at Balmore?' she asked.

He turned to look at her and she felt the full effect of his smoky blue eyes.

'Another week. I'm surprised to hear a London accent here, tonight. Are you on holiday too?' He spoke pleasantly and his manner had just the right amount of polite interest, very different from Callum's polite indifference.

'In a way,' she answered, and went on to tell him why she was staying on Stornish, ending with the rueful comment, 'But I'm afraid Callum Black doesn't like me being

145

there.'

'I think I can tell you why,' he said softly, in an almost conspiratorial manner. 'At first glance you have an astonishing resemblance to Marguerite Reddish. In fact when I looked over and saw you sitting here I thought for one fantastic moment that the clock had been put back for six years and that you were her.'

'Oh, I didn't know,' said Gail weakly. She felt slightly sick with shock. That must be how Callum had seen her the morning he had found her in his bed. Her likeness to Marguerite must have been the reason for his antagonistic attitude towards her in particular, apart from the difficulties her father's ownership of Gartbeg had created.

'Did you know Marguerite?' she asked. He was really far more handsome than she had supposed and she imagined he must have looked devastating in ceremonial uniform.

'I met her. I can't say I knew her. I was staying with the Boyds on leave from the Army, at the time. My parents were friends of Sir Morris for years and he has always made me very welcome in his home,' he said. 'Callum brought her over to meet Sir Morris and Alice. I shall always remember Alice's reaction. She was very upset.'

His haunted blue glance strayed over the room in the direction of Alice. She was now taking her turn in the centre of her eightsome and was dancing with featherlike grace, her white arms raised above her head while the other seven circled round her.

'Why was she upset?' asked Gail.

'She had tended to regard Callum as her particular property when they were younger and she was a little taken aback when she realized he had found someone else. I was posted abroad soon afterwards, but Alice wrote to me regularly and I heard about the drowning. From the little I know about Callum I would guess he bottled up his grief. He's not the sort to invite sympathy and would reject it with hard words if you gave it to him.'

But you're not like that, thought Gail. You show your suffering in your eyes and on your face. It's all there to pull at a woman's heart-strings and it's pulling at mine now. Recognizing the familiar impulse, she gave in to it and with deft and sympathetic questioning soon had the story of his accident when playing polo. His mount had stumbled and fallen, pinning him beneath its weight and crushing his left leg.

'What do you do now that you're out of the Army?' she asked.

His smile was charming and had just the right amount of mocking self-disparagement.

'I work in my uncle's publishing company. I'm not very good at my work.'

'Oh, give yourself time,' counselled Gail. 'How long have you been in the company? Only a few months, I expect.'

'Nine, and already it seems like nine years. I tell myself I'd feel better if I had some incentive to work for, a wife and children perhaps. And I haven't taken kindly to being cooped up in an office yet. Also living in London can be a lonely business. It's so difficult to meet people.'

'But you know your uncle and his wife and family.'

'He's a crusty widower and has no children.'

'Then when I return to London I shall look you up,' offered Gail. 'I'll introduce you to lots of people. Don't forget to give me your address.'

He looked at her with interest and to her surprise took one of her hands in both of his.

'I should like that,' he said.

At that moment Alice and Patrick came up, the dance having finished.

'What would you like, Malcolm?' asked Alice sweetly, although her greenish-blue glance was sharp as she noticed he was holding Gail's hand. Still gazing at Gail, Malcolm withdrew his hands from hers.

'Gail is very understanding and is going to take pity on

my lonely state in London. We're going to meet when we both return there.'

'Quick work,' observed Patrick with a knowing grin and a wink in Gail's direction.

'I'm sure that will be very pleasant for both of you,' said Alice, still as sweet as honey, but this time Gail received the impression that the sweetness was simulated to hide an acid reaction to Malcolm's words. 'When do you have to go south, Gail?'

'I have to be back at work on the fifteenth of September. I'm hoping my father will be here soon. He goes back to work on the same date, so there isn't much time left for him to see Gartbeg.'

'Do you really believe Callum will let him keep it?' asked Patrick.

'What can he do to prevent Mr. Collins from keeping it? Gail's father is the legal owner,' said Malcolm.

'I wouldn't be trusting a Black if I were Mr. Collins. Callum is sure to have ways and means to make living on Stornish uncomfortable for someone he doesn't want there. And no one is going to convince me he's happy the island has been split in two,' replied Patrick.

'He's already used some of his ways and means on me, and I've survived,' said Gail lightly.

'Except for a sprained ankle. I wonder what other accident will happen before you have to leave?' murmured Patrick suggestively.

'Now, Patrick,' cautioned Alice in a brisk elder-sisterly fashion, 'you shouldn't make remarks like that about Callum.'

'He may be restrained and subdued when you're around, but there's a Gaelic devil in Callum which he's inherited from old Adam. Don't forget the old man got rid of the Reddish woman by making staying in his house uncomfortable just because he thought she was unsuited to the way of life of the island and also an unsuitable mate for Callum. Yes, Callum grows more like his grandad every day, silent and secretive and just a little mad, although I'll concede he's not such a puritan as the old man.'

'He's not mad!' protested Alice.

'Must be, if he's more interested in animals than in human beings. He'd rather count seals than come to see you,' taunted the unrepentant Patrick. 'I see Hughie Murdoch is beckoning to me. I promised him I'd go to the hotel with him for a drink. Coming with us, Malcolm?'

As Malcolm declined a furious Alice hissed at her brother,

'I'm thinking you've had a drink too many already, Patrick Boyd, judging by your talk!'

But he paid no heed and with a wave of his hand went off to the entrance to the village hall.

'Please do not be thinking he always behaves like that,' Alice excused Patrick primly. 'He comes to the island merely out of a sense of family duty and finds staying here very dull. He's studying law in Edinburgh and once he's called to the bar I expect we shall see very little of him. Is your aunt not here?'

'She brought Eileen, Ron and me in her car and she's gone to visit Eileen's aunt while we're dancing,' replied Gail. 'Did you want to speak to her?'

'Only to issue an invitation. I was talking earlier this evening to Callum on the phone and he was saying how much she would like to see Balmore House and the gardens. I was thinking that you and she might like to come over to meet my father and to have tea.'

'Yes, we would,' said Gail, showing enthusiasm on Aunt Jane's behalf.

'Then shall we say next Friday? Your ankle should be a little better by then.'

'And even if it isn't Gail could always stay and keep me entertained while the rest of you tour the gardens,' put in Malcolm blandly.

For a second Alice looked nonplussed. Then she sent a hard assessing glance in Gail's direction. But the hardness was soon obliterated by her sweet smile.

'It must be wretched for you to have hurt it so badly. I'm sure there must be some way in which we can help you. Maybe I can persuade Patrick to take you out when he goes fishing. Sometimes he likes to borrow one of Dougie Lean's boats and to go pottering about amongst the islands. I'll speak to him. It would be a way of keeping him entertained while he's here.'

Alice was true to her word. Two days after the dance on Monday morning, which was sunny and calm, Patrick arrived at Gartbeg to invite both Gail and Jane to go with him on *The Islander*, one of Dougie's boats.

'I thought I was going to have you both to myself, but Malcolm has decided to come too. It's not a good day for fishing . . . too bright . . . but it's ideal for sunbathing and sightseeing. Don't bother to bring any food. Alice has provided everything. She loves to organize people. She thinks you and I will keep one another out of mischief,' he said with a grin at Gail. 'She seems to think we have something in common.'

'I wonder what it can be?' countered Gail.

'Our age. What else could it be?' he retorted cheekily.

They returned to Stornish in the tranquil golden glow of late afternoon having spent a pleasant day seeing the famous basalt columns of the island of Staffa, the unusual lava terraces of the Treshnish Isles, and having spent a sleepy restful afternoon at anchor in the beautiful Calgary Bay on the north-west corner of Mull where the clean white sands, deserted and unspoilt, were backed by cliffs and woodland.

When Gail and Jane stepped ashore at Stornish and turned to say goodbye to their escorts before Dougie ferried them back to Sorasay Malcolm said surprisingly,

'We must do this again. What do you think, Patrick?'

'It depends on the weather. Is it too good to last,

Dougie?'

'We might get another two days,' replied the fisherman.

'Then shall we say Wednesday?' said Malcolm, looking at Gail.

She thought quickly. Now that she knew him a little better she realized how dangerously attractive he must be to Alice. Amenable and gentlemanly in his behaviour, he was a pleasant companion, and Alice, who was being neglected by Callum at present in favour of seals, must find such companionship balm to hurt feelings. So he must be kept away from Alice.

'I should like to go again,' she agreed. 'It's a good way of seeing the islands without having to walk far.'

'Good. Then we shall see you about ten o'clock on Wednesday morning.'

On Wednesday Jane decided not to go on the proposed cruise because she had a headache and felt she would be poor company, but she drove Gail down to the jetty to await the arrival of Patrick and Callum. When Dougie's boat bumped alongside at the jetty, however, Malcolm was the only passenger. He explained that Patrick had received an unexpected phone call from a friend who had put in at Tobermory on a sailing boat and had decided to go over on the steamer to see him.

'What will you do if we don't go cruising?' asked Gail.

'Go back to Balmore and wander around after Alice,' he said.

'Could you handle the boat?'

'Yes,' he said diffidently. 'If Dougie will give his permission.'

'Aye, you can have the boat,' agreed Dougie. 'But I wouldn't be staying out long if I were you. We're due for a change in the weather.'

'Then let's go round Sorasay and come back for lunch to Gartbeg,' suggested Gail enthusiastically. With a

151

bit of luck she would be able to persuade Malcolm to stay the rest of the day with her and perhaps make further arrangements to keep him away from Alice during the rest of his stay at Balmore.

'I can think of nothing I'd like better,' replied Malcolm courteously.

Several hours later Gail sat in the open cockpit of *The Islander* and gazed miserably through the increasing drizzle of rain. Up in the bow Malcolm was being sick for the third time since the boat had stopped.

So much for keeping him away from Alice, thought Gail. Why, oh, why couldn't she leave well alone? It had seemed such a good idea to go for a cruise this morning and everything had progressed smoothly for a while. Malcolm had handled the boat just as well as Patrick had done.

It was when they were opposite the raised beaches on the western side of Sorasay that the engine had begun to race. Neither of them had thought there was anything wrong until there was a smell of burning and Gail noticed that the boat was not moving forwards. She mentioned as much to Malcolm. He had looked puzzled, but had taken no immediate action.

'Don't you think we'd better stop the engine and find out what's wrong with it?' she had asked. He seemed to be one of those people who are excellent company when everything is going well but who are incapable of taking the initiative when anything goes wrong, and she realized ruefully she would have to take all the responsibility for this escapade and make all the decisions.

He had obediently stopped the engine and the silence which had followed had been shattering. There they were drifting on the current on a wide expanse of the Atlantic with the coast of Sorasay seemingly floating further and further away as the morning haze had thickened and the sun had gone out.

'I know nothing about engines, I'm afraid,' said Malcolm, looking charmingly apologetic in a way which had reminded her of Karl. 'I suppose this one is under this boxlike affair.' He had patted the bulky wooden box which took up most of the space in the cockpit.

'Yes. But if you know nothing about it there isn't any point in removing the cover.'

'No,' he had agreed humbly. 'Shall I start it again? Maybe the rest has helped it to cool down.'

She had nodded and the engine had started accommodatingly, but as soon as he had put it into gear it had begun to race again and the boat had remained stationary except for a sideways drifting motion.

'We'd better stop it or we might damage it,' Gail had said, and again silence had enveloped them. Staring at the wooden box, she had tried to marshal all the little knowledge she had of boats and engines.

'If the propeller was broken or had fallen off, would that mean we would make no progress?' she asked.

Malcolm had snapped his fingers and had looked at her with respect dawning in his eyes.

'That's it! The propeller isn't turning.'

'That means we're stuck here until someone comes by and sees us which might be never,' Gail had said gloomily, and then she had noticed Malcolm's pallor. His pale face definitely had a tinge of green. Surely he wasn't going to be sick? Why, there wasn't any wind and the boat was hardly moving. But it was moving, because although there weren't any ripples on the water yet there was an ominous slow swell rolling in from the west.

'Do you feel ill?' she had asked sympathetically.

'Well, I don't feel in the pink,' he had replied rather testily. 'We should never have come.'

'My fault,' she had replied, and he had actually agreed. She had thought suddenly of Callum. He would have agreed that it was her fault too. He would have called her wilful, impetuous, foolish. But he wouldn't have sat there looking sorry for himself. He would have tried to do something. Then she had put a brake on her thoughts. She was being unfair. How could Malcolm do

153

anything?

Soon afterwards he had gone to the bow to vomit over the side, and it was then that she had noticed that Sorasay had disappeared completely and that the sky was covered with lowering grey cloud. It wasn't long before the first drops of rain had begun to fall and she had been forced to take shelter under the canvas dodger which protected the cockpit from flying spray when the boat was moving. Malcolm had returned and had also huddled under the dodger, his face white, his eyes closed.

And now she was thinking,

'No one will ever find us. If only there was some way of attracting attention!'

As usual with Gail the thought was father to the act and impulse sent her to the stern locker. She opened it and congratulated herself that for once impulse had been right. In the locker she found a tin box marked with the word 'Flares' and in it she found six red signal lights. Each one was a cylinder about ten inches long which resembled a rather thick firework and on the outside of each the instructions of how to use them was printed.

Gail took them over to Malcolm to show him.

'What's the use of trying? No one will see them,' he groaned.

'There might be a fishing boat in the vicinity,' replied Gail hopefully.

'We'd hear its engine if there was. I tell you, Gail, you'll just be wasting them if you set them off now.'

'Well, I'm going to try one at least, to see if it works. It will be better than doing nothing.'

Following the instructions, she tore off the piece of tape attached to the cylinder to expose the igniting composition. Then she removed the striker which was attached to the underside of the tape. That done, she struck the exposed surface firmly with a striker and was rewarded with a big ball of flame which lasted about five minutes. Pleased with her effort, Gail decided to take Malcolm's advice and not waste the flares but to put them

154

into use if or when she heard the engine of another boat.

The swell was becoming noticeably steeper and waves were beginning to break against the side of the small boat. Malcolm departed to the bow and Gail realized that her own stomach was beginning to feel queasy. It occurred to her suddenly that they were probably drifting on the tide and that they should have anchored immediately the engine had stopped. She said as much to Malcolm when he returned to the cockpit to flop down weakly in a corner, but either he was too miserable to take any action or he hadn't heard her.

Shivering a little, she tried to think about something pleasant. It wasn't easy with the boat rolling from side to side one minute and then pitching and tossing the next. She would rather act than think. She took out another flare and prepared to set it off. While she was pulling off the tape she thought she heard the sound of an engine and she sat still and listened. The only sounds she could hear were the hiss and splash of the sea, and the creaking of the boat's timbers. Then it came again, the dull throb of a boat's engine. Quickly she removed the striker from the cylinder and struck the exposed surface of the igniting material. The flame shot out and she stood up and waved it in the air. When it went out she took another flare and ignited it and did the same. To her surprise and delight an answering flare came from out of the murk and it was followed by the shadowy hull of another slightly larger boat. As it came nearer she had no difficulty in recognizing Dougie's other boat.

It came alongside *The Islander*. She could see Dougie enveloped in oilskins at the tiller, and poised on the boat's rail was Callum, a rope in his hand. As Dougie put his engine into neutral Callum jumped and landed in the cockpit of *The Islander*. At once he turned and went up to the bow where he made the rope fast to a bollard on the deck and then shouted something to Dougie. Then he came back to the cockpit.

'What happened?' he asked, gazing at Malcolm's figure and greyish-green pallor.

'We think the propeller's fallen off,' said Gail, and he flicked a glance in her direction.

'How do you feel, Fraser?' he barked next.

'Terrible,' groaned Malcolm.

'Then I suggest you go aboard Dougie's boat, and lie down on one of the bunks. When we start towing this it's going to roll badly.'

'Isn't it doing that already?' grumbled Malcolm as he stood up and staggered over to the side of *The Islander*. Helped from behind by Callum and from in front by Dougie, he was soon aboard the other boat and out of sight.

Callum turned to Gail. His dark eyes roved over her wet bedraggled hair and dripping clothing.

'You'd better go too,' he ordered.

She was so pleased to see him that the thought of being parted from him immediately was too much to bear. She shook her head.

'No. I want to stay with you,' she said honestly.

He didn't argue with her but pulled off his oilskin and threw it on the floor, then tugged his thick sweater over his head. When it was off he pulled it ungently over her head and commanded her to put her arms in the sleeves. It was deliciously warm although it hung on her like a sack. Callum put his oilskin coat on again and leaning over the side of the boat shouted something to Dougie. In response an oilskin jacket landed in the cockpit of *The Islander* and Gail was ordered to put it on and to keep under the dodger out of the rain.

Callum took the tiller in his hand and yelled again at Dougie. The engine of the other boat stopped idling and the boat moved forward slowly. When the tow rope grew taut and tugged at *The Islander*'s plunging bow, Callum pulled the tiller across to bring the boat into line behind the other one.

Not until he was sure the tow rope was holding and *The*

Islander was moving forward did he spare another glance for Gail. She was still shivering. He put a hand in his oilskin coat pocket and pulled out a flask, unscrewed the top and handed it to her.

'Take some of that. It will warm you up,' he ordered.

Taking the flask from him, she obeyed. Fiery liquid caught in her throat and she spluttered, but some of it coursed down inside her. She handed the flask back.

'Ugh! That was horrible,' she said with a grimace.

'I'll have you know, Goldilocks, it's good malt whisky you're condemning!'

'The product of your own private still, no doubt,' she quipped. How much better she felt now that he was there. She didn't mind how long the journey back to Stornish might take as long as she was with him.

'What if it is?' he challenged. 'Are you going to report me to the Customs and Excise?'

'No, I wouldn't. Oh, Callum, have you really got a still? May I see it one day?' she said eagerly.

He didn't reply, but she saw him grin mischievously and guessed she'd never know whether he had an illicit still or not. He took a drink from the flask, put the top on and put it away in his pocket. Then ordered her to put the tin box holding the flares in the stern locker.

'Who set off the flares?' he asked.

'I did. Malcolm was helpless. He's been sick most of the time.'

'You took a chance coming out today with him. As far as I know he has very little knowledge of this area and even less about boats and engines.'

'He didn't want to come at first, but I persuaded him.'

'That damned wilfulness of yours! When will you learn?'

'I was trying to help. Callum, you must see how attractive he is.'

'Why didn't I guess? He's another of those lame dogs you find so attractive. He has a limp, a general air of

157

helplessness and seems to have suffered more than his fair share of the slings and arrows of outrageous fortune. Oh yes, he's dangerously attractive.'

Although the heavy sarcasm in his voice puzzled her she was glad he had grasped the message she was trying to get through to him.

'Then you should understand why I asked him to come to-day and to take me out. The more I can keep him away from Balmore the better. While he's there he's with Alice and under her feet.'

'So you're helping Alice too.'

'Well, yes, in a way. But I can't say you're very co-operative.'

He flashed a surprised glance in her direction.

'Aren't I? Then you must tell me what I should do while we have a few moments to ourselves without fear of any interruption.'

Gail looked round. They were entering the strait of water which separated Stornish from Sorasay.

'We weren't very far away after all,' she said.

'No. Although the boat had probably drifted on the tide. A word of advice, Goldilocks. Next time you're stranded in a boat and have no means of getting back to port put out an anchor. It will stop you from drifting.'

'I'll remember,' she replied seriously. 'How did you know where to look for us?'

'We didn't, although we probably would have found you earlier if we'd set out earlier. But Dougie and I didn't get back from the Treshnish Isles where we'd gone to look at the seals until one o'clock. He missed his boat and said something about you having said you'd be back in time for a meal at midday. I went up to Gartbeg and Jane knew nothing of your whereabouts, so I phoned Balmore, to learn that you hadn't gone there either. There was nothing left for us to do but to set out in search of you. It was more luck than good management that sent us that way round Sorasay so that we saw your flare.'

'I'm sorry we caused so much trouble,' said Gail

humbly. He didn't reply, seeming too interested in watching Dougie's boat as it chugged up the middle of the strait against the ebbing tide. Feeling miserable again as she realized how Callum must be deriding her for her foolishness, she sat crouched under the dodger with her arms clasped around herself to hug warmth to her. Callum noticed that she had turned pale and that the light had gone from her grey eyes and so he asked gently,

'Now what is it I should be doing to be more co-operative?'

His question dispersed the misery a little and roused her interest in the problem of how to prevent Alice from preferring Malcolm to him.

'You should go to Balmore more often.'

'Is that all?' He sounded very surprised.

'No, it isn't,' she snapped wondering how anyone as intelligent as Callum could be so blind. 'But it would be a way of showing that you care. How else can a woman tell when a man is interested in her if he doesn't make any effort to be where she is, if he seems more interested in counting seals than in her feelings?'

His glance strayed momentarily from the tow line and the boat in front to her face.

'Is that how I seem?' he murmured. 'Obviously I've been guilty of indifference and neglect.'

'Yes, I'm afraid you have, and if you don't act soon it may be too late and history may repeat itself, as Eileen has prophesied. Oh, Callum, can't you see? If you're not careful he'll take her away from you just as Ian took Marguerite.'

He didn't seem to be unduly perturbed by her warning and he kept his gaze steadily on the boat ahead. They were now approaching Stornish jetty and Dougie was signalling with one hand to Callum.

'Here, Goldilocks, hold the tiller while I untie the towrope. Keep it steady in the middle like that,' he instructed briefly. He went up to the bow, undid the tow rope and gathering some of the slack rope into a coil threw it to

159

Dougie. Then he heaved the anchor overboard and *The Islander* came to a gentle stop. Dougie turned his boat in a wide sweep and came back towards them.

'I'll away to Sorasay to put the Major ashore,' he yelled. 'I can see there's a car over there waiting for him.'

Callum made a thumbs-up sign to show that he'd heard and came back to the cockpit, where he sat down beside Gail.

'Someone has set off from the jetty in a wee boat to take us off. It won't be long before you're at Gartbeg in front of a fire. You know I thought that ankle of yours would keep you out of trouble this week.'

'It was Alice's idea that Patrick should take us out in a boat. She thought it would be a good idea for me to see the islands without having to walk.'

'Then where was Patrick today?'

'He couldn't come.'

'And Malcolm came of his own accord?'

'Yes, but only to tell me the trip organized for today was off. He would have gone back to Balmore if I hadn't urged him to stay with me.'

He leaned his elbows on his knees and rested his chin in his cupped hand and gazed down at his feet. Eventually he said,

'Thank you for your advice. Often someone outside a situation can see everything much more objectively than a person who is involved. I can assure you it won't go unheeded. Alice has invited me to go over to Balmore on Friday when you and Jane go for tea. I shall make every effort to be there for at least part of the time.'

Gail was so pleased that she clapped her hands together.

'And I know Alice will be glad to see you. She was disappointed when you didn't go to the dance last Saturday, and quite rightly so.'

He didn't reply but continued to stare at the floor of the cockpit. A troubled frown pulled his thick eyebrows

160

together to form a bar above the bridge of his nose, and Gail wondered whether she dared ask what was troubling him. *The Islander* swung round on the anchor chain as a squall of wind buffeted it, and she had a sudden glimpse of the jetty and a dinghy being rowed across the water towards the fishing boat. There was a small group of people standing on the jetty and she could see Jane's car parked on the road. She realized how much anxiety she had caused by her impulsive decision to go to sea with Malcolm, and putting a hand on Callum's arm she said huskily,

'Thank you for coming to our rescue. If you and Dougie hadn't come, if you hadn't seen the flare, I hate to think what would have happened.'

'I hate to think of it too,' he answered in a low voice. 'One drowning in a lifetime is enough for anyone.' And she knew he was thinking of Marguerite.

He sat up straight and looked at her. There was that strange glow in the depths of his eyes which she had noticed before, and as their glances met and held she had again the odd feeling that they were walking along the white sands together under the stars like the lovers in the song Ron had sung at the McCaigs' house.

Then the dinghy bumped against the side of *The Islander*, a man's voice hailed them and the spell was broken.

CHAPTER 6

THE day was sunny but cool. As Gail and Jane drove to
Balmore House the wind shook the pale gold barley
which stood in the fields. As always Gail was entranced by
the glimpses of sheer beauty which a drive across Sorasay
offered. On the moorland heather blazed against a blue
sky streaked with white feathery clouds. Beside a small
loch, green with waterlily leaves, a grey heron stood motionless on one leg. In the natural deciduous woodland
which clustered around the driveway up to Balmore
House the occasional conifer stood out, dark and angular.
Jane was talking about Sir Morris Boyd.

'He's become a legend in his own time.'

'Oh, why?' asked Gail, pulled out of her musings about
the island.

'He bought this island twenty years ago. Its acquisition
would have been enough for most people, but not for Sir
Morris. He decided that Sorasay would not only be his
country estate but it would also be his home and that the
islanders would be his people in the same way that Stornish has been for the Black family. Quite an effort for a
man who's not island bred and born.'

'I thought the Boyds belonged here.'

'Sir Morris does now, and I have a feeling his daughter
does too. But they came originally from Glasgow.'

'Then what has he done that's so marvellous?'

'He has shown what can be done by a beneficent and
understanding landlord. He's built new homes and byres
for the people where necessary, but he's made them do
their bit too. This means that the islanders can make a
reasonable living and that the young people haven't had
to leave in such large numbers as they have in the past.
And in addition he has created the most exquisite
gardens.'

162

'How do you know so much about him?' asked Gail, amazed as usual by her aunt's knowledge of out-of-the-way affairs.

'I read, dear, and I ask questions. Mr. Gorrie has been a mine of information.'

Balmore House was much bigger than Gail had expected. Mostly Georgian in design, it boasted a very un-Georgian square tower in the middle, in which the front door was set. When Jane rang the bell the door was opened by an elderly gentleman who was dressed in grey flannel trousers and a navy blue blazer. His small greenish eyes twinkled at them from behind the thick lenses of his glasses as he introduced himself as Morris Boyd and welcomed them.

'Come in. Alice is already entertaining in the drawing room or she would have been answering the door. This way.'

He led them through the hallway into an oval room whose doorways and windows were shaped to fit the curves of the walls. Saying he would join them in a few minutes, Sir Morris departed. As she stepped into the room Gail had an impression of pale blue walls which were perfect backgrounds for the heavy dark frames of the paintings and for the red and gold striped material with which the settee and armchairs were covered.

Through another door she noticed a book-filled room before her roving gaze met Callum's dark, unrevealing eyes. He was standing in front of the fireplace looking just as much at home as he would in his own house. Alice, who had been speaking to him when Jane and Gail entered the room, stood up and came forward to greet them in her most gracious manner.

'Malcolm will be with us soon and then we can all set off together,' she said.

'I hope he's recovered from Wednesday's little escapade at sea,' said Jane.

A faint frown spoiled the smoothness of Alice's brow and she glanced sideways at Gail.

'Yes, he has. I can't understand why he went.'

'I went because I wanted to go with a very charming person,' put in Malcolm as he entered the room looking very spruce and debonair. He was also dressed in flannels and blazer and wore a paisley patterned scarf tucked into the open neck of his pale blue shirt. He walked straight up to Gail, took one of her hands in his and said with his most charming smile,

'How are you, my dear?'

Gail, who was thinking he couldn't have behaved better if she had asked him to, smiled back and said she was well.

'Good. I hope you're going to walk round the gardens with me. I think our paces should be well matched.'

'Surely you're not going to walk all that way? Your ankle can't possibly be strong enough yet.' Callum's voice had lost its lazy lilt and sounded curt and critical. Gail glanced at him quickly. For once his eyes weren't blank. A little fire seemed to be smouldering in their depths. But before she could speak Malcolm answered for her as he drew her hand through the crook of his arm.

'Not all the way. When we tire Gail and I are going to sit on the lawn and entertain each other until the rest of you return.'

'An excellent arrangement which should suit both of you, I'm sure,' remarked Callum, and the dryness of his tone drew not only Gail's attention but also a curious frowning glance from Alice.

At that moment Sir Morris came into the room all ready to lead them round his estate. He asked Alice what her plans for the afternoon were.

'I thought we'd start with the rose garden and work gradually through the others and end up at the cheese factory,' she replied.

'The cheese factory is my daughter's pride and joy since she became the secretary of the company,' explained Sir Morris to Jane. 'We had such vast quantities of milk we had to do something with it, so we started

164

making cheese.'

'Quite successfully too,' said Alice, showing more vivacity than Gail had ever seen her show before. 'We've just had another thousand-gallon tank installed which you must see, Callum. We'll go out this way through the library.'

From the rose garden they progressed to the Italian garden, and it was there that Gail managed to lag behind, causing Malcolm to lag with her. She did it deliberately because it seemed to her that Callum would never have Alice to himself as Alice seemed determined that the four of them should stay together.

When she complained quite truthfully to Malcolm that her ankle was aching he reacted in the way she had hoped and suggested that they went to sit on the front lawn which was very sheltered from the wind.

Once they were lounging on long wicker garden chairs Malcolm admitted that although he appreciated the gardens he wasn't sorry to avoid seeing the cheese factory.

'To tell the truth I can't stand the smell of the place. It has exactly the same effect as that damned boat had the other day. Which reminds me, I forgot to thank Callum for rescuing us. I hope you felt none the worse afterwards.'

Gail assured him that she had felt no ill-effects and he looked at her admiringly.

'You were very brave and so resourceful too,' he commented. 'I'm actually beginning to look forward to going back to London knowing that you'll be there. It's going to make all the difference.'

He went on talking. He was a good talker and she was reminded of Karl again because it was obvious that Malcolm liked an audience too, preferably a sympathetic audience who would assure him that he would succeed eventually. Yet having spent the best part of an hour describing how he would reorganize his uncle's business if it were his to reorganize he suddenly surprised her by saying,

'But my heart isn't in publishing. What I would really like is a place like this.' He waved his arm in a wide gesture towards the house. 'I have a little money left to me by my father, but it's not quite enough to buy an estate. You know, Patrick hasn't the slightest interest in Balmore or Sorasay. Alice has done all the work. Fortunately her father has a good sense of justice, so she should inherit the place.'

'Would you like to marry Alice?' asked Gail.

'That's what I like about you. You're very direct,' he said, smiling. Then he shrugged his shoulders. 'The thought of marriage has crossed my mind several times during the past year, but I haven't a chance against the man on the spot.'

'You mean Callum?'

'Yes. He's here and he has far more knowledge and experience of the islands than I could ever hope to acquire.'

'Then why chase a will o' the wisp? Alice and Callum are well suited, and Eileen McCaig tells me that everyone expects they'll marry soon,' said Gail. She placed a hand on his arm and said urgently, 'Living in London can be fun, you know.'

'I should think living anywhere with you would be fun, Gail,' he replied, taking the hand which rested on his arm in his. 'Perhaps you're right. I am chasing a will o' the wisp. I'd begun to hope that Alice wrote to me regularly because she regarded me as a little more than just an old friend of the family. But being the fine person she is she probably wrote out of the kindness of her heart, knowing that I was alone in the world.'

His sigh, the lost-little-boy expression on his face touched Gail's soft spot and immediately danger signals flashed. How like Karl he was, handsome, charming, long-suffering, searching for someone on whom he could lean for the rest of his life. How unlike Callum. A strange feeling of revulsion swept over her and she longed to pull her hand out of his grasp and run from the garden.

'Two love birds on the lawn. How touching!' said a light mocking voice, and they both turned to see Patrick standing behind them.

'Where are the others?' he asked.

'Looking at the cheese factory,' replied Malcolm blandly as he released Gail's hand and lay back in his chair. 'Just back from Tobermory?'

'Yes. There's a stiff breeze out at sea to-day. The old steamer rolled like a pig coming across,' said Patrick, as he sat in a chair on the other side of Gail and looked down the length of the lawn. 'I didn't know our nutty naturalist was coming today. I wonder what's he's up to now?'

Following the direction of his gaze Gail saw Callum crossing the lawn making for the house, apparently unaware of the group sitting in the corner partially screened by a neat box hedge which formed a right angle. He was carrying something and as he came closer she could see that it was a seagull. Perturbed because he had left Alice, Gail was out of her chair without hesitation and limping after him.

'Where did you find the bird? What's wrong with it?' she asked breathlessly.

He stopped and showed her the bird which cheeped mournfully.

'It has a broken wing. I found it on the shore of the loch.'

'But I thought you'd gone to the cheese factory?'

He gave her a strange enigmatic underbrowed glance. He didn't look a bit nutty as Patrick had so unkindly suggested. In fact in comparison with the long-suffering Malcolm and the brittle sharp-witted Patrick he seemed very much the level-headed man of action.

'I've had my fill of seeing cheese being made. And although I love all things that grow, formal gardens are not in my line, so I skipped out. I don't think they'll have missed me.'

'Alice will,' said Gail exasperatedly. 'Oh, Callum,' she

167

thought, 'how could you pass up an opportunity to be with her even if it meant going to the cheese factory? Independence is all very well, but as you once told me it doesn't do to go to extremes. How can you expect to win Alice if you don't show her that you want to be with her?'

But she kept her thoughts to herself.

'Will she? I wonder?' he remarked. Glancing over her shoulder, he noticed Malcolm and Patrick. 'Please excuse me,' he added coldly. 'I want to put this wing in a splint. With care it might just heal.'

He started to move away. She followed, limping hastily to keep up with him.

'Don't let me take you away from your admirers,' he cracked unpleasantly.

'*You* aren't,' she retorted quickly. 'I want to see what you're going to do with the poor bird.'

'Of course, I should have guessed. I was forgetting you're far more interested in a creature which is lame than in one which isn't,' he observed sarcastically. 'You know, the islanders are going to miss you when you leave, Goldilocks. You've provided them with more gossip than they've had for years. They've followed closely every move you've made from the time they heard that you spent your first night on Stornish in my bed. Your holding hands with the handsome Major at the dance last Saturday and your subsequent adventure with him at sea have been discussed with relish. They can hardly wait for the next romantic episode in your life.'

His sarcasm puzzled her as well as grated on her nerves.

'We didn't hold hands,' she defended hotly.

'The way Annie tells the tale you did, and I've just seen you holding hands with him yourself. Here, hold this bird while I look for a suitable piece of wood for a splint and a box to put the bird in.'

They had reached a stone-built outhouse at the back of the house. It appeared to serve as a storage place for wood and boxes. Gail, who had never held a bird in her life before, held out her cupped hands and Callum placed the quivering creature between them.

'Hold it gently but firmly,' he instructed. 'Don't be afraid of it, because it's really more afraid of you. It's frightened because it has lost its freedom and doesn't trust us.'

He went into the shed and Gail sat down on a bench which was set against the wall of the shed. The bird moved restlessly in her hands as if it wanted to escape and she held it more firmly, although its bones which she could feel through its feathers and its skin seemed so fragile she was afraid she would crush them.

When Callum reappeared he was carrying a cardboard box and a few small pieces of wood. He placed the wood in the box and set it on the ground. Then he sat down beside her. Pulling a handkerchief out of his pocket, he began to tear it into narrow strips. As she watched Gail was reminded of the time when he had bound her ankle.

'You must be very heavy on handkerchiefs if that's how you're always mistreating them,' she observed. 'I must remember to send you some for Christmas.'

'The lame creatures I have to treat occasionally would welcome that,' he replied lightly.

They didn't really have to talk to each other, thought Gail. It was enough just to be sitting there with him watching the deft movements of his hands, knowing the pleasure of being near to him.

So she was quite unprepared when he spoke abruptly.

'Have you heard from your father this week?'

'Only a picture postcard from Italy.'

'No mention of Gartbeg?' he asked, taking the bird from her. He held it carefully on his knee with one hand and spread the broken wing out with the other.

'No, there wasn't.'

'Then I have news for you. I received a phone call from my solicitor yesterday. He has received a letter from your father's solicitor saying that he had been instructed by your father to sell Gartbeg back to me at slightly more than the price paid for it. I told him to agree immediately. All being well, the property should change hands at the end of September, and then Stornish will be whole again.'

The satisfaction in the tone of his voice depressed Gail. Phil had taken notice of her letter and Callum had got what he wanted.

'You must be pleased,' she said in a low voice.

'Very pleased, even though I shall be out of pocket as a result. Now Ron can come back to the island and Eileen won't have to leave her sheep.' He gave her an oblique glance and smiled.' I'm thinking I have you to thank. You did as I asked and told your father of the situation on Stornish, didn't you?'

'Yes, I did,' she mumbled, wondering why she was having difficulty in swallowing a lump which seemed to be blocking her throat and making speech almost impossible.

Callum was busy binding the makeshift splint to the bird's wing with strips of handkerchief. Glancing at his face, she saw that he was completely engrossed in the humble task he was performing and having given her his news and expressed his gratitude he had apparently forgotten her.

'I love you, Callum,' she thought. 'I love your gentle strength and your singleness of purpose. I know you can be high-handed and sometimes unpleasant and that possibly you have other bad as well as good qualities which I don't know about, but I love you just the same, for love's sake.'

The thought stunned her to silence. She sat there feeling helpless, knowing the blood had drained from her face. She watched him place the bird in the box. It fluttered its good wing a little, but when it discovered it couldn't move its broken wing it lay still with its dark eyes blinking.

Callum leaned back against the sun-warmed wall of the shed, behaving as if he had all the time to sit and stare or dream. He would always find time to dream, she thought, and then wondered what he was dreaming about now. About Alice, possibly, and his future life with her? Gail noticed he hadn't bothered to dress conventionally to come to tea with Alice. He was wearing brown corduroy trousers, a checked sports shirt over which he had pulled a crew-necked sweater. His brown brogues were scuffed and dusty and she guessed he had walked to Balmore from the Stornish ferry.

'You're very quiet for you,' he commented suddenly. 'What's the matter?'

'I was wondering what you look like when you're dressed properly,' she replied evasively.

He glanced down at his clothing and then looked at her, puzzlement narrowing his eyes.

'I'm dressed properly now, aren't I? Come to think of it, this is the first time I've seen you without the inevitable pants. The difference is very stimulating,' he countered. 'So you want to know what I look like when I'm in my glad rags? I'll call on you one day when I'm in London and you shall see.'

Although she was slightly unnerved by his comment that he found her appearance in a dress stimulating, the fact that he had even considered the possibility of calling to see her in London surprised and delighted her.

'Is that a promise?' she asked eagerly, conveniently forgetting Alice.

'It would be if I knew where you're going to live when you get back there.'

The delight faded. She had forgotten that particular problem too. Where would she go when she left Gartbeg, when there was no longer a reason for her to stay on at Stornish? She couldn't go and live with Phil and Priscilla. It wouldn't be fair to them or to herself.

'I don't know myself yet. I'll go with Aunt Jane next Wednesday – unless you would like us to leave sooner?'

It had come to this after all. She was offering to leave, something which he had wanted her to do ever since she had arrived.

'No, you don't have to do that. Wait until you hear from your father. I expect you'll receive a letter from him by the next delivery,' he answered quietly. 'After all, the house is still his until the contract is signed and the money is paid over. And that will be the end of your Hebridean adventure. Do you regret the impulse which brought you here?'

'It wasn't impulse. It was an arrogant letter from a man which brought me here,' she retorted, and he laughed.

'I'm beginning to think I shouldn't have written that letter. I should have let my solicitor deal with the matter. But I was so wild at the dirty trick Ian had played on me. Little did I know I was letting myself in for more trouble.'

'Have I been very troublesome?'

'What do you think?' he challenged, and the fiery gleam was back in his eyes. It was as if a fire long damped down had begun to smoulder. 'You've been a damned nuisance, and you know it,' he added forcibly.

She shouldn't let it hurt so much that flat outright rejection of her, but it did hurt terribly, ripping through the flimsy façade of her sophistication, penetrating deeply to her vulnerable heart.

'Then I shall definitely leave with Jane,' she replied, 'And then you won't be troubled any more. We'll be able to give Malcolm a lift to London. He's thinking of going back next week too.'

'How very convenient for him,' said Callum, coming as close to sneering as she had ever seen him. 'But I must warn you, Goldilocks, he's not for you. Stay away from him.'

Infuriated suddenly by his automatic manner, she sprang to her feet. Eyes sparkling, hands on her hips, she stood in front of him.

'Why should I? What right have you to tell me what

172

to do?'

'I haven't any right. But I can say what I think, just as you do. You didn't hesitate to give me some advice the other day. I'm giving you some now. Whoever takes on Fraser needs to be as hard as nails. You're too sensitive, too soft.'

Her anger subsided almost as quickly as it had risen, as she realized it was concern for her that had made him speak as he had done.

'But don't you see, Callum, if he leaves with Jane and me it will be a great help to everyone concerned,' she reasoned.

She expected the fire to fade from his eyes and to be replaced by an expression of relief as he realized Malcolm would be leaving Balmore and Alice sooner than he had expected. But it didn't fade. It seemed to glow more brightly, and he put out a hand and grasped her wrist so tightly that she almost cried out, and pulled her slowly towards him.

'What are you trying to do, Goldilocks?' he demanded. 'Court disaster again by following your impulse to help every lame dog which crosses your path? Fraser doesn't need your help. He's very capable of managing his own affairs.'

'How do you know?' she stormed, trying to pull her wrist free from his grasp. 'Please let go, Callum. You're hurting me!'

He released her at once and pushed his hands into his pockets while his mind searched for ways with which to divert her from the course on which she seemed so set. She was rubbing her wrist and the sight of his own finger marks, dark on her pale skin, made him angry with himself.

'What do you know about people needing help?' she said furiously. 'You don't know when you need help yourself. You believe yourself to be so self-sufficient that you don't need anyone.'

He rose slowly to his feet and stood over her.

'That depends on how you would be defining the word need,' he said softly, and the Hebridean lilt was very noticeable in his voice. 'Here's my definition.'

His hands gripped her shoulders roughly then they slipped across her back as he pulled her against him. His kiss was a bruising, burning happening and it overcame all opposition. It was fire which threatened to scorch and consume her. Then it stopped and, still helpless, held hard against him, Gail heard the sound of footsteps approaching on the gravel path. She tried to pull free. She was too late. Patrick's light voice held a sneering note as he said,

'Found you both at last! Tea is about to be served in the drawing-room. Try not to look too dishevelled, Gail. You might arouse suspicion. You're certainly going the rounds today.'

Callum did not stay to tea. Carrying the box with the seagull in it under his arm, he accompanied Gail and Patrick to the front door and left them there after instructing Patrick to make his excuses to Alice and Sir Morris. Then he turned on his heel and set off down the driveway. He hadn't gone far when he heard the sound of running footsteps behind him.

'Callum, wait!' called Alice breathlessly.

He stopped obediently and turned to look down at her.

'Well, Alice?' he asked gently. He had always dealt gently with Alice because he had always felt sorry for her. She had so little appeal for him.

'There's something I must say to you,' she began nervously. 'There hasn't been time this afternoon and I didn't think you'd be in such a hurry to leave.'

'I want to reach Aird's Bay before dark to make the day's count of seals.'

Alice licked her lips and twisted her white hands together. She did not look at him but kept her gaze fixed steadily on the wrought iron gates at the entrance to the drive.

'It isn't easy for me to say this, Callum. I've thought about it for days and hesitated because ... well, because of what happened six years ago and I didn't want to be responsible for hurting you. But today I've come to the conclusion that it must be said. I don't want to marry you. I'm sorry,' she said stiffly.

For a moment he was silent. Above their heads the tree tops soughed softly in the wind and in the depths of the shrubbery, birds twittered. Then Callum laughed, a surprised spontaneous laugh. Alice tossed her head and looked at him.

'It isn't funny,' she scolded.

'It is for me,' he retorted. 'Since I've never proposed to you in so many words there's no need for you to apologize for jilting me.'

Alice drew an exasperated breath.

'I know you haven't proposed, but for the past year everyone has been saying, everyone has assumed that one day we would marry,' she explained.

'I know, and we've let ourselves drift along on that assumption. It was a nice tidy arrangement, the sort which is dear to the hearts of people like Eileen McCaig and Annie Rankin, and even liked by your father. The union of the ancient almost extinct Black family with the wealthy Boyd family which has done so much for the island of Sorasay, and I'm afraid I've been guilty of falling in with the idea. Call it taking the line of least resistance, if you like. You seemed to have no objections – at least none that I was aware of.'

A faint pink stained Alice's cheeks.

'You're not very complimentary, Callum,' she remonstrated.

'The truth seldom is,' he replied bluntly. 'If it's any consolation to you, Alice, let me say this. I'm very glad you've had the courage to come out into the open and to tell me that you've decided a calm, unadventurous, loveless marriage is not for you after all, because you've solved a problem for me.'

175

'Loveless?' she exclaimed, cutting him short when he would have amplified his statement.

'Yes. Don't let us deceive ourselves that we've ever been in love with each other.'

'You haven't been in love with me, I can see that,' she returned tartly. 'But I was with you . . . once.'

He was surprised and curious.

'You say once. What happened?'

'I discovered during this past year that love can't flourish when it isn't returned. At least mine couldn't.'

'Then it's I who should be apologizing to you,' he said gently. 'I'm sorry. To hurt you has never been my intention. In fact that's why I did nothing to deny or oppose the gossip and rumour which started up soon after my return to Stornish . . .'

'You were sorry for me!' she hissed, suddenly angry. 'Oh, that's worse than your indifference. I wonder if you know, Callum, how emotionally dead you are? You have been for the past six years. Marguerite did that to you. Oh, you've been gentle, pleasant, polite to me during the past year, but totally indifferent.'

At the mention of Marguerite his face went pale and the skin tautened across his cheekbones.

'Shall we call it a day, Alice?' he said wearily. 'You've spoken your mind and I'm glad you have. One of us had to clear up the situation and possibly you have more reason to do so than I have. But may I offer a word of friendly advice? Go back now to your tea-party, otherwise you may find your effort has been in vain. Malcolm is fast finding a new interest.'

When Gail entered the drawing-room after having washed her hands and tidied her hair she noted with a strange mixture of relief and disappointment that Callum wasn't there. Alice was absent also, but she appeared shortly following the housekeeper, who was wheeling a tea trolley laden with gleaming cutlery and china into the room.

176

'Has Callum gone to count seals again?' asked Patrick mockingly. His eyes were bright and inquisitive and he was obviously enjoying Gail's discomfiture at having been discovered by him when being embraced by Callum.

'I believe he has,' answered Alice briefly. Then with a complete change of manner, sugary sweetness coating the acidity, she turned to Malcolm and asked him to help her with the serving of the tea. He obediently stood up and taking a cup and saucer from her with one hand and a small tray bearing a milk jug and sugar basin in the other he went across to Jane who was sitting by a window talking to Sir Morris.

'You'll never bring Callum to heel,' needled Patrick. 'He just isn't a domesticated animal. What do you think, Gail?'

He was baiting her, but she mustn't rise while she was sitting here with Alice on the watch, thought Gail. Keeping her gaze on the lovely deep wave of russet-coloured hair which half hid one of Alice's cheeks as she bent over the tea-pot, she answered him quietly,

'Oh, I'm sure Alice has all it takes to handle Callum. I'm told that wild animals take kindly to gentle treatment.'

Malcolm, who had returned for another cup of tea to take to Sir Morris, chuckled.

'For wild animals substitute men, Patrick, and you have Gail's philosophy. She's been handling me gently most of the afternoon and I've loved every minute.'

At that moment Alice turned to Gail to offer her a cup of tea. The expression in her eyes was cold and inimical and spoke more loudly than words. 'She knows,' thought Gail, agitatedly. 'That devil Patrick must have told her that he saw Callum kissing me. Oh, why did I taunt Callum? Why couldn't I keep my mouth shut for once?'

To her relief Jane decided at that moment to ask Alice a question and after that the conversation became general so that Patrick had no more chance to do any baiting. At

177

last Jane stood up and announced that it was time she and Gail were leaving if they were to cross the causeway before the tide was high and it became dangerous. As the rest of them rose to their feet Alice murmured to Gail,

'Before you go there's something I want to show you in the library.'

Puzzled by the urgency in Alice's voice, Gail followed her into the library. As soon as she had entered the room Alice closed the door and leaning against it said coldly,

'I haven't really anything to show you, but I do have something to say to you.'

Gail turned and eyed her anxiously. Judging by the bright hardness of her eyes Alice was seething.

'I'm sorry. You see, it was all my fault, Alice . . .' she began.

'Of course it's your fault, although I'm surprised you have the grace to admit it. Unless this is just another of your tricks to disarm me. Oh, please don't be putting on that wide-eyed innocent look. It may work with the men, but it has no effect on me. You know what I'm talking about.'

'I'm afraid I don't,' replied Gail, her pride returning as she reacted to the tirade of abuse.

'Then I'll tell you. Ever since you laid eyes on him you've been trying to attract him away from me!'

'That isn't so. Please believe me. Oh, how can I convince you? Listen, I'm leaving next Wednesday with my aunt. Does that convince you?'

'Never to return?'

'Yes, I promise. My father is selling Gartbeg back to Callum. Once it's sold there'll be no reason for me to come back here.'

There was still doubt in the greenish eyes which studied her.

'From now until Wednesday is a long time. I must ask you to promise not to see him again between now and then.'

'Not even to say goodbye?'

'No. I'm sorry, but I can't afford to let you have that opportunity.'

'Very well. If it will make you feel less anxious I agree. But it will seem very rude to leave without saying good-bye.'

'Then you must seem rude. You haven't minded much more unpleasant things being said about you while you've been here, so you shouldn't mind being considered rude. And now I'll let you go.'

Sitting beside Jane in the car as they travelled the now familiar road to the Stornish causeway, Gail felt exhausted. She was glad that for once Jane was too preoccupied with her driving to talk. Slumped in her seat, she gazed out across the flat fields of the eastern side of Sorasay to the mountains of Mull which were pale saffron as they reflected the tranquil light of the late afternoon sun.

Tranquillity. It was a mood she had come to associate with the long fine evenings of the Western Isles and she tried now to achieve that mood. But peace of mind had gone and she feared it had gone for ever. Callum had destroyed it that afternoon.

Gail bit one of the knuckles of one of her fingers to try and stop the tears from coming. He had communicated his need very clearly by his ruthless embrace. For him need had only one meaning, physical desire. It was the only way he needed her, yet she had thought and had hoped once or twice during their brief relationship that they had been moving towards something deeper.

But she had been deluding herself. When he had once referred to the danger of liking her too much he had meant she attracted him physically, and that was a temptation he wanted to avoid because he was going to marry Alice. That was why there was no room for her in his life.

At least she was now well aware of Alice's feelings concerning Callum. While the woman felt so possessive about him there was no danger of him losing her to Malcolm.

But to make sure that history did not repeat itself at the last minute it would be as well to ensure that Malcolm left Sorasay when she and Jane did, and to do that she must have Jane's co-operation, which meant telling her the news about Gartberg being sold back to Callum.

Although she was surprised to hear that her brother had agreed to sell Gartbeg Jane was quite agreeable to take Gail back to London with her and also to inviting Malcolm to accompany them. She decided she would extend the invitation when she went over to Balmore again the following Monday.

The week-end was wet and windy and kept them indoors most of the time. Monday morning was spent cleaning up the house so that they could devote their time on Tuesday to packing. The afternoon brought the expected letter from Phil while Jane was away at Balmore. The letter informed Gail that her father and Priscilla had returned from Italy the previous Thursday and had found Gail's letter awaiting them.

'Reading between the lines,' Phil had written, 'I gather that Black is a formidable personality and that if we moved into Gartbeg we would never have any peace from him. We'd be harassed all the time. That is not the sort of atmosphere conducive to artistic creation and so I've decided to sell the place back to him. Priscilla thinks Cornwall more suitable, in any case, and has a cottage down there which was left to her by her mother.

'However, nothing in this world is wasted and I'm sure your stay on Stornish has been interesting and a good experience. We hope you'll come back with Jane and we'll be glad to see you both. Remember, love, you can live with us for as long as you want, but I've a feeling you'll want a place of your own.'

Gail had hardly finished reading the letter when Jane arrived back from Balmore just as Eileen walked up the path to Gartbeg. It was quite obvious that both of them were bursting with news, but Eileen managed to get hers out first.

'Callum has said Ron can have Gartbeg. Ach, I'm so happy I could cry!' she exclaimed.

'Cry away then, dear. We could have told you on Saturday, but thought it would be better if he told you,' said Jane.

'I can't help feeling a wee bit disappointed too,' said Eileen with a quick change of mood.

'Whatever for?' asked Jane.

'I'm thinking we won't be having Mr. Collins to give us some advice for the choir and I was looking forward to that. And then you'll be leaving Gail and I'll be missing you and all the talks we've been having. But before you go we'll have a grand *ceilidh* tomorrow night and Annie will sing *Land of Heart's Desire* for you because Ron isn't here, and Dougie'll play his pipes and maybe Callum will come and tell us one of his ghost stories.'

'He may not feel like coming to a *ceilidh*,' said Jane. 'Not when he hears about Alice.'

'What's happened to her?' asked Gail and Eileen simultaneously.

'She has gone away with Malcolm Fraser. Sir Morris is very upset. He has no idea where they've gone. They left on Saturday's steamer.'

'Eloped, that's what they've done,' said Eileen, her romanticism getting the better of her. 'I told you history would be repeating itself if Callum didn't take care. Ach, who is going to tell him?'

'He probably knows by now. I should think Sir Morris will have told him,' said Gail dully.

They talked for a little while longer in subdued tones almost as if someone had died. After fixing a time for the *ceilidh* Eileen left and Gail did a little half-hearted packing. All the time she kept thinking about the news Jane had brought with her from Balmore House, and as she remembered her well-intentioned but feeble attempts to detach Malcolm from Alice and the advice she had given Callum she squirmed inwardly. How useless it had been! She might as well have saved herself the trouble.

181

But what of Callum? He had seemed to take her advice quite seriously and his behaviour at Balmore on Saturday had been that of a jealous man even though he had made no attempt to stay with Alice. Had he guessed then he had lost her? Was that why he had been so unpleasant about Malcolm? And when he had kissed her, had it been the kiss of a man who had just been rejected and who had decided to take it out on the nearest female?

How unhappy he must be, and now that he needed help she was preparing to leave. But she hadn't left yet. There was still time to go and see him to tell him how sorry she was. She wouldn't be breaking any promise to Alice because she realized now that everything Alice had said to her in the library at Balmore House had concerned Malcolm and not Callum.

She decided to go and see Callum the next day after lunch. She told Jane she was going for a last walk by herself and set off along the road towards the causeway. When she came to the stile over the drystone wall she climbed over carefully and struck off across the field to the plantation of trees. Picking her way through them, she recalled vividly every word Callum had spoken that first morning as she had followed him. When she reached the field of heifers she crossed it cautiously. The high wall between her and the farmyard gave her some trouble, but eventually she was over, and without knocking one stone down.

She decided to go to the back door because the front door was always used by Marguerite's ghost. She laughed a little at her flight of fancy, but there was something about the house and this part of the island on a grey windy day like today which excited the imagination. It was on a day like this that Marguerite had left the house and had gone to her death.

By the time she reached the back door she was in a fever of expectancy. How would he look? Grim and brooding, or blank-eyed and distant? Or would he laugh

182

at her for being concerned about him, shrug off her sympathy and her farewell, and say good riddance?

Annie answered the door.

'Is it himself you are wanting, miss?' she asked.

'Yes, I've come to say goodbye. We're leaving tomorrow.'

'Aye, I know. Ach, you've walked a long way for nothing. He's away to Aird's Bay again. Now that September is in the seals are coming ashore. Come in and sit down and rest your ankle a wee bit.'

Gail entered the kitchen and sat down on the nearest chair.

'Will you be taking a cup of tea and a scone?' asked Annie.

'No, thank you, I'll not stay. Did Eileen tell you about Miss Boyd and Major Fraser?'

'Aye, she did, and I can't say I was surprised. For all I'm wanting himself to marry and settle down and rear a brood I'm thinking these past weeks she wasn't the wife for him.'

'Oh, why not? I thought you believed like Eileen that their marriage would be the best possible arrangement.'

'Aye, I did for a while. But I've been thinking lately that Miss Alice is a wee bit stiff and bossy, and not much sense of humour, and believe me, you have to have a sense of humour as well as some imagination to live with Callum Black.'

'I see. Is he upset because she's gone away with the Major?'

'Now I wouldn't be calling him upset. He's a wee bit absent-minded during the last few days. He forgot to milk the cow this morning. There she was bellowing her head off when I arrived and he was asleep on the sofa in the other room as if he couldn't be bothered to go to his bed last night. But I wouldn't like to be saying what is on his mind. You can never tell with him any more than you could tell with his grandfather. It could be anything from the seals to the young trees in the plantation. No, Callum isn't one for sharing his problems.'

Gail rose to her feet, having decided what she must do.

'I'd better go before Aunt Jane thinks I'm lost. I'll be seeing you tonight at the *ceilidh*?'

'So you will. You'll be leaving a message for himself?'

'Yes. Please tell him I called to say goodbye.'

'I'll tell him if he's back before I leave, but if he's not I'll leave a wee note for him.'

Once out of the house Gail glanced at the path which went over the moors. Could she find her way to Aird's Bay alone? She would like to see the seals coming ashore as well as see Callum. She was sure she could manage. She let impulse take over and in less than ten minutes she was struggling through the heather in the teeth of the wind, hoping that she was going in the right direction.

Callum lay in the grass on top of the headland and gazed through the binoculars at the big fat bull seal which was heaving itself over the narrow foreshore of the bay, its belly muscles contracting and expanding, its hands gripping the rocks as it heaved itself forwards and upwards from the narrow sandy beach to the grassy slope behind the shore. The seal's resting period was over and it had come ashore to search for a suitable territory away from the sea's edge where the swell was dangerous. It had had its last meal for a month or two and once on its territory it would make very few returns to the sea. It would live on its blubber, the thick layer of fat beneath its skin.

Callum lowered the glasses and rubbed his hand over his eyes. He hadn't slept very well last night and his recumbent position was producing a desire to sleep now in spite of the coolness of the day and the strength of the wind. Still holding the binoculars, he folded his arms on the ground and rested his head on them and closed his eyes. Immediately he felt wide awake. He cursed softly to himself. Being a person of action he resented heartily the occasional periods of introspection which afflicted him when everything he had done or said recently went in review past his mind's eye to be analysed.

He opened his eyes and raised his head. Something was moving on the opposite headland. He raised the glasses to his eyes. Someone was on the edge of the eroded cliff. Whoever it was stood and stared down at the sea and then to Callum's horror began to scramble down the cliff face. The wind pulled at the gaily coloured scarf the climber was wearing and it slid off to reveal golden hair.

Callum dropped the binoculars, stood up, cupped his hands round his mouth and yelled as loudly as he could,

'Go back! It isn't safe. Go back!'

But she didn't seem to hear. By this time Luran was barking excitedly, disturbed by his master's behaviour.

'It's no use, Luran. She can't hear because of the wind and the sound of the sea. We'll have to go round. What the devil does she think she's doing climbing down a cliff face which has been falling away in lumps for years?'

He picked up the binoculars and put them in their case, then glanced over at the cliff again. As he looked Gail, who was only a few feet from the ground, slipped, hung precariously for a second and then fell and rolled down the cliff to the bottom. But Callum didn't wait to see her body reach the ground because he was on his way down the path which led to the shore, moving swiftly but with innate caution, with the barking dog at his heels. It didn't take long for him to reach the shore, but the walk across to the other side of the bay seemed to take an age and then he had to pick his way through the boulders at the foot of the cliff before he could reach Gail.

To his relief he found she had fallen on to a small patch of shingly sand. She lay on her back and as he approached she moved her head and moaned. He knelt beside her and took one of her hands in his and the taste of fear was sour in his mouth.

185

'Goldilocks,' he said softly.

She opened her eyes and looked at him directly.

'I came to say goodbye. Alice said I wasn't to see you again, but she didn't mean you, she meant Malcolm. I got everything mixed up. Oh, my head hurts!'

'Don't talk,' he cautioned. 'I'm going to see if you've broken anything. If you haven't after a fall like that, you're lucky.'

A quick examination assured him that no legs or arms were broken, but he couldn't be sure about ribs. However, Gail did not complain about any pain when she breathed, so he guessed she was all right if a little bruised and suffering from slight concussion.

'You're going to sit up now and then you're going to stand up and we're going to walk back to my house. It's becoming very obvious to me that you're not fit to be let out alone,' he said, deliberately curt to stiffen her spirit.

Once she was standing he took the scarf which had slipped off her head and tied it over her hair again. Then with his arm round her waist he guided her through the boulders.

'That isn't fair,' she retorted eventually. 'I've managed to take myself about London most of my life without any accident. I only have accidents on your island. How was I to know that cliff was unsafe? You should put a danger sign there.'

'I've no intention of despoiling my island with ugly signs,' he replied. 'I've warned you that you weren't to wander where you liked. What were you doing over there anyway?'

'I got lost,' she admitted. 'I came to find you, but I lost my way on the moors and came out on the wrong side of the bay. It seemed quicker to climb down the cliff than to walk all the way round.'

'A quicker way to kill yourself,' he said curtly.

After that they were both silent as she tried to concentrate on walking, which seemed strangely difficult and would have been impossible without his assistance.

Once they had climbed away from the bay and were on the moors he let her rest on an outcrop of rock.

'I thought it was quicker to Gartbeg over the hill,' said Gail.

'It is. But I'm not taking you to Gartbeg. I'm taking you to my house, as I've already told you.'

'Why?'

'Because I'm going to make sure your ankle is rested properly before you go walking anywhere again.'

'It will take a long time.'

'I know. It will take weeks, months, years.'

'But I'm going back to London tomorrow.'

'No, you're not. You're not leaving Stornish until I say you can,' he replied imperturbably.

He was behaving in the most peculiar manner. No wonder Patrick called him nutty! Maybe the fact that he had lost Alice had affected his brain. He isn't one for sharing his problems, Annie had said only this afternoon. Well, he should be made to share them. Being too proud to talk and share one's troubles was a sure way of going mad.

'I was sorry to hear about Alice,' she offered diffidently.

'What have you heard about Alice?' he asked politely.

'She's gone away with Malcolm. I tried to prevent it from happening, but it was no use. There's a rumour that they may marry.'

'There was once a rumour that she and I might marry,' he said. 'It came to nothing.'

'That's why I'm sorry.'

'I'm not,' he said drily.

'But, Callum . . .'

'Alice told me on Friday just as I was leaving that she didn't want to marry me, even though I'd never proposed to her. I was never more glad to hear anything in my life because I decided that I couldn't marry her either and was trying to find a way to tell her without hurting her. I'm very glad Fraser came to stay at Balmore for his hol-

187

idays this year and that she transferred her attentions from me to him, although there was a time when I thought you were going to foul everything up because you had your eye on him, and even asked for my co-operation. I presumed you asked me to see more of Alice because you wanted the road kept clear for yourself.'

'That isn't so,' she gasped. 'I was trying to help you by keeping Malcolm away from Alice. I wouldn't have gone on that cruise with him otherwise. I thought you'd stand more chance of marrying Alice if you co-operated a little by paying her more attention. Eileen was afraid history might repeat itself and that you might lose the woman you loved to another man again.' She suddenly noticed a gleam of amusement in his eyes. 'Oh, why should I bother to explain? You knew what I was trying to do.'

She was furious with him. She had spent the day feeling sorry for him. She had walked over the moors, had got lost, had fallen down a cliff, all because she thought he would be unhappy and would need comforting. And he didn't care a damn about Alice, or anyone else for that matter. He didn't need her.

Rising to her feet, she started to limp away. Her foot caught in a root of heather and she tripped and fell. She tried to struggle to her feet, but her head was swimming. Strong arms closed about her and lifted her. 'Sometimes I hate you, Callum Black!' she muttered, and heard him answer almost gaily,

'That's a start, anyway.'

About an hour later Gail lay on the big sofa in the living-room at Stornish House and gazed dreamily at the peat fire which flickered in the hearth. Her freshly-bandaged ankle rested on a cushion and several more cushions supported her back. On a small table beside the sofa was a tray bearing a tea-pot, a cup and saucer and milk and sugar. She stretched out a hand, lifted the cup and drank some more of the hot sweet tea. It made her feel distinctly better. The shock she had felt when she had twisted her ankle again and had fallen down the cliff face was receding and she was experiencing the pleasant sense of euphoria which often follows being hurt. She had been cared for and made comfortable and no demands had been made on her. All she had to do was lie there and take it easy until Jane came for her.

She could hear Callum talking in the hall. He was phoning Jane to ask her to come over in the car. Soon the moment of farewell would be on her and she hadn't any idea what she should say. The pleasant dreamy feeling fled, chased away by a feeling of desperation. Meaningless phrases flashed through her mind ... 'Thank you for having me. So nice to have met you. Hope we'll meet again some time. I'll never forget my stay here.'

She had used them all at some time or other when saying goodbye. They had tripped easily and politely off her tongue and had meant little. But if she used any of them when saying goodbye to Callum she would mean every word, especially, 'I'll never forget,' because she would never forget waking up in this house and seeing him sitting on the end of his bed. She would never forget laughing with him, being carried by him, being kissed by him. So she would probably say nothing because her feelings were too deep to be expressed in trite phrases, too deep for tears.

He had finished talking and she could hear him returning to the room, so she leaned back on the cushions and gazed again at the fire. He came up to the sofa and stood over her.

'Jane will be here in about an hour. She'll finish your packing and bring your cases here,' he said authoritatively.

'But there's no need for her to bring my cases,' she replied.

'You'll need your clothes unless you intend to wear what you have on now all the time. Your pants are torn as a result of the fall and your windcheater isn't in very good shape either.'

'But I'll be going back to Gartbeg with Jane. We're leaving tomorrow, so why should I need my clothes here?' She heard her voice rise a little hysterically.

'I thought I'd made it clear to you that you're staying here until your ankle is properly better. Jane is agreeable to stay in this house until Saturday when she must leave. By then your father and your stepmother will have arrived, so you need not worry about the proprieties.'

Gail swallowed and looked up at him. As usual his face and eyes gave nothing away.

'I wasn't worrying about the proprieties,' she said weakly.

He raised his eyebrows in an expression of simulated surprise.

'Weren't you? Well, I was. I didn't want Annie to get any funny ideas again. I've just spoken to your father and invited him to come and stay for a few days. He was delighted to receive the invitation and said he'd like to see Gartbeg before he parted with it. He and his wife are flying to Glasgow airport tomorrow and they should set out for Oban on Thursday. Would you like some more tea? You've gone very pale.'

Gail let out an explosive breath.

'You ... you ... You are the most domineering, tantalizing man in the whole of the Western Isles!' she stuttered. 'Why should you invite my father to come here? Why, only a few weeks ago you were telling me you don't like strangers on Stornish and you were appalled at the thought of him coming to stay here for a few months out of every year.'

He sat down on the edge of the sofa and contemplated the fire.

'I realize my behaviour must seem a little odd,' he admitted. 'But inviting someone to come and stay as my guest is entirely different from having someone forced upon me. I've invited him because my upbringing dictates that I should do no less. I know that these days it isn't considered necessary to consult parents and that their rights and their feelings are disregarded at every turn, but I think it would be courteous to ask for your father's permission to keep you here.'

He was mad after all. Round the bend, up the wall, off his rocker.

'And what if he doesn't give his permission?' she asked sweetly, humouring him.

He turned and smiled at her.

'I shall still keep you here.'

Both his smile and his calm assumption that she should want to stay with him roused conflicting feelings within Gail. A wild dizzy happiness that at last she had found someone who wanted her for herself warred with a more usual desire to assert her independence.

'Supposing I try to escape?' she challenged.

'I shall come after you and bring you back, following the best traditions of my ancestors when dealing with recalcitrant wives.'

'But you said once that there was no room for me in your life,' she reminded him cautiously.

Was it the reflection of the fire or was that gleam in his eyes the outward expression of some intensely-felt emotion?

'So I did,' he agreed. 'Ever since I found you asleep in my bed I've been trying to convince myself of that. I had my life all mapped out and there was no room in it for a foolish, obstinate, impulsive girl who would disturb the routine of my days and nights. Also I had a slight commitment to Alice. Although I'd never asked her to marry me I knew she expected it, and after my own experience with Marguerite I didn't think I could hurt anyone in the way I'd been hurt. So I did my best to avoid you, but we met by accident and every time you roused feelings I'd forgotten I possessed. But you seemed undisturbed, and so I tried to smother those feelings as I was afraid of a repetition of what had happened six years ago.'

'You did a very good job of smothering them,' said Gail. 'I thought you were in love with Alice.'

191

He shook his head.

'No. Oh, I think I have some affection for her similar to the feeling a brother might have for a sister. I didn't really understand what was happening to me, however, until I heard of your association with Malcolm Fraser. Knowing your preference for lame dogs I was worried in case you were hurt by him. But it wasn't until you said you'd be leaving with Jane and taking him with you that the fire began to kindle. I was suddenly madly, furiously jealous of him. I wanted to kidnap you, bring you here and lock you up so that you wouldn't be able to have anything to do with him. Then you had the audacity to accuse me of not needing anyone. It was as if you'd thrown oil on the fire. Not need you? When I think of the nights I've spent on this sofa recently, afraid to go to bed in case your ghost tormented me . . .'

'Oh, Callum!' she gasped, half-laughing. 'You could have slept in one of the other beds.'

'So could you, for that matter,' he snapped, 'but you had to choose mine.'

The flame in his eyes danced and flickered as he leaned towards her. This was a very different Callum from the polite, impassive man she had known until now. This was a man whose emotions ran deeply and strongly, who was hot-blooded yet sensitive.

'And I thought you were jealous of Malcolm because you were afraid he might take Alice away from you. I thought that when you kissed me you were punishing the nearest female.'

'How foolish can you be, love?' he mocked softly. 'I kissed you because I wanted to kiss you. The urge to do so had become too strong for me to control. If you knew how many times you've been close to being kissed by me, Goldilocks, you'd be surprised. It seems you have much to learn. If that cheeky puppy Patrick hadn't interrupted us perhaps I'd have convinced you then that I'd discovered that there's room for you in my life, and I would have saved myself an uncomfortable week-end trying to

192

think up some plan of action to stop you from leaving Stornish tomorrow as well as the horrible sight of seeing you fall down that cliff.' He pushed a hand across his eyes and drew a shaky breath. 'Would you mind if I kissed you now and if we picked up where we left off last Friday at Balmore?'

'No, I've been wondering what you've been waiting for,' she teased gently, and was immediately pulled rather roughly into his arms. This time she was able to respond and it was a long time before they spoke again, while the rising wind moaned around the house and rain lashed at the windows and the firelight flickered in the darkening room.

'From the way you're behaving I gather you're willing to stay and live with me here,' murmured Callum eventually.

'With or without my father's permission, because I love you,' she replied happily.

'That's all I need to know, because I love you too,' he answered. And the rest was said in silence.

Remedy for Love

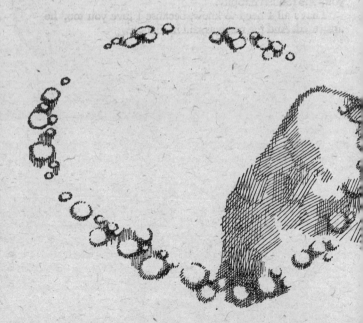

Simon Rigg's unexpected arrival created quite a stir. It had been a long time since anyone had lived at Riggholm, and the local people were curious.

Furthermore, they suspected the man was an impostor. But Susan Thorpe, sensing a need in the fatigued, enigmatic newcomer, reached out a helping hand.

But could she really help someone who had plainly stated that he'd rather she left him alone?

CHAPTER 1

THE local diesel train drew into the platform at Seaport station with a long sigh as if it was glad to come to rest at the end of the journey which had brought it across the north-west corner of Cumberland and then south from Maryport along the coast.

Susan Thorpe, who was also glad her journey was almost at an end, reached down her suitcase from the rack above the seat. Knowing she was going to step out into slanting slivers of cold rain, she had already put on her shiny red raincoat and had tied a scarf over her thick dark hair.

As she was lifting the case down she glanced at the other travel-worn, once expensive suitcase which was also on the rack, and then allowed her glance to slide downwards to the man who sat, or rather lolled, beneath it in the corner of the seat, his head tilted against the window. He was still asleep. He had been asleep when she had entered the compartment at Carlisle and he had slept, or had seemed to sleep, all the way. There had been other people occupying the Pullman-type compartment and one of them had sat between Sue and him, so she hadn't taken much notice of him.

But from Whitehaven onwards he and she had been alone in this part of the compartment—she in her corner, he in his. She had had plenty of time to observe that his clothes, although of a style she privately considered wildly unsuitable for that part of the country, were of very good quality, and that his tawny-brown, curling hair was worn far too long for her tastes. And eventually she had decided that she was very relieved that he slept because that meant she could ignore him very easily and get on with her daydreaming, a pastime she found useful on train journeys.

Now it looked as if she could ignore him no longer. She would have to waken him because this particular train didn't go any farther than Seaport. She touched his suede-clad shoulder and said loudly,

'This is Seaport!'

A pair of sleep-hazed blue eyes looked up at her out of a pale, hollow-cheeked, rather haggard face.

'What?' he muttered sleepily. 'What did you say?'

'This is Seaport. The train doesn't go any farther.'

The blue eyes narrowed and hardened as he sat up straight and pushed back his dishevelled hair in an attempt to tidy it.

'Thank you,' he said coldly. The coldness set her at a distance, as did his back when he stood up to take down one of his cases.

Not that she would want it any other way, thought Sue, with a grin, but a smile never did anyone any harm when you were saying thank you. Picking up her case, she murmured, 'Good afternoon,' and made her way to the door on the other side of the compartment, opened it and stepped out into the damp afternoon air. Rain stung her face and beat a tattoo on her raincoat, forcing her to dash for the shelter of the station buildings. The air, though cool, was tangy with the smell of the sea, damp earth and all the other subtle scents of a drenched countryside. What did it matter if it was raining as if it had been raining for decades and would go on raining for another decade? She was glad to be there smelling the sea, the damp soil and the wet undergrowth.

A familiar stocky figure loomed up to take her ticket. It was Frank Waters, his grey eyes glinting merrily behind his glasses.

'I wasn't expecting you until summer, lass,' he said.

'I've come home to help Ralph,' she answered simply, wondering how much local gossip had informed him of her brother's problems. 'Is he here to meet me?'

'Good for you! He's needing help. No, he isn't here yet. Go and sit in the waiting-room.' His glance went past her to the stranger who was walking very slowly along the platform, carrying his suitcases as if they both weighed a ton.

'Now, who's this?' murmured Frank. 'A stranger, by the

looks of him. You'd never see a local dressed like that. He travelled in the same compartment as you. Know anything about him?'

'No. Only that he slept all the way from Carlisle,' said Sue, thinking that the stranger looked even more of a desperate character now that he was awake and walking than he had asleep.

'Did he now?' said Frank softly. 'Sleeping hasn't done him much good, judging by the way he's handling those bags.'

Sue smiled to herself and went into the waiting-room. Frank was an avid reader of detective novels. No doubt by the time the stranger had handed over his ticket he would have been carefully assessed and his features and clothing would have been memorised in the hopes that Frank might hear on the radio or TV that someone somewhere was searching for such a person.

The swishing sound of pneumatic tyres passing through puddles caught her attention. Looking through the window she saw that a blue van with the words *Thorpe and Son, Ltd.* written in white on its side panel had drawn up outside the station. She turned back to pick up her suitcase. By the time she had lifted it the outer door of the waiting-room had opened and her brother Ralph, big and burly, had entered and was striding towards her.

'How's that for timing?' he asked, as he took her case from her and planted a rather hurried kiss on her cheek. 'We have to hurry. I've left Jemima with Mrs Kent and they don't exactly see eye to eye.'

'Why didn't you bring her with you?' asked Sue, as she opened the door for him to pass through. Behind her she could hear voices. It sounded as if Frank was having a discussion with the stranger.

'She won't sit still,' replied Ralph. 'I've tried one of those car seats, but she manages to climb out of it. I tell you, Sue, I'm at my wits' end. I don't know what to do with her.'

'Which is why you phoned me, I know,' said Sue, noting

new lines of strain round his eyes and mouth. 'Well, I've come, so you can stop worrying about the child.'

He slanted her an affectionate glance from bright, shrewd hazel eyes and smiled.

'Thanks, love. I knew I could depend on you.'

He opened the door of the van and she climbed up into the front seat. He banged the door shut and walked round to the back of the van to open the rear door and thrust her case in among the clutter of tools. He had just climbed up to take his seat when Frank appeared through the station door waving his hand. Sue let down the window on her side as he approached the van.

'Can you give yon fellow a lift to Riggholm?' he asked.

'Riggholm?' ejaculated Ralph. 'But it's . . .'

Frank put a finger to his mouth and shook his head from side to side as the stranger came out of the waiting-room.

'That's where he's going. And since you own the taxi service I thought it'd save him phoning for Jack. I know damn well Jack'll not go near the place anyway.'

'All right,' said Ralph with a resigned sigh. 'Tell him I'll put his cases in the back. Move over, Sue. He'll have to sit beside you. I wonder why he wants to go to Riggholm?'

Without waiting for an answer he dropped out of the van and went round to meet the stranger. Frank scurried back into the station after a final wave to Sue, who moved along the seat as she had been told. The doors at the back of the van slammed shut and one of the side doors slid back simultaneously. The stranger climbed up into the van. As his eyes met hers Sue smiled hesitantly, but he didn't respond. His cold blue glance swerved away from hers and he presented his profile for her to stare at.

He'd be quite handsome if his face wasn't so thin and worn-looking, she thought, and if it didn't wear such an expression of supercilious boredom.

'Move over a bit,' grumbled Ralph, as he took his place behind the steering wheel. 'Put your legs over that way or you'll be in the way of the gear lever.'

Giving him an exasperated look, Sue edged reluctantly

nearer to the taciturn stranger and tried to curl her legs out of the way. The van started up and the wipers swished across the rain-spotted windscreen. Ralph released the brake and the van curved away from the station and down the hill towards the village of Seaport.

As always Sue was excited by this particular view of her home town and she leaned forward to see the shining wet slate roofs of the old houses set on either side of the narrow main street so close to the shore of the wide bay which was really the estuary of a river. Seaport had long lost its right to be worthy of the name of port because the estuary was now so badly silted with sand that only very shallow draught boats could approach it at high tide, and then they had to keep to the winding river channel. In fact very few boats came to Seaport because there was no pier and no docking facilities and when the tide went out it was as if someone had pulled the plug out of a water-basin because the water all went away leaving uncovered stretches of golden sand criss-crossed by narrow channels.

Sue could see that the tide was out that afternoon and that the water had retreated beyond the long curve of Rigg's Bank, a wall of stone which stretched out from the shore at the end of the village street across the sands, and could be seen only as a hazy moving mass under the sodden grey blanket of the sky.

'How far from the station is Riggholm?'

The deep slightly husky voice speaking on her left made Sue jump. Glancing sideways at the stranger, she leaned back and let Ralph answer the question.

'About four miles. No one lives there.'

'I know.' The clipped reply pushed away any further curiosity on Ralph's part, but as always Ralph refused to be pushed away.

'It's been empty for nearly three years,' he said. 'Ever since old Matthew Rigg died. You won't be staying there tonight.' He added the last sentence as a certainty.

'I will,' was the brief arrogant reply.

They had reached the bottom of the hill and Ralph

201

stopped the van at the stop sign where the station road joined the main road coming from the north. Then as he turned the van on to the main road he said urgently with his usual disregard for another person's opinion,

'But you can't. It must be uninhabitable, damp and dirty. Why, I don't even know if there's any furniture in the place.'

'I've been assured that there's furniture.'

This time there was the ghost of a laugh in the tired husky voice and Sue glanced at its owner. The profile was still in evidence and now it was vaguely familiar. Broad forehead under clustering tawny-brown curls, straight high-bridged nose, firm chiselled mouth and square stubborn chin, like the head of a Roman warrior she had once seen on a coin in the museum at Carlisle.

'Have you bought Riggholm?' she asked, her own curiosity getting the better of her.

He went on looking through the windscreen.

'No, I haven't bought it,' he replied.

'Then why . . .' began brother and sister together, and this time the man turned to look at them. A lazily-amused glance roved slowly over Sue's pink cheeks and dark brown eyes and passed on to take note of Ralph's leaner, more weatherbeaten face.

'I inherited it,' he drawled. 'Matthew Rigg was my uncle. I'm Simon Rigg.'

Simon Rigg. He must be the son of Lupus Rigg who had been Matthew's younger brother. Lupus had left Riggholm years ago and had emigrated to Canada after quarrelling with his brother. As far as Sue knew he had never been back to Riggholm. But now she knew why the stranger's face was familiar. He was the only surviving member of the family which had dominated the life of the Seaport district for hundreds of years; a family with whom the Thorpes had enjoyed a fascinating love–hate relationship for generations, often taking different sides in any argument which affected the life of the country as a whole, such as the Civil War when the Riggs had been Cavaliers and the Thorpes had been Roundheads, but sometimes conniving together when it had been for the financial advantages of their families.

Ralph turned the van across the side road and guided it into the petrol station which stood on the corner of the village street. Beside the station was an old, tall Victorian house, well-named The Gables, which had been built by a Thorpe and where the main branch of the family had lived ever since. Ralph leaned forward and looked directly at Simon Rigg and said in his typical forthright way,

'We're pleased to be the first to welcome you to Seaport, Mr Rigg. But you can't stay the night at Riggholm. It's unthinkable. You must stay with us.'

Once again the blue eyes took an inventory of the faces of brother and sister. Simon Rigg shook his head.

'No, thank you,' he said coldly, and offering no reason for his curt refusal he turned away to look through the windscreen at the notice on the wall of the house which said, 'The Gables. Bed and Breakfast. Evening meals provided to order'.

Encouraged by her brother's hospitable attitude, Sue suggested earnestly,

'Then come and have tea with us.'

His face was so thin and haggard. Burnt out—that was how he looked. Curiosity vied with pity as she longed to know what had happened to make him look like that.

'No, thank you. Can we go to Riggholm now?'

Sue and Ralph glanced at each other. To both of them Simon Rigg's refusal was quite understandable and having made their offers of hospitality they did not press him, although they were both a little offended by his abrupt and graceless manner.

'You'd better get down, Sue,' said Ralph, 'and go and rescue Mrs Kent. I'll be back soon.'

He opened the door of the van and jumped down. With a muttered 'Goodbye' to the aloof Mr Rigg, to which he didn't bother to reply, Sue followed her brother and had entered the house before the van had left for Riggholm.

Jemima Thorpe was fifteen months old, had brown hair and eyes, fat pink cheeks and possessed her father's irrepressible curiosity. When Sue entered the big cosy living kitchen in which she had spent her own babyhood Jemima was sitting on the floor playing with the aluminium pans which she had pulled out of the cupboard under the sink.

In a wheel-backed rocking-chair beside the fireplace Mrs Kent, the Thorpes' nearest neighbour, small, slight and bespectacled, sat knitting. She looked up when she heard Sue and an expression of relief crossed her sharp-featured face.

'There you are at last! I was hoping you'd come before Jemima's teatime. I'll just go and get my hat and coat and I'll be on my way. Is it still raining?'

'Yes. Doesn't it always in March? Take your time, Mrs Kent. There's no hurry,' said Sue. 'Won't you stay and have a cup of tea?'

At the sight and sound of the newcomer Jemima, who had just learned to walk, stood up and began to waddle towards Sue waving a wooden cooking spoon in her hand and chanting, 'Mama, Mama.'

'No, I won't stay,' said Mrs Kent. 'Ee, she's a handful, this Jemima. I'm warning you, she'll give you a busy time of it. I'm not surprised her mother is ill. And her dad is that soft with her. I keep telling him he'll be sorry one day that he's not been firm enough with her.'

She went into the hall to fetch her coat and hat and Sue bent to lift her niece in her arms, at the same time removing the wooden spoon from the little plump fist to avoid being hit with it. Immediately Jemima screwed up her eyes, opened her mouth wide and let out a squeal of frustration. Then she began to squirm and wriggle in an attempt to escape from Sue's arms and return to the floor.

'Now, Jemima, that's no way to greet your only aunt,' said Sue with a laugh. 'You and I are going to see a lot of each other during the next few weeks and you'd better learn that I'm in charge!'

Noticing the high chair, she carried the still squealing,

kicking Jemima over to it and set her down in it. At once the child began to rock the chair back and forth violently, lifting it off its front legs and then off its back legs.

'Ee, don't let her do that, Sue,' shrieked Mrs Kent, returning to the kitchen. 'The other day she rocked it right over and gave herself an awful bump on the head.'

'Then I don't think she'll be rocking it over again,' replied Sue calmly, as Jemima roared deafeningly.

After casting a worried glance in the direction of the child Mrs Kent hurried to the back door and Sue followed her.

'Well, I suppose you know what you're doing,' muttered Mrs Kent, 'you being a children's nurse. But I don't envy you, not one little bit. Yon child's a demon!'

Sue laughed.

'Oh, you don't mean that, not really. She's just a healthy bundle of energy who needs guiding in the right direction. Thanks for minding her. I know Ralph is very grateful to you.'

Mrs Kent's face softened and she patted Sue's arm gently.

'It's the least I can do for him while he's in trouble,' she murmured. 'I'll never forget how good he was to me when I had that trouble with Martin. I'll be seeing you, Sue.'

Back in the kitchen Sue gave the wooden spoon back to a suddenly subdued Jemima who accepted it with a wide grin and immediately began to bang the little table which was part of the old-fashioned wooden high chair. The chair had been in the Thorpe family for generations as had many other pieces of furniture in the house.

Taking off her raincoat and scarf, Sue searched the cupboards until she found the food she required for the baby and then began to prepare it. All the time she was working she talked to the little girl who answered with a series of gurgling sounds interspersed by the few words she could say and which she repeated over and over. Having prepared a pot of tea for herself and some tiny honey sandwiches and milk for Jemima, Sue sat down in the chair beside the high chair and drank tea while watching the child stuff the sandwiches in her mouth.

Ralph in trouble. His wife ill. So that was how he was covering up the unpleasant fact that Penny, his wife, had gone away. She had walked out one day and had taken the train south to return to her mother in Manchester. The reason for her desertion of her husband and child Sue didn't know, because Ralph hadn't told her in his brief phone call asking her to come and look after his house, his child and his business while he went to Manchester to persuade Penny to come back to Seaport.

'Drink, drink,' said Jemima, leaning out of her chair at a perilous angle as she tried to reach the cup containing her milk which was on the nearby kitchen table. Sue fitted the top on the cup which enabled the child to drink from it without spilling the whole lot down her front and handed it to her. The plump hands held it capably and Jemima was soon drinking happily, stopping now and again to smile beguilingly at her aunt.

Gazing at the child, Sue could see very little of Penny in the round pink cheeks, round brown eyes and straight brown hair. Penny was tall and slender with soft shoulder-length honey-coloured hair and violet-blue eyes. She had first come to Seaport when on a caravan holiday with her parents. They had put their caravan on Thorpe's caravan site at the head of the bay and instead of moving on after two nights which had been their intention, they had stayed the whole of their two-week holiday. When they had left they had promised to come back the following year. They had, in fact, come back sooner, for a long week-end in September. The attraction, Sue realised, had not only been the fishing for salmon trout in the estuary which had first drawn Arthur Shaw to the area, or the long walks among the dales and beside the lakes which had drawn Mrs Shaw. It had been Ralph, who at twenty-six had just taken over the management of the conglomerate business which his father had built up over the years and which included not only a petrol station and car repair workshop but also a boarding house, a caravan site and a fishing-boat hiring business as well as the agency for coal and other fuel for the area surrounding Seaport.

Ralph had attracted the slim, pretty, slightly spoiled city girl and in his turn had been attracted by her. The September trip had resulted in an invitation for him to spend Christmas in Manchester and by the time Easter had come round Penny and he were engaged to be married. The marriage had taken place the following October when the busy summer season was over, and now two and a half years and one baby later Penny had left The Gables for good, or so she had threatened.

Jemima coughed, spluttered, went red in the face, hurled the cup on to the floor and squealed at the top of her voice. Sue smacked the child's hand and bent to pick up the cup which she placed on the table. Surprised by the smack, Jemima stared at Sue, then smiled. Sue smiled back.

'You mustn't throw cups, Jemima,' she said quietly.

The child stretched out her arms appealingly, wanting to be lifted out of the chair.

'No. Stay there while I find a clean nappy and then I'll change you.'

The kitchen was really no different from when she had lived in the house, thought Sue as she lowered the old-fashioned wooden clothes-rack on which Mrs Kent had hung the clean nappies to air in the warmth rising from the fire and the Aga cooker. There was no impression of Penny at all—unless the collection of indoor plants spread along the shelf beneath the window had been introduced by Penny.

She selected a nappy, held it against her face to make sure it was soft and dry and then hauled on the rope to return the rack to its position. Taking a towel from the baby basket on the dresser, she spread it on the table. Then she picked up Jemima, laid her on the towel and began to pull down the dungaree-styled pants the child was wearing.

'How your mummy could leave a poppet like you is beyond my imagination,' she said, and Jemima, apparently fascinated by this capable adult who talked to her all the time, gurgled happily and kicked out her sturdy legs.

The back door opened and Ralph walked in.

'You look at home already,' he remarked, coming over to the table. Jemima held out her arms and said, 'Dada, Dada,' then tried to roll over. Sue laid her firmly back on the table.

'You can go to your dada when I've finished dressing you,' she said, and Jemima gurgled happily again.

'You seem to know what to do. If Penny or Mrs Kent or I had spoken to her like that she'd have yelled blue murder,' said Ralph. 'Any tea left in that pot?'

'Yes. It should still be hot. She's already tried yelling at her auntie, haven't you, poppet? And it just didn't work. There you are! Another half-hour of play and then it's bedtime for you.'

Sue picked the child up and put her down on the floor. The little girl swayed on her feet for a few seconds smiling and whispering, 'Dada,' then she knelt on the floor and went off at high speed towards the pans.

Ralph leaned against the table, drinking his tea, watching Sue remove the towel, baby powder and cream from the table.

'You can put her to bed, but I bet you a pound she'll yell and will have you going up and down the stairs umpteen times before she gives in through sheer exhaustion and goes to sleep,' he said.

'So that's what's been happening,' remarked Sue coolly. 'You've been letting a fifteen-month-old female boss you around.'

'Oh, it isn't recent. She's been like that ever since Penny brought her home from the hospital. She just won't settle. Penny says she's highly strung.'

'Highly strung, my foot,' retorted Sue. 'That child is no more highly strung than you are. She's strong-willed, I'll grant you, and she needs to be handled firmly. She has to learn that you mean what you say. I suppose you and Penny have rushed to her every time she's opened her mouth and bawled, and she's had you on the run ever since. Poor Penny! No wonder she left.'

'That isn't the only reason why she left,' said Ralph quietly. 'But I'll tell you all about that after we've had supper.' He frowned and glanced at the clock on the mantelpiece. 'Five-thirty,' he muttered, and strode over to the door of the big cool larder. Opening it, he switched on the light and stared at the well-stocked shelves and then began to select items of food.

'What are you doing?' asked Sue, following him and peering in.

'Collecting some food for Simon Rigg. I'm going back to Riggholm. I tried to persuade him to return here with me, but he wouldn't. I'm worried about him. He looked all in when I left him. He wouldn't let me go into the house with him. Sent me off with a flea in my ear for being an interfering busybody.'

'Which you are, of course, and always have been. You take after Grandmother Thorpe for that,' said Sue with a grin. 'I should guess his flea had a sting to it.'

Ralph grinned back.

'Yes, it had. He's quite adept at ice-dripping sarcasm.'

'I can imagine. He's Matthew's nephew, remember. I wonder why he's suddenly turned up, literally out of the blue? I always thought Lupus went to Canada.'

'He did. But I believe he returned to this country after his wife died.'

While they were talking to the accompaniment of Jemima's band of clanging pan lids Sue had found a cardboard box and Ralph had put the food he had selected in it. Sue watched him, thinking how typical it was of him to be concerned about the unfriendly thin-faced man whom he had driven to Riggholm. As if he didn't have enough problems of his own! But Ralph had always been like that, often treading where he wasn't wanted because he felt he must help others even against their wishes if necessary.

'Did he tell you why he'd come to Riggholm?' she asked.

'No. You must have noticed he isn't the communicative type. There, I should think that will do until he's able to shop for himself. I wonder if there's any light in the house or anything to cook with? When you come to think of it, he must be pretty desperate to turn up here without informing anyone he was coming so that the house could be prepared for him.'

Desperate. That was how she had thought Simon Rigg had looked when he had walked along the platform at the station.

'Whom could he inform?'

'The lawyers who are supposed to keep an eye on the place, I suppose. Anyway, I think I'll take a couple of oil lamps and a Primus stove.'

'What about bedding?'

'A sleeping bag is the best thing. Any bedding in that place must be mildewed by now. Ugh! I hate to think of the state it must be in.'

The rest of the equipment was found and he went to load it into the van. When he returned to the kitchen Sue was comforting Jemima who had clouted herself with a pan lid and was sobbing. As soon as she saw her father she held out the sore finger to him for him to kiss and then smiled at him through her tears.

'I'll take some coal too,' said Ralph. 'I should be about an hour. I keep the pumps open until seven. Jack's gone home. Think you can manage? There shouldn't be anyone wanting petrol, but you never know. Now that spring is here we sometimes get the odd courting couple out this way.'

'On a night like this?' said Sue, grimacing at the rain which was still sluicing down the kitchen window.

'Yes. They're not fussy about the weather. All they want is love,' he replied with a grin.

No one called for petrol, so Sue was able to take her time in bathing Jemima and putting her to bed. Having tucked the child up in her cot, Sue said goodnight in a firm voice, kissed the rosy cheek, put out the light and went downstairs to prepare a meal for Ralph. She had hardly reached the kitchen door when she heard a wail from upstairs. Smiling to herself, she shut the kitchen door and went to the larder for ham and eggs. Fifteen minutes later she opened the door stealthily and listened. All was quiet. Still stealthily she crept up the stairs and went to stand outside Jemima's room. The sound of steady breathing, occasionally disrupted by a sob, assured her that Jemima was asleep.

Ralph was away a little less than his hour, but by the time he arrived back the table was set, the fire was leaping in the hearth and there was a good smell of cooking.

'Looks good and smells good,' he commented as he took off his raincoat and hung it behind the back door. 'Where's Jemima?'

'Fast asleep.'

He raised his eyebrows in surprise.

'I should have asked you to come sooner.'

'Why didn't you?' Sue took the ham and egg pie she had made from the bottom oven of the Aga cooker where it had been keeping warm, and placed it on the table.

'I didn't think Penny would stay away this long,' he muttered. 'And I wasn't sure you'd want to come.' He glanced down at his big grease-marked hands. 'I'll go and wash,' he added.

While they ate he told her about the reception Simon Rigg had given him when he had returned with the food.

'He wasn't at all pleased at seeing me again. But when I told him what I'd brought he didn't turn me away. As I'd guessed, there was no light in the house. He had a torch and he'd groped around and had unearthed some candles. He had one in his hand when he answered the door. He reminded me of Ebenezer Scrooge in *A Christmas Carol* as he stood there, sour-faced and narrow-eyed, with his candle guttering.'

'What's the house like inside? Is it like Scrooge's, all cobwebby and dirty?'

'I don't know. He didn't let me in. I just dumped the

stuff inside the door, he thanked me grudgingly and shut the door in my face.'

'And you didn't knock and force your way in?' mocked Sue, knowing how difficult it was to stop Ralph when on one of his errands of mercy.

'No, I didn't. To tell you the truth, I didn't dare. I don't think I've met anyone, since old Matthew died, who managed to convey without saying a word how much he wanted to be left alone. Something has happened to him . . . I don't know how to explain it.'

'Something has happened which has turned the milk of human kindness sour in him.'

'That's it. Scrooge again. Which reminds me, did you see the musical they made of the story?'

'No.'

'That's not like you, Sue. You usually spend all your time off at the flicks.'

'Not recently. I . . . I've been too busy.'

Ralph gave her a sharp shrewd glance.

'Don't tell me someone real has come along to put an end to your worship of film stars,' he teased, and to his amazement Sue's cheeks glowed a brighter pink, her brown eyes flashed and she hissed,

'Oh, be quiet!'

'There is someone.'

'There was,' she said flatly. 'Now tell me about Penny.'

'After you've told me who has superseded Burton and Newman and company. It's nice to think that some ordinary flesh-and-blood fellow has caught your attention at last.'

'The others are flesh and blood,' she objected.

'Not the way you see them. They're only images on a screen. Anyway, who is he? As your closest relative I have a right to know.'

'He's a doctor at the hospital. But it isn't—it wasn't— serious. I mean, he doesn't know I . . .'

'I see. Another case of hero-worship. When will you grow up?'

'I'm as much grown up as you are, even if I am six years younger. Fancy letting your wife run away and leave you holding the baby!' Sue jibed crossly.

Ralph winced.

'I suppose I asked for that. All I know is that Penny was tired and rundown after the winter. She'd been saying she'd like to go and see her mother for some time, but I didn't think she'd go alone, nor did I think she'd stay away so long. Last week when I phoned her she said...' He paused and took a gulp of tea. 'She said she didn't want to come back here, that she was sick of Seaport and our way of life here, that she wants me to sell up and go down to Manchester and find a job. She said that if I didn't agree she wouldn't come back to me.'

'And what did you say?'

'I lost my temper and told her that I'd never sell The Gables and leave Seaport and hung up.'

'Oh, Ralph, how awful! But what do her parents say? I'm sure Mrs Shaw can't approve.'

'She doesn't. She rang up almost immediately afterwards and suggested that I go down there and see Penny. She also suggested that I ask you to come and look after Jemima. She thinks that if Penny and I have a couple of weeks together without Jemima it will do us both good and we'll be able to sort everything out. I didn't agree at first because I didn't want to ask you.'

'Why not?'

'Well, you have your own life to live and I know you're enjoying your work with the children. But it was no use. Jemima was beginning to drive me nuts, too, and no one here wants to look after her, not even Aunt Emily, and you know what a good scout she is usually. So I had to ask you. How did you manage to get time off?'

'I didn't,' said Sue dryly. 'Matron wouldn't agree to let me have leave of absence for family reasons, so I just gave notice and came.'

Ralph made a face, stood up and walked restlessly round the room, coming back to rest his hands on the table and lean on them.

'And you can guess how that makes me feel,' he said. 'You didn't have to go to that extreme, Sue. I could have found a way.'

'For heaven's sake stop fussing,' said Sue, as she collected dirty dishes together. 'If your own sister can't help you no one can. I'd been looking for an excuse to leave Newcastle anyway.'

He looked at her shrewdly.

'Because of the doctor,' he said, and in a couple of strides he was beside her, looking down at his sister, who kept her face turned away from him, stubbornly. 'So it was more than hero-worship,' he said softly.

She nodded and her mouth trembled a little.

'I like to think it was. But it was just as one-sided really as hero-worship. Oh, we went out together for a while and then someone more interesting, more attractive came along and he lost interest in me.' She grinned suddenly and looked up at him. 'I'll survive.'

'Good lass. But I'm sorry, and I understand.'

'Thanks, Ralph. That helps a lot. And now hadn't we better start making plans for your departure? You'll have to tell me what you want me to do.'

They spent the rest of the evening discussing a plan of action for the next few weeks and by the time they went up to bed they had agreed that Ralph should leave at the end of the week for Manchester to arrive unannounced at his parents-in-law's home in order to surprise Penny, and that afterwards they would let events take their own course.

'Don't rush things,' counselled Sue. 'Now that you know I'm here you can take your time. Why not take Penny away for a decent holiday somewhere where the sun is shining at this time of the year? I'm sure you can afford it after last summer's success. You should have taken her away before, you know.'

'I suppose you're right. But I've been very busy,' sighed Ralph.

'It's not the only way you're like Dad,' commented Sue.

'But please, Ralph, for everyone's sake don't make the mistake he made.'

He nodded and for a while they were both silent, thinking of their parents who had set off so gaily for their first holiday in years and had never returned.

Later, lying in her bed in her own room, Sue listened to the rain beating on the window and thought of Mark Pelham, the young house surgeon with whom she had fallen, or had thought she had fallen in love just before Christmas. What a wonderful festive season it had been! Never before had she enjoyed the usual dances and parties so much. What a difference it had made to attend them escorted by the hospital's most eligible bachelor instead of going with the usual group of unescorted nurses hoping to find a suitable partner. Always shy and a little insecure in her dealings with the opposite sex, Sue had never had any steady boy-friends during her adolescence (she could hardly call her association with Derek Barnes steady) or during her years of training at the hospital in Newcastle. She supposed that was why she had passed her exams with such high marks. No one had ever come between her and her studies.

Then she had met Mark and she had thought it had been a case of love at first sight, that romance was hers. But apparently it had not been love at first sight for Mark, a fact which had gradually dawned on her during the past few weeks when he had started cancelling the arrangements he had made to go out with her. She was finally convinced the little affair was at an end, as far as he was concerned, when she saw him at the cinema with another woman one evening. Only a few hours earlier he had rung up to say he couldn't keep his engagement with her because he had changed duties with another doctor.

There was nothing she could do about it because she realised forlornly that he had never been serious and he had not expected her to be serious either. But being Sue she had been serious, and had extravagantly lavished on him all the affection of which her generous nature was capable. And when he had looked elsewhere, she had been desolate. No longer could she bear to see him or even hear his voice when their paths happened to cross. She longed to leave the hospital, to leave Newcastle where she had been perfectly content for the past four years. Homesickness had hit her and a desire to see the sun set beyond the distant rim of the ocean, to watch the slow relentless tide cover the sands and then to look away from the sea towards the dusky barrier of the Lake District mountains, had tormented her.

But who would want her at Seaport? Not Ralph, absorbed in his wife and child and his business. She could of course have transferred to another hospital in another town and she had started to make tentative enquiries. Then Ralph had phoned her. His cry for help had been a clarion call which she had answered willingly at once.

And now she was here in her own room listening to the rain and hearing the sound of the waves as they dashed against the sea wall which protected the garden of The Gables from the tide, when it was in. Never again would she see Mark, except perhaps like this, in her mind's eye before she slept, or possibly in dreams. Never more would she see his handsome face. He'd been handsome enough for a film star. Almost as handsome as Simon Rigg.

Recollection of the man who had travelled on the train with her from Carlisle changed the direction of her thoughts unexpectedly. She wondered how he was coping in the old house on the other side of the bay. With his gaunt, lined face and tired blue eyes, he had looked far from well. Yet he hadn't been very pleasant to Ralph who had only wanted to help him. But then unpleasantness had been a characteristic of the Riggs. Just because they had been in this area before anyone else had come on the scene, hundreds of years ago, they thought they could behave as they liked without any consideration for anyone else. Matthew Rigg, from whom Simon had inherited the house, had been a bachelor and a miser. During the last ten years of his life he had been more or less a recluse, hiding away in the big beautiful house, letting it deteriorate, allowing the grounds to become overgrown just because he couldn't bear to part

with any money. And since he had died it had been moul-
dering away, left severely alone by the local people, no
practical use to anyone. If Matthew had had any love for
his fellow men he could have done something with the
house. For instance, he could have turned it into a convalescent home for poor children, the sort Sue had nursed in the
children's ward in the hospital, whose parents had never
been able to afford to take them away for a holiday by the
sea or in the country; children who had never known what
it was like to walk with bare feet on golden sands, play hide
and seek among the sand-dunes or gather bluebells in the
woods. And on that thought she fell asleep.

It didn't take long for Sue to adjust to the way of life at
The Gables. After all, she hadn't ever lost touch because
she had always come home for her holidays. She soon discovered that Jemima was an early riser. Six o'clock on the
dot every morning she would be awakened by the rattling of
the cot in the room next to hers as her energetic niece shook
it. Jemima had found out some time ago that if she shook
the cot hard enough it would travel on its wheels right
across the bare wooden floor of her room. Usually if Sue
wasn't quick enough, Jemima would get the cot jammed
across the door so that it was impossible to open it inwards
and enter the room. Once the child realised no one could
enter the room she would open her mouth and squeal, and
for a while there would be pandemonium in the house while
Ralph tried to get his arm round the partially open door
and push the cot away from it. However, after being caught
out several times by this novel and exciting way that
Jemima had thought up to draw attention to herself and
have everyone in the house on the run, Sue made sure that
she got up as soon as she heard the rattling start.

Apart from such episodes, she found looking after her
young niece very enjoyable because the little girl was so
loving and so lovable. As she had guessed, it only required
firm and patient handling plus a little foresight to set the
child on the right course for life.

Ralph decided eventually to leave Seaport on Friday afternoon. After looking through his shirts and socks, Sue announced she had never seen such a dull and grisly selection and managed to persuade him to go up to Whitehaven to buy some new ones. She looked at his best suit and told him to buy a new one as well as some gay casual clothes for his holiday as soon as he arrived in Manchester, at which advice he cocked a satirical eyebrow and asked her if she wanted him to become a peacock in order to win back his wife—to which Sue replied that a little interest in his personal appearance would do no harm.

Before he left she studied the bookings which had been made for both the accommodation provided in the house and the caravans so that if any holidaymakers came on chance during the Easter week-end she would know where to fit them in. Judging by the books it was going to be a busy Easter, and she felt glad that even if he was having personal problems Ralph was at least successful in his business.

But apart from supervising the three men who worked in the petrol station and the woman who worked to keep the house and caravans clean, Sue felt there wasn't really very much for her to do besides looking after Jemima, and she couldn't understand why her sister-in-law had become tired and rundown, and said as much to Ralph.

'Well, for one thing she couldn't handle Jemima the way you can, and she hasn't had the training in management of a business that Dad gave to both you and me. Also, I think she finds Seaport dull. You have to admit it isn't very exciting here in the winter,' he said defensively.

'She has you.' To Sue with all her idealism concerning love and marriage to be with the person one loved all day and every day was the ultimate desire, if she could only find someone whom she could love and who would return her love. 'Or does she find you dull too?' she added.

Ralph's face darkened and his mouth tightened.

'Maybe she does,' he said gruffly. 'I don't know. Oh hell, it was all so perfect at first, then exciting when we knew there was a baby on the way. But these last few months have been miserable. I've done my best to help Penny, to understand her, but it got to the point when ... when she wouldn't even let me make love to her.'

He covered his face with his hands as if embarrassed at having to admit as much to his younger sister.

Sue, jolted by his exasperated confession, stared at him with troubled eyes. This was her big brother Ralph, always so confident and cheerful, admitting defeat. Looking back, she realised that his attraction for Penny, the only child of well-to-do parents, had seemed suspect at the time, too good to be true. Girls like Penny did not usually take up with unsophisticated young men from the country like Ralph, even if he was strong and kind, and handsome in a craggy rough-hewn way. On the other hand, young men like Ralph, skilled at fishing, fond of the outdoors, with a certain surprising business acumen, did not usually fall for a delicate well-mannered young lady from a suburban home like Penny. It had been truly an attraction of opposites, which was supposed to be a good basis for marriage. But was it possible that their marriage had been a mistake? Sue hoped not, not only for Ralph's and Penny's sakes but also for Jemima's.

'I think it would have helped her if there were other young women about her age and who have babies, living in the village,' Ralph was saying as he tried to explain Penny as much to himself as to his sister, 'but as you know the youngest in the village is Jack Parker's daughter Polly, and she must be over thirty now. Perhaps if you were here——?' He cocked a quizzical eye in his sister's direction.

'But I'm not married and I don't have a baby,' retorted Sue. 'How could I stay, anyway?'

'You could have a share in the business,' he said, losing his morose look and becoming enthusiastic. 'Remember Dad always wanted that, only you insisted you wanted to be a nurse. You could take charge of the house, make it into a real boarding house instead of just providing bed and breakfast. The tourist trade is growing and I've been trying to persuade Mrs Kent she needs a smaller house so that I can buy up her property next door. Then I could turn The Gables into a hotel. Now, I don't want you to commit yourself yet, but think about it while I'm away.'

'I will if you promise you'll forget all about this place and think only of Penny while you're on holiday. I've an awful suspicion you've been so taken up with your grandiose schemes for extending that you've been neglecting her.'

'I have to work, don't I?' he retorted, but a dull betraying red had spread over his face and his eyes didn't meet hers.

'Not to the exclusion of showing some consideration of your wife. She should come first and Jemima should come next.'

'They do. Isn't that why I work? It's all for them.'

'But have you shown them they come first? Oh, I know you acknowledge Jemima when she's here, but you never play with her as a father should play with his child.'

'I haven't time,' he said sulkily.

'Yet you had time to go and help Simon Rigg the day I came. Oh, Ralph, you don't know how lucky you are. You're here on the spot at her bedtime. Many fathers are still stuck in their offices or in a traffic jam or on a commuter train at baby's bedtime.'

'Is it important for a father to be there?' he asked in surprise.

'It's important for him to give some time to his child. You helped make Jemima—don't you think you should help look after her? That must be part of the trouble you're having with Penny. You and she haven't been sharing. Starting tomorrow you'll learn how to bath your own child, Ralph Thorpe, and your little sister will show you how!'

He studied her gravely for a second or two, then he smiled.

'You've learned a lot while you've been on that children's ward, haven't you, little sister? But I hope your expectations as to what a man should or should not do in the partnership of marriage aren't going to lead to disillusionment one day. Don't expect too much, Sue.' Then seeing she looked a little distressed he changed course and said, 'All right, it's a deal. But you'll have to tell me what to do if she roars at me. In return you might do something else for me while I'm away. You might walk over to Riggholm and see Simon Rigg.'

'Oh no! Why should I want to do that?' objected Sue. 'He's not the sort of person I'd want to visit. Have you seen him again? The whole village is buzzing with the news of his arrival, but everyone is a bit disappointed because he hasn't put in an appearance.'

'Yes, I've seen him, but not closely, not to talk to. I drove over yesterday to ask him how he was coping and to show a little neighbourliness. There was no reply when I knocked at the front door, so I opened it and gave him a shout. No answer. So I wandered round to the back of the house. Not a sign of him in the garden. I was just thinking of going back to the house to make sure he wasn't in it when I saw him walking along the shore. I must say I was relieved when I saw him.'

'Why? What did you think had happened to him?'

'Well, when there wasn't an answer I thought perhaps I should carry out a search for him, because he might be ill or dead. I'd like you to go over just to make sure he's all right.'

'What on earth for? What do you expect him to do? Commit suicide?'

'The thought had occurred to me,' said Ralph gravely.

'Oh, Ralph, you are the limit!' said Sue impatiently. 'Go to Manchester, attend to your Penny and forget Simon Rigg. He isn't and shouldn't be your chief concern right now. The Riggs have managed to survive without our assistance so far.'

'Only just,' murmured Ralph. 'And I think this one needs our help even if he's too proud to show it.'

That caught Sue's interest.

'What do you think he's done?' she whispered.

'I don't know. It may be that he hasn't done anything. But something unpleasant has happened in his life and I've a feeling he's come here either to hide from it or forget it. You'll go and see him, Sue?'

'I'll go. It'll make a good walk for Jemima on a fine day.'

Friday came and Ralph left. He gave Jemima a puppy as a parting gift. It was three months old and was already quite big, a mixture of collie and terrier, stiff-haired and long-nosed with pointed ears; it was a reddish brown, and Sue christened it Rusty and took it out with her on a leash whenever she took Jemima for a walk.

When Ralph had been away four days he phoned Sue one evening and announced cautiously that Penny had agreed to go away with him for a holiday to Guernsey in the Channel Islands for about two weeks. Penny also talked briefly to Sue, asking in her soft voice about Jemima. Taking a chance on offending her sister-in-law, whom she didn't know very well, Sue gave her a little advice.

'Make the most of this holiday, Penny. Ralph loves you, but you'll have to do a little loving in return if you want to keep him. I can tell you now he won't leave Seaport.'

'Oh!' gasped Penny, sounding outraged. 'He told you?'

'Yes, and this might sound trite, but it makes two to make a success of marriage.'

'How can you possibly know?' retorted Penny. 'You're not married or even engaged.'

Sue said no more. It was true. She had no right to go around handing out advice about marriage when she only knew what she had read or observed. She wasn't likely to know anything about it either. Sit-on-the-shelf Susie, she mocked herself, who was going to develop one day into spinster Susie. Ah well, there was nothing wrong in being single. Better to be single and happy than married and miserable. Still, it would be nice if some man came along some day and liked her for what she was and asked her to share life with him.

At last she found time to walk over to Riggholm. Actually it wasn't a question of not having time but of weather, because since Ralph had left it had been raw and damp and not suitable for taking Jemima for a long walk. But at last a day came when the sun shone out of a placid blue sky, and as soon as Jemima had awakened from her afternoon nap Sue put her in her push-chair, clipped a leash on to Rusty's collar and set out, intending to walk across the sands at the head of the bay to the old grey, creeper-covered house which peeped shyly through the screen of its surrounding shrubbery and trees.

She had just left the petrol station and was turning left to take the path down to the sands when she met Mrs Kent, loaded with parcels, having obviously come from the station.

'Ee, it's a lovely day, but a bit warm for carrying parcels,' said Mrs Kent.

'You should have rung up Jack and he'd have come up to fetch you,' said Sue. 'You could have charged it to Ralph. He wouldn't mind letting you have a free ride.'

'I know he wouldn't, love. Any news from him? Is his missus well?'

'Yes. They're going away to Guernsey for a holiday.'

'Fancy that! Do them both the world of good. That's what they've both been needing, if you ask me. Are you going far?'

'I thought I'd walk over the sands to Riggholm.'

Mrs Kent nodded wisely and her spectacles flashed in the sunlight.

'He was in the village yesterday,' she said, lowering her voice to the conspiratorial tones of the true gossip. 'I saw him with my own eyes. He went into Price's. Gertie said he was ever so polite, but she said he struck her as being a bit reserved-like. He wouldn't say whether he'd come here to live for good or whether he was on holiday. Wouldn't say anything about the house. Just chose his groceries, asked if they could be delivered, paid up and walked out. You didn't tell me you and Ralph drove him down from the station the day you came back,' she added accusingly.

'I didn't have time,' murmured Sue. Jemima was beginning to jig up and down in her push-chair as if anxious to be on her way and Rusty was tugging at the leash.

Mrs Kent looked round carefully to make sure there was no one else listening and then continued in her best know-all manner.

'Between you and me, I thought he looked a bit under the weather, for all he was dressed so flashy. As if he'd been on the razzle, if you know what I mean. Dissipated-looking, like Lupus Rigg used to look when there'd been a party at yon house, and I'm wondering if he's followed in his dad's footsteps. Ee, he was a wild 'un all right, was Lupus. But he got his just deserts in the end.'

Sue would have loved to stay and hear all about Lupus's wildness and what Mrs Kent considered to be 'just deserts', but Jemima had begun to squeal with frustration and the puppy was proving to be very strong for its age.

'I'm sure he did,' she gasped, as Rusty pulled her along. 'I'll have to go. I'll be seeing you, Mrs Kent.'

Pulled by the excited puppy, Sue careered down the path to the sands, much to the delight of Jemima, who gurgled and laughed all the way. The sand, still damp after the morning's high tide, was firm and so pushing the push-chair wasn't as hard as Sue had thought it might be, and after a while she released the puppy and let him run about.

As Mrs Kent had said, it was a lovely day. A fresh wind set the distant blue water rippling and flashing in the sunlight and chased small white clouds across the sky. Even the dark hulk of Rigg's Bank curving across the mouth of the estuary looked benign, and the white beacon marking its end stood out starkly white against the blue backdrop of sea and sky. Yet as she approached the Riggholm side of the bay Sue couldn't help feeling guilty. Her father had always decreed that the Riggholm shore was out of bounds for his children and Sue had never questioned his strict commands. His attitude had been the result of countless unpleasant encounters with Matthew Rigg and his brother Lupus as well as the accumulated hostility to the Rigg family handed down by the Thorpes from generation to generation.

So now, as she pulled the push-chair up the steep bank to the private road running in from the high road to the house, she felt a tremor of apprehension as she trod on what had been hitherto forbidden territory.

The road was broken, muddy and rutted, and she had difficulty in steering the push-chair along it. Trees planted by former Riggs shaded the road and on some of the low-hanging branches of chestnuts she could see that the pinkish sticky buds were already swelling. Here and there among the woodland there was a gleam of silver as the furry catkins known as pussy-willows were touched with sunlight. At her feet in the damp straggling undergrowth the bright faces of celandines twinkled. The place was quiet and peaceful, even the twitterings of the birds were muted.

Eventually she reached tall black iron gates set between two stone pillars on which a coat of arms was carved. The gates were closed. Looking through them, straight up the wide driveway, she saw the house, long and low, its grey stone face half-hidden by virginia creeper. It looked cool, elegant and very supercilious but slightly battered. Rather like its present owner, thought Sue with a humorous twitch to her lips. Like him it looked as if it wouldn't take kindly to uninvited visitors such as she was. The feeling of being unwanted added to the feeling of guilt made her pause even as she put out her hand to lift the latch of the gate.

Now that she knew that Simon Rigg was alive and kicking and had been seen in the village behaving fairly normally there was really no reason why she should seek him out. She stood there uncertainly, not knowing what to do, noting the unkempt appearance of the drive and the drifts of daffodils, newly-unfurled, pale witness to the vigour and persistence of their kind as they peered through the accumulation of dead leaves which lay around them.

Ralph had suggested that Simon Rigg might have come to Riggholm to hide from something unpleasant, and Sue couldn't help recalling that in the past there had been several Riggs who had been out-and-out rogues and who had performed wild and reckless deeds which had put them on the wrong side of the law.

There had been Riggs who had smuggled goods into England from America and anywhere else during the eighteenth century and who had hidden their illicit cargoes in the cellars of Riggholm. There was a legend told that they had dug a tunnel underground from the cellars to the seashore so that stuff could be carried to the house without anyone being seen.

Then there had been the Rigg who had supported Bonnie Prince Charlie and had tried to raise men to follow him when the Prince had marched into England. That Rigg had been executed by the headsman at Carlisle. Another had been hanged as a traitor because he had helped John Paul Jones, Admiral of the American Navy, to find his way into Whitehaven harbour one April morning during the War of American Independence in his warship. The alarm had been given and Paul Jones had only just escaped with his life and his ships. But the Rigg involved hadn't.

Even later when the family had gone into the coal-mining business in a big way in the north of Cumberland and had become very wealthy there had always been an impetuous, reckless member of the family, different from the rest, and always in trouble. In more recent times that person had been Lupus. Was it illogical to assume that his son, the only surviving Rigg, was the same?

Although she had often been secretly fascinated, when younger, by stories about the wilder members of the Rigg family, Sue now felt she didn't really want to meet Simon Rigg again. She knew he was alive and she had seen the house. She would go back home to the safe unexciting law-abiding ways of the Thorpe family.

She had just swung the push-chair round when she realised that Rusty wasn't with her. She called and whistled. A seagull passing overhead mocked her with its croaking call. Rusty didn't appear, and Sue accepted with a sigh of resignation that she would probably have to open the gate and enter the grounds of Riggholm to search for the puppy if he didn't come soon.

CHAPTER 2

SHE was just wondering whether to leave Jemima by the gate in order to go to the edge of the bank to look down on the shore to see if she could spot Rusty when the little dog charged down the driveway, making for the gate where she was standing. Jemima greeted him with a squeal of delight and he sat on the pathway, head on one side, tongue lolling out, looking up appealingly, obviously waiting for the gate to be opened.

Guessing that once she opened the gate the mischievous puppy would go rushing off in some other direction, Sue put her hand to the latch of the gate and opened it a little way.

'You managed to get into the garden without using the gate, why can't you get out of it?' she admonished. 'Come on, you naughty pup!'

As he pushed his head through the opening she grabbed his collar and hooked the leash into the metal ring. Then she pulled the gate wider and he came through his tail hanging down dejectedly.

Footsteps sounded on the gravel of the driveway and she pulled the gate towards her quickly, intending to close it and be on her way before the owner of the house could detain her. But she was too late. The gate was pulled back rather roughly so that she had to release it and she turned to encounter heavy-lidded blue eyes which regarded her with a sort of weary hauteur.

Simon Rigg held on to the gate with one hand, put his other hand on his hip and drawled icily,

'Are you the owner of that destructive creature?' He was wearing a navy blue shirt tucked into corduroy pants which were belted low on lean hips. His hair was dishevelled, the skin of the well-shaped hand holding the gate was ingrained with soil, and soil caked his shoes. But for all he looked slightly disreputable and even vaguely piratical there was no mistaking the authoritative manner in which he spoke, inherited no doubt from generations of Riggs who had ruled the roost at Riggholm and in the surrounding countryside.

Sue felt tempted to retort rudely and stalk away, but Jemima forestalled her by chuckling and holding out her arms to him and saying, 'Dada, Dada,' as she did to all men. Also, after her first initial rebellious reaction Sue was experiencing a strange flutter which started somewhere below her ribs and moved upwards, threatening to cut off her breath. It was a new and very strange feeling and she wasn't sure whether it was caused by fear because of what Rusty might have done in the way of destruction or by this sudden face-to-face encounter with Simon Rigg.

'Yes,' she said weakly, at last. 'What has he done?'

'He's been digging holes in my garden, all over the place. He nearly uprooted some daffodils!' He made the latter sound like a crime punishable only by death.

'Oh, I'm sorry,' she defended breathlessly. If only the flutter would go away! 'He isn't used to things. This is his first long walk in the country and he isn't sure what he is yet. I thought it would be safe to let him run across the sands and in the woods. I didn't think he could get into the garden.'

'I expect he got in where the wall is broken down. You'd better start training him so that he'll learn what he is, or one day when he goes trespassing he may come to a particularly unpleasant end,' he replied severely.

'Oh, you wouldn't!' gasped Sue, then stopped. The blue eyes were quite cold and hard and the set of the firm, chiselled mouth was grim. There was no doubt that Simon Rigg would have no compunction about putting down a dog which he found destroying anything on his property.

'He's only a baby,' she added, in defence of the recalcitrant dog.

'All babies have to be trained, as you should know,' he replied, his cold glance dropping to Jemima who was showing off abominably by hanging over the side of the push-chair as far as the straps which held her in would allow her.

'But I haven't had time to train him yet,' explained Sue. Somehow it was most important that he should understand that she was not normally careless about other people's property. Anyway, she thought mutinously, she wouldn't have come this way if it hadn't been for her brother's concern for Simon Rigg himself. 'Ralph only brought him home last Friday.'

'You woke me up on the train, didn't you?' he said.

'Yes. I'm Susan Thorpe.'

He was cross, she thought. But he looked less haggard than when she had last seen him and the greyish tinge was missing from his face.

Jemima howled suddenly, causing the dog which had been resting quietly, keeping a wary eye on Simon, to jump to its feet and start barking.

'Quiet, Rusty! Sit!' ordered Sue brusquely, determined to show Simon that she could control the dog when she wished. But Rusty took no notice. He rushed off at high speed and she had to pull with all her might on the leash to avoid being pulled after him. The violent jerk on the leash seemed to bring the puppy to its senses and Sue was able to turn her attention to Jemima.

To her surprise she found that Simon was squatting in front of the push-chair holding one of the little girl's plump hands in his and was in the act of kissing it. As he was about to raise his head Jemima shrieked with ecstasy and grabbed a handful of his hair and pulled hard. He smiled, and the difference the smile made to his thin face caused that strange fluttering to start again below her ribs. He detached Jemima's hand from his hair and holding both of her plump hands between his, clapped them together as he chided her gently,

'No, darling, you mustn't pull. It isn't the sort which

comes off. It's real,' he said gently, and this time it was the difference in his voice which made Sue feel all wobbly. No longer icily crisp or wearily indifferent, it was warm and caressing like the sun on the back of her neck. But she had hardly noted the difference when it changed as he looked up at her. The ice was back as he informed her,

'She caught her finger in the spokes of the wheel.'

Both his eyes and his voice rebuked her. Apparently he thought it was her fault that Jemima had hurt herself. Not only did he think she was incapable of keeping a puppy under control but he also thought she couldn't look after a child either! Righteous indignation boiled within her.

'Jemima's howl is always far louder than the pain merits, and I can see you've been as easily fooled as her father is by the performance she puts on. Don't you recognise a big production about nothing when you see one?' she retorted coldly.

'You call this nothing?' he exclaimed, holding out Jemima's chubby middle finger for her inspection.

A small piece of skin had been torn off the inside of the finger leaving a raw red patch. Immediately all Sue's irritation with the man faded and squatting beside him she took Jemima's hand in hers.

'Oh, poor poppet!' she murmured sympathetically.

Jemima, pleased to have the attention of two adults, beamed benignly at them and kicked her heels on the footrest of the push-chair. Simon straightened slowly to his full height.

'I'm glad to see you aren't totally devoid of feeling when your child is hurt. Isn't it true that a child only behaves badly, or puts on a big production, as you call it, when it isn't getting enough attention?' he said.

Again he sounded accusing. Standing up too, Sue faced him and was annoyed to find her head was no higher than his shoulder.

'Yes, it is true. Possibly that's why Jemima does it. But please don't think it's because she hasn't been getting attention from me. She isn't my child. She's Ralph's and

Penny's.'

Surprise flickered in his eyes and then was doused and replaced by the expression of tired indifference. He stepped back and leaned against the old stone wall and she noticed that the grey tinge was back in his face.

'Ah yes, the estimable, all-curious Ralph on whom I slammed the door so rudely. If you aren't his wife you must be his sister. Yes, I can see a resemblance now. I called to see him yesterday to offer my apologies and to pay him for the food and equipment he brought that night I arrived, but I was told he's away.'

The change in his manner, his willingness to admit that he had been rude to Ralph knocked Sue slightly off balance and she found herself wanting to reassure him that the change was noted and appreciated.

'That was nice of you. Ralph would have appreciated the gesture, although he wouldn't have accepted payment. You see, he was worried about you. He thought you might, that you were . . .' She stuttered to a stop as she realised that with her impulsive desire to respond to his apology to Ralph she had said too much. Also it was suddenly impossible to express Ralph's opinion of Simon Rigg's state of mind on that wet evening over a week ago when she was being watched by sardonic blue eyes.

'He thought I might do myself in,' Simon finished for her. 'He asked me why I had come to Riggholm and I told him I'd come to die. Rather a melodramatic statement, but it described how I felt, and I suppose naturally enough he thought I was considering suicide.'

Sue's eyes were round with astonishment. 'Are you going to die? Is it chronic?' she whispered.

'Is what chronic?' he asked irritably, his eyebrows coming together in an impatient frown.

'The disease you have. Is it incurable?'

'Not as incurable as the curiosity about other people's affairs from which you and your brother seem to suffer,' he snapped.

But she didn't take the hint. She stayed right where she

231

was. Lifting her chin at him and looking him straight in the eyes without any affection or coyness, she retorted with spirit,

'It may seem like idle curiosity to you, but Ralph's interest in people is genuine. He really cares about others. He was concerned about you and wanted to help you. I asked about your illness because my work has been with people who have often been seriously ill and who require rehabilitation, and I thought I might be able to help too. I'm a trained nurse.'

He made a wry grimace of distaste.

'I guessed as much. Then why aren't you working in a hospital where you're needed?' he demanded crossly.

His reply flummoxed her. She was not used to people showing such obvious distaste for her profession or demanding autocratically why she wasn't doing her job, so she was stampeded into replying defensively again,

'Oh, because Ralph had to go and find Penny and persuade her to come back, so he asked me to come and look after Jemima,' she stammered.

'In that case I suggest you concentrate on looking after her and leave me to look after myself,' he said unkindly.

She looked at him anxiously. The signs of fatigue in his face, the dark shadows beneath his eyes, the sharpness of his cheekbones, the hollows beneath them, troubled her. He was too young to be looking and behaving like someone at the end of his rope. She guessed he was only a few years older than Ralph, three at the most, yet the difference between them was probably best measured in amount of worldly experience acquired than in years. Ralph at twenty-nine was vigorous and optimistic despite his present problem. This man was not only physically tired but was sick at heart too. All her nursing instinct clamoured to be allowed to care for him. She wanted to go into his house and prepare a good meal for him, and make a comfortable bed for him to sleep in. She imagined he was camping out in the house, making do, which was no way for him to live in his present condition.

But Jemima was shouting her impatience and the puppy was pulling at the leash.

'Well, if you're quite sure you don't need anything, I'll go now, because it's nearly Jemima's teatime.'

'I thought she was getting restless,' he murmured, apparently making no secret of the relief he felt that she had decided to go. Then with a sort of weary curiosity he drawled, 'Who is Penny?'

'Ralph's wife. She went to visit her mother and now she won't come back.'

'I see. It's a habit young wives have, or so I'm told,' he observed with world-weary cynicism.

With obvious effort he lunged away from the wall, turned away from her and went through the gate. Closing it, he walked slowly up the drive without a backward glance.

Despite the squealing child and the tugging animal, Sue remained standing where she was and watched the man's lethargic movements. Not until he had entered the house did she move, and then she set off at high speed along the muddy road, pushing the child and pulling the dog, her head down, not seeing the signs of spring, as she wrestled with her thoughts.

What was wrong with Simon Rigg? Why had he come to Riggholm? Mrs Kent had observed that he looked dissipated and had perhaps taken after his father Lupus, who had been a wild one. But to Sue's trained eyes the signs of fatigue on his face spelled only physical and mental exhaustion, as if the man had driven himself or had been driven by some unrelenting devil to the edge of collapse. And now he was here at Riggholm with his caustic tongue and his entrancing smile, which apparently he reserved for babies only, and no matter how much he wanted to be left alone and ignored it was going to be difficult for her to ignore someone who was so much in need of a helping, comforting hand.

Although Sue's parents were no longer alive, she and Ralph shared one grandparent with their two cousins Greta and John Carter. This grandparent was Harriet Thorpe, a formidable, strong-willed woman of seventy-eight who lived at present with her only daughter Emily Carter on a farm up in the fells to the east of Seaport. Having lived in the area all her life and having a quick and lively mind, she was an authority on the local history and knew everything there was to know about most families who lived in Seaport or round about. Above all she possessed a fierce family pride and took a great interest in the concerns of her grandchildren.

Sue wasn't surprised, then, when Grandmother Thorpe and her Aunt Emily arrived at The Gables the next afternoon just after she had put Jemima upstairs for her afternoon nap. Emily, a typical sturdy north-countrywoman, dressed in good tweeds, her naturally curly white hair cut in a serviceable style, her face plump and rosy, bustled into the kitchen followed in a more sedate fashion by her mother. Grandmother was small and slight and wore her thinning hair scraped back into a tight knot right on top of her head. She gave the impression of being a gentle, slightly delicate old lady, but her children and grandchildren knew she had the constitution of an ox and a' will of iron. She accepted Sue's kiss on her soft lined cheek, glanced round the kitchen with her bright brown eyes and said in a surprisingly deep voice,

'Where's the child?'

'Having a nap, Gran. Come and sit over here,' said Sue.

'Don't hustle me, girl. I'm not as good on my legs as I was,' objected Grandmother. She seated herself in the rocking-chair, and gave her granddaughter a sharp penetrating glance.

'You're like me at the same age. No beauty, but a good clear skin and good clean blood running beneath it. You seem to have some sense too—a rare commodity in young folk these days, if all I read is true. So you managed to make the little scamp take a rest. I told Penny that any active child of that age needs a rest in the afternoon, but she always had some excuse for not putting her down. Silly little fool, letting a baby get the better of her!'

'Now, Mother, don't be so critical. Penny did her best. She wasn't well. Having Jemima did her no good at all, pulled her down badly. Well, it's nice to see you, Sue love. Put the kettle on, there's a good girl, Mother and I are just gasping for a cup of tea,' said Emily in her quiet pleasant way.

'You may be gasping, Emily, but I'm not,' asserted Grandmother. 'Take your time, lass. Don't let her rush you. She's always been the same. Never happy unless she's got everyone on the run.'

'Now, Mother, that's not true.'

As she turned away to fill the kettle Sue hid a smile. The good-natured bickering between her aunt and her grandmother had been a part of the Thorpe family scene ever since she could remember. The deep curt tones of her grandmother's voice and the soft placating note of her aunt's were an intrinsic part of her background and for her they represented the integrity and warmth of family life. For although these two bickered endlessly they never actually quarrelled with each other. Sue often thought that they didn't because her aunt was so placid and her grandmother was so supremely imperturbable. Grandmother was always right in her own estimation, so she made statements. She never argued.

'Have you heard from Ralph?' asked Emily, as she took down cups and saucers from a cupboard.

'Yes. They're going to Guernsey for a holiday.'

'Humph. An expensive way of making it up,' commented Grandmother. 'He can't afford to be taking a holiday at this time of the year with the season just starting.'

'If it's going to save his marriage he can afford it,' said Emily. 'Besides, Penny deserves a rest. It's lucky for Ralph that Sue was able to come and look after the child. Were you able to get leave of absence, love?'

'No, I'm afraid not. I had to give notice. But I didn't mind. I needed a change,' replied Sue.

'Change, change!' snorted Grandmother. 'Don't know what's wrong with young folk today, always needing change. It was because you wanted a change that you went away to Newcastle to do nursing, if I remember rightly, and now you're wanting change again.'

'And going away has done her a lot of good. Why, I'd have given anything when I was younger to have gone away from Seaport and seen something of the world,' said Emily, smiling kindly at Sue.

'Oh, would you?' snapped Grandmother. 'First I've heard of it. You didn't say so at the time.'

'What was the good of me saying so?' returned Emily, winking at Sue.

But as if she hadn't noticed her daughter's interjection Grandmother continued in full flow, declaiming how perfect her generation had been.

'In my day we stayed put in our place, where we belonged, doing our bit for our family and for the community. In my day ...'

'In your day everything was different, Mother, very different. You weren't subject to the same pressures that young people of today are. You didn't live at the same pace.'

'No, we didn't,' agreed Grandmother with deceptive mildness. 'We had to work hard. We had no time for pace-making, or keeping up.'

There was a knock on the kitchen door and it was pushed open by Martin Kent. He was tall and lanky and his dark hair dropped in an untidy fringe across his forehead, almost into his eyes. Beneath the fringe his eyes were wide and apprehensive as he flicked an uncertain glance in the direction of Grandmother. As always when disturbed he stammered badly.

'Th ... th ... there's gent outside ... w ... wants to speak to you,' he said, and then fled.

'Needs his hair cutting,' pronounced Grandmother. 'Don't know why Ralph employs him.'

'He's a very good mechanic,' said Sue, wondering what

236

Grandmother would say if she saw Simon Rigg's hair. 'I won't be a minute. You have your tea.'

The 'gent' was Simon Rigg, elegant in a belted jacket of smooth fawn suede open over a blue high-necked sweater. He was leaning indolently against the wall of the little white-painted office and at his feet was a round metal can with a spout and a handle, the sort used for carrying paraffin. As Sue approached him he looked up, then touched the can with one foot as if to indicate it to her.

'I had to come in for some fuel for the Primus,' he said without preamble. 'There is a cooking machine of sorts in the kitchen at Riggholm, but it isn't either an electric cooker or a gas one and I'm not sure what kind of fuel to get for it. I tried to describe it to the boy, but either he doesn't understand me or he's frightened of me.'

'He's a little nervous and withdrawn with strangers,' explained Sue, and to her surprise he nodded as if he understood Martin's problem.

'I see. Anyway, he muttered something about Miss Sue knowing and rushed off to find you. I hope he didn't interrupt anything. I didn't want him to bother you,' he said politely.

'Oh, it's no bother,' replied Sue quickly, determined to use this opportunity to help. 'Perhaps your cooker uses solid fuel.'

'I've no idea. I'm quite incompetent when it comes to housekeeping,' he said with a ghost of the entrancing smile he'd given Jemima. 'What's solid fuel?'

'Anthracite. We have a cooker like that too. If you'd like to come into the kitchen I'll show it to you and then you can tell me if it's similar to yours.'

He moved away from the office. Taking his movement as agreement to her suggestion, Sue led the way across the yard to the back door of the house and he followed her. As he entered the kitchen, however, he paused in the open doorway when he noticed Grandmother and Emily. For a moment it looked as if he would turn on his heel and walk out. Reacting immediately to his hesitation, Sue put a detaining hand on his arm and whispered,

'It's quite safe. They won't bite.'

He flashed her a furious glance, taking exception to her remark. But he didn't retreat. Sue closed the back door and moved across the room.

'This is Mr Simon Rigg from Riggholm. He's come to look at our cooker to see if it's the same as the one at his house,' she announced, and was amused to see her usually imperturbable grandmother start with surprise.

Turning back to Simon who had followed her slowly, she said,

'This is my grandmother, Mrs Harriet Thorpe, and my aunt, Mrs Emily Carter. They live at Greenthwaite Farm up in the fells.'

She had to give him credit for good manners when they were required. Without any sign of the reluctance which she guessed he was feeling he shook hands first with Emily, who blushed and almost simpered as she acknowledged his greeting, and then with Grandmother, who stared at him with bright curious eyes.

'You're like Matthew,' she asserted in her gruff voice. 'Almost his living image.'

'Aren't you a little mixed up, Mother?' said Emily. 'This is Lupus's son.'

'I know, I know whose son he is,' said Grandmother. 'But he looks like Matthew. He has his bonny blue eyes and his curly hair and his firm handshake. Could be his son. I should know.' She leaned towards Simon as if she was about to impart some important piece of information. 'Your uncle was once a friend of mine, young man. He wanted to marry me, but I chose Michael Thorpe instead.'

Feeling slightly apprehensive about Simon's possible reaction to her grandmother's personal comments, Sue was surprised when he smiled at the old lady in the same way as he had smiled at Jemima the previous day.

'Obviously my uncle had very good taste,' he remarked gently. 'It's a pity that the Riggs lost to the Thorpes in that instance.'

238

Grandmother's eyes gleamed appreciatively and she chuckled.

'Not the first time they lost either, although the Riggs had their triumphs too,' she said. 'Now, that was Lupus speaking. Now I know you must be his son. He always had a smooth tongue and he could be very charming. Unlike Matthew, who for all he was so handsome could never say what he wanted to say, especially to women. Poor Matthew! He was disappointed twice in his life—first by me and then by your mother. Yet I often think if he'd only asserted himself, and shown more patience, he might have won her.'

'My mother?' A frown had replaced Simon's smile and his voice expressed sharp surprise. Sue felt that her grandmother was talking too much and tried to attract Emily's attention in the hope that her aunt might interrupt and change the subject in her usual adept way. But Emily seemed to be mesmerised by Simon. Elbow on the table, chin on her hand, she was staring at him as if he was a visitor from another planet, which with his up-to-the-minute clothes and with his longish curling hair he could have been, when you compared him with the conservatively dressed farmers with whom Emily was used to mixing.

'Yes, your mother,' said Grandmother complacently, apparently all set to indulge in a flood of reminiscences concerning the Rigg family. 'Matthew was in love with her, but when Lupus left Riggholm in a fury because Matthew refused to pay his debts, she followed him. We were never told as much, but we assumed he married her. Much good marriage to him did her. Lupus must have led her a dance.'

She saw his shoulders stiffen and his head come up sharply as he made no effort to hide that he was offended by the implication underlying Grandmother's words that his parents might not have been married and that their relationship might not have been happy.

'I believe that, although it was tragically brief, their marriage was very happy. My father never recovered from the great shock of her death,' he said, his voice still polite

239

but several degrees cooler.

To Sue's relief Aunt Emily roused from her stupor. Rising to her feet and picking up her handbag from the table, she said,

'Mr Rigg has come to look at the cooker, Mother, not to listen to you. It's time we went on our way.' Turning to Simon, she smiled and added, 'It's very nice to think that there's a Rigg back at Riggholm again. It's grieved many of us to see the place deteriorating through lack of attention. I expect we'll be seeing you about?'

'Of course we'll be seeing him,' growled Grandmother as she stood up. She peered up at Simon and tapped two fingers on his chest. 'I like a man who's loyal to his own people. Come to tea at Greenthwaite some day and I'll tell you more about the Riggs and the Thorpes. They're all descended from the Vikings, you know, who came about a thousand years ago, not directly from Scandinavia but from established settlements in Iceland and the Scottish Islands. That they were our forebears is an undeniable fact. They left signs in the Cumbrian names such as thwaites, ghylls, becks, dales and fells; words or parts of words in place names and surnames, all from the old Norse language. And did you know the Riggs were smugglers for a while? The only time Thorpes did business with them, I suspect. Aye, you'll need to know all about your family if you're going to live here.'

Her quizzical glance and her last sentence showed that Grandmother was dying to know more about Simon Rigg's business. But, as Sue guessed, he didn't give anything away.

'My staying here depends entirely on whether I get what I came for,' he replied coolly.

'And what's that?' asked the irrepressible Harriet Thorpe.

'Peace and quiet, hopefully uninterrupted by busybodies, do-gooders,' here he flicked a wicked glance in Sue's direction before adding, 'and nosy old ladies.'

Sue gasped, Aunt Emily looked astounded. But Grandmother chuckled joyfully.

'Ee, lad, you're after my own heart. You don't pull your punches. But I'm sorry you want to keep to yourself. It doesn't do any good.' She sighed heavily. 'Matthew did that. Didn't do him any good at all. Come along, Emily, time we went. Didn't I tell you he was like Matthew?'

When Sue returned to the kitchen after seeing her relatives depart she found Simon standing in front of the cooker.

'I'm sorry. I hope you'll excuse my grandmother. Meeting you must have excited her and roused her memories. Sometimes her remarks about other people are a little tactless.'

He shrugged indifferently.

'There are times when I say what I feel about other people too.' He frowned and then added rather obscurely, 'Or at least I've always wanted to, but have never done so until I came here.' The frown faded and the glimmer of a smile appeared as he glanced at her. 'Don't apologise for your grandmother. I found her very refreshing. This cooker is identical to the one at Riggholm. How does it work?'

Vaguely pleased that he had liked her grandmother, Sue explained quickly and concisely how the cooker worked.

'And where will I get the fuel for it?' asked Simon.

'We can supply it. Ralph is the agent for all kinds of fuel delivered in the district.'

'Is he now? He's built quite a little empire for himself,' he commented dryly.

'Oh, he didn't build it all. My father established most of the business when he came back from the war and decided to have a petrol station. You see, the Thorpe family had always been fishermen and seafaring people, but as the estuary gradually silted up and the coastal trade fell off, the family had to turn to other means of earning a livelihood. For my father it was either build up a business like this or leave Seaport, which he didn't want to do. You might say that necessity was truly the mother of invention in his case. In Ralph's too. He's thinking of opening a hotel now that the tourist industry is increasing. If you'll come outside I'll show you the fuel and then I can take your order in the office.'

They were just leaving the office when a small tangerine sports car swept up to the petrol pumps. It was driven by a young man with dark hair, who wore a striped college scarf around his neck. When he saw Sue, his long-jawed face registered ludicrous surprise.

'It can't be sweet Susie Thorpe, by all that's wonderful!' he exclaimed. 'It must be nearly two years since I last saw you. Our visits to this dead-and-alive hole have never coincided. How long are you staying?'

He stood up in the car, stepped over the door and came over to her. To her surprise and embarrassment he caught her up in his arms, twirled her round and as he set her on her feet he kissed her on the cheek.

'I'm here for a few weeks. I'm looking after things for Ralph,' replied Sue primly, trying to flatten her hair, wishing that her cheeks hadn't gone pink, wishing above all that Simon Rigg had not been a witness to the recent scene. 'Are you home for Easter, Derek?'

'Yes, worse luck. My job came to a disastrous end yesterday and here I am crawling home and nearly out of petrol as well as cash.' His eyes glinted over her trim figure and glossy hair. 'It's great to see you, Susie. I came home only because I'm short of cash and Mother insisted on my presence here, or I might have gone to Switzerland with some of the boys and girls. Still, if you're going to be here the holiday won't seem so bad.'

'I'm here to work, not play,' she warned laughingly. It was rather a boost to her morale to think that Derek hadn't forgotten her and wished to see more of her.

'I'd like the fuel delivered as soon as possible, Miss Thorpe.' Simon Rigg's attractively husky voice reminded her that she'd been in the middle of a business transaction when Derek had arrived. It also drew Derek's gaze in the direction of Simon, and he stared in a puzzled way at the well-cut stylish clothes and the thin, handsome face and

242

brown curling hair of the man at her side.

'I say, haven't I seen you somewhere before?' he asked brashly.

'No, you haven't,' was the cold and abrupt reply as Simon didn't even bother to glance at him. 'When may I expect the fuel, Miss Thorpe?'

'Will later this afternoon be suitable?' said Sue hurriedly.

'Perfectly,' he agreed.

He turned away and went to pick up the paraffin can. As he walked out of the station Sue remembered she hadn't warned him of the difficulties he might encounter when lighting the cooker and called after him,

'Oh, Mr Rigg, you might have some problems with the cooker. It'll be cold and a little damp. A gas poker and a cylinder of butane gas will help.'

He stopped and looked back.

'Then deliver them with the fuel,' he ordered.

'Did you say Rigg? Then that's why you seem familiar,' said Derek, sounding pleased as if he had solved some knotty problem. 'You're one of the Riggs of Riggholm. Wait until I tell my mother. She'll be so interested. We're the Barnes of Scartop, you know. My father is Brigadier-General Digby Barnes. He's a member of the Rural District Council. Mother will want to have you over for dinner, if I'm not mistaken.'

Sue saw exasperation tauten Simon's face and the glance he gave her was cold and scornful. Apparently he blamed her for Derek's brash approach.

'Any invitation your mother is likely to issue will be ignored,' he said, and ice crackled in his voice. 'I've not come here to go on the local gentry's visiting list. You and I have never met. Remember that, please, Mr Barnes.'

He turned away and walked off round the corner of the road, bound for Riggholm.

Derek looked at Sue and his feelings were expressed in the lugubrious raising of his eyebrows and the downward curve of his wide mouth.

'Whew! Old Matthew to a "t" in more ways than one. Yet I have a funny niggling feeling that I've seen him somewhere else,' he said. 'Don't you think he's familiar?'

'I did at first, but once I learned that he's a Rigg I decided his familiarity was due to the fact that he resembles Matthew,' replied Sue. 'How many gallons do you want?'

'Make it five and put it on Dad's account. No matter what Rigg said I must tell Mother about him. She'll want to call on him. So will Christy, when she knows what he looks like.'

'No, Derek, don't.' Sue's objection was spontaneous and involuntary.

'Why not? He'll soon stop being stand-offish when he meets Christy. She can get round anyone when she wants to. So can Mother, come to think of it.'

Now Sue's opinion of Christy Barnes, Derek's teenage sister, was not very high. She considered her to be a spoiled, selfish brat who would pester anyone to get her own way. Also she knew that Mrs Barnes, a tireless social climber as well as being the fund-raiser for many local charities, would have no hesitation in harrying Simon Rigg once she knew he was in residence. And in view of Simon's remark to her grandmother that he'd come to Riggholm for peace and quiet she felt she must try and protect him from the Barnes mother and daughter if it was at all possible.

'Please don't tell them,' she urged, as she put the petrol hose back on its bracket after filling the tank of Derek's car.

'Regarding him as your special property already?' needled Derek unpleasantly. 'I was always led to believe that the Riggs and the Thorpes were daggers drawn.'

'Not always. But apart from that I think we should try to respect his desire for privacy. He's come here for that.'

'Another Matthew, eh? Oh well, I won't tell Mother and Christy if you'll promise to do something for me,' said Derek.

'What is that?' she asked cautiously, knowing of old his propensity for mischief.

'Come sailing with me on Easter Monday. The old dinghy is still in good shape.'

'But I won't have time. I'm here to look after the business while Ralph is away. I'm not expecting him back until the week-end after Easter.'

'You'll find time if Simon Rigg's desire for privacy is so important to you,' he threatened cheekily. 'See you, Sue.'

Sue delivered the fuel to Riggholm herself, because she forgot to tell Roy Beck, who drove the lorry and made the fuel deliveries for Ralph, to take the bags of anthracite to Simon Rigg. The afternoon had been busy because the warm sunshine had brought a steady trickle of motorists into Seaport. They were mostly shopkeepers from the nearby towns who had come out to spend their early closing day enjoying the first warm day of spring.

It wasn't until she was giving Jemima her tea that she remembered, and then it was too late to ask Roy because he had finished for the day. She managed to persuade Jack and Martin to lift the heavy bags into the back of the van together with the cylinder of gas and the poker, but neither of them would agree to drive the stuff over to Riggholm. Both had a strange antipathy to the place. She knew that Jack's dislike of the Riggholm property stemmed from a tongue-lashing he had received once from Matthew Rigg when the latter had caught him poaching pheasants on his land and she could only assume that the nervous, autistic Martin had been influenced by the stories he'd heard from his mother, and possibly Jack as well, about the miserly bad-tempered squire of Riggholm.

She couldn't say she was exactly drawn to the place herself, knowing that Simon didn't want callers and having felt the lash of his tongue yesterday. But she had promised she would deliver the fuel that afternoon and deliver it she must. So having put Jemima to bed she went across to the Kents' house and persuaded Mrs Kent to baby-sit for her, assuring her that the child was fast asleep and that she wouldn't be any longer than half an hour at the most.

It was a lovely still evening. The bay was a bowl of rose-coloured water in which the houses of Seaport were reflected almost perfectly. The main road north was a golden path leading to mysterious hidden places. But she had to leave that golden road and turn into the muddy, rutted, tree-shaded road which led to Riggholm.

When at last, after a jolting uncomfortable ride, she reached the gates of the house, she found with relief that they had been set wide open in readiness for the delivery of the fuel. She drove up the driveway carefully and parked the van in front of the house. As she descended and walked up the flight of stone steps it seemed as if every blackbird and thrush in the vicinity had chosen to sit among the Riggholm trees to sing their evensong.

There was an old-fashioned bell-pull beside the panelled front door. She pulled it and heard the bell clang quite clearly. After waiting a few seconds she pulled it again and once more heard the bell clang within the house. But no one came to the door. She put her hand on the door knob, turned it slowly and pushed. The door opened. She put her head round it and called,

'Mr Rigg, I've brought the fuel!'

Her voice echoed hollowly through the high shadowy hallway. She waited, but no one appeared.

Where was Simon Rigg? In the garden, perhaps. Closing the door, Sue skipped lightly down the steps and went round the side of the house through the shrubbery to the back garden. The smell of newly-cut grass tickled her nostrils and she sneezed. Simon Rigg had been busy. The circular lawn edged by rhododendrons, silver birches and gracefully, drooping willow trees, was half cut. Sunlight glinted on something which lay on the grass beside a rather ancient grass-cutting machine. She walked over to investigate. It was a newly-sharpened sickle. Simon Rigg was doing things the hard way with the old-fashioned tools which the gardener who had once worked for the Rigg family had used.

But where was he?

Sue glanced once more round the garden and then called his name. He didn't appear, and an odd feeling of panic swept over her. Perhaps he had overdone the gardening and had taken ill. Perhaps he was lying in the house dying. Panic lent wings to her feet and she hurried through the shrubbery, ran up the steps, pushed open the door and entered the house.

It smelt damp and musty and once more she sneezed as dust tickled her nose. The hallway was pleasantly panelled in oak. On the left a door was open. Sunlight slanted through it across the parquet flooring of the hall and dust motes danced in the shafts of yellow light. Sue went slowly towards the open door, a little afraid of what she might find within the room.

It was a big room and had an enormous bay window facing west overlooking sand-dunes beyond which the sea glittered. It was furnished with old-fashioned velvet-covered armchairs and a huge chesterfield on which was thrown the sleeping bag which Ralph had lent to Simon Rigg. There were two glass-fronted cabinets filled with all sorts of silver and china ornaments and there were several occasional tables. On one of the tables Sue noticed some cutlery and a cup and saucer, and on a high-backed chair beside the chesterfield some articles of clothing had been tossed. As she had guessed Simon Rigg was camping out, using only one room and possibly the kitchen.

But where was he?

Panic took hold again and retracing her steps to the hall she walked to the bottom of the curved stairway and called,

'Mr Rigg, Mr Rigg, where are you? Are you all right?'

Once again her voice echoed through the house.

'I'm perfectly all right, thank you.'

Sue whirled, clapping her hand over her mouth to stifle the involuntary cry of fright. Simon was standing just inside the closed door which she guessed led to the back regions of the house.

'You frightened me,' she accused.

'I intended to,' he replied coolly. 'I'm not sure I approve of young women who invade my house and screech at the top of their voices. I was in the garden when the bell rang, but before I reached the front door you had left it and had gone round to the back garden. I heard you calling me, so I made my way through the house to the garden only to hear you enter the house at the front as I was about to leave it at the back. Couldn't you have waited after you'd rung the bell until I answered the door?'

He was extraordinarily adept at making her feel in the wrong, and she didn't like the feeling.

'You were so long in coming I thought that something had happened to you,' she retorted.

'What could possibly happen to me here?'

'You could overtax your strength and have a heart attack.'

'But a weak heart is not a complaint from which I suffer,' he said with the exaggerated patience of one explaining to a person whose intelligence was suspect. 'It seems to me that your chosen occupation has made you hypersensitive where illness is concerned. Do you go around labelling people with various diseases?'

'No, I don't,' she snapped angrily, her face flushing as she realised he was making fun of her. 'I've been working in a children's ward and...'

'That fits,' he interrupted. 'You look at me sometimes as if I'm a child in need of care. Perhaps I ought to warn you that I'm a fully developed adult, and male into the bargain. Don't come too near or you might regret it.'

Although disconcerted by the glint in his eyes Sue had to retort,

'But you'll admit that you're in need of care.'

He shook his head.

'I'll admit nothing. I can take care of myself, so I hope you haven't been making secret plans to help my rehabilitation by being a sister to me, or the mother I've never known.'

Remembering the longing she had experienced yesterday to cook for him and to make his bed, Sue writhed inwardly in reaction to his irony. But on the heels of embarrassment came more anger.

'Who'd want to be a sister to you?' she countered. 'You're cold and unkind, and yesterday you were very rude to Derek Barnes.'

'You think so? I don't. I was merely making it quite clear to him that I hadn't come to Riggholm to socialise. I think he got the message.'

'Then why have you come here?' she demanded.

'I've come here because it's my home,' was the surprising reply.

'Oh, you can't expect me to believe that,' she scoffed. 'You weren't born here and you've never shown any interest in the place before, although you must have known about it for nearly three years.'

'Even so, it's true. One morning I woke up and I said to myself, I'm going home to Riggholm.'

Sue stared at him closely. Blue eyes regarded her steadily, directly. He seemed quite sincere.

'But you'd been ill,' she said, hoping to prise more information out of him.

His gaze didn't waver.

'No, unless you call exhaustion an illness. There's nothing as debilitating as working hard and playing hard at the same time, which I've always had a tendency to do,' he replied smoothly. 'And now perhaps you'll explain why you've come here when I thought I'd made it clear I wished to be left alone. It would be as well if you explained before it goes dark and we have to light the candles.'

'But haven't you had the electricity switched on yet?' she asked.

'How would I do that?'

'There must be a master switch somewhere. Didn't you tell the electricity board you were going to come and live in the house?'

'I didn't, but I expect my uncle's lawyer did. Where will I find the master switch?'

'Near the fuse box, which should be in a cupboard

somewhere, possibly in the kitchen.'

'Then I shall look for it when you've told me why you've come.'

'I've brought the fuel for the cooker. Do you think you can help me to lift it out of the van?'

The expression on his face was compounded of exasperation and rueful amusement.

'Surely one of the men at the garage could have brought it?'

'I forgot to ask Roy who does the deliveries, and neither of the other two will come near this place because they remember what your uncle was like,' she explained, 'so that left me.'

'I see. They think I'm tarred with the same brush that he was,' he remarked with a twist at the corner of his mouth.

'Well, in the country old prejudices die hard,' she defended, 'and until you've proved otherwise they'll think you're like him. I made a promise to you this afternoon and I had to keep it.'

He gave her another of his sardonic glances.

'Tomorrow would have done. Remember always you don't have to kill yourself keeping promises you've made to me. Another night without the cooker wouldn't have harmed me. However, since you've brought it we'll heave the stuff round to the coalshed.'

It was a struggle, but they managed to drag the sacks of fuel along the path through the shrubbery to the coalshed. Then they entered the house through the back door into the big cavernous kitchen, where Simon sat down on a chair and wiped his brow with a handkerchief.

'You really hit rock bottom before you woke up that morning and decided to come here,' Sue said, eyeing him professionally. 'How did it happen?'

'I thought I'd told you,' he snapped irritably, 'I worked too hard. I don't propose to go into the morbid details.'

'It might help me to understand if you did,' she replied.

'Why bother to understand? Why not accept me for what I appear to be? Another slightly eccentric, irascible Rigg

250

who wants to be left alone.'

'Because I'm not sure you should be left alone,' she answered gravely.

He gave her a quick wary glance and pushed the handkerchief into his pocket.

'Which cupboard do you think the electric meter and fuses are hiding in?' he asked, and she knew a keen and startling disappointment that he had decided not to confide in her.

They searched the cupboards and eventually found the right one and switched the master switch on. Sue tried a light switch and the one naked bulb hanging from the middle of the ceiling in the kitchen glowed with weak yellowish light.

'Not exactly suitable for reading small print, but it's a light,' remarked Simon. 'The marvels of modern science are wonderful if only you know how to use them. Thanks for your assistance.'

It sounded like dismissal, but now that she was here Sue didn't want to leave. There was so much to be done to the house to make it comfortable. Surely she could help in more ways?

'What about the cooker?' she asked.

'I'll tackle that tomorrow, I think I've had enough excitement for one day.'

'I could light it for you,' she offered eagerly. 'It won't take long with the poker.'

He looked down at her serious pleading eyes and steeled himself against her offer.

'If you're going to be so insistent about doing everything I'll never learn from my own experience, will I, Nurse?' he said lightly.

'And if you never learn to accept help from anyone graciously you'll develop into a cross-grained old bachelor like your uncle and then no one will want to help you,' she countered. 'I'm going to light that cooker and tomorrow you'll find you'll have hot water for washing and you'll be able to cook your breakfast on it.'

'All right, for once you win. I'll show you just how gracious I can be and let you light it.'

Lighting the cooker, however, took much longer than she had anticipated because first of all it had to be cleaned and then it let off such obnoxious fumes that they had to try and open the kitchen windows which seemed to have been jammed for years. By the time they had opened them and had the back door open as well and had wafted the fumes out into the calm evening air they were both half coughing and half laughing.

'This wouldn't endear us to the anti-pollution league,' he said, and then burst out laughing. 'You should see your face! You look like a Black and White Minstrel.'

'You should see yours,' she retorted, laughing too. 'It's zebra-striped!'

They both laughed again and then were suddenly silent, eyeing each other. Very much aware of him, she stood under the stark electric light bulb in the smoky kitchen as through the open window came the blackbird's final flawless song of the day.

Sue broke the silence first, glancing away from his intent gaze to the window and asking hurriedly, almost nervously, as if she could cancel with a spate of words the sudden strange intimacy which had sprung up between them.

'It's almost dark. I must go. Mrs Kent is looking after Jemima and she'll be wondering where I am. I said I'd be only half an hour.'

'Did you tell her you would be coming here?' he asked.

'Yes, of course. I could hardly come without telling her where I'd be. Something might happen while I'm gone and she might have to send for me.'

'I suppose so. But I can't help wishing you'd left the delivery of the fuel until tomorrow. I can't help wishing that you hadn't come and hadn't stayed so long,' he said coolly.

It was silly to feel hurt by his remarks, especially when she had known he had wanted her to leave earlier and she had more or less forced herself upon him. But she was sure

252

she wouldn't have felt hurt before this evening's rather odd and somewhat humorous episodes, and would have regarded his withdrawal as normal. Now she could only stare at him in bewilderment.

He was leaning against the kitchen table in the same way that he had leant against the wall yesterday, as if he could no longer stand upright without any support. And as she stared at him she realised suddenly that he was warning her off in the same way that he had warned Grandmother, and less gently, Derek Barnes that afternoon.

'I see,' she said slowly. 'You don't want me to come here any more.'

'Put bluntly, yes, I'd rather *you* didn't come here again.'

The inexplicable sense of hurt gave way to a sudden desire to inflict pain on him. In a burst of uncharacteristic vindictiveness she countered by referring to his own slashing remark to her grandmother.

'Which category do you place me in? Am I a busybody, a do-gooder, a nosy old lady or local gentry?' she flashed.

His steady underbrowed stare was intimidating, and immediately she found herself regretting her impulsive unusual reaction. The blackbird's trilling ended abruptly and she was conscious that twilight had thickened to darkness outside. She should have left long before this, but it was dawning on her gradually that this man with his handsome haggard face and steady blue eyes possessed a strange compelling attraction for her.

'I place you in none of those categories,' he said softly. 'You are much more troublesome and disturbing than any of them.'

Troublesome. Disturbing. She had gone out of her way to help him because she had felt strongly that he was in need of help, although perhaps he himself wasn't aware of that need. And here he was, having in some measure accepted her help, telling her he found her attentions troublesome and disturbing! He hadn't actually slammed the door in her face as he had when Ralph had tried to help, but his attitude had the same effect.

253

'I'm sorry,' she said stiffly. 'My intention was only to help.' Then across her inward vision there flashed a picture of Matthew Rigg, tall and proud, stalking along the road, looking neither left nor right, acknowledging no one, keeping a whole community at arm's length, and again anger shook her and she burst into a torrent of words.

'Gran was right about you. You are like your uncle! You think as he did that you can live without other people. Like him, you're mean and selfish, and you're going to let this house be wasted and you're going to waste all that money when you could be using both to help others less fortunate than you are. Oh, you're a Rigg all right. How many times have I heard my father say that neither your uncle nor your father considered anyone but themselves? One always considered how much it would cost before he did anything and the other made sure he did nothing which interfered with his pleasure. You seem to have inherited their worst traits!'

She ran out of breath unexpectedly and stood there, her brown eyes sparkling, her breasts rising and falling under her yellow ribbed sweater.

'Have you finished?' he asked quietly. Then when she didn't reply, he added, with a quiver of amusement, 'That was quite a speech!'

His calmness had the effect of disarming her and before she knew what she was doing she was apologising.

'I'm sorry. I don't know what came over me.'

'I do. I know. I irritate you just as you irritate me. A mutual feeling which we share like so many other things such as Norsemen as ancestors, smuggling and a sense of family loyalty.'

He watched dispassionately as the expression of embarrassed shame on her face was chased away by one of puzzlement. 'It's not that I don't appreciate your help and your interest,' he said. 'I do. But I would prefer it if you would just accept the fact that for the time being I don't want to associate with other people.' He paused and then murmured more to himself than to her, 'Lately the world has been too much with me and I would be glad of privacy.

254

I have to find myself without any help.'

A few minutes later, driving along the rough road, Sue tried to put her chaotic thoughts into some sort of order. Never had she behaved in her life before as she had behaved in Simon Rigg's kitchen. But then never had she met anyone like him. One minute she was furious with him, the next abject, falling over herself to apologise, a slave to his charm.

As she drove along the main road back to the village the words of the poem to which he had referred obliquely repeated themselves in her head. How well she knew them, having learnt them by heart at school. They had been written by William Wordsworth, who had been born not very far away, in the town of Cockermouth.

> *'The world is too much with us late and soon,*
> *Getting and spending, we lay waste our powers.'*

Had Simon Rigg been laying waste his powers getting and spending and in an act of revulsion had come to Riggholm? Was that his way of explaining why he had come?

She drove into the petrol station and parked the van in its usual place, jumped down, locked it and hurried to the house. As she entered the kitchen she could hear Mrs Kent's voice in the hall. She was evidently answering the phone. She called out to Sue,

'Is that you, Susan? Come quickly! It's Ralph. It's the second time he's rung up. He says it's very urgent.'

CHAPTER 3

RALPH sounded harassed. He came straight to the point when he had acknowledged Sue's greeting.

'Penny's in hospital—peritonitis. She wasn't well while we were in Guernsey, so I brought her back to her parents.

255

It blew up early this morning. She was in terrible pain and we called the doctor. She was in hospital within half an hour, and they operated right away. It was touch and go whether she'd survive. I've never spent such a dreadful day in my life.'

'Oh, Ralph, I'm so sorry. Is there anything I can do?'

'Only go on with what you are doing. Stay there for the next few weeks, because Jemima is going to need you. I'll come back to Seaport on Wednesday and I'll stay over Easter so you won't have to cope with that on your own, then I'll return here. Do you agree?'

Sue agreed at once. Ralph thanked her and blessed her. They had a few more words about Penny and he rang off.

Although Sue was sorry his holiday with Penny had been cut short by illness, she was relieved he was coming back for Easter because she knew from the increase in bookings that the week-end was going to be busy. The southern part of the Cumberland coast had been a secret long kept by the Cumbrians to themselves, which was just as well because now the magnificent sands and small historic villages could be enjoyed by the growing number of visitors from the industrial areas. Ralph's return also meant that she would be able to spend more time with her friend Jill Thomas, a fellow nurse who was coming to Seaport on Thursday to stay for four days. She hoped she would be able to make the visit a pleasant one for the cheerful happy-go-lucky girl from Newcastle who had been such a kind friend.

Ralph duly arrived home on Wednesday afternoon just as Sue was supervising Jemima's usually sticky teatime. The problem was to make sure at least as much went into Jemima's mouth as went on to the floor. But as soon as she saw her father the little girl swept the plate of honey sandwiches, which was on the little table in front of her, on to the floor and jigged up and down shouting, 'Dada, Dada!'

Ralph came across and to Sue's surprise picked up his daughter and hugged her closely as if he had really missed her. It was the first spontaneous gesture of love she'd seen him show to the child and she wondered whether the anxiety he had just experienced over Penny's health had made him appreciate the child more.

'How's Penny?' she asked, as she cleared up the mess Jemima had made.

'As well as can be expected, I suppose,' he replied, rather morosely. 'What a fright she gave us all! It'll be some time before she'll be able to take over looking after this scamp.'

'Perhaps it was her appendix which was bothering her, making her feel ill and rundown. Aunt Emily said that Penny hasn't really been well since she'd had Jemima.'

'No, she hasn't. And I feel really guilty about it. I should have noticed.' Ralph sighed heavily. 'Anyway, it's over now and I hope the worst is past.'

'And is everything all right between you and her, now?' Sue asked cautiously.

He put Jemima back in her chair and she let out a bellow of frustration.

'I'm not sure yet. She hasn't agreed to come back to Seaport yet,' he replied rather grimly. 'But all that matters now is getting her back to good health. I'll worry about the other when she's well again.'

During the course of the evening Sue told her brother everything that had happened since he had gone away, including her visit to Riggholm and Simon's visit to the petrol garage and subsequent rudeness to Derek Barnes. At the mention of Derek's name Ralph glanced at her sharply.

'Did he ask for petrol?' he said.

'Yes. He was on his way home for the Easter week-end. He said his job had just come to an end. He asked me to charge the petrol to his father's account.' Then noticing a stiffening in her brother's face, she added, 'Shouldn't I have let him have credit?'

'No, you shouldn't, but you weren't to know that. Last time he did it I had a visit from the Brigadier. He told me on no account was I to charge Derek's purchases, and that I was to make him pay cash. They've had a great deal of trouble with him since he left university. He's been fired from one job after another. He's supposed to have been

257

working in Preston, but I wouldn't be surprised if his sudden appearance on home ground means he's been fired again, and he's come back to sponge on his mother. Derek isn't exactly one of the world's workers, you know.'

'I know. But I'm sorry he's having difficulties.'

Ralph considered her thoughtfully, then said seriously,

'Be careful where he's concerned. I know you and he used to be friendly, but I always felt that he asked you to go out with him when there was no one else around. Don't let him take you for a ride, Sue. It's just possible he might take advantage of that one-time friendship.'

Ralph's warning about Derek worried Sue a little. Having a strong streak of loyalty in her make-up she found it hard to distrust someone who had been a friend, off and on, since childhood. She supposed it was true that Derek had only asked her to go sailing with him or hiking when he had had no other companion. But what harm could he do her? She decided that Ralph was taking his position of being her much older brother far too seriously. He seemed to have forgotten she was twenty-three and for the last five years had been working in a big city hospital. Admittedly she had taken a tumble when she'd fallen in love with Mark. But she was quite convinced she had learned from that experience and would not be easily taken in again. At least she hoped she wouldn't be.

But worry about herself didn't last long. Jill was arriving the next day and plans had to be made for her entertainment. Sue met her off the train on Thursday afternoon. A tall girl with short straight hair and rather short-sighted grey eyes, Jill had a tendency, when off-duty, to dress in the extremes of fashion, and when she stepped off the train wearing a bright red trouser suit, high-heeled red shoes with enormous brass buckles on them and a wide-brimmed white hat, Frank Waters' eyes were wide and he was unusually silent as he collected her ticket.

Jill greeted Sue with a gamin grin and then cast her eyes heavenwards.

'Is this the best you can do in the way of weather?

You're looking well, cherub. Could it be that life on the home range is agreeing with you?'

'Could be,' said Sue, as she led the way out to the van. 'Where did you get that hat?'

'I made it, out of white felt. Isn't it gorgeous?'

'Gorgeous, but most unsuitable for a holiday by the Cumberland coast. If it doesn't rain it might blow, although the forecast does say sunny periods and temperatures in the sixties.'

'Not to worry. I've brought my raincoat, my stout walking shoes, a good tweed skirt and a pair of jeans. But I had to travel looking my best. You never know, cherub, I might have met "the man"!'

To meet 'the man' was Jill's undisguised ambition. She had quite decided ideas about him. He would be in his mid-thirties, have a good private income, be sophisticated and good-looking. So far she hadn't met any man who possessed any of those attributes, or if she had, he hadn't shown any interest in her.

But for all her odd ways she was good-hearted and when she heard of Sue's plans for the week-end she was happy to fall in with them as long as she didn't have to get up too early.

'Sleep is what I crave,' she said. 'Hours and hours of it. I've just come off nights and I feel like a wrung-out rag.'

Good Friday morning dawned grey and still. A thick white mist hung over the calm water of the bay. It was so thick that when she looked out of her bedroom window Sue couldn't see Riggholm.

It had become a habit with her to look across to the long, low house half hidden by its screening trees and shrubs. When she questioned herself about the habit she shied away from the question guiltily and tried to think of something else, because she knew that her interest in the present owner of Riggholm had grown out of all proportion.

Was it distance lending enchantment? Or was it because he had told her to stay away from him that made her want, contrarily, to go and see him again? Whatever the reason for her interest she found herself thinking about him during the course of every day, wondering what he was doing alone in the big house and puzzling about snippets of their last conversation.

What had he done to make him so exhausted before he came to Riggholm? What had he meant when he had said he had to find himself without any help? How childish and tiresome he must have thought her when she had had the effrontery to do the very thing she had warned Derek not to do—invaded his privacy. And then to add insult to injury she had blurted out her opinion of him. Why, when she had read the signs so clearly, had she intruded where she had known she wasn't wanted?

The questions circled through her mind daily and remained unanswered because the answers lay in the unknown part of Simon Rigg's life and in the depths of Sue's own character, depths which she was afraid to plumb, afraid in the same way she had been afraid of that strange moment of awareness, almost of recognition, which she had experienced in the kitchen at Riggholm.

Ralph's voice calling to someone outside roused her and she pulled her gaze away from her bedroom window and her thoughts away from Simon Rigg. The heavy mist meant the day would be fine and if she and Jill were going to get out and about there was much she had to do before awakening her friend from her much-needed sleep.

Having persuaded Ralph to let her have the van for a few hours Sue decided to drive Jill to Wastwater, the deepest lake in England. They packed some lunch, put Jemima in the car seat between them and set off along the main road to the north. The mist had cleared and the sun shone out of a pale blue sky in which the occasional fluffy white cloud hung motionless. On one side of the road newly-ploughed fields, neatly-ridged and bordered by tidy hawthorn hedges, rose in gentle folds to green tree-topped hills. Here and there, in clusters of elms, rooks were busy building nests high on the slender elegant branches, the sign of a good summer to come. On the other side of the road rough grass sloped down to the yellow sands at the head of the bay.

'I walked there this morning,' said Jill, pointing to the sands. 'Just as the tide was going out. I met the most gorgeous man. He was tall, had a mane of brown curly hair and one of those wonderfully interesting faces, all bone structure and hollows, and he walked as if he owned the earth.'

'Simon Rigg!' exclaimed Sue. 'You've described him very accurately.'

'I looked at him very accurately. He fascinated me. So you know him. When can you introduce him to me?' said Jill.

'Never, I should think. He wants to be left alone.'

'And that makes him more fascinating than ever, of course,' said Jill. 'Now I'm all agog. Where does he live? What does he do?'

'He lives, at present, in the house you can see from The Gables, across the bay. I don't know what he does or has done. I suppose you could call him the local squire,' replied Sue.

'Doesn't that mean he owns all the land around here?' Jill sounded thoroughly excited.

'It used to mean that, and the Riggs once owned the village. But now there's only the house and an estate of about a hundred acres.'

'Mm, sounds big enough for me,' mused Jill. 'Is he rich?'

Sue laughed outright as she recognised her friend's attempts to assess whether Simon Rigg could possibly be 'the man'.

'He should be. He inherited Riggholm from his uncle and presumably inherited the Rigg family fortune, too, which his uncle who was a miser inherited from his father. They made it from coalmining. One of the Riggs back in the eighteenth century was wise enough to buy some land in the area to the west of Cockermouth which became a great source of wealth for local land-owning families. Anyway, according to my father the Riggs made quite a packet.'

Jill was ticking off items on the fingers of one hand as she murmured,

'Devastatingly good-looking, owns big house in country beside the sea, is wealthy without apparently having to slave for his living. It could be him. Sue, you've got to introduce him to me.'

'Knowing you, I'm surprised you didn't introduce yourself.'

Jill smiled.

'Well, it wasn't for want of trying. I said good morning, but all I received in return was a frosty glance as he walked by, which put me off.' She was silent for a few minutes as she stared frowningly through the windscreen at the ribbon of grey road. 'I can't help thinking I've seen him somewhere before,' she said slowly, and Sue gave her a sharp glance. 'Do you think he's ever been to Newcastle?'

'We know very little about him, only his name. He's only just come to live here. Both Ralph and I have tried to find out more, but he's very good at not answering direct questions, and he's made it very plain that he wants to be left alone.'

'I wonder what he's done wrong to make him feel like that,' murmured Jill.

Sue gave her another sharp glance but said no more. When it came to romancing about people Jill was even worse than herself, and for some reason she didn't want to share her own views on Simon Rigg with her friend.

At the village of Holmrook they turned off the main road and followed a country road which led inland towards the blue-grey barrier of mountains. Soon the road was winding beside the lake which lay cool and placid, tinted turquoise and gold where it wasn't shadowed by the massive eminences of the Scafell range. Long and narrow, the lake was bordered on the other side by the screes which plunged steeply and dramatically into the calm waters. On dull days this sheer wall of rock could look forbidding, but today under the benign spring sunshine it looked serene, revealing a variety of colours from vivid splodges of green to subtle shades of rose pink glinting from crannies and crevices.

Sue drove part way along the road which went to Wasdale at the head of the lake. She ran the van off the road on to the grass and parked under some trees.

The next hour passed pleasantly enough. They walked along the stony shore and skimmed pebbles in the clear deep water for Jemima's entertainment and then sitting on a travelling rug spread on the grass they ate their lunch. When they had eaten Sue laid Jemima down on the seat in the van to sleep and Jill went off by herself to explore.

Having put the picnic equipment away Sue lay down on the rug and sunned herself, listening to the quiet murmur of the trees and to the almost imperceptible trickling sound of water lapping gently against stone. Wastwater was one of the wildest and most solitary places she knew, a place outside the touch of time. In wet cloudy weather its brooding silence could be unnerving, but today its mood was serene and soon Sue's eyelids drooped and she dozed.

She was awakened suddenly by the sound of Jill's voice.

'Sue, Sue! I've remembered where I've seen him!'

Sue sat up groggily as Jill flung herself down on the rug.

'Seen whom? Whatever are you talking about?' she demanded. Jill knelt beside her, her eyes dancing with excitement.

'I've remembered where I've seen your squire before. He's the Duke of Monmouth!'

Sue made a grimace of exasperation.

'Now I know you're cuckoo! I always suspected it ...' she began, but Jill cut in quickly.

'Oh, not the real Duke, silly. He's an actor and he played the part in a film about the Monmouth Rebellion. He was awfully good. The critics raved and everyone predicted a great future in films for him. He was in other films before that one in a supporting role. But he's been mostly in live theatre ... Shakespeare and all that, and his name is Simon Fell.'

'But he can't be,' objected Sue, feeling utterly confused.

'His name is Simon Rigg. I know it is. Grandma wouldn't make a mistake. She'd know a Rigg.'

She hadn't seen the film that Jill had mentioned and she knew very little about the live theatre, so she couldn't really argue with Jill. Yet she kept recalling that Derek, too, had thought he'd seen Simon before and Simon had denied too vehemently that it could not be possible.

'If what you say is true,' she said slowly, 'why is he calling himself Simon Rigg and living at Riggholm?'

Jill lay back on the rug and gazed up at the sky through the branches of the larch trees on which buds were already swollen.

'Perhaps he murdered the real Simon Rigg, knowing he had inherited a house and his uncle's wealth, and now he's masquerading as him. That would be why he wants to be left alone,' she mused fantastically. 'He acted the part of that sort of murderer in the first film he made. No, I expect the explanation is more simple than that. Fell is probably his stage name, and he's come up here to relax, get away from it all, for a few weeks' holiday.'

'He's come to get away from something, I agree there,' said Sue.

'Well, there's one sure way of finding out. You must go and ask for his autograph,' said Jill.

'Oh no, I couldn't do that,' replied Sue quickly.

'Why not? All you have to do is go to the house, say you've recognised him, that you admire his acting and would like his autograph, and then stand back and watch his reaction.'

'But that wouldn't be true. You recognised him, not I. I've never seen him in a film,' objected Sue. 'Besides, I don't want to go to Riggholm and see him again, and I don't want you to go there either.'

Jill glanced at her curiously, but before she could question her Jemima wailed and that was the end of the conversation.

Saturday remained fine and although busy Sue found time to take Jill and Jemima over to Seascale where they sat on the firm sands and watched the waves creaming in from the Atlantic, and afterwards drove home by way of Drigg nestling behind its sandhills, skirting the gullery nature reserve, the first local nature reserve to be established in England.

On Sunday they visited the gardens at Muncaster Castle, the imposing embattled and towered family seat of the Penningtons which dated from the thirteenth century, and from there they drove along the valley of the Esk to the village of Boot, terminus of the narrow-gauge railway familiarly known as the Ratty. From Boot they branched off down another road which led through the fells to another valley and eventually arrived at the whitewashed house snuggling in a fold of the hills which was known as Greenthwaite Farm.

Sunday afternoon tea at Aunt Emily's had been an institution for as long as Sue could remember and it was no different on that Easter Sunday than it had ever been. Besides her aunt and uncle and grandmother there was John, Emily's and Tom's eldest son, a tall quiet man with the distant dreaming blue-grey eyes of the fell sheep farmer. At thirty-one John was still a bachelor and his mother had given up all hope of him marrying. His sister Greta was also there, with her husband Howard, who surprisingly was no farmer but a scientist working at the experimental nuclear plant which lay to the north of Seascale. The eldest of their three children, Judy, was fascinated by Jemima and took her off to see the hens in the farmyard.

With such a family gathering the conversation was naturally gossipy. In the absence of Ralph, Greta pressed Sue with questions about Penny, and above the general flow of talk Grandmother Thorpe's deep voice boomed as she held forth to Howard about the ugliness of his place of work and how it must have frightened people away from the district.

'But don't forget, Mother, it's also brought work,' said Emily.

'Aye, for outsiders,' said Grandmother.

'Like me,' put in Howard, his eyes twinkling good-naturedly. 'Just think, Grandma. Greta would still be a spinster if I hadn't turned up to work at that detested place.'

'Don't you believe it, Howard Jones,' retorted his wife. 'There were other fish in the pond before you arrived, you know.'

'But it's the stranger fish that always gets hooked,' said John quietly, and everyone laughed, and Sue noticed that Jill who had been sitting very quietly listening, flashed him an interested glance.

Tea was taken as usual in the big dining-room at an enormous oval table on which a white cloth had been spread and on which the Crown Derby tea service glittered and gleamed in the afternoon sunlight. First there was cold Cumberland ham served with Cumberland sauce and salad, which was eaten with quantities of freshly-baked bread and farm butter. Then there were several cakes to choose from, including gingerbread and a currant cake flavoured with rum. And all through the meal the teacups circulated regularly round the table back to Aunt Emily to be refilled and passed again to their owners.

Sue sat next to Jemima who had been seated in the old high chair Aunt Emily had kept for the use of her grandchildren when they visited her. She noticed with amusement that Jill had been seated next to John and was doing her best to draw that taciturn individual into conversation, and was having some success. And when Jill's attention was distracted by Grandmother who was sitting on her other side, Sue noticed her cousin eyeing his neighbour surreptitiously out of the corners of his eyes.

When the meal was over Sue, as usual, volunteered to help with the washing up. Howard had taken Jemima off with him and the other children to inspect parts of the farm with his father-in-law. John, to everyone's surprise, had rather awkwardly offered to show Jill round the farm. So Sue found herself in the kitchen, with Greta at the sink, while Aunt Emily acted as putter-away of the clean dishes and Grandmother sat in the corner and held forth. As always washing up time was the best for truly feminine conversation and they covered a lot of ground while the water swished in the bowl and the crockery and cutlery rattled.

'A very good Sunday tea, Emily,' said Grandmother, unexpectedly handing out praise to her only daughter. 'One Sunday you must ask yon lad from Riggholm. He looks as if a good square meal wouldn't do him any harm.'

'Lad from Riggholm? Don't tell me you'd invite a Rigg to tea, Grandmother Thorpe,' teased Greta.

'Aye, I'd ask that one, because he reminds me of when I was young and because he isn't afraid to stand up to an old woman when she's being nosy, and most of all because he has a bonny smile.'

'And because he looks like Matthew Rigg when he was young,' said Emily softly. 'But I doubt he'd come, Mother. What do you think, Sue?'

'I agree with you, Aunty. He made it plain to me the last time I saw him that he wanted to be left alone.'

'But he mustn't be left alone.' Grandmother smote the arm of her rocking-chair forcibly with her fist. 'Matthew wanted to be left alone, and we left him alone and look what that did to him. He developed into a selfish, crotchety old miser without a good word for anyone, and he died by himself.'

Grandmother's voice shook with scarcely-controlled emotion and Sue looked at her with interest. The old lady had just voiced her own feelings concerning Simon Rigg's desire to be left alone, and yet how was it possible to intrude where you weren't wanted?

'But we can't force ourselves upon him, Gran, if he doesn't want us,' she said.

'I don't see why not,' answered Grandmother. 'Knowing what I know now I realise I should have forced myself on Matthew, but it was difficult because I was married and your grandfather didn't like the Riggs. But you're in a different position. You're young and single, and the young can be forgiven anything. If Ralph didn't have so many problems of his own, he'd do it.'

'But how?' demanded Sue. 'I've been twice and he wasn't very nice.' She remembered Simon's intimidating blue gaze, the icy tone of his voice when he had dismissed her, and then she recalled with a sudden quickened thudding of her heart that it was possible that the man at Riggholm was not Simon Rigg at all.

'Just keep going to see him for any reason at all. Persist. It's the only way,' said Grandma. 'I know the Rigg temperament. They're a proud, stiff-necked lot. Matthew wouldn't admit that he'd been hurt, wouldn't admit that he needed help. And if I'm not mistaken this one's the same. He's taken a beating somewhere over something dear to his heart and he's come here to hole up and lick his wounds. It's there in his face. You'll have to make him feel he's wanted. Involve him in the life of the village. That's why I want Emily to ask him to tea. I want to tell him what a great worker and philanthropist his great-grandfather was and all that he did for Seaport.'

'My, my, Grandma, fancy a Thorpe wanting to help a Rigg! I always thought the two families didn't see eye to eye,' joked Greta.

'I was a Faller before I was ever a Thorpe,' retorted Grandmother haughtily.

'Supposing he isn't Simon Rigg at all?' said Sue quietly. 'What then?'

They all stared at her as if she'd said something totally incomprehensible.

'What do you mean?' rapped Grandma.

Sue told them quickly about Jill's conviction that the man at Riggholm was an actor by the name of Simon Fell.

'Fell?' pounced Grandmother sharply. 'Fell was his mother's name. Mildred Fell. She did a lot of amateur acting in her day in local shows. Perhaps Lupus didn't marry her after all. But one thing I'm sure of, that lad's father was a Rigg. There's no denying the family looks. Matthew or Lupus—could have been either.'

'Mother!' Emily's voice was shocked and Greta exchanged a surprised glance with Sue, who shook her head in denial of the implication in Grandmother's statement.

'Don't be so mealy-mouthed, Emily,' snorted Grandmother. 'Of course it could have been either of them. Whatever Matthew might have become in his old age he was still handsome and hot-blooded and possessed what your generation call sex-appeal and I prefer to call masculine magnetism, when he was in his prime, and that was when Mildred Fell was such a regular visitor at Riggholm, just before the war.'

'So Simon Rigg and Simon Fell could be one and the same person,' said Greta.

'Not could be, they are,' insisted Grandmother.

'Well, isn't that interesting now?' said Emily mildly. 'To think he's an actor!'

'Wait until the village knows,' warned Greta. 'There'll be a queue at the gates of Riggholm for his autograph.'

I hope not, oh, I do hope not, thought Sue, as she imagined Simon's irritable reaction.

As they drove back to Seaport through the lovely valley in the clear light of late afternoon Jill was very quiet, so quiet that in the end Sue asked,

'I hope you weren't too overwhelmed by the family?'

'No. They were lovely, all of them. How lucky you are!'

'What makes you say that?'

'Lucky to have lived here among all this beauty and with people like that. Why you ever came to work in a hospital in Newcastle when you could have stayed here beats me.'

'I suppose it must seem strange,' replied Sue, thinking of the narrow street of terraced houses which Jill had once shown her as the place where she had grown up. 'But you see I had a great urge to help people less fortunate than myself. I wanted to nurse, and there didn't seem any way of doing that living here.'

'I suppose not,' said Jill absently, then after a moment she observed, 'I like your cousin John.'

'He's very shy.'

'Not really. I don't think so. He told me all about the

sheep and the lambs and about the Herdwick breed of sheep being one of the hardiest in the country. He told me too of the legend that the breed is descended from a flock of Spanish sheep which swam ashore from a wrecked galleon. Do you think it's true?'

'The galleon bit is, but I'm not sure about the sheep. Is that all you talked about?'

'No. We talked about the advantages of Friesian cattle over Ayrshire cattle. He's very knowledgeable,' replied Jill quite seriously.

'Oh, I've no doubt of that,' remarked Sue dryly, with a mischievous grin, 'especially about sheep. Now let me tell you what I've learned this afternoon. The name of Simon Rigg's mother was Mildred Fell.'

'So Fell is his stage name and he isn't a masquerader. In a way I'm disappointed. It would have been exciting to have unearthed a mystery.'

'There still is a mystery. Why has he come here and why does he want to be left alone?' said Sue.

'I'm going to leave you to solve that for yourself, cherub,' said Jill. 'But if it's any help I seem to remember reading somewhere that a girl who was involved with Simon Fell died in suspicious circumstances about six months ago. Maybe he was in love with her and is having trouble with his conscience. Do you know, a most curious thing has happened. Now that I know who he is I've lost all interest in him?'

'But why should he have trouble with his conscience?' queried Sue.

Jill shrugged indifferently.

'Sorry, can't help you there. I can't remember the details, but funnily enough I can remember the name of the girl. It was Caitlin, which is Welsh, I think.'

If the death of someone he had loved was the reason for Simon having come here to hide it would fit in with everything Grandmother had said about him looking as if he had taken a beating over something dear to his heart, thought Sue. It would also mean that he was even more like his

Uncle Matthew, since the loss of the woman he had loved to his brother had been the cause of Matthew's seclusion from the world. And Grandmother had said on no account were they to allow Simon to become like Matthew. He was not to be left alone.

But how, in what way could she on her own overcome such stubborn determination on Simon's part to remain aloof?

Next morning, the high tide being at a convenient time, Sue went for her promised sail with Derek while Jill looked after Jemima on the shore. Although there wasn't much wind Sue found it pleasant to be sailing again in Derek's old fourteen-footer and to watch the village slide slowly past as they made for the open sea. They never reached it because they spent their time tacking back and forth against the slight breeze trying in vain to reach the long arm of Rigg's Bank which Silas Rigg, grandfather of Matthew and Lupus, had erected to give some protection to the bay in stormy weather.

When time dictated that they should turn back and run before the wind to reach the village before the tide went out Derek observed as he stared at the looming wall of stone which curved like a dark monster across the glittering water,

'One day that wall is going to be breached by the tide, and then there'll be trouble for those houses which were built at the end of the village after the bank was erected.'

'I haven't heard that before,' murmured Sue, thinking dreamily how she loved this view of her home village, its white and grey houses clustered along the edge of the water which went right up to the wall protecting their back gardens. Behind the houses the tree-crested hills of Lythedale presented a backdrop of green curves against the blue of the sky.

'My father's often mentioned it,' said Derek importantly. 'In fact he thinks the local improvement association should have it strengthened or have the houses knocked down and find the occupants alternative accommodation. But no one seems to listen. They say a Rigg built it so it must be all right. It's incredible to realise that in this day and age people still trust in something a man had built nearly a hundred years ago just because he was the squire and his name was Rigg.'

'I don't find it hard to understand. It's better to have trust in something than none at all.'

His glance was impatient.

'You're more of a square than I'd thought,' he gibed.

'What if I am? I suppose you think a person should trust only himself and no one else and should keep looking out all the time for people who might betray his trust.'

'Something like that,' he conceded sheepishly.

'Well, I can't live like that. I'd rather have trust and be betrayed than never have trust at all. If I'm square, you're cynical before your time. Supposing I said I didn't trust you?'

'All right, all right, Susie. Pax!' he laughed. 'You haven't changed a bit, and when you start crusading I'm the first to give up.' He gave the mainsheet a twitch in an attempt to free the mainsail more and then grumbled about the lack of wind.

'If it dies away altogether we won't be able to reach the shore before the tide goes out, and you know what that means,' he said.

'Yes. We'll have to pull the boat along the river channel. It wouldn't be the first time either,' said Sue.

And suddenly they were remembering all sorts of escapades which had taken place during their youth and the argument about trust was soon forgotten.

That evening, which was the last of Jill's holiday, Sue had just put Jemima to bed and was about to prepare the evening meal when her cousin John Carter arrived. He muttered something about having come into the village for something and having decided to call in before returning to the farm. Surprised by his unexpected visit, because John hardly ever came by himself to The Gables, Sue asked him to sit down and then on a sudden impulse invited him to stay for a meal. He agreed with such alacrity that she gave him a sharp glance. He was looking round the room as if he had lost something. Not finding it, he looked straight at her and asked abruptly,

'Happen your friend has gone back to Newcastle?'

'You mean Jill? No. She's gone for a drive with Ralph. He had to deliver some fuel over at Ghyllthwaite because Roy is on holiday today. They should be back soon. Do you want to see her?'

'Happen I do,' he replied slowly, and sat down in the rocking-chair and began to fill his pipe.

Secretly amused by the sudden turn of events, Sue concentrated on preparing the meal while he sat and smoked and glanced through one of Ralph's motoring magazines.

What would Jill think when she found him there? Would she consider him worthy of being 'the man'? It was true he had a few of the attributes. He wasn't bad-looking with his smoke-blue eyes contrasting with dark eyebrows, and he wasn't poor by any means because he was one of the more successful farmers in the district. But no one in their right mind would ever say he was a sophisticated man of the world.

While they were eating, Jill brought up the subject of Simon Rigg again. She had been walking on the shore during the afternoon and she had seen him again.

'I'm even more sure he's Simon Fell, the actor,' she said.

'Did you speak to him?' asked Sue.

'Not on your life! The way he looked at me I began to think the shore belonged to him and I was trespassing. I didn't dare open my mouth.'

Ralph laughed.

'Sounds like Simon. But what's all this about him being an actor?' Sue explained to him about Jill's suspicions and Grandmother's admission that his mother had been called Fell and had acted in local theatricals when she had lived in the Seaport area.

'Seems to add up then, doesn't it?' said Ralph, then

added to Jill, 'If you'd been here yesterday afternoon you'd have had plenty of chances to speak to him.'

'You mean he was here, at the garage?' said Jill. 'Oh, why didn't you tell us?'

Ralph grinned impishly.

'You seemed too taken up with sheep farming to be interested,' he scoffed, and Jill flushed and glanced warily at John, who did not seem to be paying any attention to the conversation.

'What did he come for?' asked Sue.

'He noticed I was back and came to thank me for the stuff I lent him and he paid for the fuel you'd taken to him. That's all. He was very civil, much more so than the last time I saw him. But I can't say he's my idea of an actor.'

'What do you expect an actor to be like?' asked Jill.

'Oh, a bit of an exhibitionist, always showing off, acting a part,' replied Ralph.

'Well, I suppose some are like that, but others are quieter, and quite self-effacing in their private lives,' said Jill.

'Do you like plays and films and such like?' asked John abruptly, looking directly at Jill. She opened her eyes wide and stammered that she did.

'Then eat up and we'll go up to Whitehaven to the flicks.'

'We?' repeated Jill weakly.

'Aye. You and me. That was a grand meal, Sue. You'll make some man a fine wife one day. Give me another cup of tea, lass, to drink while I'm waiting for Jill to get ready.'

Vainly trying to hide her grin, Sue took his proffered cup and in doing so met her brother's gaze. Ralph winked and she almost collapsed with laughter. As she poured the tea she noticed that Jill, always a slow eater, was 'eating up' fast. Then, her meal finished, she stood up and excused herself and almost ran out of the room in her haste to get ready.

Ralph was just thinking of locking the pumps and packing up for the day after one of the busiest Easter week-ends

274

he had ever known when a small dark car glided to a stop in front of the petrol station. A small undistinguished man got out of it and came to ask Ralph if he knew of anywhere he could stay for bed and breakfast.

Ralph said, 'Right here,' and told him the terms, and the little man, who had small, round black eyes which didn't seem capable of staying still but flicked this way and that, taking in every detail of Ralph's face and figure as well as every detail of the petrol station, agreed to the terms. Ralph showed him where to park his car and then took him into the house where Sue showed him the dining-room and the sitting-room, then took him up to the bedroom where he would sleep.

Once she had accepted the paying guest Sue forgot about him, presuming he would make himself comfortable in the sitting-room for the evening, and she and Ralph settled down to discuss how long he would be able to stay near Penny in Manchester and what business Sue could expect to deal with while he was away.

At eleven o'clock a happy but rather bemused Jill arrived back, accompanied by John who stayed to have a cup of tea before driving back to Greenthwaite Farm. Later in her bedroom Jill confided to Sue that John had said he would drive over to see her in Newcastle the following Friday evening and would stay for the week-end, and that he had invited her to go and stay with his mother at the farm as soon as she was able to get another long week-end's leave from the hospital.

'I'm more flummoxed than I've ever been in my life,' she added. 'He's so different from what you'd expect.'

'I've never expected anything from John,' laughed Sue. 'He's just my silent cousin who knows everything about sheep and knows nothing about anything else.'

'Don't you believe it,' retorted Jill. 'He knows how to treat a woman. He's been very well brought up.'

'Three cheers for Aunt Emily,' said Sue facetiously. 'Wait until I tell her.'

'Don't you dare!' hissed Jill furiously, at the same time

blushing unexpectedly, and Sue stopped laughing to stare.

'Jill, you don't mean you're seriously attracted to John?' she exclaimed.

'I like him very much. And I'm going to accept his invitation to go and stay at Greenthwaite, and one day, if he asks me, I'll marry him,' said Jill defiantly. And for once Sue was silent.

Sue was amazed by her friend's sudden and serious attraction to her cousin, and his obvious liking for Jill, and long after Jill had left on Tuesday morning she continued to think about it. How had it happened? How had they known? Had there been a sudden flash of recognition at some time on Sunday when they had been at Greenthwaite, a brief moment of awareness such as she had experienced in the kitchen at Riggholm when she and Simon Rigg had stared at each other in silence? No, it couldn't have been like that because they had followed up, or at least John had, and in the old-fashioned phraseology of the North he'd 'come a-courtin'' and Jill had been ready to be wooed. Whereas Simon had sent her packing, calling her troublesome and disturbing, and she had been only too glad to run away.

Once again Sue made a great effort to push the enigmatic owner of Riggholm from her mind and attend to her work. Ralph had left for Manchester and the only people in the house were herself, Jemima and the small dark man who had stayed for bed and breakfast.

She served him his breakfast in the dining-room where he sat at a table in the window and stared out mournfully at the rain which was cascading down the window-panes.

'I suppose we mustn't grumble, eh?' he said, and she noticed he spoke with a London accent. 'We had a good Easter. First for years. Record temperatures in Scotland, of all places.'

'Are you touring the Lake District or just passing through?' asked Sue politely.

'Passing through, after a fashion. How long I stay depends on whether I find what I'm looking for.'

276

'Are you looking for a place to buy, a cottage perhaps?' Sue knew that many people from the south of England searched the area for old houses to buy and renovate as country holiday places.

'No. I'm looking for a man.'

His flat statement had sinister undertones and a peculiar chill fluttered down Sue's spine.

'I hope you find him,' she said uneasily.

'I hope so too. I've been on the hunt for over three weeks. That's too long to be away from home. Now you look the sympathetic sort and might be able to help. Have you ever seen him?'

He had taken a photograph from his wallet and he laid it on the table. Sue knew before she looked down that it was a photograph of Simon Rigg. It was a good picture and had obviously been taken for publicity purposes when he hadn't been quite so thin.

'Why do you want to find him?' she asked, hoping that the wobble in her voice hadn't given away that she recognised him. 'Has he done something wrong?'

'I don't know what he's done. I only know I'm paid to find him and inform my boss where he is.'

'Who's your boss?'

'I work for a private enquiry agency. Missing persons mostly. Husbands who've made off with the wages and wives who've run away.'

'No murderers, or anyone like that?' queried Sue, her natural curiosity getting the better of her.

He gave her a scathing glance.

'Not on your life! Well, have you seen him?'

'No, I'm afraid I can't help you.' She'd done it. She'd told an out-and-out lie. But to have told the truth would have been to betray a trust. Even though Simon had never actually asked her to keep his presence at Riggholm a secret from anyone who might come looking for him she could not tell this man where to find him. 'Have you any idea at all where he might be?'

The man was putting the photograph away.

'North of England,' he said acidly. 'Now I ask you, where would you look if you were told that? It's a big place when you're looking for someone. A country house beginning with the letter "R". That's all the client could tell us. It's near a place called Sea ... something. You'd think that would confine it to the coastal areas, wouldn't you? But you'd be surprised how many Sea ... somethings there are, nowhere near the coast. I've been up the east coast to Seaham, Seahouses and Seaton Delaval, and now I'm working my way down the west coast. I've been to Seascale and now I'm here in Seaport. Who knows, tomorrow I might be at the end of my journey at Seaforth near Liverpool. I suppose there are no country houses around here beginning with the letter R?'

He cocked a bright black eye at her. She shook her head woodenly.

'Stranger here, eh?' he queried. 'Funny how I always seem to pick on a stranger to ask.'

When he had finished his breakfast he paid for his night's stay and left. Sue went about her household chores, her mind in a turmoil. Why had she lied? Why should she defend Simon Rigg? For all she knew the enquiry agent might have been employed by Simon Rigg's wife to find him. Why hadn't she told the truth? Because she didn't want to be the one who split on him, to give him away. Let someone else tell the agent that there was a house near Seaport which began with R, and that the man in the photograph was living there.

But having settled her conscience in that way she began to come to the conclusion that she must use the time gained to warn Simon that someone was looking for him. When she had told him, he might go away, move on somewhere else. He might admit that he was not Simon Rigg after all.

So after lunch instead of putting Jemima in her cot for a sleep she dressed the little girl in her waterproof, put on her own raincoat and wellington boots and set off on foot, crossing the sands at the head of the bay and hoping that no one would see her going that way.

By the time she reached the house she was very wet and Jemima was grizzling miserably. She pushed open the gate and struggled up the drive, noting that it had been almost cleared of weeds. She went up the steps and rang the door-bell and waited patiently, remembering that the last time she had come her impatience had earned her a tongue-lashing.

At last the door opened. Simon stood there looking at her with surprised blue eyes which gradually hardened as he realised who she was.

'I must talk to you. It's very important,' she said urgently, afraid that he might slam the door in her face.

At that moment Jemima stopped grizzling, held up her arms to him and smiled beguilingly. He looked down at her and smiled too, that quick entrancing smile which he reserved for babies and old ladies.

'Hello, Jemima. You look very wet,' he said gently. Then, the smile fading, he glanced at Sue. 'You too,' he added curtly. 'Come in.'

He helped her to lift the push-chair through the door into the hall. Then while she took off her own raincoat he lifted Jemima out of the push-chair and stood her on the floor. He knelt in front of her and removed her waterproof coat and hood, talking to her all the time, a special kind of rubbish which Jemima seemed to understand but which left Sue out. Then carrying her clothes over his arm he stood up and reaching down took one of the child's hands in his and said,

'Come on, darling, we'll go to the kitchen. It's warmer in there.' And Jemima, staggering a little because her plump legs were a little stiff after sitting in the push-chair, went with him.

Feeling more than piqued because he paid more attention to the child than to her, Sue followed with her raincoat over her arm. In the kitchen Simon hung the child's wet things over the rail in front of the cooker, then taking Sue's raincoat he hung it on a hook conveniently placed in the alcove in which the cooker stood.

'Please sit down,' he said politely, waving a hand in the direction of a fine windsor-backed chair, and she sat down and took Jemima on her knee to prevent the little girl from wandering about.

'I expect you'd like some coffee,' Simon added. 'There's some left in the percolator. It isn't long since I had my lunch, so it should be hot.'

'Thank you,' said Sue, suddenly feeling very shy. As he turned away to a cupboard to take out a mug, a bowl of sugar and a cream jug she glanced about the room. There was a difference in it since her last visit. The walls and ceiling had been washed and a shade had been found for the light. On the dresser against the far wall the willow-pattern plates gleamed. The table was covered by a thick chenille tablecloth he had unearthed from somewhere, and most surprising of all, in the centre was an old soup tureen filled with flowers and greenery from the garden.

But the difference wasn't only in the room, she discovered as she watched Simon pour coffee into the mug. It was also in her host. Although he was obviously still some pounds short of what must be his normal weight he looked much better. The sunshine of the week-end had tanned his lean cheeks, so that when he looked at her to ask if she took milk and sugar in her coffee, his eyes seemed bluer and brighter.

The coffee prepared, he carried it over and set it on the table near to her and then took Jemima from her. Sitting in another chair slightly larger than the one she was seated in, but of the same elegant style, he nursed the little girl on his knee.

'I'll hold her while you drink your coffee and tell me what is so important. She'll stay still with me,' he said.

And Jemima did stay still, leaning back against him, trusting him completely.

Sue took a gulp of coffee and wondered where to begin. Now she was with him she felt desperately shy. She hadn't been shy at their previous meetings because she hadn't known as much about him as she did now.

'At the door I took your word that what you have to tell me is very important, thinking that you wouldn't have walked all that way in such weather if it wasn't. If I hadn't believed you I wouldn't have let you in,' he said cuttingly, and the impression of gentleness which had been conveyed while he was preparing the coffee and dealing with Jemima was destroyed at once. 'I hope it wasn't another excuse to intrude.'

The taunt stung. Sue sat up straight, all shyness gone.

'No, it wasn't. I wouldn't have come at all if I hadn't thought you should know at once what has happened. Last night a man stayed at The Gables for bed and breakfast. This morning he produced a photograph of you and asked me if I'd ever seen you around here.'

His eyes narrowed slightly and she noticed that the knuckles of one of his hands, resting on Jemima's arm, whitened.

'What did you say to him?' he asked.

'I told him I hadn't seen you. Then he asked me if there was a country house near Seaport beginning with the letter R. I told him I didn't know.'

'But why did you lie?' He spoke so sharply she thought he must be rebuking her.

'I ... I ... well, you said you wanted to be left alone and I didn't want to be the one who betrayed your whereabouts. I tried to find out why he was looking for you, but he didn't know himself. All he had to do was find out where you are and report back to his agency.' She leaned forward and whispered urgently, 'You haven't done anything wrong, have you?'

For a moment Simon stared at her in puzzlement. Then heavy eyelids hid his eyes as he looked down at Jemima's head and he wound a strand of her silky hair round one finger.

'I've done many wrong things in my time,' he drawled laconically, evasively.

'I mean criminally wrong, like murder, or armed robbery, or kidnapping?' She couldn't think of any other criminal activities because he was regarding her with that intimidating underbrowed glance, and it occurred to her suddenly that if he was a criminal he could be violent, and in coming to warn him she had placed herself at his mercy.

'Would it matter very much to you if I had done something criminally wrong?' he asked.

'Well ... er ... yes, it would.' She was nervous now. 'You see it wasn't until the enquiry agent left that I realised that by lying to him I might have ...' She couldn't go on.

'You might have been preventing the law from taking its proper and just course,' he finished for her. 'You'll be glad to know, then, that I've not done anything criminally wrong.'

Sue's sigh of relief was loud and uninhibited.

'Thank goodness for that!' she said with such heartfelt fervour that the man's mouth twitched with amusement as he watched her take another gulp of coffee. She placed the coffee mug on the table and leaned forward to ask earnestly,

'Are you married?'

He stiffened with resentment and the amusement faded from his face.

'If I'd known you were going to conduct an investigation into my private life I certainly wouldn't have let you into the house,' he replied haughtily.

'Oh, please understand,' she pleaded. 'I'm not being nosy. I asked only because the agent said most of his work was searching for missing husbands.'

'And you were afraid you might be aiding and abetting an escape from the shackles of matrimony, which would have lain heavily on your conscience. Is that it?'

She nodded and he added with a touch of the amusement he had shown a few minutes earlier,

'Then you may sleep easily in your bed. So far I've managed to avoid that particular trap.'

She was tempted to argue with him about his sardonic reference to marriage as a trap, but decided against it. At the back of her mind was her grandmother's forcible denunciation of Simon Rigg's desire to be left alone. Persist,

persist, Grandmother had said. You can do it, Susie. And now that she had gained entrance once more to his house she was going to persist. So at the risk of being snubbed again she asked another question.

'Didn't you want anyone to know you had come to Riggholm?'

'No. I think I made it clear the last time you were here that I want to be alone for a while. One of the best ways of doing that is not to tell any friends or acquaintances where I'm going or where I'll be.'

'But if that man learns from someone else in the village that you are here and goes back to tell his boss, will that bring trouble to you? Will it bring someone here whom you don't want to see?'

'It might,' he replied, still evasive. 'Who will tell him? Your brother?'

'No, Ralph's gone to Manchester to see Penny. She's in hospital there. But anyone else who has seen you might tell him—Derek, or Mrs Kent or Mrs Price.'

'Or the girl who inspected me so closely twice when she passed me on the shore.'

'No. That was my friend Jill. She's gone back to New-castle. She was looking at you closely because like Derek she was convinced she had seen you somewhere before, and not knowing the Riggs she wouldn't know of your re-semblance to Matthew Rigg.'

He didn't move. The hands still holding Jemima, who soothed by the warmth and security in which she found herself was gradually falling asleep, were quite still. But Sue knew by the intensity of his gaze that he was alert to the implication that Jill had recognised her.

'Did your friend remember where she had seen me?' he asked lazily, as if it was of no consequence.

'Yes. She said she'd seen you in two films and that your name is Simon Fell. I told Grandma, and she said your mother's name was Mildred Fell. Is it true? Are you really Simon Fell as well as Simon Rigg?'

'It's true,' he admitted equably. 'I wondered how long it

283

would be before anyone recognised me and I was hoping that here no one would.'

'And now that the truth is out what are you going to do? Go somewhere else to hide?'

It was her turn to taunt and he didn't like it.

'What concern is it of yours if I do?' he countered.

'It will be such a waste ... a waste of your life.'

'I was aware that you were concerned about the fate of this house and the money, but now it seems you're worried in case I waste my life. Isn't that a little presumptuous on your part? After all, it is my life to do with as I please, which is one of the reasons why I came here in the first place, to prove to myself that I have some control over it and over my future.'

'Had you lost control?' she couldn't help asking.

His eyes were long slits of blue narrowed against some sort of pain or unpleasant memory.

'Almost, or at least it was beginning to seem like that,' he replied, and the familiar sardonic curve of his mouth was in evidence again.

Excited by the thought that she was perhaps getting nearer to his reasons for coming to Riggholm, Sue persisted.

'What happened?' she asked.

Immediately his eyes widened and the glance he gave her was pure ice, but she willed herself to be immune and returned his steady gaze with a candid stare of innocent curiosity.

'Seems to me you've asked that question before,' he replied sarcastically. 'Is asking questions part of a nurse's work these days? Is that how you quiz a person when you're looking after him in hospital? Perhaps I should remind you this is not a hospital and I'm not your patient.'

Sue flushed and bit her lip. So much for the persistence Grandmother had advised! Now it looked as if her persistence had made her more unpopular than ever with her host, which wasn't her aim at all. She watched him, saw the quick frown which was immediately chased away by the expression of rueful amusement as he glanced down at Jemima and wondered, not for the first time, how anyone with such a cruel tongue could be so gentle and patient with a child.

'Grandma says your mother was a very keen amateur actress,' she said, trying again to rouse a spark of interest.

'Was she?' he drawled, making no attempt to hide his boredom with the subject. 'Since I never knew her I can hardly say she influenced my choice of career.'

It was useless, Sue thought as the silence was heavy again between them. She couldn't do what Grandma had asked her to do. He resented her questions. He resented her presence. She could almost feel him willing her to go. She was sure that if Jemima hadn't fallen asleep in his arms he would have shown her to the door by now.

She would make one last effort. She couldn't sit there in unbearable silence waiting for the child to wake up any more than she could disturb a sleeping child. She had to say something, anything to stave off that strange feeling of intense awareness of his physical presence which was creeping up on her and making her feel curiously giddy and irresponsible.

'Have you any idea who is looking for you?' she asked.

He flicked a bored glance in her direction and shrugged one shoulder.

'Might be a theatrical agent,' he replied.

'Then I suppose I should have told the enquiry agent you were here after all,' she said despondently, thinking that her effort in coming here had been in vain. She'd done nothing to help after all, had probably dramatised the coming of the enquiry agent beyond the limits of reality, had interfered unnecessarily and so caused him to lose a part in a play or a film.

'Someone else will tell him, as you've pointed out,' he comforted carelessly.

'Do you think he has a part for you in a play? Will you want to try for it?' she asked eagerly.

'No. For the time being I've had acting up to here.' He

made an expressive gesture with the side of a flat horizontal hand against his throat. 'I'm tired of being Simon Fell. I want to find out what it's like to be Simon Rigg, landowner and shareholder.'

'And perhaps become a recluse like Matthew Rigg, and make no contribution to the community at all. You'd be more use acting,' she taunted, and struck a spark at last.

He looked up and his eyes blazed at her for a moment and she braced herself for a broadside. It came in a cold, clipped voice.

'Listen, Miss Do-Gooder Thorpe. I've no intention of becoming like my Uncle Matthew or anyone else. I came here for peace and quiet, to rest and think. Apart from four notable interruptions by you and your brother I've found that peace and quiet. I haven't yet finished resting or thinking, so I'm going to stay here until I have. And when I'm ready, not before and not because any bossy little know-it-all nurse has told me, I shall decide what to do with this house and all that odious money in which you appear to be so interested. And then, if you're still around and are still interested, it's possible I might ask your opinion. But until then I'd be glad if you would keep your opinions to yourself and stay away from here!'

Some of his annoyance must have transmitted itself to Jemima, because she stirred and wailed. Without hesitation Simon set her down on the floor, stood up and went over to the cooker alcove where he had hung Sue's raincoat. He lifted it down and passed it to her without a word. Then taking the child's clothing from the rail in front of the cooker he squatted before her and dressed her.

Jemima blubbered noisily and sniffled unhappily.

'Don't cry, darling,' Simon comforted her brusquely, and she stopped crying to stare with round brown eyes at this adult who usually spoke to her softly. 'We all have to be taught a lesson now and again,' he said. 'This time you've outstayed your welcome.'

Struggling into her still damp raincoat, Sue felt her cheeks flaming with embarrassed shame and anger. She had no doubt that his words to the child were meant for her. She longed to strike back with more words, but deep down she had to admit that perhaps she had asked for that final snub.

Later, as she pushed the push-chair over the sands in the teeth of the driving wind and rain, she wished again that she hadn't gone to Riggholm that afternoon, and wondered miserably why she had twice defied Simon's request to be left alone. If it hadn't been for Grandmother insisting that he shouldn't be left alone she would never have gone back to Riggholm. Never, never. And now she would never go again.

CHAPTER 4

THE enquiry agent didn't return to The Gables that evening, so Sue came to the conclusion that he had found the information he sought from someone else. That her conclusion was right was borne out by Mrs Kent, who came the next morning with the specific intention of imparting the interesting piece of news that Simon Rigg was Simon Fell, the actor.

'How do you know?' asked Sue, pretending ignorance.

'Well, it was like this. I was in Price's yesterday afternoon. The shop was busy and I had to wait to be served. In comes a stranger and stands around looking and listening. Soon after him, who should come in but young Barnes with his sister to do some shopping for their mother. The stranger started to talk to them about the change in the weather and such-like, and then he brought out a photograph and asked them if they recognised the man in the picture. By this time we were all listening.'

'And did they recognise him?' asked Sue.

'The Barnes girl screeched in her posh accent, "Ooh, that's Simon Fell! I've seen him on the films." So I looked over her shoulder and I said, "It never is. It's Simon Rigg from Riggholm, over t'other side of bay." And the stranger looked at me sharp-like and said, "Are you sure?" I said, "Of course I'm sure," and the Barnes girl said, "So am I sure." So then young Barnes said, "Here, let me look." And he said, "It's Rigg all right. But it's Fell too. I've seen him on the stage." Well, to cut a long story short the stranger said, "Riggholm, did you say?" and he wrote the name down in a book. Then he thanked us very much and walked out.'

Mrs Kent paused, sipped some tea and then continued.

'I've been a bit worried since,' she confessed. 'Do you think we should have told him? I mean, we didn't know who he was. I wouldn't have said anything if that girl hadn't blurted it out as if she knew everything.'

'Yes, I think it was all right for you to tell him,' said Sue. 'You see, he asked me first and I told him I didn't recognise the photo. Then I went to tell Mr Rigg.'

'Ee, that was nice of you, lass. What did he say?'

'He didn't seem to mind the man knowing he was here.'

'Is it true that he's an actor and has been in films?'

'Yes, it's true.'

'Fancy that! I can hardly wait to tell Gertie. She said the Barnes girl was film-struck and sees film stars where there aren't any. She fancies herself as an actress, so you can depend upon it she'll be round at Riggholm with her mother to see what he can do to help her. She's not one for letting grass grow under her feet, nor is her mother.'

When Mrs Kent had gone Sue wondered what sort of reception Christy Barnes and her mother would receive from Simon. She imagined it might be short and sharp, unless of course he found the young and pretty Christy a more interesting visitor than the 'bossy, know-it-all nurse' who had a habit of asking awkward questions and offering forthright opinions. The memory of his scathing comments made her cheeks burn again and anger bubbled within her. Oh, what had possessed her to lay herself open to such an attack? Why had she gone knowing that he didn't want visitors?

The answer to such questions which was forming in her mind she didn't like, and she denied it hotly. Nothing would make her admit that she was becoming more and more attracted to Simon Rigg, like a planet to its sun, especially when she considered that there were probably many other planets in orbit around him, all resembling Christy Barnes, with whom she would have to compete for his attention. And to prove that she wasn't attracted she would never have anything to do with him again. Never.

Derek called in just before noon to have the tank of his car filled up.

'I've been given the push,' he announced mournfully. 'My illustrious father thinks I've hung round long enough, so I'm off to London to knock on the door of one of his friends to find out if he's truly a friend and will offer the Brigadier-General's son a job.'

'Can't you find work nearer to home?' asked Sue.

'Not the sort of work which would keep me in the standard of living to which I'm accustomed. Would you like to ask me in for a cuppa, or some other form of stimulant? I've something to tell you of great interest.'

'I bet I know what you're going to tell me,' said Sue as they went into the kitchen. 'It's about Simon Rigg being an actor.'

'Now, that's not fair, Susie. You've pinched my line,' he complained. 'Mmm, what a good smell! Come with me to London and cook for me, Susie?'

'Don't be an oaf. If you haven't a job you can't keep a cook.'

'Or a wife,' he supplied ruefully. 'But you could work for both of us, and cook as well. Several of my friends had that sort of set-up at college. Their girl-friends had good jobs and kept them while they finished their studies.'

'But you aren't studying, Derek. Anyway, I don't like that sort of set-up, as you call it.'

'I had a feeling you wouldn't,' he said with a grin. 'Susie Square, that's you, waiting for Mr Right to come along and pop the question in the good old conventional way. But for all you're square, I like you, and who knows you might be waiting here for me when I come back having made my million, and you'll be ready to fall into my arms.'

'That'll be the day,' scoffed Sue, placing a cup of tea in front of him. 'Here's your stimulant.'

'How did you know about the Rigg–Fell bit?' he asked as he heaped sugar into the cup.

'My friend Jill recognised him at the week-end.'

'And you didn't tell me,' he accused. 'There's friendship for you. Why didn't you tell me?'

'Because—oh, because I didn't want you to tell Christy,' she excused herself lamely.

'Well, she knows now, and after this afternoon's performance I almost wished she didn't.'

'What did she do?'

'Pestered me into taking her to Riggholm, where she put on the most frightful act of stage-struck innocence you've ever seen. I could have curled up with embarrassment. The look he gave her when she told him why she was there would have shrivelled my mother, and usually very little gets through her tough skin. But Christy must be pure rhinoceros all the way, because she didn't notice.'

'Did he say anything?'

'He told her he wasn't interested in toad-eaters and that he hadn't set himself up as a consultant on the film industry, and closed the door. She didn't understand what he meant, of course, and she burbled all the way home that he was all she'd hoped he would be and that she was going to see him again.'

Derek frowned and then added very seriously,

'I tell you, Susie, I'm afraid of what she might do when I'm gone. She's a bit headstrong, and only sixteen, and after reading about the Hughes girl I'm not sure I trust Mr Simon Rigg where teenage girls are concerned. He didn't come out of that with an unblemished reputation from all accounts.'

'What Hughes girl?' queried Sue, thoroughly mystified by his remarks.

'I read about her in one of Christy's film magazines. She unearthed all those which had a mention of him. Her name was Caitlin Hughes. She was about sixteen or seventeen. She was very friendly with Simon Fell, but very, if you get my meaning. Then suddenly she dropped out of the picture, wasn't seen in his company any more. A month or so later she was found dead at her home. The usual thing—an overdose of sleeping pills, balance of mind disturbed. Then the rumours started. She'd taken her life because she'd been upset because he'd dropped her.'

As he listened to Derek's rather staccato account of the information about Simon he had discovered, Sue recalled Jill's mention of Simon being involved with a girl called Caitlin who had died in suspicious circumstances. At the time she had thought he had been in love with the girl who had died and had come to Riggholm to grieve, alone and secluded, much as his uncle had done when he'd been disappointed in love. But now Derek's story shed a different light on the man who lived in the house across the bay. Even so, she had difficulty in believing that anyone who could be as gentle as Simon was to Jemima could treat anyone young as badly as Derek had implied.

'I don't believe it,' she said sturdily.

'Don't want to believe it, you mean,' jeered Derek. 'Oh, I remember all your crusading words about having trust, but isn't that taking it a bit too far? Or are you no better than my kid sister when it comes to actors and film stars? Are you so bedazzled by the glamour you can't see them clearly?'

'No,' she denied vehemently. 'It's nothing to do with him being an actor. I just find it difficult to believe that the man I've met could deliberately hurt in the manner you've suggested anyone as young as Caitlin Hughes was.'

'So you know him well, do you? You've seen a lot of him, have you?' queried Derek with a flash of jealousy. 'Yes, I seem to remember you regarded him as your special property from the time he came.'

'That isn't true. My contacts with him have been on a

purely business level,' retorted Sue, while at the back of her mind a small voice seemed to whisper, 'You didn't have to go and deliver the fuel to him. You didn't have to go yesterday.'

'Oh, sure,' said Derek sarcastically, 'I've heard about your visits to Riggholm. It's odd that you haven't delivered fuel to anyone else around here in person in the evening and spent over two hours doing it. Even odder that you should walk over in the afternoon in a rainstorm and spend the best part of an hour over there.'

'How do you know?'

'Ever tried keeping a secret in Seaport? You should know better. There's always someone peeping out of a window watching the comings and goings.' He pulled a battered magazine out of his jacket pocket and tossed it on to the table as he stood up.

'Here, read this, and then you'll have an idea what sort of a man you've been visiting and perhaps you'll take more care in future. It's time I went. See you, Sue. I'll be coming back one day, and I'll hope to find you here.'

When he had gone Sue read the article about Simon. It was the usual sort produced by such a publication which gave publicity to actors and actresses while purporting to tell the public something about their private lives. It said a little about Simon's career as a dedicated actor in repertory after training at the Royal Academy of Dramatic Art, the great variety of roles he had played, his sudden taking of London by storm in a performance of *King Lear* when he had played of all parts that of the Fool and the following year going from the ridiculous to the sublime and acting the part of Prospero in *The Tempest*. The article then mentioned the films in which he had taken supporting roles only to steal scenes from the stars until eventually he had been cast in a leading role in the memorable film about the Monmouth Rebellion.

Having dealt with his career the article went on to mention Simon's association with Caitlin which had ended so tragically. It quoted a so-called 'friend' of both the actor and the girl, who had said, when interviewed, that it was obvious to her that Caitlin had died because she had taken 'some man's' callous treatment to heart. Simon, it appeared, had been very silent on the subject of Caitlin's death and when interviewed by the writer of the article had said he had no comment to make.

With the story there was a photograph of the girl with Simon attending some theatrical function in London. There was another woman in the picture to whom the caption referred as Diana Witham, a great friend of the actor's, who had appeared on stage with him.

Sue considered what she had read. The portrayal of Simon as an ambitious and extremely talented and versatile actor had been put over very clearly, as had the impression that he was someone who would have no hesitation in rejecting anyone who hung on and possibly retarded his rise to the top of his profession. From such an outline it was easy to infer that Caitlin had become a nuisance and had been dropped.

Then she thought about the Simon she knew; about his determined if rather weary attempts to keep herself and Ralph at a distance; about his gentleness to Jemima and her grandmother, of his own oblique reference to having almost lost control over his life and of his need to find himself, and she tried to relate the flesh and blood person she knew to the blown-up image created by words, and couldn't.

Her glance lingered on the picture. Caitlin Hughes had been pretty, that was certain. Simon was holding her hand and smiling down at her and she was looking up at him, undisguised admiration in her expression. There was no doubt in Sue's mind that they had been enjoying one another's company that particular evening and she felt a sudden painful ache in the region of her heart.

With an impatient gesture she flipped over the pages of the magazine hiding the picture from view. Foolish drooling over the picture of a film actor was not for her, so she tossed the book on to the pile of motoring magazines on the shelf in the corner, believing that by doing so she had tossed the disturbing story of Caitlin Hughes out of her mind for good.

A week later Ralph returned. His news about Penny wasn't encouraging. She was still in intensive care and he had decided he would be better in Seaport working instead of fretting in Manchester. Penny's mother had promised to keep him informed of Penny's progress and later he would take Jemima down to visit her mother and her grandparents. Meanwhile, he hoped that Sue would stay and look after her niece.

May came in. Rhododendrons and azaleas bloomed in a blaze of colour in the gardens and laburnum trees dripped yellow blossom. On still evenings the air was full of the scent of hawthorn blossom. Sue took Jemima for walks among the sandhills, visited her aunt and grandmother and received visits from them. Then one day Ralph decided to take Jemima with him to see Penny and left Sue in charge.

The day before Ralph was due to return she decided to go up to Whitehaven to do some shopping while she was still free. It was a typical May day, blustery and sunny with dark purple clouds swirling across a sky illuminated by brilliant sunshine. Jack Martin drove her up to the station and she just caught the train, flinging herself through a door as it began to move away from the platform. Breathlessly, she took the first seat she came to, sat down and looked up into the blue eyes of Simon Rigg.

She closed her eyes briefly, thinking that perhaps he was an apparition which would be gone when she opened them. But when she cautiously raised her eyelids he was still there watching her with amusement.

'Do you always catch your trains with literally a split second to spare?' he drawled. 'You only just made it at Carlisle, that time.'

Sue's eyes rounded with surprise.

'But you were asleep,' she retorted, not finding it strange that they had begun to converse as if they had seen each other only yesterday instead of three weeks ago.

'I had one eye open,' he replied easily. 'I always like to

take note of my fellow passengers before sleeping.'

He looked well. His face had filled out and was healthily tanned. The expression of weary indifference had gone. He looked intensely, vividly alive, and Sue felt the pull of attraction more strongly than ever.

'Are you going back to Newcastle?' he asked politely.

'Oh no, I'm going to Whitehaven to do some shopping and to have my hair cut.'

'That's strange, so am I,' he said. 'Where's Jemima?'

'In Manchester with Ralph. He's taken her to see Penny.'

'Isn't she any better?'

'Yes, she's better. She's been in intensive care, but she should be able to leave hospital soon. When she's strong enough Ralph will take her away for a holiday.'

'While you and Jemima hold the fort of his business. Ralph is lucky to have a sister like you.'

The unexpected praise accompanied by a glance of admiration made her shy and she looked away out of the window at the fields in which fresh green shoots were growing, at the distant bluish mountains. His attitude was so different that she searched for a cause. Perhaps it was because they weren't in his house but were on neutral ground here on the train. Or perhaps it was because he was feeling better. Unable to keep looking out of the window, pulled by the irresistible attraction she glanced at him. He was still watching her, his eyes narrowed speculatively. The speculative gleam unnerved her and she stuttered into speech.

'Did anyone come to find you at Riggholm? The enquiry agent found out you were living there, you know.'

'I had three callers. Your friend Derek Barnes with his pest of a sister, and later Mrs Barnes. They only called once.'

'Oh dear,' said Sue, 'you were rude to them.'

'I was. Very.' And suddenly they were laughing together at a shared thought.

'We shouldn't laugh, really,' said Sue. 'Poor Derek was most embarrassed by Christy's behaviour.'

'I should hope he was. But dealing with her and him was

295

easy. The mother was a different matter.' His face hardened and he looked away out of the window. 'The mothers of stage-struck girls can be the very devil,' he added in an undertone, and then lapsed into a rather brooding silence.

Sue also looked out of the window. The train had passed through Seascale and was running close to the coast. Huge breakers driven by the strong wind were breaking on the long stretch of deserted damp sand. Fascinated as always by the movement of the sea, she watched the water retreat, gather itself together and rush forward again to hurl itself at the land in a frenzy of white foam.

Sue discovered that ever since she had sat down she had been sitting upright on the edge of her seat as if ready to run away or to do battle. But there was no need to run away from or do battle with Simon this time because he was as easy and casual with her as if they had been old friends. The thought made her relax and lean back in her seat and the movement disturbed his contemplation of the sea and he looked round.

'That's better,' he murmured. 'Now you look less like a bantam fighting cock ready to scratch my eyes out.' His glance roved over her springy hair. 'Must you have it cut?'

Sue could only stare her amazement.

'Your hair,' he added by way of explanation.

'It grows very thickly and becomes very heavy if I don't keep it short and it would get in the way when I'm working.'

'You could tie it back out of the way,' he suggested gravely. What a ridiculous situation to be sitting on a train discussing the length of her hair with a man who the last time she had seen him had given her the rough side of his tongue, and who for all practical purposes was still a stranger! Sue eyed him warily, looking for signs of mockery. But he smiled at her suddenly and her knees went all wobbly and she was glad she was sitting down.

'Go on, say it,' he taunted.

'Say what?' She was thoroughly confused by now.

'Say that the length of your hair is no business of mine.'

'Well, it isn't, is it? I hardly know you, and ...'

'And our relationship so far has hardly been intimate,' he put in dryly, 'and last time we met I wasn't very pleasant to you. I had to be unpleasant for your sake as much as mine. Perhaps one day I'll be able to tell you why. Meanwhile I hope you'll forgive and forget.'

Sue, being generous at heart, was so overwhelmed by this approach that she went more than half way to meet him.

'It's forgotten and forgiven already. I understood. You'd been ill and were unhappy about something. I irritated you with my questions and with trying to help you when you didn't want help. But you see we were so afraid you might become like Matthew, and Grandmother told me to persist, so I did. Now I realise that you're not like Matthew at all. You're much ...' She stopped. Here she was getting carried away again, encouraged by his gentler manner towards her, into saying more than she should.

'Go on,' he prompted. 'I'm much what?'

She flicked a wary glance at him, and decided that he wouldn't be angry if she spoke her mind this time.

'You're much tougher, more worldly.'

He made a grimace of distaste and then laughed.

'I don't think I like being called tough. It conjures up someone inflexible. Would you mind if we substituted resilient? As for worldly—it's hardly surprising that I'm more worldly than my uncle. After all, I've lived much more in the world than he ever did. But what interests me is that you, Ralph and your grandmother have been so concerned about what might happen to me, someone you scarcely know. That I find unusual.'

'Aren't you used to anyone being concerned about you?' she asked.

A curious expression almost of pain flickered in his eyes and then he looked out of the window again.

'There was someone once,' he said vaguely, and immediately the name Caitlin flashed into Sue's mind. But before she had time to ask a question he looked at her and said, 'But all that's in the past, and there was never any real danger of me becoming a recluse like Matthew. All I needed was time to think, get everything in the right perspective, and thanks to the wonderful atmosphere of Riggholm I think I've done that now and I'm ready to change my life-style.'

'Life-style.' The phrase was new to Sue. 'What do you mean?'

'Literally change my style of living. The last fourteen years or so have been extremely hectic and I've had no time to be myself.'

'Are you going to live at Riggholm?'

'Perhaps. It's a bit big for a bachelor, don't you think? And yet the last time I shared a house with others it was not exactly a successful arrangement,' he remarked cynically. Then he glanced at her sharply and the speculative gleam was back, putting her on guard. 'You said you hated to see Riggholm wasted when it could be of more use to the community. What did you mean by that?'

The train was slowing down as it approached White-haven station, and there was really no time to tell him before it stopped. He seemed to understand the reason for her hesitation, for he leaned forward and said urgently,

'We'll meet for lunch somewhere, when you've done your shopping and I've had my hair cut. You must know of a good inn or restaurant?'

Quelling a feeling that she was being stampeded, Sue told him the name of one and where to find it.

'We'll meet there at one o'clock, then,' he said, 'and you can tell me what you think should be done with Riggholm. Think of it as being my way of making amends for being so boorish last time we met.'

Sue did not go to the hairdressers. For all that the practical side of her nature told the other more romantic side, which longed for love, that it was foolish to let herself be influenced by a man who had so recently berated her, from whom she had vowed she would stay away and against

298

whom Derek had warned her, she was so bemused by Simon's change of attitude that she refused to listen to herself. And in a hazy, dreamlike state she wandered round the town making her purchases absentmindedly and then walked down to the harbour.

It was strange how anticipation of an unusual occasion, that of going to lunch with an attractive man who happened to be a fairly well-known actor had changed her outlook. Suddenly she saw beauty where before she had seen none. It was in the graceful exteriors of the few fine Georgian houses, relics of a more prosperous era. It was in the splash of colour provided by the tulips massed in the flower-beds in front of the modern Civic Hall. Down in the harbour it was in the gliding gulls, white against purple clouds as they hovered above the fishing fleet unloading its silvery catch, in the glinting puddles left by the retreating tide and in the smooth curves of the few yachts which lay tilted, high and dry on the mud.

Beauty everywhere, filling her heart with joy. When had she felt like this before? A derrick creaked raucously as it lifted fish from a hold and Sue remembered when she had felt that surge of joy. It had been at Christmas when she had been looking forward to going to the dance with Mark Pelham and she thought she had been in love.

The memory troubled her. Joy disappeared like a burst bubble. Turning sharply, she walked away from the harbour back into the town. Was she to be caught again in the entangling web of love just because Simon Rigg had smiled at her and had asked her to have lunch with him? She shook her head, a sharp little shake to clear it of the dreamy haze. Oh no. She wasn't going to make the same mistake twice. Much as he might attract her it wouldn't be wise to fall in love with Simon Rigg because although he denied it on the train he was tough and didn't need that sort of love. She must remember he had asked her to lunch only to seek her opinion about Riggholm. A business lunch. She must remember that, and keep her distance.

One of the big blowsy clouds obliterated the sun temporarily and the town lost its sparkle. A flurry of rain flounced across the street. A church clock struck the hour. Sue quickened her steps, turned a corner and made for the restaurant where she had promised to meet Simon.

The restaurant was unpretentious but known for its good cooking. Most of the clientèle were women in from the surrounding district to do their weekly shopping. There was, however, a sprinkling of men from offices and banks, judging by the conventional suits and ties.

Sue wasn't surprised to see many curious glances directed at Simon as they made their way to a table for two situated by a window, for not only was he tall and handsome and dressed with a careless elegance seldom seen in Whitehaven, but he also moved with unselfconscious poise and grace, even though he must have been aware of the close scrutiny of several pairs of eyes.

Sitting across from him at the table while he studied the menu, she fell once again a victim to the hazy dreamlike state she wished to avoid. How she wished she had seen him in the film Jill had mentioned. She imagined him in the long, full-skirted velvet or satin coats of the late seventeenth century, a fall of lace at his throat and at his wrists, one of those long curled wigs on his head. If he grew his hair long, really long, it might look like one of those wigs. As it was, the barber had trimmed it skilfully so that although it was definitely neater and shorter the cut had no resemblance to the short-back-and-sides type of cut which most of the other men in the room sported.

His face swam into focus as she realised he had spoken to her. A blush stained her cheeks as she realised how ridiculously her thoughts had been wandering.

'I'm sorry, I didn't hear what you said,' she stammered.

'So I gathered,' he remarked. 'I asked you why you were staring at me. Is there something wrong? Don't you approve of the barber's work? Or have I a smut on my nose?'

'Oh no. I was just thinking.' If she told him her thoughts he would mock her unmercifully or merely despise her.

She would seem to him like any other star-struck adolescent. Like Christy Barnes, dazzled by his public image or by the roles he had played, having no real interest in the actual man, when in reality she had outgrown that sort of image-worship years ago, or thought she had.

'You were thinking,' he said. 'Are you sure? I think you were romancing, wishing I was someone else, perhaps. The man of your dreams? There was a very far-away look in your eyes. I suppose nurses do dream occasionally.'

The mockery, although gentle, challenged and irritated her.

'Yes, they do, but isn't it just like a man to assume that the dreams are always about men? I thought we were going to discuss Riggholm, not my dreams,' she retorted coolly. 'I think it would make an ideal holiday home for children who have been ill and whose parents can't afford to take them away for the rest and fresh air they need to recover properly.'

'Exit the dreamer and enter the nurse with the over-developed social conscience,' he remarked, with a sardonic twist to his mouth. 'Very well, we shall discuss Riggholm. Yours is a suggestion which appeals to me very much. But is the house big enough?'

Relieved that he had stepped back a pace after coming very near to reading her mind, Sue relaxed again.

'I don't know. I've never seen all of it. How many rooms are there?'

'Twenty, including the kitchen. Then, of course, there is the cellar, which I suppose could be put to some sort of use.'

The cellar, from which there was supposed to be a tunnel leading to the sea-shore through which the Riggs and their smuggling associates, the Thorpes, had once carried their contraband to the house. Sue lost her businesslike poise and became again the girl who had always wanted to see the tunnel.

'Have you been in the cellar? Is there a door in it leading to a tunnel? A smugglers' tunnel?' she asked eagerly.

Simon noticed her eyes sparkle and her face lose the prim expression which it had taken on when he had accused her of romancing, and was glad of the change. He hadn't liked the stiff set-down she had given him when he had taunted her.

'I've no idea. Should there be?'

'Well, according to all the stories about the Riggs, the ships which brought the contraband used to heave to several miles offshore and the smugglers used to go out in small fishing boats, collect the loot, bring it to the shore and then carry it through the tunnel to the house where it was kept in the cellar until the Riggs could get rid of it to their customers.'

'And the Thorpes were in on this?'

'Yes, because they were fishermen and used to the sea. But one of them loved the law better than he loved the Riggs and turned informer.'

Simon made a face.

'How unpleasant of him! I didn't notice a door when I was down in the cellar, but then my visit was very short-lived.' He grinned with a touch of self-disparagement. 'I couldn't find any light switch, so I took a candle. It went out when I was going down the steps. My imagination got the better of me and I decided that discretion was the better part of valour. You could look tomorrow if you like when you come to see the house.'

The invitation surprised her when she thought of his efforts to keep her away from Riggholm and she was on guard immediately.

'But why should I want to see the house?'

'You can scarcely give a considered opinion on whether it's suitable for a children's home until you've inspected it properly, can you?'

'No, I suppose not. But do you want me to come?'

He frowned impatiently.

'I wouldn't invite you if I didn't,' he snapped with a touch of the old irritability.

'But you said last time I was to stay away.'

'Until I'd decided what I wanted to do. Now I've decided.' He read the puzzlement in her eyes and leaned across the table. 'If you're still uncertain perhaps it will help you if I tell you that I wanted you to stay away because I was unsure of you, suspicious, if you like to put it that way?'

'But why?' She was astounded, as most honest innocent people are when they learn that someone has been suspicious of them.

'A certain cynicism. You see, during the past few years most of my private life has been public property. When I arrived at Riggholm and felt its blessed peace fold around me I was determined no one would invade my new-found privacy for a while. I'd reckoned without people like you and Ralph because I'd never known anyone like you before.'

'Then what made you more sure, less suspicious?'

He gave her one of his enigmatic underbrowed glances and then the heavy eyelids edged with bronze gold-tipped lashes hid the blue depths as he looked down at his empty dessert plate. A faintly mocking smile hovered around his mouth.

'A way you have of telling me your honest opinion of me, a lack of obsequious flattery in your attitude, unlike a certain Miss Barnes. No one would ever mistake you for a toad-eater, Susan.'

Sue's face burned as she recalled the times she had pointed out his shortcomings.

'But I didn't know who you were then,' she said faintly.

'And when you did learn you didn't change your attitude. You kept on punching where it hurt. That's why I'm sure now you're no silly, self-centred girl wanting to share in the ostensible glamour of the theatre or the films.' He looked up suddenly, his eyes challenging as they met hers. 'But I'm beginning to wonder now whether perhaps you aren't an even more dangerous kind of female.'

Sue was absolutely flummoxed. No one had ever referred to her as dangerous before.

The arrival of the waitress, already enslaved by Simon's

smile and pleasantly-worded commands, gave her a chance to search for and recover her poise. She looked round the room finding reassurance in its homeliness. The gentle murmur of north-country voices rose and fell about her ears, reminding her that she was among her own people, warm, loyal people. She was one of them. How could she be dangerous? Surely the shoe was on the other foot. It was Simon Rigg who was dangerous, had always been dangerous where she was concerned, and never would she go to Riggholm again by herself.

The waitress had gone after leaving coffee with them. Sue wielded the small silver pot and passed a full cup to Simon who thanked her absently. He was looking beyond her, a faint frown between his eyebrows. Sue made a decision and spoke crisply and concisely.

'Ralph is coming home tonight. May I bring him to see Riggholm tomorrow, please?'

He transferred his gaze from whatever was holding his attention back to her face.

'If you want to bring him, yes.'

'You see, he's very good at sizing up rooms and might have some ideas on arranging accommodation,' she explained quickly.

'Then bring him and Jemima. I'll entertain her while you two look round,' he said equably.

'She'll like that,' said Sue, relaxing now that she realised he didn't mind if she didn't come alone. 'You're very patient with her and she responds to you much better than she does to Ralph.'

His eyes crinkled at the corners as he grinned at her.

'I shouldn't have said you never use flattery,' he murmured. 'You're only saying that because you're determined to see Riggholm become a children's convalescent or holiday home, with me as a big-scale baby-sitter. Remember, I asked only for your opinion. I'm not promising anything.'

He looked past her again and asked abruptly with no sign of humour, 'Is there a theatre in Whitehaven?'

'There's one at Moresby, near by. The Rosehill. It's considered to be one of the most beautiful small theatres in Europe.'

'When is the season?'

'I think it's open from September to July. Many familiar musical companies and singers have performed there.'

He nodded. He was still looking past her. She longed to look round to see at whom he was staring. She wanted to know why he had asked about the theatre, but she had no chance because he signalled to the waitress and said smoothly,

'I think it's time we left. I've still some shopping to do.'

There was no doubt in her mind that he had withdrawn. He had had enough of her, only this time dismissal was more polite than on other occasions. Feeling a strange mixture of despondency and relief, she walked ahead of him through the tables, her glance flickering over the people sitting at them searching for someone who looked theatrical. But no one caught her attention and Simon didn't stop to speak to anyone, so she decided that she must have imagined he had recognised someone.

Outside the restaurant he made no attempt to detain her when she said she was going to catch the next train to Seaport, and after telling her to come to Riggholm with Ralph the following afternoon he said goodbye and walked away.

Sue sighed as she watched him go. She was more puzzled than ever by Simon Rigg. Today he had come out of his seclusion, had told her more about himself than ever before, and yet she had this strange feeling that he had held out the hand of friendship, of cordiality, deliberately because he wanted something from her. The little maggot of distrust which Derek had introduced was beginning to grow, feeding as it did on her lack of confidence where her emotions were concerned.

It was some time before she was able to tell Ralph of the invitation to go to Riggholm, because he had so much to tell her about Penny and her slow but sure recovery. He intended to take her away on holiday again at the beginning

305

of June. Between then and now was the spring holiday weekend at the end of May when the caravan site was fully booked. He was worried that he might be trespassing on Sue's time and said so, but she assured him that she was quite contented to stay and look after Jemima and the house and then told him about the invitation.

Ralph looked up with interest.

'So he's come alive, has he?' he commented. 'I'll be glad to go with you. I've always wanted to see the inside of that house, and I want a word with him anyway, now that he's shown signs of being human. We could do with him on the local citizens' improvement association. The Brigadier has been on to us about the Bank, but there just isn't the money available to pay for any reconstruction or repairs. It'll take a fortune, and Simon Rigg has that fortune, so we've got to get him interested.'

Sue wondered whether she had done the right thing in asking Ralph to accompany her when she realised he was going to put pressure on Simon for money. She wasn't sure how the owner of Riggholm would take to being told how he should spend his inherited wealth. And anyway, she thought, she had been given the first go at offering an opinion on how the Riggholm estate could be best used for the benefit of the community.

They were greeted pleasantly enough by Simon and were told to take their time looking at the house while he took Jemima off with him to help in the garden.

The house was in mellow mood. Warm afternoon sunlight shafted in through its windows burnishing wooden panelling, glinting on a collection of lustreware jugs on the white-painted mantel of the fireplace in the big sitting-room. This time there were no signs of 'camping' and, although the carpet was worn in patches and the chairs and chesterfield needed recovering and possibly re-springing, the room possessed a genteel elegance. In the dining-room silver gleamed and winked on an enormous oak dresser which went with the long refectory table and carved chairs. Everywhere had been swept clean of cobwebs and already

Sue could tell the house was responding to the interest and care bestowed on it by someone who obviously liked it.

Upstairs, however, the story was different. The bedrooms were stark and almost empty and the sunlight, so kind downstairs, showed up the peeling paint and damp patches. She noticed that Simon had chosen a front bedroom as his own, and as she looked out of the window she realised that she was looking straight across the bay to The Gables and her own bedroom window glinting with reflected golden light.

When they had finished looking round upstairs they went down to the kitchen and found the door to the cellar, an empty cavernous place with damp streaming walls. There was nothing in it except some old barrels and a sailor's strongbox which was locked. Sue carefully inspected the walls and came across a place where there were bricks instead of stone and knew that the story about the tunnel had been true, but at some time someone had removed the door and had had the aperture bricked up.

When they went outside again they found Simon in the back garden weeding. He had given a small trowel to Jemima and she was weeding too, or so he said, but it looked as if the child was treating the soil of the border as she did sand, piling it into little hillocks resembling sand castles and occasionally attempting to eat it.

Sue was so excited at having found where the door in the tunnel used to be that she blurted out her find to Simon immediately. He leaned on the long handle of the hoe he had been using and looked down at her, an expression of indulgent amusement on his face. He had discarded the sweater he had been wearing when they had arrived and his loose blue shirt was undone down the front almost to his waist, revealing a muscular chest on which hairs glinted. His face slightly flushed from exertion, his tawny hair dishevelled, his eyes bluer than the placid May sky arching above, he seemed to Sue to be more attractive than ever and she had to look away quickly in case she was caught staring at him too long and he guessed the effect he had on her.

Staring fixedly at an enormous crimson rhododendron blossom, she watched a large fuzzy brown bumblebee fly delicately first into one wide-mouthed finely-veined trumpet of the blossom and then into another while she tried to control the strange leaping of her senses which being near Simon had caused. She had never felt like this in the whole of her life before. Not even the sight of Mark had ever produced this breathless longing to touch and to hold. Thank goodness Ralph was with her!

'Of course it needs a lot doing to it,' she heard Ralph saying in reply to Simon's query as to what he thought of the house. 'But it would make a grand hotel. One of those select places known for its cuisine. With the right decorations and the right sort of service it would attract people from all over the place. Wealthy people wanting to get away from the rat-race, big businessmen as well as honeymooners looking for a quiet secluded spot. Seaport needs a hotel and I've been thinking of starting one.' His bright glance roved round the garden. 'But this place would be perfect. You've made a difference to the garden. You've been working hard.'

Simon executed a mocking stage bow.

'Thank you. It does me no end of good to have my puny efforts appreciated. I've found the gardening very soothing. So you'd like the place converted into a hotel? That's rather a different scheme from what your sister has in mind.' He gave a sidelong glance in the direction of Sue's studiously averted face. 'What do you think of that, Nurse Thorpe? A profit-making concern instead of a philanthropic one, with Ralph as manager?'

'I'd like to have a shot at it too,' said Ralph enthusiastically, forgetful of the need for money for the repair of Rigg's Bank. 'With the sort of capital you could provide I could make a go of it, I know I could.'

His enthusiasm for his own suggestion had the effect of curing the knee-shaking, tummy-fluttering sensations from which Sue had been suffering as she saw her own plans for Riggholm being swamped by his. She swung round and caught the two men in the act of eyeing each other. In Ralph's eyes challenge and excitement glowed. In Simon's shrewd speculation gleamed. It was that gleam of speculation which roused her anger.

'Oh, if profit is all you're interested in and can talk about, I may as well leave!' she exclaimed furiously. 'Come on, Jemima, let's go.'

She swooped in the unsuspecting child, who immediately squealed loudly because she had been taken away from the nice messy soil. Anger lent strength to Sue's arms and in spite of the kicking and squirming and the pathetic yells of 'Dada, Dada!' she managed to carry the child round to the front of the house where the van was parked. She flung open the back doors of the van, took out the folded push-chair, jerked it open and dumping her outraged niece into it, set off at a furious rate down the driveway.

She wasn't sure with whom she was most angry, Ralph for suggesting the hotel or Simon for suggesting that Ralph might like to manage the hotel. Or was her anger really against herself for behaving so foolishly at the sight of Simon? Was it just an excuse to flee before she succumbed to that compelling, glamorous attraction. Even when he had been weary and sick at heart he had possessed a certain physical dynamism difficult to resist, but now that he was back to full strength, his virile allure was devastating.

Jemima was still yelling. Sue gave the push-chair a little shake.

'Be quiet!' she ordered. 'You're no better. Your aggressiveness collapses as soon as you see him, so be quiet!'

Surprised by the sharp tone of her aunt's voice, Jemima stopped yelling and looked at Sue with wide tear-filled eyes.

'The sooner your mummy is well again and can come back the better for me,' muttered Sue. 'I'll be able to go away from here, back to my work.'

But the thought of going away depressed her. To leave

309

this place in the fullness of spring when the trees were newly green and the hedgerows were full of wild flowers and the distant purple mountains were etched against pale skies would be hard, especially when she had come close to finding someone for whom her shy heart had been searching.

Her eyes brimmed with tears too, but not for long. Dashing them away with the back of her hand, she said aloud,

'Stuff and nonsense! Can't you see it's the same old thing? Image-worship? A one-sided business, and I'd thought you'd grown out of it.'

Fortunately Ralph made no mention of her sudden departure from Riggholm, nor did he make any mention of the hotel although he stayed with Simon a long time after she had left, and in the busy preparations for the spring week-end holiday the visit to Riggholm was temporarily shelved.

The Tuesday after the holiday Aunt Emily and Grandmother dropped in for their weekly visit.

'I expect you know your friend Jill is coming next week-end to stay at Greenthwaite,' said Emily. 'John has invited her.'

Sue said she knew, having had a letter from Jill only that morning.

'Seems a funny choice for a farmer to make,' grunted Grandmother. 'A town-bred girl who looks as if she has no stamina.'

'He hasn't chosen her yet, Mother. They're just friends,' said Emily.

'Humph! Seeing as it's the first time he's ever asked a lass to come and stay it looks to me as if he's made his choice,' retorted Grandmother.

'What do you think, Sue love? Do you think it's serious?' asked Emily.

'It could be, and I hope it is, because Jill is one of the best—and you needn't worry about stamina, Gran. Jill's a nurse and has to be strong. John needs someone to love and to love him. He can't spend all of his life doting on sheep,' said Sue.

'I'm sure you're right. Anyway, love, we'd like you and Ralph and the child to come up for tea on Sunday so that you can see Jill.'

'Aye, and what about the lad from Riggholm?' said Grandma. 'Time we had him to tea. Have you seen him lately, Susie?'

'Yes. I had lunch with him in Whitehaven on Wednesday,' said Sue stiffly.

'Ah, what did I tell you? Persistence. There's nothing like it for prising a hermit out of his shell.'

'You were wrong there, Gran,' answered Sue rather tartly. 'He had no intention of becoming a hermit. And as for your idea about him having taken a beating over something dear to his heart, I doubt very much whether he has a heart.'

'Ho-hum. Like that, was it?' chuckled Grandmother. 'Well, I'm glad to hear the lad has spirit. And when are you seeing him again?'

'I'm not,' replied Sue stiffly. 'We met on the train by accident and he asked me to have lunch with him because he wanted my opinion on how he could put Riggholm to use for the community. I told him my ideas and Ralph and I went over to look at the place. Then Ralph said it would make a good hotel. I left them to talk about it. Obviously my idea was out because it was non-profit-making.'

'What was it, love?' asked Emily kindly, seeing that her niece was upset about something.

'I thought it would make a good convalescent or holiday home for children,' said Sue.

'And you were miffed because he didn't catch on to it straight away,' commented Grandmother. 'I can't see why he has to do anything with the place except live in it.'

'But he finds it too big for himself,' explained Sue.

'Then he should take a wife and sire a brood,' grunted Grandmother, with her usual earthy outlook on life.

'Maybe he doesn't want to.'

'Why shouldn't he? He looks virile enough.'

'It isn't the fashion to have large families these days, Mother,' said Emily. 'I think Sue's suggestion is a lovely one.'

'You would,' growled Grandmother, 'but it isn't wanted here and Matthew wouldn't approve. He wouldn't have liked a hotel either.'

'Matthew is dead now, so it's none of his business, is it?' said Emily gently. 'Mr Rigg, I'm sure, is quite capable of deciding for himself what he should do with the house.'

'Then what does he want to ask Susie's opinion for?' countered Grandmother. 'And what has fashion got to do with having a family? You have a family when you feel like having one.' She stood up suddenly and banged with her stick on the kitchen floor. 'I'll tell yon lad what he should do, if he's wanting opinions. We'll go now Emily and call on him and invite him to tea on Sunday.'

'But he might not want to have tea at Greenthwaite,' objected Sue faintly, afraid that her outspoken grandmother might say too much on the subject of marriage and families to Simon Rigg and receive a caustic set-down as a result.

Grandmother gave her a long considering look and her brown eyes twinkled suddenly with mischief.

'I think we'll find he's just longing to be invited,' she said. 'And anyway, it's time he learned a little more about his family.'

The possibility that Simon might be at Greenthwaite for tea on Sunday had the most peculiar effect on Sue. She could only describe the state of agitation into which her grandmother's suggestion had sent her as the 'dithers', as she hesitated about going to the farmhouse to tea herself. Whenever she thought of Simon being there in Aunt Emily's comfortable sitting-room, leaning back in one of the wing chairs, his blue eyes agleam with some private amusement as he watched, and listened to the homely family conversation, the flutters started somewhere below her ribs. She wanted him to be there and yet she didn't,

312

because she didn't know whether she would be able to sit there in the same room and appear casual and unconcerned. Consequently she began to think up ways of opting out.

Perhaps she could pretend she had a cold and Ralph could take Jemima on his own. But then would she feel any better sitting alone at The Gables imagining the pleasant tea-party she would be missing? Of course, there was always the chance that Simon would refuse Grandmother's invitation. If he was consistent, he would. 'I'm not here to socialise,' he had said to Derek. But that had been when he wanted to be left alone, and apparently that period of seclusion was over.

She wished she knew what his answer to Grandmother had been. Should she telephone Aunt Emily and ask her? She had almost reached the telephone to put thought into action when another thought stopped her in her tracks. No. It wouldn't do to show too much interest in Simon in front of her family or they would be up to their usual trick of drawing conclusions, in this case imagining that she and Simon had reached the same stage in their relationship as Jill and John had, a stage which Sue was convinced never would be reached.

She was still undecided whether to go on Sunday or not when John brought Jill in to see her on Saturday evening. There wasn't much chance to talk to her friend privately and she had to invent an excuse in order to invite Jill up to her bedroom for a few minutes.

'This is a lovely view,' said Jill, going over to the window to watch the play of light on the dimpling water in the bay. 'Oh, you can see the house belonging to Simon Fell. John's mother tells me he's coming to tea tomorrow. I can hardly believe it. To think we're going to have tea with a film star! Your grandmother says you had lunch with him in Whitehaven one day. I must say you manage things very well, Sue Thorpe, in your own quiet way.'

'I didn't manage anything. We met by accident and our lunch was a business affair,' retorted Sue stiffly.

'Business? Don't tell me you're thinking of going on the

stage or breaking into films?' teased Jill.

'No. He wanted my advice about his house, that's all.'

Jill, who was more alert than she appeared to be, glanced at her friend's averted profile. The slightly retroussé nose and one plump pink cheek was framed by a fall of straight thick hair which was longer than she had ever seen it. The new length, below the ears almost to the shoulders, suited Sue, softening as it did the fullness of her face and the squareness of her chin, but Jill didn't like the new stiff hands-off attitude her friend had displayed when teased about Simon. Normally Sue would have treated such teasing remarks with a flippant good-humoured retort and they would have giggled together.

But being a sympathetic sort she didn't persist with her teasing and went on to talk about John's visits to Newcastle to see her and how nervous she was about staying at the farm.

'Oh, surely you're not afraid of Aunt Emily and Uncle Tom?' exclaimed Sue, glad of the change of subject now that she had learned what she wanted to know about Simon going to tea.

'No, they're both dears, but I'm afraid of doing something wrong or of making some ignorant remark about the farm because I'm sure your grandmother is just waiting for me to make a fool of myself so that she can show me up in front of John. And then when he realises just what a goof I am he'll think twice.'

'If he loves you the fact that you know nothing about farming won't matter. Why, Aunt Emily wasn't born on a farm either and knew nothing about it when she married Uncle Tom.'

'But at least she grew up locally, and that must have helped.'

'Oh, Jill, you mustn't let Gran frighten you. Her growl is far worse than her bite. She's a dear, lovable old lady and is entitled to her opinion, which usually differs from that of everyone else, but that doesn't mean she's invariably right or that we should all do what she says. John probably doesn't listen to her at all. He has a mind of his own and when he decides to do something there's no stopping him. Surely you've learned that over the last few weeks?'

Jill nodded and smiled rather shyly for her.

'Yes, I've learned that. I'm glad I told you, and I hope you're right about the loving bit. But it will still be nice to have you there tomorrow, Sue, to give me some moral support.'

The knowledge that Jill expected her to be at Greenthwaite the following day to give her moral support put an end to Sue's 'dithers'. She would go and in supporting her friend she would forget her own trepidation at the thought of seeing Simon in the family circle. However, they occurred again when she was dressing Jemima ready for the outing when she realised that Ralph had probably offered to give Simon a lift to the farm as his only means of getting there, and that there was the possibility of having to sit beside him in the van for eight miles there and eight miles back.

'Are we giving Simon a lift?' she asked.

'No, why should we? He has his own transport now.'

'Oh.' She felt very deflated by this piece of news. 'I didn't know.'

'If you'd stayed a little longer the day we went to Riggholm you'd have known. He asked me who was a good dealer in cars in the district. As a matter of fact that's why I went up to Carlisle on Wednesday. I took him with me and we had a great time looking at cars. It's a grand pastime when you're helping someone else to spend their money. He chose a nice little job in the end. Nothing fancy. By the way, I meant to ask you—why did you go off in a huff that day?'

'Because he seemed more interested in hotels than in helping children,' she replied coolly, and Ralph gave her a curious considering glance.

'Well, for once, Miss Know-all, you were wrong. He's very taken with your suggestion, and thought your refusal to stay and talk about it most odd. The hotel idea is out

315

because it would mean him giving up the place as a home completely, whereas he thinks that if it was a holiday home or convalescent home or whatever you like to call it, for children, he'd be able to live in part of the house and would also be able to participate in the running of the home. Anyway, I daresay he'll have something to say to you about it today.'

The 'nice little job' to which Ralph had referred turned out to be an expensive-looking blue affair, neat and compact, not showy as Ralph had said, but definitely powerful and efficient. It was parked in the farmyard at Greenthwaite next to Howard Jones' cream Morris, and at the sight of it Sue felt her heart jolt and the palms of her hands go clammy. She would have preferred to have arrived before Simon and to have been thoroughly settled, in the middle of a conversation or perhaps helping Aunt Emily in the kitchen, so that she could have ignored his arrival. Now she would have to enter the sitting-room and be greeted by him as the family watched curiously.

But when she did go into the room with Jemima she found he was being monopolised by her grandmother and was listening so attentively to the old lady that he didn't notice at first that she and Ralph were in the room until Grandmother, coming to the end of some long discourse, turned to greet them. Then Simon spoke only to Ralph, giving her a slight cool nod, in passing, so to speak, and immediately and contrarily Sue's blood boiled as she wondered why she had bothered to wear her new spring dress and to brush her hair until it shone when he paid so little attention to her. For once he was dressed more or less conventionally in a light grey suit with a blue shirt and the only touch of flamboyance was his tie.

During the next fifteen minutes Sue had time to notice, since nobody talked to her, that Simon seemed very much at ease with the family. There was no sign of indifferent boredom on his face and gradually she realised that her relatives were treating him as if he was no one out of the ordinary and that he was accepting them as if they were the

316

sort of people with whom he had mixed all his life, and gradually her blood simmered down. After all, she hadn't wanted him to single her out in front of the family in case such behaviour would lead to conjecture on their part, and she should be glad that he hadn't.

Relaxing, she sat back and listened to Ralph holding forth about Rigg's Bank and watched Simon as he leaned forward, his forehead wrinkled in creases of concentration as he tried to understand the portent of her brother's complaint. Ralph's voice stopped and her uncle took up the story with occasional interjections from Grandmother and John. Then suddenly, as if he had become conscious of her gaze, Simon flicked a glance in her direction and smiled, a slight but strongly intimate smile, which faded almost as soon as it had appeared.

It seemed to Sue that her heart leapt up and out of her body in response to that brief recognition of her presence. But remembering her resolve to keep her distance she didn't smile back, turning away deliberately to speak to Greta.

At the table she was pleased to find that Simon had been placed beside her grandmother near the top end while she had her usual place near the door which led to the kitchen and had Jemima beside her. With a bit of luck, she thought she might be able to avoid any direct conversation with Simon.

It was as the meal was coming to an end that John surprised everyone by standing up and announcing in his abrupt way,

'While you're all here I may as well say my piece and put an end to all the guessing that's been going on in this family for the last few weeks. This morning on the way back from church I asked Jill to marry me and she said she would. Happen we'll be wed in t'autumn when t'harvest is in.'

CHAPTER 5

JOHN'S announcement was greeted, of course, by a great
deal of noisy excited chatter which didn't stop until it was
time for him to drive Jill down to Seaport to catch the train
to Carlisle so that she could return to Newcastle. When the
couple had departed, the women of the party all disappeared into the kitchen to wash up dishes and to discuss the
latest event at their leisure, while the men went off either to
look round the farm or to entertain the children.

Her contribution to the dish-washing done in unaccus-
tomed silence, Sue went out into the garden to make sure
Jemima was being cared for by her cousins. Satisfied that
the child was happy for the next half hour, Sue slipped out
of the garden, walked down the road and turned off into a
lane which wound across country.

The lane, known locally for obvious reasons as Lovers'
Lane, was not a place where you hurried. It went up and
down hill between tall leaning hedges heavy with May blossom and garlanded with briar roses. It was full of surprises
and secrets. There were noises which you could never quite
place, twitterings which couldn't possibly be produced by
birds and grunts which couldn't possibly be made by sheep,
or so Sue always liked to think. It was for her a magic
place, a place to which she had often escaped as a child and
as a teenager, where she had often found solace when upset,
and of whose quiet sympathy she now felt in need.

As so often after a day of fine drizzling rain the clouds
had lifted and now the sun was shining. Above the feathery
tops of the high hedges the sky was a pale eggshell blue.
Sue walked, warm and safe, deep in her dreams. Suddenly
there was a break in the hedge on her right and across the
moss-grown bars of an old gate she saw the lovely land
sweeping down, then rising slowly again to soft green wood-
land-shrouded curves and on to grey-blue crags.

Stopping at the gate, she leaned on it. Behind her a

thrush was singing and down in the valley the rooks were cawing. From the garden she had just left came the sounds of children shouting and laughing. But here she was alone with time to spare to enjoy the tranquillity of the lane and to dream of what might have been and what could be.

'May I share the view with you, or do you prefer to keep this one to yourself?'

It was Simon. He was beside her, leaning grey-clad arms on the top bar close to hers, his shoulder touching hers, closer than he had ever been. At once her tranquil dreamy mood was suffused with dangerous sensations.

'I usually manage to enjoy it alone because no one knows I come here,' she explained, inwardly warning herself to keep calm and cool. 'How did you know I was here?'

'Your uncle and I were returning to the house after a rather strenuous tour of some of his fields and I happened to glance down here and saw you dawdling along. As soon as I could escape I came after you because I wanted to talk to you.' He looked across the quiet valley. 'This country is full of surprises, and I find it difficult to believe my family lived here for generations and yet until a year ago I knew nothing about it.'

'Didn't your father tell you about it?'

'No, never. He told me nothing about Riggholm, my uncle or my mother.'

'But didn't you ask?'

'I learned early in life that my father didn't like questions about matters which were close to his heart, so I stopped asking them,' he replied curtly, then after a pause he added more gently, 'This place is so different from the world in which I've lived until recently. Its pace is leisurely, beyond the edge of things.'

'It's the roots of heaven,' said Sue softly, gazing up at the mountains now gilded by the sun, and forgetting her resolve to keep her distance, influenced by the dreamy atmosphere of the lane.

'An apt description. Is it your own?' he asked, turning to glance at her.

'No. It comes from a story told in Westmorland about the place between heaven and earth through which men used to pass quite freely. So that men's minds shouldn't be dazzled by the beauty of heaven, the in-between place was made in the image of heaven shrouded in soft mist. It was of the earth and yet it was filled with a spirit beyond the range of men's minds. It was so perfect that it couldn't be anything else but the roots of heaven.'

He was silent, staring out over the rain-washed valley which twinkled here and there with reflected light as the sunlight was trapped by lingering raindrops on tree and bush.

'But if this place is truly the roots of heaven,' he murmured at last, 'what am I doing here? A few months ago I was beginning to believe that heaven was not for me.' Then as if startled by his own musings he turned sharply to her and said abruptly, 'Did you know I'd be here today for tea?'

'Yes, Jill told me last night. But I was surprised you'd accepted the invitation. Sunday tea with a large garrulous family isn't the sort of entertainment I'd have expected you to enjoy,' she replied honestly.

'Why shouldn't I enjoy it as much as any other human being?' he demanded.

She moved away from him a little uneasily, sensing that he was displeased by her comment.

'I suppose,' he continued, 'you've a preconceived notion, based on what you've read somewhere about actors, that I prefer a more sophisticated type of entertainment. Bacchanalian parties perhaps, or dalliance with various beautiful women.'

The scathing tone of his voice made her stiffen guiltily, involuntarily, as she recalled the article Derek had given her to read. She looked away from the mountains, along the green and purple valley where the river wound like a silver-ribbon among overhanging willows, turning her face away from him so that he wouldn't be able to see the tell-tale blood which had risen to her cheeks.

He stared at the wealth of reddish brown hair presented for him to look at. 'Hair of night and sunshine spun'. Swinburne's lines flashed through his mind and his mouth curved in a slightly bitter self-mocking grimace. He reached out a hand, took a handful and pulled hard. Her head came back and she gasped with pain.

'Oh, please Simon, let go!'

'Not until you promise not to turn your back on me as though you consider me beneath your contempt,' he threatened.

She turned to look at him at once and the hair slid out of his hand. Her eyes were dark brown and velvety.

'Sunflowers,' he said, and the dark eyes widened even more.

'W-what do you mean?' she stammered, and there was no sign of the stiff and starchy nurse. She was a young woman with a soft tremulous mouth and bewildered, beseeching brown eyes.

'Your eyes remind me of the centres of sunflowers, deep brown, flecked with yellow, wide and innocent, yet warm and compassionate, reflecting the inner soul, perhaps? At least I thought so when I first met you. But lately there has been a difference, a certain coolness in them, and they've had a tendency to avoid meeting mine directly, as if you've found out something about me you don't like.'

Her eyes darkened almost to black before her eyelids covered them. Shining white teeth appeared to catch her reddened lower lip.

'So you've been delving in mud and you've uncovered something nasty,' he jeered rather wearily.

The lustrous gloom of her hair glinted in the soft evening sunlight as she tossed back her head to look at him again.

'Oh no, I haven't delved. I guessed that something unpleasant had happened to make you feel sour, but when you didn't tell me yourself I didn't try to find out what it was. It was Derek. When he found out you were Simon Fell he gave me an article written about you to read. You see, he was worried about his sister.'

His mouth took on a grim line and he stared at her with narrowed eyes.

'And he hoped you'd get the message too,' he said. 'Did it come through loud and clear: "Beware the big bad wolf of Riggholm who swallows little girls whole"?'

His words flicked at her sensitivity. Her hands tightened on the top of the gate. Before her eyes the fields and trees blurred a little. He had invaded her magic place and it would never be the same again.

'I didn't want to believe what it said about you,' she said desperately, hoping that when he saw she was willing to give him the benefit of the doubt he would open up and tell her about Caitlin Hughes.

'Most of it was true, so why shouldn't you believe it?' he retaliated. Most of it was true. That meant surely that some of the article hadn't been true. Although Sue's trust was badly shaken, it survived. Turning, she looked directly into his eyes.

'Why did you come to tea today?' she countered.

His puzzled frown was a familiar impatient quirk of his eyebrows, but he answered without hesitation.

'I came because your grandmother invited me and I find it very hard to refuse anything to the very old. I came because it gave her pleasure to invite me, to see me, to call me Matthew occasionally and to see me eat what she calls a good square meal. I came also,' his pause was infinitesimal as a faint mischievous smile appeared, 'I came because I hoped Jemima would be here.'

'Then there's the answer to your own question,' said Sue seriously. 'I didn't want to believe that you'd deliberately hurt someone like Caitlin Hughes because I've seen you be gentle with Jemima and have known you to treat my grandmother with tolerance and consideration.'

He stared at her thoughtfully for a few seconds and then turned to look across the valley again, and his profile was as uncommunicative as that head of the Roman warrior she had seen on a coin.

'Isn't this flattery a little out of character?' he queried

322

lightly. 'You'll be saying next that you'd prefer to have Riggholm made into a home for old people instead of a holiday home for children, just because I've accorded an elderly lady the respect and courtesy she deserves.'

She felt a keen stab of disappointment as with the deftness which came of long practice he avoided the chance to confide in her about the circumstances surrounding Caitlin Hughes' death. In a few words he could have explained his involvement with the girl instead of leaving her to believe the worst of him. But there was nothing she could do about it, so she followed his lead.

'A home for old people would be as good as one for children,' she said earnestly.

'And would satisfy your social conscience admirably. But it wouldn't find favour with your grandmother any more than Ralph's suggestion of a hotel found favour with you a few days ago, you little spitfire,' he mocked. 'Did you know your grandmother has very definite views on how Riggholm should be used? She thinks I should get married and rear a family there.'

'Oh, I know,' sighed Sue, wishing her grandmother would keep her mouth shut on certain subjects. 'She has the oddest and most impractical suggestions.'

'Now what, may I ask, is odd and impractical about me getting married and having a family?' he enquired with a touch of exasperation.

'Well, you once referred to marriage as a trap, and if you feel like that it would be better if you didn't get married.'

'I held that view for a number of years, partly because I felt that personal freedom was essential if I were to make a success of my career and partly because of the mess I've seen some of my acting colleagues make of marriage,' he observed. 'But recently I've had cause to change my mind because my circumstances are different.' His eyes narrowed and his glance roved over her face and figure assessingly. 'I should think your approach to matrimony must have been very different from mine and hasn't changed much since you discarded your puppy fat. You'll believe that it's the

323

only possible way in which a man and woman can live together.'

Suspecting that he was making fun of her conventional appearance and outlook in the same way that Derek teased her for being square, Sue raised her chin and looked him straight in the eyes.

'Supposing that it is my view?' she retorted. 'Is there anything wrong in wanting a lasting and stable relationship with someone who wants the same?'

'No, there's nothing wrong. It's what most people are searching for. But it doesn't describe the marriages which I've seen which have tended to be brief and unstable.'

'That's because the couples involved haven't taken marriage seriously. They haven't thought initially beyond the glamour of the ceremony and the honeymoon. For them marriage has been only an ending, whereas ideally it should be the ending of one relationship and the beginning of another new and more exciting one which should develop and deepen over the years.'

He stared at her in silence for a moment and then his eyes crinkled at the corners as he smiled indulgently.

'A very mature view,' he scoffed softly, 'lifted right out of a marriage guidance counsellor's textbook. So marriage is a beginning. Of what, I wonder? A field of battle or a bed of roses?'

'Both,' asserted Sue, a little shaken by his mockery of her dearly held ideals. 'Like life itself.'

Interest flickered in his eyes.

'Only a realist could profess such idealism,' he murmured. 'But what do you really know about marriage, apart from what you've read or dreamed about?'

'I've seen how marriages in my own family work. Aunt Emily and Uncle Tom, Greta and Howard, my parents ...' Her voice trailed away and her eyes darkened with grief.

'What happened?' he probed.

'They went away on the first holiday they'd had for years. Ralph and I persuaded them to go. They hadn't gone very far. Instead of taking the motorway they'd decided to take the old road over Shap, thinking to miss the fast traffic. Their car went out of control when they were going down the steep part and went over the edge. If we hadn't persisted they wouldn't have gone and maybe they'd still be alive,' she said in a small voice.

She felt the warmth of his hand as it covered hers where it rested on the top bar of the gate.

'They went together,' he comforted. 'Better that way than for one of them to be left behind to grieve and be lost for the rest of his life, which is what happened to my father.'

Although she appreciated his comforting gestures the touch of his hand on hers was doing strange things to her insides. Cautiously, stealthily, she pulled her hand from under his and folded her arms to lean again on the top of the gate.

'Since you have such faith in the institution of marriage you must be pleased by your down-to-earth cousin's decision to marry your lovely and rather spectacular friend,' he remarked. 'Do you think they've thought beyond the glamour of the ceremony and the honeymoon?'

'I hope they have. But they've only known one another for about six weeks and then they've met only briefly at the week-ends. It seems very sudden.'

'"No sooner met but they looked, no sooner looked but they loved; no sooner loved but they sighed; no sooner sighed but they asked one another the reason; no sooner knew the reason but they sought the remedy,"' he quoted. 'Rosalind's description of love at first sight from *As You Like It* seems to fit the situation. And doesn't your idealism allow for love at first sight?'

His question troubled her because it touched on her own confusion concerning the recognition of love. Glancing away from his suddenly bright and observant eyes, she stammered,

'I don't know how they can tell they love each other when they haven't known each other for very long. I mean, love is more than just physical attraction or even a sharing of interests or background. It must be because Jill and John are very different from each other.'

'And doesn't your textbook provide an answer to that one?' he jeered gently. 'Doesn't it lay it down in black and white how to recognise your true love at first sight? Perhaps Shakespeare is a better guide after all. "Love looks not with the eyes but with the mind," he says. Outward appearance, difference in age and background, gossip about the loved one's shortcomings aren't supposed to affect your judgement. Your mind is supposed to recognise instantly the other mind with which it desires to be united. "And therefore is wingèd Cupid painted blind." '

He spoke as if he knew, as if he had experience of love. Had he loved Caitlin Hughes after all? A queer little flash of jealousy rocketed through Sue, making her more confused than ever.

'But if only one mind does the recognising—what then?' she argued.

'So there is a man in your life,' he pounced suddenly, curiously.

'There are several,' she replied with a shaky flippancy, as she realised she had given herself away. 'There's Ralph, Jack, Martin, Uncle Tom.'

'I said man, not men,' he said acidly, apparently very annoyed by her answer. 'A man with whom you wish to have that lasting and stable relationship you talk about so glibly. Is it Derek Barnes?'

The question surprised her. Wherever did he get the idea that she was interested in Derek?

'Derek and I used to play together when we were children. We used to meet occasionally during the holidays when we were teenagers to go sailing or to play tennis. Our relationship has been very intermittent and casual.'

'That wasn't the impression I received the day he arrived back in Seaport,' he commented sardonically.

Recalling Derek's exuberant greeting, Sue flushed for the second time that evening, then seeing the mockery gleaming in Simon's eyes she felt annoyed with herself for being so vulnerable to his taunts.

'That was only high spirits,' she replied coolly.

'Then if he isn't the man in your life there must be one in Newcastle.'

She flinched and he knew he had touched a wound only lightly healed as yet.

'I thought so once,' she admitted, 'but he fizzled out.'

He burst out laughing, making her feel juvenile and gauche.

'Like a damp squib,' he scoffed. 'What a way to describe the departure of a former lover! What a blow to his masculine vanity if he knew he had fizzled out in your estimation. It's possible, of course, that you may have dampened his ardour. There are times when you're like a shower of rain, refreshing but definitely dampening.'

She wasn't sure how to take this last personal remark. She had a suspicion that he was taunting her to get some unspecified but violent reaction from her. But one thing she was sure about.

'Mark wasn't my lover. I've never had a lover. We went out a few times together, that's all.'

Her answer seemed to amuse him again and she found she was having the greatest difficulty in preventing herself from slapping him. He moved closer to her and she retreated from his advance. She was stopped short by the hedge where it met the gate, driven into a corner by Simon, who stood before her, one hand nonchalantly resting on the top of the gate, the other stretched out to twist a piece of blossom from the hedge.

'That you've never had a lover except perhaps in your dreams is becoming more obvious by the hour,' he remarked, 'and it's high time somebody made up for that deficiency in your life.'

His eyes were like blue flames flickering with mocking challenge. The piece of blossom came away from the bush and he held it to his nose to sniff at it.

'It's unlucky to pick May blossom,' said Sue in a faint panicky voice.

'Who cares? I'm not superstitious,' he replied. 'Would you like a lover, brown-eyed Sue?' he added softly.

Her heart beating madly, Sue tried to assert herself.

'Not at the moment, thank you. Now will you stop behaving in this ridiculous fashion,' she said coldly.

'It's raining again,' he mocked.

'I can't understand why you should think that I should like a lover,' she said exasperatedly.

'Perhaps I think that way because this lane has a magic about it. Perhaps because it's the bewitching hour?'

'Bewitching hour?' she queried.

'Dusk,' he said quietly, still watching her.

Looking round, she saw with surprise that while they had been talking twilight had crept up. The sun had almost gone. Pools of blue shadow had collected in the folds of the hills. The mountains looked like giant elephants sleeping, nose to tail, their wrinkled grey backs hunched to the soft sky which was already bleached by moonlight. The thrush had stopped singing and down in the valley the rooks had gone to their rest.

Once before she and Simon had stood together and had been very aware of each other. Then she had gone from his house, afraid of what that awareness might mean. Now she could not go because he had deliberately cut off her escape.

'Isn't this the time when the elves come out and make fairy rings upon the grass, and lovers steal away down country lanes to kiss in the moonlight?' he murmured suggestively.

How did he know she had stood in this place many times and had seen the fairy ring of fungus in the wet vivid grass and had watched the moon creep up the sky and had longed for someone to love her?

He was too close. All the things she had read about him in the article, all she had heard about Lupus loving and leaving, jumbled in her mind. That he wanted to kiss her and that it would be a pleasant experience she had no doubt. She wished she could receive his embrace in the lighthearted spirit he would give it, in the spirit in which probably all the other kisses had been given and taken in this lane. But she couldn't. She was suspicious of the change in his attitude towards her and most of all she was afraid of her own responses.

'Sue, Sue, come on! It's time we went home. Jemima's nearly asleep.'

Ralph's voice was near and coming nearer. Sue closed her eyes in relief and in that moment Simon leaned forward and kissed her with a brief efficiency which left her shaking.

'Goodnight, brown-eyed Sue,' he whispered in a laughter-ridden voice, adding more seriously, 'Thanks for having trust.'

Her eyes flew open in surprise at his last remark. But he had turned away and was walking round the bend in the lane. A few seconds later she could hear him and Ralph talking, then the sound of their footsteps retreating up the lane.

For a while she lingered, elbows on the top bar of the gate, hands over her hot cheeks. When she looked down at the grass in the field she saw a fairy ring. On impulse she opened the gate, slid through it and stepped into the ring, recalling the old myth that if you stood in the ring and listened hard enough the fairies would answer your question. Head tipped downwards, she asked her usual question—how would she know when someone loved her? and waited to hear if they had anything to say to her. But all she heard was the whine of a car engine starting up followed by the crunch of gravel as wheels moved over it. Quietly she listened to the noise of the departing car, guessing it was Simon's until it faded out of earshot. But even then she could hear no answer to her question.

Ralph left Seaport three days later for Manchester. Penny was well enough to travel and he intended to take her back to Guernsey for a week before hoping to persuade her to return to Seaport. Although his mind was set on making sure Penny had a good holiday he was worried about leaving his business at a time when many people were thinking of taking their holidays. Sue assured him that she could manage to supervise everything for him, but his glance still held doubt as he considered her over the breakfast table.

'And when I bring Penny back, if I bring Penny back,' he said, betraying his uncertainty where his private life was concerned, 'will you stay?'

'I haven't come to a decision yet,' she faltered, avoiding his glance.

'Good. That means you're still open to persuasion. Stay the rest of the summer anyway, Sue, please. It will help me very much if you would. If ... Penny comes back, she's going to have problems with Jemima.'

'It would help if Jemima had company and competition in the form of a brother or a sister,' she countered.

Ralph examined his hands closely, a frown darkening his face.

'It's easy enough to say that, another matter entirely providing the brother or sister to order. Penny's been warned that she shouldn't have another child.'

'But you could adopt. Another child to care for would take Penny's mind off herself and off Jemima.'

'Hey, hold your horses, little sister!' laughed Ralph. 'Don't I have a say in all this? If you're so keen to provide Jemima with company and competition the best thing you can do is give her a cousin.'

'And who would be the father? It's usual to get married before having a child,' replied Sue primly.

'Well, now let's see,' drawled Ralph mockingly. 'Who's available? I can't say I'd take kindly to young Barnes as a brother-in-law. How about Simon Rigg? You have to admit he's easily the most eligible bachelor hereabouts, and it seems to me you and he were a long time together in Lovers' Lane on Sunday night.'

'I might have known you'd bring that up sooner or later. Talking to someone in Lovers' Lane doesn't mean a thing,' said Sue, wishing that she hadn't developed the stupid habit of blushing every time Simon's name was mentioned.

'Only talking?' gibed Ralph with a knowing twinkle in his eyes. 'I saw him kissing you.'

'Oh, that,' Sue tried to shrug carelessly, and failed miserably. 'What's in a kiss?'

'Now, Sue, you can't deceive me into believing you're that hard-boiled. There's not much in a kiss, but one usually leads to another and so on until ...' He paused suggestively and watched anger flash in her dark eyes.

'Ralph Thorpe, if you really want me to stay and help you for the rest of the summer you'll stop teasing me about Simon Rigg,' she threatened furiously. 'He means nothing to me and I wouldn't marry him if ...'

'I know, I know,' he cut in swiftly. 'You wouldn't marry him if he was the last man on this earth. Famous last words, Sue, so watch your step. All right, I'll keep mum, but it won't stop me from drawing my own conclusions about all I see and hear.'

Now that she had given her word to Ralph she couldn't really go back on it, thought Sue when she studied the booking for the caravans after lunch the next day. Jemima was having her afternoon nap and for the time being the house was quiet. For the next two weeks the caravans were fully booked by couples with young children not yet old enough for school. There were also several bookings for bed and breakfast and evening meals at the house. That meant Mrs Kent would be in to cook and that Jack Parker's eldest daughter would come over to do her usual summer job of cleaning the house and changing the bedding. Sue's job was to supervise them and to be on the spot when guests arrived and departed. And that was how it would be all summer.

She laid down the book and stared out of the window of Ralph's small study which was on the ground floor of the house at the back, overlooking the small walled garden. On the high sea-wall a rambling rose clambered. Already its small pointed buds were being coaxed to open by the warm June sunshine to which it was fully exposed at this time of the day.

April, May and now June. How long had she known

331

Simon? A little longer than Jill had known John. Long enough to fall in love with him? He had told her that love looks with the mind, not with the eyes, so it was no use believing the reaction of her senses to his physical appearance. If that were the case to see Simon was to love him at once. Then how did her mind look at him? She closed her eyes and immediately was reminded of the time she had closed them in Lovers' Lane and he had kissed her. The magic of the lane was all about her, the strong scent of May blossom was in her nostrils and Simon was before her, his eyes like blue flames, his smile white and tantalising.

She opened her eyes again, banishing the vision. What was the use? Every time she tried to think about the essence of the man and look at him with her mind his outward appearance bedevilled her. What was he like? And why had he come so close to making love to her the last time they had met when only a few weeks earlier he had sent her packing from his house?

A bell rang. It was the one which sounded when anyone wanting petrol drove into the yard. Knowing that Martin was busy working on a car engine and that Jack Parker was still having his lunch, she went to answer the bell. A black car was drawn up to the pumps. Behind the steering wheel sat a man whose brown hair touched the collar of his elegant suit and whose eyes were hidden by dark glasses.

'Fill her up,' he ordered casually.

She unhooked the hose from its bracket, undid the cap of the car's petrol tank, inserted the nozzle of the hose and switched on. When the tank was full she reversed the process and went to tell the customer the price.

He had removed his glasses. Curious brown eyes looked at her out of a thin ascetic face. He handed her two pound notes.

'You're the girl I saw recently with Simon Fell in Whitehaven,' he stated rather than asked.

His calm matter-of-fact approach made her jump and she was unable to hide her surprise, completely betraying herself by the wide wary glance she gave him as she took the money.

His mouth curled rather unpleasantly as his glance roved over her again.

'I'm glad you haven't bothered to deny it. I recognised you straight away. You're so unlike the usual style of woman Simon associates with that I felt sure you were worthy of attention.'

Not liking the way he referred to Simon's usual style of woman, or his cynical smile, Sue went to the office to get change. He must be the person Simon had recognised in the restaurant and to whom he hadn't bothered to speak, presumably because he wished to avoid him.

She returned to the car and gave him his change, but didn't say anything. He pocketed the change, considered her carefully, then said abruptly,

'I believe he's living around here in a house called Riggholm?'

'Who told you?' she countered.

'Someone in London when I was there a couple of weeks ago. Someone who is very interested and has always been interested in Simon's whereabouts.' He beat a little tattoo with long thin fingers on the steering wheel. 'By the way, if you should be seeing him again you might tell him that Paul Hurst stopped by for petrol and sent this message: the huntress is free and is stalking her prey again. I'm sure he'll understand.'

Paul Hurst. The name was familiar, but she couldn't place it.

'Why don't you go and see him yourself, Mr Hurst, and tell him?' she said coldly.

He took out a cigarette case, selected a cigarette and lit it before he answered. The glance he gave her through the smoke was rather rueful.

'Because I wouldn't be very welcome. Simon and I are not what you'd call bosom friends. In fact there is a distinct possibility we might be considered as rivals. Oh no, don't get me wrong. I'm no actor. I'm a musician. Piano accom-

333

paniment, a very exacting profession not receiving sufficient acknowledgement, if I may say so. I've just been appearing with Madame Sybil Roska, the soprano, a very polished performer. We were at the Rosehill Theatre, a delightful place.'

'Then in what ways are you and Simon rivals, Mr Hurst?' she asked.

His smile was slightly strained.

'To put it delicately, an old affair of the heart. At least my heart was in it, but I doubt very much if his was. Yes, it's very interesting to find him here consorting with the local maidens, becase he never bothered very much with women unless they were actresses or associated in some way with the acting profession. I'm not surprised he's shaken the dust of the big city from his feet, for a while, after that dreadful business of the Hughes child. You know about her, of course?'

'I know she died rather tragically.'

'Simon didn't tell you, though?'

Sue shook her head negatively. She didn't like this person very much. He was too unctuous, but she was unwilling to let him go because he knew Simon.

'I thought not,' he said with a knowledgeable nod. 'That's a little mystery he prefers to keep to himself—not that he was ever one to talk about matters concerning himself. But his silence in this instance has given weight to the rumours which spread after the girl's death that they had an affair and that he used her obvious affection for him to further his own ambition. Then having attained his object he dropped her, and the poor little soul was too sensitive to take it in her stride.'

'Did you know Caitlin?' asked Sue, trying to ignore the cold numbness which was creeping round her heart.

'Since she was born. Her mother is a cousin of mine. So naturally knowing Simon too I watched their little affair with interest, from the wings, as it were. It all started when her father brought him home one evening. Like any other young girl Caitlin was fascinated at first. Simon had always

334

had a great way with young people. Gradually, however, infatuation replaced fascination and she used to go to see him at the theatre where he was acting. Then she began to go to the house where he lived. He'd rented a house that year. He said he was tired of living in apartments. It wasn't long before it was a home-from-home for any young and struggling actor in London. And Caitlin was there too ... cooking for them.' Paul Hurst made a faint grimace of disgust. 'I'm sure I have no need to go into more details for you to get the idea. But Simon was like that, carelessly generous with anything he possessed.'

'Possibly he remembered what it was like to be young and struggling himself,' murmured Sue, clutching blindly at any kindly thought or action on Simon's part which would bolster her badly battered trust in him.

'Possibly,' drawled Paul Hurst, giving her a searching glance. 'Anyway, that was the set-up. Poor little Caitlin infatuated, and nothing any of us said to her made any difference. But after the film contract was signed it was noticeable that she didn't go to the theatre quite so much and that she was no longer such a regular visitor at the house. It was enough to keep the gossip writers busy for weeks.'

'But what had the film contract to do with her?' asked Sue.

This time Paul Hurst looked at her with an air of disdainful surprise.

'Oh, I thought you'd know. Caitlin was the daughter of Evan Hughes, producer and financial backer of several great movies. The contract Simon signed was with him. Get the point? Of course, I was out of the country when she died, but I heard the rest of the story from ... er ... a very great friend of mine who knows Simon well. He'd used the poor little soul's friendship to put the screw on Evan in order to get that contract, and never once has he denied those rumours I told you about.'

The numbness was complete now. She felt as if her heart would never beat again with the old joyous carelessness.

She had trusted blindly for the last time in her life. However, there was just one point which wasn't quite clear.

'But if he wanted the contract so badly why does he say he's given up acting?' she queried.

The narrow brown eyes were suddenly very shrewd as they looked at her.

'Does he say that? Well, well,' he drawled as he stubbed out his cigarette in an ash tray opening out of the dashboard. 'Yes, I agree it seems very strange, and I've often wondered myself why he broke that fabulous contract, walked out of a play which had been a roaring box-office success since it had opened but which folded as soon as he left it, and just disappeared from view. You have no idea?'

'Me? Oh no, I know hardly anything about him.'

'It's a good thing I happened to call in, then, isn't it? You're a lot wiser about him now,' he suggested unpleasantly. 'Time I moved on. I'm on my way to Manchester, by a devious route, I know, but I like to see as much of the countryside as I can. Don't forget to give Simon the message if you see him, will you? It'll give him something to think about. I'm glad we had this little talk. Makes me feel good to know that my assessment of a person is occasionally right.'

'You mean your assessment of me?' asked Sue, round-eyed.

'Yes. You're not a bit like Simon's usual style of woman, and that gives me a little hope where that little affair of the heart I referred to earlier is concerned. Goodbye.'

Later, when the nasty taste he had left behind him had worn off a little, Sue was able to consider clearly all that Paul Hurst had told her. She was glad, she realised, that he had recognised her and had stopped to talk to her. At last she had met someone who had known Simon and the world in which he had lived before he had come to Riggholm, that fascinating world of stage and screen celebrities, rife with jealousies and rivalries and odd personal relationships. She had learned that Simon had always had a way with young people, that he was carelessly generous towards young actors struggling up the ladder of fame, two characteristics which endeared him to her and to which she could easily give credence. But on the discredit side she had learned that he was also capable of ruthlessly using the affection bestowed on him by a young girl who had known no better to achieve his ambitions.

'You're a lot wiser now,' Paul Hurst's remark haunted her through the next few days. Had he been warning her not to be taken in as Caitlin had been, thus confirming the suspicions aroused originally by Derek and then later by Simon's changed attitude towards her in Lovers' Lane? Was the Simon who had taunted and kissed her in Lovers' Lane the real Simon or had he been acting a part to obtain something he wanted? And what could he possibly want from someone like herself? Would she ever know?

Then there was the strange message Paul Hurst had passed on. How could she relay it to Simon? Riggholm still didn't possess a telephone, as far as she knew. Gone were the days when in her innocence she could go over there uninvited. She could only wait and hope to catch him one day when he came for petrol.

But when he came he was on foot. She was just setting out with Jemima for an afternoon walk when he walked into the yard. At the sight of him Jemima shrieked her welcome and held out her arms. He squatted before her, smiled at her and took her chubby hands in his.

'Hello, darling. Although I appreciate your rapturous greeting it isn't you I've come to see. It's that stiff and starchy nurse who claims to be your aunt.'

The overwhelming desire to greet him as rapturously as Jemima had which had shaken Sue to her depths was chased right out of her mind by the oblique taunt and by the time he straightened up to look at her she was just as stiff and starchy as he had described her, finding the prim façade useful to hide behind.

Immediately the expression of warmth and gaiety left his

face and was replaced by a puzzled frown.

'Where are you going?' he demanded abruptly, as if he had a right to know.

'To the sandhills,' she replied coldly.

'I'll come with you,' he announced arrogantly, and she panicked.

'Oh no, please don't bother. If you've something to say, say it here.'

He glanced slowly round the yard at Martin who was filling a car's tank with petrol and then at Jack who was sitting in the office. Then his gaze came back to her and it seemed to her that anger sparked in his eyes.

'Afraid to be alone with me?' he jeered softly, and at once she thought of their last meeting and the stolen kiss in the lane.

'No, of course not.' It was her best nurse voice, crisp, no-nonsense, denying the implication that he had the power to disturb her when they were alone. 'But I . . .'

'But me no buts, woman,' he interrupted autocratically. 'We shall walk together in full view of curious village eyes and on the way we shall talk. When we get there who knows what will happen when we're hidden among the sand-dunes, quite alone and unseen. Come on, Jemima.'

He jerked the push-chair out of Sue's loose hold and began to push it out of the yard. She had no alternative but to follow, hurrying a little to catch up with him, trying not to notice Mrs Kent staring open-mouthed from the other side of the street at the strange spectacle of the squire of Riggholm dressed casually in gaudily-striped flared pants and a bright blue shirt pushing a child's push-chair down the village street.

Once she had caught up with him Simon began to talk.

'I've been seeing people who know about children, sick children, poor children, convalescent children,' he said tersely. 'Local public health and welfare people, hospital authorities. They're all very interested in your idea, especi-ally if the place can be subsidised by a private fund and if a house could be donated in a suitable locality. Some of them

338

have already condescended to look at Riggholm and have pronounced it ideal, with certain renovations and modifications, of course. I've also been to see the family lawyer. He was very sceptical at first, but eventually I persuaded him that I was sincere in wanting to set aside some of Uncle Matthew's fortune to finance the home.'

Carelessly generous with anything he possessed. Here was evidence of that characteristic proving once and for all he was not like Matthew at all. All she could say was,

'Oh, Simon!'

'Oh, Simon,' he mimicked unkindly. 'Is that all you have to say after my efforts to try and do as you suggested? If you're careful and behave yourself I might recommend you to the directors of the home and you might swing a job as head nurse or matron or something, and then you wouldn't have to go back to Newcastle.'

'But what will you do? Where will you live?' she asked.

He gave her a mocking sidelong glance.

'You sound as if you really care. Originally I had thought the house could be arranged with part of it for me. That, however, seems to depend on the success of my next move. All is not yet accomplished because those authorities I've been talking about have doubts about my respectability. You see, when I told them I should like to participate actively in the organising of the home they became very suspicious and asked for my qualifications. I told them what I'd been to date and they were very dubious. One of them suggested, however, that if I were married their doubts would not have arisen. Strange how marriage immediately makes a man respectable in the eyes of some people.'

Although he spoke lightly, almost sneeringly, Sue guessed he had been a little hurt by the local authorities' suspicions of his intentions.

'And if your next move isn't successful, what will you do then?' she asked.

'Hand over the house and the money to them and let them get on with it,' he said rather surlily.

'And go back to the theatre?'

'Perhaps,' he replied non-committally.

They had come to the end of the village street. Ahead of them were the sand-dunes, mile upon mile of them stretching along the coast. The soft sand made pushing the push-chair difficult, so Simon pulled it behind him. The sun was warm and small blue butterflies fluttered above the bent coarse grass growing out of the sand. From the shore, hidden by the dunes, came the soft slurring sound of waves breaking on sand and withdrawing again.

Soon they came to a hollow surrounded on all sides by the sandy banks of grass. Simon stopped, turned and lifted Jemima out of the push-chair and put her on the sand. Sue knelt beside the child and gave her the bucket and spade she had been carrying. Jemima immediately began to bang a noisy tattoo on the bottom of the bucket with the spade, looking up at Simon and chuckling as she did so. He sat down beside her, took the spade from her and began to fill the bucket with sand. Jemima helped him by grabbing handfuls of sand and pushing it into the bucket.

Sue watched man and child for a while, half listening to the rather one-sided conversation which Simon carried on with Jemima. This wasn't a part he was playing, this relationship with the child. This was the real Simon, patient and yet firm with a little girl whom he didn't have to keep at a distance, with whom he could be himself.

The flash of insight comforted her and she realised she could carry it further. She could imagine him with a sixteen-year-old like Caitlin Hughes, being the same, listening sympathetically, perhaps, to confused adolescent thoughts and possibly offering advice, and receiving in return, all unknowingly, an abundance of worship. At least she could imagine it if she hadn't been told differently; if Derek hadn't given her that article to read; if Paul Hurst hadn't been an onlooker of part of the affair; if Simon hadn't been so silent on the subject, dodging it whenever she brought it up.

Sue sighed. It was suddenly very important that she

should hear about Caitlin from Simon himself if only she could find some way to open it up. It was important because if ever she was to trust anyone again she had to have her initial trust in him vindicated. And that could only be done by him.

'A man called Paul Hurst came to the garage for petrol the other day,' she said. 'He recognised me. He'd seen me with you in the restaurant in Whitehaven. I think you noticed him. Do you remember?'

He went on patting sand into the bucket as if he hadn't heard her, and she had to admire his self-control. The bucket was full so he turned it upside down and then pulled it up to reveal a very crumbly sand castle which Jemima promptly destroyed.

'Yes, I remember,' was the smooth reply. 'Is he still at Rosehill?'

'No. He's gone to Manchester. He asked me to give you a message. He said, "The huntress is free and is stalking her prey." He said you'd understand.'

'The huntress,' Simon repeated slowly as he began to fill the bucket with sand again. A faint smile twitched his lips. 'How like Paul to be subtle! So I can expect a visitor. I wonder what line she'll take this time?' He looked up and his eyes were wary. 'Did he talk much to you?'

'He said you'd once been rivals in an affair of the heart.'

Simon laughed heartily and Jemima chuckled with him.

'Hardly rivals,' he said when he had stopped laughing. 'Paul just had to blame his lack of success with the woman in question on someone and I happened to be handy. It didn't matter that my affections were not engaged.'

'Yes, he said your heart wasn't in the affair,' she said rather acidly, and he looked at her sharply.

'There wasn't an affair,' he retorted coldly. 'You seem to have had a good gossip. What else did he tell you?'

'He said he'd often wondered why you'd broken a fabulous film contract, walked out of a play which was a big box-office success and disappeared. Why did you, Simon?'

He stopped shovelling sand, stretched out on his stomach, folded his arms and laid his head on them.

'I was tired,' he murmured briefly, tantalisingly, and closed his eyes.

Back to square one, thought Sue ruefully, deciding that his reticence about himself was one of his most irritating characteristics. It was as if he didn't want anyone to know or understand him.

She tried again.

'Was it because of the way Caitlin died?'

He was silent so long she thought she wasn't going to answer her. Then he opened one eye to look at her.

'You show a very morbid interest in her,' he remarked. 'I wonder why. I do hope you aren't considering identifying with her too closely.' He was doing it again. Dodging the issue instead of explaining and answering her question.

'Of course I don't want to identify with her. How could I? I know nothing about her.'

He looked at her with two eyes, bright with mockery.

'Tut, tut, Paul is slipping. I'd have thought he'd have told you all about her.' The mockery faded and was replaced by a darker, more obscure expression as he added softly, 'I agree it would be difficult for you to identify with her because you aren't at all like her. She didn't have eyes like brown velvet. Do you know, I always assumed that Vikings were fair or red-haired and had blue or grey eyes.'

Another red herring to entice her away from the subject of Caitlin! She was tempted this time to retaliate physically by pushing sand down the front of his shirt where it was unbuttoned to reveal a glimpse of bare chest below the arch of his neck. It was the sort of impulse she might have given in to if he had been Ralph or even Derek, and she recognised it as wholly youthful and mischievous. But her imagination leapt ahead to the tussle that might result and she experienced such a pang of desire she had to look away quickly and clench her hands to stop herself from grabbing sand.

'Grandmother Thorpe's family have Spanish blood. Her maiden name is Faller, taken from Falla. There's story that when the Spanish Armada was scattered by the storm which blew up during the battle with the English fleet, some of the galleons were blown north and one of them was wrecked on the coast just south of here. Some of the survivors were taken in by local families and were eventually absorbed into the community. But variations of their names and some of their physical characteristics keep cropping up,' she stated in a flat monotone.

'Thanks for the history lesson,' he replied drily. 'Spanish and Viking. No wonder you're such an enigma, promising warmth one minute and blowing cold the next. Just now I would guess the wind is sitting in the north.'

Sue sat stunned, open-mouthed. She was an enigma? What did he think he was, with his taunting caustic remarks alternating with long reserved silences, his cool arrogance at odds with that sympathetic gentleness and consideration which he had shown to Jemima, Grandmother and yes, she had to admit it, to herself.

She swung round intent on retaliation, but he had lowered his head to his arms again. Apparently he thought he had deflected her from her intention to find out more about his relationship with Caitlin. Well, he'd soon find out that the Thorpes were tenacious when they wanted to know something!

'Paul Hurst told me that Caitlin's father offered you the film contract, but he implied that you wouldn't have been offered it if you hadn't ... I mean, if you and she ...' She stumbled to a stop because when it came to the point she wasn't sure how to describe his association with Caitlin.

He raised his head to remark sarcastically,

'Which day did you say he called for petrol? Thursday, or was it Friday? I seem to remember my ears burning one of those days. Did you enjoy discussing my past with him?'

Although she flinched at the sarcasm she refused to be put off. He was annoyed and it was just possible that out of his annoyance might spring the truth.

'I didn't discuss anything with him,' she replied coolly. 'But he seemed to think it important that I should know your silence on the subject has given weight to the rumours which were spread after her death.'

'And you would like me to verify or deny what Paul implied, I suppose,' he said.

Sue nodded.

'Well, here it is, straight from the horse's mouth. Yes, Caitlin and I were good friends. Yes, her father did offer me a film contract. Anyone can infer what they like from those two statements of fact. I can't help what people think.'

His answer had told her nothing new. It merely gave the impression of supreme disregard on his part of other people's opinion, a carelessness which was indicative of that heartlessness to which Paul Hurst had referred.

'But supposing what they're thinking isn't true?' she tried again desperately.

'Then that's their mistake,' he replied indifferently.

Something of her disappointment must have shown in her face, because digging his elbows in the sand and propping his chin on his hands he made an effort to explain,

'Look, Sue, all I've ever wanted to be is a good actor, no more, no less, able to communicate the great truths contained in drama as well as I possibly could to the public. For years I worked to be just that. Nothing else mattered.'

'Not even people?'

'Only *en masse*, as an audience. Singly as individuals who might make demands on my emotions and time, no,' he replied curtly, and was silent again, staring broodingly at the sand.

It wasn't much of an explanation after all, she thought, and it didn't help her at all. It only confirmed the suggestion that Paul Hurst had made that Caitlin had been sacrificed to further Simon's ambition.

'Then why did you throw it all away?' she asked.

He turned his head to look at her. 'I was losing my integrity,' he replied briefly. 'I was no longer what I'd wanted to be, a good actor. Oh, I was acting ... too much. On stage at night, in a film during the day. Then suddenly it occurred to me that I no longer knew who I was. I seemed to be only a puppet in the hands of agents, producers, directors' publicity men. I had to get out, go away, think about it. You know the rest.'

'Did it happen after Caitlin's death?' she asked.

'Yes,' he replied brusquely. 'Do you mind if we discuss something else now? I find raking over my past mistakes ... boring.'

'But you can't run away from the past,' she objected.

'You can turn your back on it, as I have done.'

'And forget it?' she challenged.

He didn't reply, but laid his head on his arms again and closed his eyes. He was so still and silent that after a while Sue wondered if he had gone to sleep, lulled by the rustle of the stiff marram grass and the soft shushing sound of the waves on the unseen shore. She sat upright, taut with distress, wishing she could relax and forget troublesome nagging thoughts. If she hadn't known about Caitlin, or if Simon had told her more, she might have been able to enjoy this moment of quiet among the sand-dunes with him, but as it was she could feel that little maggot of distrust growing bigger as it fed on the big gaps in Simon's attempt to explain what had happened before he had come to Riggholm.

'Dreaming again?'

His voice was lazy, but the expression in the one blue eye watching her made a peculiar shiver go down her spine. He was looking at her as if he wanted to ...

'Dreaming of the fellow who fizzled out?' he prodded wickedly, and at once her dangerous thoughts were swept away by the taunt.

'No, not at all. I thought you'd gone to sleep,' she retorted.

'And you envied my peace of mind?' he suggested, with a perspicacity which alarmed her. 'Why spend time worrying about the past? The present is far more interesting. At least I find it so. I wasn't sleeping, I was letting my mind drift in pleasant idle thoughts and wondering what you'd say if I asked you to marry me.'

She felt as a boxer must feel when his opponent lands a blow near the heart. When her breath returned her good north country common sense returned with it, making her speak tartly.

'I'd say you were out of your mind, plain daft!'

He laughed delightedly, rolled over to his back and laid his head in her lap, an action which made her tingle all over. His eyes glimmered with amusement as he looked up at her.

'Another refreshing Sue-like shower of rain,' he said. 'Do you know you look quite different from this angle, less stiff and starchy. Behold then a man out of his mind. I'm asking you to marry me.'

This wasn't how she'd ever imagined a proposal of marriage, this casual half-humorous approach. Nor had she ever expected it from this man. Coming as it did on top of their recent rather unsatisfactory conversation in which he had refused very deftly, she thought, to tell her anything about Caitlin, it raised doubts about his sincerity. So she looked away from him at the sand-dunes to other dunes glinting green and gold in the sunlight.

He sat up suddenly and putting long fingers under her chin turned her face towards him.

'I meant what I said,' he informed her sternly. 'I asked you to marry me.'

'Why?'

The question was spontaneous and it betrayed her uncertainty. He frowned impatiently as he always did when she challenged him.

'Why not? Why does a man propose marriage to a woman? I thought you'd know all the answers to that. Perhaps because he wants a housekeeper. Perhaps because he wants a child. There are all sort of sensible good reasons,' he replied with a touch of irritability, as if he considered her obtuse.

He glanced over at Jemima still busy with her spade, burrowing in the sand, unaware of the tension which existed between her two adult companions.

'I'd like a child like Jemima, with Spanish dark eyes,' he added softly, and watched the blood run up into Sue's cheeks and he couldn't resist teasing her. 'Of course it could be that I want to marry you to improve my image in the local community. Marriage to Nurse Thorpe would surely make me truly respectable and no one would have any hesitation in granting me permission to establish a children's convalescent home at Riggholm.'

But the teasing note in his voice fell on deaf ears. Believing that only cold calculation lay behind his sudden proposal, Sue looked away at the sand-dunes again.

'I'm not giving the right answers to your questions, am I?' he said quietly, and she shook her head dumbly.

'Would something like this help you to make up your mind?' he offered gently, and once again she felt his fingers under her chin. But his mouth was within an inch of hers when her whole body stiffened in rejection of his assumption that he could persuade her to do what he wanted by making love to her.

He withdrew at once.

'No need to panic,' he said dryly. 'I've never forced myself on an unwilling woman yet, no matter what Paul Hurst might have led you to believe. I take it the answer is no.'

She could only nod again.

'I could ask why too, but I won't,' he said, and she noticed a muscle tensing at the corner of his mouth as he exercised self-control. Then in a low voice he added, 'Once I had the impression that you trusted me even though you knew very little about me.'

For a moment the magic of Lovers' Lane, sweet-smelling and misty, was about her, the roots of heaven.

'Oh, I did,' she cried sincerely.

'But now you're not so sure?'

'I don't know.' The magic faded instantly. 'Oh, I'm all mixed up. I don't know what to think. Please go away, Simon, and leave me alone,' she said wildly.

'Damn and blast Paul Hurst!' he said succinctly, and the

quietness of his voice made his cursing all the more effective.

Disturbed by the stridency of Sue's voice, Jemima apparently felt her security threatened and she stopped burrowing. She stood up and tottering over to Sue, sat down plump in her lap. Finding comfort in the child's soft round body, Sue cuddled her, moving a cheek against the fine silky baby hair.

'All right, Jemima. My turn to learn a lesson today,' said Simon soothingly as if he also realised that the little girl had been upset by the raised voices of adults. 'I can take a hint. I know when I'm not wanted.'

But there was a bitter undercurrent to his words which brought Sue's bewildered gaze back to his face. His eyes were dark and stormy and the lines etched originally on his face by disillusionment and exhaustion were back.

He twisted to his feet in a quick lithe movement and stood over her and the child, his hands on his hips. Sunlight picked out bronze highlights in his hair and the breeze billowed in his blue shirt. As usual his physical appearance made Sue feel slightly groggy.

He shivered a little as he looked down at her.

'Yes, the wind is definitely in the north today, and I'd thought it would be warm and was fool enough to come without my jacket,' he said. 'Which only goes to show how bad I am at predicting the weather. I think I'll go back by way of the shore. I believe it's possible to walk to Riggholm that way.'

She was suddenly perturbed and anxious about him. When he referred to the wind being cold he really meant her. He had expected her to be warmer, easier to bend to his will, perhaps, and by rejecting his proposal she had defeated some object he had wished to attain. She should feel pleased that she had had the strength of mind to refuse him, but she could only feel anxious.

'But it's a long way,' she said hurriedly, urgently. 'The tide will be turning shortly. Once it's turned it comes in quickly through the gap between Rigg's Bank and Riggholm. You wouldn't have a chance if ... Oh, Simon, don't go that way.'

He shrugged carelessly.

'Why should you care what I do?' he gibed nastily, and turning on his heel walked out of the hollow.

CHAPTER 6

IT was three o' clock in the afternoon. Aunt Emily and Grandmother Thorpe were sitting in the kitchen at The Gables. The room was dim because the spell of fine weather had broken and rain had lashed Seaport all day.

Sue scooped up spoonfuls of cake mixture and dropped it into white waxed-paper baking cases. She wished her head would stop aching. Grandmother's incessant flow of comment and observation were doing nothing to help the headache. And now to crown everything she was talking about Simon, the last person Sue wanted to hear or think about.

'Aye, I thought he was very sensible for a Rigg. A much better bet than either Matthew or Lupus, who were both slightly unstable in their different ways. He's much more level-headed. That'll be the Fell blood coming out. Good solid stock, the Fells.'

Level-headed. That was a kindly way of describing him, thought Sue mutinously. Downright calculating was her own way of describing Simon's approach to life. Calculating and unromantic. Why, even his attempt to kiss her yesterday had been deliberate. He had wanted to confuse her by awakening her senses, something which he had discovered he could do in Lovers' Lane. Well, he had failed in his attempt.

'He seemed to listen to my advice too,' said Grandmother complacently.

'What advice was that, Mother?' asked Emily, the ever-faithful giver of the right cue.

'I told him to get wed like our John. And I told him

there was a likely lass near at hand too.'

Sue experienced a sudden hysterical desire to laugh. Gripping her lips tightly together to stop the laughter from bursting out and shocking her relatives, she scraped the last of the mixture from the big mixing bowl and dropped it into the last case as Emily asked placidly while her knitting needles clicked rhythmically,

'And who is that, Mother? Knit one, slip one, knit two together and pass one over.'

'Our Susie, of course. They'd suit each other fine, and it would keep them both here in Seaport where the Riggs and the Thorpes have always lived.'

'You mean to say you told Simon Rigg he should ask me to marry him?' said Sue, her voice rising hysterically so that Aunt Emily looked up from her knitting and watched her niece carefully.

'Aye, I did,' replied Grandmother, still complacent.

After a worried restless night, tossing and turning, wondering whether she had done right in refusing Simon's proposal, going over everything that had been said in the hollow between the sand-dunes, trying to ignore the feeling that in some way she had hurt him, and trying above all to blot from her mind that last glimpse of him, alone and lonely, walking on the sands, Sue felt cross and in no mood to deal patiently with her grandmother's formidable self-assertiveness.

'You had no right to tell him that,' she burst out. 'How dare you interfere!'

'Now, love, don't be so upset,' soothed Emily anxiously. Then turning to Grandmother, she said with more severity than usual, 'Whatever made you say that to Mr Rigg, Mother?'

But Harriet Thorpe paid no attention to her daughter. Her bright eyes were watching her granddaughter's expressive face as Sue picked up the tray of uncooked cakes.

'So he's asked you already, has he?' she barked.

'Yes, he has. Yesterday. And the answer was no,' snapped Sue. She turned away to the cooker, placed the

350

tray on the top and bent to open the door of the top oven.

'Why?' rapped Grandmother. 'Why did you refuse?'

'Because—oh, because I didn't like the way he asked me,' retorted Sue as she put the try in the oven. 'Ouch!' she exclaimed as she accidentally burnt her arm on the hot oven door.

'Here, love,' Aunt Emily was beside her, 'come and sit down and drink your tea. You're looking peaked. I hope you're not trying to do too much while Ralph is away.'

'No, I'm all right. I didn't sleep very well last night, that's all,' muttered Sue, wishing for once that Grandmother wasn't there so that she could confide all her troubles to her kindly understanding aunt to whom she had taken her problems ever since her mother had died.

Emily's eyes were gentle as she poured more tea and handed the cup to Sue.

'I know it couldn't have been an easy decision for you to make,' she was saying. 'He's so handsome and so pleasant and it would have made a change to have an actor in the family. It isn't easy for any of us to say no. Just think of your grandmother when Matthew asked her. For weeks, even months afterwards she must have wondered whether she'd done right in saying no to him.'

'Don't talk about me as if I wasn't here,' grumbled Grandmother. 'It was no hardship for me to refuse Matthew. I didn't love him. Now, what didn't you like about yon lad's way of asking you, miss? What's made you so particular all of a sudden? I suppose because he didn't go down on his bended knees and swear he'd love you for ever you thought he didn't mean what he said. I'm warning you, Susie, if that's the sort of proposal you're wanting from a man, you'll wait for ever.'

If he'd said he loved me, first, I'd have told him to publish the banns straight away, I'd even have married him by special licence, thought Sue wildly. But he didn't say it, not once.

'He was too deliberate,' she said aloud. 'And now that I know you suggested it to him I'm glad I refused.'

'Humph. You're a fool, Susie. I'd thought better of you. Of course he was deliberate. Marriage is a serious step not to be undertaken lightly. If you think you'll get another chance and that he'll come again asking you the way you want to be asked I can tell you now, your thinking is wrong. A Rigg never asks twice for anything. I know the breed, and that one is as proud as any of them,' said Grandmother severely.

'But remember, Mother, you said yourself he has Fell blood in him, too,' said Emily gently, noting how white Sue had gone.

'And you've just admitted that you refused Matthew because you didn't love him,' attacked Sue, rather shakily. Her grandmother's reprimand worried her, pointing out as it did that Simon had been deliberate because he had been serious. 'He asked me to marry him because he wants a housekeeper, a child and someone to help him establish a children's home, not because he loves me. And I refused because—well, because I don't love him.'

'If that's how you feel, Sue, we'll say no more about it, shall we, Mother?' said Emily, giving Grandmother a warning look because she had noticed the tears brimming in Sue's eyes.

'I'm sure I'm sorry I ever opened my mouth,' replied Grandmother huffily. 'Not love him, indeed! Never heard such nonsense in my life. Why, you know nothing about love, and you won't ever know if you go around expecting people to be perfect.'

And that was really the trouble, thought Sue, later, when they had gone. She didn't know anything about love. She didn't know whether the leap of delight she had felt when Simon had walked into the yard yesterday afternoon was love or just the physical reaction to his physical presence. She didn't know whether this awful aching sadness she was feeling because she had rejected him was love for him or merely a silly yearning for something which she had denied herself by her own words and actions.

Surely if she loved Simon she would have accepted him

no matter how he proposed to her, no matter what mistakes he had made in the past. If only the ghost of Caitlin Hughes hadn't raised its head, she would have fallen in love with him, but as it was until the ghost was exorcised she didn't think she could trust him enough to love him.

So she spent her spare moments in futile speculation about her own feelings, wishing she had someone in whom she could confide, someone like Jill who knew about love.

Ralph returned and brought Penny back with him, a Penny who was still thin and who had dark shadows under her violet eyes but who seemed glad to see her child and who was more settled and happy. Obviously Ralph's and her love had withstood the test which it had just undergone, for they seemed very pleased to be together again.

Sue decided it was no use confiding in Ralph about the situation between herself and Simon because she imagined he would call her a fool as Grandmother had done, and at the moment she felt too sensitive about the subject to take any more criticism. As it was she had difficulty in meeting his eyes when he asked her if she had seen anything of Simon recently.

'Only once. He came to tell me he'd talked to various authorities about a children's home. I haven't seen him since,' she said.

'No?' Ralph's right eyebrow took on a wicked slant. 'And I'd thought you two would be as thick as thieves as soon as my back was turned.'

'Oh, do I smell a secret romance?' said Penny eagerly. 'Is there something between you and this Simon Rigg, Sue?'

'There's something,' Ralph answered for her with a mocking grin, 'but I'm not sure whether you'd call it a romance. A love–hate relationship is more like it, and it usually goes on when I'm not here.'

'Remember what I said I'd do if you didn't keep quiet about it,' threatened Sue.

'I remember,' he said. 'Sorry, love,' he added to Penny, 'I've been blackmailed into silence.'

But Sue guessed he would tell his wife all about the 'romance' as soon as he was alone with her.

With Penny's return, Sue's routine changed. No longer entirely responsible for Jemima, although she still dressed her in the morning and gave her breakfast, so that Penny could rest, she was able to concentrate on the work connected with the bed and breakfast business. Sometimes she found herself thinking nostalgically of hospital life and knew that she could never dedicate herself wholly to running a boarding house or hotel in partnership with Ralph. However, as always taking pride in whatever she undertook to do, she worked hard and before she knew what had happened it was almost the end of June and the tourist season was well underway, making business brisk.

It was with a faint shock of dismay she realised one evening that she hadn't seen or heard anything of Simon for over three weeks. Not that she hadn't thought about him. She had. In the quietness of her room at night the last action of her day was to look across the bay to make sure he was still at Riggholm. And every night the yellowish light would twinkle back at her through the trees, assuring her he hadn't left.

But when she heard from Mrs Kent that he hadn't been seen in the village since that time he had gone to the sand-dunes with her and Jemima she began to feel anxious. Supposing, after all, he behaved as Matthew had done when Mildred Fell had turned him down in favour of his brother? Supposing he did what she had tried hard to prevent him from doing, cut himself off from everyone, it would be her fault. She would be just as responsible for what happened to him as he had been for what happened to Caitlin.

Time and again the sight of him as she had last seen him, a solitary figure against a backdrop of flat sand and glittering sea, returned to haunt her. Would he always be like that, alone and lonely, becoming more and more reserved?

She became so worried about him that in the end she asked Ralph if he had seen Simon since he had come back.

He gave her a slow assessing glance before answering.

'Yes. I've been over to see him a couple of times about Rigg's Bank. I've been hoping he'll do something about making available some money for repairs.'

'What did he say?' She really wanted to say, 'How did he look? Was he well?' But it wouldn't do to appear too eager to know details with Ralph watching her with his hawk expression.

Ralph noticed the attempt on her part to appear unconcerned and decided to try his hand at acting.

'Gave me the rough side of his tongue. Sour as a lemon, just like when he came. Seems to have no interest in anything except the garden.' His eyes narrowed as he noticed Sue gnaw anxiously at her lip. 'What happened while I was away?' he asked. 'What's happened to make him change again? He was doing so well. But now ... well!' He made an expressive gesture with hand and shoulders as if he had given up all hope where Simon was concerned.

'How should I know what happened?' Sue quavered.

'Now stop hedging. You know very well what I mean. Something happened between you and him. If you don't tell me I'll ask Gran. She's bottling something up and she's fit to burst.'

Rather than let him hear her grandmother's biased account Sue reluctantly told him about Simon's proposal and her refusal.

'But I thought you liked him?' exploded Ralph, forgetting his part. 'I could tell by the way you kept looking at him when you thought no one else was watching that day at Greenthwaite. And then of course there was no doubt he liked you. He wouldn't have gone to tea there if he hadn't known you'd be there.'

'How do you know?' asked Sue, astounded.

'He told me,' said Ralph simply. 'He said Gran had promised faithfully that you and Jemima would be there and that was why he'd accepted her invitation.'

Sue remembered Simon's mischievous smile when he told her that he had gone to look after Jemima.

Ralph heaved a deep sigh and she looked at him anxiously. His heavy eyebrows were pulled together in a dark frown.

'Well, all I can say now is that you can say goodbye to any hopes you had of Riggholm becoming a children's convalescent home, and the local improvement association can say goodbye to any hopes of raising the money to repair Rigg's Bank. He's leaving soon. Talking about going back to London. And then we'll be back where we started—an empty house going to rack and ruin, and no money to mend the Bank, which I reckon will burst the next gale we have. Just think, Sue Thorpe, of all you've thrown away.'

'But he didn't say he loved me,' she blurted out, goaded beyond endurance, and he glanced at her sharply.

'So that's your problem. He messed it up, did he? That's odd. I'd have thought that being an actor he'd have known how to put it across to you, dressing it up with all sorts of romantic nonsense. Instead I suppose he was honest with you, and you, with your romantic head in the clouds, took offence.'

He glanced at her again. She had gone very pale and for the first time he noticed she had lost that fresh, clear-eyed look which had distinguished her and which had prevented her from looking plain. She looked downright unhappy and it occurred to him that the time had come to offer some sound brotherly advice.

'You'll have to go and see him, Sue, before he leaves. He won't come to see you again. He's a Rigg, remember. The ball's in your court and if you've any sense, you'll be returning it and not letting any stupid pride stand in your way. Need I say more?' he said gently.

She shook her head. She understood perfectly what he meant. But he didn't know about Caitlin.

The conversation with Ralph stayed with Sue all that day, nagging at her, requiring her to come to terms with herself. The most unpalatable fact that he had told her was that Simon was leaving Riggholm. Yet why should he stay? Now that he was better and had found himself there was no reason for him to stay. But if he left what was the point in her staying on in Seaport for the rest of the summer?

The thought occurred when she was brushing her hair which was almost shoulder-length, in preparation for going to bed. She stared at herself in the mirror above the dressing table. Wide brown eyes stared back at her accusingly.

'You're a fraud, Sue Thorpe, a hypocrite,' she whispered. 'You said you were staying for the summer to help Penny and Ralph. You pretended you didn't want to leave Seaport because you love it so much in the summer time. But you meant you wanted to stay because Simon Rigg is living at Riggholm and ever since he came into your life everything has been transformed, even your home village.'

She attacked her hair again, brushing it until her head hurt as a sort of punishment for deceiving herself. Then she switched out the light, went to the window and looked across the bay. The light glowed in the purple night. How many more nights would it shine out through the trees? How much longer would Simon be there in the old creeper-covered house? Would she be able to bear staying in Seaport when he had left? Not seeing him for nearly four weeks had already played havoc with her peace of mind. How would she feel when he had gone out of her life for ever?

She covered her face with her hands and groaned. She shouldn't have refused. She should have said yes because she loved him. She would never be happy until she could live with him, laugh with him, fight with him, share with him. He was her other half.

But why hadn't she realised that until she had refused to marry him? Because she had looked at him only with her eyes and through the eyes of others. She had been so busy trying to avoid being deceived by him that she'd decieved herself. Instead of being led by her own original instinctive trust in him she had allowed his silence about Caitlin Hughes distort her mind's view of him. Hadn't he once said he had learned never to ask his father questions about subjects close to his heart because he knew he wouldn't receive any answers. Wasn't it possible the same was true of him? He wouldn't talk about Caitlin because it hurt him to talk about her.

She took a last look out of the window and then climbed into bed. Staring up at the shadowed ceiling she struggled with her pride. As Ralph had said she must make the next move. But how? What excuse could she find to go over to the house which she had once vowed she would never visit again?

She was still looking for a reason the next afternoon when Jack Martin looked into the kitchen to say he had just brought a 'party' from the station who was looking for somewhere to stay, and was there any room. Sue told him to tell the 'party' to go to the front door and she went through the house to open the door when the bell rang.

The 'party' turned out to be a tall blonde woman of about thirty-five years of age, elegantly dressed in a black pants suit. A black sombrero-styled hat framed her long oval face and from under its brim a pair of clear green eyes surveyed Sue from top to toe before a well-shaped mouth smiled pleasantly.

'I'm Diana Witham,' announced the woman, as if the name should mean something to Sue. 'Paul Hurst suggested that you might be able to put me up if I decided to come here. Can you?'

Trying vainly to remember where she had heard the name before and wondering why the supercilious, cynical Paul had recommended The Gables to this well-dressed sophisticated woman, Sue opened the door wider and said,

'Yes, we can. Please come in.'

Diana Witham picked up her neat shiny black suitcase and her equally neat shiny black hatbox and entered the wide hallway.

'How long do you wish to stay?' asked Sue politely. 'I have to ask so that I'll know which room to give you.'

'About a week. I shouldn't think it will take me any longer for me to do what I have to do, and if the weather is going to continue like this I don't think I'll want to stay any longer. Does it always rain like this?'

'No. We often have very good weather this time of the year. This storm blew up during the night. It should be over by tomorrow morning. I'll give you a room at the back of the house with a view over the bay, although I'm afraid you won't be able to see much today.'

Sue picked up the case and led the way upstairs to the first floor and along a passage to the right. Taking a key from her pocket she unlocked the first door and pushed it open, suggesting that Diana Witham entered the room first.

'Why, this is lovely,' exclaimed the visitor, glancing round at the antique furniture. She walked across to the window to look out at the blurred view of the bay. 'Is the house very old?'

'Not as old as some around here. Early Victorian.'

'It has wonderful atmosphere, both restful and romantic, and you've done well to keep the furnishings in the right period and yet comfortable,' said Diana Witham. She sat down on the padded window seat and looked across the room at the patiently waiting Sue. 'Paul was right about you, too. He said you were a no-nonsense sort of person on first sight but that you had beautiful eyes, full of dreams.'

Slightly disconcerted by the cold appraisal in those clear cold eyes and by the personal comment, Sue took refuge in asking a question.

'Are you a friend of Mr Hurst's?'

Diana Witham chuckled throatily.

'Yes, but for a long time he's wanted me to be more than a friend. We met recently at a party given by a mutual friend and I was very interested when he told me he'd passed through Seaport a few weeks ago, because I had received information that another friend of mine was living near here. And then Paul told me how he'd happened to be lunching in Whitehaven when he saw Simon Fell ... with you.'

'Simon Rigg, you mean?' said Sue through suddenly stiff lips. Now she remembered where she had seen Diana

Witham's name. It had been in the caption beneath the picture in the magazine which Derek had given her to read. Diana Witham was the 'good friend' of the actor.

'Simon Fell to me, dear. Has been for years, ever since he joined the repertory company of which I was the leading lady. We were recently in a play together on the London stage.'

'Oh, you must know him very well, then,' said Sue.

'I thought I did until a few months ago,' said Diana Witham, and there was a curiously vicious note in her voice. She looked at Sue, another long appraising glance, and then rising to her feet went across and closed the door quietly. Then she came and sat on the bed.

'You look the sort of person who can be trusted with a confidence,' she said, and the warm pleasant smile appeared again, although the eyes remained as cold as the tarns, those small lakes high up in the mountains. 'You see, once, in a fit of pique, when I first knew Simon, I married someone else. It was a mistake. However, a divorce put an end to that piece of foolishness and I was hoping that the chance of working again with Simon in a play might lead eventually to marriage with him. Then that silly little fool Caitlin Hughes took an overdose, and Simon in a sudden fit of the blues threw everything away and disappeared from view. I was so mad because he'd ditched me and everyone else in the play that I decided I never wanted to see him again. But,' here the slow smile appeared again, 'he has various attractions which I've never been able to resist, so I hired an enquiry agent to find him. It took the fellow ages and cost me a fortune, but he found him in the end. And to think that if only I'd been patient and waited, I'd have learned where Simon was living from Paul! Ah well, that's life, I guess.'

Diana, the Latin name for the huntress goddess in classical mythology. Of course, why hadn't she realised it before, thought Sue. How subtly Paul Hurst had worded his message to Simon. And Simon had understood and had expected this visitor who was now lounging on the bed.

But Diana Witham was talking again and it was important that she should listen to every word.

'Yes, it was amazing really, that is to those of us who had known Simon. He'd always seemed so cold, off-stage, so untouchable. Nothing mattered to him but his career.'

'Did you know this Caitlin?' asked Sue.

'My dear, all of us in that play knew her. She was for ever at the theatre haunting him. I dropped many a hint suggesting she should get lost, but she was too starry-eyed to hear, so in the end I just told her the truth—that he wasn't in love with her and that one day he and I would marry.'

'Did she believe you?'

'I think she did. Anyway, soon afterwards she stopped coming to the theatre and then a month later she was found dead.'

'What did Simon say when he heard the news?'

'Not a word. Wouldn't even give an interview to the press. They interviewed me and I told them exactly what I thought had happened. He'd been friendly with her because through her he hoped to reach her father, the great Evan, and when he'd achieved his end, a film contract to make three big films, no less, he dropped her. How was I to know Simon would take offence at what I'd told the press and walk out on me? He'd never seemed to care what anyone said or wrote about his private life before. Ah, well, it's over now and I've forgiven him for ditching the play. It's a funny thing, you know, but time after time I find myself forgiving him.'

Everything was falling into place, thought Sue. Here was the trouble-maker, Diana the huntress, who wanted Simon and was prepared to do anything to get him.

'And now I'm here and I'm dying to know which is his house,' continued Diana, who having found a captive and docile audience was enjoying herself, playing to the galley for all she was worth. 'He never told me he'd inherited a house and a fortune, the brute. As soon as I heard about him from Paul, who is excellent at ferreting out information, I came. Paul said he was sure you'd be glad to help me and show me the way to Riggholm.'

The pleasant smile was back, but the eyes were still cat-like and watchful.

'Oh ... er ... yes,' stammered Sue. 'But don't you think ... I mean Simon won't be expecting you. Shouldn't you let him know you're here first?'

'And wait for an invitation?' said Diana. 'Oh no, that isn't my way at all. I like surprise tactics, dear. I'm hoping they'll do the trick. I'm hoping he's so fed up being there on his own, cut off from his first love, which is the theatre, and with which none of us have ever been able to compete, that he'll welcome me with open arms and will be delighted to read the new play which Tubby Shaw has sent him to read. And within six months he'll be back on the boards and I shall be Mrs Simon Fell.'

'Rigg,' countered Sue firmly. 'Rigg is his proper name.'

'Who cares? What's in a name? It's the man who counts. Now when can you take me to Riggholm?'

'But don't you want to go alone?'

'No. I've thought about this very carefully and knowing Simon and how adept he is at taking avoiding action I think it would be better if a third party were there, a witness, if you like, of our meeting, so that if in the future he should go back on anything he might say to me at our meeting I can always ask you to support me. Also I presume you know the house and where to look for him if he doesn't answer the door,' said Diana. She noticed a flash in the dark brown eyes and she laughed, a gurgling, knowledgeable laugh. 'Ah, I can see that you do, just as Caitlin knew that other house. Could it be that I've come just in time to save another lamb from the slaughter? Paul suggested it might be the case, which is another reason I made haste to come here. When shall we go, dear? This evening?'

'No, I'm afraid that won't be possible,' said Sue with a coolness she was far from feeling. The woman was frightening with her well-laid and tastily-baited trap, truly a huntress. 'I have to work here. Tomorrow morning after ten-thirty would be better.'

362

Diana stifled a yawn.

'I'm inclined to agree,' she drawled. 'I'm a little tired after that terrible journey north and I'd like to look my best. I hope the weather clears up. I have the most ravishing dress and hat I want to wear.'

The chances of Diana Witham being able to wear her ravishing dress and hat the next day were pretty slim, thought Sue, as two hours later she struggled across the wet sand at the head of the bay in the driving rain. She was on her way to warn Simon of Diana's coming. It hadn't taken her long to decide that it was only fair to warn him, although he had already been alerted by Paul Hurst's message.

Of course, it was possible that he might be glad to see Diana, as that woman had suggested, since she was a link with his first love, the theatre. But Sue had a strong instinctive feeling that he wouldn't, and from now on she was trusting her instinct where Simon was concerned.

Rain dripped down her face and she stuck out her tongue to catch some drips, an action left over from childhood. She was glad it was raining because that meant that visibility was poor and there was less chance of anyone seeing her crossing the sands. She hadn't told Ralph or Penny where she was going. To have done so would have meant too many explanations about Simon which she didn't feel free to make.

By the time she reached the front door of Riggholm she was extremely wet, and shivering. She pulled the old-fashioned bell-pull and waited to hear the bell ring in the house. Tonight the house seemed unfriendly, dark and damp. She knew that Simon must be in because his car was parked on the driveway.

Suddenly the light over the door went on, illuminating the quivering wet leaves of the creeper. The door was pulled back sharply, almost angrily, indicating the mood of the person opening it. He stood there staring down at her, dressed in the grey suit he had worn to tea at Greenthwaite and his magenta-coloured shirt and gaily patterned tie were two fantastic blobs of colour under the harsh light.

As he recognised her his eyes narrowed suspiciously and he surveyed her bedraggled state, making no move to let her in.

'Well?' he demanded.

It was going to be much harder than even she had anticipated and in the face of his hostility she almost turned and ran.

'I have something to tell you. It's important.'

'Again?' was all he said. But he stood back and motioned to her to enter.

She stepped past him into the hall and immediately noticed the smell of paint. She looked around curiously. In the hall there were step-ladders, trestles and planks of wood and all the other equipment used by house decorators.

'Ralph told me you were doing nothing to the house,' she said accusingly, swinging round to face him, speaking as if they had seen each other only yesterday.

'Did he? Then he was mistaken,' he replied coolly. 'May I take your raincoat?'

Shades of their first meetings! He was as far away from her as he had ever been then. Her heart began to sink like a lead weight.

'I'm not staying long,' she replied quickly, on the defensive.

'All right, so you're not staying long,' he retorted irritably, 'but you can't stand around in wet clothes. Take it off. Take your boots off, too. I expect they're full of water.'

They were wet and taking them off wasn't easy because there was no chair in the hall and she had to balance on one leg while she pulled the boot off the other. When the boot came off water cascaded all over Simon's suede-shod feet.

'I'm sorry,' she muttered.

'Why did you have to walk in weather like this?' he asked. 'If your journey was really necessary, why didn't you come in the van?'

'I didn't want Ralph to know I was coming here,' she said as the other boot came off and water showered out.

The boots off, she struggled out of her soaked raincoat and then removed the drooping scarf from her head. Wet hair clung to her head and she felt a mess, a miserable mess. So miserable that on meeting Simon's faintly critical gaze as it roved over her appearance she felt like bursting into tears. She wouldn't have felt so badly if he hadn't looked the last word in elegance, less like a hermit than anyone she'd ever seen.

He took her raincoat, and leaving her to carry her boots and her scarf, he led the way to the kitchen where warmth reached out and enveloped her, dispersing the misery a little. Then she noticed the changes. Instead of the old porcelain sinks there were new shining stainless steel ones. Cupboards with Formica tops stretched along the walls. The old dresser had gone and so had the old wall cupboard, pulled away to reveal plaster work in need of attention.

Sue stared at the evidence of renovation and wondered what it all meant.

Simon hung her raincoat on the hook by the cooker, draped her scarf over the rail and put her boots on the floor close to the warmth. That done, he glanced at his uninvited guest who was standing still as if awestruck by the sight of the new sinks and cupboards.

He stared his fill, noting that her face was washed clean by the rain and that her hair hung in damp strands from its centre parting. Her thin ribbed cotton sweater with its laced-up front was damp also and it clung closely to her body. Rain had also reached her short brown skirt, making a dark mark down the front. Below the skirt her shapely legs were bare and slightly tanned, slimming down to well-turned ankles and bare broad feet. As he glanced at them the toes of one foot turned upwards and then straightened again.

The bare twitching toes amused him. He watched carefully, waiting for them to turn up again, and then he noticed she was shivering.

'Sit down,' he ordered peremptorily, and she came out of her trance, gave him an apprehensive glance and sat on the edge of a chair. She sat stiffly, her hands folded in her lap, as she had sat among the sand-dunes. Stiff and starchy, he had once thought her to be, and so she looked now, sitting primly upright.

He went to a cupboard and took out a full bottle of brandy and placed it on the table. Then began the search for glasses. He found them at last and went to rinse them at the sink.

'I suppose you're doing the house up to sell it,' said his visitor in a prim little voice. 'Ralph told me you're leaving.'

'And I suppose you've come to say goodbye,' he replied, mimicking the frozen tones of her voice exactly, as he returned to the table and began to pour brandy into the glasses. When he had done that he handed one to her and said, 'Here, drink that. It'll warm you and stop that shivering.'

She looked at the glass he held out to her and then glanced at him warily.

'I couldn't,' she said.

'Couldn't what? Say goodbye to me or drink the brandy?' he said drily.

'I couldn't drink the brandy,' she said swiftly. 'How arrogant of you to presume that I couldn't say goodbye to you.'

'Why can't you drink it?' he said, ignoring her taunt. 'Suspicious of my intentions? I wonder you dare set foot in this house, you're so suspicious of me.'

'Oh no, it's not that. I'm not used to brandy and it might go to my head.'

'And you might say and do things you don't normally let yourself say and do, which might be interesting for me,' he suggested softly, insinuatingly. Then more curtly, 'Drink it willingly or I'll make you.'

'You wouldn't dare,' she retorted, leaning as far back in the chair as she could.

He leaned over her, grasped a handful of her hair at the back of her head, pulled hard and held the glass to her mouth.

'Well?' he said threateningly.

366

She raised a hand, took the glass from him and sipped a little of the liquor.

'That was a very nasty way to behave,' she chided as he released her hair and sat on the corner of the table.

'But the only way to deal with you when you're in one of your stiff and starchy moods. You're very strong-willed and need firm handling,' he replied easily, and picking up the other glass he sipped some of the brandy.

Sue, feeling the warming effects of her one sip, cautiously drank some more and felt the tension, which had caused her to shiver just as much as being drenched by the rain had done, begin to ease so that she was able to look at him. To her surprise he was staring at her feet. She looked at them too. The sight of her own toes, all bare, stretched out for him to inspect, shocked her a little and she sat up straight again and tucked her feet under the chair.

'I was fascinated by the way you can turn up your toes. Do you know when you're doing it, or is it a twitch which occurs only when you're nervous?' he asked.

'I'm not nervous.'

'Not now,' he agreed. 'But you were when you came into the house and into this room. You were all tensed up. Why?'

She looked down at the rest of the brandy in her glass. How could she tell him her nervousness had been caused partly by excitement at seeing him again and partly by anxiety about how he would receive her? He seemed to be so unaffected by her arrival. He was handsome and confident, cold and heartless, just a little out of reach. She realised ruefully that she had been hoping to find him desperate and weary as he had been the first time she had come to Riggholm so that she could have offered comfort and then love to him. But how could she offer love where it wasn't even missed?

'I can only assume by your silence that you were nervous because you were afraid I might propose marriage again to you or try to kiss you,' he was saying. 'Well, let me put your mind at ease. I shall do neither. I don't believe in repeating myself.'

That hurt far more than it should. But instead of rousing her to retort as it might have done once it brought tears to her eyes and she remained crouched in the chair gazing down at her brandy.

Simon finished his drink and set the glass down with a click on the table, then studied the girl crouched in the chair. Her hair was beginning to dry and red lights were appearing in it. Normally she would have been out of her corner fighting in reaction to his taunt, but tonight she was unusually subdued.

'Was your journey really necessary?' he prodded.

She sniffed, searched wildly for a handkerchief, but it was in her raincoat pocket. So she dabbed ineffectually at her face with her fingers, hoping he hadn't seen the tears which had escaped to creep down her cheeks.

'I think it was,' she said gruffly. 'I came to tell you the huntress has arrived. She's at The Gables and tomorrow I'm bringing her over here to see you. She wants to surprise you, but I thought you'd like to know she's coming so that you can avoid her if you want. If you'd only had a telephone installed I could have phoned you and then I needn't have come and ...'

'Wait, wait!' he was half laughing. 'Who the hell is the huntress?'

Sue looked up, forgetful of her tears, not realising they had dried streakily on her cheeks and that her dark eyelashes were stiff and wet.

'Have you forgotten? Paul Hurst said the huntress was stalking her prey, and today Diana Witham came to Seaport. She told me it was she who sent the enquiry agent to look for you. She wants to marry you.'

He didn't seem very interested in what she was saying, being more intent on staring at her face with a rather anxious expression in his eyes.

'Why have you been crying?' he asked, quite irrelevantly, Sue thought.

'I haven't. It was the brandy. It made my eyes water.'

'I don't believe you.'

A little silence followed that exchange. Their eyes met and held, and words were forgotten temporarily. Then Sue looked away, reached forward and put her half-empty glass on the table.

'Diana was the huntress in classical mythology, wasn't she?' she asked in a tremulous voice.

'Yes. So she's finally caught up with me. I wonder where she got the idea that she's going to marry me? As far as I can recollect, and my memory is fairly accurate, you're the only woman to whom I've ever proposed.'

'Then why should she say such a thing if it isn't true?'

'Diana has always worked on the principle that if you say something often enough it'll come true,' he remarked cynically.

'She's also brought a play for you to read. A man called Tubby Shaw sent it, and she predicts that before six months is up you'll be back on the stage.'

She noticed how his eyes lit up when she mentioned the play and acknowledged to herself rather bitterly that Diana had known what bait to use.

'Is she right, Simon?' she whispered.

'Possibly she is,' he said evasively. 'It seems that acting is all I'm fit for, and after my most recent and unproductive encounter with the local authorities on the business of making this place a children's home I feel like dropping the whole idea and going back to London tomorrow with Diana. How long did she say she was staying?'

'A week. She said she thought that would be long enough.'

'If she'd waited a little longer I could have saved her the journey,' he said in a hard voice. He cast a quick under-browed glance at Sue, noting the averted face, the stiff upright pose, and his eyes narrowed speculatively. 'But now that she's here,' he continued in the same hard voice, 'I may as well make use of her. I'll marry her. She looks respectable even if she isn't, and she could put on an act of being

369

very interested in this scheme for helping the underprivileged child. In fact, if I know Diana and what she really wants, her act will be good enough to fool anyone into thinking that to establish a children's convalescent home was all she'd ever wanted to do. It'll be good publicity, now I come to think of it, and should go down well if Tubby wants us to do another play together. I'll put it to her tomorrow. What time will she be here? I hope the weather clears up and then I can show her what I've accomplished in the garden.'

As he warmed to his theme his voice lost its hardness and the cold lump which Sue was beginning to regard as her heart grew heavier and heavier. So he would be able to show Diana, who would be wearing her ravishing dress and hat, the wonders he had performed in the garden. Oh, yes, she could imagine them, both tall and graceful, strolling on the lawn proposing and being proposed to. And later they would go up to Carlisle together and Diana would put on an act to convince the authorities that she sincerely wanted to help poor sick children.

Sue felt suddenly ill with jealousy and hate. Jealousy of Diana who would become Mrs Simon Fell or Rigg after all and hate for Simon's cold planning ahead. She couldn't stay with him a minute longer. She drew a shaky breath and stood up.

'We'll be here after ten-thirty. I'd better go now,' she said woodenly. She lifted down her raincoat. It was still unpleasantly damp. When she had put it on and fastened it she sat down to pull on her boots.

'I'll drive you back,' offered Simon, and there was a strange urgency in his voice.

'No, thank you. I prefer to walk,' she snapped.

'Not in this storm. It's getting worse. I can't let you go.'

'I'm used to this weather and I'd rather be out in the wind and the rain than sitting in a car with someone as despicable as you are,' she said proudly, her head high.

She stalked out of the kitchen and along the passage.

With his longer strides he overtook her and reached the front door before her. He stood with his back against it so that she couldn't open it. It seemed to her that he was unusually pale and his eyes glittered with an anger which frightened her.

'Why am I despicable?' he demanded.

'Because you use people,' she accused, and his face seemed to go paler. 'You were going to use me, now you're going to use Diana to get your own way over the children's home. You used Caitlin...'

'I did not!' The denial rang out furiously.

'Everyone says so.'

'You mean Paul Hurst said so, and he said so because that's what Diana told him, that's what she told the press or anyone else who would listen. She spread the rumours which you, like everyone else, believe.'

'But why?'

'Because she was so damned jealous of Caitlin and of me that she had to strike at us both somehow. She was jealous of Caitlin because I was sorry for the child and tried to help her, forgetting that any attention I gave to anyone female would be noticed by Diana, marked down and used later against me.'

He paused, breathing hard.

Sue stared at him, realising that she was near the truth at last.

'Why were you sorry for Caitlin?' she asked.

'She was an only child neglected by both her parents, both of whom are brilliant in their own lines. Caitlin wasn't brilliant. She was an ordinary, lonely little girl. I'd known what it was like to be lonely and unwanted at that age and I used to find time to listen to her and talk to her. She gobbled up the attention I gave her like a hungry bird gobbling up crumbs and came back looking for more. I couldn't turn her away. It would have hurt her too much. That was my mistake. If I'd kept her at a distance she wouldn't have come so often to see me and no one would have listened to

Diana and drawn the wrong conclusions about Caitlin's death.'

'She loved you,' Sue accused.

'In the way, perhaps, that you love Ralph, as a brother. I loved her too, but not enough to save her. She became ill soon after I signed the film contract. She had to stay in hospital to have a series of tests. She came to tell me the results one evening just before the play started. She said she had an incurable disease and that she had a couple of years to live. I didn't believe it, but I had no time to discuss the problem there and then because I had to go on stage. When I came back to the dressing-room she'd gone. Next day she was found dead after taking some of her mother's sleeping tablets.'

'But if that's what really happened why didn't you deny the rumours?'

'You know so little of the world in which I lived that it'll be difficult for you to understand. Have you ever tried to change the way of thought of a group of people? Have you ever tried to change overnight the image of yourself which had been built up over the years by clever publicity? No, I can see by your expression that you haven't. It was the discovery that I was completely helpless, at the mercy of Diana's spite, that made me realise I was no longer in control of my own life.'

'Why was she jealous of you?'

'Long-standing professional jealousy plus an overwhelming desire she has always had to possess me. It came to a head when I received better notices in the press for my performance in that play than she did. She was wild, and always looking for ways to pull me down. Well, she succeeded in a way, because when I realised that everyone believed her story that I'd used Caitlin to get that film contract, I was sick, sick to death of the whole set-up, the string-pulling and the mud-slinging. So I walked out. But you know that.'

'I didn't know about Caitlin before,' she whispered. 'You wouldn't tell me.'

'I couldn't, because I felt I'd failed her, and that hurt. She took her life because the balance of her mind was disturbed and I shall always regret that I didn't love her enough to stop her. Do you still think I used her?' Again there was an urgency in his voice.

Sue nibbled her lower lip. She had reached the truth at last. The ghost was exorcised and her original trust was vindicated. But the fact remained that in spite of what Diana Witham had done to him he had said this evening that he would marry her.

'I believe you,' she said. 'Please will you open the door now. I'd like to go home.'

'Not across the sands,' he said firmly. 'The tide's coming in and I'll drive you home. I'll see Diana while I'm over there.'

That did it. But she didn't argue and he opened the door, letting her go through first. Once outside Sue skipped down the steps and started to run along the drive. Around her the trunks of trees creaked as they swayed slightly in the increasing wind. Raindrops from their branches showered down, hitting her head with a force she could feel through the thin stuff of her scarf. Behind her she heard the car start up and she increased her speed.

Running blindly, she turned out of the drive on to the muddy, rutted road, splashing through the puddles. She slipped in one of them and crashed to the ground just as the car swung on to the road and came straight at her, its two headlights like great eyes boring through the grey murk, hypnotising her. She tried to scramble to her feet, to hurry to the side of the road before the car should hit her, but she slipped again and fell.

Gasping for breath, she saw the headlights illuminate the bushes at the side of the road as the car braked and swerved. It skidded, plunged off the road to the right, crashed through the thick undergrowth and came to a sudden stop against a tree trunk. The lights went out and the engine died.

This time she made it when she tried to stand up because

fear greater than any she had ever known gave her strength; the fear that Simon was either badly injured or dead.

'Simon,' she shrieked. 'Simon!'

She slithered and scrambled down the bank through the wet grass, oblivious of the bramble thorns which caught at her clothing. Below the bank she could hear the sinister hiss of water being driven on to the shore by the wind and was thankful that the car hadn't gone any farther and plunged into the raging tide.

She reached the car and wrenched open the nearest door just as Simon emerged from the other side. The relief at seeing him alive hit her somewhere in the solar plexus and made her feel giddy.

'Simon, are you all right?' she gasped faintly.

He was rubbing his forehead with his hand, but at the sound of her voice he turned and shouted furiously,

'Yes, no thanks to you, you stubborn little fool! What were you trying to do? Make me into a murderer? As if I hadn't enough on my conscience.' Then with a change of tone, anxiety taking the place of anger, 'Stop, Sue, stop it!'

Everything was swaying around her. She was going to fall. She knew she was going to fall because she couldn't stay upright any longer. Then someone's arms were around her and she was being held tightly against something hard and yet not hard, something covered with smooth material which was alive, moving, throbbing. Dazedly she realised she was in Simon's arms and her head was against his chest and it was his heart she could hear beating. She listened carefully. One, two, three ... Surely it had missed a beat?

'Don't pass out on me, Sue,' he was murmuring urgently in her ear. 'My experience with swooning females is limited to the theatre where they only counterfeit the fainting. Anyway, I can't really see that there's anything for you to swoon for.'

She raised her head and looked at him although she would really have preferred to stay leaning against him, feeling the caressing comfort of his fingers in the tangle of

374

her damp hair from which the scarf seemed to have slipped, listening to the magic of his voice which even when he was anxious held a subtle hint of mockery as if he couldn't take her predicament seriously.

'Yes, there is,' she retorted. 'I thought you'd been killed and that it was my fault. That's enough to make anyone swoon. Oh, Simon!' The grogginess was receding fast, but she couldn't stop the tears which gushed forth suddenly at the thought of what might have happened.

'Oh, Susan,' he mimicked shakily, and then suddenly, impelled by the same overwhelming force, they were touching each other, stroking each other's faces, gripping arms and shoulders, making sure no damage had been done. Gradually the feverish movements stopped and Simon's arms slipped round her again and then they were kissing, hungrily straining close to each other as if fearing someone or something might come and part them. And all the time the raindrops fell around them and on them, pitter-pattering on to the leaves of the trees, then sliding off to drench their hair and clothes.

At last they became aware of the wet grey world about them and drew apart.

'Oh, Simon,' said Sue, the all-practical woman, as she touched his wet jacket, 'your lovely suit will be ruined.'

He let out a crack of laughter.

'Oh, Susan! It's remarks like that which a man might find extremely unromantic when he's just kissed you with all the passion he can muster after having narrowly missed running over you with a car and having suffered a crack on his forehead in consequence.'

'I'm not unromantic,' she defended. 'It's you. You've no idea how to propose to a woman.'

'I'll not argue the point here and now. But let me say this—I have other suits, but there's only one you. Now let's go back to the house and drink brandy, to recover from shock, of course, and to find out why you were running away from me.'

He seized her by the hand and began to pull her up the

375

slope to the road.

'But the car——' she spluttered.

'Will you stop worrying about goods and chattels? That can stay there until morning and then your big brother can do something about it.'

They reached the road and he turned in the direction of Riggholm. Sue pulled back reluctantly.

'I'd better go home,' she muttered. 'They might be wondering where I am.'

'Let them wonder. Riggholm is home and it's nearer than The Gables,' he argued. Then seeing she was still hesitant he went close to her and put his arms around her and whispered, 'You're cold and wet and in a state of shock, not fit to be out alone on a night like this, for all that it's Midsummer's Eve and we should be wandering in the woods together. Come home with me, Sue, and I'll tell you how much I love you.'

'Oh!' She was startled. 'Do you really love me? I mean do you know?'

'I've known for some time, but I refuse to elaborate here with rain dripping down my neck while you catch pneumonia. In spite of indications to the contrary I do have my romantic moments, but I prefer to have them in comfort.'

'But I thought you'd decided to marry Diana after all?'

'That was something I thought up on the spur of the moment to see if I could get a reaction from you. I did, slightly more than I bargained for, but it cleared the air between us, which had become a little foggy recently. Now, are you coming, woman? Or do I have to drag you by the hair?'

He twined one hand in her wet locks and pulled.

'I'll come,' she agreed in surrender.

Some time later when the storm was at its worst and early darkness had closed in on that Midsummer's Eve which had no resemblance to summer, Sue sat in the corner of the enormous shabby chesterfield in the sitting-room at Riggholm. She was swathed rather than dressed in an elegant

376

dressing gown belonging to Simon made of peacock blue silk, the feel of which against her skin gave her sensuous pleasure.

Leaning back, she watched Simon who had also changed out of his wet clothes into hip-hugging fawn pants and a blue sweater, kneeling before the big hearth in which he had lit a fire which so far had refused to burn properly. Using a huge pair of old-fashioned brass tongs he was moving pieces of charred wood around when a gust of wind swept down the chimney and grey smoke puffed out into the room.

He swore and flung the tongs down in disgust.

'I can't understand it,' he complained. 'I had a marvellous fire going in here a few days ago.'

'It's the direction of the wind,' said Sue calmly. She knew all about the vagaries of chimneys in old houses. 'You should have these old fireplaces taken out and central heating installed.'

He turned and scowled at her as he picked up the heavy poker.

'Take this out? I'll have you know it's genuine Adam. Also I happen to like open fires.'

'They're wasteful and they pollute the atmosphere,' she replied primly.

'Maybe they do, but they provide a much more romantic setting for a declaration of love. I had it all planned. If we can't have starlight and a carpet of bluebells in the woods this Midsummer we'll have flames leaping in a darkening room, and now look at this murky mess.'

Sue couldn't help giggling as she glanced at the new spiral of smoke which had curled out from under the arch of the fireplace.

'We'll both be kippered soon,' she said. 'We could sit in the kitchen.'

The poker went down with a clatter and the springs of the chesterfield twanged as Simon flung himself beside her. He leaned towards her, his eyes blazing with blue fire.

'The kitchen is not a convenient place for making love,'

377

he grated between clenched teeth, and her heart hammering madly, having lost its leaden feeling for some reason or other, Sue shrank back in the corner and played with the tassel at the end of the dressing-gown sash.

'You don't believe I love you, do you?' he said more quietly. 'You think I'm acting, playing a part, pretending in order to get something I want. Well, I do want something. I want *you*.'

His last three words were said loudly and they echoed round the big room. Sue glanced fearfully into the shadowed corners, half expecting Matthew Rigg to appear and object to such uninhibited behaviour on the part of his only nephew.

Then her shoulders were seized by rough hands and she was forced to look at Simon again.

'But Diana ... you said ...' she stuttered. 'The children's home.'

His mouth twisted in a grimace of self-disparagement.

'I seem to have been my own worst enemy,' he said. 'You see, when I began to feel better and I began to think logically again it occurred to me that I could still be a good actor if I could escape from the world of the theatre and the films occasionally, if I had a real home, a bolt-hole like Riggholm where I could be myself. And I decided that it would be more of a home if there was someone here, someone who cared for me and for whom I could care; someone who wasn't connected with the theatre and who wasn't dazzled by the glamour. And I realised that very person had been here in the house. You were the person.'

'But why did you send me away?'

'Because, as I told you later, I was still unsure. You see, the unpleasant publicity after Caitlin's death made me wary in regard to personal relationships. But gradually I realised you had trusted me when you hadn't known who I was. Do you remember the night you came and lit the cooker and we laughed with and at one another? I think it was then that recognition took place for you as well as for me. But unlike your cousin and your friend, you and I had both had recent unhappy experiences and so we shied away from each other. Anyway, when I decided that you were possibly the person with whom I wanted to share my life, and I set out to know you better, I found that you'd changed and had become more suspicious of me, all because of an article in a magazine.'

'If only you'd told me about Caitlin the way you told me tonight!'

'I couldn't, then, and in any case, to my obtuse masculine mind I couldn't really see what my relationship with her had to do with you and me. Then that day in the sand-dunes I wanted you so badly I tried to rush you, and I sought the remedy for love too soon. I should have waited until you'd recovered from Paul Hurst's visit. You refused, and quite honestly, Sue, I didn't know what to do. I couldn't believe that you didn't love me as I loved you.'

'But you didn't say you loved me,' she objected.

'You didn't give me a chance. I was going to tell you when I kissed you, but you rejected me so fiercely I knew there was no point in persisting. I wasn't sure whom I should blame most, Paul Hurst for gossiping or that fellow in Newcastle for petrifying your emotions. Sue, I asked you to marry me because I loved you and I knew that was the only way I could have you. I need someone in my life like you to give it stability, to give me an anchor, and I think you need someone like me.'

'Oh, I do, I do!' Her emotions suddenly became un-petrified. 'Oh, if only you'd said you loved me before you asked me to marry you I wouldn't have refused,' she cried.

'And we wouldn't have wasted three whole weeks,' he said dryly, and gave her a little punishing shake. 'Remember in future that when I kiss you it's because I love you.'

'But what about Diana?'

'She'll have to be handled carefully because she has that play in her luggage and I want to read it. But I think that can be done, and a certain Mr Paul Hurst will be for ever grateful to us for sending her back to him.'

'You mean she is his affair of the heart?' queried Sue.

'But definitely. Always has been.' He gave her a curious narrowed glance. 'Tell me, Sue, would you have come here tonight if Diana hadn't appeared on the scene?'

She tangled her fingers in the tassel of the sash again.

'Well, I was looking for an excuse to come because Ralph said you were miserable like you were when you came and that you were leaving, and I knew I couldn't bear it if you went away.'

'So Ralph had a hand in all this too, and I wouldn't be at all surprised if Paul told Diana about you and that brought her hot-foot in pursuit of me, giving you your excuse to come here. And now it's up to me to devise a way to send Diana back to Paul.' He laughed suddenly. 'It has all the subtleties of a Shakespearian plot! All's well that ends well. It is going to end well for us, isn't it, Sue?'

'A beginning, not an ending,' she reminded him.

'You realise, I hope, that the other reasons I gave for wanting to marry you still stand. I still need a housekeeper, I still want a child with Spanish dark eyes and I still want to realise your dream for you and turn Riggholm into a children's home or something equally useful. With your help I should be able to have all three, if they're what you want too and you won't mind me spending some of my time in the theatre. Are you willing to try?'

He released her shoulders and moved away from her, making no attempt to sidetrack her with lovemaking. He was playing fair, telling her how it would be if she married him. She would have to share him with his other love, the theatre. Would her love be strong enough? It had wavered badly, but had survived and was perhaps now stronger for having been tested early. There was only one way she could decide.

'If I agree to try will it please you?' she asked.

'It will please me very much.'

'Then the answer is yes, this time.'

He kissed her then. It started as a gentle kiss, but somehow it got out of hand and it was some time later that they both became hazily aware that the front door bell was clanging and at the same time the wrought-iron knocker on the door was being used with great effect. They had only time to glance at each other enquiringly when the front door was opened, heavy footsteps tramped through the hall and Ralph appeared in the doorway of the room.

'Are you there, Simon?' he said urgently. 'Rigg's Bank's burst and the homes at the lower end of the village are flooded. We're having to evacuate them. Oh, I'm sorry, I didn't know you were busy.'

By now Sue had disentangled herself from Simon's arms and they both stood up to face Ralph.

'Don't be silly, Ralph,' she said. 'It's me.'

'So it is. I wondered where you'd gone. Come to your senses at last, I see.' He slanted a mocking glance in Simon's direction. 'You'll have to marry her now, lad. You realise that, I hope? I'll insist.'

'Oh, why don't you tell us why you've come here instead of making insinuations and playing the heavy father,' said Sue, blushing furiously.

'I've come to ask Simon if he'll put up the five families here for a few nights until flood goes down. I've brought one family with me. If you could welcome them with a cup of tea and make them comfortable it would go a long way to calming them,' he answered. Then noticing that Simon was staring at him as if he was crazy he added, 'Well, after all, lad, you are squire and it's your bank . . . at least it has your name on it, so you should do something to help. And maybe this accident will convince you once and for all that we need money to repair it.'

Simon grinned at him.

'All right, Ralph, you win. Bring them in. The more the merrier tonight, because it's Midsummer in spite of the weather, a truly festive occasion, especially since Sue has agreed to be my wife.'

Ralph grinned back.

'Good!' he said gaily. 'But just think of all those old Riggs and Thorpes turning over in their graves in the churchyard at the thought of a Rigg marrying a Thorpe.'

He glanced critically at the smoking charred wood in the fireplace. 'A right mess you've made of lighting that fire. Happen you need a wife,' he added mockingly, and left the room.

Simon drew Sue into his arms and kissed her again.

'Happen I do need a wife,' he murmured, mimicking Ralph's way of speaking. 'As soon as possible, please. And so begins a new and exciting relationship. Never to end.'

'Never to end,' Sue repeated dreamily, 'because it's the remedy for love.'

THE LEGEND OF THE SWANS

The Legend of the Swans

Will Fox's keen glance disturbed Gina. "You're the kitten-soft kind of woman who likes comfort," he said, rousing her from the lethargy that followed her fiancé's death.

Well, she'd shown his overbearing brother that she had stamina. She'd accept Will's challenge to work in the wilds of Scotland.

Gina's arrival coincided with the return of the swans, which, legend decreed, would keep her in the glen forever. Surely that couldn't be true?

CHAPTER ONE

It was seven-thirty in the morning. Shafts of yellow sunlight, filtering through fine net curtains, touched the pale face of the young woman who was asleep in the bed, and brought to life a faint sparkle of red in the ruffled mass of curling brown hair which was spread across the pillow.

The bell of the alarm clock on the bedside table began to sound. It was a pleasant mellifluous chiming, designed to make waking up a joy. It stopped and music took its place, filling the room with gay noise composed to make any sleeper want to bound out of bed to greet the April morning happily.

Long brown eyelashes, which were spread out on the pale cheeks, fluttered and were raised to reveal the gleam of green-shot golden eyes. A long slim arm appeared from under the bedclothes, stretched out and the music was turned off. With a groan the young woman turned in bed and buried her head into the plump soft pillow.

The door of the room, which was partially open, swayed slightly as a blue Persian kitten sidled through it. The kitten paused in the doorway, his whiskers quivering. Suddenly he yawned widely, revealing a tiny pink tongue and sharp white teeth. Gathering himself together, he sprang forward and landed on the bed. Purring loudly, he began to knead the bedclothes with his padded paws. The expression on his face was ecstatic, the eyes half-closed, the black line of the mouth turned upwards at the corners.

Georgina Marriott, known to her friends and relatives as Gina, opened her eyes properly this time, looked at the kitten and then at the clock. Had she imagined hearing the alarm? She peered at it. Seven-thirty-five. April the twelfth. Memory came surging back and she groaned again, not wishing to face up to it, trying to escape from the knowledge that Oliver was dead and that she was not married. Once more she buried her head in the pillow as if by doing so she could forget, but the kitten continued with his kneading and his purring, knowing that if he did so his owner would be forced to wake up properly.

Listening to Blue's familiar purring, Gina kept her eyes stubbornly closed. In the back of her mind she knew that she had set the alarm purposely last night to wake her early because today she was going for an interview for a job and she wanted to spend the morning preparing her clothes so that she would look her best.

But, as on every morning since she had received the news that Oliver Fox, her fiancé, had been killed in a car crash, inertia claimed her. Of what use was it to get up and dress, to put on an act, to attempt to be interested in a job, when all she wanted was to die?

The door was pushed open more widely and a tall blonde girl, dressed in a blatant purple woollen suit which she wore with a white high-necked sweater, entered the room carefully carrying a cup and saucer. Gilt bracelets jangled on her wrists, gilt chains swung between her firm breasts and gilt ear-rings glinted wickedly amongst her blonde curls. An expression of concern marked her normally cheerful face as she glanced at the recumbent figure in the bed.

'Wakey, wakey, Gina love. Here's a nice cup of tea. Remember you're going for that interview. Make the most of yourself. Why not wear that new suit, the wheat-coloured one?'

'I'm not going,' mumbled Gina from the depths of the pillow.

Lynette Brown, affectionately known as Birdie on account of her first name, looked troubled.

'But, Gina, it'll do you good to go out. Remember what Dr Lambert said? You must have a change. Go away from here. Make a complete break with the hospital and everything associated with Oliver. Only that way will you recover from the shock quickly.'

388

Still Gina did not move. Only the back of her ruffled head was on show.

'Birdie, will you please do me a favour?' she asked in a muffled voice.

'Of course I will, love,' said the generous kindly Birdie.

'Go to work now,' said Gina flatly.

Exasperation took the place of tender anxiety on Birdie's face.

'Oh, Gina, what am I going to do with you?' she exclaimed.

'You don't have to do anything,' replied Gina. 'I've got to work this out by myself. Thanks for the tea. Now, please leave me alone.'

'All right. But I still think you should go for the interview. Don't forget I'm giving a party tonight for Pam Harwood.'

Gina groaned, 'Must you?'

'Yes, I must. I promised. And remember it's Mrs Chadwick's day for cleaning the flat, so you'll have to get up some time.'

'Leave the front door unlocked so that she can get in,' muttered Gina. 'G'bye.'

' 'Bye,' replied Birdie, and shrugging her shoulders helplessly she left the room.

Gina did not move. On the bedside table the tea grew cold. Blue, the kitten, stopped kneading, and curling round and round several times to make a warm spot, he settled down to have a snooze.

The minutes ticked away. The shafts of sunlight grew stronger and their angle altered slightly. The outer door of the flat opened and a small woman entered the hallway, removed her coat and hung it in a cupboard. She went into the kitchenette and clucked her tongue at the pile of dishes there. Then, humming to herself, she began to run water into the sink.

In the bedroom all was quiet except for the purring of the dozing kitten. Suddenly the telephone on the bedside table rang persistently. The kitten sat up, eyes wide, ears twitching. The telephone continued to ring. Gina moaned, stretched out an arm, lifted the receiver and, with her eyes still closed, murmured sleepily into the mouthpiece.

'Hello.'

'Did I wake you up?'

The question was asked by a masculine voice with a lazy lilt to it. The voice was completely strange to Gina. Her eyes flew open and she sat up straight in bed.

'Who's speaking?' she asked.

'Will Fox. I almost became your brother-in-law. I'd like to come and see you.'

The voice was crisp now, autocratic in tone.

'Oh—er—Mr Fox,' stuttered Gina, caught with her defences down. 'That's nice of you, but I'm sorry, I'm not receiving visitors yet. I haven't been very well and...'

'That's too bad,' the voice interrupted her, rudely, Gina thought. 'I won't be this way again and I'd like to see the girl Noll chose to be his mate. Also I've something to suggest which might be of interest to you. Sure you won't change your mind about inviting me round?'

'Mr Fox——' Gina began.

'Captain,' he corrected curtly.

'Then, Captain Fox, I've said I'm sorry I can't see you,' she said in a cool clear voice. 'Oliver's death was a great shock to me. The doctor recommended rest and then a complete change. He said I was to have nothing to do with anything or anyone connected with Oliver.' That wasn't entirely true, but it was all she could think of on the spur of the moment. 'Besides,' she added, 'I don't think you would gain anything by meeting me at present.'

There was silence at the other end of the line. She was just thinking that he had hung up or that they had been cut off, when he spoke again, softly and yet clearly, almost as if he were beside her in the room and was whispering into her ear.

'I think you should let me be the judge of that,' he said.

'I don't know what you mean,' she stammered.

'I mean I prefer to be the one who decides whether I shall gain anything by meeting you.' He was crisp again. 'I could be at your flat in a few minutes.'

'Oh no, Mr—I mean, Captain Fox, I couldn't possibly be ready to meet you. I don't want you to come here. I want to be left alone, I've no wish to see anyone.'

She became suddenly aware that the ringing tone was sounding in her ear. He'd hung up on her.

Gina set the receiver back on its rest and leaned against the pillows. Two patches of brilliant colour glowed in her cheeks, fantastic blobs of red on her pale cheeks. When she glanced downwards she saw her breast was rising and falling rapidly as her heart beat faster than normally.

Captain Fox. Captain William Fox. Captain of what? She tried to recall what Oliver had told her about his elder brother, but her mind was foggy on the subject. She could remember sending a wedding invitation to him, against Oliver's wishes. The address had been somewhere in the Highlands of Scotland. He had replied, but she could not remember whether he had accepted or declined the invitation.

Her forgetfulness acted as a spur. Before she realised it she was out of bed and standing at her dressing table, searching through the papers in the top drawer. Small and slender, but with softly-rounded seductive curves, her legs shapely below the hem of her short diaphanous nightgown, her brown hair cascading about her shoulders, she looked much younger than her twenty-three years and gave an initial impression of someone who was helpless and vulnerable.

The replies to the wedding invitations were not where she expected them to be. Then she remembered they were in a folder in the drawer of the bedside table. She padded over the shaggy orange carpet, gently chastising Blue, who had left the bed and was rubbing himself against her bare legs.

She was leafing through the correspondence in the buff folder when there was a knock on the door. It struck Gina that Mrs Chadwick was extraordinarily noisy that morning, then she called to her to come in.

Behind her the door opened and closed just as the letter from William Fox appeared. The name leapt out from the paper, bold and authoritative-looking, just as Blue hissed and spat, and jumped up on to the bedside table, knocking the cup of cold tea over and scattering letters, cup and saucer to the floor.

'Naughty Blue!' scolded Gina, lifting the kitten from the floor. 'It's only Mrs C.'

'No, it isn't,' said the masculine voice she had heard only a short time ago over the phone. 'It's me.'

Gina whirled round. Above the kitten's blue fur her face was white, her green-gold eyes were shadowed, deeply sunk in their sockets, but they blazed with indignation as they met those of the man who leaned against the closed door of her room.

'Who let you in?' she demanded.

Big-shouldered and slim-hipped, he was built like a heavyweight boxer. His nose looked as if it had once been broken and re-set and a white, wicked-looking scar, which could have been caused by a knife wound, angled across one lean cheek. He wasn't handsome with a suave regularity of feature, as Oliver had been, but neither was he ugly. His face suggested a rugged rock-like personality and she guessed he could be rough when he wanted.

'Mrs Chadwick did,' he replied with an urbanity which contradicted his looks. His light blue eyes, deep-set under thick dark eyebrows, were busy taking in her appearance, making her feel very conscious of the brevity of her gown. She hugged Blue close to her as if for protection from that curious gaze, but the kitten objected to being detained, struggled free and, jumping down, went to hide under the bed.

'She had no right! How dare you come in here! Go

away!' The words came out with the rapidity of machine-gun fire as Gina, furious by now, clasped her arms across her bosom.

He grinned and his face changed miraculously. She was looking at a mischievous boy who would never take no for an answer.

'Surprise tactics have always been my speciality,' he said calmly. 'I told her I was a close relative of yours and that I'd come to see you to commiserate with you in your loss. We had quite a little chat together about you. You've sunk pretty low in her estimation.'

Gina was surprised.

'Oh! Why?'

'You've been lying in bed until all hours, opting out.'

Gina discovered she was shaking. How dared Mrs Chadwick discuss her with this rude man! She tried to object, only to find she was so angry she couldn't speak. So she just stood there by the bed, pale and trembling, as her unwanted visitor strode over to the dressing table and picked up the photograph of Oliver. He stared at it for a moment and then swung round to look at her.

'And how long have you been wallowing in self-pity?' he asked in easy conversational tones, as he replaced the photograph.

Her body stiffened, her head came up and her eyes sparkled dangerously.

'You may not have realised it, Captain Fox, but the days of keeping a stiff upper lip are over. None of us have to pretend we're not hurt any more,' she retorted. 'The man I loved was killed two days before our wedding day. Is it any wonder I'm shocked and sorry for myself?'

In one stride he was standing over her, his light eyes cold, his wide expressive mouth curling into a sneer.

'It isn't any wonder Mrs Chadwick is disappointed in you,' he jeered. 'No spunk, she said.' His glance shifted to the bedside table and he reached out a hand to pick up the bottle of sleeping pills which had been recommended by Dr

393

Lambert. He read the label and his scornful gaze came back to hers. 'Is this the drug you use to help you to escape from reality?' he demanded sternly.

Anger was now an insistent throb, beating through her mind, thrusting aside the torpidity which had claimed her body and mind for the past week. She longed to strike at this man who had invaded her room. Why, even Oliver had never been in this room and had never seen her in such a dishevelled state, and she had been engaged to marry him!

'I don't take drugs,' she flung at him icily. Hands clenched by her sides, shoulders back, she stood up straight, no longer concerned about how she looked. 'Now, will you please go before I call the police?'

The sneer faded from his face and was replaced by the mischievous grin. He folded his arms across his chest and rocked back and forth on his heels.

'Why do you want to call them?' he asked mildly.

'You've invaded my privacy and I wish to dress,' she retorted haughtily.

'Oh, is that all that's bothering you?' he murmured, letting his glance rove again. His gaze come back to hers. Devilment was in his eyes now, blue and twinkling, dancing between soot-black lashes. 'Go ahead. I can turn my back. It won't be the first time I've been present in a woman's room when she's not dressed.'

'That I can believe,' she hissed, and reached blindly for the telephone receiver. Her hand never reached it because he caught and held her slim fingers in his much bigger hand. Furiously she tried to twist them free, but shock and unhappiness had weakened her and she was no match for his superior strength. Suddenly very near to tears, she found herself leaning against him helplessly, rather appalled at her own violent behaviour.

'I'll go from the room on one condition,' he offered softly, and she felt his breath stirring her hair.

'Yes?' she whispered. 'What is it?'

'If you'll come into the other room when you're dressed

and listen to a suggestion I have to make to you.'

The roughness had gone from his voice. It was kind, almost tender. She lifted heavy eyelids and gazed up at his rock-like jaw. It was difficult to believe that he was Oliver's brother. Oliver's hands had never grasped hers bruisingly, like this. Oliver's mouth had been chiselled, almost perfect in shape. Above the rock-like jaw this man's mouth was wide and curving and the lower lip was full and sensual.

'Well? Do you agree?' he asked.

Her glance went past his mouth, past the jutting broken nose to his eyes. They were not the soft pansy blue of Oliver's, but the cold clear blue of ice-girt seas, and beyond them the craggy, lined forehead was framed by close-clinging slightly curly hair, several shades darker than Oliver's had been, almost black.

'I agree,' she submitted, thinking she had no alternative but to agree when held like this.

'That's better.'

He released her and left the room. Alone, Gina took several deep breaths, examined closely the marks left by his fingers on her wrist. Then she went over to her wardrobe and began to take out the clothes she intended to wear.

She guessed that Oliver had told her very little about his elder brother because their relationship had not been a very close one. After all, there had been a difference of eight years in their ages. Oliver had just celebrated his twenty-seventh birthday before he was killed, which meant that the big brute in the next room was thirty-five. He looked every day of it too, thought Gina waspishly, and then she wondered at her own strong feelings. She had not felt any strong emotion for days.

Having chosen a pair of sleek wheat-coloured pants and a matching angora sweater to wear, she went off to the bathroom. For fifteen minutes she soaked herself in the perfumed water. Then she dried herself in a leisurely fashion, trying all the time to recall anything that Oliver might have told her about his brother.

If she remembered rightly Oliver's father had been killed in some sort of accident when serving with the British Army. William had been seventeen at the time and had followed in his family's tradition by joining the Army, much against his mother's wishes.

His mother had married again, choosing as her second husband a man who followed a much more peaceful profession, that of the law. When her younger son had shown an interest in medicine as a career, she had encouraged him. Gina had met Oliver and William's mother, now Mrs Ann Simpson, and she had the utmost admiration for her calm well-organised attitude to life and her active participation in the various voluntary associations in the town of Leamington, where she lived.

Oliver had studied medicine at Birmingham University, and it was while he was in his fifth and final year there and she was in her third and final year at the local domestic science college that they had met.

The only daughter of fairly wealthy parents, Gina did not really have to work, but she had always been interested in cooking and in household management, so her parents had thought the training would be useful to her.

When she had qualified, with honours in institutional management, she had gone to work in the hospital where Oliver had been working as a house surgeon. It was at that time she had left her parents' home and had moved into a mews flat, in the still-elegant suburb of Edgbaston, which she shared with her old school friend Birdie. Six months later she and Oliver had become engaged.

Quickly, plans had gone ahead for a wedding. It was to have been the spring wedding of the year, between Oliver, son of the late Lt.-Colonel Geoffrey Fox and Mrs Ann Simpson of Leamington, and Georgina, daughter of Mr and Mrs David Marriott of Henley-in-Arden. Birdie was to have been the only bridesmaid and John Oldham was to have been best man. They were to have gone to Malta for their honeymoon, returning to live in a pleasant modern detached house in one of the better suburbs of Birmingham.

Everything had been ready. She had given up her job at the hospital to spend the last week of her life as a single woman preparing herself mentally and physically for marriage. Although there had been moments, terrifying moments, when she had wanted escape from her commitment to Oliver and run as far away as possible, she had never admitted those moments to anyone.

Then the blow had fallen. Returning by car from a Rugby Union game, which he had gone to see at Twickenham with some friends as his last fling as a bachelor, Oliver had been killed in one of the multiple crashes caused by fog on the motorway, and the dream of the perfect marriage had been shattered.

Suddenly the door of the bedroom was hit by the flat of someone's hand. It trembled and Gina spun round from the dressing-table mirror, fully expecting William Fox to march in. But the door didn't open. He merely called through it.

'Hurry up. I haven't got all day to waste waiting for you to titivate.'

Grimacing at the door, Gina controlled a desire to throw something at it, and with an effort she sang out sweetly,

'Coming!'

She turned back to the mirror, finished applying her lipstick, tilted her head this way and that to survey the way she had arranged her hair, high on her head in a smooth chignon with a few corkscrew curls dangling tantalisingly in front of her ears. Then, satisfied that she looked cool and sophisticated, she opened the door, went down the passage and made what she hoped was a stunning entrance into the living room.

The effort was wasted. The living room was empty. From the kitchenette came the most delicious smell of bacon and eggs cooking mingled with the aroma of percolating coffee.

Gina's stomach gurgled noisily. She hadn't eaten properly for days and now she felt ravenously hungry. Surely Mrs Chadwick wasn't cooking breakfast? She wasn't paid to cook, just to clean.

Quickly Gina crossed the room to the door leading to the kitchen. She looked round it. William Fox, seeming much bigger because of the smallness of the room, was standing by the cooker. His shabby tweed jacket was off, the collar of his checked Viyella shirt was undone and its tail was half in and half out of the waistband of his thick Army pants. His tie was dangling over the back of one of the kitchen chairs.

'What do you think you're doing?' demanded Gina in her most supercilious tones.

He glanced round.

'Cooking breakfast. Want some?' he asked genially. 'I've set a place for you, working on the theory that the smell of someone else's bacon cooking always makes me feel hungry and so the same might apply to you.'

He opened the oven door, took out two plates which had been warming, and expertly scooped bacon and eggs from the frying pan on to them.

'You've no right——' Gina started, then changed her mind and exclaimed, 'Where's Mrs Chadwick?'

'I sent her home. Told her to come back on Monday. I hope you don't mind.'

'Mind!' Gina discovered she was shrieking in a most unbecoming shrewish fashion. 'Of course I mind. She hasn't finished cleaning yet, and she won't be able to come on Monday because she works for someone else then.'

'Well, you're doing nothing these days, so it won't take you long to make the beds, vacuum and flutter a duster about,' he replied easily, setting the plates on the table. 'There you are. Eat up,' he ordered. 'How do you like your coffee, black or white?'

'I don't. I prefer tea,' she seethed.

'Ah well, *chacun à son gout.* You'll have to make the tea yourself.'

He sat down on one of the spindly kitchen chairs and

Gina wished quite viciously that it would disintegrate beneath his weight and land him on the floor.

'Come on, George,' he invited. 'Sit down and be friendly.'

She sat down and tried not to be interested in the food. He cocked a dark eyebrow at her, pursed his lips and gave a wolf whistle.

'My mother told me you were beautiful,' he murmured, 'but I didn't believe her because she'd always had a tendency to exaggerate about anything connected with Noll. He was her blue-eyed boy and he always had to have the best of everything, even if in actual fact, he didn't always choose the best. This time, however, I'm willing to concede she's right. He really picked a winner in you when it came to looks. You are beautiful, or you will be when you've matured a bit more. That outfit you're wearing is the latest, I suppose.' His grin flickered wickedly. 'I must say I prefer you in a nightie. Are you sure you won't have some coffee?'

'Captain Fox——' began Gina, speaking through gritted teeth.

'I shan't object if you call me Will, George,' he put in generously.

'My name isn't George!' she flared, goaded beyond endurance and stamping her foot on the floor.

'Tut, tut, what a temper,' he reproved her. 'You'll feel much better when you've eaten. Then we'll talk for a while, then we'll go out. I thought we'd go for a drive somewhere. I'd like to go to Stratford. I've never been there. Later we could have dinner together at some country pub. By then I think we'll know each other pretty well. Don't you, George?'

'I've no wish to know you any better,' she replied coolly.

Picking up her knife and fork, she began to attack the food which she could resist no longer. He stared at her bent head with narrowed observant eyes, picked up the coffee pot and poured coffee into the second cup. He pushed the cup and saucer across to her.

'Georgina's a heck of a name,' he remarked. 'What did Noll call you?'

'If by Noll you mean Oliver, he called me Gina like everyone else does,' she replied haughtily.

He made a face at her.

'I prefer George,' he said.

'I don't really care what you prefer since I have no desire to be acquainted with you any further,' she said silkily, wondering how she could get rid of him.

'You may not have any desire to be, but you're going to be. I need a woman.'

Her head came up in shocked reaction to this blatant statement and he grinned at her.

'One who can cook for large numbers of people and knows how to cater for them,' he continued easily, although his eyes twinkled with devilment again in acknowledgement of her shocked reaction.

Looking down at her surprisingly empty plate, Gina wondered what he had in mind, but told herself that she wasn't going to show the slightest interest.

'Aren't you going to ask me why I need a woman who can cook?' he prodded.

Slowly she raised her eyelids to give him a bored glance from under her long lashes. He grinned again knowingly and pushed his empty plate aside.

'Devastating! I bet you've practised that for years,' he murmured mockingly, and to her annoyance blood rushed to her cheeks. He leaned across the table and brushed a long forefinger down her cheek. 'Now that is real and gives me hope,' he commented. 'Your mother tells me you cook very well.'

'*My* mother?' she exclaimed.

'Yes, I called to see her. She gave me your address and phone number.'

'Why do you need a cook?' she asked. 'You cook very well.'

He inclined his head in mock appreciation of the compliment.

'Grudgingly admitted, but at least you admitted it,' he said. 'Have some more coffee while I tell you why.'

Meekly Gina passed her cup. It was the best coffee she had ever tasted.

'Soon after I left the Army I bought a small estate in the Highlands of Scotland. My intention was, and still is, to farm it,' he explained. 'It's good sheep country and I already have a sizeable flock. There are fertile fields and the possibility of rearing some dairy cattle. One day it occurred to me I could share the beauty and peace of the place with others and make a little money on the side. I decided to run an adventure camp for young people of both sexes. I ran into an old friend from my army days who was very interested in the scheme. Last summer we organised our first two camps. They were a great success, but from the point of view of some of the parents of the youngsters attending they had one drawback.'

'What was that?'

'There was no woman on the premises.'

'I understand,' said Gina. 'Couldn't you or your partner get married?'

'He did. Last November, and we thought our problem was solved,' he said drily. 'His wife was very enthusiastic at first. She'd been a social worker in a slum district of Glasgow and she thought up the idea of having groups of poorer youngsters come to the camps. We decided to run one for them this Easter. Now Madge is expecting a child and can't cope. Twenty youngsters are due to arrive next week and we need someone to cook for them.'

'Aren't there any local women willing to help?'

'No. You see the place is situated on the shores of a sea loch which is practically inaccessible from the landward side. There's no electricity. Cooking is done by Calor gas, which I haul in myself from Ullapool. Not many women these days are willing to put up with such conditions. I've interviewed a few and once they've learned that there's no

401

electricity, they've refused. Not many of them have measured up to my standards either,' he added cynically.

'Why don't you get married?' she asked curiously.

His face turned to stone and his eyes went blank.

'What makes you think that having a wife solves anything?' he retorted coldly. 'I tried marriage once. It didn't work.'

Gina raised her eyebrows. He met her glance squarely and smiled.

'I'm not going into details,' he murmured. 'Now when your mother told me that you'd trained in institutional management, and that the doctor had prescribed a complete change of scene for you to recover from the shock of Noll's death, I thought that you might be interested in, and possibly suitable for, the job. That's why I had to see you.'

He paused and glanced round the pretty kitchenette. Then he looked at her, his keen glance taking in the smooth crown of burnished brown hair, the smoothly applied make-up, the close-fitting expensive sweater and the fine white hands holding the coffee cup, and his wide mouth curled jeeringly.

'But now that I've seen you in your nice cosy little nest I realise I'm off-centre,' he said. 'You're the kitten-soft kind of woman who likes comfort, who likes to be adored and waited on, and who likes to be loaded with worldly goods. You're loaded too, aren't you, with money? I suppose that's why Noll wanted to marry you. I daresay you were going into marriage with a handsome annuity behind you, bestowed on you by your old man.'

Gina's fingers gripped the coffee cup. She longed to hurl it at him. His jeers pricked her pride and stabbed painfully at the vulnerable romantic heart she hid beneath her sophistication. It was just possible that Will Fox had hit the mark more closely than she wanted to admit.

'Oliver loved me,' she retorted. 'And I loved him. He would never have wanted to marry me for any other reason.'

Again he raised that infuriating right eyebrow at her.

'You think not?' he queried. 'Naïve, aren't you? Noll was like my mother.'

'And she's one of the most charming people I've ever met,' defended Gina.

'Charming, I grant you, but with an eye to the main chance. Ambitious to the core. You should have seen what she did to my father because he refused to climb any higher in his career. She was the reason why he was always volunteering for jobs where there were no married quarters,' he said, his mouth curving cynically. 'But far be it from me to destroy your illusions about people. Would you come and cook at the spring camp?'

Gina's eyes widened in bewilderment.

'B ... but you've just said I'm not suitable.'

'No, I didn't say that. I said that I didn't think you'd be interested in coming to the back of beyond, now that I've seen you in your setting. But I'm getting pretty desperate now. The boys are due to arrive next Monday. If you decide to come you could travel with me tomorrow, and stay until Madge can cope again. I expect she'd like to have company.'

'I ... I'll think about it,' Gina evaded the issue because it was surprisingly difficult to refuse.

He sighed heavily.

'That means you're not interested. All right, think, and while you're thinking we'll go to Stratford.'

'Oh, no, I can't. I have an appointment in Warwick at two o'clock,' said Gina, glad she had an excuse for retreating.

'An appointment for what?' he demanded.

'A job. With the county education committee's school meals service.'

'Then you can go there after we've been to Stratford,' he replied coolly. 'Do you have a car?'

'Yes, a Triumph Sports.'

'You would,' he remarked drily. 'A present from Daddy,

403

I've no doubt. We'll go in that. I'm driving a small truck at the moment. Very useful, home on the farm, but not really suitable for driving round the Warwickshire country lanes. Now, you go and make your bed and I'll wash up and then we'll go.'

'I . . . I . . .' stuttered Gina, who was not used to receiving orders.

He stood up and began to gather the dishes together.

'Come on, George, look sharp. It's a lovely spring morning and we're going to miss the best part of the day if you don't get a move on. By the way, who uses the other bedroom?'

'My flat-mate, Bir . . . I mean Lynette.'

'Now there's a name I could like,' he murmured. 'What's she like?'

'Blonde, five feet nine inches. I'm not sure of her other dimensions,' replied Gina with a touch of acidity. She was sure Birdie would like Will Fox. He had the physique and easy confident manner the blonde girl always admired in the opposite sex.

'What does she do for her living?' asked Will casually.

'She's assistant buyer in the women's fashion department of a big department store. Why do you want to know?'

'I'm just trying to find out what she's like and whether she'd object to moving into your room while I use hers tonight. Do you think she would?'

Gina stood there with her mouth agape as the water swished into the sink.

'Mr—I mean Captain Fox, it isn't a case of *her* objecting,' she said at last, 'it's whether I object. This is not a lodging house, nor can it be commandeered as a billet for the Army on the move.'

His grin flashed out and he lifted his shoulders in a careless shrug.

'All right, don't get all upstage at the thought of another woman sharing your bed. I could have offered to share it with you instead, but I thought that would be presuming on

404

our almost close relationship too far. If you don't like the idea I'll sleep on the sofa,' he said.

'You could sleep in a hotel,' sniped Gina, and he gave her a glance of mock-disapproval.

'Now, now, George, that isn't very hospitable of you. Your mother wouldn't approve. I slept in the spare room at your parents' home last night. Very comfortable, too. Go and change your pants for a skirt, and bring a raincoat. There just might be a shower while we're out.'

There was nothing she could have done to prevent it from happening, thought Gina defensively, when she sat in her car half an hour later and watched Will's hands on the steering wheel as he guided the vehicle skilfully through the traffic on the main road going south through the suburb of Solihull. Harking back to the conversation which had taken place at the flat, she realised she hadn't tried very hard. She had gone and changed into the skirt which went with the golden-coloured suit, and she had brought a raincoat, a scarlet one.

The hood of the car was down and the soft spring air lifted the curls at the sides of her face, making them swing. It was, as Will had said, a lovely day. With a strange shock of surprise she noticed that the season had been working its magic in gardens and on the countryside while she had been moping in the flat.

Moping—that was exactly what she had been doing, and she would still be lying there in her bed, her eyes closed against the sunny day, wishing she could die, if this outrageous man had not come this morning and forced her to come with him. No, not forced, he hadn't done that, but it was difficult to describe what he had done. By a series of taunts and suggestions he had made her leave the bed, get dressed, eat and come out with him.

What a misery she must have been during the past week! She had behaved like a spoiled child who had had her favourite playmate taken away from her. Not that she and Oliver had played much together. Theirs had been a serious courtship as suited a young ambitious doctor and the daughter of the managing director of an engineering company.

Yes, Oliver had been very conventional, but his brother was not. Having now met Will it was easy to understand why Oliver had talked so little about him. Understandable too was Mrs Simpson's silence on the subject of her elder son. He just did not fit in the comfortable middle-class community in which Ann Simpson lived and moved. She would always have to be explaining his odd behaviour and comments to her neighbours, who might look askance at someone who preferred to live in a wild inaccessible part of the country and who had tried marriage, but had found it didn't work.

She pondered his terse statement, wondering what matrimonial tangle lay hidden behind it. She imagined Will Fox could be quite difficult to live with and would require a lot of loving. He would also be difficult and demanding to work for. She had said she would think about his suggestion that she should go and cook for his adventure camp more as a way to put him off than anything else, hoping he would leave the flat and go north without her.

But he hadn't left, and it looked as if she was going to be saddled with him for the rest of the day, so any refusal to his offer of a job would have to be made to his face, a task she didn't relish as she was sure he wouldn't accept any excuse she made.

By evening it should be easier to give him a straight flat refusal. She was sure she would be offered a job by the county education committee. Her references were excellent and she had her father's influence behind her. Her mother, too, was well known. Yes, there was really no decision to make. It would be made for her that afternoon at the county offices, and later, safe and sound in the knowledge that she had a job, she would be able to send Will Fox on his way.

Pleased with her thoughts, Gina relaxed in her seat. They had passed through her home town of Henley-in-Arden and were now speeding along the road to Stratford.

The wooded slopes and neatly ploughed fields of the countryside were very familiar to her. Here she had often wandered as a child and, later, as an adolescent searching the woods and hedgerows for the wild flowers, so beloved by Shakespeare, who had wandered here himself, that he had scattered their names liberally throughout his plays. Violets, oxlips, woodbine, musk rose.

'Why do you want to go to Stratford?' she asked Will.

'Although I was born in Leamington, I've never been to Stratford,' he replied. 'I think it's time I went there, because I was christened William Shakespeare.'

Gina exploded into spontaneous laughter. Anyone who looked less like the Bard of Avon than Will Fox was difficult to imagine. It was the first time she had laughed since Oliver had been killed. She didn't know the difference laughter made to her. It drove the serious, slightly supercilious expression from her face and turned her into a natural, fun-loving girl with sparkling eyes, rosy cheeks and glinting white teeth, all of which her companion noticed with approval in his glance.

'Oh no,' she gasped. 'You'll be saying next that Oliver was named after Oliver Cromwell.'

'He was. Ironic, isn't it, that I turned out to be the soldier?' he said.

'He didn't tell me,' she exclaimed.

'He wouldn't,' he commented drily. 'No more than I used to tell anyone my full name for fear of being laughed at. Now I've reached the age when I don't care who laughs at me.'

'Whose idea was it? Your mother's or your father's?'

'I owe my name to my mother. She chose it in a rare moment of romanticism. You see, her maiden name was Hathaway, and that, combined with her christian name of Ann, gave her ideas. She was never able to find a Will Shakespeare to marry, so she called me after him. I think at one time she had a hope that I might live up to the name and become a poet or a playwright. She soon lost that hope

407

when it became very obvious that I was more interested in out-of-door activities than in reading or writing. My father, whose family had always had members in the British Army, retaliated when Noll was born by having him christened after his hero, Oliver Cromwell.'

Gina was laughing again.

'I wonder why he didn't tell me?' she said, when she had her breath back.

'I suspect he went all out to make an impression on you. Probably Mother told him not to tell you. He always tended to follow her advice.'

'He didn't tell me much about you, nor did your mother.'

'For the same reason, I expect. They'd rather you didn't know about me. I've been a great disappointment to them,' he replied cynically.

'Black sheep?' she queried, and saw his crooked grin appear.

'That's as good a description as any,' he said non-committally. 'Do you know Stratford well?'

'Every nook and cranny.'

'I hoped you might, because I want to see all the places —Anne Hathaway's cottage, the Grammar School, Holy Trinity Church, Clopton Bridge, the theatre, the lot.'

'Anne's cottage is at Shottery, and it wasn't really hers. It was called Hewland Farm and belonged to her father. She was just born there.'

'Then we shall go to Shottery too.'

Stratford was busy, but not as crowded as it would be later in the year when the hordes of visitors from overseas would cram into every hotel and guest-house. Gina and Will visited the house on Henley Street where Will Shakespeare's father had lived, then lingered for a while in the old Grammar School with its wooden beams and diamond-paned windows. In the church they stood in silent worship beneath the stone bust of the poet, in the chancel. Soft light, colour-mottled, filtered through the stained glass windows, adding to the sense of peace and timelessness.

It was peaceful too at Shottery. The cottage, built of mellow brick and timber and roofed with brown thatch, in that combination of various materials which is a feature of Tudor houses, basked in the April sunlight. Daffodils danced in the garden and birds twittered happily as they flew amongst the many trees and shrubs. Inside, in the kitchen, Gina and Will sat side by side on the narrow wooden settle on which, it is said, Anne Hathaway and Will Shakespeare had done their courting.

'It's more likely that they did their courting in the fields. To quote Shakespeare himself, "Between the acres of the rye,"' said Gina, with a touch of dryness.

'You sound disapproving. What's wrong with courting in the fields in springtime?' asked Will, raising an eyebrow at her.

'Nothing, I suppose,' she said, feeling the blood creep warmly into her cheeks as she encountered the knowing twinkle in his eyes. 'But I suspect he had to marry her because of the consequences of their courting.'

'Poor Will!' he murmured. 'If that was the case, *he* has my sympathy.'

Back in Stratford they paused on the grey Clopton Bridge which spans the river Avon. Once more side by side, they leaned on the old stone wall and watched two white swans glide downstream. Then they drove out of the town to the theatre, finding its bulky twentieth-century structure very different from the Tudor buildings in which they had spent most of their time.

There was no more time to linger. Leaving Stratford, they set out for Warwick. As they drove along country lanes, whose hedges were beginning to burst into leaf, the sky clouded over and rain threatened. In the county town, the walls of the still-inhabited castle loomed grey and formidable over the narrow thoroughfare.

Will left Gina at the front door of the County Council offices, saying he would come back for her in an hour. As he drove away Gina felt suddenly cold and nervous. For the first time since Oliver had been killed she was alone in the world outside her flat. The next step she would make by herself.

Suddenly she realised how much she had enjoyed the time spent with Will in Stratford. She was surprised how much she had known about the place and its famous playwright and how much she had enjoyed sharing that knowledge with Will. He had listened to her attentively, drawing out her knowledge with skilful interested questions, and she had a feeling he had enjoyed the tour as much as she had.

Pulling herself together, she told herself there was no need to be nervous. There would be several people on the interviewing committee whom she would know and she was sure the interview would go easily.

An hour and ten minutes later she emerged from the offices with an expression of bewilderment on her face. Across the road she could see the Triumph parked. Will 'Shakespeare' Fox was lounging behind the steering wheel.

Gina crossed the road quickly and slid into the seat beside him.

'Do you mind if we go back to Birmingham by way of Henley-in-Arden? I must go and see my mother,' she said breathlessly.

His eyes were shrewd as he slanted a glance at her.

'You didn't get the job,' he said.

'No. And I can't think why.'

'For once the magic formula didn't work,' he remarked drily, as he started the car and eased it away from the curb.

'What magic formula?' asked Gina.

'The right surname, the right contacts as well as the right qualifications,' he replied, with a touch of sarcasm. 'I presume you have all those for this area, and yet they chose an experienced stranger.'

'Yes, they did. But how do you know?'

'Fortunately it happens all the time, otherwise the taxpayer might have good reason to complain,' he remarked drily. Then, more gently, as he noticed the expression of distress on her face, 'The job as cook for the spring camp is still open.'

Gina looked out at the fields and woods, blurred now as the rain became more than a threat.

'I'm still thinking about it,' she said lamely.

'But it would have been much easier if the decision had been made for you by the offer of that job with the county,' he jibed. 'All right, think away.'

They reached Green Willows, her parents' house, just as the rain began to fall heavily. Gina left the car to run into the house, leaving Will to adjust the hood to keep the seats of the car dry.

Her mother came to the door in answer to her ringing and regarded her with surprised brown eyes.

'Gina, how lovely! Oh, how much better you look,' she exclaimed. She glanced past her daughter at the car. 'Who's with you?'

'Will Fox,' said Gina shortly, stepping into the hallway and removing her raincoat.

'He did call you, then. I rather hoped he would. Such a pleasant man. We had a very jolly evening with him. Your father was most impressed by him.'

'Mother,' said Gina, interrupting the flow of her mother's words which, she knew from experience, would go on for ever if no one interrupted, 'I've just come from an interview for that job with the county education committee. I didn't get it.'

Dilys Marriott was a slightly built, dark-haired Welsh woman. She wore a perpetually surprised expression on her fine-boned face. This expression did not alter as she turned to look at Gina and it was difficult to guess whether she knew anything about the interview or not.

'Didn't you, dear?' she said smoothly. 'Well, don't be too disappointed. It wouldn't have been much of a change for you. You'd have still been here in Warwickshire, near all

411

the places you used to visit with Oliver.'

Will came in, closed the front door and Mrs Marriott went forward to meet him.

'How nice to see you again, so soon,' she said warmly. 'Let me take your raincoat. My goodness, you did get wet! It started off such a nice day. We're just going to have afternoon tea in the lounge. Come and join us. Then you'll both stay to dinner, of course. Your father will want to see you, Gina dear.'

They followed her across the thick pile carpet and down two shallow steps into the big lounge which was a long, low-ceilinged room with wide windows at each end looking out on to well-tended gardens.

To Gina's surprise and secret horror there were already several women in the lounge, all of them engaged in different forms of needlework. With a cold feeling of dismay she stopped short and stared at them. They stopped talking and stared at her, and then beyond her at Will.

'We're sewing for the church bazaar,' explained Mrs Marriott.

'Then we'll go into the library,' said Gina desperately, in full retreat, wanting to escape from that curious sympathetic battery of eyes.

'No, of course not,' said her mother firmly. 'They'll all be so pleased to see you and quite delighted to have Will to tea with them. Come along now and I'll introduce you, Will.'

While Gina stood uncertainly, Dilys took Will by the arm and led him forward. He didn't seem at all ill at ease, although Gina suspected that inside he was laughing to himself. Reluctantly, her face burning, she followed in their wake.

'Nice to see you, Gina,' boomed a voice on her left. 'Come and sit beside me and tell me what you've been doing with yourself, girl.'

She glanced sideways and recognised, with relief, the vicar's sister, who had once been a teacher of gymnastics at the local grammar school. She sat down beside her and was immediately swamped with local news because the vicar's sister didn't really want to hear about Gina Marriott, but required merely a receptive ear for her gossip.

At five o'clock the women were seen off by Dilys, who lingered in the hall to speak to each one in turn. In the lounge Gina took a biscuit from one of the plates and curled up on the big chesterfield. She glanced at the broad back of the man who was standing in the window embrasure looking out at the rain.

'Your behaviour was exemplary,' she said. 'How did you do it and not laugh?'

He swung round and came slowly towards her. Hands in his pockets he stood over her. His mouth was grim and his eyes were like blue flints. Gina shivered a little.

'If mine was exemplary, yours was disgraceful,' he said softly. 'You deserve to be spanked, you spoilt little cat.'

He didn't tell her why she deserved to be spanked because her mother came back into the room. Gina thought she had never been spoken to by anyone like that before, nor had she ever been spanked. And what was more, she couldn't think why he thought she deserved such treatment. As far as she knew she'd done nothing wrong. She'd sat beside Miss Berry and had listened to her ramblings, knowing she was safe there and wouldn't have to face up to the expressions of sympathy which would have been her lot if she had spoken to any of the other women.

In the half-coma produced by the effort of pretending to listen to Miss Berry she had been vaguely aware of Will handing round tea for her mother, passing plates of sandwiches and cakes and generally making himself useful as well as pleasant, much to her surprise. She had thought, judging him by his behaviour in the flat that morning, that he would have sat apart, silently ridiculing the bazaar ladies' type of conversation, as Oliver would have done. But, instead of doing that, he had joined in.

Even now he was helping her mother to remove the remains of the tea party, carrying out a laden tray and coming back for another. As he passed by the end of the chesterfield he glanced at her and ordered brusquely,

'Come on, George, look alive. There's plenty to do. Your mother isn't getting any younger, you know. In fact she's just gone upstairs to have a rest before dinner.'

She blinked up at him.

'But Mummy hardly ever rests.'

'Well, she's resting now. Her legs are aching, she says. You and I are going to rinse the crockery and put it in the dishwasher and put away the food, and then you're going to cook the dinner, just to show me whether you're any good at it or not,' he announced calmly.

'But Mrs Brooks always...'

'Mrs Brooks has the 'flu, and isn't here today. Nor has she been here all week. And it's time you stopped depending on the older generation to do your work for you. Now, are you going to move voluntarily, or am I going to make you?' he threatened, coming to stand over her again.

Gina moved. Head held high, she went through to the kitchen and started on the dishes. He came to help her and they worked in silence. Secretly worried about her mother, Gina worked quickly and efficiently, conscious all the time of waves of disapproval being relayed from Will to herself. She kept telling herself that she didn't care whether he approved of her behaviour or not and that he had no right to be so critical of her, but she could not help wondering whether he was right, and she was spoilt.

As soon as the dishwasher was going and the food had been put away, she excused herself, saying she was going to see her mother to ask what was for dinner. Glancing at Will in her most supercilious manner, she suggested that he went to sit in the library or the lounge and to make himself at home until her father returned.

Upstairs her parents' bedroom was as it had always been, a pleasant comfortable haven; a place to which she had scurried in the night as a child disturbed by nightmares, to climb into the big bed beside her mother, knowing that she would be safe there.

Dilys was lying on the bed idly turning the pages of a magazine.

'Mummy, are your legs really aching?' asked Gina, approaching the bed.

Dilys glanced at her, an amused twinkle in her eyes.

'Yes, they really are. So nice of you to offer to clear up after the tea party and to say you'd cook the dinner. Poor Mrs Brooks isn't at all well. The 'flu left her with bronchitis.'

Gina opened her mouth to say that she hadn't offered to clear up or to make the dinner, then closed it again as she realised the offer had been made on her behalf by that infuriating, interfering man downstairs.

Then remembering his criticism of her, she sat down on the side of the bed, fiddling with the gold charm bracelet which had been a twenty-first birthday present to her from Oliver.

'Mummy, would you say I'm spoilt?' she asked suddenly.

'A little, yes. But it's natural for you to be. You're our only daughter and perhaps your father and I have been easier with you than with the boys and have given you most of the things you've asked for. You've been easy to spoil because you've always been so pretty and good-natured. Why do you ask?'

'Something which happened today made me wonder if I am.'

'Not getting the job?' Dilys's eyes were shrewd.

'Yes, but not only that. You see, when Will Fox made me go out with him, I realised for the first time since Oliver was killed how awful and miserable I'd been and how badly I've been treating everyone. You, and Daddy, and Birdie and Mrs Simpson, you must have all been terribly fed up with me.'

'No, dear, not fed up. None of us could ever be that. But

415

we have been very concerned about you. I suppose I showed my concern to Will when he called to see us yesterday. I thought it was nice of him to call. He'd been to see his mother to give her his sympathy on the death of Oliver and to explain why he wasn't able to arrive in time for the funeral. Apparently the road where he lives was made impassable by the spring rains. It must be a very remote place. He did tell me its name, but I can never remember those Scottish names.'

'It's somewhere in the Highlands,' muttered Gina.

'That's right, and he's allowing it to be used by some organisation for underprivileged youths over the Easter holidays. Very good of him, I thought. Anyway, he asked for your address and said he'd call on you and try to persuade you to go for a drive somewhere. I'm glad he succeeded. You look so much better. Your cheeks are quite pink and your eyes are brighter.'

Persuasion! So that was William Fox's name for the tactics he'd used that morning, thought Gina, suddenly indignant again.

'You like him better than you liked Oliver,' she accused her mother.

Dilys sighed and closed her eyes. Then, opening them, she looked rather pityingly at her only daughter, the child on whom she had lavished so much of her love. She knew that Gina was innately shy and affectionate, yet she also knew that the young woman could be very stubborn at times. The stubbornness had shown itself particularly over the matter of her marriage to the punctilious, ambitious Oliver.

'I didn't dislike Oliver,' she explained slowly. 'I just thought you should have waited longer before deciding to marry. After all, Gina, he was the only young man you'd ever known. You can't say that they've been queueing up to take you out over the years, can you?'

That was true. Although attractive to look at, Gina had not had any boy-friends because she was shy, and she hid that shyness under a façade of sophistication which had tended to frighten young men away. Only Oliver had persisted in getting to know her and, because of that persistence on his part, she had believed him to be in love with her and had consequently fallen in love with him.

'Oliver and I were ideally suited to each other,' she defended shakily, tears springing to her eyes as they often did since Oliver had died. 'We liked the same things. We never quarrelled. Our marriage would have been perfect.'

'No marriage is ever that,' murmured Dilys. 'Not at the start, at any rate. It might grow to perfection over the years as the partners learn what love is all about.' Then seeing that Gina was very upset, she patted her hand comfortingly. 'I just felt that sometimes Oliver's approach to you was rather calculated and that your relationship seemed cut and dried. Arid, almost. No surprises, no excitement. There was nothing unpredictable about Oliver. You would always have known where you were with him, which might have led to dullness later. I suppose I'm an old-fashioned romantic at heart, but I used to feel that you weren't in love with each other, at least not in the way David and I were, and still are. There, we won't talk about it any more because I can see it's upsetting you. Will you stay the night? Michael will be home from Oxford for the week-end. He's bringing a college friend with him. Captain Fox is welcome to stay the night with us again.'

'No, thank you. We won't stay,' said Gina hurriedly. 'I promised Birdie that I'd help her with a party she's giving. I'll come down again tomorrow. I'll have to start looking for another job.'

'Have you anything in mind?'

'No. I was so sure I'd get the job with the county. Of course I could take the job that Will Fox has offered me.'

'What is that?'

'He needs a cook for the spring camp. His partner's wife is expecting her first baby soon and can't manage very well. I've a feeling he doesn't expect me to take it. He thinks I'm too soft.'

'He's probably right. From what he told us last night about the place I can imagine that it's very hard work cooking under such conditions for large numbers. Imagine, Gina, what life is like without electricity. No dishwashing machine, no automatic washing machine. Everything done by hand. You wouldn't like it because you've always been accustomed to the best equipment, both at home and at work.'

'So you think I'm soft too,' complained Gina.

'I think you wouldn't like working in such conditions,' said Dilys.

'Then I think I'll go, just to prove to you as well as to Captain Fox that I can work under those conditions. Honestly, to hear you both talk you'd think I'm incapable of hard work! Well, I'll show you, and him too, that I'm not a spoilt little cat!' flared Gina, her eyes sparkling like topazes.

'Oh, dear. Is that what he called you?' asked Dilys with a chuckle of delight. 'He's not a bit like Oliver, is he?'

'No, he isn't. Not one little bit,' grated Gina, through clenched teeth.

CHAPTER TWO

'BUT you're not a bit like Oliver. You can't be his brother.' Birdie's exclamation, when Gina introduced Will to her at the flat, was an echo of Dilys' remark.

He had accompanied Gina to the door of the flat, much to her surprise because she had thought he would have left her outside the building. He had come with her, he said, because he had left his briefcase in the flat.

'I can assure you I'm his brother. Same parents, just a different combination of genes,' said Will jovially, his glance roving appreciatively over Birdie, tall and Junoesque in a long clinging black evening gown with a deep plunge neckline which left little to the imagination. 'Where have you been all my life?' he added provocatively.

Birdie's wide knowledgeable blue eyes twinkled back at him.

'Right here, Will, waiting for you to turn up. I hope you'll stay for the party. Come into the kitchen and help me sort out the drinks while Gina goes and changes. It's as good a way as any I know of getting to know one another better.'

'Lead the way, Birdie. I'd love to know *you* better,' he replied with a grin, and Birdie chuckled delightedly as she tucked a long white arm through one of his.

'Oh, William, you're just the boost this girl's morale was needing.'

They went off to the kitchenette together apparently having forgotten Gina, who went on to her own room. The bed was still unmade and Blue was curled up on the corner of the eiderdown which trailed on the floor. He greeted her excitedly when she flopped down on to the bed.

'Oh, Blue,' she whispered to the furry, purring animal, 'what am I going to do? I think Will Fox has forgotten that he offered me a job.'

She had hoped to bring up the subject of the job as cook at the spring camp during the drive back to Birmingham, but she had found it difficult to communicate with her companion, who had been silent and reserved, concentrating on driving in the pouring rain.

His withdrawn manner came as a surprise because during dinner with her parents, her youngest brother Michael and his college friend, Will had been pleasant and talkative.

But in the darkness of the little car she had felt once again that he disapproved of her, even disliked her. His dislike had arisen, she guessed, from his observance of her behaviour at the tea-party. He had seen her at her worst, he thought, and now he wanted nothing more to do with her. She longed to tell him that she hadn't behaved badly deliberately, that she had only shrunk from the social occasion, in the same way she was shrinking from Birdie's party now, because she didn't want anyone to pity her. But she had found it completely impossible to communicate with him when he had ignored her.

And now he and Birdie had met the chances of approaching him were fading fast. They were obviously attracted to one another on sight. 'No sooner looked than loved.' Was that how it would be with them?

Impatient with her thoughts, she pushed Blue to the floor and stood up. If she didn't go to the party she wouldn't be able to rest because of the noise. Birdie's parties were always very gay and very noisy, which was why she and Oliver had always avoided them. Also, she had to make sure Will Fox did not monopolise Birdie too much. Robin Carlton, who had been taking Birdie out for some months, would be coming, and Gina was convinced he was in love with Birdie.

Going to the wardrobe, she selected one of the evening dresses she had bought for her trousseau. It was made of fine wool and was patterned in deep greens and blues. A pleat from the seam just under the high bustline gave it a

420

mediaeval effect. It had a simple low curved neckline and full three-quarter-length sleeves. With her hair let down from its chignon and drawn back from her face to hang in rippling curls down her back, Gina looked elegant yet youthful as she entered the living room.

She did not realise that the dress emphasised her softness, giving her a pampered look in the eyes of Will Fox, who surveyed her with a slight sneer curving his mouth. He was lounging on the settee with Birdie. One of his arms rested on the back of the seat behind his hostess and his hand touched the top of Birdie's bare arm. Noting the intimacy with which he was already treating her friend, Gina determined to be as pleasant and as kind to Robin when he came.

When Robin did arrive he looked rather dumbfounded by the sight of Birdie on such good terms with the lively Will, and immediately Gina's determination increased. For the first time in her life she exerted herself to hold a man's attention. Robin responded rather half-heartedly, but as the party became noisier and noisier, he seemed to grow more and more disheartened as Birdie ignored him, finding in Will someone who could cap her own humorous remarks with outrageous witticisms which set everyone roaring with laughter.

Then at one point someone asked Will where he was staying for the night in Birmingham. He considered the question with apparent seriousness and looking straight at Gina said,

'I'm staying here. As a matter of fact I'm hoping to move into Birdie's room.'

No one took his remark seriously except Gina herself and Robin, who muttered,

'I can't stand any more of this,' and left the room.

Hurrying after him, Gina tried to persuade him to stay, but he was too angry to listen and left the flat banging the door behind him.

If Birdie noticed his absence she said nothing, and the

party went on, although, without Robin, Gina lost interest and eventually retired to her bedroom.

There she made the bed and began to undress. What a day it had been! She felt as if a whirlwind had entered her life when Will Fox had entered her room. Nothing had been the same since then. All her preconceptions about people had been upset. He had made her start questioning about herself, about Oliver and now about Birdie.

She had known Birdie since her days at the Grammar School. They had spent holidays together. Yet what did she really know about her? She had always thought her kindly if a little scatterbrained. But after this evening she was beginning to wonder about Birdie's morals.

Realising the direction her thoughts were taking, Gina found her face burning. Was Will Fox really going to stay the night in the flat? There was only one way to find out. She must go and see if he had left with the others. The noise from the living room had died down now although she could still hear the record player and, above it, people calling out good night, followed by the sound of the flat door closing.

Opening the door of her room a crack, she listened. All was quiet except for the sound of soft music. Gina stepped out into the passage and went along to the living room. She walked in and stopped dead. On the settee were two people entwined in a close embrace. Birdie and the ex-Army Captain, of course.

Her heart beating fast, Gina whirled and retreated along the passage to her room. Closing the door, she leaned against it, trying to calm her agitation. What could she do? Nothing, really. Birdie and Will were adults and what they did together was none of her business. Why, then, did she have this strange sense of disappointment? She had thought better of Birdie. As for Will Fox—well, there wasn't anything she would put past him.

The rest of the night seemed interminable. She couldn't sleep. Every time she turned on the bedside lamp and stretched out her hand to the bottle of sleeping pills prescribed by the doctor there flashed across her memory the image of Will's mouth twisted into a sneer and she heard his voice, almost as if he were there in the room with her, asking her if they were the drug she used to forget reality. Immediately her hand withdrew from the container, she switched out the light and flung over on her other side to woo sleep once more.

The trouble was her imagination was too vivid. She kept thinking of Birdie and Will as she had last seen them kissing on the settee in the living room. It was strange that it should bother her. Over the past few months Robin Carlton had stayed late with Birdie in the living room and Gina hadn't given it a thought.

Ruefully she had to admit it was because Will Fox had been there tonight. He was unpredictable. She couldn't be sure what he was really like. She had changed her mind about him several times already.

Dawn crept stealthily into the room, filling it with pearl grey light. Gina gave up trying to sleep and decided to go into the kitchen to make herself a cup of tea. It was only six-thirty. That meant the day was going to be long, a wasteland without Oliver. Perhaps she would go home and spend the day with her parents, and maybe tomorrow she would visit her eldest brother Luke and his wife and their new baby. Anything to fill in the empty hours.

To her surprise the living room was tidy, all the debris of the party having been swept away as if by a clean broom. Cushions had been plumped and ash trays had been emptied. Everything had a shining look. The settee did not look as if anyone had slept on it, and immediately Gina's heart plummeted. Where was Will Fox?

She went to the kitchen, and this time her heart leapt up. Someone was there before her, someone who was whistling a familiar tune, a folk song she had once heard with a slyly seductive lyric, something to do with lifting a woman's petticoat to buckle her shoe.

'Good morning, George.'

Will was pouring boiling water into the tea-pot. He was clean-shaven and was wearing a different shirt. He was alert and bright-eyed and, apart from a few tell-tale lines under his eyes, she would have thought he had slept a full eight hours during the night. He made her feel more jaded than ever and she resented him.

'Good morning,' she replied coldly. 'So you did stay the night after all.'

'I did. But it's time I was on my way north. I've dallied in the lush pastures of the enervating south long enough. Have you finished thinking yet?'

'About what?' she countered.

'My suggestion that you should come north with me.'

'After last night I'd have thought you'd have asked Birdie to go with you,' she said, still cold.

'Miaow,' he retorted with a grin. Then, sobering, he added, 'I didn't mention it to her. She's a great girl, lots of fun to be with. She and I...' he paused and gave her an enigmatic glance. 'Do you think she'd come if I asked her?' he queried with a touch of earnestness which was oddly disarming, giving her the impression that for once he was uncertain and needed encouragement.

But Gina was not disposed to encourage him in that direction. Birdie must not be given the chance to go north with him and cook at his adventure camp. There was Robin Carlton to be considered. Besides, Birdie couldn't cook!

'No. I don't think she would,' she replied firmly. 'You see, she likes her work here and she's in line for promotion soon. Actually I had finished thinking and I'd come to the conclusion that perhaps I could help you out, on a purely voluntary basis, until your partner's wife is able to tackle the work again. Would that be of any use to you?' she asked, in the manner of someone conferring a great favour.

He was busy pouring tea into three cups, and he did not answer at once. When he'd finished pouring he glanced at her thoughtfully.

'You're not exactly the sort of person I had in mind,' he said slowly, 'but I'm inclined to accept your magnanimous offer because I've always worked on the theory that one volunteer is better than several pressed men. Thanks, George, I'll be glad of your help. And now I must take this cup of tea to Birdie. I think I owe it to her.'

He didn't say why he owed the cup of tea to Birdie, but left the kitchen before Gina could remonstrate. She followed him into the passage just in time to see him go into Birdie's room and close the door behind him. A few seconds later she heard them laughing together. She had the most uncomfortable feeling that the joke they were sharing was on her. Hands clenched by her sides, she returned to the kitchen to drink her tea and give Blue his morning milk.

As she set the saucer on the floor for the kitten, the enormity of her recent impulsive decision to go north with Will Fox that day and stay in his wilderness to cook for twenty youths became more apparent. Whatever had she been thinking of? What had goaded her into offering to help him for nothing? She must be out of her mind. Going over the conversation which had led up to her making her offer she realised, with a sense of astonishment at her own peculiar behaviour, that she had offered merely because she hadn't wanted him to ask Birdie.

The telephone shrilled suddenly in the living room. Almost tripping over her dressing gown, she rushed to it to make sure she answered it before Will did. It would never do for him to answer it at this time of the morning.

Robin answered her breathless greeting. He wanted to speak to Birdie. Gina told him to hang on and, glad to see that Will had gone back to the kitchen, she went into her friend's room.

Birdie, looking curiously angelic in a white crocheted bed-jacket with full sleeves, was sitting up in bed. She greeted Gina with a smile and raised her tea cup.

'Look what William the Conqueror brought me,' she said.

'The Conqueror? Why do you call him that?' exclaimed Gina.

'Oh, he just strikes me as being the sort of man who sees and conquers,' replied Birdie, airily.

'Birdie, did you ... I mean ... did he ... Where did he sleep last night?' stammered Gina.

Birdie's eyes widened.

'On the settee in the living room, I suppose. That's where he said he'd sleep.' Then as understanding dawned on her she exclaimed, 'You didn't really believe him when he said he was going to move in with me? Oh, honestly, Gina, how could you?'

'Quite easily. The last I saw of you both you were in a very convincing clinch, and he hardly left your side all evening. In fact poor Robin was—oh, heavens, I forgot! Robin is on the phone. He wants to speak to you urgently.'

'Why didn't you tell me? Here, for goodness' sake take this cup and saucer. Oh, it worked, it worked! It must have worked. Oh, darling William the Conqueror, however can I thank you enough?' sang Birdie as she got out of bed and sped from the room, leaving a completely bewildered Gina holding the cup and saucer.

Pulling herself together, Gina went along to the kitchen again where Will was eating his breakfast and reading the Saturday morning newspaper.

'Your tea is going cold. Better pour some more,' he said practically. 'And eat well. I don't stop for snacks when I'm driving.'

'But I don't think I can be ready to leave today,' said Gina.

'Why? What is there to do except pack a few clothes and your toothbrush?' he asked. 'Take jeans and shirts and loads of sweaters, if you have any. And warm pyjamas. We have plenty of draughts up north. You won't need an evening dress, much as I liked the one you wore last night. There aren't any bright lights where I live.'

'Captain Fox——' she began, but he raised his voice above hers and continued to issue orders.

'Let's see, it's now seven-fifteen. We should be able to leave at nine. I'll make some sandwiches. Have you a thermos flask? Good. We can take coffee too. I can eat while I'm driving with you there to hand me the food. That means we can keep going and should reach Loch Lomond this evening. We can stay the night there with a relative of mine. Now, as soon as Birdie stops talking to Robin...'

'How do you know she's talking to him?' interrupted Gina, and he gave her an irritated, slightly scornful glance.

'Do you think she'd leave her bed in such a hurry to speak to anyone else?' he countered. 'As I was saying, as soon as she gets off the phone you telephone your parents and tell them where you're going. Then pack your bags while I bring the truck round. Anything else you have to do?'

Gina felt panic rising within her. Wildly she looked for reasons to delay their departure.

'Yes, of course there is, and I'd just like to make it clear here and now that I'm not a subordinate soldier whom you have to brief before sending him on a mission,' she said coldly. 'I know perfectly well what I have to do before I can leave here. I need more time. I can't give up half a flat just like that.' She snapped her fingers. 'Someone will have to take over my share of it. And what about Blue, my kitten?'

'What about Blue?' he drawled, rather menacingly, she thought.

'I can't desert him. Oliver gave him to me.'

'Won't Birdie look after him for you until you come back?'

'I don't think he'd stay with her or anyone else,' she replied, seeing a loophole through which she might escape.

'No cats,' he returned tersely.

'No cat, no me,' she retorted grandly.

For a moment there was deadlock as they stared at each

other. Then with a careless shrug of his shoulders Will said,

'All right, bring him. But don't blame me if he gets lost, or drowned, or is shot. Well, that's the cat sorted out. I don't think you'll have any serious trouble in getting rid of your share of the flat. Young Robin will be moving in soon.'

'Young Robin,' she repeated. 'You talk as if you were old enough to be his uncle.'

'That's how I feel, sometimes—like an uncle, giving the younger generation the benefit of my hard-won experience of life,' he remarked, and bitterness carved lines beside his expressive mouth.

'But not Birdie's uncle,' observed Gina with pseudo-sweetness. 'Uncles don't usually embrace their nieces passionately.'

His quick grin was shameless.

'I thought I heard you come into the living room. You can blame that little incident on my proximity all evening to a beautiful blonde. She went to my head and I got carried away by the part I was playing,' he replied blandly, rising to his feet. 'If you've finished eating I'll clear away while you phone your parents. If you have any problems in explaining to them, let me talk to them.'

She had no problems. Her father seemed delighted by the idea and told her not to worry about the flat or any other business because he would look after that for her.

'It'll do you good to get away. Nothing like a change to help you forget,' he said.

She was about to say that she would never forget Oliver and didn't want to forget him when she realised that she had not thought of him since yesterday. She had been too busy. Oliver hadn't even been the cause of her sleepless night. His brother had taken over in that respect.

Her mother was also enthusiastic about her decision to go north.

'Three or four weeks should do the trick,' she said comfortingly, 'and then you'll be ready to come back and face up to normal life again. Write to me as soon as you get there and let me know what it's like.'

Her telephoning done, Gina went in to see Birdie again to tell her she was leaving that day. She found her friend in an ecstatic mood, trying to decide what to wear.

'Oh, Gina, I'm so happy! Robin has asked me to marry him. He said he couldn't wait until he got here. See what a little competition does for a man, even if it was only pretence.'

'You mean you and Will behaved as you did last night deliberately in order to make Robin jealous?'

'Yes. As soon as I met Will I guessed he would be the sort of person who wouldn't mind playing up to my lead. He did it very well, don't you think?' laughed Birdie.

'Too well. I was the only spectator for the big love scene,' remarked Gina drily. 'Robin had left long before that.'

'Oh, that,' said Birdie, and to Gina's astonishment she blushed rosily. 'I suppose it wasn't really necessary, but somehow it happened so naturally, and it was nice.' The expression on Birdie's face changed to one of grave seriousness. 'Gina, are you sure about going to this place where Will lives? It might be a bit rough, not like living here, you know.'

'I know. I'm going to prove to him that I'm not spoilt and pampered, and that I can work as hard as anyone. At the same time I'll be helping his partner's wife. She'll probably be glad of the company of another woman. It isn't a permanent job. I volunteered to do it and can leave when I'm ready. I'll probably be back here in time to be your bridesmaid.'

'I hope so. I was going to ask you, but I didn't like to because it isn't long since you were going to be the bride and I was going to be the bridesmaid,' said Birdie. 'I wish it had all turned out differently for you, Gina, and I hope you won't let losing Oliver stop you falling in love with someone else.'

'I'll try not to, but at the moment I feel as if I'll never

429

fall in love again,' sighed Gina, her eyes filling with tears. 'It's so painful when you lose the one you love.'

The journey to the wilds of Scotland was worse than a nightmare to Gina. Accustomed to travelling in comfort, she found the cab of the small truck which Will owned noisy and draughty. The seat was hard making it difficult for her to relax. Her companion's determination to reach Loch Lomond that day meant that he drove at a steady fast pace once they were on the northbound motorway. He did not bother to entertain her with small talk and there was no radio.

Lunch was taken somewhere between Manchester and Lancaster as they roared along at a steady seventy miles per hour. It was impossible at that speed to pour scalding hot coffee into a plastic cup without spilling it on to her light beige pants. It was almost impossible to drink the stuff because every time she raised her cup to her lips the truck lurched quite unnecessarily, she thought, and she and the cup failed to make contact.

The simple needs of nature seemed not to affect the Army at all, and then, when Will did condescend to stop, he did so on a windy, rainswept stretch of road amongst the bleak fells of Westmorland. She had to climb over a dry stone wall, only to land in a swamp the other side in which she dropped Blue so that the Persian complained bitterly.

When she finally fought her way back across the road to the truck and its waiting whistling driver, she had to brave his derisive glance which took in her dishevelled hair, coffee-stained, rain-soaked pants and muddy, bedraggled animal.

'You might as well get used to living close to nature,' he mocked, 'because where we're going there's nothing else but moors and mountains and water.'

As they forged forward through the mist-laden fells Gina began to feel the effects of her sleepless night. She tried to doze, but there was nothing for her to rest her head against. It kept nodding forward. She would feel as if she were falling and she would jerk it up again and peer blearily out of the rain-spotted windscreen, then doze off again. The jerking happened several times, making her feel thoroughly wretched.

She wished she was at home curled up on the chesterfield at Green Willows, watching the Saturday afternoon sports programme on the television, looking forward to afternoon tea as served by her mother, or alternatively, shopping in Birmingham and then going on to the cinema or to the repertory theatre to see a good play.

'You can try my shoulder, if you like.' Will's voice came as a shock, breaking through the cloud of sleepiness which hovered around her. She glanced at the shoulder in question. It looked sturdy and stable. Having made his offer he seemed unconcerned as to whether she tried it or not. Shifting a little closer to him, she leaned her head against the upper part of his arm, her eyelids drooped, and in no time she was asleep.

The sound of voices roused Gina. Opening her eyes, she blinked in a puzzled way, wondering where she was. Beneath her cheek the tweed of Will's jacket was rough, yet comforting, and she was loath to sit up.

Eventually she became aware that they had stopped for petrol and that the boy attending to the pump was staring through the window at her in an interested way, a cheeky knowing smile curving his mouth. He had a long-jawed freckled face and, from beneath his cap, tufts of sandy hair stuck out. Something about his face spelt Scottish to her.

'Where are we?' she muttered, sitting up and trying to tidy her hair with her hands. Leaning down, she picked up her handbag and brought out her compact. Snapping it open, she glanced at her face and hair, and nearly passed out with shock. One of her cheeks, the one which had been resting against the hospitable Harris tweed, was red and the other was quite pale. Her hair was straggling down from its chignon and her eyes looked slightly bloodshot. Her lipstick was non-existent! She looked literally as if she had been pulled through a hedge backwards. No wonder the boy was grinning!

'Lockerbie,' answered Will briefly, flexing his shoulder and arm as if they were stiff from having supported her.

'In Scotland?'

'Yes.'

He turned away to pay the boy. Since they had stopped perhaps there was a chance that he would let her go to the women's room to clean up, if the petrol station had such a place. If not, perhaps they could go for a cup of tea at a café in the town. Hurriedly she asked him as he stuffed his wallet back into his inside pocket. As if he hadn't heard her he reached out to turn on the ignition, and the engine roared into life. Before releasing the brakes he glanced at her critically.

'You have a comb, haven't you?' he asked, and she nodded. 'Well, use it,' he barked. 'And let's get this straight before we go any further. Where you're going no one is going to worry if you don't look like the latest model out of a women's magazine. Least of all shall I worry. Cleanliness and neatness is all that is required. You're coming to work, not to stand around looking decorative.'

The truck lurched forward and turned out into the road. Gina had a confused impression of a narrow rain-washed street lined with plain-fronted shops and houses, all huddled together as if for comfort, and then they were on a fairly new wide road, still heading north.

On either side of the road green fields, looking dank and desolate under a grey sky, stretched away to gently curving hills. Beyond the hills she could just see the bulk of higher hills, also grey like the sky. Here and there a row of dark pines marched up a hillside and in the corners of fields, bare deciduous trees spread forlorn, dripping branches.

With an exaggerated sigh for the benefit of her companion, Gina peered once more at her reflection and struggled to comb her hair. It wasn't easy to do with one hand, so in the end she unpinned the chignon and tied the released long tresses with a chiffon scarf she had brought. Using a freshening pad, she cleaned off her old make-up and didn't apply any more. Then she sat back and looked out of the window.

They seemed to be quite high up now and the rain was more like mist swirling around them. Water sprayed up from the wheels of traffic passing in the opposite direction, flinging mud at the windscreen of the truck.

Whatever happened to springtime? thought Gina, as she looked out at the bleak scene. The hills had crowded closely about the road now and she could see water cascading down the dark glistening rock. She thought of the daffodils nodding their heads in the garden of the cottage at Shottery the previous day and of the fresh tufts of green sprinkling the hawthorn hedges in Warwickshire. Here there were no hedges and no daffodils, only the dark primeval walls running across the open land and a few weirdly-shaped pine trees. And the villages through which they passed had none of the warmth of mellow brick or golden stone, but were pale grey and secretive-looking.

From the rear of the truck came the plaintive cry of the cat, but Gina knew better than to ask the uncommunicative driver of the vehicle to stop. Nor did she wish to get out of the truck in this weather to duck behind a stone wall again only to return to some derisive remark. So she sat silent, once again wondering what had possessed her to go north with him.

The rest of the journey was miserable in the extreme as she grew more and more cramped and more and more hungry. Hamilton was a mass of factory chimneys and endless dark streets, then they were on the outskirts of Glasgow, then in the city itself beside a muddy turbulent river, crossing a bridge amidst slow-crawling traffic which made her companion curse vividly and fluently with little concern for her gently-reared ears.

Once over the bridge they turned left along a main thoroughfare where lights were glittering and the Saturday afternoon shoppers were still crowding the pavements. Then back to the river they went. It was charcoal grey now, under low tumbled clouds.

Gradually the city was left behind. Ahead Gina could see the dim outline of mountains beyond a wider stretch of water. Lights flashed, sometimes red and sometimes white. Something vague and shadowy, ablaze with light, floated on the water and she realised it was a ship moving down the estuary.

Soon they were passing through another town past an old castle, turning right up a hill into the darkness of the countryside again. Lights once more ahead and they were in the town of Alexandria. There were people queueing up for a cinema, pubs opening their doors, a fish and chip shop where she could see people leaning on the counter waiting to be served. She could almost smell the fish and chips and her stomach gurgled suddenly, noisily.

'Not far now,' murmured Will comfortingly, the first time he had spoken since he had sworn on the bridge. She couldn't see him properly now. He was only a bulky shape in the dim light; a profile occasionally illuminated by the lights of a passing car.

How did he do it? she wondered. How did he keep up the steady pace without stopping or flagging? It must be the Army training, this ability to go on until the destination was reached. He would be terrible to work for, making the same demands on her that he made on himself, and expecting her to respond. Whatever had possessed her to volunteer to come with him?

One more town to go, smaller this time, and then the countryside again and to the right a wide expanse of nothing. No, not nothing. She could just make out the faint gleam of water. It must be a lake. Careful, Gina, they call them *lochs* in this part of the world. Could it be Loch Lomond at last? she asked her companion. His answer was brief. It was.

They turned off the road on to another narrower one. A

house glowing with light loomed out of the darkness. It was long and low.

They stopped before a flight of shallow steps leading to a black-painted door. The engine of the truck was stopped. The silence was blessed to Gina's ears, but it was split almost immediately by the harsh impertinent blare of the truck's horn as Will announced their arrival to whoever was in the house.

The black door swung open. Light poured out showing up the slanting silvery rain. Two figures appeared, slim and adolescent, both with fluffy hair, both in pants. It was difficult to tell whether they were boys or girls or one of each. One of them began to jump up and down with excitement, and when Will opened the door of the vehicle, the jumping figure turned and scampered back into the house. Gina could hear a shrill voice yelling.

'Mum, it's Will! He's come after all!'

The other figure skipped forward, not seeming to mind the rain. Will jumped down, picked whoever it was up in his arms and whirled it round. There were squeals of delight.

Gina supposed she had better get out and see to her poor neglected kitten. She opened the door at her side and, moving rather stiffly, stepped down, splosh into a puddle.

The voice she could hear speaking to Will was that of a girl, and as she walked carefully round the back of the vehicle, she could see Will walking with the girl towards the house. As he put a foot on the lowest step he turned and called out,

'Come on, George, don't be shy.'

It seemed to Gina that he phrased everything he said to her deliberately so as to annoy her.

'I'm coming,' she snapped back. 'But I'd like to let Blue out first, if you don't mind.'

Saying something rude, which was almost inaudible but not quite, about the cat, Will strode back to the truck, opened the canvas cover which protected the back of it, and reached in for Blue. The kitten wailed miserably as it felt the rain on its fur, struggled a little and jumped from Will's hands. It ran away into the wet darkness.

'Oh, Blue!' wailed Gina, who was feeling damp, stiff and miserable herself and had no desire to go searching an unknown garden for her pet.

'Don't worry. I'll find him,' said the girl in a lilting voice, and she disappeared into the gloom.

A woman, tall and angular, appeared in the doorway and peered out into the driving rain.

'It's good to see you again, Will. Who's with you? Who is it?' The well-modulated English voice rose on a note of excitement and expectancy.

Gina felt Will's hand grip her elbow as he urged her forward up the steps.

'This is George, new chief cook and bottle-washer for the camp,' he announced firmly.

'Oh,' there was some disappointment in the woman's voice. 'I thought for a moment it was someone else. Come in, then.'

She turned into the house and they followed her into a wide hallway through an archway into a big pleasant room.

'It is Will, Drew, and he's brought a lad he calls George,' the woman was saying. The man lounging in a deep arm-chair burst out laughing as he looked past her at Gina and he was joined in his mirth by the other adolescent, who was a boy of about fourteen years of age. The woman swung round saw Gina and exclaimed,

'Oh! It isn't a boy at all.' Her blue eyes sparkling in her handsome big-featured face, which was somehow familiar. She rounded on Will. 'You mischievous devil,' she rebuked him. 'George, indeed! Now, what sort of a name is that for a wisp of a girl?' She smiled kindly at Gina.

'My name is Georgina,' said Gina, encouraged by that smile. 'Most of my friends call me Gina.'

'Which means you don't count Will amongst your friends, I should guess,' replied the woman. 'I'm Meg

Maxwell, Will's aunt, and this is my husband Andrew and my son Gordie.'

The man, who was tall and slim and had iron-grey hair, unfolded himself from his chair to greet Gina pleasantly and to shake hands with Will.

'We've been waiting for you for two days, now,' he said, in a soft lilting accent. 'What kept you?'

'The small business of finding someone to help Madge Anderson at the camp,' replied Will briefly. 'Who won to-day?' He settled down in a chair opposite to his host. Gordie immediately climbed on to the arm of the same chair to hang over him.

'Wales took a licking, I'm glad to say,' replied Andrew.

Meg touched Gina on the arm.

'Listen to them,' she murmured. 'Rugby Union fans, both of them.'

'Just like Oliver,' said Gina, who was still grappling with the fact that this woman was also Oliver's aunt and she had never heard of her before.

'Oliver?' queried Meg. Then light dawned in her eyes. 'Then you're *that* Georgina?'

'Yes. I was going to marry Oliver. He never told me about you.'

Meg's smile was wry.

'I'm not surprised. Ann, Will's mother, broke with us after she married again.'

'You are Oliver's father's sister, then?'

'Yes, I'm Geoff's sister. Much younger than he. I remember him as a young dashing officer, very gay and lively. Will is like him, or he used to be.' She glanced at her nephew rather anxiously. 'But there I go chattering on and you must be wanting a cup of tea. When did you eat last?'

Gina told her and Meg clucked her tongue disgustedly. This time the glance she sent in Will's direction was neither anxious nor affectionate.

'No wonder you look so pale and tired! Come upstairs and I'll show you where the bathroom is and the room where you'll sleep tonight, and you can explain why you've come all this way with Will.'

Gina followed her from the room and up a wide open staircase. The very contemporary style of the house surprised her and she said so.

'I suppose you were expecting to stay in an old grey stone house with quaint dormer windows set in the roof, typically Scottish in design,' said Meg with a laugh. 'Well, you see, Andrew is an architect by profession and this house is his own design. We bought this land overlooking the loch a few years ago to get away from the city, and we love it. Nan, my daughter, is especially happy to live out here. She's horse-mad and we have two in the paddock nearby. By the way, where is she? I thought she went out to greet you.'

Gina explained and Meg smiled again.

'Your kitten will be in good hands, don't worry. Nan loves all animals. I'm surprised Will let you bring him.'

'I told him no Blue, no me, and he gave in,' said Gina coolly.

'You surprise me,' murmured Meg, giving her guest a slow assessing glance. 'He must have wanted you to come very badly. Will rarely gives in to anyone. If people won't go his way he usually ditches them. He can be very ruthless at times.'

'I'd noticed,' said Gina, following her hostess into a small bedroom decorated in bright colours and furnished with simple white furniture.

'Why did you come with him?' asked Meg.

'To prove to him that I'm not as soft as I look, and that I'm quite capable of cooking for twenty boys, more if necessary,' replied Gina, and again Meg looked at her curiously.

'I can see why Will thought you were soft,' she said, then added gravely, 'You won't let him down, will you, Gina? He's been let down rather badly. Another time might be once too often. I've noticed a tendency in him to become rather withdrawn and dour lately. I'll leave you now. When you're ready, come down and we'll have a meal. We'll be able to chat afterwards because Andrew is taking Will to see a friend who is interested in sending his boys to the camp.'

When Gina eventually went downstairs feeling refreshed after a wash in unbelievably soft water, she found that Nan had come in and was trying to coax Blue to drink some milk from a saucer. The kitten was backed up against the kitchen wall, his back arched, his eyes wide.

'I found him in the stable. All the cats go in there because it's warm and cosy in the hay. He's lovely, so he is, but frightened of us,' said Nan, in her soft lilting voice. She was tall like her mother and her dark hair waved about her oval-shaped face which was lit by the blue eyes which were her inheritance from the Fox family.

Gina picked up the trembling kitten and stroked his damp fur.

'His name is Blue. Thank you for finding him.'

'You ... you're not Bridget, are you?' stammered Nan shyly, her eyes grave and questioning.

'Of course she isn't. She's Gina,' said Gordie in a whisper, glancing over his shoulder at his mother who was busy at the cooker.

'Who's Bridget?' asked Gina softly.

Two pairs of blue eyes regarded her steadily. Then Nan said quietly,

'She used to live here. She's the daughter of a friend of Mummy's who died. Bridget ran away.'

'Dinner is ready, so if you'd like to tell your father and Will, Gordie, Nan can take Gina through to the dining room,' said Meg, coming over to them. 'Leave the kitten here. I'll see that he gets something to eat.'

Recognising that Blue was amongst friends, Gina went with Nan and took her place at the dining-room table, where she was joined by Andrew and Will. The meal passed pleasantly, almost gaily. There was obviously good rapport between Will and his relatives and the conversation was scattered with family jokes.

As Gina ate she wondered about the terse whispered conversation which had taken place between herself and Nan. Who was Bridget, and why had she run away? And what had she to do with Will Fox?

When the meal was over the two men excused themselves to go and see the friend of Andrew who was interested in the adventure camp.

'You'll be all right, I hope,' Will said brusquely to Gina as he passed her on his way out of the room. 'Meg will look after you. In case you've gone to bed by the time I come back just remember that we want to make an early start again, about nine o'clock.'

She almost said 'Yes, sir,' and saluted him, Army fashion, but instead she confined herself to making a face at his retreating back.

'Don't you like Will?' asked the curious all-observant Nan, who thought the world of her grown-up cousin.

'Not much,' admitted Gina cautiously, thankful that Meg had left the room too.

'Bridget did. She thought he was a hero. That's why she ran after him and married him,' announced Nan.

Gina swallowed this amazing piece of information without a tremor, hoping she did not look as astonished as she felt.

'But her liking for him can't have lasted, because she ran away from him, so Mummy says,' continued Nan, who like many girls of her age was fascinated by the complicated relationships of adults. 'We haven't seen or heard from her since. Mum keeps hoping she'll turn up one day, but Daddy thinks she's dead.'

So that was why Meg's voice had risen in hope when she had noticed that Will had someone with him.

'When were they married?' asked Gina.

'Oh, years ago. About seven years, I suppose. Bridget was only eighteen. She went to London and then to Germany where Will was stationed then. She sent Mummy a photograph taken after they were married. It's upstairs. Mummy daren't have it down here in case Will sees it. Bridget was very pretty. She was always combing her hair and making up her face. I can remember watching her when I was little. Would you like to see the photo?'

'Perhaps you shouldn't take it from your mother's room,' Gina demurred. 'She might not want me to see it.'

'She won't mind. I expect she'll tell you all about Bridget because you're going to work for Will. I mean, it wouldn't do for you to fall in love with him, seeing how he's married, would it?'

Gina repressed a desire to inform Nan in her tartest tones that there wasn't the slightest possibility of her falling in love with Will, and the girl went off to get the photograph.

While Nan was away Meg reappeared and took Gina off to the living room where Gordie had settled on the floor in front of the television. Meg took out her knitting and, with a few questions, soon knew how Will had found Gina and had asked her to go and cook for him.

'I think I can understand the way his mind was working,' she said. 'He would be thinking it would be good for you to get away from Birmingham and the associations with Oliver. He would be understanding how you felt. He knows what it's like to lose a loved one.'

'You mean Bridget?' asked Gina.

'Has he told you about her?'

'Very little,' replied Gina, thinking of Will's terse comment about marriage and how it hadn't worked for him.

'It was such a shock to us when he wrote to tell us she'd run away from him,' said Meg. 'She had lived with us for about two years. I gave her a home when her mother, a good friend of mine, died quite suddenly of a heart attack. Her father disappeared into the blue years ago. And now it seems as if Bridget has inherited his vanishing tricks. I found her stubborn and very difficult to handle, but I assumed that she was awkward because she had lost her mother at a crucial age. She was always wanting to stay out late at night. Then Will came here on leave. She thought he was wonderful and he took her out several times. He went back to Germany and soon afterwards Bridget ran away from here. I didn't hear from her until she wrote to say she'd met Will again and they were to be married.'

Meg sighed and took the photograph from Nan, who had come back into the room. She showed it to Gina, who gazed at the small pretty young woman with curling long hair and wide-set eyes, laughing up at a younger Will, in uniform, who looked rather serious on his wedding day.

'Hasn't he tried to find her?' she asked.

'Yes, whenever he could. Four years ago he left the Army and we didn't hear from him for a while. Then one day he turned up here to say he'd bought a place in the Highlands and that he intended to farm there. Not a word about Bridget, then or since. If I mention her he always changes the subject. We've no idea whether he found her or not. She could be dead for all we know.'

Meg concentrated on her knitting until she finished a row. Then she looked up and gazed at Gina with those clear observant eyes.

'Bridget wasn't unlike you,' she said. 'She was small and soft.'

Kitten-soft, Will had called her on their first meeting, thought Gina, and she wondered uneasily whether she had reminded him too of his wife.

But the warmth of the room was making her feel drowsy, and Meg noticed.

'I heard you being given orders about an early start to-morrow morning,' she said, with a humorous twitch to her lips, 'so I think you'd better go to bed. The journey has taken a lot out of you today, and Will won't have noticed. Basically he's a good person, but he tends to forget that others aren't as strong as he is. Now I've put the electric blanket on in your bed and I noticed Will had put your cases in the room for you. I hope you've some warm night-wear for sleeping in when you get to the glen. It can be cold at night up there, even in May and June.'

Gina found the bed blissfully warm and she was soon asleep. She slept dreamlessly and heard nothing until some-one banged on the door hard enough to make it tremble.

'Eight-thirty, George. Want some breakfast before we go?' called a familiar masculine voice.

'Yes, please.'

'Then show a leg!'

The rain had stopped and the view from the bedroom window showed her the famous loch shimmering in pale sunlight with wreaths of pearly mist rising from it. In the distance, rising above the mist, she could see the sharp out-line of a snow-covered mountain peak shining against the sky.

Shivering in the cool air, she dressed quickly in warm woollen pants, a sweater and suede jacket. In the mirror her face looked surprisingly rested, the skin glowing faintly, the eyes bright and alert. Her hair was a tangle and she had time only to give it a few sweeps with the brush before tying it back with the chiffon scarf. No time for titivating with Will Fox waiting for her or he'd have no compunction about invading the room to hurry her along. A hard man who drove others hard and who had possibly driven his wife away from him.

Breakfast was a good wholesome meal at which the whole of the Maxwell family were present. Gina ate everything, remembering the hunger during the journey of the previous day. As soon as she had finished eating Will rose from the table saying it was time they left. Blue was placed in his basket under the canvas cover of the truck along with Gina's suitcases, and soon the truck was turning away from the house and Gina was waving goodbye to the assembled Maxwells.

The road north wound close beside the lake and offered fascinating glimpses of the smooth stretch of water from beneath the down-curving branches of leafless larch trees or through the interlacing branches of dark pines. Feeling rested and comfortable, entranced by the serene beauty of scenery so different from that of her home county, Gina asked questions, and her companion, also in a better mood than on the previous day, answered her pleasantly and informatively. Soon she knew that the name of the snow-capped mountain rearing up on the opposite shores of the loch was Ben Lomond: that the names of all the islands she could see began with the word Inch; and as the loch narrowed and they twisted through a village called Tarbet, that the name meant small neck of land or isthmus and that the village was in fact on an isthmus created by the closeness of the head of Loch Long at that point to Loch Lomond.

With the lines of communication open Gina was encouraged to ask more questions about their destination, and learned that they were bound for a place called Glengorm.

'It means green or blue glen,' explained Will, 'and that describes it pretty well. In the summer it's all greens and blues.'

'How far is it from here?'

'Close on a hundred and twenty miles by road. If you'd like to see exactly where it is there's a map book underneath your seat. Look at the map showing the north-west of Scotland and you should be able to find it. It's in the area north of Ullapool.'

She did as he suggested and eventually found the glen, a narrow strip of green winding between masses of grey, which gave way to a strip of pale blue called Loch Gorm which opened on to the bigger mass of blue, representing the sea. Looking at the key to the map, Gina discovered that grey in all shades represented land above five hundred feet above sea level. There didn't seem to be any road of any importance leading to the glen or through it. Only a white line, which, according to the key, meant 'narrow country road, unsurfaced'.

'Why, it's miles away from anywhere,' she exclaimed. 'Whatever made you choose a place like that to live?'

'I didn't. It chose me,' was the laconic, bewildering reply.

'How?'

He was silent, seeming more interested in manoeuvring the vehicle round a bend on the outskirts of Crianlarich than in answering her question. Loch Lomond was now behind them and they faced the gradual pull up to Rannoch Moor.

Not receiving an answer, Gina glanced up from the map at Will, wondering whether to repeat her question, but the expression on his face prevented her from speaking. He was staring ahead, his eyes narrowed, his jaw ridged and rock-like, his mouth bitterly curved as he dealt with obviously unpleasant thoughts.

He spoke suddenly in a harsh voice.

'A few years ago, not long after I came out of the Army, I felt a great need to get away by myself. I decided to explore the Highlands alone. There I hoped to find glens, moors and mountains unblemished by dams, pylons and ski-lifts, and if I found any people, I hoped that they would be simple kindly souls untouched by the rat-race.'

He stopped speaking almost as abruptly as he'd begun, and Gina, surprised by the savagery of his outburst, was able to ask,

'Did you find what you hoped for?'

'Yes, I did. I found rest and peace, unchanging stability and a sense of the importance of old values, none of which I'd ever known before. I spent two days climbing in near-blizzard conditions in the area near Glengorm because an old man I'd met on the road said that I would see paradise from the top of a certain mountain. I was on the top of Ben Searg when the cloud broke suddenly. Sunlight appeared and glinted on a sheet of water. It was like a momentary glimpse of paradise, of a promised land. I hurried down the mountain and made my way towards the loch. That night I

445

slept in my tent beside the loch in a copse of birch trees to the sound of a torrent roaring in the glen.'

He paused again, and this time Gina didn't ask any questions. She was too busy grappling with yet another new aspect of Will Fox. Why had he found it necessary to get away alone? Had the disappearance of his young wife affected him more deeply than he had cared to admit to anyone?

'Next day,' he continued more quietly, 'when I awoke and looked out not a ripple broke the smooth blue surface of the loch, which reflected silent white hills and the dark ruins of an old tower built on a promontory. Near the tower I found a house, deserted but in good repair. There were fields around it that had once been tilled. In a state of great excitement I decided I would live there and farm. As soon as I could I went down to Ullapool and enquired about the place. It was for sale—house, fields, moors and half a mountain, the whole glen, in fact. In the grip of a strange fascination I made an offer for it. It was accepted immediately. I've lived there ever since.'

'How long?'

'Four years this coming Easter. Eighteen months by myself, except for Lachie Munro, who is the only crofter in the glen. The rest of the time Gavin Anderson has been there with me setting up the buildings for the adventure camp.' He chuckled reminiscently. 'We had a great time erecting the huts which I bought at an auction. We finished them just before the first batch of youngsters arrived last year.'

'What do you do with the boys?' she asked.

'Try to pass on to them skills which have given me so much pleasure in life.'

'What are they?'

'Climbing, camping, sailing, canoeing, fishing, forestlore, also simple rules for survival in the wilderness. That reminds me—I didn't ask you. Have you any other skill besides cooking?'

Gina thought of the dinghy sailing which she'd done

since she was ten, sharing the boat with her brothers. She hadn't done much since she'd met Oliver, but she knew it was a skill which she would never lose.

'I can sail a dinghy,' she offered diffidently. 'Luke, my eldest brother, and I once won a junior championship.'

He flashed her an interested glance.

'Good for you,' he murmured. 'You'll be of more use than I'd hoped. You can help out with the sailing instruction when the weather is suitable.'

Gina forbore to remind him that she would not be staying very long in Glengorm, only until Gavin's wife was able to cope again.

She was finding that she had no wish to fight with Will Fox this morning. Knowledge of his failed marriage was making her view him quite differently. He wasn't just a rough, tough ex-soldier accustomed to giving orders and getting his own way. He was a man who had loved and lost, who had made a mistake and had paid for it.

His mood also was softer, as if he was feeling the influence of the place he had made his home. He was less relentless in his desire to reach it and even condescended to stop at the Bridge of Orchy. For a while they leaned together on the ancient stone structure watching the river swirling down from Loch Tulle, comparing it with that other more placid river they had watched in Stratford. The air was cold and sharp but invigorating. The brown moors were silent, stretching away endlessly to the distant mountains. No traffic passed them. They had all that Sunday morning to themselves. They could have been the only people alive in the world.

Lunch was taken leaning against the truck where it was parked on a grassy sward beside another river further north, beyond the ramparts of Ben Nevis. Blue, sniffing and curious, trampled the grass happily. There were few signs of spring even though the sunshine was warm.

The afternoon was spent travelling deeper and deeper into the mountains along a winding road, past solitary crofts and remote dark forests. There was very little traffic, although Will assured Gina that the same road would be busy with caravans and cars in the summer. The lack of traffic and of people gave Gina a sense of aloneness and insignificance, which was increased by the strange shapes of some of the mountains.

By the time the sun was slipping down the sky she was a willing prisoner to the image of the Highlands as presented to her that day of April. There was enchantment in the landscape as burns, forests and mountains unfolded before her when the road wound on past Achnasheen and Loch a Chroisg, through the lifting, lilting land.

When the sun had gone the light lingered long in the west, but darkness came inevitably and there were still many miles to go. Steadily the truck ground onwards. Hunger gurgled noisily in Gina's stomach and her head nodded. She felt rather than saw the last bend in the road because she was pitched towards Will and then away from him again. Then they were gliding downwards towards the faint shimmer of water. She could just make out the bulk of a tower against the clear starlit sky. She saw a white house gleaming amongst the delicate tracery of branches. The vehicle stopped, the engine was cut and in the silence she could hear the lowing of a cow from a barn.

There were no lights shining from the house and she sensed an uneasiness in her companion as he sat still for a moment.

'I wonder where everyone is,' he said at last, and opened the door on his side.

He jumped out. Gina left the truck more slowly and stiffly. The air was cold and crisp and she could hear water lapping on an unseen shore.

She was aware that Will had gone to the house and was opening the porch door. She heard him yell rudely, his voice abrasive.

'Gavin, Madge! Where the hell are you?'

Only the echo of his own voice answered him. He disappeared and Gina waited. From the back of the truck came the inevitable pitiable mewing of the kitten. Remembering how he had run away the previous evening Gina decided to wait until Will came back to her before she attempted to take the kitten out of the truck. She felt the would like a little light on the subject before she made any move.

Standing there in the starlit dark, listening to the soft lap of water on a shore, hearing the faint soughing of the wind in the branches of trees she was aware of a strange dread forming in her mind. Where were Gavin and Madge Anderson? Why hadn't they answered Will's call? Why were there no lights in the house?

There was probably a perfectly reasonable answer to her questions, but she could not help recalling Meg Maxwell's anxious remark about Will having been let down rather badly once and that the next time he was let down might be once too often and have a detrimental effect on him. Was it possible that the Andersons had let him down?

Gina shivered and would have given anything in that moment to have been back in Birmingham in her own comfortable flat instead of standing in the damp darkness of a Highland glen waiting for the reappearance of the man who had brought her there.

CHAPTER THREE

LIGHT flickered out from one of the ground floor windows of the house. Gina guessed it came from an oil lamp which had just been lit. The faint glow grew in strength as she waited and watched.

Then Will spoke from the doorway. His voice was loud and harsh, shattering the silence and making her jump.

'Aren't you coming in?' he barked.

'Yes, yes, of course,' she called back, thinking he didn't sound very welcoming. 'But I'd like to get Blue out first. I can't see a thing.'

'You'll have to get used to the darkness. We don't have street lighting in the glen,' he replied sardonically.

Gina's heart sank a little. His softer, more kindly mood had evaporated. Once more he was the tough Army captain issuing orders. He reached under the canvas cover for Blue. swore and withdrew his hand quickly as the kitten scratched him.

'Here, you get him out,' he growled at her. 'I'll take the cases.'

Blue felt soft and warm. Gina was comforted by the feel of her pet who was a familiar friend in that unfamiliar place.

Cautiously she followed Will along a path to the door of the house and stepped into a porch and then through another door into a narrow hallway. From there they went into a room from which the light came.

It was a big room with bare stone walls which had been painted a cheerful yellow. The wooden floor had been sanded and varnished and it was scattered with bright rugs. The furniture was mixed; comfortable armchairs set about a stone fireplace; a big roll-topped desk; a pretty oval-shaped gate-legged table on which the oil lamp hissed and flared.

Gina stood hesitantly, hugging Blue close to her, rubbing her cheek against his fur as Will set down her cases beside the desk. He glanced across at her and his mouth quirked sardonically.

'I'm beginning to feel a little sorry for Noll—in retrospect, of course,' he murmured.

'Why?'

'He had to compete with that kitten for your love.'

'He didn't have to do anything of the sort,' she retorted indignantly, surprised by this sudden attack. 'I loved him just as much as I love Blue.'

The sardonic twist became more apparent.

'Just as much? Not more than?' he queried jeeringly. 'Then I reckon Noll is better off where he is. At least he won't suffer disillusionment finding out that you loved him only as much as you love your pet.'

'That isn't what I meant at all,' she flared. 'I loved Oliver in a totally different way from the way I love Blue. He didn't have to compete with anyone. Anyway, he wasn't like you. I would never have had to run away from him as your wife ran away from you.'

The words were no sooner out of her mouth than she regretted them. She didn't usually go in for wounding people deliberately. She couldn't think why she'd said them except that there had been an overriding need to retaliate, to hurt him as much as he seemed intent on hurting her.

His eyes were a hard soulless blue, making her doubt whether it was possible to hurt him.

'So Meg talked, did she?' he said coolly. 'Just as well, really. Saves me the trouble, and maybe it'll stop you from getting any sloppy ideas. And now to find out why Gavin and Madge have skipped. There should be a note somewhere.'

Her heart sinking even lower Gina followed him out of the room because he took the lamp with him. Shadows pranced on the walls of the hallway as they went down it into another big room, which was obviously the kitchen. It was well equipped with cupboards and cooking facilities and in the middle of the floor was a long table with benches on either side. Obviously the campers ate their meals there.

The note was on the table, a single sheet of paper held down by a water jug. Gina looked round the room while Will read it, not daring to watch the expression on his face change.

The sound of the paper being scrunched by a hand drew her attention and, fascinated, she watched Will's long fingers curled round the note with a viciousness which frightened her. She expected him to swear, but all he said was,

'I might have guessed. The little. . .!'

She never heard what he intended to call either Madge or Gavin because he didn't finish the sentence, but she guessed it wasn't complimentary.

'What's wrong?' she asked hesitantly. His face was dark, his eyes looking paler and harder than ever. He tossed the crumpled note on to the table.

'Read it,' he barked, and went out of the room.

Still clutching Blue, Gina picked up the note and straightened it out. It was written in a rather schoolboyish scribble.

Dear Will,

I've had to take Madge down to her parents' home. She feels she can stand this place no longer. Personally, I think that it's her condition which is making her hyper-sensitive to atmosphere, but there's nothing I can do about it. If I don't take her away she says she'll leave me. I'd like to say that we'd be coming back once the child is born, but somehow I don't think that will happen.

Sorry to let you down. I hope you'll understand why I've had to put her first. It was good while it lasted, Will, for me at any rate.

Good luck.
Gavin.

So her intuitive feeling that the Andersons had deserted Will had been right, thought Gina, as she placed the note back on the table. Once again Will had been let down. They must have gone while his back had been turned because they had been unable to tell him to his face that they wanted to leave. In order to get her own way with her husband Madge had used a weapon Gavin had known that Will would appreciate. She had threatened to leave him if he did not do as she wished. No wonder Will had been tempted to call Madge rude names!

Instead of standing there clutching her pet and shivering she should be showing some spirit and doing something to help soften the blow which the desertion of the Andersons must be to Will. Meg Maxwell had been afraid of how another let-down might affect him. Well, the new cook and bottle-washer was going to make sure that it brought him nothing but benefits.

Setting Blue down on the floor, Gina went over to the cooker. It was big and shiny and possessed several burners on one of which was a kettle. She filled the kettle with water. Instinctively she found matches and the gas storage cylinder. She turned on the regulator to release the gas from the container, then turned on one of the burners and lit it before placing the kettle on it. Soon she was searching cupboards for food and cooking equipment.

Her weariness evaporated miraculously as she worked and soon she was humming to herself as she pottered about. Blue was silenced with some tinned milk and by the time Will returned to the kitchen, after bringing in all the luggage from the truck, the table was set at one end for two people. The smell of soup being heated and something savoury being cooked in the oven made the kitchen seem the homely, welcoming place it should be.

Hearing Gina humming a tune he often whistled himself, Will grinned at her.

'I never thought I'd hear someone as prudish as you singing a song like that,' he teased her. 'Do you know what it's about?'

'Seduction?' she guessed, colour flaming wildly in her cheeks as she met his amused glance. He looked less violent now, she was relieved to see.

'In the nicest possible sense,' he replied, 'and with a happy ending. The food smells good. How soon can we eat?'

'In about fifteen minutes. I've made some tea. I expect you could do with a cup. I know I could,' she said.

'After that blow beneath the belt from the Andersons I think I'm in need of something stronger,' he remarked, going over to a cupboard and taking down a bottle of whisky. He poured some into a glass, then leaned against the table and sipped some of it, and watched her pouring tea.

'You look very much at home,' he commented, noting how the effort of preparing the meal had loosened some of her hair from the chiffon scarf which tied it back, so that corkscrew ringlets dangled tantalisingly about her flushed cheeks.

The expression in his eyes disturbed her, making her suddenly very aware of her position alone with him in his house miles away from anywhere, preparing his evening meal as if she were his wife.

She looked away from that disturbing blue gaze and squeaked a question from a throat which was dry.

'What are you going to do now that Gavin and Madge have gone?'

'Carry on. What else can I do? With twenty lively youngsters and their two social workers arriving tomorrow I can hardly change everything now. Anyway, you're here, and a good cook on the premises means that half the battle is won. I can manage the instruction courses myself and we can organise the lads to help with the washing up.' He paused and gave her a strange underbrowed glance. 'Unless it's in your mind to do a disappearing act, too,' he tacked on.

Bitterness made his voice harsh again and etched lines

454

round his mouth, but she noticed there was no self-pity there.

'I'm not in the habit of letting people down,' she returned loftily, looking at him down her straight shapely nose. 'I said I'd help you out until...'

'Until Madge was able to cope again,' he reminded her drily. 'But you see Madge won't be coming back, ever, and there's the camp in May to get through as well as the summer camps, and all those letters to answer from hopeful youngsters wanting to come and cupboards to stock with food.'

She sent him a wide-eyed glance. His gaze met hers steadily. He was not appealing to her for himself. He was making her feel that if she didn't stay she would be letting down all sorts of people she had never met.

'I'll stay until you find someone else to help you, no longer,' she said.

His mouth twitched and dark eyelashes hid his eyes as he looked down at his drink.

'Good for you, George,' he said softly. 'Now I know where I stand.'

'But what about other help? Who will take Gavin's place? Do you know anyone else who would be willing to come and live here?' she asked.

'I know of someone who is interested,' he replied vaguely, and tossed off the remains of his whisky. Then he gave her another penetrating stare. 'No one, I repeat no one, is irreplaceable in this life, George. Neither a partner, nor a wife, nor yet a fiancé.'

That stung. Again her wide glance flew to his and stayed briefly, only to fall away before the intensity of his. Her distress must have shown in her face because he put out a hand and touched her gently on the cheek. She flinched away from his touch and turned on him like an angry cat. He smiled gently.

'All right, kitten,' he soothed. 'My intention was only to comfort you—I know you believe that no one can ever take the place of Oliver. But that isn't true. Someone else will come along one day and the old chemistry will start working and before you know where you are you'll be wanting to share his bed...'

'Never!' she spat at him. 'Anyway, that isn't why I wanted to marry Oliver. We both agreed that the physical aspect of marriage was the least important part. We wanted to marry for other reasons too.'

He raised his eyebrows and whistled jeeringly.

'Did you now,' he drawled, and devilment danced in his eyes. 'How very civilised of you both! I had a feeling that might have been the way of it. You're remarkably unawakened for a young woman who was about to be married only ten days ago. Far be it from me to criticise Noll's methods of wooing you. I suppose he knew what he was doing. After all, he was a doctor.' He sniffed and jerked his head in the direction of the cooker. 'Something seems to require your attention over there. I'll go and wash my hands and hope that when I come back the grub will be ready to eat. I'm famished.'

He left the room again whistling that tantalisingly familiar tune which, she realised now, she had been humming to herself. Hand to the cheek he had touched, which seemed hotter than the other, she attended to the soup which had been about to boil over. She wondered if she would ever learn to avoid falling into the traps Will Fox set for her to fall into during the course of conversation. He set them, she was sure, for his own amusement because her innocent serious replies made him laugh. How on earth was she going to work for and live with him for most of the summer?

Live with him! The words screamed through her mind like warning. That was just what she was going to do. She was going to live alone with him in this house without the chaperonage of the Andersons, unless there was another house where she could live.

While they were eating she approached the new problem in a round about way, wary of any scoffing remarks he might make. She asked first of all where the Andersons had lived.

'Here, in this house, on a temporary basis. Gav was going to build a house, but he kept putting it off. I think he knew as much as I did that Madge wouldn't stick it out here,' he replied tersely.

'Did you sleep in one of the huts?' she asked diffidently.

He looked up, puzzled.

'No, why should I? This is my house, and it's big enough to house three families, let alone one. They had the third floor. I sleep on the second floor.'

'But when the campers are here don't you sleep in the bunkhouse then?'

He gave her a rather pitying glance.

'Look, George, some of the lads and lasses who come are almost twenty. None of them is younger than fifteen. Even if they come without an adult leader, I reckon they're quite old enough to sleep in the bunkhouse without supervision. Now, come clean and tell me what's really on your mind. You're not very good at a flank attack.'

'Living alone here with you,' she gulped hastily, and her face burned red again.

He stared at her for a few seconds, obviously taken aback.

'I'm not sure how to take that remark. Seems to me you're casting aspersions on my character,' he said in frost-bitten tones.

'I'm sorry,' she muttered. 'I didn't mean to. I just thought it might look odd to other people, you and I living in the same house when we're not married or anything.'

Under the dagger-swift glance of his eyes her spirit quailed and her voice trailed away to silence.

'I see,' he said, and although there was still a sprinkling of frost, his voice was slightly warmer. He rubbed his chin reflectively with one hand. 'Without Gavin and Madge here, there might be gossip. Is that what you're getting at?'

She nodded and couldn't prevent her face from flaming again.

'Well, there's nothing we can do about that,' he replied calmly. 'I must say the thought hadn't occurred to me and I can assure you that it won't occur to our nearest neighbour, Lachie Munro. But now that you mention it I can see that it might create difficulties later.' He paused and frowned, rubbing his chin again, gazing with narrowed eyes at nothing, as if a new thought had struck him. Then he shrugged and looked at her. 'Not to worry, George. If anyone is unpleasant I'll deal with them. Of course, if you'd really prefer to sleep in the bunkhouse, you can, but don't expect me to move out of here.'

She hesitated, not knowing what to say. His calm attitude was making her feel as if she had made a fuss about nothing. His eyes had begun to twinkle again as he noticed her hesitation and she wished she'd kept her mouth shut in the first place.

'No,' he cautioned, 'don't decide yet. Wait until I've shown you the room where you're going to sleep. Madge decorated it all ready for the new cook. I've put your luggage up there and it's a flight of stairs above mine, if that makes you feel any easier. The bunkhouse is all right, but a bit rough, and once the campers come you'd have no privacy there.'

She went with him meekly up the stairs to the third floor. There were two large attic bedrooms, one of which had been the Andersons'. Will led her into the other and in the soft light cast by the oil lamp which he placed on the high Victorian chest of drawers she could see that the room had been recently decorated.

'Well? What do you think? Here, or the bunkhouse?' he asked.

'Here,' she muttered, avoiding his mocking gaze.

'I thought that would be the way of it,' he remarked drily.

She pushed her hand across her forehead in a gesture of

weariness. The bed under its old-fashioned patchwork cover looked inviting, and she longed for nothing more than to climb into it and sleep.

As she lowered her hand Oliver's diamond ring which she still wore on the third finger of her left hand caught the light and flashed brightly. Will's eyes narrowed and hardened when he saw it.

'You're tired,' he observed brusquely. 'I'll get the sheets for the bed. You may as well turn in now.'

His concern surprised her. She had thought he didn't notice when anyone was tired.

'But the dishes——' she began.

'I'll do them,' he replied curtly.

He left the room, returning within a few seconds with clean sheets and pillow slips. He was followed by Blue, who entered stealthily, ears cocked and tail on high.

'What shall I do about Blue?' asked Gina.

'Do you really want to know what *I* think you should do with him?' he asked, looking down at the kitten menacingly.

'No, no,' she said quickly.

'Then don't ask foolish questions. He's your responsibility, not mine, and as long as I don't find him curled up on *my* bed I don't care a hang where he sleeps. Good night, George.'

He went out closing the door behind him, but the old-fashioned latch had hardly settled into place than it lifted again and he put his head around the jamb. Devilment was back in his eyes, blue and twinkling.

'I'm afraid there's no lock on this door, but I know of a trick which I've found useful in the past, when I haven't wanted to be disturbed.'

He came in, closed the door, strode across to an old chair with a tall ladderback, picked it up and going back to the door tilted the chair against it so that the top rung of the ladderback rested under the latch.

'It won't keep a determined intruder out, but it will slow

him down considerably,' he said with a grin. Then lifting the chair away, he opened the door and went out again, the grin still wickedly flickering as he murmured, 'G'night. Sleep well.'

She did sleep well, worn out with the journey as well as the strange emotional upheaval coming north with Will Fox had caused within her. She did not wake until the flat of a hand hit the old door, making it tremble and causing Blue to jump up on to the bed, spitting and growling with fright.

'Show a leg George!' Will sounded as vigorous as usual. 'It's seven-thirty. Breakfast is ready and this is the last time I cook it this week. If you're not down in ten minutes I'll come and drag you out of bed!'

The air felt chilly to the end of her nose and she was reluctant to move from the warm bed, but she couldn't risk having him come in and pull her from the bed as he had threatened.

No wonder Bridget had run away from him if that was the sort of treatment she had had to put up with, she thought, and then she reprimanded herself for her unkind thought. Will was probably just as capable of treating someone he loved as gently as the next man was, and considering the circumstances perhaps it was best if he were rough with her.

Blue was rubbing against the door asking to be let out, so, flinging back the bedclothes, Gina braved the chilliness of her first morning in the Highlands and hurried to open the door. The kitten slid through the opening and padded away downstairs.

Opening the flower-printed curtains, Gina gazed out. Four slender silver birches, their trunks gilded by morning sunlight, made a frame for a picture of winter-bleached moorland, sloping down to a blue loch beyond which a mountain reared, a perfect cone topped with sunlit icing where the snow reflected the morning light. While she stared entranced by the wild alien landscape, a pair of swans flew over the loch and slid heavily into the water, spattering it with silver ripples.

Excited by the sight of them, she dressed quickly and went downstairs. Will was sitting at the table eating and looking at some letters. Gina went over to the oven and took out her breakfast, then sat down at the place set for her.

'I've just seen two swans land on the lake—I mean the loch,' she announced, unable to keep the excitement out of her voice.

His reaction surprised her. He looked up sharply, his eyes widening.

'Say that again,' he ordered.

She repeated what she had said and added, 'Is that so unusual? You look very surprised.'

With an obvious effort he collected himself and shrugged.

'Just a sign that spring is on its way,' he murmured evasively.

'Oh, it does come here, then? I was beginning to wonder whether it ever came when I saw the snow on the mountain top,' she said drily.

'You'll find other signs, if you care to look,' he replied with a grin.

'Such as?'

'Flowers hiding in warm sheltered crannies.'

'Oh, what sort?' Gina was delighted. She glanced at the bare formica top of the table and imagined it covered with a pretty cloth and an arrangement of spring flowers in the centre.

'Primroses. When you've finished eating, grab a jacket and I'll show you round the place. I might even show you where the primroses are.'

Outside the air was sharp but fresh. There was no sound other than that of cold water running here and there through rocks and lank brown heather or lapping at the shores of the loch. Will showed her the copse where he had

461

camped the first time he had come to the glen and made her listen for the sound of the torrent inland, which had lulled him to sleep.

'Just four years ago,' he said. 'There's quite a difference in the place since then. Come and see the bunkhouses.'

On their way to the timber huts which were situated on a plateau of land close to the lochside to the right of the house, they passed a barn. A tall man with a shock of greying hair who was wearing denim dungarees over a thick woollen shirt appeared in the doorway.

'Good morning, Lachie,' Will greeted him. 'This is George. She's come to cook for the campers.'

'Good day to you, miss,' said the other man. His round innocent blue eyes had a slightly dazed look in them as he regarded her pants.

'When did the Andersons leave?' asked Will.

'I'm thinking it would be a day or two after you left,' said Lachie, wrinkling his forehead. 'She was after giving him no peace. She'll be no loss to the glen.'

'Perhaps you're right,' said Will. 'But I shall miss Gavin.'

'Aye, he was a grand lad. It's a pity, so it is, that he was caught,' murmured Lachie, who was still furtively eyeing Gina. 'Have you been seeing the swans?'

'Not yet. But George has. When did they come?' Will sounded a little uneasy at the mention of the big white birds.

'The evening before last, just as the sun was setting. Ach, I couldn't believe my own eyes,' said Lachie, and chuckled suddenly, the expression in his eyes now decidedly impish as he looked from Gina to Will and then back to Gina again. 'I should have known you'd be bringing a bonny lass with you.'

He turned back into the barn, and they continued on their way to the bunkhouse. Will led the way, striding quickly, a frown on his face.

'What did he mean by saying he should have known

you'd be bringing me with you?' asked Gina as soon as she could catch up with him. She had read that the Highlanders often believed in second sight and she wondered whether Lachie possessed the ability to see into the future.

'He was referring to an ancient legend about the glen,' said Will curtly. 'You'll find that Highlanders usually have some tale to tell about the places in which they live. They use them to explain anything which is strange about the place. It's best to listen to them with a grain of salt. I've no time for such stories myself.'

No, you've no time for them, but this one has disturbed you for some reason, thought Gina, grimacing at his broad back as he opened the door of the nearest bunkhouse, and she decided that she would ask Lachie Munro as soon as she could to tell her the legend of the swans.

Although there was a certain amount of pride in Will's bearing as he showed her the bunkhouses with their rows of camp beds, showers, wash basins and drying rooms, which he had erected with the help of Gavin and Lachie, the enthusiasm with which he had set out had waned. His withdrawal became more and more noticeable as they returned to the house. His mind was obviously not on what he was doing and he had forgotten to show her where she would find primroses.

Perhaps it was just as well, thought Gina with a sigh as she looked round the clean well-equipped kitchen after she had finished clearing up the breakfast dishes. After all, she was not there to decorate the place, as Will had pointed out, nor to soften the house's uncompromising austerity and masculinity. She was there as a volunteer to help out until another partner could be found to help run the camps.

After a midday meal which Lachie shared with them, Will went off to Lochinvie to collect post which might have arrived while he had been away. He didn't invite Gina to accompany him, but gave her instructions about making sure the beds in the bunkhouse were ready and to prepare dinner for the hungry youths expected that evening.

When she had done all she could in the way of preparation Gina realised that Blue was missing. Going outside, she found the afternoon was mild and sunny. Down the slope from the house the loch dimpled under the caress of a slight breeze and the dark tower had lost some of its dour aspect. aspect.

She called to Blue and wandered down the path to the loch. Near the small curving beach of shingle the two swans sat. At her approach they reared their necks and hissed, then waddled down to the water and took off to swim sedately away.

From high above her head Gina heard the plaintive but unmistakable cry of her kitten. Looking upwards at the tower, she saw a cheeky blue-grey face peeping out of an opening in the ruin.

'Oh, Blue, you naughty kitten! How did you get there? Come down at once!' she called.

Blue merely put his head on one side and looked mischievous. Gina approached the tower more closely.

'Come down, Blue,' she ordered.

'Do not be worrying about the wee cat, miss,' said a voice nearby, and looking round, she saw Lachie sitting on a rough stone bench near the entrance to the tower. He was enjoying the sunshine and quiet smoke of his pipe. 'If you'd be after sitting down for a wee while the cat will come down in its own good time,' he added. 'Ach, it's a lovely day, so it is, and we're in no hurry, no hurry at all.'

Listening to the lazy drone of his voice and seeing the expression of permanent pleasure on his lined weatherbeaten face, Gina guessed that Lachie had never been in a hurry in his life.

Accepting the invitation to dawdle with him for a while, she sat down on the bench next to him and leaned back against the rough stone of the tower. The sunshine was warm on her skin and when she closed her eyes it glowed behind her eyelids.

'Aye, it's a free and easy life, so it is,' continued Lachie, his voice making slow music in the soft air. 'I can shoot a deer if it comes on my croft and I can fish in the burns and in the sea. If I need extra money I can come and work for Will Fox or go to Ullapool to mend fish boxes. You'll be knowing the old Gaelic saying, perhaps?'

'No. I know nothing about the Gaels,' said Gina humbly.

'Then there's a lot for you to be learning,' he said. 'It goes like this: "When God made time he made plenty of it." Remember that and you'll never be suffering from indigestion,' said Lachie wisely. 'And now you'll be telling which part of England you come from.'

She told him, and then listened to a long story about the time he had visited Birmingham during the second world war.

'And is that big market place, the Bull Ring, still there?' he asked, coming to the end of his tale.

'Yes, but it's all been rebuilt since you were there. You wouldn't recognise it now,' she replied.

'And there'll be too much traffic, I'm thinking, and people in a hurry,' he murmured. 'Ach, you're better off living here where it's quiet and no one is in a hurry, not even Will. For all he has the ways of a conqueror, he can take it easy and slow when he's a mind to it.'

Easy and Slow. That was the title of the folk song which Will whistled. But the song wasn't about work. It was about the slow, sly seduction of a young woman, suggestive in its lilting melody and phrasing. Yes, she could imagine Will Fox conquering a woman by easy, slow methods if he found his usual direct method of attack failing to win him what he wanted.

'How long have you lived in the glen?' she asked Lachie.

'Since I was a young man. I took over my grandfather's croft just after the war.'

'Are you married?'

'I was, but my wife went away. The glen cannot hold a woman, or it couldn't until two days ago.'

'Oh? Why is that?' asked Gina, her interest caught.

Lachie pointed with the stem of his pipe at the swans which were still sailing slowly on the water.

'They have come back after being away for almost three hundred years,' he intoned.

'But I thought they came here each spring?' said Gina.

'There has been no swan seen in Glengorm since the chief of the Macneal clan lived in this tower,' he replied.

'When was that?'

'In the seventeenth century. He was a soldier too, fighting for King Charles the Second. Once when he came back to his inheritance, which included this glen, all of that mountain and the big castle on the other side of it, he brought a young bride with him. She came from the south, like you. Lovely she was, but as shy and timid as a roedeer. She preferred living in the tower here to living in the castle. She liked to feed the swans when she felt lonely, and she was often lonely because she was barren and bore no children and her husband the chief of the clan was often away.'

Lachie paused to relight his pipe. Gina, enthralled by the story which she guessed was the legend to which Will had referred, watched the swans and imagined the slight figure of a young woman dressed in a long gown, with ringlets of hair falling over her shoulders, standing on the shore throwing pieces of bread to the big birds.

'Then one day she disappeared,' said Lachie, his pipe going to his satisfaction. 'In the autumn it was, when the leaves were gold and russet and the heather turned brown. She went when the swans flew south. All winter she was away. The people of the glen said she had gone with the swans she loved, back to her own place and people, turning into a swan maiden and flying with the birds. They said she would come back when the swans returned in the spring. They said that to comfort the chief, who was brokenhearted when he could not find his dear one.'

'Did he ever find her?' asked Gina in an awed whisper. She was finding the similarity of the story to the little she knew about Will Fox's marriage rather disconcerting.

'No. All that winter he waited, and when the spring came he watched, but the swans never came, nor did his wife. The next year it was the same, and in all the years that followed neither his wife nor the swans were seen in the glen again. After a while the chief married again, but his new wife would not stay in the glen. Gradually all the women left the crofts, and since then no woman has been able to stay in the glen. My own grandfather did not take over his croft until his wife had died, and my father did not dare to live here because his wife would not come.'

'What a strange story,' murmured Gina. 'But surely there was some reasonable explanation for the young woman's disappearance. Perhaps she drowned in the loch, or something like that?'

'She flew away with the swans,' said Lachie stubbornly. 'And the glen has been cursed ever since then.'

'Are there any of the Macneal's descendants living near here?' asked Gina, deciding not to argue with him.

'Ach, yes. Mistress Macneal comes to the castle at Easter and stays there until the autumn. The rest of the time she's away in some warm climate, Florida, or the Mediterranean, or some such place. She's the chief of the clan now, since her old father died, leaving no male heir. She married a star-spangled Scot for his money and persuaded him to change his name to Macneal.'

'Star-spangled Scot?' repeated Gina with a laugh. 'What do you mean?'

'He's an American with Scottish ancestors and a Scottish name,' replied Lachie, imperturbable as ever. 'Aye, the Macneals did well when the chief married him.'

'Do they still own the glen?'

'Ach, no. Will owns it. When the Macneals were poor, a while back, they started to sell off the land. This part was bought by a man called Henderson who hoped to turn it into his country estate. He built the house yonder and called it White Lodge, but his wife would not stay, no more than

Madge Anderson would. She said she felt the glen didn't want her, that the spirit of the young bride was pushing her out.'

'You mean she saw the ghost of the woman?' exclaimed Gina.

'Aye.' Lachie puffed contentedly at his pipe.

'Did Madge say she had seen it too?'

'It suited her to say she had,' said Lachie drily. 'But do not be worrying about it. You'll not see it because you've come with the swans, and the curse says that no woman will rest in Glengorm until the swans come back in the springtime when the true mistress of the master of the glen returns.'

Gina looked closely at his long-jawed face. He seemed quite serious and his innocent blue eyes returned her gaze openly.

'You're not sure whether you believe me or not, are you lass?' Lachie queried softly.

'No, I'm not. Who is master of the glen now?'

'Will Fox. He bought it from the Henderson family.'

No wonder Will had looked at her sharply when she had said she had seen the swans that morning. No wonder he had been disturbed by their return.

'Lachie, do you know what the name of the Macneal's wife was?' she asked.

'I mind she was called Bridie, the Scottish version of the name Bridget, common enough in the Highlands and Islands. Look now, there's your wee cat. Wasn't I after telling you he would be coming to join you if you didn't hurry him? Ach, it's a fine wee pussy you have there, and you'll have to be taking care of him and not letting him roam too far, and him not used to the land yet.'

If he was still disturbed by the return of the swans to Glengorm, Will gave no sign of it on his return from Lochinvie. He brought many letters, applications he said from people wishing to attend the camps in the summer and he expected her help in going through them and answering them.

Not long after his return the first group of campers arrived, having walked over the moors from Ullapool as part of the adventure course. Most of them were boys between the ages of fourteen and sixteen, excited by their first visit to the Highlands and grateful for the meal to which they helped themselves in the kitchen. Another group including some girls followed half an hour later.

The youngsters were accompanied by two social workers; one was a burly bearded young man called Steve Harris who was the outdoor projects officer of the youth association to which the youngsters belonged, and the other was a slim fair young woman named Janet Fines.

Janet confided in Gina that she was really a teacher of art in a school in Glasgow but that she gave some of her free time to the youth association which had been organised in the slum area in order to help youngsters, disorientated by their removal from old condemned tenements, to new housing estates.

'How do you help them?' enquired Gina.

'By teaching them pottery amongst other skills, taking groups of seven to eight of them after school is over. The classes serve a dual purpose. Apart from learning a skill they talk to me, and that's a contact with them, and I learn to know them and to understand something of what they're up against, the despondency of decay and demolition. This place is a marvellous contrast to the place where they live at present and we're lucky that Captain Fox has made it available to them. I'm sorry though that Madge had to give up, and I hope her desertion won't set him against social workers as a whole,' said Janet anxiously.

'He may not have very kindly feelings towards her personally,' replied Gina, 'but I don't think he's the sort of person to allow her behaviour to prevent him from doing something which he considers worthwhile.'

'I hope you're right. Anyway he has you to help him now. I must say that meal was very good. If you're going to feed us all like that during the next two weeks I'm going to put on weight,' laughed the lively, energetic Janet.

During the next few days Gina worked harder than at any time in her life. Up early every morning, obeying the summons of Will's hand on her bedroom door, she cooked twenty-six breakfasts, then cleared away and washed up. After that she prepared the food for the evening meal and also for the packed lunches which the campers took with them on the various expeditions. Admittedly she had help, but there were times when she thought nostalgically of the various electrical gadgets her mother had possessed to assist in the preparation of meals.

One evening half way through the camp, feeling particularly tired as she tidied up after finishing all the preparations for the next day, her mind wandered to the strange legend of the swans as told to her by Lachie Munro. It was probably only coincidence that the name of the wife of the Macneal who had once been master of the glen had been Bridie, the Highland version of Bridget, but it could be enough of a coincidence to raise Will's hopes about the possible return of his own wife, now that the swans had come back.

She hadn't had much private conversation with him since the campers had come. He usually spent the evenings with the social workers discussing the plans for the next day's activities, and by the time he returned to the house Gina was in bed fast asleep. Not once had she been kept awake at night by thoughts of Oliver and what might have been if he had not been killed. Nor did she think of him much during the daytime. She was too busy.

The youngsters attending the camp were a lively bunch, and all were grateful for their opportunity to enjoy the beautiful scenery and to participate in recreations which might otherwise have been denied to them. When it came to showing them how to sail, Will enlisted Gina's help and she gave dry land instruction on the simplest points of sailing before showing them how to rig the dinghies and launch them.

470

She enjoyed seeing the bright red sails of the small boats fluttering against the blues and greens of the loch on a fine day and often wished she had time to go sailing herself. Hearing Will enter the kitchen behind her, she voiced her wish aloud to him.

'There'll be plenty of time when they've gone,' he said, then to her surprise he brushed her cheek with the back of his hand in that strangely affectionate gesture he had used once before. This time she didn't flinch away from him.

'You're looking better,' he remarked. 'Behaving better, too. Not so your cat, though. Look at this!'

He held out his arm and pushed back his shirt sleeve to reveal a long deep scratch on the inside of his wrist.

'Oh, how did you get that?' exclaimed Gina.

'Rescuing your foolish animal.'

'When? Where? You didn't tell me.'

'I'm telling you now, aren't I?' he retorted. 'He seems to be fascinated by high places. The more dangerous they are the better. He had somehow scrambled down the cliffs at the end of the loch and he was stuck on a ledge, and letting out the most ear-splitting cries. I climbed down and managed to grab him. The scratch was my reward for effort.'

'Thank you,' said Gina, faintly. She had a sudden vision of the cliffs, dark and forbidding, as she had often seen them, rearing up against the backcloth of the sunset. At the foot of them the sea flung itself against tumbled rocks. If Blue had fallen he would have been dashed to pieces against those rocks. If Will had slipped he would have gone too, his body hurtling over and over through the air into the heaving smashing water.

Her mouth trembled suddenly. Tears brimmed in her eyes. He had said she looked better, but she was still easily upset by the thought of death.

'Are the tears for me or for the cat?' he asked derisively. She blinked furiously and glared at him.

'For both of you. You could have been killed.'

'Not I. I'm too experienced a climber to take any unnecessary risks. If I'd thought there was a chance of me slipping I'd have come back for a rope. But you'll have to watch him. He likes this place and he's beginning to run wild. There's nothing to stop him from straying on to the Macneal estate and if Grant Parker, the game warden, sees him he might shoot first and ask questions afterwards.'

'Oh, surely he wouldn't shoot a kitten?'

'Oh, yes, he would. Those grouse moors are the Macneal pride and joy and Parker raises some of the finest game in the country. He won't take kindly to a stray cat amongst his special pigeons. So keep your precious Blue near you, if you can.'

'I'll try, but I've been so busy, and it isn't always possible to keep him in with the door forever opening.'

'I know. That's why I didn't want you to bring him. And don't think I haven't noticed how hard you've been working. You're not feeling so sorry for yourself now, are you?'

'No, I'm not,' she admitted. 'I must have been a pain in the neck after Oliver was killed,' she added, unconsciously using one of his own phrases to describe her miserable behaviour.

'You were,' he agreed. 'And your mother was at her wits' end wondering what to do about you. Are you glad you came here to try Fox's remedy for all ills?'

'Now that isn't a good question to ask at the moment. Ask me when my back isn't aching and my hands are restored to their normal state,' she riposted.

He laughed and, putting his arm round her shoulders, hugged her gently.

'Mrs Chadwick was wrong. You have plenty of spunk, and anyone who says otherwise will have me to reckon with,' he said softly.

Surprised by the hug, and more than a little perturbed by the effect being close to him was having on her, she sought refuge in flippancy.

'Kitten-soft, you called me,' she accused.

'And so you are,' he murmured. His hand slipped down

over her shoulder and slid under her arm.

She looked up to object. He bent his head swiftly and kissed her on the mouth. Gina sprang away from him, startled and quivering.

'How dare you!' she exclaimed, unable to think of anything else to say, knowing she sounded ridiculously prudish.

'I dared because I wanted to kiss you to thank you for all you've done recently. You won't let me pay you because you volunteered to come, so I have to find another way of expressing my appreciation,' he explained coolly. 'Now come off it, George, stop behaving as if I'm the villain in some Victorian melodrama. What's a kiss between friends?'

He was laughing at her, and she could not bear his laughter any more than she could bear his kiss, no matter how lightly it had been given. Turning, she fled up the stairs, every nerve tingling. Blue chased up after her, as usual, but for once she had forgotten him and, inadvertently, she shut him out of the room in her desire to be alone with her tumultuous thoughts. His scratching and mewling took her back to the door again. She opened it impatiently and let him in.

'It was all your fault, you silly kitten,' she muttered. Ignoring her, Blue strolled across to the mat on which he slept every night, stretched out full length on his side and blinked drowsily at her.

'If you hadn't been on that ledge,' Gina continued, 'he wouldn't have had to rescue you. Then you wouldn't have scratched him and he wouldn't have told me about the scratch. Then I wouldn't have said what I did and he wouldn't have been tempted to do what he did.'

It all made sense to Gina, but Blue didn't think much of the explanation and yawned disgustedly before licking his forepaw and passing it over one ear.

Still quivering, Gina undressed and quickly climbed into the cold bed. The effect of Will's kiss on her was alarming. Viewing it now from the shelter of her room, she knew that he had given it as he had said, in friendliness, as a way of showing his appreciation. Her violent over-reaction had been quite uncalled for.

It would have been different, she agreed with herself, if they hadn't been alone in the house. It would have been different if she hadn't been all keyed up to marry Oliver only to have her desires frustrated by his sudden death. It would have been different if Will hadn't married a girl called Bridget, who might turn up any day because the swans were back in the glen, a sure sign that the true mistress of the master of the glen would return soon.

Gina groaned, tired of the tug-of-war of argument, and fell asleep surprisingly quickly and slept as soundly as she had always slept in that bed.

To her relief Will made no reference to her odd behaviour when she met him briefly before serving breakfast the next morning, and during the next few days there were no more conversations alone with him before bedtime.

Storms blew in from the Atlantic and the water in the loch was churned up under the onslaught of wild wind and sleety rain. Two of the campers out on their four-day camp returned sodden and miserable, their tent having been washed away by a rushing torrent of water which had suddenly developed on the mountainside where they had been spending the night. Another lost his way on the moors and a search party had to be organised to find him when he didn't turn up. He was found and brought back triumphantly by the boys whom Will had taken with him on the search and who had all apparently enjoyed climbing perpendicular rock for the first time in their lives.

Will took all the crises in his stride, turning each 'adventure' into an object lesson for the entire group. His calmness and foresight were remarkable, thought Gina. He was always able to think his way out of a difficult situation, but he never took unnecessary risks. He handled the young people easily and with humour, but when they had all gone he admitted that he had missed Gavin, and that it was important that he found someone suitable to take Gavin's place before the next group arrived in May because they would have no social workers with them, but would be private individuals paying for the chance to participate in some 'adventures'.

It was with that in mind that he left her and Lachie in charge of the farm and drove down to Glasgow to look up an old Army acquaintance. Feeling rather pleased that he trusted her sufficiently to stay and look after his home, Gina took the opportunity to relax and explore the glen.

The weather had changed again and was mild and sunny. There were many more signs of spring than had been visible when she had arrived. The icing was still on the summit of Ben Searg, but it had shrunk and in the woodland, which covered the lower slopes of the mountain, there was a glow of pink as buds swelled.

Gina fed the swans every day. They were becoming more used to her and no longer reached out their necks in ugly attack. They did not like Blue, however, and the frisky kitten was sensible enough to keep a safe distance from those snapping beaks and muscular necks.

One day when feeding time was over Gina wandered along the edge of the loch, intending to go as far as the opposite shore which had always attracted her. As usual Blue accompanied her, occasionally disappearing into the undergrowth of brambles and reappearing ahead of her.

After one disappearance he did not come back. Having found that the distance to the opposite side of the loch was much further than she had anticipated, Gina wished to return to White Lodge. The absence of the kitten, however, made her unwilling to return without him as she remembered Will's warning about the possibility of the kitten being shot by the game warden of the Macneal estate.

Calling to Blue, she walked on a little further until she came to some wire fencing. It didn't look like electric fencing, so she ducked through the strands and went on, still calling to the cat.

After a while she decided it was silly to walk any further,

so she sat down on a convenient boulder of rock and awaited Blue's reappearance. As Lachie would say, there was really no need for her to hurry. She might as well relax and enjoy the view. From her position she could see another aspect of the dark tower and behind it, winking through the screen of birches, the white walls of the house.

The afternoon was still and quiet. No cry of seagull or whaup disturbed the peace. Even the water was silent.

'I suppose you realise you're trespassing?'

The voice was masculine and rather husky. She turned to find a young man of her own age standing a few feet away from her. He was tall and too thin. His handsome face was a pale wedge framed by a tangle of longish black hair. His eyes were as dark as his hair, opaque and unwinking. He was dressed in well-cut tweed pants and a beautiful cream-coloured Aran sweater. Between his hands was Blue.

'Is this yours,' asked the young man, not waiting for her to answer his first question.

'Yes. Where did you find him?'

'Stalking a pair of robins who are busy building their nest. You'd best take him. If Parker sees him he'll shoot him.'

He spoke gently and his smile was diffident yet disarming. Gina took Blue from him and thanked him.

'I wouldn't have trespassed if I hadn't lost him,' she explained apologetically.

'I couldn't care less whether you trespass or not,' he replied. 'You're from the White Lodge, aren't you?'

'Yes.' Gina pushed some tendrils of hair back from her face and the sunlight caught in the diamond on her finger, making it flash. 'I'll go back now that I have him,' she added.

'Do you mind if I walk with you? I've nothing else to do. Mother sent me out to get some air, but there's nothing more dull than walking by myself. Before the storms started I used to come down to the beach here and watch you through the binoculars.'

'Oh.' She was dismayed. He grinned rather sheepishly.
'Do you mind?'

'Yes, I do. Why didn't you come over and make yourself known to us instead of spying?'

'I wasn't really spying. It was just something to do. I suppose I should have come over. Andrea keeps saying I should meet Will Fox, and Mother thinks an adventure course would be good for me. Make a man of me, she says.' He laughed rather mirthlessly. 'But I'm a man already and I don't want to be done good to. I've been ill.'

She could see that he had. His face had the pallor of someone who had recently spent a long time in hospital.

'What was wrong?' she asked gently, feeling a surge of sympathy towards him.

'Car accident,' he said gruffly, as if it hurt him to talk about it. 'Multiple fractures, then pneumonia. Oh, don't be too sympathetic. It was my own fault. I was driving too fast on a wet greasy road and the car skidded. I always drive too fast,' he added in a low, defiant voice.

He was really desperately unhappy, thought Gina, in need of help in the same way she had been after Oliver had been killed.

'Was there anyone else in the car at the time of the crash?' she asked, thinking it might help him to talk to a complete stranger about it.

'Yes. That's why I didn't want to go on living afterwards,' he mumbled.

Exactly as she had felt. Then Will had appeared on the scene and had forced her back into life.

'A girl?' she persisted.

'Yes.' He closed his eyes tightly as if to prevent her from seeing tears brim in them. 'My girl-friend. We'd just decided to split, or at least she'd decided. She knew my mother didn't approve of her. Now she's in intensive care and may not live.'

'Who is Mother?' asked Gina, deciding to ignore the break in his voice.

477

'I thought you'd know,' he exclaimed.

'I've only been at White Lodge for just over two weeks, and I've been so busy that I haven't had time to find out about neighbours.'

He was staring at her curiously.

'Then you must have come with the swans,' he said.

'Yes, I did.'

'How odd, but it fits in with the legend, doesn't it?' he exclaimed.

Gina was startled. She couldn't see how her coming to the glen fitted the legend at all.

'Does it? I don't see how.'

'Oh, never mind. Forget it. I'm Gregor Macneal,' he said as they moved side by side back along the shore. 'My mother is the chief of the clan and you've been trespassing on her estate.'

'Will it be yours one day?'

He shook his head with a glimmer of a smile.

'No. My eldest brother is the heir. I'm just the no-good youngest son,' he replied. 'It'll be his when she dies, and that won't be for years and years. Like Victoria Regina, she'll outlive everyone. She's a tough nut, and the only person I've heard of who doesn't seem to be afraid of her is Will Fox. As a result she has it in for him.'

'Why?'

'Because he goes his own way without consulting her, but mostly I suppose because he owns the glen and she would like to see it as part of the Macneal estate again. She was furious when she learned that the Hendersons had sold it behind her back. She tried to buy it back off Will, but he wouldn't sell. Then he started the adventure camps. She'd love to find out some black mark against him so that she could hold it over him and make him dance to her tunes, but she can't. His Army career was without blemish. His dealings with the local authorities are above board, and as far as anyone can tell his morals are of good repute. So she's been trying something else.'

'What is that?'

'My young sister, Andrea, has taken a liking to him, so Mother is encouraging her. She thinks that as her son-in-law Will Fox might be more amenable to her ideas.'

'Oh, but——' began Gina, and then stopped short. She had been about to say that Will was already married, then she had realised that that piece of information was not hers to pass on, and that Will would be annoyed if he learned she had been talking about his personal life, especially since he did not do that himself. It was quite obvious that the Macneal family knew no more about Bridget than Lachie did.

'But of course when Mother sees you she'll realise that he's scotched that move on her part too.'

'Sees me?' Gina was absolutely mystified.

'Yes,' said Gregor with a grin which seemed to gloat over the possibility of his mother being discomfited. 'She's not going to like you one little bit. I'm going to leave you here because it's quite a long walk back to the castle and I'm not up to walking a long way yet. Thanks for letting me talk to you.'

There was light in his dark eyes now, a gleam of admiration as they roved over her smoothly coiled red-glinting brown hair and creamy-skinned heart-shaped face.

'Please come and see us at the Lodge whenever you feel like a change. There won't be any more campers for another month,' said Gina impulsively.

'I'd like to come,' he said simply. 'But perhaps I should warn you, now I've found someone like you in this wilderness where nothing ever happens I'm likely to make a nuisance of myself. You haven't told me your name.'

'It's Gina.'

'Gina, the nut-brown maiden, who came with the swans,' he murmured, and his smile appeared, not so diffident this time, but infinitely charming. 'Yes,' he added, 'the glen is going to be quite different now that you're here.'

The meeting with Gregor Macneal made Gina feel light hearted. It was nice to know that there was someone about her own age living near with whom she had something in common, even if it was only a fatal car accident. She thought about him several times during the next two days while she was busy about the house. He was handsome and cultured, yet had a touch of wildness which was attractive. She was looking forward to seeing him again when he came on his promised visit to the Lodge.

Sunlight and soft winds made cleaning a must. Gina swept away winter cobwebs and washed everything that was washable. She had never had this urge to make everything clean before, but then she had never had a house to herself before. And if she didn't spring-clean White Lodge, who would?

In a frenzy of energy she washed blankets and curtains and strung them on the line in the garden to blow in the gentle breezes. Later she beat the dust out of rugs and mats. In the house she washed paintwork and floors.

Astonished by her burst of activity, Lachie, who was taking his time to plough Will's fields ready for sowing grain, shook his head at her and told her that if she wasn't careful she'd be getting indigestion. She laughed at him and told him she didn't care. The house was going to be clean and sparkling before Will returned.

'He won't notice,' muttered Lachie, in pessimistic mood.

'Think not?' challenged Gina. 'Want to bet?' He looked surprised.

'Ach, now, and me not a betting man,' he moaned, shifting his pipe from one side of his mouth to the other.

'I'll tell you what we'll do, then,' said Gina. 'You know that lovely old pewter jug you have sitting on the mantelpiece in your cottage?'

'I do that. It was my grandmother's and her mother's before her. Family heirloom, that's what it is.'

'Then will you lend it to me?'

'Now why should I being doing that?'

480

'I want to arrange some flowers in it.'

'And where will you be after getting the flowers?'

'You're going to show me where the primroses grow,' replied Gina.

'Primroses? That's easy.'

'Not today—tomorrow morning. I'm going to arrange them in the jug and I'm going to put it on the kitchen table. If Will notices them and the clean house I keep the jug. If he doesn't you can have it back. Do you agree?'

Lachie's eyes twinkled as he looked down at her.

'Ach, it's a winning way you have with you lass, for all you're a sassenach. I agree.'

By evening that day Gina was tired with her efforts at house-cleaning, but there was one last job to do, and that was to tidy the big roll-topped desk in the living room where Will kept all the correspondence pertaining to the camps. She had been wanting to tidy it ever since she had started to help him to answer the applications.

It took quite a long time because she discovered, to her dismay, that Will's private correspondence was mixed up with the business stuff. There were letters from his mother, letters from Meg Maxwell, postcards from friends on holiday in various parts of the world. Gina decided that she must suggest to Will that if he was going to continue with the adventure camps he should obtain a proper filing system.

Then she brought her thoughts to a full stop.

'Stop it, Gina,' she said. 'You're only a volunteer. Don't get too involved because one day you'll be leaving.'

She threw away the clutter of unwanted paper and then began to sort the remainder into neat piles. While doing so she came across the invitation to her own wedding. The sight of it brought tears to her eyes and held up the job of tidying for a few minutes.

When she began again she came across several letters written on pink perfumed paper. The postmark on the envelope was German. Her curiosity getting the better of her, thinking they might be letters once written to Will by Bridget, Gina took the sheet of paper out of one envelope. To her surprise the letter was written in a language she recognised as being German. It was signed with the name Irma.

She was glad she didn't understand the language because she was sure she would have been tempted to read the letter if it had been written in English. As it was she felt slightly embarrassed, as if she had stumbled upon a secret in Will's life, and she pushed the pink envelopes away in a pigeon-hole, and spent the rest of her hours awake, wondering who Irma was and why she should write so many letters to Will.

CHAPTER FOUR

NEXT morning Lachie showed Gina where the primroses were hiding in warm secret places near a burn where it rushed down to the loch. Delighted to find the pale yellow flowers protected by their oblong leaves, the surfaces of which were wrinkled and furry, Gina picked as many as she could with fairly long stems, and took them back to the house. There she arranged them in the pewter jug which she discovered had been designed in the reign of George the Second and had the lovely curves and decorated handle of that period.

There were no tablecloths in the house big enough to cover the long table, but she had found a length of the cotton cretonne which someone, she guessed it was Madge Anderson, had used to make curtains. Placed cornerwise on the table it added colour and brightness to the room. In the middle she set the jug of primroses and birch catkins, which she had also collected, and stood back to admire the effect.

'I mind my wife used to do the same,' said Lachie with a sigh.

'And didn't you like her doing it?' asked Gina, interested.

'Aye, I did, but I never said so to her.'

'Oh? Why not?'

'Ach, she would have had flowers all over the house, even in the privy, and what use are flowers to a man when all he's wanting is good food after a hard day in the fields? And when I'd be reminding her of that she'd look at me and she'd quote the Bible at me. "Man shall not live by bread alone," she'd say. She was very knowledgeable about the Bible. She was a Sunday school teacher at the kirk.'

'She was right too. There are more important things in life than eating all the time.'

'Aye, but not when you're hungry, lass.'

'Where is Mrs Munro now?' asked Gina. Lachie would never let her have the last word on principle and could be as exasperating as any other man when he wanted to be.

'Under the green sod in Lochinvie kirkyard, God rest her soul,' he intoned with mournful reverence.

'But I thought you said she left the glen because it couldn't hold a woman?'

'So she did leave, in a box made of elm wood. Beautiful, it was,' murmured Lachie, his blue eyes smoky as he looked into the past.

'When was that?'

'Let me see now. Kirsty is almost thirty—aye, it must be thirty-one years ago. She was lovely, so she was, but the bairn was too strong for her, whatever.'

'Bairn? You mean she died in childbirth?'

'That was the way of it. We couldn't get her to the hospital in time. My sister took on the rearing of Kirsty. It wouldn't have done to let her stay in the glen. Now she's married to Kenny Ross, a fisherman in Ullapool, and has bairns of her own. She serves in the chandler's shop. You'll be going there and having a wee talk with her one day.'

He drifted out of the kitchen into the warm sunshine of late April and Gina watched him go, feeling bemused, as she always did after a conversation with Lachie. He was so contented with his lot here, living alone in the glen, and it was difficult to imagine him as a young man. Even more difficult was it to imagine him as a father and grandfather. The similarity of his story to that of the chief of the glen whose wife had disappeared and also to that of Will, whose wife had left him, worried her a little. She wouldn't like Will to become like Lachie, she thought.

She was in her room sewing the zipper which had worked loose on her jeans when she heard the sound of a vehicle coming down the road. Flinging the jeans aside, she went across to the window. It was the blue truck, dusty after its journey. To her surprise close behind it came a shiny black car—a Rolls-Royce.

If the black car had not been there she would have rushed down the stairs to fling open the door to welcome Will home, but instead she lingered in her room to finish the sewing.

Once it was finished she could contain herself no longer. She had to find out who had come in the car, and to find out if Will had noticed the primroses. Changing into the smooth wheat-coloured pants and fluffy sweater she had worn the first day she had met Will, she swathed her hair into its chignon. Thinking how much her complexion had improved with the use of the soft water of the glen, she applied a touch of make-up to eyes and mouth, and then, with a sudden urge to look her best, she hung golden hoop ear-rings in her ears.

Half way down the narrow stairs she paused on hearing a woman's voice, clear and autocratic.

'So when Gregor came with a tale that he'd met the young woman who was staying here, when he was out walking, I just had to come and see her for myself.'

Gina froze where she stood and waited for Will's reply.

'And see her you shall.'

There was a lilt of laughter in his voice, which put her on guard at once. Will Fox was up to mischief.

He came out of the living room into the hall, and the sight of his waving blue-black hair above the breadth of his tweed-clad shoulders made her feel suddenly weak and she caught hold of the banister to support herself. She had not reckoned on being glad to see him.

His foot on the bottom stair he raised his head and saw her.

'Oh, there you are. I was wondering what had happened to you,' he said, his glance taking in her pink-tinged face and the soft curves of her figure outlined by the clinging knit pants and sweater. 'My word, you are dressed up. Expecting company?' he asked cheekily.

Oh, he was on form all right. Unholy glee seemed to be

dancing in his light blue eyes and all her pleasure at seeing him was pushed aside by irritation with his mischievous mood.

'No. I dress to please myself,' she retorted.

Creases appeared in his cheeks as he grinned.

'The get-up isn't wasted,' he drawled. 'We have company. The local gentry, all three of them. They've come to size you up, and also to find out if you and I are living in sin, so watch how you go.'

Warning was implicit in his words and he closed one eye in an outrageous wink. Immediately she was reminded of the act he and Birdie had put on the night of the party at the flat.

He swung away down the stairs again. Apprehensively she followed him. As she reached his side he placed a possessive arm about her shoulders and urged her into the room.

'Here she is, Mrs Macneal. Georgina Marriott, my fiancée,' he announced.

Gina was aware of several things at once; the sudden tension in the room as Will swept her into it; the painful grip of his hand on her elbow as he held it after her attempt to slip out of his casual hold on her shoulder; the violent emotional upheaval his announcement caused within her, which made her turn her head to glare up at him.

His eyes laughed down into hers and with just the faintest sardonic twist to the corner of his mouth he murmured,

'This is Mrs Elena Macneal of Castle Duich, sweetheart, chief of the Macneal clan, her youngest son Gregor, whom I think you've already met, and her daughter Andrea.'

Sweetheart, indeed! Anger sizzled within Gina. She would get her own back on him for his presumptuousness somehow, she vowed.

Across the room she saw Gregor leaning against the wall behind one of the armchairs. He smiled at her and nodded. In the armchair was a tall slim girl of about eighteen years of age. She had a mop of black hair, a dark-browed sulky face, and was dressed in stained jodhpurs, muddy riding boots and a high-necked white sweater.

'Never mind them. I'm the one who has come to see you,' the autocratic voice which had spoken before belonged to the small woman in her late fifties who sat perched on the edge of another armchair. She was wearing a magnificent kilt with a white blouse and a jacket of dark tweed. Her face was modelled on austere lines and wore an expression of imperiousness. The only resemblance to her two youngest children lay in her fine dark brown eyes. Her hair was grey and was cut short.

Her training in good manners asserting itself, Gina moved forward with her hand stretched out.

'I'm very pleased to meet you, Mrs Macneal,' she said.

Her hand was taken and shaken and the dark brown eyes looked her over.

'I can't say the same,' retorted Elena Macneal, 'because it would be untrue. But you're better than I expected, much better. Where do you come from? I don't think I know anyone called Marriott. Sounds English to me.'

'From Warwickshire. My father is the managing director of a machine tool company. You may have heard of it—Marriott and Edwards,' returned Gina, her back up and the light of battle in her eyes as she recognised an attempt to discomfit her.

She had the pleasure of seeing the dark brown eyes widen, before they looked past her at Will.

'You've done well for yourself, Will Fox, perhaps not as well as you could have done if I'd had my way,' said Elena Macneal. 'How long have you been engaged?'

The question was shot at Gina and almost caught her off balance. She turned appealingly to Will.

'Sorry, darling,' she said softly. 'I can't remember how long. Does it really matter?'

He came forward and slipped an arm round her waist.

'I can't remember either,' he murmured, gazing down at her. 'About two or three weeks, I think.' He gazed at the all-observant chieftain of the clan Macneal. 'When one is blissfully happy one tends to lose count of time,' he added.

Gina had the greatest difficulty in controlling her laughter. Will was the last person she would expect to use such sentimental language. But it seemed to go down surprisingly well with Mrs Macneal. Her face softened and a faint smile appeared.

'I'm glad to hear someone is happy these days. So many young people seem to want to flout convention and not go in for engagements, or even marriage.' She sent a fierce glance in the direction of Gregor, who turned away and went to look out of the window. 'When are you thinking of getting married?' she asked Will.

'In the autumn, some time. We haven't set a date yet.'

'Very sensible,' replied Elena with a nod. 'You're going up in my estimation, Will Fox. It isn't good to rush into marriage. You need time to get to know one another.'

'That's why Gina came back north with me to stay for a while,' Will said suavely. 'You may have heard that the Andersons have gone, leaving me in rather a difficult position. Fortunately Gina is trained in institutional management and has been able to help out with the camp.'

Gregor moved restlessly and looked round at his brother.

'Now you've found out what you wanted to know don't you think we should leave?' he suggested. 'After all, Captain Fox has only just returned home and he and Miss Marriott must have a lot to talk about.'

Mrs Macneal sent a scathing glance in his direction.

'I'll leave when I'm ready and not when you tell me. Go and wait outside if you don't like the conversation,' she barked.

A dark mutinous expression crossed Gregor's face and for a moment it looked as if he might retaliate. Then he turned and walked swiftly out of the room and out of the house.

'Please excuse Gregor's lack of manners,' said Mrs Macneal. 'He's been very ill, poor boy. We thought we'd lost him. And now he doesn't seem to want to face up to life at all. I was wondering whether you could do anything to help him, Will. He did some climbing and sailing when he was at school. In fact he was very keen on outdoor activities when he was younger. I thought that perhaps he could help you run one of your camps. It would get him out of doors and give him something to think about other than himself and that ... that young woman.'

'No,' replied Will firmly, his eyes glinting like steel. There was no mischief in him now. Nothing of the fond lover either, thought Gina.

Mrs Macneal drew herself even more upright. Her eyes flashed and her bosom heaved, in reaction to his insolence, and Gina decided it was time she took a hand in the proceedings.

'Surely this can be discussed sensibly before any decision is made,' she said softly. 'I'll make some tea. I spent the morning baking and I'm longing to try out my chocolate cake on someone. Please won't you stay and have some?'

She turned to Andrea Macneal, who until now had been silent and sulky, but the young woman deliberately ignored her, an expression of boredom on her patrician features.

'Afternoon tea has always been one of my weaknesses,' said Mrs Macneal, suddenly gracious. 'You've been well trained, lass, by your mother. Take note, Andrea.'

Gina turned to Will.

'Will darling,' she purred, giving him one of her up-from-under looks, 'please make Mrs Macneal feel at home while I go and make the tea.'

He gave her in return one of his dagger-bright glances, which told her more than anything else that he didn't take kindly to being told what to do by her. She had more than got her own back for being called sweetheart by him.

Gina was just filling the kettle when she was surprised by the appearance of Andrea, who strolled into the kitchen her hands in the pockets of her jodhpurs. Now that the young woman was standing up Gina could see that her figure was flat and boyish and that there was a certain awkwardness in her manner. Andrea was really not much more than a schoolgirl.

'It's strange that Will has never mentioned you to us,' said Andrea, leaning against the table and watching Gina's busy hands as she set crockery on a tray. The girl's voice was deep like her mother's and had the same slight suggestion of Highland sibilance in it.

Gina looked up and smiled brightly as she recognised an attempt to put her on the spot.

'He's never mentioned you to me either,' she replied coolly. 'But then he isn't a very communicative man. Possibly he forgot all about you when he was staying in the south with us.'

Andrea scowled, an expression which did nothing to help her face, bringing, as it did, her thick dark eyebrows together across the top of her bold prominent nose. The edge of her straight white teeth explored her full lower lip. Obviously she didn't like being blocked in her attempt to disconcert Will's suspiciously new fiancée.

'You're not at all the sort of person I'd have expected him to want to marry,' she persisted.

'What sort of person did you expect?' asked Gina.

'Someone used to the outdoors, who would enjoy the activities he enjoys, who would know about farming and like living close to nature. You're so obviously more used to the city, and you look too soft and cuddlesome, like a pet,' replied Andrea, with a sneer.

A cup rattled in its saucer as Gina set it down. Careful, she warned herself. She must not let this abrupt sulky girl upset her.

'But then it's well known that men and women often choose their opposites as their partners for life,' she said gently. It was surprising how useful her own mother's comments on life could be. She had never thought she would be passing them off as her own philosophy.

'I think that to have interests in common is much more

important if a relationship is to be successful and survive,' said Andrea sharply, anger burning in her dark eyes. 'You know nothing about farming or about living here.'

'I can learn,' replied Gina quietly, noting the unhappiness in Andrea's face. It seemed that the chief of the clan Macneal had more than one unhappy ill-adjusted child!

There was no doubt that Andrea was very upset. She was not only suspicious of Will's engagement, she was hurt by it because, encouraged by her mother, she had probably come to regard him as her property.

'What will you do here when winter comes and the road is washed away?' demanded Andrea agitatedly. 'How will you manage with no entertainment, no shops, with Lachie as your only neighbour? Madge Anderson wasn't able to put up with life in the glen, and she had lived in the Highlands before, so how do you think you will manage?'

The deep voice was thick with scorn. Gina stared helplessly as understanding of this new complication hit her.

'I'm sorry you've been disappointed. I wish I could help you,' she said impulsively and rather foolishly.

Andrea, whose wits were quick, noted the foolishness and pounced on it immediately.

'Help?' she exclaimed harshly. 'How can you help me? The only way you could do that would be to return your engagement ring to Will and to go away from here and never come back.'

Her voice choked suddenly, she whirled on her heels and ran from the room. Staring down at Oliver's ring, Gina heard voices in the hall, then the front door closed noisily and the house was ominously silent.

'Make that tea for two only, you and me,' said Will drily as he came into the kitchen. 'Mrs Macneal has left too.'

'Oh, you were rude to her again,' exclaimed Gina as she poured water into the tea-pot.

His grin was unrepentant as he leaned against the table and helped himself to chocolate cake.

'Not rude, just honest. I told her I didn't want her play-

491

boy no-good son helping me, least of all if she's going to push him at me. I've had enough of her pushing Andrea at me. By the way, the daughter looked as if the world had come to an end as she went out of the house. What did you say to her? Were you rude? Or just honest, like me?'

'You should know why she was upset,' retorted Gina. 'She's in love with you, and she can't bear the thought of you being engaged to me.'

He let out a crack of scornful laughter.

'Love? Is that what you call it? More like a schoolgirl crush just because I've noticed her and have talked to her a few times.' His mouth twisted bitterly. 'I've had enough of that sort of love in the past and I can do without it now. It has a way of fading fast when faced with the reality of living with the object of worship.'

Gina looked at him sharply, but he didn't elaborate and went on eating his cake. When he had finished it he said,

'Now it's time you explained why you told Gregor we're engaged.'

'I didn't,' she replied indignantly. 'When I met him on the shore he did most of the talking.'

'Then where did he get the idea?'

Gina pushed a cup of tea across the table to him and as she did so noticed Oliver's diamond flashing on her finger.

'He must have noticed my ring and drawn his own conclusions,' she said in a stifled voice. 'Oh, what a mess! *You* could have denied it,' she rebuked him.

He stood up and came across to her, lifted her left hand and examined the ring.

'Yes, I suppose it was the ring that convinced him,' he murmured, ignoring her rebuke. 'Strangely enough I'd thought of suggesting to you that you stop wearing it or put it on your other hand. Diamonds—a girl's best friend. Did you choose them?'

'Oliver and I agreed that they were the most suitable,' she replied faintly, wondering why she felt peculiar whenever he came close to her.

'Oh, eminently suitable,' he commented ironically. 'As well as being a good investment. I've no doubt, either, that that was how Noll regarded *you*. A good investment.' He looked up and met her wide hurt gaze, and said softly, 'Now, if I were really engaged to you I'd give you topazes to match your eyes.'

Perturbed by the remark as well as by the expression in his eyes, she snatched her hand away, picked up the tea pot and began to pour tea for herself.

'But you're not engaged to me,' she retorted shakily. 'May I know why you didn't deny it?'

He gave her one of his bright stabbing glances, finished drinking his tea and said with uncharacteristic evasiveness,

'I'll tell you later. Just now I have work to do and I've no more time for chit-chat. Lachie's fallen behind with the ploughing.'

He went from the room and she heard him dash up the stairs, presumably to change into working clothes. She stared at the primroses and felt the first stirrings of disappointment. He hadn't noticed them after all.

Will was busy out of doors until twilight and Gina could hear the monotonous sound of the tractor which pulled the plough as it crossed and re-crossed one of the fields. When he came in he brought Lachie with him to share the evening meal Gina had prepared, and she sat silent all through the meal listening to Lachie's voice droning on about this and that, hoping he would go when he had finished eating so that she could confront Will about the question of their 'engagement'.

But Lachie was in no hurry to leave, and Will, in a relaxed and easygoing mood now that he was back in his home, encouraged him to stay and play cribbage. They invited Gina to join them in a game, but she refused, pleading that she had some sewing to do.

Leaving them in the kitchen she went into the living room and tried to be interested in doing some petit-point embroidery. It was one of a set of seat covers for the dining room chairs which her mother had given her for a wedding present.

Sewing, however, made her restless. She found herself recalling Oliver's and her plans for their future together. It was the first time she had thought consciously about him since she had left Birmingham and she discovered she was now able to look at everything in a much more objective light. Her view was no longer obstructed by that terrible aching sense of loss.

Cut and dried. So her mother had called those plans, and had suggested that Oliver had not been in love with her. That afternoon Will, in a strangely mean and cynical mood, had said that Oliver had probably regarded her as a good investment. It was odd that he, Oliver's brother, and her mother should think alike about Oliver. Did that mean it was true, that Oliver had not loved her ecstatically and passionately, above all else, as she wanted to be loved, but had seen in her only a suitable wife for an ambitious doctor who would do all the right conventional things?

But then had she loved him ecstatically, and passionately, above all else, or had the great distress she had felt at the time of his death merely been the result of the blow her ego had suffered because she had not been married after all that big build-up?

Gina made a small sound of distress. She did not wish to think about it any more. Casting aside the petit-point, she wondered where Blue was. She hadn't seen her pet since just before supper.

She went into the kitchen. Lachie was still talking and she wondered, a little unkindly, if he ever stopped. Will, who was lounging indolently in his chair, looked rather somnolent, and she wondered if the whisky was affecting him. Certainly the level in the bottle on the table had gone down considerably since she had left them, but she knew that Lachie had an amazing tolerance for his native drink and could absorb large quantities of it without any visible effect.

She asked them if either of them had seen Blue. Will shook his head negatively without glancing up from his cards. Lachie, after a brief thought, said he hadn't either, but he was minded of a legend concerning cats and the island of Raasay a story into which he launched with fervour.

Irritated, Gina left the room abruptly and went upstairs. Blue wasn't in her room, so she took a jacket and scarf, went downstairs and let herself out of the house.

The evening air was soft and mild. A hazy moon peeped from behind a cloud so that finding her way down the path to the loch was made easy. Calling Blue occasionally, she walked slowly and thought about the two men playing cards in the house.

She was sure, now, that Will had brought Lachie in for a meal and had asked him to stay and play cards because he did not wish to be alone with her, and possibly because he still wanted to evade having to tell her why he hadn't denied they were engaged. But she was determined to have it out with him, and as soon as she had found Blue she would return to the house and think up some reason to get rid of Lachie.

Shingle crunched beneath her feet as she reached the shore. Wavelets were falling in moonlit frills in the narrow beach. To the north the sky was still streaked with light and she wondered if she would be in the glen long enough to see the northern lights.

It was such a remote place; a place of almost fairy-tale beauty, and there were times when she wondered whether she was really there or whether she was having a dream. Perhaps she was in one of those deep drug-induced slumbers which she had known after Oliver's death. Perhaps soon she would awake in the dark, sad and lonely, and would weep when she found that Glengorm did not exist and that Will Fox and all the other people she had met recently were but shadows, existing only in her imagination.

The crunch of footsteps on the shingle behind her was not dreamlike. Someone else was there with her. She turned and saw him dark and bulky against the sheen of moonlit water.

'Are you there, George?'

She was tempted to play a game with him, to remain silent and creep off into the shadow of the birches and hide from him.

But even as she turned to do so he was beside her, more used to seeing in the dark than she was. His hand was on her arm, turning her to face him although she was sure he would not be able to see her face.

'What are you doing here?' he asked.

'Looking for Blue.'

'He came in just as Lachie was leaving,' he replied. 'I gave him some milk and the fish you'd cooked for him. I shut the door when I left the house so he can't get out again.'

'Thank you,' she said, and then sighed. 'I thought Lachie would never go.'

'Did you want him to?' He sounded surprised. 'And there was I thinking you'd be sorry for him because he's lonely. I thought you liked listening to his tales.'

'Not when I want to talk to you. You have something to explain,' she said shortly.

'I suppose you want to know if I had any success in finding someone to help with the May camp. The answer is no, I'm afraid, but Clarke Robertson has said he's willing to come for the summer.'

'Who is Clarke Robertson?' she asked with a touch of exasperation.

'The chap Andrew took me to see when we were down at Loch Lomond. He's a physical education teacher at a private school. His wife is willing to come and help too and they'll bring their two boys with them. It's probably better than having someone staying here permanently. I don't really need anyone here all winter.' He paused and added rather facetiously, 'Now that you and I are engaged I've no hesitation in asking you to stay on during May to help me with the next group of campers. When you go back south I can always say you changed your mind about marrying me and jilted me.'

Gina drew a slow breath and gritted her teeth. She supposed she should be grateful that he had brought up the subject of the engagement first, but his facetiousness found no echo in her.

'Will, it isn't like you to dodge an issue. Please tell me why you didn't deny what Gregor said,' she pleaded.

He didn't answer immediately. She could hear, the sound of the torrent falling over the rocks high up in the glen, and behind that sound was the muffled thunder of the sea breaking at the foot of the cliffs at the entrance to the loch.

'I thought I was backing you up,' he said eventually. 'I thought you'd told him we were engaged to protect yourself. Then I decided it was as good a way as any to protect my own good name as well as yours. It also created a suitable barrier between me and Andrea, who was becoming a bit of an embarrassment before I went to England.'

'Why do you want to protect your reputation?' she asked, thinking that all he had to do to keep Andrea at bay was to say he was married already.

'Well, you see, Mrs Macneal, as head of the clan, tends to rule the roost hereabouts. She has a great deal of influence with the local people. She doesn't like me because I'm an "incomer" and because I've taken over some land which she regards as still being Macneal property. She would love to find a way of making my life here uncomfortable and would go to any lengths, even so far as besmirching my reputation. Once she heard that there was a young woman living here and that the Andersons had left she thought she had the advantage. Fortunately for us her own son jumped to the wrong conclusion and saved me the trouble of having to think up some story to cover up.'

'But supposing Bridget, your wife, turns up?' she asked, voicing the worry which bothered her most.

His fingers bit cruelly into her arm, which he was still

holding.

'Bridget will not be coming back,' he said harshly. There was a short tense silence. Gina waited, hoping he would explain why Bridget would not be coming back, but when he spoke his voice was quiet and he made no reference to Bridget.

'Now that Clarke and his wife have promised to come I won't need to hold you to your promise to stay in the summer, but I'd be glad if you'd consider staying until they come at the beginning of July. Of course, if you feel like it you can stay on after they've come. You're welcome to stay as long as you like, George, until you're fully recovered from Oliver's death. Is that clear?'

She nodded silently because she was having difficulty in controlling the quiver of her lips as tears spurted to her eyes. When he spoke kindly like that it was her undoing. She could see quite clearly why he had brought her here and she knew that his cure was working.

But he had not seen her nod and the pressure of his fingers increased again as he peered at her and asked,

'Well? Is it clear?'

'Yes, yes, it's clear, Will, very clear. Thank you for explaining and for being so kind.'

Fingers touched her cheek and explored upwards moving against her wet eyelashes.

'Tears again?' he jeered gently. 'Softly!'

After that it seemed quite natural to be in his arms and held closely, while she sobbed her heart out as pent-up emotion overflowed.

Eventually her sobs subsided and she searched frantically in her jacket pocket for a handkerchief, only to find she had none.

'I haven't one either,' he said with a chuckle. 'You'll have to use your knuckles. Are you all right now?'

'Yes, thank you,' she sniffed. 'I'm sorry I broke down. It was just that you ...'

'Don't bother to explain, I understand,' he broke in

498

sharply. 'It had to happen sooner or later. Let's go back to the house now and on the way you can tell me what you think is wrong with Gregor Macneal.'

He took one of her hands in his as they walked side by side. The moon's radiance was growing stronger, striking sparks of light from the ice cap of the mountain, lining the outline of solitary trees and bushes, silvering the barks of the birches.

'He told me he'd been in a car crash. His girl-friend was hurt and may not survive, and it's his fault. He needs help, in the same way that I needed help that morning you came to see me.'

'Well, well,' he drawled lightly, 'you're coming on. You've actually admitted you were in a bad way. So now you're sorry for Gregor, are you?' His voice rasped queerly on the question. 'Beware of sympathy, George. Too much of it has a way of killing.'

'You could help him,' she said.

'What makes you think that?'

'You helped me.'

'But you, my dear almost sister-in-law, were only sunk in grief and merely needed rousing from it. Gregor's problem goes deeper than that. He's never been much good. You were good material to work with. The spunk was already there. It had just been smothered by soft living.'

'Couldn't that be true of Gregor too?'

They had reached the house. He opened the door and let her go through first. In the lamplit hall she turned and was shocked to see that his face was pale and drawn. His mouth was set in a hard controlled line and his eyes were narrowed as if he were in pain.

'Will, what's the matter?' she asked impulsively, placing a hand on his arm.

'Nothing much.' He shook off her hand impatiently as if he didn't like her to touch him. 'Just a twinge from an old wound. Let's hope you're right about Gregor because I've a feeling we're going to see a lot of him. Now that he's met you, he'll be round here by the hour, like his sister used to be. But don't expect me to welcome him with open arms. The best therapy for him is a certain amount of humiliation until he starts wanting to be recognised as someone who can do something positive.'

He turned back and opened the front door again and added,

'I've just remembered I forgot to close the barn door. Good night, George.'

She was sure he hadn't left the barn door open. He just wanted to be out of the house, away from her curiosity. She went up the stairs with a vague feeling of regret because he kept her shut out from his personal feelings. It was all right for him to comfort and help her, but she must not be allowed to comfort him. She was convinced the wound to which he had referred was not a physical one. Something she had said out there in the lovely spring moonlight had touched a sensitive spot.

Had it been her reference to Bridget? Why was he so cagey about his missing wife? Why was he so sure she would not be coming back to him?

The questions circled around Gina's mind as she prepared for bed, and remained unanswered, as usual. It was not until she had switched off the light and lay waiting for sleep to come that she realised that she was still saddled with the ridiculous complication of being 'engaged' to the man who had almost become her brother-in-law.

Next day she paid her first visit to Ullapool. The main reason for going was to stock up on gas and food. Gina sat beside Will in the front of the truck and was able to see the scenery through which she had travelled the night she had come to Glengorm.

Now that the month of May was in, changes were everywhere. It seemed to her that an artistic magician was at work, touching up the landscape with new colours. The dark pine forests were suddenly streaked with fresh light green as larches came into leaf. Birch catkins were like golden tassels, swinging in the breeze. A shower of rain danced across the scene. Sunlight followed it and at once mountains and moors sparkled joyously as raindrops reflected the light.

Ullapool was quite a big village. Situated at the end of a large sea-loch, it had been built mostly in the eighteenth century to the order of the British Fishery Society. Its name was Norse in origin and meant Ulla's Home. It was as tidily arranged as only a planned settlement could be, with rows of whitewashed terraced houses sparkling in the sunlight.

Will parked the truck behind the curved seawall and pointed to the quay where the fishing boats huddled together.

'That's where I worked the first summer I owned Glengorm,' he said. 'I loaded lorries with fish.'

'Why?' asked Gina, surprised.

'No money,' he answered with a grin. 'Buying the estate cleaned out my bank balance. I used the little my father had left me, plus my savings. It was while I was working here that I had the idea for the adventure club.'

He opened the door and jumped down into the street. Gina got out her side of the vehicle, thinking that he would never cease to surprise her.

They went straight to the chandlers for the gas and were greeted by Lachie's daughter Kirsty, a rosy-cheeked, plump woman with her father's blue eyes. Those eyes turned to Gina and sized her up.

'A wee birdie brought me a piece of news this morning, and I'm thinking this is the young woman it concerns,' said Kirsty, her eyes twinkling.

'Oh, and what was the news?' asked Will casually.

'That you and she are engaged to be married. Is it true?'

'Yes,' said Will, before Gina could think. 'And who told you?'

'Mistress Parker, the gamekeeper's wife from Castle

Duich. She heard from the chief herself. Ach now, Will, aren't you going to introduce me? I feel I know the lass well already because Feyther has talked to me about her.'

Will introduced Gina, and Kirsty's sincere congratulations were accepted easily by him, but less easily by Gina.

'Feyther was right then, and there I was thinking he was having one of his daydreams. He told me the swans were back and that the curse had been lifted from the glen because they had brought with them the true mistress of the master of the glen. Ach, it's wonderful, so it is, after all those years.'

'A coincidence, nothing more,' said Will drily.

'Now isn't that just like you to be unromantic,' said Kirsty, sending a sympathetic glance in Gina's direction. 'Coincidence, indeed! If it is, Will Fox, it's a well-planned one.'

It was the same everywhere they went that morning. In other shops, on the quay where Will paused to greet some of his fishing acquaintances, in the hotel where they had their lunch. Mrs Macneal had done her work well in telling Mrs Parker, for it seemed that everyone who knew Will knew that he was engaged to Gina and there was nothing Gina could do about it.

'What are we going to do?' she wailed, as soon as the waitress had served them with their roast lamb.

'Nothing,' replied Will calmly. 'The fuss will soon die down. When you go, they'll nod their heads at one another and say they never expected yon young Sassenach lassie to stay in the glen. By then Andrea will have got over her infatuation.'

'And how will you like that? You'll look as if you've been let down again,' hissed Gina, suddenly furious with him.

His eyes, cool and wary, met hers across the table.

'Since I'll know it isn't true it won't worry me,' he said evenly.

'Well, how do you think I'll like it, having everyone think I couldn't put up with life in the glen and so I jilted you?' she exclaimed.

'The alternative is to have everyone talking about you now and saying something else which isn't true.'

'And that is?'

'That you and I are living together as man and wife without being married,' he said coolly. 'Take it or leave it, George. Perhaps you'd prefer to back out now and go back to Birmingham.'

She was caught. She supposed she could have walked out on him and gone back home, but it would mean letting him down, and she had agreed to stay to help him with the next group of campers. She had boasted once that she wasn't the sort of person who let people down, and at the back of her mind was Meg Maxwell's warning that Will had been let down too often in his life.

'No, I'm not backing out,' she heard herself saying firmly. 'I said I'd stay for the next camp, and stay I shall.'

He looked up at her and grinned.

'I thought you'd say that,' he said with maddening complacency, so that she wanted to shake him. He went on to talk about the rest of the shopping they had to do and she had to assume that he considered the matter settled. She was staying as his fiancée in the eyes of the neighbours, until such time as she wished to leave.

There was so much she didn't know about him, she thought, so much he kept hidden. When she had first met him she had believed him to be a roistering ex-soldier used to making easy conquests where women were concerned. Now she knew that his marriage had failed for some reason and that its failure had hurt him so much he could not talk about it, even to Meg, to whom she guessed he was closer than he was to any of his other relatives.

After the trip to Ullapool life settled down to comfortable routine. At that time of the year there was a great deal to do on the farm and often Will asked Gina to help by taking on such simple jobs as feeding the hens. She even learned how to milk a cow, and when he brought her a little lamb to look after because its mother had died, she was delighted.

The attention she gave to the lamb tended to make Blue jealous and one day the kitten roamed too far away, with the result that Gregor Màcneal used his discovery of the cat on the grouse moors to come and make his first visit. He found Gina in the garden, perched on some rather shaky stepladders, trying to fix the clothes line which had become detached from one of its posts. He offered to fix it for her and she came down the ladder thankfully and took Blue from him.

When he had done the small job she thanked him again.

'For that you deserve a reward. Come and have a cup of tea and some home-made scones, and tell me what you've been doing since we last met.'

'I've been doing precisely nothing,' he replied. 'I've been bored to distraction and boring everyone else around me.'

'Then why didn't you come over as I suggested?' she asked, going into the house through the back door.

'I didn't like to intrude.'

'Intrude?' she was surprised.

'On you and Will. You're an engaged couple, remember.'

'But that needn't stop you from coming if you want to.'

'You're sure?'

'Oh, Gregor! How often do I have to say it? I'm sure. You're welcome to come any time.'

He didn't look any better than he had the last time she had seen him. If anything his cheeks were hollower and his eyes were more sunken, but he followed her into the house and wandered about the kitchen after her while she made tea and set out cups and saucers. Before the afternoon was over she knew all about his affair with Audrey, the girl who had been hurt in the accident, his dislike of his mother and her overbearing ways and his rather dismal attempts to free himself from her dominance.

'Every time I think I've escaped from her something awful happens like that accident and I'm dragged back to her,' he complained. 'She smothers me,' he added, with a twisted grin at his own pun. 'I wished I'd never been born with a silver spoon in my mouth. I might have grown up with a sense of responsibility if I had. But everything has been too easy and now I've reached the point when I can't find any reason for living.'

Gina didn't make any comment. She just let him talk, and after that first afternoon visit he came, as Will had predicted he would, every day. Some days he walked over, some days he came in a sports car which he said really belonged to Andrea. His had been smashed up in the accident and he hadn't bothered to buy another. In fact he was doubtful as to whether he was entitled to drive any more.

Every time he came Gina endeavoured to have a job for him to do, which helped her. At first he was diffident about helping her because he was afraid of what Will might say, and in fact the times when Will was present at the time of Gregor's arrival, he often made a disparaging remark about the young man. Gregor took these remarks with a meekness which Gina found alarming, but one day he blew up after Will had left the house.

'The trouble is, I know he's right,' he seethed. 'I am good for nothing. But since I've met you and him I've wanted to be good for something. Gina, isn't there anything I can do to show him that I can be positive and do things, that I'm not just a playboy and a parasite? Do you think he'd let me help him run his next camp?'

'I don't think so. Not unless you can show him what you can do before the campers come,' replied Gina, thinking of Will's blatant refusal to Mrs Macneal when she had suggested Gregor might help him. 'Do you have any skills you could pass on to others?'

'Apart from crashing cars, you mean,' he said with another twisted smile. 'I've done some rock-climbing. I used to swim for my school. I've done some sailing.'

'Could you rig a dinghy and launch it?' asked Gina, her eyes lighting up.

'Of course I could.'

'Then come on,' she cried gaily. 'I've been longing to go sailing, but there's been no one to go with.'

'What about Will?' he asked.

'He's been too busy. There's a lot to do on the farm and he has only Lachie to help him. Come on, let's go and get one of the dinghies out of the storage shed now, and rig it.'

He followed her out into the sunny afternoon. There was a breeze, enough to make a ripple on the water, enough to test a person's skill in sailing without the sail being too strenuous.

'You and Will are a strange couple,' Gregor ventured to comment while they were sorting out the rigging of the mast prior to stepping it on the deck of the dinghy.

Gina cast a wary glance at him.

'Why do you say that?'

'You don't act as I would expect an engaged couple to act.'

'How do you expect an engaged couple to act?'

He grinned at her and she realised suddenly how attractive he was now that his face was filling out and his eyes had lost their hunted look.

'I'm probably off course,' he said, 'but I thought you'd be much more ... Help! I don't know how to put it ... much more loving, I suppose. I've never seen him touch you, except on the day we came with Mother, and I've never heard him call you anything but George. The same goes for you too.'

'You must remember you're not here all the time,' she said quietly, hoping she sounded convincing.

He gave her a sharp glance and then had the grace to blush.

'I see. No, I'm not. Sorry, Gina, I didn't mean to probe, I suppose you and Will are just as much in love with each other as the next engaged couple is. You wouldn't be here helping him if you weren't in love with him. I mean, it isn't the sort of place a woman like you wants to be buried in unless . . .' He was floundering badly and he realised it. 'Oh, hell, why don't you tell me to shut up and mind my own business?' he exclaimed disgustedly.

'Shut up and mind your own business, Greg,' she said, and her gay laughter trilled out, catching the attention of Will who was on his way to the bunkhouse and causing him to stop and stare for a moment at the two young people standing close together beside the dinghy.

The sail down the loch and back again was a success. Gina and Gregor took turns at the tiller and at jib-handling and were soon working together as a team. When he was leaving to return to the castle in Andrea's two-seater, Gregor asked her if they might sail together again the next day.

'If the weather is suitable I don't see why we shouldn't,' she replied, aware that Will was standing at the front door watching.

'And will you ask Will if I can help him with the camp?' was the next question, asked appealingly.

'Now that is something *you* must do for yourself,' she said, and he made a face at her before slipping into gear and roaring off in a cloud of dust.

That evening for the first time in days, Lachie did not come for the evening meal. He had gone to Ullapool, driven there by Will, who said he would go in later to pick him up and bring him back to the glen.

As they ate their meal Gina noticed that Will was very quiet. She supposed he was always quiet at that time of the day, but she hadn't noticed because of Lachie's presence at the table. Certainly breakfast was never a quiet meal because Will was always lively in the morning, banging on her door to wake her up and then making outrageous remarks about her inability to get up early in the morning of her own accord.

She sat there wondering what she should talk about, growing more and more aware of tension. When she glanced up at last she found he was staring at her almost as if he had never seen her before. He had often stared at her, sometimes speculatively, sometimes with mischief dancing in his eyes, sometimes curiously, but she had never known him stare at her with such intensity before. It seemed as if a blue fire glowed in his eyes. Disconcerted, she burst suddenly into speech—anything to break the silence which had become unbearable.

'Gregor and I had a lovely sail today. Those dinghies handle very easily. What design are they?'

He blinked, looked away and answered her absently.

'You didn't mind us taking one out?' she asked, rather timidly. It hadn't occurred to her before that he might be annoyed about her taking the dinghy, without asking his permission first.

'No. You seemed to be handling it quite competently. How did Gregor manage?'

'He sails well. Will, don't you think he's getting better? Don't you see a difference in him this past week?'

'I'd be blind if I didn't,' he said drily. 'But then he's having a good time of it. He has a pretty young woman to talk to and sail with, all the home-made cakes and scones he can eat. There aren't many who have it so good. Better watch your step, George. He'll be falling in love with you next and then you'll be in a fix, and you an *engaged* woman.'

She decided to ignore that crack, although she wondered what had caused him to make it. It seemed to her that the dryness in his voice had verged on bitterness for a moment.

'He'd like to help you with the next camp,' she said quietly, watching him carefully for his reaction.

He looked at her sardonically.

'Then he'll have to ask me himself, won't he?' he said.

'That's what I told him. But you'll let him, won't you? I think it would do him good. You see, he wants to prove to

508

you that he can do something positive, and you said that when he felt like that he'd be making progress.'

'Prove to me?' he queried, raising one eyebrow. 'I thought it was you he wants to impress.'

'It was at first, but now it's you.'

'I'll believe that when he comes and asks me if he can help,' he replied, still sardonic. 'It seems he's succeeded where you are concerned and you're suitably impressed. Isn't that so?'

She looked at him, her golden eyes wide and slightly puzzled. In the glow from the oil lamp her skin had a creamy sheen and the red in her hair glinted. Although she did not realise it, the weeks in the glen had brought her latant beauty into full bloom.

'I'm not sure what you mean. I like Gregor very much,' she said slowly.

'Well, that's a start, isn't it?' he remarked, pushing his chair away from the table and leaning back in it so that his face was in the shadow. 'I'd say it's a sign you're almost recovered. Do you ever think of Noll these days?'

She hadn't thought of Oliver for days, but as she reached for an empty plate she noticed the ring on her finger.

'When I notice his ring,' she retorted sharply.

'Then perhaps you should get rid of it,' he suggested softly

'When the camp is over, not before,' she replied, rising to her feet and taking the plates over to the sink. She returned to the table with the pie she had made. She cut it into wedges aware that he was watching her again. He was in a strange mood, she thought. If anyone ever asked her in the future if she had known Will Fox, she would never be able to answer with a straight unqualified affirmative. It would take years to get to know him.

He took the plate she passed to him and set it down on the table in front of him.

'I shall miss your cooking when you go,' he said.

'Not me, just my cooking?' she challenged lightly. She

509

did not wish to think about leaving the glen, not yet, and it seemed to her that he was wishing to get rid of her.

He didn't answer her challenge, but began to talk about how he intended to organise the next camp. He asked for her opinion, which she gave, but all the time she had the feeling he was discussing the camp because he wished to keep away from any further intimate or personal conversation. When he had finished eating he helped her clear the table and then went off to the living room to answer some letters.

After pottering about the kitchen for a while, Gina realised she was doing nothing really except putting off the moment when she would go into the living room too, to sit and sew. It was silly to behave in this way just because she was alone with Will in the house. They had been alone before and she hadn't felt this oddly restless feeling.

She went up to her room and glanced out of the window. Spring had brought longer days with it and light still lingered in the sky behind the mountain. Gina sighed involuntarily as she felt her blood stir. So far it had been an untasted spring for her because her love had been snatched away from her by an untimely death.

She looked down at Oliver's ring and thought of the strange conversation she had just had with Oliver's brother. What had he meant when he had said she should get rid of the ring which tied her not only to Oliver but by a strange freak of circumstance tied her to Will too. If she had not worn the ring Gregor would not have assumed she was engaged to Will and the whole complication would not have happened. Was it possible that Will was finding his pseudo engagement to her irksome? Had he been suggesting that if she got rid of the ring he would be rid of her?

It was useless to let herself be tortured by such questions. She would go and ask him outright. Picking up her embroidery, she went down to the living room and sat near the small table where the second oil lamp had been placed. Will was still at his desk. He had not looked up when she had entered.

With Blue curled at her feet, Gina pushed the needle in and out of the canvas seat cover. All was quiet except for the purring of the kitten and the scratching of Will's pen on paper. Then that noise stopped too. She looked up. Will wasn't writing any more, but was leaning back in his chair and staring at her as he had stared at her in the kitchen. She moved a little uneasily, as he stood up and walked slowly over to her.

'What are you doing?' he asked.

'Petit point.'

'What is it for?'

She spread the embroidery out on her lap. The formalised design of roses glowed in the lamplight.

'It's a cover for the seat of a dining-room chair. Mother gave me a set of reproduction Regency chairs for a wedding present,' she replied.

'Are you always going to let the past dog you?' he asked suddenly. 'Wearing a ring which means nothing, sewing a seat cover on which he'll never sit. You're young and beautiful, and it's time you came alive.'

The seat cover was snatched from her knee and flung across the room. The violent action startled the kitten, which reared up and clawed at Will's trousers, was picked up and dropped on to the seat of another armchair.

Gina, astonished by Will's behaviour, was on her feet without realising it.

'Will Fox, your manners are atrocious!' she spluttered.

He grinned down at her, and she became aware that she was trapped between him and the chair on which she had been sitting.

'Yes, they are, aren't they?' he conceded. 'That's why my mother tries to pretend I don't exist. I might embarrass her some day. It's also why Noll didn't want me to attend his wedding. Did you know he wrote to me saying he didn't expect me to accept the invitation you had sent, and that he'd understand if I refused? If I'd come to the ceremony

511

he'd have been on pins all the time in case I made some awful gaffe. And now, George, I'm going to give you another taste of my atrocious manners.'

He jerked her forward roughly and kissed her. Unlike the last time she didn't pull away from him, acknowledging ruefully that this was what she had been wanting him to do. Giving in to the desire which flared suddenly within her, she responded, holding him closely, luxuriating in the warmth and possessiveness of his embrace.

After a while, still holding her, he rubbed his cheek against the silkiness of her hair and whispered into her ear.

'Aren't you going to say "How dare you?"' he asked mockingly.

'No.' Her voice was shaky. 'But I'm beginning to wonder if you've let yourself be carried away by the part you're playing.'

He laughed and his arms tightened about her.

'You know what the next step is?' he queried suggestively.

'Yes.' She tried to move away from him.

'Do you want to take it with me?' he asked.

Her whole body stiffened in reaction and he released her at once.

'Don't panic, George,' he said, suddenly cool. 'We'll take it slowly. After all, that's what an engagement is for, isn't it? Though it seems to me Noll didn't use his time very well. You are ridiculously innocent for your age and only half alive.'

'But we're not engaged,' she retorted frantically, appalled at the way her senses were clamouring for him to take her in his arms again.

'In the eyes of our immediate neighbours, we are,' he reminded her, and there was a touch of steel in his voice. 'It struck me today that young Gregor was becoming suspicious and that maybe we ought to behave in a more lover-like way when he's about the place. I'm going to fetch Lachie now. Be sure you're in your bed before I get back,

512

won't you?'

His mockery flickered her on the raw. With a toss of her head she turned away to look for her embroidery. She could hear him whistling his tantalising tune, then the front door closed and she was alone in the silence of the house.

She made sure she was in bed before he returned. In her room she buried the embroidery at the bottom of one of her suitcases: She would not sew again while she was staying at White Lodge. She was also tempted to remove Oliver's ring from her finger and put it in its velvet-lined box at the bottom of the suitcase too, but the thought of the remarks its absence from her finger might bring forth stopped her.

Once in bed she closed her eyes determined to sleep, but for the first time since she had come to the glen sleep avoided her. She was fidgety and restless, thinking about Will, of the quick searching ruthlessness of his kiss which had discovered her innocence, of the roughness of his cheek against hers, of the warmth of his hands and body. Oliver had never kissed her like that, and the trouble was she had wanted it to continue, had longed to take the next step.

But how could she take any step which would involve her with Will when there was always the shadow of Bridget hovering in the background? How could she go any further with him without love in her heart?

And she wasn't in love with Will. Nor was he in love with her, and what had happened down there in the lamplit dusk of the living room had been merely the result of the spring, the time of the year when, as everyone knew, the fancy turns to thoughts of love.

CHAPTER FIVE

'AND what makes you think you can help me? As far as I can see you've been nothing else but a parasite ever since you came into this world.'

Will's voice had that abrasive quality with which Gina was only too familiar. Memory of the first time they had met in her flat came flooding back. She felt herself cringing inwardly, a feeling which was followed almost immediately by a strong desire to strike back at him.

But he wasn't speaking to her. He was speaking to Gregor who had come at last to ask if he could help at the next camp. It had taken him two days to pluck up the courage to ask Will, and now he was there outside the kitchen window which Gina had opened to let in the fresh morning air.

Holding her breath, she waited for him to answer Will's searing attack. Would he retaliate or would he run away?

'I can sail.' He said that confidently enough. Then came the staggering challenge. 'I bet I can climb the cliffs at the mouth of the loch in a faster time than you can.'

A cold hand seemed to clutch at Gina's heart. Surely Will wouldn't take up that challenge. The thought of them clinging to that wall of rock, high above the foaming water, horrified her.

'Do you now?' Will's voice had changed. It sounded amused, interested. 'All right. Are you game to try this morning?'

'Yes. Only I haven't any boots,' said Gregor hesitantly.

'The weather has been dry, so those plimsolls you're wearing will do,' replied Will easily. 'I'll ask George to come and stand at the top of the cliffs to time us and see who reaches the top first. Does that sound fair to you?'

Again Gregor's answer was a nervously spoken agreement and Gina had a desire to scream through the window, 'No, you mustn't. You'll both be killed.'

By the time they came into the kitchen to tell her their plan and to ask for her co-operation, she had controlled her desire to scream at them, but she was still pale and she stated her opinion of them concisely.

'I think you're both crazy, and I refuse to do what you ask.'

Will laughed at her.

'A purely feminine reaction,' he said, flicking her cheek with his fingers, an action which did not go unnoticed by Gregor. 'Come on, now, sweetheart. Be at the top to greet the winner with a kiss. We'll climb without you even if you won't come, but it won't be half so much fun without a reward, will it, Gregor?'

Gregor swallowed nervously, smiled a trifle wanly and agreed that it would not be so much fun without the promised kiss as a reward.

Will took a bunch of keys out of his pocket, chose one of them and held it out to Gregor.

'Here, take this. It opens the door of the storeroom in the first bunkhouse. You'll find ropes there. Bring two. I think we should both take one in case we need them. While you're gone I'll try and persuade George that she'll miss a great adventure if she doesn't come and then I'll ask Lachie to come with us to the bottom of the cliff with us to say "go".'

It was the first time he had ever spoken to Gregor as if he considered him to be a rational intelligent person and the young man noticed and reacted accordingly.

'I'll go right away,' he said, taking the key. Then with a smile in Gina's direction he added, 'Be ready with that kiss, Gina, when I reach the top of the cliff first.'

Alone with Will, Gina turned on him.

'You can't let him do it. His nerves are still bad.'

'He issued the challenge, remember,' he replied coldly. 'You once said he wanted to prove himself. Well, this is his chance.'

'But those cliffs are so dangerous,' she quavered.

'They're not as bad as they look,' he said.

'Not to you, perhaps, but you're an experienced rock-climber and assault leader. Gregor isn't.'

'If he isn't able to climb that rock then he should never have challenged me,' he retorted. 'If he fails it will prove better than anything else would that he's unsuitable to help at the camp and that he's not able to take responsibility. On the other hand, if he makes it to the top in front of me or behind me, I'll be willing to have him as an instructor.'

He was hard and ice-cold. This was the side of him Gina disliked heartily and could never like. It had been developed by his service in the Army, she realised, and was the reason why he would always be a leader and not a follower.

Her dislike showed in her face and made her eyes shimmer with green-shot golden light. He returned her gaze coolly, completely unmoved.

'Oh, you're so hard!' she exclaimed. 'No wonder Bridget ran away from you. Being married to you must have been like being married to a piece of granite!'

She might just as well have kept her mouth shut for all the effect her words had on him.

'*You* wanted him cured,' he said curtly. 'Well, he is, almost.'

'But supposing he falls?'

'He won't because he'll know that you're waiting at the top to greet him with a kiss when he comes roaring over the edge,' he retorted drily. 'See you there in about an hour and a half.'

An hour and twenty minutes Gina stood at the top of the cliffs. Behind her several sheep and their lambs grazed on the short sweet grass which carpeted the rocky headland jutting out into the sea and forming one side of the entrance to Loch Gorm.

Peering cautiously over the edge, she could see no one climbing the sheer rock which flashed pink in the sunshine.

About twenty feet below she could see a small ledge and wondered if it was the one from which Will had rescued Blue. But when she looked away to the right and then to the left she realised that the cliffs were so extensive that there could be many small ledges. Here and there small bushes and stunted trees grew out of crevices and she wondered how they managed to survive in such a wild windswept place.

It was a lovely day and when she turned away from the edge of the cliff she could see far out to sea to a line of land on the horizon, dark blue and mountainous. She guessed it was a distant Hebridean island. High above the sky was a pale washed-out blue, across which small clouds were drifting. Far below the water heaved and rippled, glinting with reflected light.

Turning back, she peered over the edge of the cliff in time to see Gregor reach the ledge. She told herself she was glad he was ahead of Will. Although it was just five minutes short of the time Will had said it would take him to climb the cliff, there was no sign of him. Jamming her hands into the pockets of her suede jacket, she turned her back on the cliff and looked out to sea again.

Keeping her gaze fixed on three fishing boats which were chugging steadily north, she forced her mind away from pictures of Will lying unconscious somewhere with a broken limb or crushed ribs. Or Will hurtling down into the fangs of the turbulent water at the foot of the cliffs. It was Gregor she should be worrying about, not Will. Gregor, who was young, soft and easily hurt like herself, not Will, who was as hard as the rock he was climbing.

Two hands curved round her waist. She stiffened as if an electric shock had shot through her. The hands slipped across her body and she was pulled against a wide chest which was rising and falling rhythmically after recent exertion.

'I've come for the reward,' Will whispered laughingly in her ear.

517

She twisted in his arms to face him. He gave her no chance to say anything, but took the reward before she had offered it.

'I didn't see you,' she exclaimed when he released her at last from that ruthless embrace. 'I thought Gregor would be first.'

'I was further over to the east of him. Are you disappointed?' She shook her head, her bruised mouth slightly tremulous.

'No. Only very glad to see you safe,' she whispered, betraying her recent anxiety on his behalf.

'You're coming on, George,' he mocked, then turned as, with a scrabbling sound of shod feet against rock, Gregor heaved himself pantingly over the edge of the cliff and lay there laughing breathlessly in the sunshine.

'I did it. I did it!' he cried exultantly. 'I knew I could!'

He rolled over and sprang lithely to his feet. With his dark hair blowing about his flushed face, his black eyes sparkling with triumph and his white teeth showing in a triumphant grin, he was suddenly the epitome of vigorous attractive youth, and Gina felt the strong pull of his attraction.

'I suppose Will has taken his reward,' he said ruefully.

'Yes, he has,' she replied, smiling at him, 'but you're going to be *given* one.'

Reaching up, she put her arms round his neck. He responded instantly. His lips were warm and sweet against her own and his arms held her close as he recognised the spontaneity of her kiss.

'Break it up,' urged Will drily. 'You have another spectator besides me. Lachie is coming, and he has a way of telling tales around the countryside.'

Gregor sprang away from Gina as if he were guilty of some grave misdemeanour, and Gina turned to see Lachie loping across the grass towards them.

'Ach, that was a fine effort, lad, just fine,' he said as he clapped Gregor on the shoulder. 'Sure and I knew you'd be doing it in record time. I mind the day when I climbed a cliff like that. In the summer of forty-one, it was. I was doing my Commando training near Ben Nevis and ...'

'You didn't come here to tell us about your assault training during the last war,' Will interrupted him rather impatiently.

'So I haven't,' agreed Lachie mildly. 'There is a young woman down at the house asking for you by your first name. She's come in a wee grey car.'

For the second time that morning Gina felt as if icy fingers had seized her heart. Had Bridget come back? She glanced at Will. His face was as impassive as usual, but mockery twinkled in his eyes as they met hers as if he had guessed at her thought and was amused by her consternation.

'Then I must go and see who this young woman is,' he murmured, and he set off down the well-worn path towards the house.

'Wait!' commanded Gregor, hurrying after Will. 'Are you going to let me help at the camp?'

Together, he and Will went down the path. Matching her step to Lachie's lope, Gina followed them, reluctant to face the woman who had come and had asked for Will by his first name.

As they approached the house she could see the woman pacing beside a grey Volkswagen. She was tall and blonde and from a distance she looked rather like Birdie, not at all like the picture Gina had seen of Bridget. With relief surging through her, Gina watched the woman turn, see Will and hurry towards him with her arms outstretched. They met, their arms going round each other in an affectionate embrace. Gina's steps faltered for a moment, but she couldn't retreat because Lachie was there clucking his tongue and asking her whether she was going to stand for yon man kissing another woman like that. Greg was also looking at her, presumably wondering how she was reacting to that fond greeting.

519

By the time she reached the grey car the embrace was over and the woman was talking to Will in German, the words pouring out excitedly, her white teeth flashing in her tanned face.

Will turned to Gina and smiled. There was affection in that smile and he reached out his hand to her. She put hers into it, glad to feel the warm comfort of his grasp.

'Come and meet Irma Brandt, an old friend of mine from my time in Germany,' he said, and in a daze she heard him introducing her for the second time as his fiancée.

Smiling, Gina held out her hand and welcomed Irma who, looking slightly disconcerted, responded vaguely in attractively-accented English and then shot a sharp question in German at Will, who answered lazily in the same language. Then he added in English,

'No one else speaks German here, Irma, so you'll have to practise your English. Let's go into the house. I'm in great need of liquid refreshment after climbing that cliff and I expect Gregor is too. How far have you come today?'

His arm round Gina's waist he urged her forward into the house. Once in the hallway Gina turned into the kitchen and suggested that he and Irma went into the living room and she would bring refreshments to them. Gregor, however, followed her into the kitchen.

'That was a surprise all round, wasn't it?' he remarked, sitting on the table and swinging his legs.

'What do you mean?' asked Gina cautiously as she prepared to make coffee for herself and Irma.

'Surprise for Will, surprise for you and surprise for Irma,' he replied.

'I didn't realise Will was surprised. I thought he behaved as if he was pleased to see her.'

'Do I detect a note of jealousy?' mocked Gregor. 'Because someone out of your fiancé's past love-life has turned up?'

'What makes you think she's been one of his loves?' asked Gina sharply.

'I'm just guessing from the expression on her face when he introduced you as his fiancée. For a moment she looked as if she'd been shot down in flames.'

'Oh, dear. What a muddle!' sighed Gina.

'Why do you say that?'

Her remark had sprung from genuine regret that her pseudo-engagement to Will might be causing more unhappiness, and she was now so used to Gregor being with her that she had forgotten he did not know the truth.

'I don't like being the cause of unhappiness for others,' she explained rather lamely, aware he was watching her with bright observant eyes.

'I was rather puzzled by something she said to him after he had introduced you to her. Did you notice? She spoke to him in German,' mused Gregor.

'Do you know German? Oh, tell me, what did she say?' asked Gina.

'I'm not fluent in the language, but I did study it at school and I've been to Germany on a couple of holidays. She said something about not having realised he was free, and how long he had been free. It made me wonder whether he'd been in prison at some time.'

'Don't be silly. Of course he hasn't. What answer did he make?'

'He was non-committal, I thought. He said he'd been free quite a while and then suggested she spoke in English. He wasn't pleased by the question.'

Had the question referred to Bridget? Had Irma been asking how long Will had been free to become engaged and marry again? And did his answer mean he was no longer married to Bridget?

'Any idea what they were talking about?' prompted Gregor.

'No, not at all. But I expect Will will tell me later. Would you like to have some beer and take him some before he comes in here roaring for it. I'll follow with coffee as soon as it's ready. Did Lachie come in?'

521

'No. He hasn't taken to Irma. Said she was an incomer and he doesn't hold with incomers.'

'Then what does he think I am?' exclaimed Gina.

'You came with the swans and so you are the true mistress of the master of the glen. Had you forgotten?' said Gregor with a chuckle. Then, unable to keep his own concerns to himself any longer, he burst out with his news. 'Will is going to let me help with the camp. I'm to start this morning, looking over the rigging of the dinghies and making sure it's all in good order, and inspecting the canoes for holes. He even suggested that I move into the bunkhouse and come and take my meals here before the camp starts on Monday.'

'Are you pleased?'

'Yes, I'm pleased, although that's rather an understatement of the way I feel after climbing that cliff this morning. I'm very pleased, thanks to you, Gina.'

'And to Will,' she insisted, worried by the ardent expression in his eyes.

'Thanks to you both, then, but I can't help wishing . . .'

He stopped talking abruptly in mid-sentence and immediately she was curious.

'Can't help wishing what?' she asked.

'That you weren't engaged to him.'

'Oh, Gregor,' she wailed, 'don't you start! Everything is in such a muddle as it is. What am I going to do?'

'You mean you're not sure any more whether you want to be engaged to Will?' he asked eagerly.

'I'm not sure about anything any more,' she said a little wildly. 'Now go and take this beer into the other room.'

After drinking his beer and listening a little while longer to Irma's discourse on all the places she had visited during the extended holiday she had taken, Will excused himself and took Gregor with him. As he left the room he kissed Gina on the cheek, to keep up appearances, of course, suggested to her that Irma might like to stay for the day, then went out trailing a rather thunderous-looking Gregor behind him.

Gina found it easy to entertain the unexpected visitor, who was interested in everything to do with the farm and talked enough for two. They went to feed the swans and lingered on the shore beside the rippling water. The silent mountain basked tranquilly in the sunshine, its cap of ice gradually diminishing in size, and the moors glowed purple and gold.

'You will not mind if I say something a little personal to you, Gina?' asked Irma.

Gina glanced sideways at her companion. In the clear light she could see faint lines under Irma's smooth make-up. The woman was older than she had at first thought, nearer to Will's age than to her own.

'No. At least I don't think so. How can I tell until you've said it?' she countered, with a laugh.

Irma joined in the laughter, throwing her head back, her white teeth flashing, her blonde hair glinting metallically. She was a vigorous person who did everything with great gusto.

'That's true,' she agreed. 'Then I will say it. I find it strange that you are living here alone with Will before you are married. Is it the custom?'

In spite of her resolve not to let herself be disconcerted by anything Irma might say, Gina felt the blood seeping slowly into her cheeks.

'No, it isn't. I came to stay here and to help with the cooking for the Easter camp. When we arrived we found that his partner had walked out on him, taking with him his wife who usually did the cooking. Will asked me if I would stay just the same and help him until he found someone else. I could hardly refuse, could I?'

'But why didn't you marry straight away?'

Gina was a little flustered by this question and wondered uneasily whether it had already been out to Will and what his answer had been.

'Why don't you ask Will?' she countered.

Irma's high shoulders rose in a shrug.

'I ask him many questions which he does not answer. He is very good at, how do you say it? At the fencing. I hoped you would be more straightforward.'

'Then I say that we did not marry immediately because we did not wish to. An engagement is a time to get to know one another better before taking an extremely important step. And that's what Will and I are doing. We're getting to know one another,' replied Gina, her thoughts winging back to Will's easy and slow philosophy. Little had she guessed that she would be using it in self-defence.

'I see. I can understand Will wishing to be careful this time. His first marriage was such a disaster, wasn't it?' said Irma.

'I don't know. He never talks about it. Did you know Bridget?'

'No. She had left him before I met him. I was his German teacher. It was a language course for young Army officers. Will was my best pupil. He has a very good ear for language. Ah, we had many happy times together in Luneburg,' Irma sighed reminiscently. 'After he left the Army we kept in touch, through letters. I hoped that one day he would be free. He told me nothing of you in his letters,' she added sharply.

Gina hoped that the expression on her face was not giving her away as she thought of the letters, written in German on pink perfumed paper, which she had found amongst the other correspondence in Will's desk. There was a vague similarity between this conversation and the one she had once held with Andrea. Yet Irma was no adolescent with a schoolgirl crush on a man much older than herself. She was a mature woman who had seen her hopes dashed that morning when Will had introduced his new fiancée to her; hopes that one day, when he was free of Bridget, she could become his wife.

'I'm sorry,' Gina muttered, as she had once apologised to

Andrea. At the first opportunity she must speak to Will and tell him that the pseudo-engagement was over. It was causing too many complications. 'You must stay here for the rest of your holiday,' she suggested impulsively.

Irma glanced at her, puzzlement shadowing her clear grey eyes.

'Thank you. I would like to do that,' she said slowly. 'I'm very fond of Will and I would not like to see him make the same mistake again.'

'What do you mean?'

'Please forgive me for being frank. It is my nature to say what I think. You seem soft and helpless, as I believe Bridget was, lying in wait to catch a man like Will, who is strong and confident and so often compassionate towards those who are weaker than he is. He was caught by that helplessness once before, and I have read that a man often falls for the same type of woman over and over again. I shall stay here for a while and make sure that he is not going to make the same mistake twice.'

Irma turned away and walked back to the house. Alone, Gina finished feeding the swans. She found she was shaking with anger. Soft and helpless like Bridget, was she? And that was why Will had taken pity on her and had brought her to the glen to recover from the shock of Oliver's death. Was it also the reason why he had asked her to take the next step with him the other night? Had he wanted her only because she reminded him of Bridget?

It was a thought she could not bear. She must find out what had happened to Bridget and why Will was free of her.

Irma stayed for lunch and spent the afternoon following Will around the farm. She left before the evening meal to return to Ullapool where she was staying the night in the hotel.

'Irma tells me you've invited her to stay here,' said Will as he helped Gina to clear away dishes after the evening meal was over. 'It's a good idea. She can help you with the cooking while the campers are here.'

'I'd rather she didn't,' replied Gina, more sharply than she had intended, and he gave her a searching sidelong glance.

'Why?' he asked.

'You know the saying about too many cooks,' she retorted.

'I do. But I thought you'd like some help. After all, it's very hard work and this time there'll be thirty campers.'

'Didn't I manage all right for the last camp?'

'You did. Remarkably well considering you were not exactly up to scratch after the shock you'd had,' he murmured placatingly.

'I may look soft and helpless,' she rushed on, 'but I can assure you that I'm not. I'm not like Bridget.'

'No one knows that better than I do,' he said quietly, his face like stone, his eyes two pools of blue ice. 'Who said you're like her?'

'Irma did.'

'Why were you discussing Bridget with her?' he demanded frostily.

'Oh, because she brought up the subject that you'd been married before.' Then seeing his face darken with anger she went on, 'Oh, Will, don't you think I should leave now and jilt you? This phoney engagement is creating such a lot of complications.'

'No.' The negative came out forcibly and called her to order. She looked at him rather timidly and waited.

With an effort he smiled at her.

'Sorry to bark at you, but I had to make you pay attention somehow. Now listen to me. We shall keep up this phoney engagement, as you call it, at least until the campers have gone. After that you can leave if you wish to.'

'But I can't see how it's helping anyone.'

'It's helping me. You can take my word for that.'

She glanced at him dubiously. He smiled at her and

lifted her left hand from her side and looked down at the ring.

'Thanks to poor old Noll, this makes the engagement look convincing to outsiders, even though it would not be my choice for you. Has anyone ever told you that when you're upset or angry your eyes blaze like topazes, sweetheart?'

'Will, stop making fun,' she said huskily, pulling her hand from his.

'I'm not.'

'I wish I knew what game you're playing.'

'A waiting game,' he murmured. 'Easy and slow. Remember? Are you going to do as I ask?'

'Only if you'll tell me about Bridget, please. I think I've a right to know.'

He turned away from her to put some dishes away in a cupboard. He came back to her and put his hands on her shoulders, holding her so that she had to look up at him. His mouth was set in a grim line and his eyes were shadowed, reminding her of the way he had looked the night he had told her he had a twinge of pain from an old wound.

'If I tell you will you promise to keep it all to yourself?' he asked gravely.

'I promise.'

'Then come into the other room. We may as well be comfortable while I unfold the details of my lurid past.'

His self-mockery did not mislead her. He was about to tell her about something which had hurt him, she was sure of that; something which had bruised his emotions, driving them underground; something which had made him what he was now, a little tough and enigmatic in his dealings with women.

In the living room she sat on the window seat and looked out. Down on the loch one swan swam, a lonely shape silhouetted against the golden water. The woods were dark now, the shapes of the trees blurred. Beyond them the moors still reflected the radiance of the setting sun and Ben

527

Searg's sharp summit was violet, laced with silver, glinting against the pale evening sky.

Will searched in his desk, throwing crumpled paper to the floor, muttering something about having to tidy it one day. Gina hid a smile, thinking of how many times he said that and did nothing, leaving her to attempt to make order out of chaos.

At last, finding what he wanted, he came across to her and tossed a long buff envelope on to her lap.

'Read that,' he ordered tersely. 'I'll fill in the background when I've locked up the hens.'

He went out of the room. Gina stared at the envelope. It was addressed to Will at White Lodge. Her throat tight with apprehension, she drew out the single sheet of paper which the envelope contained. The heading on the paper was the address of a hospital in the south of England and the date was the seventeenth of August four years previously.

Quickly she read the letter. In terse direct terms it informed Captain Fox of the death of his wife Bridget and requested him to attend her funeral. After that announcement the language of the letter changed slightly as if the writer of it, a certain Dr Lilian Vance, had known Will personally. She assured him that everything had been done for his wife and that he must never blame himself for the condition into which she had sunk, but should regard her death as a blessing in disguise because she had been hopelessly and incurably addicted.

Her hands shaking, Gina folded the sheet of paper and replaced it in the envelope. Bridget was dead, and had been for almost four years. She had been a drug addict and had presumably been in a mental hospital. Suddenly, quite clearly, Gina could see and hear Will as he had looked and spoken in her bedroom at the flat when he'd asked her if she had taken a drug to escape from reality. Now she understood what had been behind his jeer. Now she understood, also, his silence on the subject of Bridget, so that even Meg, who had known Bridget, still did not know she was dead or how she had died.

Will re-entered the room and sat down beside her.

'I'm so sorry,' she murmured.

'Don't be. It wasn't much of a marriage. I married her for all the wrong reasons,' he replied grimly.

'What were they?' she asked.

'Pity, a wish to help someone weaker than myself. It's always been one of my shortcomings and verges on arrogance, I suppose. Add to that physical desire and you have a bad mixture,' he replied cynically.

'Meg told me that you met Bridget at her home.'

'Yes. I was on leave and interested only in having a good time. She was pretty and also interested in a good time. She was easy to make love to—too easy. I took what she offered, went back to Germany and never gave her another thought. Then she ran away from the Maxwells'. She told me afterwards she found their way of life too strict. Six months later she turned up in Germany and begged me to marry her. I told her to go home to Scotland, but she wouldn't. She threatened to commit suicide if I didn't marry her. I didn't realise then what was wrong with her and, as I still found her physically attractive, I married her and created my own hell.'

'But why did she run away from you?' asked Gina.

'I discovered that she was helping to smuggle drugs from Holland into Germany. I threatened to expose her to the police if she didn't stop, so she ran away. Sickened and disillusioned by then, not only by her bad habits but also by her inability to love anyone other than herself, I told myself that I didn't care. I let two years slip by without trying to find her. Then Meg wrote to me asking why she hadn't received any letters from either Bridget or myself and I realised I would have to try and find her.'

'Where did you start to look?'

'It wasn't difficult, because in the meantime I received a letter from that hospital. She had been taken there after a suicide attempt while under the influence of drugs. I went to see her. She was in a pitiful state. They said there was hope for her if I'd take her back and provide her with a good home, somewhere in the country, they suggested, away from the city and all its distractions. A farm with animals she could take an interest in. Sympathy and kindness was what she needed, they said. Remembering what she'd been like, I didn't really believe them, but I did as they suggested. What else could I do? I'd married her. She was my wife for better or for worse, and even though I didn't love her I couldn't desert her just then, because she had no one else.' He stopped talking abruptly, his voice choked with bitterness.

'So you found the glen,' said Gina softly.

'Yes, and bought it and went to work in Ullapool, thinking that it was possible, when the hospital released her and allowed her to come north, she would soon recover in such peaceful surroundings where nature is all-important. Then that letter came. It was all over and I had only the future to look forward to. My marriage was an ugly mess which I preferred to forget. I couldn't even talk about it to anyone, not even Meg. You're the first to know.'

'Thank you for telling me.'

'Does it help you to know?' he asked, taking the letter from her and going over to the desk to push it into a pigeonhole.

'Of course it does. I've been terribly worried in case she turned up unexpectedly and found us "engaged".'

'You shouldn't have been. I thought I'd told you she wouldn't be coming back.'

'Yes, but you didn't say why she wouldn't be coming back and your attitude didn't make it easy to ask questions. Why have you kept it all hidden, Will? Wouldn't it have been better to tell someone?' she queried.

He moved away from the desk and came to stand beside her.

'That's a hard one to answer,' he murmured. 'I suppose

the answer lies somewhere in my nature. I've always tended to keep my problems and my failures to myself, and my marriage to Bridget was a problem and a failure from start to finish. In being too sympathetic towards her when she came to me in Germany I almost destroyed myself as well as contributing to her destruction. If I'd been tougher with her from the start we would never have married and it's just possible she might have survived.'

He murmured something about having to go and see Lachie and went from the room, leaving Gina to stare out at the shadows deepening in the glen.

The next day Irma returned and moved into the bedroom which had been the Andersons' when they had lived at White Lodge. She said she would stay for as long as the campers were there in order to give Will some help. She was a Girl Guide leader and had had much experience in camping and in the use of the compass. She also knew some geology and was willing to give talks on the subject to the campers. Will seemed very pleased to have her there and had no compunction in making use of her.

Later the same day Gregor arrived in Andrea's car and moved into one of the bunkhouses, and that evening there were four for supper in the big kitchen at White Lodge. The long quiet evenings were over.

On Monday the campers arrived. This time they were a mixed bunch, mostly young men whose ages ranged from seventeen to twenty-five. They came not only from Britain but also from different parts of the continent, and after their arrival there was no more time for personal conversations between Gina and the other inmates of the house.

The days passed by quickly, sometimes sunny and mild, sometimes grey and boisterous as the wind whipped the water and shook the trees. Sea-birds driven inshore by the wild weather shrieked and chattered as they circled and hovered over the loch and surrounding fields and moors. In the garden, obeying the summons of the season, huge purple flowers bloomed on the rhododendron bushes and the two

531

laburnum trees dripped yellow blossoms.

Gina cooked meals, packed up lunches, organised washing-up parties and gave instruction in sailing. Every night she fell into bed and slept deeply. During the day she was aware of Gregor, smiling and growing more confident by the hour; of Irma and Will laughing and joking together in German as they enjoyed each other's company.

Towards the end of the second week of the camp she began to think about leaving. In a few days she could leave, if she wished. Will would not bind her.

The thought of leaving made her heart ache in a strange way, yet the more she saw of Will and Irma together the more convinced she became that she was in the way of their happiness. Once the camp was over she would break off her pseudo-engagement to Will, return to Birmingham and take up the thread of her life again from where it had been broken before her real engagement to Oliver.

The necessity for her to leave soon was brought home to her by a letter from Meg Maxwell, who had already written to Will to tell him that she and her husband were taking a few days' holiday and would call to see him. She had written separately to Gina to say she had heard that Will's 'chief cook and bottle-washer' was still with him and that she looked forward to meeting her again.

The letter came as a slight shock, but a necessary one. It would never do for Meg to come and find her engaged to Will, Gina decided. It was all very well keeping up an act for the benefit of neighbours and outsiders, but it would never do to deceive someone belonging to Will's family. There she drew the line, even if he didn't. She would have to leave that week-end before the Maxwells arrived.

The sight of Irma and Will in close conversation as they returned slowly to the house in the dusk on the last evening of the camp confirmed her in her decision. She must leave before Irma did and give both Irma and Will the chance of happiness which had been denied them while Bridget had lived.

Such thoughts gave her no pleasure and that night she slept badly, with the result that she overslept and did not waken next morning until she felt a hand on her shoulder as someone shook her. She opened her eyes to find Will bending over her. Behind him bright sunlight streamed through the window.

'Oh. What's happened?' gasped Gina, sitting up in bed.

'You didn't hear me bang on the door,' he replied curtly.

'Oh, dear, the breakfast!' she said ruefully.

'Don't give it a thought. Irma is cooking it and doing a great job at such short notice. You should have let her help you with the cooking before this, then you wouldn't have become so tired.'

There was no sympathy in his attitude. He was just stating a matter of fact, and although she knew he was right Gina did not feel any better.

'She's welcome to cook here whenever she likes, all summer if she wishes,' she said haughtily, her chin up and her eyelids drooping. Then she wished she had kept quiet because his eyes began to gleam with mockery.

'She doesn't want to stay. She's leaving this afternoon,' he said calmly.

'I don't believe it. She told me she would stay here as long as she could,' she retorted.

His eyebrows went up in surprise, but all he said was,

'Well, she's stayed, and this afternoon she's leaving.'

'So am I,' announced Gina, rather breathlessly, and saw the mockery fade from his eyes as their expression sharpened.

'How?' he asked.

She nibbled her lower lip, in a quandary. How she would leave had not been one of the questions she had asked herself during the night and so she had no answer ready.

'With Irma, if there's no other way,' she said. 'I'm sure she'll be delighted to give me a lift.'

Will turned away from the bed and walked over to the door where he paused, his hand on the latch.

'I didn't think you'd be in such a hurry to leave,' he said. 'I hoped you'd stay a few days longer and meet Meg and Drew again. They'll be here by Monday afternoon.'

'And that's why I must leave soon. How can I stay when they're coming?'

He gave her a puzzled glance over his shoulder.

'I thought you liked Meg,' he murmured.

'I do, that's why I can't deceive her. We can't tell her we're engaged. She's your relative and she still believes Bridget is alive.'

'Perhaps the time has come for me to tell her about Bridget. Now that I've told you it won't be so difficult telling her,' he said slowly. 'Then she won't find our engagement strange.'

'But I don't want Meg to believe we're engaged,' she insisted rather desperately, wondering why he was being so obtuse. 'I don't want to deceive her. I want to go home.'

He turned back to the door and opened it slowly, apparently considering her rather wildly spoken request.

'All right,' he said at last. 'Then it shall be as you wish. Stay one more night and I promise that tomorrow I'll drive you south to catch a night train to Birmingham.'

He left the room closing the door behind him. Gina sat slumped on the bed, vaguely aware that something was wrong. Telling him that she wished to leave had been much easier than she had anticipated. One more night in the glen and her period of recuperation would be over. Oliver was not forgotten, but he was now part of a past which didn't hurt any more because the present and future were showing signs of being much more painful. She was well and whole again, but she had the most miserable feeling that she did not want to leave Glengorm after all. She wanted to stay here in the White Lodge and be chief cook and bottle-washer for its master.

When she went down to the kitchen she found Irma saying cheerful farewells to campers who were leaving and giving crisp guttural orders to those who were helping to clear away dishes. There was no doubt that she was in charge of the kitchen this morning.

'Your breakfast is in the oven,' she said to Gina after giving her a brisk good morning, and her cheerfulness grated on the nerves.

'Will tells me you're leaving today,' Gina said, taking the plate of food from the oven and placing it on the table. 'Couldn't you stay a little longer? I'm sure Will would like you to meet his aunt. She's coming here on Monday.'

'I would like to meet her very much. Will has told me how good she has been to him, making a home for him to go to when he was on leave from the army and he was not welcome in his mother's house,' said Irma, 'but I'm afraid I must return to Germany. I have liked it here. The glen is a beautiful place in which to live. I hope you realise how lucky you are. Excuse me, please.'

She left the room hurriedly. Alone, Gina ate her breakfast and thought. She was convinced that Irma had gone from the room quickly because she had been overcome with emotion at the thought of having to leave Will. Surely there must be some way in which she could help her to stay. If only she could leave that afternoon before the German woman, perhaps everything would work out happily after all. But how could she leave the glen and go south when she had no means of transport.

Just then Gregor came into the kitchen and she saw a way of solving her problem.

'I must speak to you alone somewhere,' she said to him. He looked surprised and then mischievous.

'You sound very mysterious,' he whispered. 'Come down to the loch where the dinghies are pulled up. My job for this morning is to make sure they're all intact. Maybe we could go for a sail. There's a small breeze wafting in from the sea.'

The small breeze, however, brought a smirring of rain with it so that Gina and Gregor were forced to retreat from the lochside to the shed where the dinghies, canoes and all their equipment were usually stored.

'We couldn't be more alone than we are here,' said Gregor. 'And there's no chance of us being disturbed by Will or Lachie because they've both gone to Ullapool this morning. What is it you want to tell me?'

'Ask, not tell,' Gina corrected him. 'Could you and would you take me to the nearest place where I could catch a train going south today?'

His black eyes widened and he whistled his surprise.

'I could and I would, but I'd like to know why,' he replied.

'I want to go to Birmingham,' she said.

He noted a certain tenseness in her manner and his eyes narrowed again, speculatively.

'Does Will know?' he queried warily.

'Yes, but he won't take me until tomorrow, and I want to go today.'

'Irma is leaving and should be driving through England. Why don't you ask her for a lift?' he suggested, looking thoroughly puzzled by now.

'I know she is, but you see I don't want her to leave. I want to stay here, and I think she will once I've gone,' replied Gina earnestly.

Gregor's expression of puzzlement changed to one of anxiety. He touched her forehead with his hand.

'Hot and feverish,' he announced. 'I guessed as much. You're not talking sense, Gina.'

'Yes, I am,' she insisted impatiently. 'At least it makes sense to me. Please will you do as I ask? Please, Gregor.'

'When you look at me like that I'm tempted to agree, out of hand,' he murmured. 'But I'm afraid of Will, so I'd like to know more before I do as you say. What's the matter? Are you fed up with Glengorm?'

'Yes.' Although her answer was far from the truth Gina seized on the reason he offered because she knew that it was one he would readily understand and accept. Other women had left the glen because they had been fed up with the way

536

of life there and Gregor knew that Madge Anderson had left for that reason.

'You can't be thinking of jilting Will,' Gregor said, hope lilting through his voice.

'Yes, I am,' she replied, gazing at him steadily, hoping that she sounded convincing and that the terrible ache of sadness she felt at the thought of leaving would not last too long.

'I can hardly believe it,' he murmured, and a strange little glow lit his dark eyes. 'Gina, say it's true and I'll drive you all the way to Birmingham,' he offered excitedly.

'It's true. Why are you so pleased?'

'Don't you see? You'll be free, and that gives me a chance. One day perhaps, you and I could...'

Aware that he was approaching closely, an ardent expression in his eyes as their glance shifted to her mouth, his arms reaching for her, Gina backed away from him.

'I'm not promising anything, Gregor,' she said sharply. 'Just help me to leave without Will knowing that I've gone.'

He lowered his arms to his sides but continued to stare at her intently.

'I don't understand,' he said. 'Are you sure you're doing the right thing by leaving?'

'Quite sure. You see, Irma is in love with Will and I think it's possible that he's in love with her. At any rate he's very fond of her. They're also very suited to each other. She's strong and clever and she knows all about camps and compasses, as well as how to cook, so she'd be a great asset to him in organising the camps. They've a great deal in common and have known each other for ages, much longer than he and I have known each other. Anyway I've decided that marriage between Will and me wouldn't work. After all, that's what an engagement is for, isn't it? To find out whether you're suited to one another before taking the next and most important step.'

Gina realised suddenly that she was babbling in her effort to convince Gregor and that he was looking even more worried and perplexed, so she stopped talking.

'I suppose you're right,' he murmured, but his manner lacked conviction. 'When would you like to leave?'

'As soon as possible after lunch. Oh, thank you, Gregor —I'm awfully grateful to you.'

A strange expression crossed his face and for a moment she had a brief impression of a different, rather malevolent Gregor. Then it passed and he gave her a twisted smile.

'You're very trusting, Gina. Knowing myself as I do I think I ought to warn you to keep your gratitude until you've arrived at your destination. Anything could happen between here and Birmingham when you travel with me,' he said.

She realised he was making an oblique reference to the accident for which he had been responsible and which had caused severe injury to his ex-girl-friend. Leaning forward impulsively, she placed a hand on his arm. Immediately he covered her hand with one of his.

'It's a chance I'm willing to take,' she said sincerely. 'I do trust you and I'm sure you won't let me down.'

'I'll do my best not to let you down,' he replied huskily, and a dull red colour stained his face. 'Thanks for trusting me, Gina. Now I'd better go and see to those dinghies for Will.'

Will did not come back in time for lunch, so there were only Gina, Irma and Gregor at the table for the midday meal. When it was over Irma said she would go and pack in readiness to leave as soon as Will put in an appearance.

'I hope he comes soon,' she said. 'I must leave at two o'clock and I do not want to leave without saying good-bye to him.'

'I'm sure he'll be back in time,' soothed Gina. 'Have you by any chance seen Blue this morning?'

'I think I saw him wandering off towards the cliffs,' replied Irma vaguely, as she left the kitchen.

Hoping that her pet would turn up soon, Gina went into the living room and tried to compose a letter to Will. The words would not flow and after several attempts which all found their way to the waste basket she wrote only:

Dear Will,
 Gregor has taken me to Birmingham. Thank you for having me.

She signed it simply with the name George and left it lying on the open desk. It didn't express at all her feelings about her stay in Glengorm, but she daren't write any more in case her emotions got the better of her. She recalled her first night at the White Lodge when Will had found the note from Gavin and felt suddenly guilty as if she were in the process of letting Will down too, and Meg Maxwell had warned that Will must not be let down again.

Shaking the feeling off, she left the room quickly before she could change her mind about the terse little note. She went upstairs, put on her red raincoat, picked up her cases, gave a last look round the room where she had slept so well for many nights, and then crept downstairs and out of the house. She hoped that Irma was too busy with her own packing to hear or notice anything unusual.

Outside she found Gregor leaning against Andrea's two-seater sports car, obviously ready to set off. He took the cases from her and put them in the space behind the seats where his own zipped holdall was already in position.

'I can't find Blue,' said Gina. 'Irma says she saw him going off towards the cliffs. I'll have to go and look for him.'

'I'll come with you,' offered Gregor, noting how white her face was and how wide and strained-looking her eyes were.

The smirr of rain had increased to a steady drenching downpour and by the time they reached the cliff top they were both soaked. Gina's bright hair was dark with rain and Gregor's hung in rat's tails over the collar of his short waterproof jacket.

There was no sign of the kitten and Gina went cautiously to the edge of the cliff to peer over down to the tossing, foaming water.

'Once he climbed down to a ledge and Will had to rescue him,' she explained to Gregor, and then she began to call the kitten.

Gregor shivered slightly as he also looked down the severe slope of the slippery shining rock.

'He could be anywhere,' he muttered. Then he grabbed her arm and added, 'Shush! Listen, I think I heard him crying.'

Gina stopped calling and listened intently. Below the sea crashed incessantly against the rocks at the foot of the cliffs. A solitary seagull glided by on a current of air, its screeching call seeming like a mocking echo of a cat's meow.

'It was the gull you heard,' she said miserably.

'No,' he insisted. 'Look—there's the kitten, down there, on that little ledge.'

She looked. Today there was no sunshine to make the rock flash with pink sparks. Instead it was dark grey with tiny rivulets of water streaming down it. About twenty feet below on a narrow ledge of rock which jutted out, something moved.

'Blue!' she called, and there was the unmistakable plaintive howl of a cat in trouble.

'He is there,' she exclaimed. 'Oh, the silly little thing! Why did he go down there just when I want to leave? What shall I do?'

'Keep on calling him. If he was able to get down there he should be able to get up. Cats rarely go to places from which they can't return,' suggested Gregor.

'But I've no time to wait for him. I must leave before Will comes back and Irma leaves,' moaned Gina desperately, seeing all her plans to help Irma and Will find happiness together disintegrating just because her kitten was too adventurous.

'Then you'll have to leave without him,' replied Gregor,

impatiently. 'He isn't all that important, surely?'

'Yes, he is. Oliver gave him to me,' said Gina, then realised suddenly, as she noticed puzzlement flash across Gregor's face, that he didn't know anything about Oliver and had never heard of him. 'I can't go without him. You must realise that,' she insisted. 'I'll have to stay and wait for him after all.'

He gave her a strange glance and then looked over the edge of the cliff again.

'If Will could climb down there I can,' he said with a touch of arrogance, and before she could remonstrate he had lowered himself over the edge of the cliff and was searching with his feet for suitable footholds while he clung to the edge with his hands.

'Oh, please be careful, Greg. It's very wet and slippery,' Gina urged anxiously, wondering what Mrs Macneal would say if she knew her youngest son was risking life and limb to fetch a silly little kitten from its precarious perch on the face of a cliff to safety, just because an equally silly young woman could not bear to go away without it. 'Perhaps you should get a rope first,' she added, as an afterthought.

He looked up at her his dark eyes glittering with some undefinable emotion.

'If we want to get away before Will comes back from Ullapool and Irma leaves, there isn't time for me to fetch a rope,' he retorted. 'Did Will use a rope?'

'No. But it was a fine day and he's much more...'

'I know,' he interrupted fiercely. 'He's much more experienced than I am in more ways than one, but he's not going to have you, if I can help it. If he didn't need a rope then neither do I. I'll show you that I'm as good as he is any day.'

Realising the futility of arguing with him when he was in such a strange stubborn mood, Gina walked away from the edge of the cliff, unable to stay and watch him climb down. She hoped he knew what he was doing, and began to wish she had agreed to leave the glen without the kitten.

After pacing up and down several times and succeeding only in soaking her feet in the wet grass, she gathered up enough nerve to go back and look over the edge again. To her relief Gregor was near the ledge. Leaning against the face of the cliff, he was reaching sideways with one hand to grasp the kitten. Spitting and snarling, Blue backed off, just out of reach.

'Oh, you stupid cat!' wailed Gina. She knelt on the wet grass, regardless of the damp patches such an action would leave on the knees of her elegant wheat-coloured pants. 'Can't you see that someone has come to rescue you?'

Watching tensely, she saw Gregor reach sideways again and fail to grasp the ball of wet, greyish-blue fur which was Blue. Then to her horror she saw him slip. He clutched desperately with his fingers to the wet rock as he tried to find new footholds, but without spikes on the soles of his shoes he was unable to get an adequate grip on the slippery surface. Slowly he began to slide down the cliff in the direction of the pounding, smashing sea.

CHAPTER SIX

PETRIFIED, her hands to her face, Gina knelt in the grass and watched Gregor's body gain momentum and begin to roll over and over down the cliff. Suddenly, with an unpleasant jolt, he came to a stop, his fall broken by a clump of bushes which grew out of a crevice in the rock. The branches of the bushes shook in reaction to the jolt and Gina prayed that they would hold him.

He lay still and she wondered if he had lost consciousness. She called to him, but her voice came out as a croak which the hovering seagull mimicked as it swooped down the cliff face, a flash of white against the dark grey.

Clearing her throat, she cupped her hands round her mouth and called again.

'Gregor, can you hear me?'

The kitten mewed plaintively and the seagull chattered mockingly. Gregor lifted an arm and waved it and Gina thought he called to her.

'Stay there!' she shouted. 'I'll go and fetch help.'

He waved again as if to acknowledge that he had heard her. She stood up and began to run down the path to White Lodge. The skirts of her raincoat caught at her legs and the wet grass seemed to suck her feet down, impeding her progress. As she ran she said over and over to herself, 'Please let Will be back from Ullapool. Please let Will be back.' Then she told herself not to waste her breath.

Panting for breath, she slithered down the last slippery stretch of the path to the house. With relief she saw that the blue truck was parked in its usual place near the barn.

'Will, Will,' she started to shout breathlessly, 'where are you?'

He could be anywhere on the estate, she realised. On the other side of the loch, on the moors, in the barn. Or he could be with Irma in the house.

Frantically she flung herself at the front door, opening it and almost falling into the hallway.

'Will!' she called.

He came out of the living room almost immediately. She had a brief impression that he was rather pale and that the expression in his eyes was one of cold wicked anger. Then she was in his arms and gasping out her story about Gregor.

'Now, George, this is no way to behave when someone needs help.' His voice was calm, as reassuring as ever. His hands were on her shoulders, holding her away from him. When she looked up she saw he was no longer pale and his eyes, though cold, did not flicker with that livid violent emotion.

'Pull yourself together,' he ordered crisply, 'and tell me slowly what happened exactly, when he slipped and where he is now, while we go and choose some ropes from the storage shed. Then you'll have to go and tell Lachie that I'll need his help.'

He turned and opened the front door and pushed her before him, out into the damp drizzle.

'And Irma too,' she suggested. 'She's strong, and could help.'

'Irma has gone. She left about ten minutes ago,' he replied curtly, as he strode ahead of her towards the bunk-houses.

Looking round, Gina realised that the grey Volkswagen was no longer parked beside the two-seater which belonged to Andrea Macneal. Her plan to leave before Irma had mis-fired after all. Irma had gone. Was it possible that her departure was the reason why Will had looked so pale and angry when he had come out of the living room?

As she caught up with him she described once again, as clearly as she could, what had happened to Gregor. By the time she had finished they had reached the storage shed, where only a few hours earlier she had made plans to leave the glen, and Will was selecting lengths of terylene rope.

He gave her a sidelong glance, said something vitriolic and unkind about Blue, then, when she would have retaliated in defence of her pet, smiled at her in a way which made her heart lurch suddenly and pink colour storm into her cheeks, and added gently,

'You're all of a dither, aren't you, love? Don't worry, I'll rescue Greg for you and bring him up all in one piece. Now go and tell Lachie to come here. Then take Andrea's car...'

'No keys,' she interrupted him. 'Greg has them in his pocket.'

'Then take the truck.' He dropped the keys into her outstretched hand. 'Go to Castle Duich and tell Mrs Macneal, or whoever is there, what's happened. Say you need the help of some strong men, preferably some with climbing knowledge. Grant Parker and a couple of the shepherds would do. Ask for arrangements to be made for Greg to be taken to hospital as soon as he's brought up. He may have broken ribs or limbs after a fall like that. Now, hurry!'

'I don't know the way to the castle,' she gasped, thinking how much better she felt now that he had taken charge.

'Go to Lochinvie, right through the village and take the first road to the left. The castle is signposted and you can't miss the way.'

'Thank you. You'll be careful, Will, please,' she begged earnestly. 'The rock is awfully slippery. I wouldn't like you to fall too.'

His clear cold eyes appraised her and he lifted an eyebrow in sardonic appreciation of her remark.

'Nice of you to care, George,' he drawled drily. 'Unlike Greg, I shan't take any unnecessary risks, not even for you. Now off you go to Lachie's cottage.'

He turned his back on her. She hesitated a moment, gazing in puzzlement at his broad shoulders. Once again she realised how little she knew about him; about his real feelings. She could only guess that something had happened to upset him, and her guess was that he was regretting Irma's departure.

Leaving the shed, she walked down to Lachie's cottage. She found him in his kitchen sitting in front of a peat fire, smoking his pipe and reading the newspaper. Lachie did not like to work on a wet day. He listened to her carefully and courteously, then without a word, he stood up, took down an old oilskin coat from the hook behind the door, put it on, clapped a disreputable tweed hat on his head, ushered here out of the cottage, and strode away in the direction of the bunkhouses.

Gina hurried after him and went straight to the truck. After a few false starts she managed to get it going and guided it gingerly along the narrow road through the glen, lurching and bumping over potholes, brimful of muddy water.

Lochinvie was a single deserted street of squat thatched cottages. Thin spirals of smoke rose from the chimneys adding to the grey cloud which hovered over the whole area. Beyond the cottages Gina found the road to the left and turned on to it, thankful to see that it was surfaced and in good repair so that she was able to accelerate.

After twenty minutes of driving round innumerable bends as the road wound, a dark grey ribbon of wet tarmac across dank dismal moorland which stretched drearily for miles under heavy purplish-grey clouds, Gina was glad when she saw a signpost which indicated that Castle Duich was only half a mile away.

At last the road straightened, cutting through a forest of gloomy dripping-wet spruce trees. Imposing stone gate-posts appeared on the left and she turned the truck to drive between them up a wide driveway which led to a massive pile of stone masonry. Turrets and battlements reared up against the cloudy sky, giving the castle an authentic Gothic appearance and bringing to mind stories of vampires and ghosts. The yellow gleam of electric light glowed here and there from latticed windows, deep-set in the thick walls.

Gina parked the truck and jumped down. She ran to the

great oak door which was under a curved archway. She pulled on the old-fashioned doorbell handle and was relieved when the door swung open silently to reveal a tall man. Judging by his green suit, which was fastened by large brass buttons, he was some sort of servant, although the glance he gave her down his nose was extremely supercilious, as if he considered she had no right to approach the castle by the front entrance.

She explained why she was there. Without hesitation he invited her into a wide hall which had a stone floor. Ancient banners hung from authentic smoke-blackened beams. Colourful woven tapestries depicting hunting scenes decorated the thick stone walls. Light from wrought iron chandeliers glinted on shields and heraldic crests, which decorated the stone canopy of the huge fireplace.

The footman told her to sit on one of the high-backed Jacobean oak chairs which lined the walls, and went off to find Mrs Macneal. Sitting on the edge of the chair her hands in her pockets, Gina gazed around in awe at her surroundings and wondered how she was going to explain to Mrs Macneal that her youngest son was lying in a precarious position half way down a cliff.

In a very short time the click of a woman's high heels on stone flooring announced the coming of Mrs Macneal. She came through an archway on the right, small and imperious, wearing her magnificent kilt with a plain black woollen sweater.

Her dark brown eyes took in Gina's wet dishevelled hair and mud-stained raincoat in one comprehensive glance before she started to speak.

'Where is Gregor?' she rapped.

The words tumbled out of Gina as she explained. As when telling Will about the accident she left out the part that she and Gregor had been about to set off for Birmingham together, thinking that it would only cause Mrs Macneal to ask more questions.

'It's all my fault,' she ended in a low voice. 'I shouldn't

547

have let him climb down the cliff. He might be seriously hurt or even...' She caught her breath shakily, unable to say the word *dead*.

The austere lines of Mrs Macneal's patrician face softened slightly and she sat down on the chair next to Gina.

'You mustn't blame yourself, my dear,' she soothed, the pride of generations of Macneals preventing her from showing any extreme emotion on hearing that her son might be badly hurt. 'He *chose* to go for your kitten and I'm pleased that he felt he wanted to help someone at a risk to himself. There was a time, you know, when he would not have lifted a finger to help anyone, but you've changed all that.'

'I?' exclaimed Gina, raising surprised golden eyes to the imperious fine-featured face of the chief of the Macneals. 'What have I done?'

'You have been here in the right place at the right time,' insisted Mrs Macneal. 'When he met you Gregor was rudderless, incapable of steering in any direction for more than a few hours at a time. In order to impress you he has made an effort to come to terms with himself. I'm grateful to you, Gina, for giving him help when he needed it most, and I'd like to think that you'll always be his friend. I wish you could be more, but unfortunately Will Fox stands in the way of that wish coming true, just as he stands in the way of a few of my wishes. Now I'm going to take you to Andrea and she'll see that you have some tea while I go and arrange for some men to go over and help Will to rescue Gregor.'

From then on everything happened so quickly that Gina was slightly bewildered. Andrea appeared and took her off to a pleasant sitting room where a young man was lounging before a fire listening to a record player. Andrea introducd him as Blake Fraser, her cousin from the States, and then bombarded her with questions about Gregor's fall. They were just drinking tea when Mrs Macneal walked into the room. She was dressed in a white riding mackintosh and wore a coloured headscarf over her hair.

'I'm going over to the cliff now,' she announced. 'Everything is arranged. An ambulance will be sent to White Lodge immediately.'

'I hope it can get through,' said Gina. 'The glen road is like a river.'

'Then it's high time the County Council did something about it,' snapped Mrs Macneal, every inch the chieftain. She had probably never given a thought to the road, which she had hardly ever used, until today, when it was essential that access to the glen should be as easy as possible so that her youngest son could be transported to hospital. 'There should be a decent road now that there's someone living permanently at White Lodge. I'll take the matter up with the Council personally.'

She swept out of the room, leaving Gina to the tender mercies of Andrea, who talked almost vivaciously about the show-jumping competitions in which she had participated over the years. The vivacity was put on, Gina realised, for the benefit of the laconic Blake, and not for her. As soon as she could, she excused herself saying she must go back to White Lodge to find out what was happening. To her surprise Andrea said she would go with her in order to bring back her car, and soon Gina was driving back across the moors with Andrea sitting beside her.

The rain had stopped temporarily and the mist-like clouds had rolled up to reveal the severe rocky ramparts of the mountains which they had been hiding most of the day. Watery sunlight shone for a few minutes, striking diamond-like flashes of light from the wet trunks of trees and from the glistening dry-stone walls.

Inside the cab of the truck Andrea was silent, obviously ill at ease now that she was alone with Gina. The vivacity had been left behind at the castle along with the American cousin. It was not until they had begun to descend towards Lochinvie that she found her tongue. Then she spoke roughly and jerkily.

'Greg's in love with you,' she announced.

549

Gina gripped the steering wheel hard and kept her glance directed at the stretch of road in front of her.

'I don't think so,' she replied coolly.

'Then why has he spent so much time at White Lodge recently?' challenged Andrea.

'He wanted to prove that he could do something positive, and he has,' replied Gina firmly.

'By falling down a cliff?' Andrea was scornful. 'If the kitten hadn't been yours he wouldn't have gone after it. He's in love with you,' she asserted. 'You must be feeling very pleased with yourself. You stole Will away from me, and as if that wasn't enough, you have my brother dangling after you and climbing down cliffs for you, behaving like a knight in some chivalrous romance, doing dangerous deeds just to please his lady.'

Gina gritted her teeth. She must not allow herself to be upset by anything Andrea said, reminding herself that every word the girl uttered was the product of sour grapes. On the other hand she decided that it was time Miss Andrea Macneal learnt the truth.

'That is untrue,' she said coolly. 'In the first place I couldn't steal Will from you because he wasn't and never has been yours to steal. He regards you as a schoolgirl, and any feeling that you have for him he sees as mere infactuation, which he can do without because he finds it embarrassing.'

She heard Andrea draw in her breath sharply as if in pain and realised ruefully that she would have to pay for making that remark. Andrea was too spiteful to let it pass unpunished.

'And in the second place,' she continued, 'Gregor and I are good friends, nothing more. He's not in love with me.'

Unfortunately her voice faltered a little as she made the statement about Gregor. She had just recalled the ardent glow in his eyes that morning when he had heard she was about to jilt Will. He could not and must not be in love with her, she thought rather wildly, because she was certainly not in love with him. She found him attractive and good company, but she was not in love with him or anyone else. She wasn't even in love with Oliver any more.

But Andrea had noticed the quaver in her voice and with her usual quickness she pounced at once.

'You don't sound very sure,' she sneered. 'You needn't keep up appearances with me, you know. I expect you're sorry that you're engaged to Will now that you've met Gregor. Perhaps you'd like to jilt Will? Why don't you? Why don't you give him back his diamond ring and marry Gregor instead? I can assure you you'd please my mother if you did. She thinks you're the best person to ever cross my playboy brother's path, so you wouldn't find any opposition there.'

'And I suppose if I did jilt him you'll be ready and waiting to comfort Will?' retorted Gina tartly. 'Catch him on the rebound—is that your little plan? Yes, I can imagine that's the only way you could get him.'

Again Andrea drew a sharp breath and again Gina wished she had said nothing.

'Yes, I would like to comfort him,' said Andrea. 'And if you like I'll tell him for you that you're in love with Gregor and that he loves you. Then Will can do the right thing by you and release you from your engagement to save you from jilting him. Of course, you must realise that it's possible he knows you've been two-timing him during the past few weeks ever since you met Gregor!'

Gina seethed in silence. There was little use in denying Andrea's accusation and telling her that it was impossible for Will to be two-timed by herself when she was not properly engaged to him. To do so would involve her in a long explanation which she was not free to make, for the simple reason that their 'engagement' was Will's secret as well as her own, and he had used it to protect himself against gossip as well as from Andrea and her mother.

Fortunately Andrea accepted her silence as a sign of defeat and made no more scathing comments or suggestions, so the rest of the journey was made without a word being said by either of them.

They reached the white house amongst the birches just as rain began to fall again. There was a big ambulance parked close to the path coming down from the cliffs, and its rear doors were open ready to receive a stretcher. Two other vehicles were parked in front of the house—Mrs Macneal's Rolls-Royce, and a Land-Rover with the words Castle Duich painted on its dark green door.

Gina was about to start walking up the path, with Andrea close behind her, when she saw a group of people coming towards her. With a word to Andrea she turned back and they both stood and waited beside the ambulance.

Mrs Macneal headed the procession. With her hands at the pockets of her riding mackintosh and her headscarf soaked with rain she still managed to look regal and self-confident. Behind her came the stretcher to which Gregor had been bound. It was carried by the two ambulance men and was followed by two other men, both wearing dark green tweed suits, obviously the gamekeepers from the Castle Duich estate.

'Is he badly hurt?' asked Gina urgently, looking down at Gregor's white face which was blotched with purple bruises. His eyes had been closed, but when he heard her voice he opened them and they looked like dark empty caverns in his pale face.

'One broken leg. Could have been worse,' said Mrs Macneal brusquely.

'Oh, Gregor, I'm terribly sorry. It was my fault. I should have gone without the kitten,' said Gina softly, walking along beside the stretcher.

He smiled faintly, a ghost of his attractive flashing smile.

'Not your fault,' he murmured, with some difficulty because the pain-killer which the ambulance men had given him was beginning to take effect and make him drowsy. 'I wanted to show you that I'm as good as Will. At least I thought I was as good as him. I'm nothing but a show-off. I always have been. Next time I'll do as he says. I'll think first and act afterwards.'

He was being lifted into the ambulance and he raised his head a little so that he could still see her.

'Thank Will and Lachie for coming to the rescue, please, Gina. Come and see me in hospital. You mustn't leave the glen. You mustn't go to Birmingham. You must stay.' He sounded suddenly desperate. 'Mother, tell her, please. She's not to go away.'

His voice faded as he disappeared into the ambulance. Mrs Macneal entered the vehicle and Gina could hear her saying something to him. Then the rear doors were closed, the ambulance men took their seats in front and the heavy vehicle lumbered away along the road.

Gina and Andrea stood side by side and watched it go.

'I suppose I'd better go to the hospital too. Mother seems to expect it,' muttered Andrea sulkily, having looked around and made sure that Will was nowhere about. 'Do you want to come with me?'

'No, thank you,' replied Gina, who was determined to do nothing which would make Andrea think she was interested in Gregor.

The girl glanced past her up the path, but no one was coming from the cliff, so with a shrug of her shoulders she turned away and went off to the two-seater car.

Soon the car was leaving with a roar of exhaust, closely followed by the Land-Rover. Gina watched them go and then turned to the path, intending to find Will and Lachie.

She did not have to go far. They were strolling towards her, ropes coiled over their shoulders, moving in a leisurely fashion in spite of the rain, as if they had all day. At the sight of Will's damp tousled hair and his wide shoulders under the old green Army sweater he was wearing, Gina felt a sudden lift of relief mingled with delight. He had dared danger to rescue Gregor and he had succeeded in his usual calm competent way.

As he came nearer she saw that he had also rescued Blue,

for he was carrying the wet and miserable kitten between his hands. He came right up to her and held the cat out to her.

'This is yours, I believe. I'm surprised to find you here. I thought you'd be away in the ambulance holding Greg's hand,' he remarked drily.

She took the kitten from him and held it close to her. A little hurt by his taunt about Gregor, she gazed at Will, her eyes wide and troubled. She noticed that the rain had made his hair curl more closely to his head; that the skin was taut across his cheekbones and round his jaw, emphasising the strong clean angles of his face; that his eyes were as cold and clear as the water in a burn; and that the curve to his mouth was sardonic as he returned her gaze. Once before, in her parents' home, he had shown disapproval of her and now she could *feel* that same disapproval travelling like an electric current from him to her. She had done something which he disliked and for the time being he hated her.

'I'll be on my way,' Lachie was muttering, as if he sensed there was trouble brewing between them and he wished to be gone before it broke. 'That was a fine piece of rescue work you and I were doing on the cliff there, Will. Not that Macneal's men weren't a help, they were, but without you and me they wouldn't have known where to start. And I'm thinking yon kitten has nine lives, so it has.'

He went off, and in the silence he left behind him Gina could hear rain pattering on the leaves of the rhododendron bushes, on the roof of the porch and on the stiff shiny material of her red raincoat.

Will started off towards the house. She fell into step beside him.

'Gregor asked me to thank you for rescuing him,' she said hurriedly.

'Why haven't you gone to the hospital with him?' he asked coolly, ignoring her thanks.

'I was afraid Mrs Macneal might misunderstand if I did,' she replied.

He raised that infuriating eyebrow at her, making her feel as if she had spoken illogically.

'Really?' he remarked with a touch of irony. 'You shouldn't worry about that. She thinks very highly of you. She keeps telling me that you're far too good for a bawdy-minded ex-soldier like me. She seems to think that in time I'll believe that she's right and I'll break off our engagement so that her beloved Gregor can try his chances with you. I gather she doesn't know you were about to elope with him.'

'We weren't eloping,' she stormed at him, eyes blazing with green-gold fire as her anger was roused by his sardonic needling. Then suddenly remembering she gasped, 'Oh, you found my note!'

'Yes, I found your note. You intended that I should find it, didn't you?' he jeered. 'I seem to go through life finding notes left by people who walk out on me as if they're afraid to tell me the truth. Gregor's accident seems to have put paid to your plans, so what are you going to do now?'

Gina licked her lips which were suddenly dry. Surely he wouldn't turn her away from his house just because she had intended to leave with Gregor instead of waiting for him to take her. She searched his face for some signs of mockery, but it was quite hard and his eyes were still cold.

'I thought I could——' she began, then changed her mind. 'Please could you let me stay another night?' she asked in a small voice. 'And please could you take me south tomorrow as you promised?'

He regarded her narrowly, his mouth twisting unpleasantly.

'You can stay the night,' he agreed curtly, 'but I'm not making any promises about tomorrow. That's another day and anything could happen between now and then.'

Gina felt fear prickle her skin. Threat underlined his words. He was going to make her pay somehow for attempting to leave without telling him.

He thrust open the door.

'Go in,' he ordered brusquely, 'and feed your damned cat. I'll go and dump these ropes and when I come back you and I are going to have a straight talk.'

Gina went into the house quickly and the door closed behind her. In the hall she set Blue down, took off her raincoat, kicked off her shoes and went into the kitchen to find milk and food for the kitten. All the time her mind was busy searching for ways to placate Will when he came in so that he wouldn't punish her too severely.

He would be wet, as she was, and he would be tired after the physical and mental effort of organising Gregor's rescue. He would want hot water to wash in and something hot to drink. She would change out of her damp clothes and then make some tea.

Her thoughts skidded to a stop. All her clothes were in her cases which were in Andrea's car. She would have to make do with towelling her hair and making it tidy.

While she was combing her hair she heard Will enter the house. He was whistling, a sound which made her relax a little. He wouldn't whistle if he were still in a bad mood. He bypassed the kitchen and went upstairs, and soon she could hear the sound of water running in the bathroom.

When he came to the kitchen she would attack first, she decided. She would ask him why he had let Irma go. She was sure that the departure of the German woman was the cause of his dourness. Then, when she had the advantage, she would tell him the real reason for her decision to leave the glen before Irma left.

Footsteps on the stairs warned her of his approach. She made the tea and set the pot on the table, turning to greet him with a smile.

'Why haven't you changed out of those damp clothes?' he rapped, and immediately her advantage was lost before she had even opened her mouth.

'All my clothes are in Andrea's car,' she explained.

'So you were eloping,' he accused.

His hair was still damp and ruffled. The taut skin across

his cheekbones was aglow from exposure to the rain that afternoon. He had changed into a blue shirt which she had not seen before, and he was still in the process of buttoning it down the front, so that she had a brief tantalising glimpse of his white-skinned muscular chest, blurred by dark hair.

He was different, or so she thought, not realising that the difference was in herself, changing her view of him. He was no longer just Oliver's rather unconventional elder brother, who had been concerned about her and had wanted to help her. He was a vigorous, powerful man with whom she had lived for almost six weeks and who had once held her in his arms and had asked her to take the next step with him. He was Will, dear and familiar to her; someone she could love with all her body and soul.

'Come on, George, stop day-dreaming!' his voice seemed to come from a long way off, rallying her, tormenting her. 'Admit that you and Gregor were running away together.'

'But we weren't,' she retorted. 'I asked him to take me to the nearest train going south and he offered to drive me all the way to Birmingham.'

'For nothing?' he gibed. 'I can't imagine young Gregor not wanting payment of some sort. Why couldn't you wait for me to take you?'

'Because I thought it might help you and Irma if I left before she did,' she quavered, watching one muscular forearm appear as he turned up the long sleeve of his shirt in neat Army-like folds, noticing how the hair-blurred skin rippled and ridged as he clenched his fist. Strange how she was noticing far more about his physical appearance than she had ever noticed before. It was as though she had come alive and was seeing properly for the first time since she had met him.

'And what little romance have you been weaving about Irma and me?' he asked dryly, as he started to roll up the other sleeve.

'I thought that once I'd left you'd be able to tell her that you weren't engaged to me any more, and then—and then...'

His eyes had begun to dance with mockery, their colour changing to a darker, warmer blue, making her forget what she had been going to say next.

'Go on, George. This is most interesting,' he urged, coming to stand close to her. The thin stuff of his shirt was taut across his shoulders and his chest emphasising their muscularity. In the hollow below the strong column of his throat she could see a pulse beating regularly. He smelt of spicy soap and she found his powerful, vibrant virility almost overwhelming. It made her feel slightly groggy and she wished wildly that he would move away.

'When I told Irma that you and I weren't engaged any more what was supposed to happen then?' he prompted scoffingly.

'You could have asked her to marry you. I know she's very fond of you. She told me so herself, and I think you're fond of her,' she stammered, her glance meeting his only briefly before sliding away from that amused twinkle in his eyes.

'You believe that fondness is sufficient basis for marriage?' he probed.

She didn't answer because she was experiencing strong desire to fling her arms around him and to stop his mocking taunts with kisses, letting such an embrace lead her willy-nilly to the next step.

'No answer?' he jeered. 'Then let me answer for you. It isn't. I've no wish to marry Irma, nor has she any wish to marry me. In fact I think she might marry a very good friend of mine who's still in the Army.'

Gina looked up then, her eyes wide and startled.

'Then what was she doing here?' she demanded, feeling very foolish and naïve.

'Just visiting, as she said. She was on holiday and while she was in Britain she thought she'd look me up and bring me news of people I used to know in Hamburg. She didn't intend to stay, but you invited her to, and I must admit she was a great help while the campers were here.'

'Oh.' Gina felt deflated. 'But she told me she was staying to make sure you didn't make the same mistake twice. She thought I was like Bridget and that you'd been attracted by the same type of woman.'

'If it's any consolation to you, George,' he said gently, 'I can tell you that she'd decided by the end of her stay here that you aren't as soft and helpless as you appear. Now let's get back to you and Gregor. Have you told him we're not engaged?'

'I told him that I was going to jilt you so that you could marry Irma. Oh, what a mess! Another mess! I thought I was helping you and Irma and all I've done is cause Gregor to be hurt badly,' she moaned.

'Never mind,' he comforted. 'It was his own decision to go after Blue, and he recognises that. He's come a long way in these past weeks. Why don't you stay a little longer so that you can visit him while his leg is mending? Now that you've jilted me you needn't worry how it will look,' he suggested.

He was her kind friend again, trying to help her by making it easy for her to visit Gregor because he thought that was what she wanted to do most. His kindness, however, was hurting much more than his unkindness had, and she pushed it away.

'No, thank you. You'll have to take me to that train tomorrow,' she said. 'It's time I left, Will. You've been very kind and helpful, but I'm better now. I can face up to life again without any help.'

Her voice shook and she had to turn away quickly. Then his hands were on her shoulders and sliding forward over her breast so that she was pulled against him. Held like that against his warm body she was a prisoner who had no wish to escape. She felt his cheek against her hair. He whispered in her ear,

'I'll miss *you*, when you've gone, not just your cooking,'

559

Gina closed her eyes and held her breath as she searched for the right words to say before the magic of the moment was lost; words which would lead her to the next step.

The front door opened and closed. Andrea's deep husky voice called Gina's name and brought the search to an abrupt end. Will released her suddenly and she went rather blindly from the kitchen into the hall.

Andrea's dark eyes were bright and inquisitive as she looked past Gina to Will and then back again to Gina.

'I've brought your cases,' she said. 'I thought you might need them.'

'I'll go and fetch them in,' murmured Will, passing Gina and going out of the house.

'I thought you'd like to know too, that Gregor's leg is broken only in one place and that he should be up on crutches soon,' said Andrea. 'He told me to tell you he'd like you to visit him, and Mother said I was to tell you that you'll be welcome at the castle any time.'

'I'm afraid that won't be possible,' replied Gina stiffly. 'I'm going to Birmingham tomorrow. My home is there, you know, and I'm not married to Will yet. Gregor was just being helpful by taking me down there instead of Will.'

'I see,' drawled Andrea, her disbelief showing in her arched eyebrows. 'In that case I'll say good-bye, and hope that you'll never come back.'

She turned on her heel and went out of the house back to the car. Gina paused long enough to watch her talking to Will, then she went back into the kitchen to drink cold tea. Eventually Will came into the house and she heard him go upstairs with her cases as the sports car roared away. When he came downstairs again he put his head round the kitchen door to announce gruffly that it was time he did some work on the farm, then left the house again, banging the front door behind him.

She did not see him again until he came in for the evening meal, and then he was uncommunicative, the expression in his eyes distant. When she spoke to him he answered absently and in the end she withdrew into silence herself, hurt by his withdrawal.

Evening sunlight, breaking through the clouds, slanted into the room and Gina wondered where she would be the same time the next day. Still travelling south, she supposed, her back turned on Glengorm and all that it had offered.

Her throat grew tight and the room blurred before her eyes. Excusing herself from the table, she began to collect dishes in readiness for washing up. Through the window above the sink she could see the swans swimming on the loch, taking advantage of the evening sunshine after a day of rain. Later she would go and feed them.

She heard Will leave the kitchen. A few moments later he came back with Lachie.

'I was just passing the door and it came to my mind that I should be telling you what I was doing this morning in the town,' Lachie was explaining in his sing-song voice.

'Sit down and tell me, then,' replied Will easily, going over to the cupboard where he kept his whisky. 'Would you take a dram while you're talking?'

'Aye, I will,' sighed Lachie, settling into one of the chairs at the table. 'I've been feeling a wee bit chilly this evening. We were after getting awful wet this afternoon. A wee dram would be fine, that is if you're taking one yourself?'

He would be there for the rest of the evening, thought Gina, with a sinking heart. His voice would drone on and on like the bagpipes. Will, patient and forbearing with him, would sit there listening to tales he must have heard many times. Occasionally he would say a few words, but it would be Lachie who would hold the floor. Then when the older man had taken his fill of whisky he would decide it was time he went to bed and would leave. Even his leave-taking would be a long-drawn-out affair because he would linger on the doorstep, talking about the stars, if there were any to see, or the weather forecast, and always he would 'mind' a day when something or other had happened and off his drone would start again.

She supposed he would be here tomorrow evening, and every evening after that. In her mind the evenings stretched into weeks, months, years, with Will sitting there listening to Lachie, until *his* dark hair began to turn grey, *his* broad straight shoulders began to stoop a little and he lost his gaiety and enthusiasm and became just another elderly man, alone and lonely in the glen with only memories for company.

Tears dimmed her eyes again as she finished drying the last dish. Lachie could have stayed away for this last evening with Will, the first time they had been alone together without the ghosts of Bridget and Oliver standing between them.

She put the dishes away and wiped down the draining board. Already the two men were on their second dram of whisky and Lachie's voice was chanting away.

'Well now,' he was saying, 'I'm going to tell you what has been in my mind these past six weeks. You'll be knowing Flora Kennedy who works as housekeeper at Castle Duich?'

Will murmured that he did know the woman.

'A fine woman, so she is. I've been knowing her all my life,' said Lachie. 'We went to school together. She buried her husband five years ago. Ach, he was a fine fisherman, was Angus. I mind the day when he and I were fishing the Gorm Water.'

Lachie was off on a tangent, reminiscing for all he was worth. Heaven only knew when he would tell them what had been on his mind for these last six weeks concerning Flora Kennedy.

Taking a bag of bread she had saved for the swans, Gina slipped out of the room, unhooked her raincoat from the peg in the hallway put it on and stepped out of the house.

Crimson-tinted bars of cloud streaked the primrose-coloured sky in the west as the sun slid below the horizon, and the glen was full of green and blue shadow. In the twilight the birches were silvery ghosts as she passed through them and the smell of damp earth tangled with the smell of the sea.

At her approach the swans swam over to the beach, and because Blue wasn't with her, they waddled ashore and came close to take bread from her fingers with their orange and black beaks.

When the swans return to Glengorm the curse will be lifted and the true mistress of the master of the glen will come back. Until that time the glen will not hold a woman.

That was the curse associated with the long absence of the swans from the glen, and Lachie had thought it had been lifted when the two swans had flown into the glen one day in April and she had come with Will, wearing an engagement ring on her left hand.

But she wasn't Will's true mistress. She was only his pseudo-fiancée and tomorrow she would be going away. The swans would stay, so there was the possibility, if one believed in legends and curses, that another woman would come to the glen; someone who would be willing to take that further step with Will, the step he had asked her to take one evening in the lamplit dusk. It was possible some other woman would know his strength and his kindness, his roughness and his gentleness, and would learn to love him.

Gina shivered suddenly. Will had said that he would miss her. She would miss him too. She would miss his noisy banging on her bedroom door in the morning, his often caustic comments about her sleepiness, his whistling of a certain saucy song which told a story of slow seduction. Above all she would miss that dangerous delight which being alone with him in the quiet house brought to her.

She couldn't go. She would have to stay and take that next step with him no matter where it might lead. Maybe she would have to leave eventually, in September when the swans winged south again, but September was a long time ahead and the important time for Will and herself was now, while Mary was still painting the glen with the fresh greens and blues which gave it its name. Together they would watch the summer months bring their own deeper richer colours to the glen and see the offspring of the swans learn to swim and fly.

There was hope in her thoughts; hope for the future of the glen as well as for the future of herself and Will. Her mind suddenly crystal clear about her next move, Gina threw the last of the bread on the water. The swans waddled forward and slid silently into the loch. Swinging on her heel, she walked up the path through the ghostly birches to the house, and there was a lightness in her step which had not been there for many weeks.

Now her thoughts picked back over her relationship with Will. It had begun explosively and unconventionally in her bedroom at the flat. It had continued to be unconventional proceeding at an easy pace set by Will as he had nursed her back to normality, taunting her and then tempting her, he had coaxed her out of the protective cocoon she had spun round herself when Oliver had died. Now she was alive again, reborn and ready to love him if he would let her.

When she reachd the house she saw to her surprise that Lachie was leaving. He was loping down the road, singing to himself one of those long Gaelic ballads of which he was so fond. Forty-two verses and all of them the same, she had once heard Will jokingly describe the lilting songs.

She watched Lachie going, and smiled to herself, no longer resenting him. When Will was as old as the crofter he would have more to remember and, if luck was with her in the future, he would not sleep alone because she would be with him.

She entered the house quietly, and took off her raincoat. Creeping to the kitchen door, she looked into the room. Will was still sitting at the head of the table. He was shuffling a pack of playing cards and in the mellow glow of the lamp light his craggy face was all angles and shadows, difficult to read.

As she approached him he looked up briefly, a lightning flicker of pale blue eyes, and said curtly,

'I was just coming to look for you. I'd like you to do something for me.'

'What would you like me to do?' she asked, her voice slightly husky with excitement.

'Give up any idea of leaving here tomorrow and stay for the rest of the summer,' he said, still very curt.

He had asked her to do just what she had intended to do, but his manner of asking was so cool and crisp that she felt slightly rebuffed.

'Any particular reason?' she asked, trying to be cool and crisp too.

'Yes. Lachie is going to marry Flora Kennedy,' he replied concisely, as if that explained everything.

Slowly and deliberately he cut the pack of cards into two. Then picking up the two separate packs he mixed them together expertly, flicking them with his thumbs so that they made a clicking sound. That done, he selected the one from the top of the pack and laid it face upwards on the table. It was the ten of spades. Quickly he laid six other cards in a row besides the first one, their patterned backs showing upwards.

'But what has Lachie's plan to marry Flora Kennedy got to do with me staying for the rest of the summer?' she asked, feeling disappointed because he was not asking her to stay for a more personal reason.

He continued to set out the cards in rows, each row one card shorter than the row above it.

'He's wanted to marry her for years but hasn't dared to ask her because he believed in the curse. He was afraid to ask her to come and live in the glen in case she died suddenly as his first wife did,' he murmured, not lifting his glance from the cards.

'Couldn't they have gone to live elsewhere?' said Gina.

He shook his head slowly from side to side. He had finished setting out the cards and now he was picking up the ones which lay with their backs upwards, one by one.

'Not Lachie. He couldn't live anywhere else but Glengorm. He would always be hankering to come back here,' he replied. 'When the swans came back and you came to the glen with me he assumed that you and I were going to be married. Like Gregor, he saw Noll's ring on your finger and assumed it was mine. He's been waiting and watching ever since. Now he's decided that you're here to stay and that his problem is solved. He thinks the curse has been lifted so he's asked Flora to marry him. She's accepted his proposal and they'll be married three weeks from tomorrow. He came to tell me tonight. I hadn't the heart to tell him that you would be leaving tomorrow and would probably not return. I'm asking you to stay, George, please, for Lachie's sake, at least until they're married and Flora is settled in the glen.'

Her mind in a turmoil, Gina gazed at his big hands moving amongst the cards. Down by the loch everything had been clear. She had recognised that she could love him and live with him and she had come to tell him, expecting nothing in return except his rousing kisses, which would have led inevitably to the next step in their relationship. Now she was in a muddle again and wasn't at all sure whether he wanted her after all.

Suddenly she was reminded of the evening when he had stood and watched her working at her embroidery. Something of the irritation he must have felt then rose up within her as she watched him calmly picking up cards and laying them down in new positions. Apparently he was far more interested in the outcome of his game of Patience than he was in her.

Leaning forward, she snatched the few cards he was holding in one hand and flung them across the room, startling the kitten which was sleeping in its basket. Then with a sweeping movement of her hand she scattered the cards on the table in all directions.

For an electric moment green-shot golden eyes blazed

down into frost-blue eyes, which slowly darkened and began to dance with devilment.

'Well, well,' drawled Will softly, pushing back his chair and rising to his feet slowly. Coming round the corner of the table, he began to walk menacingly towards her, forcing her back against the wall. 'I wondered when you'd come alive. What caused that little display of temper?'

'You did!' she seethed. 'You're so smug, so confident that I'll stay. But why should I stay for Lachie's sake? Why don't you ask me to stay for your sake? Don't you ever want anything for yourself?'

'As a matter of fact, since you ask, I do want something for myself,' he replied tranquilly, standing over her, his brawny arms crossed over his chest. 'I want you, but only when you're ready, and not half alive.'

'Supposing,' she whispered shakily, putting a hand upon his forearm to caress it with her fingers, lifting her eyelids slowly to look up at him, feeling the blood rush to her face as for the first time in her life she made a deliberate attempt to entice a man, 'Supposing I told you that I'm ready now, what would you do?'

He left her in no doubt about what he would do. In a second she was in his arms and crushed against him. His kiss was all she had anticipated it would be and she responded readily to it, feeling desire scorch through her, its flame devouring any final doubts she might have had herself. When they drew apart at last they were both breathless.

'We'll have to be married,' Will murmured huskily into her hair. 'That's the next step for us.'

Once again he had surprised her. She had been sure that when he had originally asked her to take the next step with him marriage had not been his intention. She pulled away from him so that she could see his face. He returned her searching gaze steadily, an expression of such tenderness in his eyes that for a moment she wondered whether this was really her familiar rough and sometimes rude friend.

'You said once that you'd tried marriage and that it didn't work,' she exclaimed.

'I know I did. At the time I meant every word because I didn't want you or any other woman to get any ideas about tying me down,' he said with a touch of cynicism. 'It didn't work for Bridget and me and I vowed after she died that I'd never marry again. Brief affairs with no emotional involvement and no regrets at parting would be acceptable, but nothing permanent any more. That was how I had it all planned, and so it was, with a reasonable amount of success, until I fell in love with you.'

'Oh!' gasped Gina, highly diverted by this admission on his part. 'When did you fall in love with me?'

His teasing grin appeared. Pushing his hands into his trouser pockets, he rocked back and forth on his heels.

'I'm not sure. I was attracted to you from the first time I laid eyes on you in your bedroom at the flat, but I thought you were just another attractively packaged parcel, all show and no depth, soft and silken to the touch, but cold and empty underneath.'

'As Bridget was?' she whispered.

'As Bridget had been,' he answered dourly. 'I offered you the job here more to please your mother than for any other reason. I didn't think you'd take it and was a bit taken aback when you volunteered to come, especially after my behaviour with Birdie. But not even my rudeness seemed to put you off during the journey to Loch Lomond, although I half expected you to refuse to come any further. I think it was when I came back into the kitchen the night we arrived here that I began to realise that there was more to you than met my eye. Although you must have been tired and cold and hungry, and although I was in a filthy mood after being let down by the Andersons, you rose to the occasion, cooked an almost perfect meal and sang to yourself while you did it. I had a flash of insight of what life with you might be, and from then my due aim was to keep you here until the shock of Noll's death had worn off and you came alive again. I knew you wouldn't return my love until you were free of him. I could only go slowly hoping that time would heal and that then you'd notice that I was here. The phoney engagement helped a little to make you more aware of me, but unfortunately Gregor, who brought it about, became a regular visitor and I was afraid that he was going to reap the benefit of all my patient efforts.'

His face tautened and darkened when he spoke of Gregor and Gina had a glimpse of a passionate possessiveness which sent a strange little quiver of excitement through her.

'When I came in today and found your note,' continued Will tersely, 'I was furious, mostly with myself for having allowed you to get under my skin to such an extent that the thought of you going anywhere with Gregor made me feel murderous. I suppose I should be grateful to your kitten. If Gregor hadn't decided to rescue him you'd have left the glen before I returned from Ullapool. As it was I was very tempted to push Gregor down the rest of the cliff into the sea, instead of rescuing him.'

'Oh, you were jealous of him!' accused Gina, clapping her hands together, feeling rather pleased that she was capable of rousing such an intense emotion in such a self-contained man as Will.

'I admit it,' he ground out savagely, 'And Andrea didn't help at all when she brought your cases back here. For one thing she interrupted us at a rather special moment and for another, she told me that you were afraid to tell me that you preferred Gregor to me and wanted to discontinue our engagement. Are you in love with him, George? If so say so, and I'll take you over to the castle now.'

'Would I have said that I was ready to take the next step with you if I were in love with him, silly?' she retorted, smiling up at him, sensing suddenly that he was very uncertain and had been made so by his experience with Bridget. 'I love *you*, Will. Look!'

She held out her left hand to him and he glanced down at it. It was ringless.

'Where's Noll's ring?' he demanded, looking directly at her, his eyes darkening.

'I've decided not to wear it any more,' she replied, laughter bubbling up inside her. 'I've developed a liking for topazes because someone said once that they match my eyes. If I thought you'd give them to me I'd stay here for ever, even when the swans fly south, I'd stay with you, Will.'

'Then you shall have them, sweetheart,' he said, laughing with her, grasping her hands and drawing her towards him. Her fingers rested lightly for a moment on his chest and she felt passion stir and ripple through him, then she was swamped again by his embrace.

The lamp on the table flickered a little as if running short of oil, making black shadows dance on the walls of the room. From his basket, which was still scattered with playing cards, the kitten gazed drowsily at the closely entwined figures of the man and woman. When they turned and walked slowly from the room he was tempted to follow them and to go where they were going, but the day on the cliff had tired him and he was loath to move. Yawning widely, he circled round several times in the basket to make himself more comfortable, curled up and closed his eyes, content for once to stay alone in the kitchen for the night, and gradually the flame of the lamp died down and went out, leaving the room in darkness.

4
FREE
Harlequin Romances

Get this book FREE!

Mail to:
Harlequin Reader Service

In the U.S.
1440 South Priest Drive
Tempe, AZ 85281

In Canada
649 Ontario Street
Stratford, Ontario N5A 6W2

YES! I want to be one of the first to discover the new **Harlequin American Romances.** Send me FREE and without obligation *Twice in a Lifetime.* If you do not hear from me after I have examined my FREE book, please send me the 4 new **Harlequin American Romances** each month as soon as they come off the presses. I understand that I will be billed only $2.25 for each book (total $9.00). There are no shipping or handling charges. There is no minimum number of books that I have to purchase. In fact, I may cancel this arrangement at any time. *Twice in a Lifetime* is mine to keep as a FREE gift, even if I do not buy any additional books.

Name _____ (please print)

Address _____ Apt. no.

City _____ State/Prov. _____ Zip/Postal Code

Signature (If under 18, parent or guardian must sign.)

AM 304